DUTY, HONOR, COUNTRY

by

Bob Mayer

Who commanded the major battles of the Civil War? ------ There were 60 important battles of the War. In 55 of them, graduates commanded on both sides; in the remaining 5, a graduate commanded one of the opposing sides.

Required Plebe knowledge at West Point.

Dedication

Dedicated to the men and women of The Long Gray Line.

Letter from Ulysses Grant 1839

Military Academy
West Point, NY
Sept 22d 1839

To R. McKinstry Griffith from Ulysses Grant

Dear Coz,
I was just thinking that you would be right glad to hear from one of your relations who is so far away as I am, so I have put aside my Algebra and French and am going to tell you a long story about this prettiest of places, West Point. So far as it regards natural attractions it is decidedly the most beautiful place I have ever seen; here are hills and dales, rocks and rivers; all pleasant to look upon. From the window near I can see the Hudson; that far famed, that beautiful river with its bosom studded with hundreds of snow sails. Again if I look another way I can see Fort Putnam frowning far above; a stern monument of a sterner age, which seems placed there on purpose to tell us of the glorious deeds of our fathers and to bid us remember their sufferings—to follow their examples. In short this is the best of all places—the place of all places for an institution like this.

I have not told you half its attractions. Here is the house Washington used to live in—there Kosciuszko used to walk and think of his country and ours. Over the river we are shown the duelling house of Arnold, that base and heartless traitor to his country and his God. I do love the place. It seems as though I could live here forever if my friends would only come too. You might search the wide world over and not find a better. Now all this sounds nice, very nice, "what a happy fellow you are" you will say, but I am not one to show false colors the brightest side of the picture. So I will tell you about a few of the drawbacks.

First, I slept for two months upon one single pair of blankets; now that sounds romantic and you may think it very easy. But I will tell you what coz, it is tremendous hard. Suppose you try it by way of experiment for a night or two. I am pretty sure that you would be perfectly satisfied that is no easy matter. But glad am I these things are over. We are now in our quarters. I have a splendid bed and get along very well. Our pay is nominally about twenty-eight dollars a month. But we never see one cent of it. If we want anything from a shoestring to a coat we must go to the commandant of the post and get an order for it or we cannot have it. We have tremendous long and hard lessons to get in both French and Algebra. I study hard and hope to get along so as to pass the examination in January. This examination is a hard one they say, but I am not frightened yet. If I am successful here you will not see me for two long years. It seems a long while to me. But time passes off very fast. It seems but a few since I came here. It is because every hour has its duty which must be performed. On the whole I like the place very much. So much that I would not go away on any account. The fact is if a man graduates here he is safe for life. Let him go where he will. There is much to dislike but more to like. I mean to study and stay if it be possible. If I cannot—very well—the world is wide. I have now been here about four months and have not seen a single familiar face or spoken to a single lady. I wish some of the pretty girls of Bethel were here just so I might look at them. But fudge! Confound the girls.

I have seen great men plenty of them. Let us see. Gen. Scott. M. Van Buren. Sec. of War and Navy. Washington Irving and lots of other big bugs. If I were to come home now with my uniform on. The way you would laugh at my appearance would be curious. My pants sit as tight to my skin as the bark to a tree and if I do not walk militarily. That is if I bend over quickly or run. They are apt to crack with a report as loud as a pistol. My coat must always be buttoned up tight to the chin. It is made of sheeps grey cloth all covered with big round buttons. It all makes me look very singular. If you were to see me at a distance. The first question you would ask would be: "Is that a Fish or an Animal"? You must give my very best love and respects to all my friends particularly your brothers. Uncle Ross & Sam'l Simpson. You must write me a long, long letter in reply to this and tell me every thing and every body including yourself. If you happen to see my folks just tell them that I am happy, alive, and kicking.

I am truly your cousin
And obedient servant
U. H. Grant
(West Point class of 1843)

Letter from Sidney Albert Johnston in 1862

Vicinity Shiloh, TN 23 years later
Grant's invading Army of the Tennessee

5 April 1862

To The Soldiers of the Army of the Mississippi:

I have put into motion to offer battle to the invaders of your country. With the resolution and discipline and valor becoming men fighting, as you are, for all worth living or dying for, you can but march to decisive victory over the agrarian mercenaries sent to subjugate and despoil you of your liberties, property and honor. Remember the dependence of your mothers, your wives, your sisters, and your children on the result; remember the fair, broad, abounding land, the happy homes and the ties that would be desolated by your defeat. The eyes and hopes of eight millions of people rest upon you; you are expected to show yourselves worthy of your lineage, worthy of the women of the South, whose noble devotion in this war has never been exceeded in any time. With such incentives to brave deeds, and with the trust that God is with us, your generals will lead you confidently to the combat—assured of success.

C.S.A. General Sidney Albert Johnston
(West Point class of 1826)

FOR HONOR

27 May 1840, West Point, New York

"TO, DUTY, HONOR, AND COUNTRY," William Tecumseh Sherman proposed, raising his mug of ale.

He shoved his chair back, along with his classmate who sat at the same table. The mugs were clunked together, whereupon the two turned their backs to each other and imbibed. Done, they turned to the table and reclaimed their seats inside the tavern on the west bank of the Hudson River, just outside of the Military Academy post limits.

"Tell me, Mister Sherman," a young cadet leaning against the bar asked, "why do you say honor in the center as the linchpin between duty and country, and not loyalty?"

Before Sherman could respond, his classmate, a lean young man with a hatchet face under short, thick black hair, drawled in a low, southern voice. "Why, honor is all a man has, Mister Cord."

Cord laughed. "Where I come from, we couldn't afford honor, Mister King."

The three cadets were the only customers left in the dimly lit tavern, with dawn less than an hour off. A rough wooden plank bar stretched across one side of the room. Behind it, head slumped onto the scarred surface, was the proprietor, Benny Havens. His loud snoring sawed through the room. Clanking noises came through the curtain behind him, where his daughter, Lidia, was cleaning up the remains of the party that had covered most of the night as many members of the class of 1840 had celebrated their pending graduation. Cord was not a member of '40, but finishing his plebe year, class of '43.

King shook his head, but didn't immediately pursue Cord's observation. "A toast without a fine cigar is practically wasted." He unbuttoned his dress grey tunic and withdrew a pair of cigars. "Direct from my home in Charleston, where they came straight from Havana." He extended one to Sherman.

The two Firsties went through the lighting ritual, to add to the lingering cloud from the night's revelries.

King blew a puff of smoke Cord's way. "With your grades and conduct record, Mister Cord, one could not expect any different."

"Here, here." Sherman slapped a hand on the scarred wooden table. "None of that. It's not fair." He had fiery red hair and thick sideburns that tapered toward the point of his chin, not quite meeting.

"Cord is the Immortal in every section, Cump," King said. "Last in every one! An honorable man would not hold such a record. He should have more pride. He should have the decency to study."

"Mister Cord studies," Sherman said. He turned to Cord with a grin. "You do, don't you?"

Benny Havens lifted his head off the bar and blearily gazed about, like an old hound dog sensing trouble at a distance.

Cord was of average size and tightly built. His face was pleasant, made more so by a wide mouth that was most amendable to a cheerful expression. His nose had a slight crook to it, broken long ago in some waterside tavern and set as well as a drunken ship's doctor could manage on a drunker patient. He had pale blue eyes and pale blond hair from his family's Nordic ancestry.

His dress grey tunic, unlike the others, had the top three buttons unfastened, and was lacking the starched white collar the other two wore.

"No need for you to step in, Mister Sherman, and defend my lack of schooling. I could study every minute and I believe I'd still be the Immortal in every section. So why fight such a futile battle?"

"It's your duty," King said. "All of us share the same duty as cadets." He turned to Sherman. "Perhaps, Mister Cord is just dull in the wits. And it's more than academics being indicative of lack of character, there are the demerits, his inattention to duty and his shabby appearance. And his presence at a gathering of firsties when he is just a plebe."

"Well, none of us really are allowed to be here." Sherman held up his mug in a token of peace. "I say we take another draft, then make our way back to our rockbound highland home and get some rest before First Call."

He and King stood once more, raised their mugs, no toast this time, turned their backs to each other, and drank. The turning of the backs had both a logical and traditional purpose. It was illegal for cadets to drink alcohol. They were also bound by the honor code to report another cadet they saw breaking regulations. So the practice had begun years ago at Benny Havens to turn backs to each other when drinking in order to be able to truthfully say, if questioned, that one had not seen the other drink. They turned to the table and thumped the mugs down, King with a bit extra force.

Sherman grabbed his cadet hat. "Time to be off."

"Perhaps I am just sorta stupid," Cord said as he peeked at the curtain, hoping for one last glance at Lidia before departing. "To the barracks and--"

"I believe," King said, his low voice cutting Cord off, "that an honorable man is one who judges himself accurately."

Cord smiled. "Why thank you, Mister King. That's the nicest way anyone's ever agreed when I said I was stupid. Kind of. Sort of."

King's eyes narrowed. He placed both fists on the tabletop, as much for balance as emphasis. "Are you saying I don't know the judge of a man?"

"I say no such thing, Mister King," Cord said, brightening as Lidia came out from behind the curtain.

Lidia had curly red hair, fair skin and sparkling green eyes. An enticing allure, like the dark blue water of a small harbor in the Bahamas that Cord had sailed by as a younger man. A harbor with such sublime depth and surrounded by perfect sand and palms, it wanted to draw you in, but the ship's master had warned Cord that such apparent havens often held hidden reefs and shoals that could cause the vessel to founder and be trapped forever.

"You spoke out of turn, plebe," King said. "As we say in South Carolina, if the dog is slapped, it barks."

Sherman sighed. He once more grabbed his mug, trying to douse the growing tension with more alcohol. "One *last* toast, George. To country at least. We can all agree on that."

"I might not be the best judge of every trait in a man," King continued, ignoring Sherman, "but I know honor and I can clearly see lack of honor."

Cord's grin disappeared. "Because you believe you're honorable, you question it in others?"

"You question *my* honor?" King demanded, face flushed.

"Honor," Cord said, "is a mirror in front of you and loyalty is a pane of glass that must be carefully nurtured and kept clean."

King's eyes narrowed. "What the devil does that mean?"

"It means you don't quite see me," Cord said. "You only see me as reflected by you."

"So you do say I am not honorable?" King pressed.

"No. You've had too much to drink, sir," Cord said, "as have I. We can continue this conversation some other time."

"Gentlemen," Sherman interjected, "we must be off. We've all had too much to imbibe."

King slapped the table. "I demand clarification!"

"Hey now!" Benny Havens called out from the bar. "Enough of that."

Unseen by her father, Lidia placed a hand on Cord's forearm and shook her head.

"We are speaking of honor," King said, dismissing Havens as uninvited to the argument.

"You can have whatever honor you want to claim for yourself, sir," Cord said with a shrug.

"I claim that which I have earned," King said, "which is more than can be said of you. You are no gentleman, sir."

"Now, now!" Benny Havens came from around the bar and his daughter quickly pulled her hand back. He was a florid-faced, full-bodied rock of a man. He sported close-cropped salt and pepper hair atop a craggy face. His apron was dirty from a night of serving food and drink to cadets. He pointed at a large flagon on the end of the bar, trying to defuse the situation. "How about I rustle the three of you up a hot flip?" The concoction of rum, beaten eggs, sugar and spices, heated by a red hot poker shoved into it, was his specialty, especially for cadets trying to beat the inevitable hangover.

King folded his arms across his chest. "I will have an apology or satisfaction."

"There isn't going to be any duel," Sherman said. "And the insults are the result of spirits, not bad intention."

"You southerners," Cord said. "You take things that aint important, awfully serious, but I apologize."

King opened his mouth to speak, but before he could, Havens' wife, Letitia, came through the curtain. Tears stained her cheeks. She walked up to Benny and held out her hands. Stretched across her palms was a limp white cadet collar.

"Where did you find it?" Havens demanded.

Letitia responded by turning to her daughter. "On her bed."

Benny Havens staggered back as if he'd been punched in the chest.

Sherman hurried forward to the tavern keep. "Mister Havens, I understand your anger at the trespass into your daughter's quarters by Cadet Cord. Let me take him back to the barracks for now and we'll deal with the matter later, when cooler heads might prevail."

The old man was slowly shaking his head, as if to dislodge the last few moments. He ignored Sherman and looked at his daughter. "Lidia, did you lay with Mister Cord this night?"

Lidia closed her eyes for a moment, and then met her father's gaze. "I did not lie with him tonight, father." She swallowed. "I wished to speak with him. He took the collar off to be more comfortable in the heat."

Letitia spoke: "What could you have to speak to him about that it needed to be in the sanctity of your room?"

Lidia looked at her mother, then her father, and finally the young cadet. "It's a private matter, but I couldn't bring the subject up with him. I couldn't bring it up with anyone." Tears began to flow as did the pent up words. "I made a mistake. Three months ago. And now—" she began sobbing and Letitia hurried to her daughter and wrapped her arms around her.

It took a moment for the implications to sink in to Benny Havens brain. When it landed, he howled with rage.

"Sir!" King was at Havens' side. "Allow me the privilege of defending your daughter." Before the old man could respond, King stepped forward and slapped Cord across the face. Hard. "You truly have *no* honor, defiling a young woman's reputation. In thirty minutes, on the river field, with pistols, which I will fetch from town." He stormed out of the tavern, brushing off Sherman's attempt to stop him.

Havens glared at Cord. "I'm going to let Mister King shoot you like the dog you are. And if you run, I'm sending my man for the Superintendent right now. One way or the other, I'll have you, Mister Cord!"

Cord was blinking, trying to sort the rapid series of events through his drunken haze.

"Mister Havens!" Sherman exclaimed. "Dueling is illegal and if the Superintendent comes, that'll at the least cost Mister Cord his cadetship, if not entail a court-martial. And if they duel, *both* Mister King and Mister Cord will be dismissed immediately from the Corps."

"So be it." Thunder rumbled in the distance, as if to punctuate Havens' resolve.

"Sir, let the Vigilance Committee take care of the matter," Sherman suggested. "At least for Mister King's sake. His anger and the alcohol have gotten the better of him."

"It's beyond the Vigilance Committee's scope," Havens said. "It happened here, in my house. To my daughter."

Sherman gave a slight bow, both in actuality and to Havens' resolve. "With all due respect, sir, then I'll make my way back to the Academy as I'm not involved and I have a busy day ahead. Perhaps I'll come back when things are peaceful."

Havens vaguely nodded. "You'd best be on your way then."

Sherman ran outside and jumped on his horse, galloping off, not in retreat, but in search of reinforcements.

Fifty miles up the Hudson River from New York City, the river narrows and makes a sharp bend to the west. The craggy highland on the left bank is called West Point and was first fortified to keep the American colonies united during the Revolutionary War. The placement of a military outpost at West Point was dictated by both strategy and terrain. The strategy insisted that the fledgling colonies stay connected and the British had seen the obvious: control the Hudson River and they could sever the particularly troublesome New England colonies from the Confederation of rebelling states to the west and south.

The terrain was the dictate of geography on military tactics. At West Point, the narrow twist in the Hudson causes any sailing vessel to tack and slow to a crawl. Add a massive chain floated across the river on rafts, covered by heavy artillery lining the bluffs above, and the small American garrison at West Point kept the colonies united throughout the Revolution.

After the Revolutionary War, the founding of the Military Academy at West Point had been dictated by necessity. The country's third president, Thomas Jefferson, detested the idea of a standing army, but accepted the reality that the country had to have such a beast. So Jefferson determined to place a leash on the animal. To keep the officer corps from becoming filled with sycophants who would support a particular party or person over the country, in 1802 he ordered the establishment of an Academy to train a professional cadre of officers that would draw its cadets from across the country and across the strata of society. As West Point was a chokepoint in the geography of the new country, the Academy located there was to be a chokepoint to the power of the military that had to sustain a democracy. Cadets would swear an oath— the very first law the First Congress enacted, an indication of its importance to the young country—to defend the Constitution, not any party or individual.

Thirty-eight years after the founding, two of these cadets, one from Ohio and the other from Mississippi, were in the Academy stable, preparing horses for a ride on a rare day exempt from duties and training.

"You can surrender now, sir, or you can fight me and suffer inevitable defeat," the young Mississippian, clad in West Point dress gray, declared. "This is going to happen, one way or the other."

Standing with arms folded across his broad chest, the boy-man considered his opponent. The massive horse had refused to be bridled for ten minutes and Lucius Kosciusko Rumble was beginning to take it personally. Rumble desired to be the first to ride York, but the magnificent beast wasn't being agreeable. He'd tossed a coin with his friend, Sam Grant, for first try at York, and gotten what he'd thought was a lucky break. Grant had dawdled saddling the horse in the next stall, giving Rumble some leeway to have his chance with the Hell Beast.

This early morning, in the midst of the summer of 1840, was not the best to go for a ride. To the northwest a dark halo of clouds gathered round Storm King Mountain's forested slopes. Flashes of lightning preceded the thunder from summer squalls scattered across the Hudson Highlands with dawn yet twenty minutes off.

Rumble was a solidly built young man, filling out the dress gray coat as if his body had been tailored for it. Broad shoulders cut in to a tapered waist. His dark hair matched his dark eyes. For all his strength and intensity, he had met his match. York was a bay stallion, at least a hand taller than any other horse in the stable, well muscled and newly arrived. It had already achieved a reputation as intractable and unridable, thus the Hell Beast. There was a gleam in the horse's eye that indicated more resistance would be forthcoming.

Rumble cautiously took a step into the stall, bit in hand. As he reached for the horse's mouth, thunder reverberated through the stables and York reared, lashing out with a massive hoof, narrowly missing Rumble's head and splintering wood. Rumble beat a hasty retreat, bumping into the young Ohioan who'd finished equipping the other horse.

"You can't force him," Ulysses S. Grant said in a level tone. "You have to lead him."

While Rumble filled out his uniform coat, Grant was lost in his. He was slender to the point of emaciation, his frame slightly stooped, and the dress gray tunic hung loosely from his shoulders as if they were a thin hanger. He was several inches shorter than Rumble's six feet and dwarfed by York.

Rumble shifted uneasily as Grant took a step toward the horse. "Careful, Sam."

Grant was focused on the horse. His piercing blue eyes stared deeply into the bay's. Grant took another step closer, within hoof range, but it was also close enough for something to pass between man and beast.

The horse twitched, began to rear, but stopped, nostrils flaring. The bay shivered, took a step back and glared at Grant. Outside the stall, Rumble remained perfectly still. Grant slipped the bit in the horse's mouth, whispering all the time to the beast, calming, forceful, reassuring. The horse's ears had been laid back, but now they relaxed, twitching forward to catch the young man's soft voice.

Grant led York out of the stall, Rumble making sure to get out of the way.

"Where's your former roommate, Cord?" Grant asked as he ran a hand over York's neck.

"Restricted to quarters."

Grant gave a low laugh. "Again?"

Rumble shook his head. "He's no Robert Lee," he said, referring to the legendary cadet from ten years prior who had graduated without a single demerit. It was a feat most cadets viewed as a result of divine intervention of some sort. Either God or Satan, depending on one's perspective of the disciplinary system, and the touchstone by which many cadets could clearly gauge their own lack of self-discipline. "Cord's never going to get ahead on demerits. He'll spend the next three years restricted to his room if he has any hopes of graduation. Superintendent Delafield has him in his sights."

"And it causes you no great trouble that Cord is locked up," Grant said.

"That is true," Rumble allowed.

"Because he's your rival for young Lidia's attention or because he's over on demerits and deserves the punishment?"

"Both."

Grant was heading toward the stable doors. "Bring the other mount, if you don't mind, Lucius." Grant said it casually, one friend to another, but Rumble followed as if it were an order, unaware of his reaction. Such was Grant's way with people as well as horses.

"The storm will be upon us soon," Rumble said, leading the more compliant, and smaller, horse Grant had saddled toward the stable doors.

"We're the first to bridle York," Grant said, making Rumble feel part of something special, the type of comment as natural to Grant as breathing was to the horse. "Waste not to ride him."

They stepped out of the stables into the dark pre-dawn, occasionally illuminated by the approaching lightning. Rain was pounding on Storm King. Rumble resigned himself to getting wet soon. Grant had decided to ride, and ride they would.

"That Hell Beast will kill you," a cadet coming down the road called out. He was instantly recognizable by his size, towering over his classmates.

Grant grinned at his best friend. "Well, I can't die but once, Pete."

James 'Pete' Longstreet addressed the small cluster of upper-class cadets who had gathered upon hearing his deep voice, always a herald of some interesting activity. "I bet that Sam here eats dirt within a minute of mounting."

Some of the cadets nervously peered about, checking for the duty officer, or of greater consequence, the Superintendent. Major Delafield was a good soldier, a solid officer who had the cadets' respect, but also a leader who had little tolerance for rule breaking. Not that Longstreet seemed to care as he took the bets, as good with the money as Grant with horses.

Rumble spotted Cord's current roommate and couldn't resist a needle. "Too bad Cord's restricted, Fred. He'd love to get in on the action."

Frederick Dent hunched his shoulders, looking particularly guilty. "Cord snuck out of the room earlier."

"I told you that would happen," Rumble said.

Longstreet let out a booming laugh. "Cord's a marked man. Crazy Virginian. Supe finds out he's gone, he's done here."

The cause of Dent's discomfort was that officially he should report Elijah Cord's disappearance to the duty officer or risk an honor violation. The saber's edge of duty and honor that cadets tiptoed around almost every day because strictly following the honor code might entail betraying a classmate.

It was more personal for Rumble. "Did he 'run it' to Benny Havens?"

Dent shrugged, wanting no part of this. "He left after midnight. He didn't say where he was going, but he'd been imbibing most of the night, so where else but a run to Benny Havens?"

"Many cadets made a run to Benny's last night," Grant noted.

"Many firsties," Rumble said, referring to the senior cadets who would graduate shortly.

"Easy," Grant said to Rumble in a low voice. "You know Cord. Maybe he just went for a flip?"

"I do know Cord," Rumble said, "and that's exactly what worries me. Lidia's a good girl but—" he shook his head, focusing on the more immediate problem. "Be careful." He pointed toward York, who had that look back in his eye and whose nostrils were flaring.

Grant put a foot in the stirrup and York sidestepped away, twisting and turning, trying to rip the rein from Grant's hand. His foot slipped out of the stirrup and he stumbled, but didn't fall. Grant's grip on the rein was tight though the horse outweighed him by a thousand pounds. Grant kept whispering to the horse the entire time, a low soothing tone. York tried to jerk his head back, but Grant anticipated the move and pulled sideways, surprising the horse. Grant's foot was back in the stirrup and then he was swinging the other leg over the saddle as York reared, trying to throw the interloper off.

However, Grant was firmly on board. York bucked and spun as if chasing its own tail. Grant was leaning forward, his slight body melding into the horse's back, his mouth next to York's right ear. The horse stopped spinning for a moment and glared at the cadets. Grant twitched the reins and gave a slight kick of his boot heels. Grant and York raced off as one, sprinting along the dirt road between stable and riding hall.

"You should've known better and been more careful with your money," Rumble said to Longstreet, tightly clutching the rein of the other horse as it strained to follow Grant and York.

The Georgian laughed once more. "Damnation, Lucius, I just wanted to see him ride the Hell Beast. It was worth it. Besides, I took all the bets on Sam conquering it."

In a minute, Grant returned, the horse at a steady trot, the young cadet's face split in a wide grin. "York is superb." He swung down off the horse and held the lead. "Come, Lucius, let's walk him off post and put him through his paces on an open trail. We'll switch off once we get a few miles under us."

"I think we should pay a visit to Benny Havens," Rumble said, desiring to find out what Cord was up to, and no longer as concerned about taking a turn on York.

Grant laughed. "In search of Mister Elijah Cord and his latest adventure? Certainly. At least we're authorized to leave post today."

The two, horses in tow, walked away from the other cadets. They headed toward the south gate and the path to Benny Havens. Grant nodded toward the Library, where he was known to spend a considerable amount of time, curled up with some novel, rather than reading the texts and military treatise a cadet ought to. "Maybe Cord is in there studying, rather than at Benny Havens?"

"You jest," Rumble said. "You know where he is and what he's trying to do."

Grant's blue eyes focused on Rumble. "Cord enjoys himself. You, on the other hand—" Grant stopped, concerned he had gone too far.

"It's true, I've no claim on Lidia," Rumble acknowledged. "Nor could I have one. But she's a good friend and I fear Cord might take advantage. And I do take things seriously." There was more tension on the lead. "Sometimes I look at my life as one of those novels you read, Sam. The book of Lucius Rumble is written—and not by my hand. I'm just following the words as they've been determined for me. I accept Lidia isn't my future because there's another woman who's been chosen for me, even though a future with her is an empty one in the most important of ways. Still, Lidia is dear to me."

"No one's life is written like that," Grant argued. "You can always rewrite it." Grant considered Rumble a grave and dependable man, and dependable went a long way in his book.

Rumble shook his head. "I'm truly not the author of my own life. I must do my duty to my family."

"Certainly you write your own life. And your family back in Mississippi is as rich as Midas, aren't they? What do you have to be concerned about?"

"They're not as rich as they appear," Rumble said. "And what money they do have is tainted."

"Tainted how?"

"By the blood of slaves."

"All money is tainted, and usually by blood," Grant said. "My father makes his running a tannery. Have you ever been in one? I will never go back inside such a place as long as I live. Blood and guts all over the place; it's disgusting to see. But what's worse, what's unbearable, is the stench. It's indescribable." Grant shook his head. "Graduate, Lucius, serve your time in Army blue, go back to your plantation and enjoy your life and the woman to whom you are betrothed."

"How important is family to you, Sam?" Rumble asked.

Grant considered the question. "I would like to find a woman who is lively, have children with her, and raise a family. I can think of nothing better, especially raising children." He grinned. "And perhaps attain the rank of major and be able to retire some day."

Rumble nodded glumly. "That's the—" he began, but paused as a mud-splattered rider came racing toward them. York began to shy, and Grant put a hand on the horse's head, murmuring to it.

Sherman reined in his horse, both breathing hard. Sherman was the mouthpiece of a small dark angel flitting about in his brain, always predicting the worst. Unfortunately, he was almost always right.

"You best get down to Benny Havens," Sherman called to Rumble. "It's going to be bad."

"Steady now, Cump," Grant said. "What's going on?"

"Elijah Cord," Sherman got out between gasps. He took a deep breath. Like a scout coming back with a report, Sherman spit out the essential information. "King and Cord got into an argument. Then Lidia came into the room and it seems Cord was in her quarters. Then it turns out, Lidia is with child from a previous visit by Mister Cord. King challenged Cord to a duel and Havens sent his man for the Supe."

"With child!" Rumble was shocked.

Grant took the information calmly. "Let's ride."

"Now Benny, please allow me my—" Elijah Cord searched for the word in the murky recesses of his brain—"freedom."

"And then what?" Havens demanded. He had an old flintlock pistol in his hand and it was pointed at Cord. Letitia and Lidia were huddled in the corner of the tavern. "You're done for boy."

Cord was seated in the corner furthest from them and Havens held court in the center. Benny Havens was a legend among cadets. Not just for his service during the War of 1812, but after it, for the small cottage he'd occupied just west of the Cadet Hospital where he'd dispensed hot flips, ale, cider and wheat cakes to home-sick young men. Among cadets, the oft-repeated story was that Edgar Allan Poe, during his short stint at the Academy, had found Benny Havens to be the only congenial soul in the entire place. Many in the years that followed agreed.

The Academy had not looked at either Poe or Havens with similar empathy. Poe departed within a year of his arrival at the Academy, dismissed for 'gross neglect of duty' and 'disobedience of orders'. The rumor in the Corps was that Poe had shown up for parade formation, the uniform order to be 'with cross belts and under arms'—wearing just cross belts and carrying his musket. True or not, it made for a good tale and good tales made many a gray night pass by a bit lighter.

Benny Havens was also banished from the military reservation. Only to set up a new tavern down by the Hudson River, just south of post limits. It was a magnet for the young cadets, many of who were away from home for the first time and thrust into a harsh disciplinary environment that reshaped their boyish spirit into captains of war. Everyone needed an occasional break from that and Benny Havens was the person to give it.

Right now, though, all the old man wanted to do was break Elijah Cord.

"You best hope the Superintendent gets here before Mister King," Benny Havens said, "although I'll be hoping for Mister King and his pistols." He waved the barrel of the gun toward the door. "Let's move to the river field and wait for whoever shows up first."

As Havens gestured for Cord to move to the door, the cadet whispered a prayer. "Please, God. I've never asked for much. And I never got much, neither, if you really look at it. I asked you to spare mother, but that wasn't to be, though she really believed in you. I know that's the way things are and that you and I have never been close. But if you can help me out of this, please, I'll be a better man. And besides," he added, as he stumbled outside, "Lidia rejected me today, but you can't blame a fellow for trying one more time especially after, well, I suppose you know about that last time. Surely I shouldn't be punished for that?"

"What was that?" Havens demanded, catching a bit of the last.

"Nothing, sir."

"You best be praying, boy. You're gonna need all the help you can get."

The storm broke upon the three riders, sheets of rain descending. Grant led the way, galloping cross-country toward Benny Havens, ignoring the road that followed a more gentle, winding route that switched back several times to the river's edge and the tavern.

Rumble was using every ounce of horsemanship and strength to keep his horse from tumbling headfirst down the steep slope. Sherman was behind, muttering darkly. They both kept their focus on Grant's slight form on top of the huge horse. Grant came to a sudden halt at the edge of a creek.

Normally a small, insignificant trickle of water, it was now a torrent, sending water cascading toward the Hudson to begin a journey downstream to New York City and thence the Atlantic Ocean. Sherman pulled up beside Rumble and Grant, his forage cap drooping over his deep-set, solemn eyes.

"We can't cross," Sherman said flatly. "It'll kill us. We have to go back to the road."

Rumble shifted in the saddle. "The Superintendent will be taking the road. He'll likely get to Benny Havens before us. And King stores his guns with the smithie in town and will make it back to the river field quickly."

"No point going if we don't get to Cord first," Grant said mildly. "Besides, we set out to get there, we get there. No turning aside."

"I don't like water," Rumble said, hands clutching the reins. "I had a bad experience."

"You won't make it across," Sherman repeated.

Grant turned and placed a hand on Rumble's shoulder. "We'll make it." He looked closer, reading Rumble's eyes. "You really do fear the water, don't you, Lucius?"

Rumble bit his lip, looking between Grant and Sherman.

"If you can't make it," Grant began, "then—"

"Let's do it," Rumble said.

Grant spurred York forward into the surging water. Rumble glanced at Sherman who shook his head. Summoning every ounce of will, Rumble directed his reluctant horse into the stream.

"Damn fools," Sherman yelled. "I'll see if I can delay Delafield." He headed for the road.

The horse shook beneath Rumble as they hit the torrent. He was being shoved down-creek despite his best efforts. Ahead of him, Grant almost got swept away, but mighty York managed to hold against the force of the water. Rumble cried out in panic as his horse lost traction. In a second he was dismounted and underwater, one hand gripping the rein, his only anchor from being washed away.

Grant leaned forward, his head against York's neck, exhorting the horse in a calm, yet firm, voice. Hooves caught in mud and rock deep beneath the water and with a powerful surge, York hauled Grant onto the far bank.

Grant twisted in the saddle and looked back. The only sign of Rumble was a hand above the turbulent water gripping the rein. Grant jumped off York.

"Hold!" he ordered his horse. Using the lead as a safety line, he leapt into the water. The current grabbed his slight frame and tried to rocket him downstream, but York was like a rock. Grant pushed forward to Rumble's horse.

"Steady." Grant grabbed the other rein and held it in place, while staring into the horse's terrified eyes, calming it. Rumble splashed to the surface, blood pouring from a gash over his right eye, flailing to get out of the stream.

"Easy, Lucius," Grant urged, as if he were talking to York, not Rumble.

Using all his strength, Rumble reached out and also grabbed York's lead. He pulled, hand over hand, to York and the shore, while Grant maintained contact with the terrified horse caught in the current.

As soon as he had his feet on solid ground, Rumble turned. There was no sign of Grant, just the horse, head above water, eyes wide with fright. The horse's taut bridle disappeared under the churning water.

Rumble used York's lead as Grant had done. He jumped back into the water, reaching with his free hand for his friend. His fingers grazed across cloth and he grabbed. Hauling with all his might, he lifted the slender Grant up.

Grant spit out water, but he didn't let go of the other horse's bridle. Together, Rumble and Grant heaved on the lead.

"Come on," Grant urged the horse. "Come on."

York must have picked up the urgency because the large bay took a step back. Together, the two men and York pulled the other horse to shore.

Grant tumbled onto the creek bank, breathing hard. Rumble collapsed on his back, staring aimlessly up at the rain pouring down through the leaves.

Grant turned his head, blinking water out of his eyes. "Thank you, Lucius. You saved my life."

"The obligation is mutual," Rumble said.

Grant got up and knelt next to his friend, noting the gash. "I think you're a bit worse for the adventure."

Rumble blinked. He reached up and touched his face. Pulling his hand back he saw the blood. "It's nothing." He stood and shivered like a dog, trying to shake off water and a bad memory. Neither were completely expunged.

Rumble wiped the blood off his face with his sleeve. They both jumped back in their saddles. Grant turned down-slope and galloped toward Benny Havens as fast as the terrain would allow. At neck-breaking speed if they had another mishap, but Rumble followed, blinking blood out of his right eye.

They raced past Benny Havens tavern and down the path to the riverbank. A clearing, thirty feet long by ten wide bordered the Hudson River. To the north, Cord stood alone, his blond hair plastered to his skull, a pistol lying on a flat rock in front of him.

To the south, King had pistol in hand, arm straight down at his side. And in the middle, but not directly between, was Benny Havens, old flintlock in his grip.

"Pick up the pistol and defend yourself with what little honor you have," King called out to Cord.

"Their powder might be wet," Grant observed.

"I wouldn't gamble lives on it," Rumble said.

As suddenly as it had started, the rain ceased. Above the opposite bank of the Hudson, the glow of approaching dawn brightened the sky.

Cord glanced at the pistol and folded his arms across his chest. "I will make amends, but I will not duel."

"Gentlemen," Grant called out. "I suggest we make haste back to the barracks and sort this out later, when cooler heads might prevail."

"This isn't your business, Mister Grant," Havens yelled back.

"Major Delafield has made quite clear his stance on dueling," Grant said. "And the Superintendent is on his way," he reminded them as if mentioning it was no longer raining, a fact they were all aware of.

"Sherman will slow him a little bit," Rumble said as he dismounted. Most likely with some tale of misery and woe that would touch the old man's heart. Sherman could predict darkness on a sun-lit field, but a cloud would invariably show up to prove him right.

"Let's get on with this," King said. "Mister Cord. On the count of three, the duel will begin, whether you have pistol in hand or not."

"Aint that kind of dishonorable?" Cord said.

"One." King was perfectly still.

Rumble started to move forward, but Havens raised his pistol. "Don't be getting involved in something that's not yours to get involved in."

"Lidia is my concern," Rumble said. "And my friends are also my concern. Mister King is a distant cousin and Mister Cord was my roommate."

Cord held up both hands in surrender. "All right. Enough. I apologize."

As they spoke, Grant spurred York, riding him wide to the north to gather speed.

"You owed me an apology," King said, "but you cannot take back what you have done to Miss Lidia. Two."

King raised his pistol, aimed at Cord, and cocked it. He opened his mouth to utter the last number, but galloping full tilt toward Cord's back, Grant jerked back on the reins and York leapt into the air, right over Cord's head and landed with a splash in the mud directly between the two cadets, the massive horse blocking any chance of a shot.

"Move, sir, on your honor, move!" King cried out. "Let me finish the cur."

Two horsemen galloped into the clearing. In the lead, Major Delafield was easily recognizable not just by rank and uniform, but by the carefully shaven fringe of white beard that encircled the lower half of his face. Sherman was behind him.

"Everyone hold fast," Delafield called out. His gaze went from person to person, assessing, judging and deciding.

"Mister King. You are dueling?"

"I am, sir," King said, "and I am not finished."

"With Mister Cord?" Delafield demanded.

"Mister Cord never took up the pistol," Rumble said, walking over to Cord.

Letitia and Lidia appeared on the path from the tavern and that gave Major Delafield pause. "What is the cause of this duel?"

"A moment with my friend, sir, please," Rumble said. He leaned close to Cord. "Is it true, Elijah? About Lidia?"

Cord let out a deep breath, almost causing Rumble to step back from the stink. "If she says she's with child, it's so. She is an honest girl."

"And it is yours."

"I suppose, given nature's realities." Cord turned his bloodshot eyes toward his friend. "I can't be boarded out. I can't go back to Norfolk."

"Always about you," Rumble said angrily. "What about Lidia?"

Cord blinked.

Rumble pressed. "You should have never gone off quarters. And you should've never been with Lidia."

"Should have's serve no purpose now," Cord said, shaking his head and wincing in pain. He peered blearily at Rumble. "What happened to your face? Are you all right?"

"Don't concern yourself with that right now," Rumble said. "We have to get you out of here. And we must uphold Lidia's honor."

Cord closed his eyes in surrender. "I'm sorry, my friend. I've done the deed, I must pay the price. Perhaps Benny will allow the marriage to wait until after I graduate and the Supe will go easy on me."

Rumble knew if the Superintendent found out Cord had lain with Lidia, there would be a storm much greater than the one nature had surrounded them with. Cord was caught between being drummed out of the Corps for being out of quarters or the same fate for being in Lidia's bedroom and transgressing her honor.

Cord's shoulder slumped. "I'm done for. You can have my full dress gray. Split out the rest of my gear as you see fit." He gave a hint of the rakish grin. "Let Old Pete Longstreet have my tar bucket—it won't fit his big head and it will drive him crazy because he won't want to give it to anyone else."

Rumble shifted his focus to the two women standing at the edge of the clearing. Lidia met his gaze. Her eyes flickered momentarily to the wreck of a young man that was Elijah Cord, then locked in on Rumble. One red eyebrow arched in quiet supplication. The movement wasn't lost to Cord either, and the grin was gone.

Rumble turned to Benny Havens. "I am sorry for causing dishonor to your family and am grateful that Mister Cord interceded for my honor. I respectfully request your daughter in betrothal, sir." A vast emptiness opened up inside of Rumble, as wide as the Mississippi and as mysterious and dangerous.

Benny Havens looked as if he'd been slapped. "It was you?" He turned to Lidia. "But you said you lay with Mister Cord."

"She said she lay with a 'him'," Letitia corrected. She nudged her daughter. "Isn't that so, darling?"

Lidia nodded.

Cord put a hand on Rumble's shoulder. "You can't do that. It's my responsibility."

"I certainly can," Rumble said. "And I am."

"I don't—" Cord couldn't form any more words as his brain tumbled in drunken freefall.

Grant dismounted and walked up to Rumble. As if talking to a horse he needed to calm: "Are you insane, Lucius? You'll lose everything."

Rumble nodded. "Exactly. But I will also gain much."

Grant hesitated for the first time all day. "Are you certain?"

"Very much so, Sam." He looked over at Lidia and met her eyes. "A lot of blank pages now to be written."

THE VIGILANCE COMMITTEE

12 September 1840, West Point, New York

THEY CAME IN THE MIDDLE of the night while Cord's roommate, Fred Dent, was on guard duty. An obviously timed frontal assault for cadets skilled in the art of the attack. However, the odds, six to one, were in their favor, so surprise was not high on their tactical agenda.

Elijah Cord was waiting, seated on the edge of his bunk, stripped to the waist and wearing a pair of cast-off pants he'd scavenged from the laundress for just this occasion. The bottle of rum he'd been fortifying himself with was tucked up in the fireplace flue, out of sight.

The six wore their full dress grey uniforms, giving the impression they were on Academy sanctioned business. As they crowded into the room they were taken aback by Cord's informal attire and his readiness for their visit.

Nathaniel Lyon, a First Class Cadet in the class of '41, stepped to the forefront, flanked by the plebe representative of the Vigilance Committee, Simon Bolivar Buckner. The other four stood in the background, arms folded across their chests.

"As the representatives of the Vigilance Committee of the Corps of Cadets," Lyon began, "we demand that you resign from the Academy for actions bringing discredit upon the Corps and conduct unbecoming a gentleman. We demand you tender your resignation immediately."

Buckner placed a piece of parchment down on Cord's desk and pointed at the pen resting in its inkwell. "We've done you the courtesy of already writing it," he said. "Just sign, sir."

Cord slowly got to his feet. It was early September and warm in the room. The academic year was getting into full swing. The barracks was still as death as the members of his company were in their bunks, awake, waiting to hear what would happen. Cord did not move toward the desk.

The seconds ticked by. Lyon glanced over at Buckner. A couple of the second rank figures fidgeted. This was not playing out the way they had anticipated.

"You will not comply?" Lyon asked.

"What exactly have I done that requires your visit?" Cord asked.

"You were absent from your room without permission," Lyon said. "You failed to take responsibility for bringing dishonor on a young woman, and your actions caused Mister King to be discharged from the Academy just a week before his graduation."

"Is it not true that Lucius Rumble, now a private in the Army, resigned to take responsibility for the very event which you now lay at my doorstep?" Cord asked. "Is it not true that Mister King's own action brought about his dismissal?"

"Everyone knows—" Lyon began, but Cord cut him off.

"Everyone knows nothing. Has Lucius Rumble made a claim against me that you're acting on? Has Mister King? I wish to know my accuser."

"Your accuser is the Corps," Lyon said. He took a step closer. "Your options are limited, Mister Cord. Resign."

"I'm afraid I must disappoint you gentlemen," Cord said. "Although I am indeed guilty of several mistakes, I will never resign."

Lyon and Buckner exchanged a glance. Lyon took a few steps forward until he was right next to Cord. He lowered his voice to a harsh whisper. "You bring disgrace on all of us with your lack of honor. Do the right thing."

"You equate right with honor?" Cord asked. He shook his head. "Never."

Lyon stepped back and raised his voice. "Then you must face the wrath of the Corps and experience the 'Silence'. No one will speak to you or acknowledge you. You will not exist."

Cord stood fast as the four cadets in the back row began to remove their full dress coats. Lyon and Buckner stayed back as the four approached, spreading out. Still, Cord made no move to defend himself. When they charged, he stood still, arms down.

The beating was quick and vicious. For half a minute they pummeled, but then the attackers slowed their fists, disconcerted by the lack of defense offered. A blow to the side of the head dropped Cord to his knees, blood pouring from cuts on his face. His lip was split, his nose broken anew. One of the attackers swung his boot, catching Cord in the chest and a rib cracked, causing him to double over in pain.

The four cadets stepped back, fists bruised and covered in Cord's blood, but otherwise unmarked.

Cord slowly straightened, then staggered to his feet. He attempted his trademark smile, causing more blood to flow from his lip. "Is that all you have to offer me?"

"You must resign," Buckner said. "That is unconditional."

"Is it now, Gentlemen?" Everyone turned to the door where Sam Grant stood, wearing dress gray and the white sash of the cadet in charge of quarters. Grant made a show of checking his pocket watch. "Unconditional, Mister Buckner? I do believe there are cadets in this room who are absent quarters after evening reveille."

"Grant," Lyon said, "mind your business. We're the Vigilance Committee."

"This is my business," Grant said. "But I am a lenient man. If you depart now, I won't have to write this up or summon the cadet officer of the day, Cadet Dent. Whose room, I believe, this is."

Lyon pointed at Cord. "He's been 'Silenced'."

"Time's passing," Grant said.

"We should go," Buckner said to Lyon.

"Stand your ground," Lyon ordered the plebe.

"Buckner's giving good advice," Grant said. "I *will* do my duty if you do not retreat."

The six departed with many a glare at both Grant and especially Cord. When it was just the two of them, Cord finally lowered himself onto his bunk with a groan of pain.

"You need to go to the surgeon," Grant said.

Cord shook his head "No. Then the Supe will find out. It's just pain."

"They didn't seem much the worse for the affair," Grant noted. "Except for their fists."

"I didn't fight." Cord was running his fingers over his bloody nose.

"Why not?"

"Because I *was* wrong," Cord said. "But I will not resign."

"Being 'Silenced' by the Corps will be most difficult to bear," Grant said. "No one has survived it for more than six months."

Cord squeezed his fingers on the side of his nose and with a sickening crack it settled back into it's previously offset position. He closed his eyes from the pain and tears rolled down his face. "You won't 'Silence' me, will you, Sam?"

Grant shook his head. "The Vigilance Committee holds no official sway. Most of the Corps, though, will follow their dictum and ignore you for the rest of your tenure here. Three years like that will be a long time."

"I did two years before the mast," Cord said.

"This'll be different, besides longer," Grant said.

"I won't get seasick at least." Cord lay back on his bed with a groan. "Why won't you honor the Silence?"

"It's a false honor they enforce," Grant said. "I was there that morning at Benny Havens. Rumble is content with his new place with Lidia. Happier than I've ever seen him. I don't think you were dishonorable, just drunk and confused."

"And now I'll pay for it," Cord acknowledged. "But I will not resign."

"That kind of spirit is what the Corps needs more of," Grant said.

Cord held out his red-stained hand. "But you will talk to me, won't you, Sam?"

Grant shook the hand. "I don't shed classmates so easily. I don't think that is honorable."

A NEW YEAR; A NEW LIFE

1 January 1841, West Point, New York

WINTER GREETED THE FIRST DAY of 1841 by howling off the Hudson River and screaming among the leafless trees on the high bluffs. Inside the Academy stable, three cadets, bundled against the cold, fumbled with frozen fingers to gear up their horses. York was still the pride of the stables and Grant still the only one to master the Hell Beast. In adjoining stalls, Elijah Cord and Pete Longstreet worked on preparing more amendable mounts in complete silence.

Sam had been born Hiram Ulysses Grant, but was now stuck with Ulysses S. Grant. The congressman from Ohio who had given Grant his appointment to West Point had gotten the name wrong on the paperwork he sent the

Academy. In the military once a piece of paper changes your name, the name is changed. So it was written and so it would be, despite all Grant's efforts to right the mistake.

Grant and Longstreet had the Superintendent's blessings to depart post on this particular day and for this particular mission. Cord, as always, was on restriction, but for the first time since the incident at Benny Havens half a year ago, he was going to break the rules once more. The months since his beating and Silencing by the Corps had been sufficient time for his wounds to heal and for the effect of the Silence to settle in. As his body grew stronger, his spirit grew weaker.

Everything took twice as long in the cold and the cadets were focused on their tasks until all three horses were ready. Grant led the way to the stable doors, where the Master of the Horse, Sergeant Herschberger, hastened to open the gate, holding it against the wind, then slamming it shut as they rode into the darkness. They were three ghosts in long gray overcoats, forage caps, and mufflers wrapped around their faces.

"Taking the road this time, Sam?" Cord asked as they trotted out the Academy's south gate, no sentry posted in such severe weather to challenge him.

"We take the road." Grant's words were grabbed by the wind and dispersed into the surrounding woods.

Leaning forward, the three made their way through the thin layer of snow on the ground until they reached the turn for the switchback to the river and Benny Havens' tavern. As they slipped below the crest of the highlands, the wind was less severe and more amendable to conversation. Cord had little experience at discourse lately, but Longstreet could not bear the lack of conversation any longer. "Sam. Excited about your summer furlough?"

Grant glanced over his shoulder with a wry grin. Only Old Pete would be asking about the summer furlough coming in five months whilst in the midst of a snowstorm and on the eve of such an important event. After two years at the Academy it would be the first time Cord and Grant would be allowed to depart for an extended period of time. Longstreet, a year ahead, had gone on furlough the previous summer.

"I'll be going home," Grant said. "It should be pleasant enough."

"Such excitement and anticipation," Longstreet said dryly.

"It's a ways off," Grant said, his focus on the road ahead.

Longstreet turned in the saddle toward Cord, the question forming, then he paused as he remembered the Silence. Torn between the informal injunction and his desire for conversation, the latter finally won.

"What about you, Elijah?" Longstreet asked. "Going back to Norfolk? I thought you never wanted to return there?"

Cord stiffened in the saddle, in no mood for idle chatter this evening, especially not on this topic, but appreciating the gesture on Longstreet's part. "I don't want to. But there's something I must do in Virginia, so I might as well swing by my home also."

That caused Grant to look over his shoulder. "What do you have to do in Virginia?"

Cord pulled back on the reins. "Try to partially repay a debt."

"It's to Lucius Rumble you owe a great debt," Grant said in a level tone.

"I know, and this touches on that," Cord said. "I talked briefly with Rumble and he's received news from George King. He's in need of some assistance."

"What can you do for him?" Longstreet asked.

"I've made arrangements to visit Major Robert Lee on my way back to Norfolk," Cord said. "He has connections to my family in business via one of his relatives. I will plead with the Major to help Mister King get into the Navy midshipman program."

"You think that makes what you did acceptable?" Longstreet said in a tone as harsh as the wind. "And what of Lucius?"

"Lucius is content," Cord protested weakly.

"You aren't Lucius," Longstreet said. He shook his head in disgust and moved into the blowing snow.

They were halfway to the river when there came the howling of wolves, louder than the wind. Grant pulled up, Longstreet and Cord behind.

"They're right in front," Grant said.

Cord slid a hand inside his long overcoat. All he had was the whalebone knife stuck in his belt, but it was better than nothing.

Longstreet spurred forward. The others hesitated, then reluctantly followed.

"How many do you think there are?" Longstreet asked, as if discussing a matter of no consequence.

"Perhaps twenty," Grant offered.

"Care to wager on the number?" Longstreet asked. The howling was louder, closer.

"I suppose no one thought to arm themselves with a pistol?" Grant asked.

"We're going to a lying in, not a hunt," Longstreet said. He was still moving forward and Grant, being Grant, was right at his side. "A wager?" Longstreet was nothing, if not persistent.

"How many say you?" Grant asked.

They hit a place where the road switch-backed and Longstreet pointed. Two gaunt wolves sat on their haunches near the side of the road, gleaming eyes peering at the travelers for a few moments, before they bounded off into the woods.

"There are your twenty, Sam," Longstreet said. "There are always more of them before they are counted. Their noise is much greater than their true strength."

Cord halted his horse as they reached the edge of the wood-line just above the tavern. "I'll wait here as I have not been invited."

"A prudent move," Longstreet said dryly. He moved forward.

Grant edged York close to Cord. "I'll step outside and give you a signal when all goes well."

"And if it doesn't go well?" Cord asked.

"Now you sound like Cump," Grant said. He slapped a mittened hand on Cord's shoulder. "It'll be fine." He reached into his coat and pulled out a cigar. "Here."

"A bit premature, don't you think?" But Cord accepted it.

The wind slicing off the ice-cluttered Hudson battered, but could not penetrate, the log cabin Rumble had built in the woods behind Benny Havens tavern. It was solidly constructed, no chink left unfilled between logs, and the fire was built up, bathing the interior with warmth. A large black kettle hung over the flames. A thick curtain separated the single room. On one side was a plank table at which Lucius Rumble and Benny Havens sat. On the opposite side of the curtain was the bed in which Lidia was preparing to give birth. Letitia was assisting the West Point Post Surgeon, sent on order from Major Delafield to attend to Lidia.

Lucius Kosciusko Rumble was from just south of Natchez, the wealthiest city in the United States. Cotton was king and Natchez funneled the cotton onto the Mississippi River. Rumble was the eldest scion of the family that owned Palatine, a rambling plantation along the eastern bank of that mighty river, extending miles inland. His middle name had caused him considerable grief his plebe year as Thaddeus Kosciuszko, a Polish officer, had designed the original fortifications at West Point during the Revolution and was revered in Academy lore.

Rumble had gained the Polish officer's last name third-hand from a town that had taken it incorrectly second-hand. His mother had been pregnant and on her way back to Palatine from her family's home in Clarksville, Tennessee, when biological necessity had caused her to stop in a small Mississippi town short of home: Kosciusko. Out of gratitude for the kindness shown her during her labor, she'd given her newborn son the town's name in between the last name forced on by family and the first name forced on by spouse. She could not have known the misspelling by the founders of the town would cause her son to be hazed twenty years later. All for lack of a Z.

There was a knock on the wood door. Rumble hastened to the door and held it against the wind as Sam Grant and Pete Longstreet slipped inside, stomping to get the snow off their boots. He slammed the door shut and secured it.

Grant smiled as he pulled off his long gray overcoat. "Corporal Rumble."

"Cadet Grant." They clasped hands, neither withdrawing the grip for long seconds. Then Rumble greeted Longstreet, warmed as much by their presence as by the fire. He asked them to join him at the table.

Grant nodded toward the curtain. "How goes the campaign?"

Rumble grimaced as they all sat down. "Fraught with peril. The Surgeon says her carriage isn't the most felicitous for birth."

Benny Havens poured generous portions of rum into mugs and shoved them around the table. He had his own halfway to his mouth when there was a cry of pain from the other side of the curtain. He downed the entire cup. Rumble idly picked his up, but his focus was on the curtain and the cup remained in his hand. His other hand rubbed the scar over his right eye.

Grant demurred, waving his hand at the cup as if it were about to attack him. "I have never partaken of spirits. It has a bad history in my family."

Longstreet finished his off in one long gulp and slammed it down. He turned to Grant. "Don't be such a stick in the mud, Sam."

Reluctantly, Grant picked up the mug and took a sip.

The cry from beyond the curtain was not repeated and there was the murmur of voices: the post Surgeon, Letitia, and occasionally Lidia's weaker, anguished whisper. None of the words could be understood so the men had to wait in ignorance.

"I remember when Letitia had Lidia," Havens said, a slight slur indicating he had been at the jug for a while. "Damn mid-wife said same thing about Letitia. They always warn, try to get you to think the worst so you'll feel better when all goes well. They distribute warnings like I do rum. Don't you fret. Lidia will be fine. She's made of fine stuff." He slapped his belly to emphasize the point.

Rumble was not consoled. He got up and began to pace back and forth in front of the curtain.

Grant rubbed the edge of the mug, and like the tactician he was, tried a diversion. "Lucius, you'd have enjoyed the lecture old Pete had to give the other day. The military science instructor caught him sleeping. No one could miss that snoring."

Rumble tore his eyes away from the curtain, allowing his friend the weak attempt at a flanking movement. "What did he have you speak on?" he asked Longstreet.

"First," Longstreet said, holding out his mug to Havens for more rum, "I was not sleeping. I was merely resting my body while my brain was engaged deep in thought about the subject matter at hand."

"Which was?" Rumble asked, playing along.

"The strategy of war," Longstreet said. "The old Clausewitz thing. Hannibal, Cannae."

Rumble shook his head. "The battle of annihilation is a thing of the past."

"It's the strategy being taught," Grant noted mildly. "Army on army until one prevails. That is war, or so the 'experts' say. Who are we to disagree with the masters like Clausewitz?"

"How come no one ever mentions that despite killing fifty-thousand Romans at Cannae and obliterating their army, Hannibal never defeated them?" Rumble asked. "And he eventually lost the war and Carthage was no more? Strategy is not about destroying the other's army."

"What is it then?" Longstreet challenged. He punched Grant lightly on the shoulder. "If we're going to argue, you might as well drink."

Grant took a deeper draft from his mug.

"You must destroy their will to fight," Rumble said. He looked to Grant. "Correct, Sam?"

Grant inclined his head, his eyes slightly unfocused. "You might well be right."

"I don't think he is," Longstreet said. "Rome should have surrendered after Cannae. The Romans were insane not to."

That got Grant's attention. He drained his mug and held it out to Havens for a refill. "But the fact is, the Romans did not surrender. I think when engaged in war, sanity is lost pretty early. Would you surrender, Pete, if you suffered a serious defeat?"

Longstreet stared into his mug as if the answer were in there, but said nothing.

Rumble leaned over the table toward Grant, almost knocking over the freshly filled mug in front of his friend. "Do you want to know something, Sam, since we're speaking of Rome?"

Grant nodded and took a drink. There was another short cry of pain from beyond the curtain. Longstreet and Havens looked in that direction, but Grant kept his eyes on Rumble.

Rumble spoke in a low voice. "My father's name is Tiberius. His grandfather named his plantation, Palatine, after the tallest of the seven hills of ancient Rome and began the tradition of Roman names in the family. Ostentatious don't you think? My father named me Lucius. And my younger brother Seneca. He'd have renamed my mother something awful, like Servilia, if she'd have allowed him."

"Why your family's fascination with Rome?" Grant asked.

"It's a way for us to feel we're more important than we are and that things are grander than they are."

"But aren't things rather grand at Palatine?" Grant asked over the lip of his mug.

"They appear to be," Rumble said, "but appearances can be deceiving."

"And if it is a son?" Grant asked, draining the mug. "What name will you give him?"

"If I have a son, I will name him Ben Agrippa Rumble."

Grant frowned. "But why the odd middle name? It sounds as if you don't fancy your family's habit of Roman names."

Around the table, the others were following the conversation.

Rumble shook his head, his dark eyes seeming to withdraw deeper into whatever pit consumed his past. "I'm not doing it for my father, I'm doing it because of my father. I had a friend on the plantation, a dear friend, who was named Agrippa. He—" Rumble paused—then continued: "died. But he had also saved my life years before that. I'm doing it in his honor."

"You never wanted to go back to Palatine," Grant said with a slight slur, finally understanding. "That's partly why you—" he paused, glancing at the others, and abruptly switched the topic back. "And if it's a girl?"

Rumble almost smiled, shaking off memories. "I wouldn't saddle a young girl with a Roman name. I think—" he was interrupted as Letitia came hustling from behind the curtain, to the black kettle over the fireplace, and dipped the ladle into the boiling water. She didn't spare the men a glance. As soon as the small pot she carried was full, she disappeared back behind the curtain.

The men could hear heavy, pained breathing. In the half year since he'd been forced to resign his cadetship because of the incident at Benny Havens, Rumble had worked in the stables, accepting the Superintendent's gracious offer to remain at the Academy as an enlisted man while Lidia grew with child.

He'd seen Cord only occasionally at the riding hall when the cadets were doing cavalry training and the two had not had a chance to exchange many words, not that there seemed much need to. The deeds were done all around and now it was all playing out.

The sound of deep and ragged breathing continued, each man at the table remaining still, as if hypnotized. Grant turned to Rumble to speak, but then stopped as he peered at his distraught friend. Rumble could take it no longer and abruptly jumped to his feet. He grabbed his overcoat and stomped into the snowy night, embracing the blast of cold wind on his face. He felt the wetness on his cheeks and reached to brush away the snow, and then realized tears were mixed with the snow.

Rumble looked up into the sky. The storm was tapering off. There was a small hole in the clouds and he saw a single star. "Let this page be a good one," he whispered. As he lowered his gaze he saw a small glow in the forest above the tavern. A taut figure was standing there smoking and Rumble stiffened as he recognized his former classmate. He was about to call out when the door swung open behind him and light spilled out of the cabin.

The Surgeon held up a hand and beckoned. "Come in and meet your son, Corporal Rumble."

Rushing into the cabin, Rumble almost knocked the Surgeon over. Grant and Longstreet were waiting for him and followed as Rumble darted behind the curtain where Benny and Letitia Havens hovered on one side of the bed. Lidia was luminous, glowing with pride and happiness. There was a bundle on her chest, making little mewling noises, and all that was visible were the tiniest of hands, reaching as if they could pluck something out of the air.

Rumble went to the side of the bed and slid his pinkie inside the slightly curled fingers of the child. He looked at Lidia and smiled. "Welcome to the world, Ben Agrippa Rumble."

Cord started forward when the door opened, but then recognized Rumble's form. Cord remained still, the cigar clutched in his hand. He saw Rumble look in his direction, but the door opened once more and the Surgeon gestured Rumble back inside.

The howl of a wolf was somewhere to Cord's left. He'd welcome the beast right now. Have it leap, tear into his flesh, devour him, take away the hole in his chest as he looked down at the log cabin and the bright glow from the small windows, openings into a world where things were safe and cordial.

He could not blame Longstreet or the others for the way they treated him. The entire Corps had an idea of what had happened. There was no such thing as a secret, especially one involving Benny Havens and his tavern. No one would ever speak of it openly, but the whispers were always there and the Vigilance Committee had issued its decree and the Silence.

Cord had excuses for last summer: he'd been drunk; he'd been tired; he'd been confused; he'd been surprised—four points of a compass framing a hurricane around his life. But in the center, in the eye of the hurricane, where there was stillness, it was the void inside of him that had caused this.

Cord looked up. "All right, God. You kept George King from shooting. Maybe I did a wrong thing that day. And three months before that day. But don't take it out on the child, please. I can bear any further wrath you wish to bring down on me, just spare the child."

Hooves clattered on the frozen ground above. Cord stepped off the path. The storm had dispersed and the night was colder. A slight tinge of dawn showed to the east across the Hudson and a few more stars glittered among breaks in the clouds.

A thickset rider swathed in a heavy black cloak and sporting a brown slouch hat came ambling down the path. The man had a wide black sash tied around his waist. Not a cadet. Cord reached under his long overcoat and grabbed the handle of his whalebone knife. He drew it and hid the blade up his left sleeve.

The way the man rode indicated he'd never fallen under the verbal lash of Master of the Horse Herschberger's commands on how to be one with the horse. The wolf howled again and the rider paused, hand snaking inside the sash and coming out with a large revolver in his meaty paw.

Cord stepped out of the darker shadow of the trees. "The wolf won't attack."

The hand, with gun, swung around and Cord was faced with not one barrel, but two, a smaller one on top of a larger. Cord held his hands away from his sides. "No harm, my friend, no harm."

The stranger said nothing for several moments and the barrels didn't waver, pointed right at Cord's heart. "Who you be, boy, and what you be doing skunking about in the dark?" The voice was deep southern, Alabama or Mississippi, and one used to issuing orders.

Cord took an instant dislike to the voice and the speaker, because there was also something in the tone that reminded him of his father. "Who the hell are you? And lower that gun."

The gun didn't move. "I got the advantage on you, boy, so you do the answering."

"Elijah Cord, third classman, United States Corps of Cadets."

"Third class, eh? What that make you? Some kind of servant?"

"It means I'm in my second year at the Academy." Cord wished he hadn't answered as soon as the words left his mouth.

The gun slowly lowered, but the stranger didn't put it back under the sash. "So down there be this Havens Tavern, aint it? I hear tell you keydets cluster there like bees 'round honey."

Cord bristled at the mis-pronunciation. He took a step forward. The man was built like a tree trunk: solid torso, solid arms and legs. No hair poked out from under the slouch hat. His face was broad, burned brown from the sun, strange to see during winter in New York, and the eyes were like dark stones, set wide apart by a nose that had been broken badly and never set. He sat on the horse like a barrel on a plank, no love lost going either way. And for some reason he couldn't pin down, Cord had no desire to point the man in the direction of Benny Havens or any other place else for that matter.

"I think you're lost," Cord said.

"I don't never get lost." The man looked past Cord. "That it down there aint it? The big building? And the little one behind it? Who live there?"

"A man."

"What this man's name?"

"What's your name?"

A smile that didn't reach the eyes crossed the man's face. "St. George Dyer. I been traveling a long way, and waiting about here a while longer, to deliver a message. Saw that army doctor fellow head down a while ago, so I figure today's the day to do that."

"Who's the message for?" Cord asked.

"A former one of you keydets. I got a message for young Lucius Rumble, from his father, Master Tiberius Rumble."

Like George King, Rumble had been disowned by his father; every cadet had heard the story. As soon as word of the marriage to Lidia and his dismissal from the Corps had reached Mississippi, a letter had come back to West Point stating Tiberius's position in no uncertain terms. That had not helped Cord's status with many in the Corps and the Silence had tightened down further.

"I can give him the message," Cord lied.

St. George looked past Cord to the cabin. "Maybe you can, boy, but when Master Tiberius wants something done, it get done right. Damn fool boy got hisself married. Now she squirting out a young 'un. Been waiting round here two weeks for tonight. I don' like waiting." The man tapped the double muzzles of the pistol idly on the pommel of his saddle, deep in whatever passed for thought in his brain. "You suppose it possible he leave that poor tavern wench he married and come home and marry who he supposed to, when he was supposed to?"

"And who is that?"

"So young Rumble aint said nothing 'bout that. Damn fool he be." The sly grin crossed St. George's face. "But that boy always did like his secrets."

When the men were forced to retreat behind the curtain under Surgeon's remonstration, they were a much lighter lot than had sat there prior. Benny headed directly for the jug. Rumble stopped Grant and put both hands on his friend's shoulders. "I want you to be his godfather."

Grant blinked, trying to think, the slur more pronounced. "But what about Cord?"

"What about him?"

"Shouldn't he have a role?"

"He had one," Rumble snapped. "He let it go. I saw him out there earlier. In the trees. I want you to always be a part of Ben. If not for you, I would not be here. And there is no house, no palace, no spot on this world I would rather be than here."

Grant bowed his head, unprecedented tears in his eyes. "I would be honored to be Ben's godfather." He put a heavy hand on Rumble's shoulder and leaned close. "Do you want me to fetch Cord?" When Rumble didn't answer, Grant backed the question down a notch. "At least let him know all went well?"

Rumble bit his lip, then gave a very slight nod.

Havens held out a mug for Rumble, having already given one to Longstreet. "Cord should keep away. He has little honor, like Mister King told 'im."

Grant buttoned his long overcoat incorrectly; one button off, but no one mentioned it. "Now, now. Cord is a good man deep in his heart." Grant tapped his chest. Rumble and Longstreet exchanged a confused glance as Grant continued his slurred ramble. "He's just not a responsible man. He's like a wide, but shallow river. Sparkling in the sunlight and pleasing to the eye, but with little substance at first glance. But a shallow river can grow deep with time. He has courage, I've seen that. Remember, who knows where we'll all be in twenty years time and who we will be?"

"Getting sentimental on us, Sam?" Longstreet asked.

"Phew," Havens snorted, blowing the topic out of the room like stale cigar smoke.

"Enough stalling," St. George said, pulling up the reins and making to move past. "I got a job to do."

"Rumble won't leave her," Cord said.

St. George gave a sly grin. "If she dead, then it be real easy for him to leave."

"Is that a threat?"

"It a thought."

"Rumble will never leave her."

"I'll be hearing all this from young Rumble's own lips, so the Master knows I heard it first-hand-like."

"And you won't get close to her," Cord added.

"Out of my way, boy." But St. George paused, peering past.

Cord looked over his shoulder. Grant's slight, stooped figure was on the threshold, backlit by the light from inside. Grant brought a cigar out of a pocket and lit it on the second attempt. A wave of relief washed over Cord.

The baby gave a cry and Rumble picked Ben up, after giving Lidia a kiss on the forehead. "I love you," he said to her.

Lidia nodded, her red curls plastered to her scalp, wet with sweat. "I love you and he is ours."

"He is ours," Rumble agreed, holding the baby as if he was the greatest and most fragile treasure a man had ever found. "Our son."

Lidia closed her eyes, spent.

Rumble carried the child around the curtain, closer to the roaring fire. Through the open door, he could see Grant, cigar in hand, leaning against the log wall for support. Rumble held Ben up over his head, as if offering him to the Gods, marveling at the lightness of new life.

"Ben Rumble," he whispered to himself.

And little Ben let out a piercing cry.

St. George started to ride around Cord.

"I won't let you pass," Cord declared with such certainty that St. George swung the gun toward him. Cord's hand was on the hilt of his knife.

"You willing to die, boy, to try to stop me?"

Cord held the knife in a tight grip, blade glinting in the moonlight, and readied for combat. "Yes."

"Now why that be?" St. George said. "Young Rumble that good a friend of yours?"

"You cannot pass."

St. George pointed those large barrels at Cord. "Then you gonna die." With a loud click, St. George pulled back the hammer.

A baby's cry echoed up the slope.

"So it's done," St. George said. "The child made it. I was hoping she might die, pushing the thing out." St. George pondered the situation. "Can't be killing a wife and a child. At least not tonight. Better for me he not come back anyway." He gently lowered the hammer back in place and tucked the pistol inside his black sash. "I got my answer, boy, and so does Master Tiberius."

St. George pulled the reins, lumbered the horse around, and disappeared up the trail. With a shaking hand, Cord put his knife back in its leather sheath and wrapped the long overcoat tighter around his body. He looked down at the cabin, knowing it was warm inside and that Rumble, Grant, Longstreet, and Benny Havens were celebrating the birth. The concept that he had a son washed over him like a rogue wave, staggering him with its immensity.

"Easy, sir."

Cord spun around, grasping for the knife once more.

"Easy, now, sir." The voice was soft, in tone like Grant's when he was with horses, except it was deep south, similar to St. George's. But different.

Cord peered into the darkness. "Whoever you are, let me see you." He had the knife at the ready, the leather wrapping around the bone handle tight in his grip.

A giant stepped out of the woods. At least six and a half feet tall, the man was dressed in a ragged collage of blankets tied around his body with ropes. His skin was as black as the night had been during the storm. His bald scalp gleamed in the faint starlight. On the right side of his face, scars were scrolled, testament to some wicked event in the past.

"My name be Samual, sir," he said.

"Are you with St. George?"

"I been following him, sir. For a long time. For a long way. From Mississippi. Been hiding out here in woods for near on two week. Waiting while he wait in town." Samual grinned, revealing startlingly white and smooth teeth. "He think he smart. He's not. But he mean. Mean as any snake in da swamp. You need remember that, sir. He meaner than that wolf howling 'bout earlier."

"You're from Palatine?" Cord asked.

Samual nodded. "I be, sir. I be sent by Mistress Violet, Mister Rumble's mother to follow." He reached inside the collage of blankets and pulled out a worn leather Bible. "If you pardon me, I don' know how you Yankees stand the cold, sir." He opened the Bible and carefully retrieved a letter. "You please give to Mister Rumble in a few months. When the weather be warmer. When it good to travel and the baby I jus' heard be older." He shook his head. "Weren't hard to follow a fella when you know where he be going."

"You know Lucius Rumble?"

"I know'd him all his life until he left for here, sir." Samual turned to go, then stopped. "Sir, might I ask you name? So I can tell Mistress Violet when I gets back who I gave letter to."

"Elijah Cord."

"Thank you, sir." Samual paused. "This be dangerous, sir. As da good book say: 'And if any mischief follow, then thou shalt give life for life. Eye for eye, tooth for tooth, hand for hand, foot for foot, burning for burning, wound for wound, stripe for stripe.'"

A chill ran down Cord's spine, stronger than the cold wind off the Hudson. "What do you mean?"

"Bad times be coming, master, real bad times, and we all best be prepared to pay what the Good Lord will extract from us."

Cord put the knife away and took the proffered letter. Before he could speak, Samual was gone, back into the darkness of the forest just as the first direct rays of sunlight slid above the eastern horizon and struck West Point.

Benny Havens held out two full mugs, one to an obviously inebriated Grant, the other to Rumble, who had Ben tucked in one powerful arm.

"Perhaps not for Sam," Longstreet said, gently removing the mug from Grant's hand, replacing it with a cup of water, and taking the mug for himself

"To my grandson, Ben Agrippa Rumble," Benny Havens toasted.

"To Ben Agrippa Rumble," they replied.

It was a day of firsts: Lucius Kosciusko Rumble had his first taste of contentment, Ulysses S. Grant had his first taste of alcohol and Ben Agrippa Rumble entered the world.

GRANT AND LEE

June 1841, West Point, New York

CIVILIAN CLOTHES FELT STRANGE to Cord after two years in uniform. They were also too tight. He'd worn them as a boy on the journey from Norfolk two years ago and now he was wearing them on the return as a man. The top few buttons on his shirt had ripped away after he put it on and reached for something, so it was open halfway down his chest. He had no money to buy a new outfit; Old Pete Longstreet and his constant series of late night barrack card games had seen to that. They might not talk to him, but they'd take his money at cards.

Cord stuffed a few toilet articles in a sack and that was the sum total of his existence outside of what the Academy had given him and the whalebone knife, which occupied its usual position in the center of his back, covered by the tail of his shirt.

And the letter he'd been given months ago by Samual. That had weighed heavy over the months intervening. There had been times Cord had dangled it over the small fire in his room, but he always stopped.

June exams were over—Cord had passed all courses, barely—and now the cadets in the class of 1843 were free until the 28th of August. Summer furlough between the second and third years at the Academy was the highlight of most cadets' time at West Point, being a time when they didn't have to be at West Point. Finishing their Yearling year, cadets went home and came back to be called Cows, due to the additional weight most gained away from the meager fare of the cadet dining hall and the strictness of the training regime.

Cord left his room and met Sam Grant, also in mufti, in the hallway of the barracks. Grant held a small haversack containing all his non-military clothing and gear. Unlike Cord, Grant had not put on weight, although like him, Grant had gained his adult height. Over the course of two years Grant had grown six inches, but still remained a paltry one hundred and twenty pounds.

"Looking very civilian," Cord said to Grant. "To Ohio?"

Grant was enthused. "Yes. I'll be there in a few days." He slapped Cord on the back. "Be careful you don't split those britches."

"I'm moving slowly for just that reason. Already ruined the shirt."

Grant looked at the damage. "What's that?" The edge of a black scroll was visible etched into the skin on Cord's chest.

Cord grabbed the left side of his shirt, covering the tattoo. "Something I got at sea in memory of my mother. You know how the Supe feels about inking the skin."

Grant sighed, looking back into his room, like an inmate let out for a little exercise but knowing he's going to be locked up again. "I feel like I've been here forever. Gray, gray, gray. Buildings, uniforms, mood."

"I don't mind the gray," Cord said. "Better than being on some ship. I just thought some things would be different coming here."

"Different how?" Grant asked.

"I don't know," Cord said. "Why'd you come to West Point?" he suddenly asked Grant.

Grant laughed bitterly. "I didn't want to. My father arranged my appointment without consulting me. When the appointment was a given, I was informed and told in no uncertain terms that I would be going to the Academy."

"Why'd your father want you to come here?" Cord pressed.

"My father is very conscious of pecuniary matters. It pleases him to no end that I am receiving my higher education on the government's teat. He also told me that he sensed I had little skill in the world of business."

"So you are at odds with your father," Cord said.

"No." Grant shrugged. "One has to trust family. He has my best interests at heart. It's what a father does." Grant hefted his haversack over his shoulder. "Why'd you come here?"

"To escape."

"From your home?"

"My journey here is the opposite of yours. I wrangled my appointment from an uncle on my mother's side of the family who has political connections. I informed my father after it was a given."

"His reaction?"

"He was probably as pleased to hear of my appointment as you were to be informed of yours."

"And now we both go back," Grant observed as they walked out of the barracks together, mingling with other former Yearlings. They were heading for South Dock to catch the ferry to New York City, where they would scatter across the country for their few months of freedom. It was a pleasant, early summer day. The trees were green, the sky was blue and one could almost forget the misery of the dark winter and shake off the gray stone on the buildings.

Grant stopped to shake hands with Pete Longstreet. Old Pete, entering his senior year, a Firstie, was assigned to the cadre that would whip the new plebes into shape. Longstreet looked imposing in his dress uniform and crossed white belts, his brass breastplate reflecting the sun, a saber strapped to his waist. The day after the Yearlings went on leave, a group of frightened, boys about to become men would come marching up this same road and cower before upperclassmen like Longstreet. No West Pointer ever forgot their Reception Day.

"Enjoy yourself, Sam," Longstreet said, ignoring Cord. "You'll be back here to our rock-bound highland home all too soon. I remember my furlough went by like a flash."

"That's cheery," Grant said. "You sound like Cump."

Longstreet laughed. "I'll lay you odds, three to one, you'll have the fastest few months of your life."

"I'll never take a wager against you," Grant said.

"A man has to gamble every once in a while," Longstreet said.

"Only when the odds are in his favor," Grant said.

"That's not a true wager," Longstreet said, "and cautious."

"Prudent." Grant reached out, finger stopping a quarter inch from Longstreet's highly shined breastplate.

Longstreet stood his ground. "That took over an hour to prepare."

Grant pulled his hand back. "Don't be too hard on the Plebes. Remember what it was like."

Longstreet slapped the hilt of his sword. "I'll have them whipped into shape by the time you get back, count on it."

Cord was invisible. The isolation of the Silence had descended around him with the tacit acceptance of most cadets. A few, like Grant, acted as if nothing were different. Most didn't care but abided by the tradition. And a handful were outright hostile as if Cord had insulted them personally in some manner.

For a moment Longstreet grew serious. "There are strange winds brewing, Sam. President Harrison dying is an ill omen. When you return, you must tell me how people are responding. We're in our own little world here. And it's certainly not the real one. Harrison was from Ohio and you'll find out how the people there feel. The letters I receive from my kin in Georgia are disturbing."

Just a few months ago, in March, newly elected President William Henry Harrison, an old army man and hero of the Battle of Tippecanoe, had spoken too long at his inauguration, a cold and rainy day in Washington. He'd taken ill and died, an unprecedented event for the young country. The government had been thrown into upheaval as the constitutional rules of succession were found to be lacking. John Tyler, the Vice President, had eventually been sworn into office as President with all powers despite debates whether he should be acting President or true President. Of more importance, Harrison's antipathy toward expanding slavery westward, and particularly the issue of Texas, had been reversed.

Thus the potential annexation of Texas was now an issue all cadets were following closely, because Mexico still claimed the territory as part of its sovereign nation. The Mexican government had promised war if annexation happened and there was no reason to believe they would not follow through on their threat. They had given Texas a great deal of autonomy after the Battle of San Jacinto, but took the stance that the treaty the defeated Santa Anna had signed was not legitimate as the general did not have the authority to negotiate for all of Mexico. While Texans claimed independence, the reality was much murkier. France, Britain and the United States had recognized Texas as a nation, but, so far, no one had pushed the issue. Mexico claimed a good portion of the western part of the continent, from Texas, up along the Rocky Mountains and to the Pacific Ocean.

"It's a mess," Grant said. "I fear a storm brewing that will lead to worse things."

Longstreet smiled. "Now you sound like Cump. Always the worst coming."

Grant nodded. "Cump always seemed to end up being right."

"Forget I asked," Longstreet said, with a sidelong glance at Cord. "Enjoy your furlough. Both of you," he added with a slight nod toward Cord, a thawing of the Silence.

They took their leave and continued on the road.

"I must stop briefly at Benny Havens," Cord said, the letter in his breast pocket a burden he needed to be relieved of.

Grant shook his head. "They have a bar on the steamer."

"Not for that," Cord said. "I have to leave something there with Benny."

Grant shrugged. "If you must, you must."

That plan was interrupted when, just before they reached the cut off to the tavern, they spotted Rumble and Lidia strolling up it, each holding the handle of a baby basket with Ben inside. Cord fought his instinct to head in the opposite direction.

Over the past year, Rumble had grown more popular with the Corps than when he had been a cadet. Young Ben was the darling of the cadets and many stopped by the small log cabin on their way in or out of Benny Havens to see the child and visit with Rumble and his wife. Teaching riding fit Rumble and he appeared happy. As much as Cord had been pushed away by the Corps, Rumble and his family had been brought into its bosom.

"Corporal and Mrs. Rumble," Grant said, with a tip of an imaginary cap.

"Sam, almost didn't recognize you out of the gray." Rumble touched a finger to his forehead, a ghost of a salute. He looked at Cord. "Elijah."

"Lucius, Lidia," Cord said, shifting his feet uneasily. He had not been back to Benny Havens or talked to Lidia since that fateful morning.

"Off for furlough, eh?" Rumble said.

All Cord could see was the baby in the basket. Pale blue eyes stared back at him with curiosity. Lidia snatched the other handle from Rumble's hand and turned away from Cord. "Let us be on," she said to her husband.

Rumble gently put his hand on her shoulder. "Have an enjoyable furlough," he said to the two cadets. "I'm glad not to go home."

"Your home is here," Grant allowed. "But your family, the rest of your family, is in Mississippi. Even though you might not want to have anything to do with them, you should think of Ben and his future."

"That's what I'm doing," Rumble said.

Grant shrugged. "One needs all the family they can possibly have. I imagine your parents might view their grandson, and perhaps you, in a different light now."

"Perhaps," Rumble allowed.

Grant leaned forward and surprisingly gave Lidia a peck on the cheek. "Take care of my God-son." Then he headed toward the ferry, leaving Cord facing Rumble. Lidia was still turned away from both of them, the baby-basket gripped tight in her hands.

"What do you want?" Rumble demanded.

"We need to speak," Cord said.

"The time for that is past."

"There is something—" Cord began, but he halted.

Rumble rubbed the scar over his right eye without realizing it. "What?"

"The night—the night Ben was born. You know I was in the woods above the tavern."

"I do."

"A rider came down the road. He was bringing you a message. From Palatine."

Rumble stiffened. "Who was it?"

"He called himself St. George Dyer."

Rumble took his hand off Lidia's shoulder. "Wait for me over by the stone wall, my dear." His voice was hard, brooking no protest, something Lidia had not heard before. She walked away with Ben and sat down on the wall, out of earshot, but watching anxiously.

"Why are you only telling me this now?" Rumble demanded.

"I'll get to that," Cord said.

"You'll 'get to that'?" Rumble folded his arms across his chest. "What was the message?"

"He said his master, your father, Tiberius, would welcome you home if you left Lidia."

"And?"

"And then he heard Ben's birth cry. And he said he had his answer."

"What did you say?" Rumble asked.

"I told him you would never leave Lidia. That was before he heard the cry and--" Cord sputtered to a halt.

Rumble's eyes had a distant look. "Tiberius would do that. My life was his plan. He thinks everything and everyone is his to plan. And then I broke his plan; failed in my duty to Palatine. And he would send St. George, of all people, with the message. It would be like sending Hannibal to Scipio Africanus to discuss peace between Carthage and Rome. My mother must have forced him to make a gesture. But gestures are all my father is good for."

"Did I do wrong?" Cord asked.

"When?" Rumble snapped. "No. You answered truthfully. I will never leave Lidia or Ben."

"Someone else was there that night. Came up to me after St. George rode off. Do you know a large Negro named Samual?"

Rumble stiffened. "Yes. He was with St. George?"

"No. He said he secretly followed St. George here."

"Then my mother sent him without my father's knowledge. What did Samual want?"

"He gave me a letter." Cord reached into his shirt for it. "He told me not to give it to you for some months, to wait until the weather got warmer," he hastily explained as he handed it over and noted the look of anger that flashed across Rumble's face.

"Then you did as you were told," Rumble allowed. "Samual is always very exact in following instructions. He's a good man." Rumble ripped open the envelope and pulled out a piece of rose-colored stationery. "As expected, from my mother. She knew my father was sending St. George and that I would never listen to him. So she sent Samual with this." His eyes were racing back and forth as he took in the lines written in his mother's flowing script. "She asks me to visit this summer. She says that there are things that must be talked about. That my father is ill." Rumble sighed deeply as he folded the letter and slid it into his uniform breast pocket. He glanced over at Lidia and Ben. "I do not wish to leave them, even for a short trip. My duty is here."

"Benny and Letitia can look after them," Cord suggested.

"I must think," Rumble said, more to himself. He looked at Cord. "It's best if you leave."

Cord glanced at Lidia and the child and Rumble moved into his line of vision. "They're not your concern. You made that choice."

"Stop acting so damn noble." Cord stepped up to Rumble, face flushed with anger. "St. George also told me you'd been betrothed. That there was someone you were supposed to marry back in Mississippi. Have you told Lidia that?"

Rumble grabbed Cord's shirt, pulling the smaller man's face within inches and popping another button free. "What I tell my wife and what I don't tell her is none of your business either."

Cord spoke each word slowly and distinctly. "Let. Go. Of. Me."

Rumble's hand unclenched but Cord didn't retreat. "You're turning your back on your family in Mississippi and some girl there. Why do you think you can build a family here? Didn't you have a duty to those in Mississippi?"

"I did," Rumble said. "But that was before—" he stopped himself. "Don't you dare to lecture me about family."

Cord took a deep breath, turned on his heel and headed toward the ferry.

Rumble watched him for a few seconds, breathing hard. He walked toward his wife. He sat down next to her on the low wall, observing his former classmates at South Dock.

"Are you having regrets?" Lidia asked.

Rumble was startled. "What?"

"To not be going back to Palatine on furlough. To not being a cadet."

Rumble didn't have to think. "Never."

"Then what's your problem with Elijah? Ignore him like everyone except Sam does. He isn't worth it."

Rumble blinked in surprise. "What's wrong?"

She glared at him, holding Ben's basket to her chest. "You're my husband. You're our son's father. I do not want that man anywhere near Ben."

Rumble looked at his wife and the child, leaning into her ever so slightly. "Yes, my dear. But we cannot deny reality. It's the great unspoken, but known, secret among the Corps, that he was with you. It is the major reason he has been Silenced, besides what happened to my cousin, George. His lack of honor."

"I do not like him," Lidia said, her body tense under his large hands.

"You liked him well enough once," Rumble replied without forethought,

Lidia twisted away from him, toward Ben. "I wish to forget that." But Lidia's pale face was flushed.

"So do I," Rumble said, "and that's my problem with Cord." He reached around her and placed his hands over hers, taking up the weight of the baby.

Lidia relaxed, her body melting against Rumble's solid form. "There's something you must know."

"And that is?"

"I am with child."

"Thank, God." Rumble closed his eyes briefly in prayer. "And there is something you must know," he said, pulling the letter out of his pocket. "I think my mother and Sam are right. I must see to it that our children have a complete family." He looked about. "There is more to the world than West Point."

June 1841, Arlington, Virginia

The massive white door swung open and a Negro dressed in fine livery was dwarfed by the opening into Arlington House. "Sir?"

"I have this," Cord said, not quite sure of the etiquette. He held out a sealed envelope.

The servant did not accept it and Cord felt a trickle of sweat slide down his back. It wasn't just because it was Northern Virginia in July. Cord extended his arm further, practically shoving the letter of introduction into the servant's chest. Reluctantly, the man took it. He was old, with close-cropped white hair. He stared at the envelope as if it might attack him.

The servant looked up. "Who are you calling on, sir?"

"It's on the envelope," Cord said. "Major Robert E. Lee."

A voice echoed in the large center hall. "You must be Cadet Cord."

The Negro stepped aside and there stood the distinguished member of the class of 1829, who had graduated second in his class of forty-six and with zero demerits, a feat Cord couldn't manage for one week, never mind four years. Lee was resplendent in his blue uniform, a red sash around his waist, gold oak leaves indicating his rank of major on the epaulets adorning his shoulders. It didn't occur to Cord to ask Lee why he was in uniform while at home, in between assignments. And if it had occurred, he most certainly would not have asked. Lee's hair was long and dark, just beginning to show a touch of gray in the mustache.

He walked up to the door and gestured at the servant. "You may go."

"Sir." The servant held out the envelope.

"You should know better than that," Lee admonished the servant as he took it. Behind Lee, another, younger slave hovered, also dressed in the same well-cut livery.

"Yes, sir." The old servant bowed his head, like a scolded dog.

"I gave it to him, sir," Cord hastily explained.

Lee held up a single finger, hushing Cord. "Go."

The old black man limped away. Lee stepped outside, glancing at the envelope. "One would think being from Virginia, you also would know better. Giving writing to a slave. The poor wretches can't read nor do they desire to. We take care of their every desire, and reading, Mister Cord, is not something they need. It will only make them discontent with the good life we have given them."

Cord had no idea what to say, so as taught while a plebe, he said nothing. He followed Lee onto the front porch, as did the other slave. The major stopped near one of the massive columns that lined the front of the house. Six across the front, one on either side, the columns framed a portico larger than the house Cord had grown up in. It was like visiting some Greek temple and one of the gods themselves had deigned to grace him with an audience.

"Some day they will finish that," Robert E. Lee said, pointing across the Potomac, to the incomplete dome of the Capitol building.

"Yes, sir."

Cord followed Lee down the wide front steps of the house onto the lawn. He was uncomfortable in his tight and tattered clothes, stained from two days of travel. He belatedly realized he should have borrowed money from Longstreet and bought something more appropriate to the mission.

Arlington overwhelmed him. From the white columns to the extensive and well-manicured lawn and gardens that stretched down to the Potomac, it seemed less a house, than a monument. It commanded the high ground on the west side of the Potomac, and thus commanded Washington itself. Lee had married the great-step-daughter of General Washington and had thus become part of this noble place.

As if sensing his thoughts, Lee continued. "The man who designed Arlington House also made the original designs for the Capitol Building, but he got into an argument over the final form, so his vision was not fulfilled. A shame really, although it does make our house all the more special."

The slave was following five steps behind Lee. What purpose the slave served, Cord had no idea.

"And your father?" Lee asked. "Is he well?"

"I will see him tomorrow," Cord said.

Lee stopped and turned toward Cord, his gaze penetrating. "A carefully worded answer. You are not close to your father?"

"He is my father."

"Again. Evasion. I do not like that." Lee's tone was clipped. "Do you hate your father?"

That gave Cord pause. "No, sir. I try not to think of him."

"Apathy," Lee said. "You're lying to yourself. Although not technically an honor code violation, it is a violation of one's personal honor."

"Are they not the same, sir?" Cord asked.

"Personal honor is imposed from within. The honor code is imposed from without. Sometimes the two are not the same. In the end, though, one must always be guided from within."

Cord remained quiet.

Lee did not. "I understand you were challenged to a duel. That you were requested to resign by the Vigilance Committee." It not phrased as a question and Lee continued. "You refused to duel. You have been Silenced. Why should I speak with you?"

"I come not for me, but for someone I owe a personal debt to."

Lee clasped his hands behind his back and looked Cord over, as if inspecting a slab of beef to be served up at an upcoming banquet. "Why did you not resign?"

"I felt my transgression did not warrant it," Cord said.

"But it was over honor?"

"It was over a woman," Cord said. "And the matter was solved to the satisfaction of all involved. The Corps had no need to get involved."

"'To the satisfaction of all'?" Lee seemed amused. "You were beaten and Silenced."

"A small price to pay to remain at West Point."

"Interesting." The major continued. "The only reason I agreed to see you was my cousin does business with your father. And you have an uncle with his hands on some powerful strings. Powerful enough to get you into the Academy. I have never met your father, so I cannot judge him. But one should always honor one's father."

Cord thought that curious given that Lee's own father, the infamous Light Horse Harry Lee of Revolutionary War fame, had lost the family fortune and absconded to the West Indies when Lee was but a child.

"I am not close to my father."

"Better," Lee said. "But who are you here about?"

"A former cadet named George King, from Charleston."

Lee frowned. "Wasn't he the one who challenged you to the duel you refused to satisfy?"

"Yes, sir."

Lee resumed his stroll across the wide lawn and Cord hurried to keep up. "What of Mister King?"

"Mister King's family has fallen on hard times. He needs an occupation. One where he can use his military training, but also one where he can be clear of what happened at West Point. He applied for one but was denied. I was hoping that your interceding might sway the decision the other way."

"Why do you care?" Lee asked.

"The duel would not have happened if it had not been for previous actions on my part, sir."

"Go on."

"The Navy is recruiting midshipmen for a training cruise, sir. I was hoping you might put in a positive word with Secretary of War Spencer for Mister King to attain one of those positions. He tried on his own and was turned down."

"Is Mister King an honest and good man?"

"Yes, sir."

"I have heard differently about you. Beyond the event that brought the wrath of the Vigilance Committee, I have heard that your list of transgressions as a cadet is long. That you have more demerits than anyone in your class. That you lead the Immortals in every section of Academics. And, you do not present yourself well at my door."

"No excuse, sir."

"Yes, sir; no, sir; no excuse, sir. You learned your answers as a plebe well. Let us see what my cousin has to say." Lee held out a hand and the slave who had been shadowing them extracted a small blade from somewhere in his outfit and Lee neatly sliced the envelope open, handing the blade back without looking at the slave.

Lee unfolded a piece of thick paper and read quickly. Then he folded the paper, slid it back in the envelope, and placed both inside his uniform coat, every move deliberate and precise as if he were being graded by some unseen entity. "My cousin speaks highly of Mister King. Apparently he is a very studious and righteous young man of the highest character." Lee raised an eyebrow at Cord. "Too bad it was he who was dismissed from the Academy and not you."

Cord couldn't stop the words. "Was it that you were perfect in your behavior for four years at the Academy, sir, or that you were very good at not getting caught or a combination of the two?"

"I see why you receive so many demerits." Lee folded his arms over his chest. "No one is perfect, but I strove to do the best I could. I viewed my education at the Academy as a God-given opportunity. I am not sure how you view it although your perseverance deserves some merit."

"I'm not asking this favor for me, sir, but for a man who will make the most of an opportunity."

"Why was he turned down in the first place?" Lee asked. "This is an excellent letter of recommendation and his record at West Point, according to this, was exemplary up to the event which caused his expulsion."

"The governor of South Carolina used his connections to block it, sir." Cord shrugged. "I am not privy to the political machinations involved."

Lee paused and raised a hand. The slave came hurrying up. Lee pointed toward a hedgerow. "I ordered you to have that trimmed yesterday."

"Yes, master."

"I do not like disorder. You will inform your overseer and accept whatever he decides for you."

"Yes, master."

Lee turned back to Cord and spoke as if the slave wasn't there. "You have had little dealing with people of color based on the incident at the door."

Cord thought the hedges perfectly trimmed. "I have not, sir. In Norfolk, at the docks, we employ free men, usually immigrants; men who are willing to work hard."

"People of color will work hard," Lee said. "As long as one stays on top of them. What you should understand is that they need the institution. They cannot function outside of it. We take care of them."

"Yes, sir." Cord glanced over at Parks, but the dark face was a mask and his eyes were downcast.

"You think differently?" Lee asked.

"I don't know enough about it to think one way or the other, sir."

"The truth is it doesn't affect you so you don't think of it at all. That is the way with most people."

"Mister King, sir?" Cord was anxious to receive a decision and get away.

"What do you think of Texas?" Lee abruptly asked.

"Sir?"

"Annexation," Lee snapped.

Cord focused. "It's inevitable, sir. Texas must be part of the country."

"It will mean war." Lee sounded eager.

"Yes, sir."

"Texas as a slave or free state?" Lee asked.

Cord glanced at the black man standing five paces away. "Slave, of course, sir."

"It has nothing do with slavery, you know," Lee said

"Of course not, sir," Cord replied, having no idea what the Major meant.

"Slavery is a given condition from God. When God wishes it to end, it will end. It is clear God wants Texas to be annexed and to be a slave state since He struck down President Harrison, who opposed both, so quickly after taking office. And it's also about the sanctity of the State. A State must have the right to choose its own course. Those wise men who wrote the Constitution knew that."

"I believe Jefferson wrote that slavery was comparable to holding a wolf by the ears," Cord said before catching himself, "and we can neither continue to hold the wolf, nor safely let it go. Justice is on one side of the scale and self-preservation on the other."

Lee's face tightened. "For a slave owner, he had some strange thoughts. What we do is bridle our people of color and keep them in their place. Neither justice or self-preservation, but rather the natural order of things to be maintained."

"I am sure you are correct," Cord said, regaining control. "Mister King, sir?"

Lee looked irritated. "I do indeed know Secretary of War Spencer. As a matter of fact, his son, Philip, is to be one of the midshipmen aboard the *Somers*, the ship that is to conduct the training cruise. It's a new vessel, currently being completed at the naval yards in New York City. I will pen a letter to Secretary Spencer and advise him to consider Mister King and see if practical military considerations can supersede political squabbling. I will include my cousin's letter of recommendation."

"Thank you, sir."

"Why did you go to West Point?" Lee asked.

Cord considered telling the truth, but so far that had not gone over well with Major Lee. "I spent two years before the mast and decided that life is not for me."

"But it is for Mister King?"

"Mister King has spent time on his ships. His family ran a trading company in Charleston and he spoke fondly of his time at sea at the Academy. And, knowing King, I believe he might be a natural for the Navy."

"It is honorable," Lee allowed, "that you are trying to do the right thing for a man who challenged you. Perhaps there is hope for you."

Cord bridled at the comment but bit back his retort.

"You may go," Lee said, dismissing Cord like he was a plebe once more.

Cord headed away, but Lee's call stopped him. "I will probably see you somewhere in Mexico in the coming years, Cadet Cord. I suggest you attend to your martial studies with more diligence. There will be war."

NATCHEZ AND TEXAS

Summer 1841, Just South of Natchez, Mississippi

RUMBLE REINED IN THE HORSE and gazed west from the bluff, feeling the familiar sheen of sweat on his body and breathing in the fragrance of magnolias. He'd galloped south from Natchez at first light, and the sun was still ascending in the east.

The Mississippi River appeared deceptively slow and calm, but beneath its muddy surface was a twisted and tangled knot of dangerous currents. Much like Palatine. The grand house was almost grand, maintenance having been a bit slack over the past couple of years since last he'd seen it. The fields were ripe with cotton, yet he'd heard rumors in town that there were problems with shipments from Palatine being delivered on time and in the proper bulk.

To his right, steamers cruised up the river, heading for the docks of Natchez for their loads of white gold.

Natchez had more millionaires per capita than any other in the United States. The townsfolk liked to say it was cotton that brought the money, but for Rumble it was much costlier: the blood of the slaves who worked the fields and the souls of those who ruled over them. Eli Whitney had had no idea the misery he was inflicting on the world when he invented his cotton gin. Prior to that, slavery was slowly dying out due to its inherent inefficiency.

Rumble wore his uniform, proud of the chevrons on his sleeve from his recent promotion to sergeant by Superintendent Delafield. And proud of his Army blue. Also, he knew it would grate on Tiberius, who often liked to be called Colonel, though the man had never worn a uniform or wielded a weapon in battle.

"I do swear, I do not like that river," a woman's voice drawled behind him.

Rumble turned the horse, a smile lighting up his face. "Mother. You never swear. Not really."

Dressed in a dark-red riding dress, Violet Rumble sat sidesaddle on her old horse, a closed parasol in her deerskin gloved hands. A bright red bonnet with the feather of some exotic bird crowned her head. She looked elegant, as always. The horse was perfectly still, almost a statue. His mother had been riding that nag as long as Rumble could remember. It had been broken a long time ago and seemed content to stay broken and be a pedestal to Violet Rumble. He rode up to her, and she leaned over, pecking him on the cheek.

But she was still focused on the river. "It almost took you from us. I stay as far away from it as possible."

"I think that is a wise thing," Rumble said. "So you still watch the road and saw my approach?"

"It is better to watch the road than the river," Violet said. She gently nudged the reins, facing toward Palatine House. "What do you think of the old place?"

"I think it looks fine."

"You never were good at lying," Violet said with a laugh. "It's falling apart. Your father spends all his time up there—" she pointed with the parasol toward the second story porch. Rumble could make out a figure dressed in white seated in a large wicker chair. "He never goes out to the fields any more."

"You mentioned in your letter that he was ill."

"He had a spell where he could not stand for two days. He refused to have a doctor come. He can get up now, but he is not the same."

"He knows I'm here?" Rumble asked.

"He does now," Violet said.

"You did not tell him of the letter?"

"He did not tell me he was sending the message via St. George," Violet said as if the quid pro quo of deceit was the natural state of affairs and quite reasonable and normal.

"How did you know then that—" Rumble stopped. Violet knew everything. "So what will be the welcome?"

"I've already welcomed you. It's my home also, you know."

"Yes, mother."

She reached out and her gloved hand gripped his forearm with force. "It's true? You have a child."

Rumble licked sweat off his upper lip. "Yes."

"A son?"

"Yes."

"You've done well. And his name?"

"Ben Agrippa Rumble."

"Oh my!" The normally unflappable Violet Rumble, formally Violet Rudolph of the esteemed Rudolph's of Clarksville, Tennessee, was rarely shocked, but she regrouped quickly. "That will make things more interesting to say the least." She glanced back at the Mississippi. "You did it in his memory?"

"Yes, mother."

"That was noble." She flicked the reins and her horse began ambling toward Palatine House. "But short-sighted and impetuous."

Well removed and out of sight from Palatine House, over a mile and a half by dirt road, was a village; one that was not registered on any maps because it was entirely a creation of Palatine. A stoutly built log cabin, festooned with a dozen rifle ports pointing in all direction, was set on a small knoll overlooking a collection of shanty shacks. The cabin had heavy wooden shutters on the insides of the few small windows and despite the June heat, they were closed and barred, as they were every night.

John Dyer, the chief overseer of Palatine, didn't mind experiencing a little discomfort for safety. Or a lot of discomfort for safety. On pegs next to each of the twelve firing ports was a Colt-Root repeating rifle, fully loaded and ready for action. Dyer had the percussion caps and rounds checked every evening, a ritual his son, St. George, had taken over as soon as he was able to pick the weapon up. The Colt-Root was essentially a larger version of a Colt revolver with a longer barrel and a shoulder stock being added to the pistol. It gave the firer six shots, albeit not always reliably. With twelve such rifles in the cabin, the barred doors and windows, and a large supply of powder and ball to reload, aided by six subordinate overseers who slept every night in an adjacent room, also all well-armed, Dyer felt confident his cabin could stave off any attack.

Those he was concerned about in terms of attack occupied the shanty sheds at the base of the knoll. Palatine owned one hundred and forty-two slaves, and John Dyer and his son were responsible for keeping them in line. The elder Dyer had learned from his own father the easiest way to do that was fear and terror.

This morning was to be a lesson in the subject, which Dyer and his son taught best. He slid a pistol in the holster on each hip, made sure his knife was loose in its sheath, looped a coiled bullwhip over his shoulder—more for show than use; although Dyer could wield it like a master, he preferred less visible methods. Not out of any concern for humanity, but because a slave bearing scars indicated rebelliousness, and that brought less gold.

Dyer grabbed one of the Colt-Root rifles, glanced at his son, who was also similarly armed, except that instead of two Colt revolvers, he carried his unique Le Mat pistol inside the black sash he wrapped around his waist every day like a badge of rank.

"Times wasting," Dyer said. "We got to get them out in the fields. Got a big load needs to be moved tonight."

"I know," St. George muttered.

"What you say, boy?"

"They'll work hard after this," St. George promised in a louder voice as he slid up the heavy wooden bar and opened the front door.

"You take care of it," John Dyer ordered his son, grimacing as he stretched his back out.

St. George's voice dropped back down to the mutter he knew his hard-of-hearing father could hear, but not make out. "Don' I always?"

There were shouts down the hill in shantytown as the other overseers gathered the slaves.

"Count," St. George called out as they reached the small clearing at the base of the knoll, just before the first shack. The slaves were clustered about in a semi-circle.

"All here," an overseer reported.

"Bring 'im here," St. George said.

A young Negro, mid-teens, was dragged forward by two other slaves.

"I done nothing!" the slave cried. "I aint done nothing, Master."

"But you will," St. George said. "I could tell it in your eyes yesterday. You know how I could tell, boy? Because I saw your eyes. I don' never want to be seeing you looking at me again."

"I won't, Master. I swear I won't!"

"I know." St. George gestured.

The two slaves held the boy upright, their hands on his upper arms, locking him in place. Then they pressed down, forcing the boy to his knees.

St. George pulled a rag out of a pocket on his black cloak. He walked behind the boy and wrapped it around his face, covering his mouth, nose and eyes and pulling it tight in the rear. He jerked back and the boy's face tilted upward.

"Samual," St. George yelled, irritated the slave wasn't already in place.

Several slaves stepped aside and the massive Negro walked through them. Samual's face was a scarred, obsidian slab, showing no emotion.

"This is your fault," St. George said to him. "You shoulda taught this boy better."

Samual halted in front of the young slave.

St. George stepped closer. Though he was a big man, Samual towered over him. "You know what happen to your woman and girl if you don' keep your people in line," St. George hissed in a voice only the big man could hear.

A muscle twitched in Samual's jaw, but there was no other sign he registered the threat.

St. George gestured and another slave came forward, carrying a water-bucket. St. George took it from him. He lifted the bucket and poured the water on the rag covering the boy's face. Within seconds, the boy was convulsing, desperate for air as water flowed in his nostrils and mouth every time he tried to breath. The boy tried to hold his breath, but couldn't do it for more than a few seconds. He moaned in extreme agony, the sensation of drowning, of dying, searing through his nerve endings. His hands were shaking uncontrollably and the two slaves were struggling to keep him in their grip.

"More water," St. George ordered.

"James learned, Master." Samual's right hand was over his heart, as if protecting it.

St. George leaned closer. "I'm taking Mary to the House today. Do you want to make sure she comes back unhurt? I can't say nothing about what else happen to your wife there. Remember, Echo now in the big house too."

Samual half-turned toward St. George, but halted. The slave ran and came back with another bucket.

St. George poured.

James' muscles were contracting from lack of oxygen.

"You let him go you be next," St. George threatened the two holding James. He'd learned the water-rag technique in the East Indies during a two-year stint on a Clipper ship plying goods across the Pacific. The traders of the East India Company used it on people they needed information from. St. George had immediately seen the effectiveness of a technique that caused so much pain but left no marks.

Seconds passed, everyone's eyes riveted on the boy's suffering. St. George jerked the rag off the James' head. "Let him go."

James collapsed to the ground, gasping. St. George kicked the boy in the stomach and an explosion of vomit and water spewed out of his mouth.

St. George faced the slaves. "The south fields. Ten wagons loaded by sundown and ferried across the river to Vidalia."

He stalked away with his father as the slaves hustled to work. Looking down at James, Samual reached inside his shirt and pulled out a worn, leather-bound Bible. He knelt next to the teen. He placed the Bible over James' heart. "'Suffering produce endurance, and endurance produce character, and character produce hope.' It says it right here in da book."

James looked up and Samual saw the anger in his eyes. "No, boy. No. You die if you show that."

"I die if I don't," James said and then spit more water and vomit out of his mouth.

Samual nodded, before looking up to the heavens. "Our day will come."

James struggled to his feet. "We be needing our time here on this earth, not in some place the white man make up to keep us crawling."

"Hush, boy. Don't speak blasphemy."

"Your son was braver," James said. "He made his play."

"And he pay for it," Samual said. But Samual's eyes were now on St. George. If the overseer had looked over his shoulder and seen the expression, there would have been worse than the water-rag for Samual even though he was under the protection of Violet Rumble.

"Father."

Tiberius Rumble did not get up from his wicker throne. He raked his son with an angry glare. His hair was white and thick, combed straight back. His clipped beard was also pure white. Deep pockets under his eyes showed weariness. There was a twitch under the old man's right eye that had not been there two years ago. A slave girl was in the dark shadows behind him, a vague figure against the wall of the upper porch. From here one had an excellent view of the Mississippi River and the haze of Louisiana across the river.

"Greet your son," Violet urged as she sat down in the wicker chair next to her husband, the slave extending a glass of something. Rumble knew it was a powerful something. One needed powerful libations to sit next to Tiberius Rumble. The slave did not offer Rumble a drink and he knew his father had to have specified that upon seeing them ride up.

Tiberius did not acknowledge his son's greeting.

"Where is Seneca?" Rumble finally asked.

Violet's face grew pinched, as if speaking of her youngest boy pained her. "He is at Rosalie."

"At Rosalie, seeing Rosalie," Rumble said.

"Is there any other reason to go there?" Violet asked in a reasonable voice.

Rosalie was the richest plantation in Natchez, which meant the richest house in the entire country. It had been built in 1823 on the site of a French outpost—Fort Rosalie. The slight detail that the Natchez Indians had massacred the French occupying the fort in 1729 had not seemed to be an issue when Peter Little bought the land and built the house. He had subsequently named his first daughter after the house, although those not quite up on history often thought the house named after the daughter. Upon meeting Rosalie Little, one could readily believe such a spectacular house should certainly be named after her.

"So," Rumble said. "Seneca is to take my place. The wedding will still take place."

Tiberius deigned to address his eldest son. "You have no place."

"I stand here," Rumble said.

Tiberius looked away, toward the Mississippi. "Seneca is my son and my heir. I have no other son."

Violet sipped her drink. "And there will be no more Rumbles if you think Seneca and Rosalie are the answer. You know that, my husband. Let's not be short-sighted. Lucius has given us a grandson. How does that play into your precious plans, my dear?"

Tiberius snapped his head toward his wife, his already red cheeks blazing with fury. "Rosalie will bring money to Palatine and—"

"Money without blood is doomed," Violet said. The long lines in her face told how old she really was. "Calm down, dear. We can at least be civilized. And you should not strain yourself."

With a deep sigh, Tiberius slumped back in his throne. He lifted his left hand and the slave was there with another tumbler of alcohol. He downed it in one gulp. Held up his hand again.

Rumble finally got a good look at the slave girl. "Echo?"

The girl's jaw clenched, but she didn't raise her eyes or answer.

"Hush!" Violet hissed.

Tiberius glared at his eldest son. "Don't you talk to her. Don't you talk to any of the nigras here. You already caused enough trouble. No more. No more." He slumped back in the chair, the effort exhausting him.

Lucius Rumble grabbed another chair, sat in it, and realized that nothing of significance would be spoken of again. It never was at Palatine. Because it was a civilized place.

There was a clear sky and the moon was a quarter full. A perfect night for deeds to be done on the sly. Enough light to accomplish the act, but not enough for the casual observer to uncover what was happening.

At the foot of an old, abandoned dock on the south side of Vidalia, Louisiana, St. George Dyer waited impatiently. A tall, raw-boned, weather-beaten woman garbed in a black dress and wide sunbonnet walked down the dock toward him.

"Ten?" she asked, wasting no time on greetings.

"Ten wagons," St. George confirmed. "Took most of the early evening to ferry them across. Simpler if we just done this on my side of the river."

"Simple is dangerous," Sally Skull said.

"This not be a dangerous time at Palatine." St. George jerked a thumb to the north and east, across the Mississippi. "The not-so-prodigal son returned and the great house in an uproar. Those people think themselves kings and queens and princes and that sort. All worried about their blood. I could show them some blood. They don't earn their money; I do."

Skull sported a pistol on each hip in reverse grip. The holster leather was well oiled and supple. She'd gotten her last name from a husband who had disappeared shortly after their marriage. If anyone asked her about his whereabouts, her reply was short and to the point: 'He's dead.' She said it in such a tone, that no further questions were ever asked on the matter.

"If you hate it so much, why do you stay?" Skull asked. "Why be their lackey?"

St. George's hand slid toward the Le Mat tucked in the black scarf around his waist.

Skull's hands were on her hips, scant inches from her own pistols. "Be careful, man. We have a profitable business arrangement." She lifted one hand and pulled a flask out of some hidden place on top of her copious bosom and offered it to him.

St. George took the flask and sipped. "Ah! What be that?"

She retrieved the peace offering and took a slug. "It's called Tequila. From Mexico. I been looking at the prospects for trade there."

"New Orleans does us well enough." St. George held out his hand for the flask.

"True," Skull acknowledged. "But times are changing. In Texas, when you're out on the plains, you can feel a storm coming on your skin and in your hair. The cattle are the same. I've seen the flame leap across their horns just before the storm hits. And I feel a storm coming."

St. George was confused. "Any storm comes, it will be Texas and Mexico. Those fools think they got their own country after Santa Anna, but you and I know that aint true. Mexico still claims Texas."

"I suppose that makes me a fool?" Skull said.

St. George gritted his teeth. "Didn't mean you."

"Sounded like maybe you did." Skull's hands were back on her hips, close to her guns.

St. George tried to look relaxed as he leaned against one of the dock posts. His hand drifted toward the Le Mat hidden in his sash

"You say things like that down in Texas, you won't last long," Skull said. She held out her flask.

St. George took it once more, but resented the un-solicited advice. "I don't plan on ever being in Texas."

"Maybe," Skull said. "And Texans *are* their own country."

"If Tyler sends troops to Texas," St. George said, "then it be war. Don't see why you want to run trade that way."

"Wars are always ripe with opportunity," Skull said.

"They what?" St. George shrugged. "I got no interest in Mexico."

"And after that war?" Skull asked.

"Huh?"

Skull sat down on a bale of cotton as slaves hurried past, loading the steamer she'd leased in New Orleans. "You got to think ahead. Past the right now."

"I been thinking ahead," St. George protested. "My father and I been sucking Palatine's tit for near ten years now. No one the wiser."

"And ten years from now?" Skull asked.

"We could all be dirt."

"And if we aint?"

"The tit will still be here to suck."

"And if it aint?"

St. George frowned. "Why won't it be?"

"Who knows?" Skull said vaguely. "Every tit dries up sooner or later." She pointed across the river, where lights from the plantation gleamed. "You hate them, don't you?"

St. George still had the flask and took a deep drag. "They get money and land and slaves just 'cause they born to it'. Why they the lucky ones? They don't have to work for it. I been working for everything I got since I could walk. It not be fair."

Skull snorted. "'Fair'? There aint no fair, St. George. There's what you take out of this world while you're breathing." She pointed at a slave walking by with a bale on his back. "We're taking that."

St. George blinked, his eyes slightly unfocused. "That be true."

Skull stood. "Harrison dying. That was a gift from heaven. Tyler's going to stir things up. We have to be prepared. For Mexico. And after Mexico." She reached into another fold in her dress and brought out a thick wad of currency. "My flask?"

St. George held it out.

She swapped out the flask for the money. "Think ahead."

JOHN BROWN

June 1841, Norfolk, Virginia

CORD WAS SEATED IN A WATERFRONT tavern in Norfolk, Virginia. It was a narrow room squeezed between a warehouse and a boarding house, badly lit, with a single, dirt-smeared window squinting over the harbor opposite the door. There was as much room on one side of the bar as the other. The bartender had given Cord a bottle of whiskey and Cord had given up his last dollar. The bartender had also raked Cord with a strange look, as if debating whether to serve him or not.

The city was alive with commerce, the port's skyline a forest of masts, rigging and sails. The rigging was the Cord family business and Cord knew his father looked out at the port as a farmer looked to his fields. The problem was, there were less masts every year as steam ships became prevalent. It would be convenient for Cord to associate his father's ill temper with the shrinking business, but the reality was that Preacher Cord was like those few upperclassmen at West Point who tormented plebes simply because it gave them some perverse pleasure. Cord sensed that even if the great fleet Agamemnon and Achilles had sailed from Greece to assault Troy pulled into Norfolk for rigging, his father would be the same.

Cord knew he was putting off the inevitable collision with his father, but he also knew he could not approach the old man sober. That would be too hard to bear. He took another drag from the bottle. A woman was seated in a dark corner, her details impossible to make out in the gloom, but she was half-dressed, and appeared passed out. There were no other customers yet. The bartender went back to filling a spittoon with a long arc of brown slime.

Cord tilted his head back and drank deeply. When he brought his head level, he saw that the bartender had a short piece of heavy, stiff rope in his hand. Cord had seen the like before and felt its sting. Bosun mates used it to get sailors moving. They called it a 'starter' on board ship because that's what it did. It was a step below the cat-o-nine-tails because it was less painful and didn't break the skin. Still, a hard strike from one in the wrong place could break bone.

"I know you," the bartender said, taking a step closer.

"Don't think so," Cord said. His non-drinking hand drifted toward the knife in the center of his back.

"The *Acushnet*." The man spit across the bar, splattering Cord with tobacco juice and saliva. With a solid thump, the bartender brought the starter down, but Cord was a split second faster, jerking his head back out of the way and getting the whalebone knife out of its scabbard and pressing up under the bartender's chin, causing the man to tilt his head back.

"Drop the starter," Cord hissed, "or I'll jam this into your brain."

The bartender released the starter and it thudded onto the bar.

Cord kept the knife pressing into the man's skin as he reached with the other hand for the bottle. "What's this about?"

"You owe me money," the bartender said, a line of spittle running down his cheek as it spilled out the side of his mouth. "I was second mate on the *Acushnet*. You gambled. You lost. You promised to pay when we berthed Boston. But you ran."

Cord laughed and took a drink, the knife steady. "Damned if I remember. By the end of that voyage we were all going a bit crazy." Out of the corner of his eye he saw the woman in the corner stand up.

"Takes that knife away from my man," she said in a whiskey scarred voice, holding up a small derringer for punctuation.

"At this range, that pea-shooter has a chance in hell of hitting," Cord said. "And your hand is shaking."

"Might hit you just by chance," the woman said.

"The amount?" Cord asked the bartender.

"Twelve dollars."

"I don't have it." Cord pulled the knife back. He nodded. "I do remember you. And I do owe you. Let me work it off."

"Why should I trust you now?" the bartender asked.

"I give you my word, I'll work here until the debt is filled."

"And why should I take your word?"

"I'm a West Point cadet on furlough," Cord said.

The bartender snorted. "A West Pointer! Like that's supposed to mean something?"

Cord clenched his fists. "I grew up here and my father runs a business on the other side of the Naval Yard."

"Who's your father?" the bartended demanded.

"Preacher Cord."

"Get the hell out of here," the bartender snarled. "I don't want your damn money and I don't want nothing to do with those types."

"What type do you mean?"

"Trouble-makers. Trying to incite insurrecetion among the nigras. Get the hell out." He was moving to the side and there was most likely something more powerful than a starter hidden under the bar.

Cord kept the bottle and backed toward the door. He made it out into the muddy, manure-splattered street. Teamsters driving wagons loaded with cargo rattled by. He slowly walked past the Naval Yard, wondering what had caused the bartender to react that way and what Preacher was up to now. Several warships were tied up to long wharves. They were mostly in sad shape and for a moment Cord had doubts about his plan, but he knew the *Somers*, the ship on which King would serve, was currently under construction and would be the newest addition to the Navy when commissioned.

Cord halted and took a drink. He staggered slightly as he tilted the bottom high.

"Old Ironsides herself," Cord said approvingly as he took in the *USS Constitution* being refitted. Forty-four years after launching, the venerable warship was a legend among those who knew the sea.

With a deep sigh, Cord turned from the ships. He took a slug of whiskey, glanced at what remained in the bottle, and then finished the rest. Cord chucked the bottle into the harbor.

He walked to a street one block removed from the water where a cluster of shops that serviced sailors and ships lined the way. Cord looked up at the front of his father's store. The paint was faded, but the name could still be read: CORD & SON RIGGING. The sign had read the same in Cord's earliest memories, indicating a master plan, in which the son had had no vote.

The sound of the shop's door creaking open on rusty hinges reached Cord. He knew who it was just from the sense of dread he immediately felt in his stomach.

"Father."

Preacher Cord was taller than his son. His hair was pure white, including his long beard, which reached to his chest. He wore a plain black shirt buttoned to the very top and black slacks. A silver crucifix hung from his neck, resting on the black cloth covering his chest as if it could ward off wounds to the body. The left sleeve was empty and pinned back to the shoulder.

"You did not write to let me know you were coming," Preacher said by way of greeting.

"I have no plan to bother you with a stay. I was in Virginia and thought I should stop by and pay respects to mother's grave."

Preacher pointed. "Her grave is in the cemetery, not here." He frowned at the slurred words. "Have you been partaking of spirits?"

Cord stood as erect as he possibly could, although he was swaying like a mainmast in a heavy swell. "I have, sir."

Preacher Cord's jaw tightened. "It is the demon's work."

"Then why do you labor so hard at it?" Cord snapped.

"What do you think mother would say if she was alive to see you like this?"

Cord took a step toward his father, fighting for control to keep his knife sheathed. "Mother isn't here because you let her die, lying in pain in that bed upstairs, too damn cheap to call for a doctor and too damn busy drinking."

"You were too young to help in the store," Preacher Cord said. "I had to man the counter."

"You could have hired someone."

Preacher Cord halved the distance to his son with an angry stride. "Are you challenging me, child?" his spittle hit Cord in the face.

"I'm not a child any more and you're not worth challenging," Cord said.

Preacher Cord's eyes glowed with rage. He shoved his son, knocking him back several steps. People were gathering, watching the spectacle.

"I will not fight you, father."

"Because you're a coward."

"And you call yourself Preacher? How is that?" Cord asked. "Do you have a direct line to God?"

"He speaks to me," Preacher said, tapping the side of his head. "He gives me the Word. I did not choose the name. I earned it and it was bestowed upon me." Preacher Cord pointed at his empty sleeve. "I know what pain is. I'd be a ship's captain now, running my own trader, if this hadn't happened."

"You're the one who quit," Cord snapped. "You're the one who gave up trying. You're—" he didn't get the next word out as his father's powerful right hand slammed into the side of his head. Cord was staggered to his knees by the blow and he once more went for the knife, and once more he halted before clearing leather.

"Easy brother!" A tall man with thick black hair and an angular face put a hand on Preacher's shoulder, pulling him back. He looked like an undertaker, with pale skin and sunken cheekbones.

Preacher wheeled, fist raised, but lowered it when he recognized the man. "Brother Brown."

"Is this the son you spoke to me of?" John Brown asked. "The West Pointer?"

"He is, Brother Brown," Preacher said.

Cord got to his feet as Brown let go of his father and walked up to him. Brown put both hands on Cord's shoulders. His eyes seemed to glitter, alive with some inner fire. "Where do you stand on the Cause?"

Cord shook his head, trying to clear the ringing in his ears. "What are you talking about?"

Brown let go of his shoulders and reached into a pocket. He pulled out a coin and extended it. Cord recognized it: an abolitionist token. On one side it portrayed a male figure, kneeling and bound in chains with the legend, *Am I Not a Man and a Brother*. The reverse of the coin bore the clasped hands of a brotherhood and the legend, *May Slavery and Oppression Cease Throughout the World*. Cord handed it back to Brown.

"I've got no stand on it," Cord said.

"Every man must choose," Brown said. "Slavery must be destroyed."

More people were gathering and the mood was shifting.

Cord looked past Brown. "Have you fallen in with this, father?"

"It is every man's duty to fight for freedom," Preacher Cord said.

"So you let mother die but you can spend time on this?" Cord spit.

Preacher Cord pointed down the street. "Get thee from here."

Cord shook his head. "You're my father."

"You're my son and you ran away." Preacher jerked a thumb up at the faded sign above him. "You had a duty."

"Damn you!" Cord cursed, as he backed away. "Damn you to hell!"

CHARLESTON

July 1841, Charleston, SC

The Ashley and Cooper Rivers join together at the Battery, then spread out to the Atlantic. In the distance, breaking the clean horizon to the entrance to the harbor was the frowning, unfinished brick stump of Fort Sumter, being built on seventy thousand tons of New England granite dumped on a sand bar. Work began in 1827, but for seven years construction on the fort had been halted because of legal disputes, but just this January, work had resumed, albeit slowly.

George King walked along the Battery, past the cannon guarding Charleston, in the company of his mother, the former Cordelia Pinckney, now the widowed Mrs. King. She paused, as she always did, in front of their former home. Looking over the guns on the Battery, the King Mansion, with its wide verandas, occupied one of the best lots south of Broad Street in Charleston. It was a house built on the hard work and commerce of her grandfather and lost in land speculation in the crash of '37 by her husband.

"I am grateful the new owners kept the name," Cordelia said.

"They wanted the prestige," King said. "I don't think they were doing us a favor."

"Hush," Cordelia said. "You must think positive thoughts."

"It doesn't depress you to walk past?" King asked.

"I have pleasant memories," Cordelia said. "They are about all I have." She tucked her arm in his and they continued. "Now. Why did Secretary Spencer change his mind about the appointment as a midshipman?"

King shook his head. "I have no idea. I assume someone at West Point called in a favor for me since Major Lee, a graduate, wrote a letter that swayed the Secretary's mind."

"Who?" Cordelia wondered. "Your cousin, Lucius Rumble, works in the stables now, married to some tavern girl. I doubt he has any sway. A fine mess the two of you made of things. He's broken my cousin, Tiberius' heart."

"What of your heart, mother?"

Cordelia squeezed his arm. "You're the only thing keeping my heart beating after all that's happened in the past few years. I think the Navy would be an excellent place for you. You always loved being at sea."

"I did. If they'd had a Naval Academy, I'd have gone there instead of West Point. Being a midshipman on a training ship is the path the Navy has to becoming an officer."

"You know they're going to make The Citadel a military academy?" Cordelia asked.

"I've heard rumors."

"The governor wants to squeeze out the Federal troops in the Arsenal. And, he needs leaders for the state militia."

"I wonder," King said, "if the threat is greater from the Federal troops or the slaves."

"Let us pray it never becomes both," Cordelia said. "I remember after the revolt of '22, every man in Charleston enlisted in the militia. I had hoped you might get an appointment on the faculty of the Citadel, but Governor Richardson blocks any attempts on your behalf."

"He hated father so strongly?" King asked.

"Your father lost the Governor and many others a fortune in the crash. They might speak of many other things, but hit a man like that in the pockets and their memory is long and their revenge is cold." She brightened. "I am happy you have this opportunity, George, although I will miss you dearly."

"I will be able to send you money," King said.

Cordelia looked away, embarrassed.

"I will rebuild the family's reputation," King said. "I vow that."

Cordelia looked back at her son. "I do believe you will."

They walked in silence, neither looking to the right as they passed one of the many old oaks dotting the Battery. The one from which King's father and Cordelia's husband, had hung himself after the crash.

Cordelia halted at the very tip of the Battery and pointed at the pile of rocks far out in the harbor. "Do you think the Yankees will ever finish that monstrosity?"

GRANT AND LIDIA

August 1841, West Point, New York

ULYSSES S. GRANT USED SLOW and deliberate strokes with the pencil. Etched on the sketchpad resting on his knees was the image of Lidia Rumble holding young Ben in her arms, against a faint backdrop of the Hudson River.

Mother and son were seated on a wood bench, across a stone basin from Grant and his pad. He was cross-legged in the grass. A small hole in the side of the basin allowed a spring to flow through it, the water going over the east side, then down the slope to the Hudson eighty feet below. Ben always stared at the spring as if seeing it for the first time—the water had some magical, calming effect on him. They were isolated from the hustle and bustle of the Academy in Kosciuszko's garden.

Lidia jokingly called it her husband's garden; that he had earned it not only because of his middle name, but more so for the hazing that missing Z had brought upon him during plebe year. Pre-dating the founding of the Academy, set on a ledge just below the Plain and over-looking the Hudson, the tranquil garden had been designed and built by Thaddeus Kosciuszko in 1778. It had been a place of contemplation for the Polish patriot who had designed the fortifications at West Point during the Revolution. A steep set of stairs cut into the side of the Plain was the only access. The ledge was thirty feet long and only twenty feet at its widest.

Lidia, Ben and Grant had been coming to the garden the last two afternoons as Grant worked on the sketches. He had already done one, but torn it off and put it underneath the blank pages, telling Lidia it was but practice. Grant was morose after his eight weeks of freedom from the Academy and facing two more years until graduation. The class of 1843 was trickling back from furlough, many like prisoners returning to their correctional institution. A new group of plebes, the class of 1845, was finishing up their beastly summer training and the entire Corps was gearing up to transition into the academic year, moving from their encampment on the Plain, into the barracks.

"Worried about Lucius?" Grant asked.

Lidia ran her hand over her belly, feeling the life inside her. "He has told me some things about Palatine and his family that cause concern. And I sense there are dark things about the place he's holding back."

"He's spoken little of his life before the Academy to me," Grant said as he continued to sketch. He was well known in the Corps as an artist, although it was not quite as respected as his abilities with a horse. Robert Walter Weir, the Professor of Drawing, praised Grant as one of the finest cadets he had ever taught, up there with James Whistler, who unfortunately, not being as proficient at chemistry as he was at painting, had been booted out of the Academy for academic deficiency after only one year.

The Academy did not teach drawing to make artists. It taught drawing to train engineers to trace terrain features. Like every other subject, the

Academy twisted the content to fit one goal: the preparation of officers for the art of war.

"He showed me the letter from his mother," Lidia said. "And the fact St. George never delivered his message directly is troublesome to me. Who knows if Mister Cord delivered it accurately or if the encounter actually occurred as he said?"

"I believe on that, you can trust Elijah," Grant said.

Lidia ignored the comment. "Lucius talks of St. George in the most negative light. I sense bad blood between the two. I hope he hasn't had a confrontation."

"Lucius can handle himself," Grant said. The pencil paused. "May I ask you something, Lidia?"

She ran a hand through Ben's hair. "Yes?"

The boy was small for his age. He had blue eyes and his mother's red hair and a most pleasing disposition for a child.

"Why did you accede so readily to marry Lucius, knowing that Elijah was the one—" Grant searched for a polite word—"responsible?"

"It's quite simple," Lidia said. "During the crisis, Lucius was willing and Elijah was not."

Grant grinned. "Your logic is perfect."

Lidia raised a red eyebrow. "You understand? Few do."

"You made the right decision. Calmness in crisis is an admirable trait, more so than genius or courage. Elijah's not a bad man, but I don't see him as dependable to others. Perhaps that will change. I sense he has something deep inside that is made of tougher stuff than most suspect."

"One can hope, but it's not something that occupies my thoughts."

Grant drew another line on the pad. "You liked him well enough once upon a time, as they say in fairy tales."

Lidia stiffened, then reluctantly nodded. "Yes. I did. He is charming. And when he gives that smile—" she did not finish.

"Ah, well," Grant said, "that is in the past."

"It is indeed. I'm happy and our child is on the way," she added, running her hand over her belly once more. Still, she seemed uneasy about the subject. "But we are trying to hide a truth that many suspect."

Grant looked at Ben's eyes without comment, then resumed sketching.

"Am I a bad woman to try to live such a lie?" Lidia asked.

"I don't judge you," Grant said.

"That isn't what I asked."

"You aren't a bad woman," Grant said firmly.

"But the issue troubles you," Lidia said.

"It makes life hard for Elijah," Grant said. "He has undergone the Silence for a while and will continue to bear it until he graduates. And even then, it will haunt his life among graduates. The army is a small place."

A shadow fell over Lidia's face. "I've heard. But he did abandon me while Lucius stood for me."

"That is so," Grant allowed. "Although, Elijah wasn't exactly in the best condition to make a decision that morning and he was also facing the prospect of getting shot."

"Which is a point against him," Lidia noted.

Grant opened his mouth to say something, but stopped himself.

"How bad is this Silence?" Lidia asked. "I've heard of it, but as long as I can remember, no one survived it long enough to graduate."

"As I said, Elijah is tougher than he appears," Grant said. "But it's extremely hard on him. A principle to succeed in the Corps is teamwork. We cooperate and we graduate. Elijah has few he can count on. It's not a fate I would wish on anyone."

"Will he graduate?" Lidia asked.

Grant shrugged. "He was having a difficult enough time before the Silence. Now, he struggles with his studies on his own, although I help him with mathematics. Time will tell. And what about you? Would you ever consider letting Elijah into Ben's life in some way?"

Lidia ran her hand over her belly again. "Perhaps once our child is born, it might be a good time to reconsider."

"It might be," Grant agreed.

"The Corps can be harsh, can't they?" Lidia asked.

"Most of the time it's for good reason," Grant said. "They're being prepared to lead men into combat, the toughest and most chaotic environment imaginable."

"But sometimes it's all so petty. You saw how my husband suffered because of his middle name. As if it were his fault that stupid town in Mississippi spelled it the wrong way."

Grant nodded. "Some of it is petty and mean, but there are many different personalities in the Corps. Overall, they're a good bunch."

They sat in silence for a while as Grant continued sketching.

Lidia finally spoke. "Can I ask you something, Sam?"

"Yes?"

"People speak of Texas and Mexico. And then there's the slavery issue. Lucius tells me the south will never give it up willingly."

"Most likely not," Grant said.

"Then we will have war, won't we? Of one sort or another?"

Grant stared down at the drawing. He ran a finger over the outline of Lidia and Ben. "Cump Sherman says it is likely. I trust his judgment."

"Cump was a gloomy sort. I'm glad he graduated, although he was always unfailingly polite."

"I imagine he still is a tad gloomy. And polite."

"What is war like?"

Grant looked up, his face grim. "I don't know. We're taught of it and we read of it, but the reality will be something we can't comprehend until we taste the fire."

Lidia gazed at the Hudson. "You seem resigned to it. Some cadets sound eager when they talk of the possibility of war."

"I suspect those who sound most eager, might end up feeling differently when faced with the actuality."

Lidia looked back at Grant. "You make it sound so matter-of-fact. I know that's what they teach here. But what do you think you will feel if you have to fight?"

Grant closed the sketchbook. "Fearful. For those I command."

"Then why would—"

"It's my duty," Grant said simply. "I swore an oath on the Plain to defend the Constitution of the United States."

"Promise me something," Lidia said.

"And that is?"

"If there is war, and Lucius has to go, that you'll take care of him."

"The army might have a say in whether we serve together," Grant noted, "but I'll do whatever I can."

Lidia wasn't done. "And, God forbid, at some future date, by some chance, Ben has to become a soldier, that you'll take care of him."

"Now you really sound like Cump," Grant said. "It'll be many years before Ben could carry arms. And I believe Lucius would rather his son do anything other than wear a uniform. In fact, I believe that's why he went back to Mississippi. To explore possibilities."

"Yes, but look where Ben is growing up," Lidia said. "It's inevitable he'll be drawn to the army."

"Or pushed away from it," Grant said. "West Point has a different effect on different people."

Lidia stared at the Hudson. "I never thought of my son growing up to be a cadet. I must think on that." She shivered, then turned her attention back to

Grant. "Promise me you will look after both my husband and my son as best you can."

"I'll do my best. I'll always look over Ben as if he were my own. Besides Cump could always be wrong. It's—" Grant stopped and looked at Ben, whose head had turned toward the sound of boots on the stone stairs.

Rumble wore a dusty uniform and his step was weary. But his face lit up when he saw wife and child. "My dears!" He ran over and wrapped his long arms around both. He hugged them for several moments as he tenderly kissed Lidia on the forehead. "It's so good to be back."

"I can't draw you in." Grant held up the sketchbook. "You're a day too late."

Rumble let go and turned to his friend. "Sam." They shook hands. "You obviously had smoother traveling. I was delayed waiting for a steamboat."

Grant glanced at Lidia, then back. "And your visit? All is well in Mississippi?"

Rumble picked up Ben and sat down next to his wife. "It was never well. And it has not changed, except for the worse. But my mother, at least, still speaks to me and for me. My father; his stand is the same as it was before my journey. Still, I believe Ben would be welcome there."

"And St. George?" Lidia asked.

"I avoided that part of the plantation as I have no responsibilities there and he avoids the main house. St. George is not my problem, although he will soon be my brother's."

Grant packed up his gear. He removed the top sheet and handed the latest sketch to Rumble. "With my compliments."

"Thank you, Sam."

"I will leave you to your family and go for a ride."

"I hear the Hell Beast's mare has given birth," Rumble said.

"Yes."

"York must be a proud father," Rumble said. "As I am."

"What in the blazes happened to you?" Grant asked, his sketchpad tucked under one arm.

Elijah Cord was dressed in dirty clothes. He sported a black eye and was leading a saddled York out of the stables toward the riding hall. He walked with a drunken limp. His blond hair was tangled and dirty, but most telling was the defeated slump in his shoulders. Despite all, he attempted his trademark grin. "Got in a bit of trouble on the boat from New York City."

The grin didn't work. Grant reached out and grabbed his shoulder. "You need to go to the infirmary and see the Surgeon."

Cord didn't stop, heading toward the entrance to the riding hall.

"What do you think you're going to do?" Grant demanded.

"Ride York."

"You're drunk," Grant said.

"That's the point."

"What is?"

Cord halted. "I can't tame horses like you, Sam. Or be a father like Lucius. I'm not sure what I'm good at."

Grant was confused. "Then why are you trying to ride York?"

"I'm not going to try." Cord led the horse into the hall, Grant following. "I'm going to do it."

"You need to—" Grant's advice was wasted as Cord put his foot in the stirrup and swung his other leg up and over York.

The horse had mercy for a second, then bucked and spun. Cord went flying, tumbling onto the tanbark floor. Grant walked over to York, one hand held up, palm out.

"Easy," Grant whispered. He glanced at Cord. "You all right?"

Cord sat up, spitting out tanbark and dirt. "I'm alive."

Grant put his hand on the rein and got York under control. "He's not an easy ride."

Cord staggered to his feet. "Nothing is easy, it seems."

"I'll teach you to ride York, if you wish," Grant said. "But only when you're sober."

Cord ran dirty fingers through even dirtier hair. "I don't know what I wish." He paused. "I hear York has fathered a foal?"

"Yes.

"I suppose he's a better father than I."

Grant led York toward the riding hall door. "You've done well to stay in the Corps, Elijah. Focus on that."

Cord followed as Grant put York back in his stall. Before he unbridled the horse, Grant opened the pad and removed the sketch he had made the previous day. "Here. This is for you."

Cord took the piece of paper. He blinked and tried to focus on the drawing. "Ben and Lidia?"

"Yes. It's my first sketch of them."

Tears formed in Cord's eyes. He threw an arm around Grant. "Thank you, Sam." And then he passed out.

THE CORPS

January 1842, West Point, New York

LUCIUS KOSCIUSKO RUMBLE stood a vigil that eclipsed the most ardent soldier at his post: a devoted husband at his ailing wife's bedside. It was the darkest hours of the night, sunset long past and dawn still a ways off. He was alone in the cabin with Lidia. Ben was staying with Benny and Letitia for the night. As was Abigail, his daughter, born just three days ago.

Lidia had bled extensively during the delivery and despite the post Surgeon's best ministrations and the greatest amount of prayers, she had slid into a coma, not yet surfacing to see or hold her daughter.

Rumble dipped a cloth into warm water and wiped his wife's pale brow. His other hand was clenched in a fist, the nails digging into flesh, as if the pain was a power he could give to Lidia. He put the cloth back on the lip of the bucket. He gently grasped her hand with his damp one.

"Come back, Lidia. You have to see Abigail. She has your eyes. And your hair. You have to hold her. You know me. I lead a soldier's life. She needs her mother."

He froze as Lidia's eyes fluttered. He leaned over, face scant inches from hers. Feeling the shallow breath from her lips. Trying to convince himself it wasn't just the shadows from the flickering candles.

It wasn't.

Lidia's eyes snapped open, confused for a moment, then focusing on the face hovering over her.

"Lucius," she whispered, her voice so faint, the crackling of the fireplace almost drowned it out.

"Yes. I'm here." He took her hand in his. Her fingers curled around his callused skin.

"Lucius," she repeated. Her gaze went past him, to the rustic cabin he'd built for her. "Your have your life now. You got your freedom through me. An escape."

Rumble licked his lips, knowing any he could utter response would be a lie

"Your life now," she repeated. "Promise me." Her eyes closed again.

"Yes, Lidia? Anything."

Her eyes flickered. "Promise me, Lucius. Ben. He must never join the Corps."

Lucius' head drew back in surprise. "He's but a baby, Lidia."

"Promise me!" Her hand tightened around his fingers with a surprisingly ferocious grip. "He cannot wear the gray."

"But why?" Rumble asked. "It's an honorable—"

She cut him off again. "This is all I will ever ask of you. Promise me."

Rumble swallowed hard, but nodded. "I promise."

The slightest trace of a smile touched Lidia's almost white lips. Her eyes closed once more. He leaned close to make sure she was still breathing, reassured for the moment.

Rumble resumed his vigil, confused and scared.

A winter snowstorm was approaching. The air was heavy with cold and moisture portending the first snowfall of 1842. Cord wore his long dress gray overcoat over his cadet uniform. It wasn't enough to keep out the freezing wind, but he didn't notice. He stood still as the tree trunks around him, looking down at the dim light flickering in the window of the Rumble cabin. He'd been there since last quarters check, sneaking out of the barracks as soon as he could.

Cord knelt, clasped his hands and looked up at the black sky, where not a single star punched through the heavy clouds. "All right, God. You did right last time. Lidia made it through bringing Lil 'Ben into the world just fine. No reason things should change now. You're scaring us all. Lots of people care for her. So if you could see it in your heart, bring her back to us." Cord lowered his head. "Thank you."

Someone was moving on the frozen road behind and Cord jumped to his feet and turned. A slender figure in gray approached.

"Sam."

Grant flanked Cord, looking down at the faint light coming from the cabin.

"Anything?" Grant asked.

No," Cord said. "Rumble came out to get some water from the creek several hours ago, but that's all. Benny and Letitia have the children. Benny told some cadets earlier that Lucius desired privacy."

"No news is good news," Grant said. "Lidia will make it. She's a tough woman. Lots of prayers in the Corps tonight for her."

Cord stiffened as the window went dark. "Oh, God."

"It's probably just—" Grant began, but then the front door opened and Rumble stiffly walked out. He made it about five paces from the door before crumpling to his knees, his head dropping to his chest as the first flakes of snow began to descend.

Sam Grant had his hand on Rumble's shoulder, keeping him from falling into the newly dug grave. The digging had been difficult, beginning with scraping off the snowfall, then using a pickaxe to break through the surface layer of frozen dirt. Rumble had done the work by himself, despite numerous offers of assistance. He'd labored the previous night by lantern and then through the day. Grant had stood by the entire time, keeping silent watch, occasionally making the journey to the cadet mess to pick up hot coffee and warm food to sustain his friend's body.

Now, as the sun was sinking into the hills beyond West Point, all was ready, right on time, because even at West Point, in fact especially at West Point, funerals occurred on time. The West Point cemetery overlooked the Hudson from a location further up-river than the Academy and a new road had been constructed two years previously from main post to the spot as if in anticipation of a greater volume of traffic in the coming years. On the north side of the cemetery, the ground dropped precipitously to the river, presently clogged with chunks of ice.

The sound of carriage wheels rumbling on the frozen road reached the two cadets. The Master of the Horse, Sergeant Herschberger, was driving the wagon with casket, followed by Benny and Letitia Havens on foot, each carrying a child wrapped in blankets. Behind them were Superintendent Delafield and the Post Chaplain. Pete Longstreet and Fred Dent completed the group.

Benny Havens walked up to Grant and looked into the open grave. His normally ruddy face was pale and he shivered from more than the cold.

Grant reached out to Havens. "I'll hold Lil' Ben, sir."

Havens gave up the one-year old boy without protest. Letitia stood next to her husband, a lighter bundle in her arms, wrapped so heavily in blankets, not an inch of flesh was exposed to the winter cold. Abigail Violet Rumble had entered the world five days ago, preceding her mother's death by three days

Longstreet, Herschberger and Dent reached for the casket and Rumble hastened to help them. He was numb from grief and cold, but when he heard Abigail give a muted cry from inside the blankets, he stumbled and fell to his knees. He struggled to his feet and helped the others maneuver the wood coffin over the hole, using ropes to slowly lower it in, the rope burning the bare skin on his frozen hand as it slid through.

The group made a semi-circle around the grave as the Chaplain took his place at the head. He began the service, the words falling hollow and empty on Rumble's ears. The Chaplain had asked if Rumble had any particular verses he wished spoken, but he hadn't been able to think of any. He knew Samual would have found the appropriate passages in his leather-bound family Bible. Samual had conducted the services at the last funeral service Rumble had attended; when they had paid respects to the first Agrippa, even though they had not had a body to bury.

Fifty feet away, in the darkening shadows of the cemetery, Elijah Cord stood among the stone markers. He'd been there most of the day, watching Rumble work, desiring to offer his aid and knowing it would be rejected. Grant had spotted him earlier, but made no acknowledgement.

There was a sound in the distance, the heavy tread of boots hitting the ground in cadence; and growing nearer. Rumble raised his eyes from the hole that was holding his Lidia and looked over his shoulder. Like a long gray serpent, the entire Corps of Cadets was marching toward the cemetery, each cadet holding a lit candle in gloved hands.

Reaching the cemetery, the Corps split into ranks, surrounding the grave on all sides, the candles flickering in the cold evening breeze. The Chaplain uttered his last line and Rumble picked up a piece of frozen dirt. Grant was close at his side holding Ben. Rumble tossed the dirt onto the coffin. The thump when it hit wood was like a punch to his heart and he took an involuntary step back.

The First Captain took two paces forward and snapped a salute, whereupon the Corps began to sing a deep, slow-paced, familiar tune:

Come tune your voices, comrades, and stand up in a row.
For singing sentimentally we're for to go.
In the Army there's sobriety, promotion's very slow,
So we'll sing our reminiscences of Lidia Havens, Oh!

Rumble turned away from the grave. The Corps had changed the words to the song that had been written several years ago in honor of the tavern that was many cadets home away from home. *Benny Havens Oh!* was been written by a member of the class of 1838, O'Brien and Rumble had heard it sung once before here: the previous January, just after Ben's birth, for the funeral of O'Brien who had died in service with the 8th Infantry regiment in Florida, where Cump Sherman was now stationed, fighting the Seminoles. Next to Rumble, Grant joined in the singing as the Corps moved on to the next verse.

To our comrades who have fallen, one cup before we go,
They poured their life-blood freely out pro bono publico,
No marble points the stranger to where they rest below;
They lie neglected far away from Benny Havens, Oh!

Outside the circle of the Corps, in the dark shadows, Elijah Cord silently mouthed the words to the song.

And if amid the battle shock, our honor e'er should trail,
And hearts that beat beneath its fold should turn or basely quail;
Then may some son of Benny's, with quick avenging blow,
Lift up the flag we loved so well at Benny Havens, Oh!

To the ladies of our Army, our cups shall ever flow,
Companions in our exile and our shield 'gainst every woe;
May they see their husbands generals, with double pay also,
And join us in our choruses at Benny Havens, Oh!

At the last stanza, Grant put his free arm around Rumble's shoulder. Gathering his courage, Cord walked forward, shouldering his way through the ring of cadets around the grave. None interfered. He stood on the other side of Rumble, close enough that their shoulders touched. He was no longer just mouthing the words, but singing with the rest of the Corps.

When this life's troubled sea is o'er and our last battles through,
If God permits us mortals there in his blest domain to view,
Then we shall see in glory crowned, in proud celestial row,
The friends we've known and loved so well at Benny Havens, Oh!

Oh! Lidia Havens, oh! Oh! Lidia Havens, oh!
We'll sing our reminiscences of Lidia Havens, Oh!

As the last refrain faded into the darkness, the cadets blew out the candles. Led by the First Captain, they filed by, shaking Rumble's hand, then Benny Havens' and whispering condolences to Letitia. Tears were flowing down Old Benny's cheeks. Cord and Grant had taken a couple of steps back.

"Might I hold Ben?" Cord asked Grant.

Grant glanced at Rumble, who was receiving the respects of the Corps. He handed the child over and then stood right behind Rumble's right shoulder. Cord held Ben in the crook of one arm and looked down at those blue eyes. He retreated further from the funeral party, until he was alone with Ben in the dark among the gravestones. Cord reached inside a pocket on his long overcoat and pulled out a fine silver chain that he had bought off a sailor in Norfolk—the only purchase he made other than for liquor from the money he made working in the Navy yard. Dangling on the chain was a ring—Cord's West Point ring.

Cord looked up at the stars. "You're a hard fellow, God. Keep this boy safe. And his sister too." With no one watching, Cord held the ring in front of Ben's eyes. He was surprised when a small hand reached out and tiny fingers wrapped around the gold ring. Cord tenderly placed his hand over Ben's. "I'm so sorry about your mother, Lil' Ben," he whispered. "She was a good woman. I loved her. I know she didn't really love me. I know she loved your 'father'." He looped the chain over the child's head and tucked the ring inside the blankets. "You will always have two fathers."

MUTINY

November 1842, *USS Somers*, Atlantic Ocean

"ARE YOU AFRAID OF DEATH? Do you fear a dead man? And dare you kill a person?" The questions came in an excited tumble, hushed but insistent.

George King sat on the foremost boom of the *USS Somers* and restrained himself from shoving the speaker into the ocean below. "I don't believe I'm particularly anxious to die quite yet, but I do not fear death."

"And killing a man?" Midshipman Philip Spencer, son of the Secretary of War, pressed him. It was just after mid-watch, the start of the 25th of November, 1842, and the *Somers* had been at sea since early September. Stars sparkled overhead as the ship cut a course west across the Atlantic.

"If honor is involved, I could kill a man," King assured him.

Spencer appeared disappointed with the answer. "Can you keep a secret?"

Now King was in a bind. First, it was wrong to be out on the boom according to ship's regulations. The only reason King had agreed was he sensed that Spencer had something of great importance to say and the situation on the *Somers* had been deteriorating since the ship had turned around and begun its return cruise from Liberia to St. Thomas. There were one hundred and twenty souls on board the ship, a hundred of them under the age of 18. There were dark whispers that Spencer was up to something and King wanted to know what it was. The boom was one of the very few places on board where a whispered conversation could be had and not have a half-dozen over-hear it whether they tried to or not.

"I can keep a secret," he said.

There were only two men on board who could navigate the ship other than the handful of officers, and King had not only noted Spencer in the constant company of those two, he'd also seen Spencer pay them money and slip them illegal liquor. King had gone under Boatswains Mate Cromwell's verbal lashings several times and had great distaste for Seaman Small's disposition.

"Will you take an oath?" Spencer pressed. He was a tall, thin fellow of nineteen who had seemed amiable enough on the outbound voyage from New York City, but King had seen something in his eyes on first meeting that had never left—a sense of instability in the mind. He'd seen that look before in his own father's eyes just before the end, and not recognized it then for what it was.

"An oath on what?"

That gave Spencer pause. "On your father."

King smiled coldly in the dark. "Certainly."

"I lead a group," Spencer began, "who will take the ship."

"Mutiny?" King couldn't believe he had just said the word. It was unthinkable. There had never been a mutiny in the United States Navy.

"I have at least twenty who will follow. We'll have to kill all the officers, of course. But the plan is solid. Everyone has their assigned task."

"What do you wish from me?" King asked, more to gain time than anything else.

"You bring expertise with the rigging. We'll need good top men, especially among all these boys. We'll strike during mid-watch when Midshipman Rogers has the duty with me. We'll stage a fight on the forecastle and when Rogers goes to intervene, throw him overboard." Spencer's voice was low, but excited. "I can get the keys for the arms chest, then we'll cover all the hatches. I'll kill the captain while Cromwell and Small and some others take care of the rest of the officers. We'll take two of the aft cannon and train them forward. Then we'll let the rest of the crew up. Those with us, we'll keep. Those against, we will kill."

The plan had spewn forth as if a mad man were saying them as a prayer. However, upon a moment's reflection, King realized it might work. "Why do you want the ship?"

"We'll become pirates," Spencer said, slapping King on the shoulder. "Raise the black flag. We'll head for the Isle of Pine and gather more crew from among the pirates there. We'll also get some women. And rum." King could see Spencer's teeth as he smiled at the thought. "Things will be much different with me as captain. We'll have a much better time and soon all of us will be rich."

King took a deep breath of sea air as he tried to determine a course of action. The ship was under a good head of sail, but St. Thomas was ten days away. The *Somers* was the newest ship in the United States Navy, a hundred feet long, with a twenty-five foot beam at its widest. It boasted two square-rigged masts and was fast and nimble in the water. She carried only twelve cannon, but her agility could more than make up for that lack. She could run if heavily outgunned or she could fight if the situation was right, and King felt a sudden affinity for the ship.

"Are you with me?"

King didn't realize he was shaking his head as he answered. "Yes." Fortunately, the night covered his true answer.

"Good. I'll be back to you once we decide which night to strike."

King stood and made his way along the boom, his bare feet, now callused and rough, gripping the wood. On his back, was slung a boarding axe, cradled in a special leather sling he'd had one of the men who repaired sales make for him. The axe had a two-foot long handle with a wicked steel, double-headed blade. One side of the head was a razor sharp axe blade, the other a pick-like spike. It was a useful tool on board ship, as well as a very lethal weapon if the need arose.

King made it to the spar deck—the main deck of the *Somers*, which sported no other levels, being flush decked from bow to stern. He saw Small in the shadows, watching him and as he made his way aft, he realized Small was following. He'd seen Small with an African dirk, more a sword, he'd bought in Cape Mesurado in Africa, constantly honing the blade to a sharp edge. The dirk was conspicuously tucked in Small's belt.

King changed course, realizing there was no way he could get to Captain Mackenzie or First Officer Gansevoort, without Small intercepting. He slid down a hatch into the berth deck and wove his way through the hammocks holding sleeping sailors until he found his own. He climbed in and spent the rest of the night tossing and turning sleeplessly as he tried to come up with a plan.

As morning came and the watches changed, King accepted he could not get to either Gansevoort or the Captain. Both Cromwell and Small were always about, always within eye's reach, not a hard task on such a small ship. Nor did King know who else was in on the plan with them.

He went to breakfast and wrangled a seat next to the ship's purser, who had access to the officers. Speaking as quietly as he could, King relayed what Spencer had said to him the previous evening. He did this with one hand on the starter tucked under his blouse. He had no idea if the purser was true to his duty or in league with Spencer. The midshipman had claimed 20 among his mutineers among a crew of 120, which made for favorable, but still dangerous, odds.

The purser took the matter seriously. "Follow me. I'll put you in my storeroom then fetch Lieutenant Gansevoort. That'll prevent these spies from knowing that you meet."

King followed the man, weaving through the maze of the ship. He caught a glimpse of Cromwell with Small and he tapped the purser on the shoulder. "It won't work. You relay the message."

King diverged from the purser's path and went over to the conspirators. They stared at him, no one speaking a word.

King finally broke the silence. "The officers have no clue. I was just talking to the purser. All thoughts are on getting to St. Thomas."

"They'll not make St. Thomas." Cromwell folded tattooed arms over his burly chest. "I hear you are with us."

"I am."

"Good. Make sure your axe is ready. There will be bloody work soon."

Aloft in the masts of the ship, King was balanced on a high wire act both physically and mentally. His expertise had pushed the officers to send him aloft ahead of the other trainees. He found he had a natural affinity for the heights and the sails. While the ship rolled in the swell, the effect was magnified tremendously at the top of the one-hundred and twenty foot main mast. Even experienced top-men sometimes suffered sea-sickness, but not King.

There were no safety ropes or protective gear other than one's nimbleness, strength, and sense of balance. King relished the challenge and today it kept him from dwelling too much on what was developing below. He'd observed Lieutenant Gansevoort shadowing Spencer throughout the day, but no overt move was made on either side. The tension coming off the crew was a palpable wave even high in the topsails.

Then, around noon, Spencer began climbing up and King felt a moment's alarm, but the midshipman went to another top-man and sat next to him. The man began working a tattoo onto Spencer's forearm.

It was well past his watch, but King remained in the rigging. It was calmer than on the deck below, where the current of men moving about was disturbed, as if a heavy stone had been thrown into a stream. Slightly after two past the noon, the storm broke open.

Lieutenant Gansevoort came to the base of the mast and hailed Spencer, ordering him to instruct all the top-men to come down. Spencer did not relay the order, but he didn't need to. Everyone began clambering down, King included. He reached the spar deck and noted that Spencer had also finally climbed down, but had stopped on the Jacob's ladder and was staring at Gansevoort. King felt a chill go down his spine as he watched the two engage in eye contact for over a minute. Gansevoort and Spencer exchanged a few words and the lieutenant finally walked away, shaking his head. The gauntlet had been thrown down, it would now come to who would strike the first blow.

The blow came before darkness fell.

The crew was summoned to quarters, everyone reporting to duty stations as if preparing for combat, except there was no other ship in sight. Then they were called to assemble aft. King stood in the ranks, seeing the grim looks on the handful of officers standing by Captain Mackenzie.

The Captain was of middling height with thin hair, his forehead balding. He was not a tyrant as a commander, but firm when need be.

Mackenzie walked up to Midshipman Spencer and spoke in a voice all could hear. "I learn, Mister Spencer, that you aspire to the command of the *Somers*."

The words washed over the crew with electric effect, but Spencer seemed unconcerned.

"Oh, no sir." Spencer had a smile plastered to his face and his voice was not at all challenging to the Captain.

King stiffened as Mackenzie glanced in his direction. "Did you not tell Mister King, sir, that you had a project to kill the commander, the officers, and a considerable portion of the crew of this vessel and convert her into a pirate?"

King waited for Spencer to glare at him, but he was ignored as the midshipman focused on the Captain. "I may have told him so, sir, but it was in joke."

"You admit you told him so?" Mackenzie confirmed.

"Yes, sir, but in joke."

King had little sense of humor, but he was absolutely certain he had not been told a joke.

The Captain and midshipman sparred back and forth in dialogue for a quarter hour, Spencer sticking to his attempt to play it all off on misunderstood humor. The fact that Mackenzie was arguing with a subordinate in front of the crew over such a serious manner disillusioned King. This was a time for swift and decisive action, not discussion.

Finally, it seemed, Mackenzie had had enough. After another joke defense, the Captain slapped his hand on the hilt of his saber. "This, sir, is joking on a forbidden subject. This joke may cost you your life."

They found papers in Spencer's footlocker. Written in Greek. They were quickly deciphered. On one sheet the names of the crew were listed in three columns: Certain; Doubtful; To Be Kept Willing or Unwilling.

King learned his name was in the third column, which meant his subterfuge on the boom had not fooled Spencer.

The midshipman was in irons, chained to the deck, aft, and furthest from the crew.

The crew was dismissed and the ship sailed on.

King felt at peace the next day after a tense night. He was high in the royals, a hundred feet above the spar deck. The only sails higher than the royals were the skysails. Flanking the royals, further out on arms, were the studdingsails. Walking out to them was a particularly challenging feat as they were over the water. These sails produced tremendous torque on the mast and were dangerous to deploy, but Captain Mackenzie's urgency to reach St. Thomas was playing out among the canvas he ordered unveiled to the wind.

The ship was angled to the breeze, on direct course for the Bahamas. King felt invisible so high up, the wind whistling about him and the sails flapping. Too much flapping, he realized. He looked over and saw there was too much slack in the studdingsails and one side was losing power from the wind while the other side gaining too much. He stood up, one hand on a rope, the other on the mast, when an order came bellowing up from below as the officer of the deck noticed the same thing.

"Tighten down the slack on the larboard studdingsail," the officer of the deck called out.

King edged toward the rigging when he noticed Small and several other sailors climbing up the ropes like monkeys, much too eager to do a dangerous job. King joined the small group and they pulled on the brace, adjusting the sails. The task was done in less than half a minute.

King and the others let go of the brace, but not Small. He kept pulling.

"What are you doing?" King yelled, trying to be heard above the wind and sails.

Small ignored him.

"Belay!" the officer of the deck screamed. His order was echoed by Captain Mackenzie: "Belay!"

"Stop it!" King yelled at Small, who continued to haul away, then suddenly stopped. Too late for the ship.

The topgallant mast ripped away from the main mast, taking with it the rigging and sails attached to it. A spider's web of sails, rigging and wood began to tumble overboard. King slapped away the canvas that threatened to engulf him, realized his purchase on the yard was doomed and then he jumped, over a hundred feet above the deck, into the topgallant sail, sliding down it until he grabbed a stay and swung himself over to the yard. Everything above him had been torn away into the sea, but was still attached to the ship by all the rigging from spar deck and lower yards, forming a massive sea anchor on one side of the vessel.

The *Somers* heaved to, abruptly changing course, almost capsizing.

Mackenzie and Gansevoort began yelling orders, getting men aloft to cut away the wreckage. King whipped the boarding axe from its sheath and slashed at rigging. He noted that Cromwell and Small were up top, but neither seemed overly concerned about doing their duty. He had no time for them. King focused on the immediate danger. Who cared about mutineers when the ship could founder?

He stopped for a second and focused on the complex puzzle of ropes, sail, and wood. The sails that were dragging in the water were twisting the ship about. There were critical points of stress in the rigging. Taking a deep breath, King made his decision. He ran along the yard, no concern for his own safety, and began to chop away key lines, separating the ship from the former part of it that threatened to consume her. Within two minutes, with remaining ropes snapping, the wreckage ripped away from the ship and the *Somers* righted and veered back on course.

King halted, balanced on the arm, breathing hard, then suddenly realized the precariousness of his position. He scampered over to the main mast and clutched it with his free hand. He started laughing uncontrollably. It lasted a few seconds, then he snapped to, hearing Mackenzie yelling near the stern of the ship. He was upbraiding Midshipman Oliver Perry who had direct responsibility for the sails.

King climbed the rest of the way down. The sullenness of the crew was giving way to something electric as Gansevoort appeared next to the Captain with a cutlass and a brace of pistols. The Captain called out for Cromwell and Small to come aft. They were in irons in a flash, joining Spencer.

And with that the rest of the crew was like a sail with no wind. Men turned to follow orders, clearing the ship of the rest of the debris and conducting repairs.

But King had a feeling they had just passed through the eye of the hurricane, but had yet to come out the other side.

It was after dark before the work detail got around to replacing the topgallant mast, an arduous and dangerous endeavor on a ship under sail. King was aloft, guiding the rope that was lifting the mast. On the deck below a large number of men were pulling on the rope. But then, strangely, men began to let go of the rope and drift away in the darker shadows on the deck.

King's first hint of trouble was when the rope stopped moving. He heard a bosun mate berating men to get back to work. Sensing disaster, King grabbed the line. He secured the lift rope to a spar as the shouting below got louder and angrier. By the time he was done, he could just make out a large mass of men gathered in the forecastle. A bosun's mate was swinging his 'starter' to get the men moving.

It all went to hell quickly.

The mass of men charged toward the rear of the ship. Right toward Mackenzie and Gansevoort. As the Captain raced below for his Colt revolver and its six shots, Gansevoort drew his single-shot pistol and screamed at the men to halt.

"By God, I'll blow someone's damn head off if you don't halt!"

King joined a bosun mate, shoving his way into the crowd, and drawing his boarding axe. "Come men," King shouted. "Follow orders."

Someone hit him in the ribs and King blindly struck back with the flat side of axe, knocking the man to the deck. The melee ended when Captain Mackenzie arrived back on deck, standing shoulder to shoulder with his first officer. He cocked the Colt and the odds swung in favor of the officers, as other armed midshipmen joined the two senior men.

King used the axe to shove the young sailors back toward the forecastle. With much muttering and cursing, the mob broke apart and a tense peace was established.

It didn't last long.

The next night while standing midwatch, King heard shouts of alarm from where Spencer, Cromwell and Small were shackled. He raced toward the sound of trouble and arrived to discover the boom swinging wildly across the aft-deck. Low enough to knock over anyone standing, but high enough to miss the men shackled to the deck.

As officers scrambled and dove, King grabbed a rope attached to the boom, shouting orders. A few men came to his aid, but as they got the boom under control, a mob of fifteen sailors came charging.

Captain Mackenzie was ready, appearing in the hatch to his quarters, saber in one hand, Colt revolver in the other. "This is a time when you cannot disobey orders for you will lose your life if you do."

The mob skidded to a halt and once more dispersed.

Mackenzie called out. "King."

"Sir." King ran to the Captain and snapped to attention.

"I heard you taking command," Mackenzie said. "Good job."

King remained at attention.

"Go to the master-of-arms and draw a pistol and ammunition," Mackenzie ordered. "Then join me in my cabin."

"Yes, sir."

He quickly gathered the weapons, then made his way to the Captain's quarters, passing a pair of weary midshipmen on guard duty at the hatch. The ratio of officers to the rest of the crew was so low, all the officers and midshipmen were pulling double and even triple watches. St. Thomas was still days away. It was a regimen that could only work to the mutineers' advantage.

King clambered down the ladder and knocked on the Captain's door.

"Enter."

King stepped inside the cramped space. Mackenzie was sitting behind his small desk, Gansevoort standing to the side. Both were still armed, Gansevoort drumming his fingers on the hilt of the saber at his waist.

"Things stand at a precipice, Mister King," Mackenzie said. "I need to gather good men to our side. Who can we trust?"

King rattled off a few names. Too few.

Mackenzie turned to Gansevoort. "We won't make St. Thomas at this rate. We are too few and too tired. We can't keep a mutiny in check and also sail the ship with those we can trust."

Gansevoort stopped the drumming on the hilt. "We must act, sir."

Mackenzie turned to King. "What do you suggest?"

King was shocked for the second time and there was enough light from the flickering lantern for it to show.

"What is wrong?" Mackenzie snapped.

"You're the Captain, sir," King said.

"I know you went to the Military Academy for four years," Mackenzie said. "You have more military knowledge than almost anyone on board."

"Yes, sir," King acknowledged. "But I'm just a recruit."

"You're dismissed."

Mackenzie had four more men arrested and put in shackles.

It didn't change anything.

Two more nights passed, the situation growing tenser, the officers growing more tired, the crew more restless.

On the last day of November, Mackenzie had King report once more to his cabin. "I asked you once before what you would suggest," Mackenzie began.

King could see that the older man's hand was shaking.

"We will not make St. Thomas," the Captain continued as if that were a given rather than a best estimate.

"Most likely not, sir," King allowed.

"So? My officers are split."

"Between, sir?"

Mackenzie didn't answer. "You know the crew. What will stop this? Come on man. Forget the rank and give me the benefit of your training."

King took a deep breath. "You have arrested more men, but cannot keep arresting the entire crew. There are only three men outside your officers who can navigate the ship—the first three you arrested. If you eliminate them, you eliminate the possibility of a successful mutiny. The men will know that. They will bow to the inevitable."

"Thank you." Mackenzie stared down at the chart on his desk. "You may go."

"Yes, sir."

"Mister King."

King blinked sleep out of his eyes. He was surprised to see Captain Mackenzie in full dress uniform standing over him. King leapt to his feet, the aft deck rough under his feet, the blanket he had wrapped around himself to snatch a few moments of sleep falling away. He snatched up the axe and pistol.

"I want you to run three ropes over the main yardarm and be prepared for hauling up."

"Yes, sir." King paused as he realized the implications. "But there will be no drop then and—"

"Do it!"

"Sir." King went to choose the ropes.

Decisive and swift action did not seem to be Captain Mackenzie's forte.

After condemning Spencer, Cromwell and Small to death and giving them ten minutes to make their peace, an hour had dragged on. Mackenzie allowed them to argue their innocence, argue the mode of their death. At one point, Mackenzie even asked the men's forgiveness.

Small gave it, then cried out "God bless that flag!"

King watched this, one hand resting on the pistol stuck in his belt and most of his attention on the crewmembers lined up on the ropes he had prepared. The three lines lay along the deck, then snaked up over the yardarm and back down, nooses tied at the end.

Finally the three mutineers were led to their ropes.

King took lead on Spencer's rope as everyone else hesitated.

The Captain had given Spencer permission to give the order to initiate his own death. A taste of honor in the aftermath of mutiny. On the order, a cannon would be fired and the ropes would be pulled. King looked at his former shipmate. Spencer's face was pale as a hood was slipped over it.

The men waited. A few nervous coughs.

The bosun mate leaned close to Spencer, then hurried to the Captain. "Mister Spencer says he cannot give the word. He wishes the commander to give the order."

Finally, Mackenzie didn't hesitate. "Stand by. Fire!"

King was pulling on the rope as the echo of the cannon floated over the surrounding ocean.

And surprisingly, the rest of the crew also pulled. Three struggling bodies were lifted into the air. There was no drop, no quick snap of the neck, but rather a slow death by strangulation.

King reached a staple, and wrapped the end of Spencer's rope around it, securing it in place and Spencer twenty feet above the deck. His legs kicked and the body spasmed. Three martinets in a macabre death dance. Every crew member was fixated on the spectacle.

King looked past the bodies. The flag of the United States was limp in the sudden calm and the three men eventually hung just as still.

Decisive and swift action did not seem to be Captain Mackenzie's forte.

After condemning Spencer, Cromwell and Small to death and giving them ten minutes to make their peace, an hour had dragged on. Mackenzie allowed them to argue their innocence, argue the mode of their death. At one point, Mackenzie even asked the men's forgiveness.

Small gave it, then cried out "God bless that flag!"

King watched this, one hand resting on the pistol stuck in his belt and most of his attention on the crewmembers lined up on the ropes he had prepared. The three lines lay along the deck, then snaked up over the yardarm and back down, nooses tied at the end.

Finally the three mutineers were led to their ropes.

King took lead on Spencer's rope as everyone else hesitated.

The Captain had given Spencer permission to give the order to initiate his own death. A taste of honor in the aftermath of mutiny. On the order, a cannon would be fired and the ropes would be pulled. King looked at his former shipmate. Spencer's face was pale as a hood was slipped over it.

The men waited. A few nervous coughs.

The bosun mate leaned close to Spencer, then hurried to the Captain. "Mister Spencer says he cannot give the word. He wishes the commander to give the order."

Finally, Mackenzie didn't hesitate. "Stand by. Fire!"

King was pulling on the rope as the echo of the cannon floated over the surrounding ocean.

And surprisingly, the rest of the crew also pulled. Three struggling bodies were lifted into the air. There was no drop, no quick snap of the neck, but rather a slow death by strangulation.

King reached a staple, and wrapped the end of Spencer's rope around it, securing it in place and Spencer twenty feet above the deck. His legs kicked and the body spasmed. Three martinets in a macabre death dance. Every crew member was fixated on the spectacle.

King looked past the bodies. The flag of the United States was limp in the sudden calm and the three men eventually hung just as still.

GRANT SETS A RECORD

June 1843, *West Point*

IN A SINGLE LINE, THE WEST POINT class of 1843 thundered across the floor of the riding hall on their steeds, sabers glinting. They wheeled perpendicular to the stands filled with spectators, coming to a halt near one of the walls. They wrangled their horses about, so that they formed a row facing the center of the hall. They raised their sabers in salute, then lowered them. It was early June and the mounted review was part of the celebration in honor of their graduation the following week.

Rumble and another enlisted man ran out with two props and a bar. They set the base of the props on the tanbark covering the wooden floor, then began adjusting the height. Rumble had a gleam in his eyes as he pushed his prop to the maximum height. The other soldier looked at him in confusion, then shrugged, following suit. They set the bar on the props, half a foot higher than the top of Rumble's head.

The buzz among the spectators began immediately. "It has to be Grant and York," was the most commonly whispered comment from cadets to family members and others not familiar with the prized combination of the riding hall. In the reviewing stand, Superintendent Delafield leaned forward in anticipation. This was not on the program they had been given for the graduation riding review.

The Master of the Horse, Sergeant Herschberger, strode out to the bar. He looked at it, at Rumble and frowned. Then the slightest trace of a smile flickered on the stern Master of the Horse's face, gone so quickly one would wonder if it had been there at all. He called out in a thunderous voice: "Cadet Grant!" The order echoed through the riding hall.

Grant, still weighing a paltry one hundred and twenty pounds, spurred York forward from the line. The contrast between the slender cadet and the massive horse would have been greater if it were not for the relaxed way

Grant rode. He didn't seem to be controlling York, but a part of the beast, the mind behind all that muscle below the saddle. Grant saluted the Superintendent with his saber, then slid it into the scabbard. As he turned to head for the far end of the hall, he winked at Rumble.

In the reviewing stands, Benny and Letitia Havens sat with Ben between them. Letitia held Abigail on her lap. Not far from them was George King, dressed in a navy uniform, the insignia of an ensign on his sleeve. His face was tanned and his ice-blue eyes held an edge to them that had not been there when he was a cadet.

Hidden at the far end of the building, near the horse doors leading to the stable, St. George stepped into the dark shadows, and folded his powerful arms across his broad chest, his clothes dusty and worn from a long, hard ride. His slouch hat was pulled down low. His black sash was wrapped around his solid waist, and a discerning observer could see the outline of his Le Mat pistol tucked inside.

Grant galloped the Chesnut bay to the far end of the hall. He spotted St. George, hesitated, but then focused on the task at hand. He turned the horse, paused for just the slightest of moments. He leaned forward and whispered something into York's ear. The horse's ears lay back and nostrils flared. Together, they began the straight run for the bar.

Man and beast accelerated across the floor, loose tanbark flying up behind, hooves thundering on the wood underneath. Grant had the horse measuring strides based on the rapidly closing distance. At the perfect spot Grant twitched the reins and York gathered himself, seeming to shrink for a second, all muscles tightening, and then bounded smoothly into the air. With inches to spare, Grant and York flew over the bar. They landed without mishap. There was a moment of stunned silence.

"Very well done, sir!" Sergeant Herschberger cried out, acknowledging that Grant had just set an Academy record. The crowd roared its approval. Herschberger turned to the rest of the class of 1843 lined up on their mounts along the wall. "Class dismissed."

With a loud cheer, the cadets mobbed Grant and York. But standing closest, next to Grant's stirrup, was Rumble. Grant leaned over and shook his friend's hand. "Thank you, Lucius."

"You're welcome, Sam."

Then Grant looked at the mounted cadets crowding round and sought out his classmate Elijah Cord and shook his hand. Grant leaned close to Cord, just as he had whispered to York: "This evening will be your opportunity. But first, there's a fellow over by the horse door that looks like the ruffian you described meeting the night of Ben's birth."

Cord swiveled his head and saw St. George. "It's him."

The overseer gave a cold smile and waved an envelope. Cord pushed his way through the mob of cadets.

In the stands, Superintendent Delafield walked over to Benny Havens and Letitia. He rubbed Ben's head affectionately and smiled at Abigail. "How are the children?" he asked Benny.

"As well as can be expected, sir," Benny said, surprised the Superintendent acknowledged him publicly. For the past couple of decades his tavern had been off limits to cadets, even after being kicked off the military reservation, and he had waged a low level conflict with the powers-that-be at the Academy, although Delafield had been more lenient than any of his predecessors.

Delafield looked past Benny as Rumble came up. "Sergeant."

Rumble snapped to attention. "Sir."

"At ease," Delafield ordered.

Rumble leaned over and scooped up Ben, holding him in his arms.

"Let's talk privately," Delafield said.

Still carrying Ben, a puzzled Rumble walked with the Superintendent a few paces away from the rest.

Delafield reached out and placed a hand on Rumble's shoulder. "I don't know if you wish you were with your classmates graduating next week. But I think what you do have here, with your family, is a much greater accomplishment than finishing four years at the Academy. Particularly in the—" he searched for a word—" honorable way in which you acted."

Delafield looked left and right, as if about to commit an infraction he would give himself demerits for. He reached into his uniform pocket and produced a small leather pouch. He pressed it into Rumble's hand. "Something I want you to have."

Rumble opened the pouch. A ring for the class of 1843. It wasn't gold, like the rest of the class rings, but silver. Rumble looked up at the Superintendent. "Thank you very much, sir. I appreciate it. But I do not deserve it."

"I believe you do."

"Sir, I—"

"Don't make me pull rank," Delafield said with a smile.

Rumble inclined his head in acquiescence. "It's a grand gesture, sir. I think you should know that our family already has a class ring."

Delafield blinked in confusion. "How so?"

Rumble reached to Ben and pulled the chain around his son's neck, exposing the ring hanging there.

"Whose is that?" Delafield asked.

"Mister Cord's," Rumble said.

"Truly? It's Mister Elijah Cord's?"

"Yes, sir," Rumble said.

"I'm impressed for the second time today." Delafield glanced at the cadets milling on the riding floor, searching for Cord. "Indeed, I am quite surprised." He seemed deep in thought. "But it's a good surprise. So you and Mister Cord are reconciled?"

"We are cordial, sir."

"Despite the Silence? Interesting." Delafield came out of whatever thought he was lost in and touched Rumble's shoulder once more. "Still, I want you to have this ring. It is between you and I and the Academy."

"Yes, sir," Rumble said. "It means a lot to me."

"Good." Delafield looked past Rumble as heavy thumps indicated the approach of a horse.

"Superb job, Mister Grant,"

Grant saluted the Superintendent and slid off York, holding the bridle lightly in his hand. "Thank you, sir."

"I will leave you gentlemen be," Delafield said and headed for the exit.

"What was that about?" Grant asked Rumble.

"Nothing important," Rumble said, tucking the leather pouch in his pocket.

"I've never seen nothing like it, Mister Grant," Benny Havens said, joining them. "What was that, six and a half feet?"

"Roughly," Grant said, as if it were a matter of little importance. "The horse did all the work."

Rumble laughed. "No one else could make York do that work."

"I wouldn't be certain of that." But Grant turned serious. "There's a man over yonder, by the horse door. I told Elijah and he confirmed it was St. George."

Rumble's good humor was gone. He tried to look over the milling cadets but could see no sign of the overseer. "I'll go over."

Grant stopped him. "Let Elijah deal with it for now. Stay with your family."

"It's my problem," Rumble said.

"Ah, but Lil' Ben is also Cord's concern, is he not?" Grant asked. "And if St. George is a threat to Ben, I think Elijah can handle things. There are some things we can trust him on. More than you think, actually."

Rumble opened his mouth to say something, but then snapped it shut.

Outside the stables, Cord found St. George smoking a cigar. "May I help you?"

"Ah, it's the third class fellow," St. George said. He had the cigar in one hand, the other hand with thumb hooked in the sash.

"I'm a first class cadet now," Cord said, "and I'll be graduating in a week and commissioned an officer in the United States Army."

"Well, good for you, boy, but there be something in the way you say it make me think you aint too sure that happening."

Cord dropped all pretenses at being civil. "What the hell do you want, St. George?"

"Got me another letter for young Mister Rumble from his father."

"Give it to me. I'll pass it on and then you can be on your way."

St. George dropped all pretenses at being relaxed. "Who you think you are, boy, giving me orders?"

"You're not welcome here."

"You the master here? To say who and who not be welcome? That fella on the horse. Now he might be someone to listen to. That be some riding. He must be from Dixie. Only a southern boy can handle a beast like that."

"He's from Ohio," Cord said. "He's a northerner."

"Now you lying," St. George said. "No Yankee could ride like that."

Cord took a step forward, veins in his neck bulging. "How dare you—"

St. George's hand slipped inside his black sash, but he didn't pull the gun. Yet. "Careful, boy."

A passing officer stopped. "Is there a problem Mister Cord?"

"No, sir," Cord said, keeping his eyes on St. George. "Just having a discussion with my friend."

"Carry on then." The officer walked off, but glanced over his shoulder a couple of times.

St. George gave the cold smile that never touched his pig eyes. "You aint too dumb. But you, you nothing to me."

Mounted cadets were filing by, crossing the dirt road and going into the stable. A few looked curiously at the two men, but most ignored Cord as they always did. Not only because of the Silence, but also because he was currently the class 'goat'. Last in overall cadet ranking. The consensus among the Corps was amazement that Cord had managed to make it this far against the weight of the Silence and his difficulties in academics and discipline. And there was a very strong rumor that Cord would not graduate the following week—that he had been 'found' in demerits and in academics and Superintendent Delafield would be boarding him out. If Longstreet were still at the Academy he would be running a pool on the odds of Cord's graduation, and there was little doubt he'd be betting against it.

St. George took a step back. "Too many nosy folk around. I hear you keydets have honor. Can I be trusting you to deliver this letter?"

"Yes." Cord almost spit the word.

St. George held out an envelope sealed with wax. "I'll be seeing young Rumble before I be going back. I'll be knowing whether you give it to him or not."

Cord took the thick envelope. "He'll get it."

St. George took a step back. "Maybe I see you later, boy. Maybe at that saloon you keydets go to. You tell young Rumble, he got a reply, he be finding me there tonight. Won't be hard for him to do, seeing as he live next door."

St. George laughed and walked away.

Grant looked past Rumble. "I see George King, back for your graduation. I'll go speak to him. Stay here and wait for Elijah to give you a report on his scouting. I'll keep your cousin occupied."

Grant led York to the midshipman. King was watching the cluster of cadets as if evaluating everything they did.

"Mister King!" Grant saluted.

King returned the salute. "Sam Grant. I remember a similar jump you did on the same horse."

"That jump wasn't as calculated," Grant said.

"Oh, I do believe it was," King said.

"I heard about the *Somers*," Grant said. "A terrible thing."

King nodded. "It was an unfortunate lack of discipline combined with poor leadership."

"I hear they're going to establish a Naval Academy because of what happened."

"Strange, what power and effect a hanging can have, especially when one is the son of the Secretary of War," King said. "Yes, there'll be a Naval Academy. We'll keep the students on shore for a few years to get some discipline under their belts before sending them out to sea. I'll be heading to Annapolis after the wedding to help prepare that very institution."

"Your cousin's wedding in Mississippi?" Grant asked.

"Yes. I've never been there but I desire to see that part of the country, particularly the Mississippi. The Navy has responsibilities for our inland waterways also."

"It should be quite the affair," Grant said. "I also received an invitation. I'll be heading home to Ohio, then to the wedding, and afterwards Mister Cord and I will report for duty at Jefferson Barracks."

When King said nothing at Cord's mention, Grant continued. "Try not to be too hard on the incoming students at your Academy. Some discipline is good, but-"

"Discipline must be absolute," King said. "A ship at sea has no recourse beyond the Captain's iron will."

Grant mildly raised an eyebrow. "There are some who say the hanging on the *Somers* was beyond the bonds of military law."

"It was necessary," King said, before softening. "Still, things could have been handled much better. There was a lack of effective leadership involved."

"Men need to be led, not forced," Grant said. "Especially in a country like the United States where we value our individual freedom so much more than other countries."

King was looking over at Rumble, Benny Havens, his wife and the two children. "Strange how time has played out. My cousin seems very content."

"He is," Grant said. "Are you?"

"With the Navy? Yes. It suits me. It was gracious of Major Lee to intercede on my behalf."

"Do you know *why* Major Lee did so?" Grant asked.

King cocked his head. "I've wondered about that."

"Elijah went to see the Major over his furlough with a letter of recommendation for you and his own personal request." Grant watched Cord come back in the stable and speak briefly with Rumble.

"Mister Cord did that?"

"Indeed."

King pursed his lips as he pondered this development. "I was going to speak to him anyway, now is as good a time as any." He brushed by Grant and headed toward Cord.

Seeing King approach, Cord walked away from Rumble and his family to the center of the stable, next to the pole Grant had jumped.

"Mister Cord."

Cord saluted. "Ensign King."

"There are some who say you will not graduate," King said, returning the salute.

"There are some who say a lot of things," Cord replied.

"We have unfinished business," King said.

"Surely, you can't be holding a grudge after all this time," Cord said.

"There is no time limit on honor."

Cord rubbed his forehead, trying to forestall a headache.

King folded his arms across his chest. "I've heard of your stubbornness in the face of the Silence. Strange thing, my getting kicked out for speaking and your suffering, but perhaps graduating, for not speaking."

"Was it worth it?" Cord asked.

"Honor is everything," King said.

"Yes, I remember. I believe you said it's all a man has."

"Perhaps I will see you tonight in Benny Havens?" King asked. "We can discuss our unfinished business some more."

Cord sighed. "Seems everyone's going to be at Benny's tonight."

Rumble sat alone on Kosciuszko's garden, the letter from his father heavy in his hands. There was more than just paper inside. A hard, round object could be felt. Cord had given the envelope to him, saying that St. George would be in Benny Havens this evening awaiting a reply. That portended disaster. St. George amongst a crowd of drunken cadets, many eager for graduation in less than a week, was throwing a keg of gunpowder into a bonfire. And it was too damn close to Ben and Abigail. Rumble had sent Cord to find Grant, so that both could be in the tavern later, but Cord had mysteriously indicated he already had a standing engagement with Grant after which they would both show up.

Then there was the issue of his cousin King and Cord. Since arriving at West Point a few days ago, King has talked little, so Rumble had no idea where his cousin stood in regard to the unfinished duel and it was a distraction he could ill afford right now.

The afternoon sun was below the level of the Plain and Rumble was in the shadows. The sound of the small fountain was drowned out by the cries of revelry from graduating cadets and their families enjoying dinner in a pavilion erected on the Plain.

Rumble looked at the seal on the envelope. A replica of the Emperor Tiberius' imperial seal. Rumble sometimes wondered if his father realized that Tiberius was Emperor of Rome when Jesus was crucified. He doubted it. The fact his Father had used his seal meant he didn't fully trust St. George. The overseer was capable of many things and quite the accomplished liar, but betraying the seal was too obvious a breach of protocol even for him.

With a sigh, Rumble broke the wax with his thumb and opened the envelope. He was shocked when he saw a single sheet of folded rose-colored paper. Inside the paper was a ring—a replica of Tiberius's seal.

Rumble smiled as he saw his mother's flowing script, images of his mother lounging in her sitting room coming to mind. The words caused the smile to disappear:

Palatine
Natchez, MS
May 15th, 1843

My dearest son,
I must admit I am somewhat sorry we are not there for what would have been your graduation. You know we would have come if the event had unfolded as your father wished. But from seeing you two summers ago, I believe you have chosen the correct path for yourself. Your father was sending St. George with a letter to upbride you for not graduating and to once more ask you to forsake your family there to return here. He does not understand your family is our family. I intercepted the letter before he gave it to St. George. I replaced his with mine. I have always had a copy of his seal, even as he sends you one he had made for his son to ensure your reply returns to Palatine intact and safe from St. George's prying eyes.
We I mourned greatly when I heard of your Lidia's death. You have known too much death for someone so young.
It is something of which I have never spoken to you, but you had an older sister. Two years prior. She died shortly after birth of the flux. I fell into grief for almost a year. I hope you do not despair as I did then. You have your

children to think of. When you were born, it lifted my darkness. And you have kept a light in my life all the years since. I am glad you have chosen your own path in life. So few are able to do so.

Rumble had to look up from the letter imagining what his mother must have felt after the death of the sister he had never heard about before and being alone with Tiberius in that huge home. He collected himself and resumed.

Your father's condition comes and goes. He says he is well, but the facts speak otherwise. Seneca spends most of his time at Rosalie—so much so that people are saying it is odd; and it is. I know he does not want to be around Tiberius. That he feels useless here as long as John Dyer and his son run the true operations of Palatine. I do not foresee that changing with Seneca's pending marriage. Rosalie is a forceful woman. I admire her greatly. But a woman cannot run a plantation no matter how talented or powerful she is. I learned that many yeas ago.

There is much going on here that your father does not know or, more likely, does not care to know. I despise Dyer and his son. But I am powerless to do anything as long as your father keeps them under his protection.

I desire you to come home once more.

At least for Seneca and Rosalie's wedding. And, please, bring your Ben and Abigail. It would do my heart good to see children here again. They would enjoy the fountain, I am sure. I promise you my full support. I want to use the wedding reception to formally recognize both your children as Rumble's and part of the family. Your father will not be able to deny me that.

I have invited your cousin, George King, and a pair of your friends: Ulysses Grant (what an odd name) and Elijah Cord whom Samual met with my earlier letter, so you will have company here.

Please put your reply in the envelope and re-seal it with the ring, which you may keep, as it would have been yours anyway.

I pray for you and your children.

With my love.

Violet Rudolph Rumble.

Rumble folded the letter, slid it inside the envelope and put it in his blouse pocket. He looked at the seal, tossing it in his hand, feeling the weight. He reached in his pants pocket and pulled out the ring Superintendent Delafield had given him. He put them side-by-side. He had achieved neither. Yet, he had ended up with both.

BENNY HAVENS

June 1843, West Point, New York

St. George Dyer sat with his chair tipped back against the wall at a corner table in Benny Havens watching the cadets drinking. They were children, playing a game. Every time the circle of cadets prepared to drink, they would turn their backs to each other, imbibe, then turn back and resume their conversation. It made no sense.

When the owner came over with another mug of ale, St. George pointed. "What they be doing?"

Benny Havens laughed. "The honor code. They aint supposed to be drinking. So to avoid having to lie about seeing each other drink, they make sure they don't see each other drink."

"That be the stupidest damn thing I done heard."

Benny Havens shrugged. "It's been that way since I opened the place. It's harmless and more a tradition these days than anything else."

"Damn foolish."

"Where are you from, stranger?" Benny Havens asked. "You sound southern."

"You got a problem with southerners?" St. George looked up at the tavern keep.

"Not at all. These cadets are from everywhere."

St. George tossed a coin on the table and Benny Havens scooped it up. "Would you be wanting a hot flip?" he asked, pointing at a flagon in which he had been dipping a red-hot poker from the fireplace every so often.

St. George tapped a thick finger on the edge of the mug. "Asked for ale. Paid for it. I be wanting something, I be telling you."

"As you wish," Havens said coldly and moved on.

St. George could hear snippets of conversation, the tavern not much larger than his overseer's cabin. The front legs of his chair slammed into the plank floor and he leaned forward when he heard someone mention a familiar name.

"I don't know why Sam Grant still talks to Rumble," one cadet was saying. "We'll be officers soon and he's enlisted."

"Hell, Grant never honored the Silence regarding Cord," another said.

"I heard tell Grant is Lil' Ben Rumble's godfather," a third mentioned.

The second cadet laughed. "You mean Lil' Ben Cord."

"Hush," the first cadet hissed. "It's not to be spoken of."

The conversation drifted off in another direction, but St. George didn't push his chair back and relax. Nor did he drink the ale. His eyes were focused on the door. Waiting.

The riding hall was empty when Cord swung the door open. He held it as Grant led York in by the bridle. The bay was skittish, little used to being in the riding hall in the dark. Moonlight glinted through the narrow, high windows and in the distance the sounds of revelry echoed from the Plain. The bar that Grant had jumped was still in place, a temporary monument to his achievement.

Cord swung the door shut and latched it, insuring they would not be disturbed. Grant ran his hand over York's forehead, whispering to the horse, calming it.

"Are you certain?" he asked Cord.

"Yes."

"Why do you think tonight will be different from the other nights we've been here?" Grant asked.

"It probably won't be," Cord acknowledged. "But it will be my last chance, regardless of what happens with the Board."

"All right. From here," Grant said, positioning York at the same spot from which he had started earlier in the day.

Cord took a deep breath, then took the bridle from Grant's hand. He put his hand on York's forehead. "Easy now."

One foot in the stirrup. York remained still. Cord lifted himself off the floor and swung his leg over the saddle. York twitched.

Grant stepped back and nodded, the movement almost unseen in the darkness.

Cord leaned forward in the saddle, as he had seen Grant do so many times before and had been taught to do. He whispered comforting words in York's ear, feeling the tension ease slightly in the beast underneath him.

"Now!" Cord hissed and York bolted, heading straight for the bar. Air rushed through Cord's hair as the bay accelerated. Cord relaxed, settling into the saddle. His hands were loose, letting York have free rein. The sound of the bay's hooves on the tanbark covered floor sounded distant to Cord. His focus was on the bar, a dark line against a darker backdrop.

York leapt, lifting Cord into the air.

As they flew over, the left rear hoof nicked the bar and it vibrated and teetered.

Cord grunted as York landed hard. He jerked the reins to look back. Grant was staring up at the quivering bar. All was still except for the piece of wood. Then it too was still.

Grant let out a whoop, more excited about Cord's achievement than his own.

Cord slid off the horse. Grant ran up and grabbed him in a hug, pounding him on the back. "You did it!"

"The horse did all the work," Cord said with his trademark grin.

"We have to tell—" Grant began but Cord held up a hand.

"No, Sam. No one is to know. This is between you and me. And York." He looked at the bar. "I just needed to prove I could do something right."

Cord reluctantly walked with Sam Grant down the path to Benny Havens. Cord knew the place would be full of his classmates, that almost all would ignore him, and that St. George and George King would be there.

It seemed a pretty damn stupid idea.

"Cheer up, Elijah," Grant said. "St. George won't try anything with the three of us around. Lucius said he would give him the needed reply and that would be that."

"Nothing is ever that simple," Cord said, falling in step with him. "And George King said he wished to speak with me there, also. I don't think this evening will turn out well."

"Now you sound like old Cump," Grant said,

"Have you heard from him lately?" Cord asked as they hit a switchback on the trail.

"He's still with the Third Artillery down in Florida," Grant said as they approached the open door to Benny Havens. "Fighting the Seminoles. Bloody affair. He wrote that they went by the site of Dade's massacre."

"That was horrible," Cord said. "Longstreet used to say Dade got massacred by the Seminoles just like Hannibal ambushed the Romans at Lake Trasimene during the Second Punic War. Marching along a road with a body of water to the right and getting attacked from the left and trapped."

Grant stared at Cord in surprise. "You've been brushing up on your martial studies."

"Someone told me I needed to," Cord said. "I wouldn't mind going down to Florida and getting in a scrape or two."

"Don't be in such a rush to get shot at," Grant advised. "Still, it is strange that Dade would get massacred in the same way as a lesson he certainly learned in tactics class."

"Perhaps there's a difference between the classroom and the battlefield," Cord said.

They walked into the bar, cadets calling out greetings; as usual, most acknowledging Grant and ignoring Cord. Many shouted congratulations to Grant over the jump earlier in the day. It wasn't hard to spot St. George's bulk ensconced at a table in the far corner. George King was at the far end of the bar, aloof and distant from the cadets with his Navy uniform and his attitude.

Cord led the way to the table in the other rear corner.

Benny Havens quickly appeared at the table with a bottle. "On me, Mister Grant, in honor of your graduation and the jump." He placed the bottle on the table, then walked away without acknowledging Cord.

"Easy," Grant advised as King came walking over.

Conversation in the tavern dropped until it was utterly silent as King stopped at the edge of the table. "Mister Cord, we have unfinished business."

With a sigh, Cord got to his feet. "I won't be dueling you, Mister King. I'll apologize again to you for any slight, and as far as—"

King held up a hand, cutting him off. "I think our business would be concluded quite satisfactorily if I bought you a drink."

Cord blinked. "A what?"

"Do you accept my offer?" King asked as Benny Havens came over with a bottle and three glasses.

"You too, Mister Grant," King said. "You interfered that morning, so we need to settle things also."

"I'm not a fan of spirits," Grant said, taking a glass, "but for this I will certainly make an exception."

King filled all three glasses. "To duty, to honor, to country," he called out loudly, so everyone in the room heard.

Slowly, every cadet lifted their glass also.

"Here, here," Grant said. The three men clinked glass on glass and without turning their backs, drained them.

Toast completed, Grant indicated a chair. "Would you join us, sir?"

"Certainly," King said. He settled into a chair and ran his fingers over the scarred wood surface of the table. "In fact, I believe this is the exact same—" he paused as Rumble's wide shoulders framed the doorway to the tavern. En masse the cadets called out greetings, several gathering around him, trying to buy him a drink. But Rumble was like a bullet to a target, wading through the drunken cadets to St. George. He held out two envelopes.

From across the room, St. George had watched Rumble the way a swamp 'gator would watch game come to a watering hole. "You got a reply for Master Tiberius?"

"It's enclosed. And here is a letter for my mother, also sealed. I have informed my father of the second letter, so if she does not get it, he will know."

St. George's pig eyes narrowed as he took the letters and slid them inside his black sash. "You accusing me of something?"

"Not yet," Rumble said, noting that St. George's hand remained inside the sash and knowing what was secreted there. "Just giving you the lay of the land."

"I'm as smart as you, don't need no talking down to."

"Maybe you do," Rumble said.

St. George uncoiled from the seat until he stood eye to eye with Rumble. "You aint no favorite son no more."

"I don't know exactly what hold your family has on my father," Rumble said. "But your time is coming."

"Everyone time be coming," St. George said. "Some sooner than others. Maybe yours is real—" he stopped looking left and right over Rumble's shoulders.

Grant, Cord and King were flanking Rumble, their faces grim. "Buy your friends a drink?" St. George asked, flashing his false smile.

"They'll drink with me." Rumble turned his back on St. George, but the overseer wasn't done.

"Hold on."

Rumble faced him, his friends backing him up. "What?"

"Where be the seal? I need bring it back to Master Tiberius."

"It's my ring," Rumble said.

"I don' think—"

"No, you don't," Rumble said. "The ring was given to me in the letter. You cannot contradict that, unless somehow you saw the contents of the letter. And giving you the seal negates the effectiveness of sealing the letters. Good night, sir."

Rumble headed for the table with his friends.

"Who the tarnation is that?" Benny asked as he came over with another glass.

"Don't concern yourself with him," Rumble said. "He's trash."

"He's dangerous," Cord said.

Rumble glanced at him. "And how do you know that?"

"Samual told me. And I've met some dangerous men in my life. He fits the bill. They're dangerous because they're mean and angry."

Rumble nodded. "Samual knows better than anyone how evil St. George is." He grabbed the bottle Benny offered and filled five glasses. He passed them around to the two cadets, the ensign and his father-in-law. "Gentleman, let's salute our two graduates of West Point, class of 1843."

"Don't be jinxing me," Cord began. "I still have to—"

Grant cut him off, lifting his glass in the air. They clinked glasses and drank deeply.

Cord was drunk and had overstayed. King had barely sipped the second toast, placed his glass down on the bar and departed. Sam had excused himself after only the two drinks, staggering out the door as he always did when he imbibed. Rumble had kept an eye on St. George until the overseer slithered out the door and into the darkness. Then he immediately made his own good night, heading to the cabin to relieve Letitia of her duties and guard his children.

Cord stayed and drank until Benny was past ready to shut down. The tavern keep propelled Cord out the door with a bit less force than he would have liked to, locking the door behind the inebriated cadet.

In the warm summer night, Cord shook his head, trying to gain some clarity. He knew the path from Benny Havens by heart and began the trek back to the barracks. He was halfway up the hill when a figure stepped out of the trees along the side of the path.

"Hey there, boy."

Cord whipped out his whalebone knife.

St. George laughed. "You got a knife, I got a gun. How stupid be you?"

In the moonlight, Cord could see the double-barreled revolver in St. George's paw.

"It's murder if you shoot me," Cord managed.

"Who be knowing? Oh, Rumble, he'd suspect, but I be long gone before they find your body. If they find it at all. Maybe toss you in the river. Rivers eat bodies. I've fed the Mississip a few."

"What do you want?" Cord asked, sliding his left foot forward, trying to close the distance.

"What do I want?" St. George muttered, as if actually thinking about the question.

"What kind of gun is that?" Cord asked to gain time.

"One dat has killed and will kill again. Maybe tonight. Then again, maybe not tonight."

"I've never seen the like." Cord started sliding his right foot forward. He was about eight feet away. He needed to halve the distance to have a chance.

"Boy, you move another one of your damn feet, I blow it right off."

Cord stopped.

"Get rid of the knife."

Cord hesitated and St. George cocked the gun with a sound that seemed like a crack of thunder to Cord. He dropped the knife.

St. George continued. "This here be a special gun. Got it down in New Orlean. Made by some French fella named LeMat. He told me he hand made it, never sold one before. Still working on da' thing. I used to carry me one of them Colts. But had to shoot an uppity nigra one time. Took me five shots to put his dumb-ass down. So I got me this."

Cord suspected someone being so chatty probably wasn't going to shoot him. St. George did indeed want something. He waited as the man rambled on about his gun, as if it were the bones of Jesus and he were a true believer.

"Got me nine bullets in the cylinder and a big old slug in the bottom barrel. That last one will put someone down permanent like."

"So you want to kill them twice," Cord said.

St. George raised the gun and both barrels pointed right at Cord's face. They loomed as big as train tunnels. "Once be good enough for me."

"What do you want?" Cord asked, unwittingly retreating the step he'd worked so hard to take forward.

"How it feel being a daddy?" St. George asked.

Cord's blood ran cold. "I don't know what you're talking about."

"I'm talking about that boy. Rumble's boy. Who he gave middle name after that uppity nigra who tried to escape. You was standing right round here in the trees in the middle of winter, waiting on his birthing. Why would a man be doing that? Why would a man with a knife be willing to die for someone he aint even that great friends with? I got to asking myself all this on the way home. But couldna figure it out and not too concerned. Then I hear some of you keydets talking while bein' stupid turning backs on each other to drink. And now I know. So how it feel being a daddy?"

Cord took another step back and St. George took one forward.

"I'm not—" Cord stopped, trying to search through his alcohol-laden mind to find the right thing to say to deflect St. George's suspicions.

"Young Rumble. What he do? He take on being daddy? Now why he be doing that? What he up to? He know about Miss Rosalie not being able to brood children. I think young Rumble maybe smarter than I once think. Maybe he got his own plan for Palatine while pretending he want nothing to do with it, hiding out here at West Point."

"He wants nothing to do with Palatine," Cord argued, taking another step back as St. George continued his slow, deliberate advance.

"Then why he come home two year ago? Why Master Tiberius send him the letter? Why he sending two letters back, one to Master Tiberius and one to Mistress Violet?"

"I have no idea." Cord backed into a tree with a solid thud.

"Why Mistress Violet invite you to younger one's wedding to Miss Rosalie?" St. George closed the distance and placed the dual barrels less than a foot from Rumble's face. "Goodbye, keydet."

Cord cringed as the first shot exploded with a blinding flash. Cord heard nothing after the first although eight more followed, then the deeper roar of the lower barrel firing.

* * *

Cord woke in a pool of vomit. He reached up to his face, not believing it was still intact. Almost. On his right temple was a burn from a bullet passing so close it had singed the skin.

But that was all.

Cord knew there was no way St. George could have missed unless he'd done so deliberately. Cord staggered to his feet. Looking about, he saw that the bark on the tree he'd been backed up against was torn to shreds. Cord saw a distinctive shot pattern. One that matched St. George's description of his gun: nine holes in a tight circular shot pattern, then in the center, a larger cavity.

A message.

But what exactly Cord was supposed to make of it, he had no idea. He had vague recollections of St. George's talking about Rumble last night.

Cord clasped his hands together. "God, thank you. I don't know why you had that crazy fellow spare me, but then again, I don't know why you made that crazy fellow in the first place. He's a mean one. Now, if it isn't too much to ask, maybe you could nudge the Board into letting me graduate? I put in a lot of time and effort here and endured the Silence, best I could. So maybe you could give a hand if it doesn't trouble you overly much?"

He picked up his whalebone knife and slid it in the sheath. Getting to his feet, he pulled out a flask, taking a long hard drink. Wiping himself off as best he could, Cord trooped up the hill toward West Point. To discover whether he had been boarded out or would graduate.

GRADUATION LEAVE

July 1843, Cincinnati, Ohio

SECOND LIEUTENANT ULYSSES S. GRANT proudly rode into Cincinnati, his newly tailored, blue uniform fitting his painfully thin body somewhat better than his West Point gray had. His sword hung at his side. Shiny gold epaulettes dangled from each shoulder indicating his rank. The outfit had arrived at his parent's house just that morning and Grant had rushed to put it on, feeling a swell of pride at the uniform and rank he had earned. Now he was in town to show his old classmates and perhaps a girl or two, what a dashing lieutenant of the Infantry looked like.

He rode down the street, imagining everyone was looking at him, remembering how resplendent old General Scott had been when he came to West Point to review the Corps. Grant glanced over his shoulder and noticed he had indeed gathered a following. A cluster of street urchins in dirty clothes were following. One ran forward, right next to Grant's stirrup and looked up at him. At first, Grant thought the glance might be reverential, but the boy's words shattered that:

"Soldier! Will you work?" The boy's riddled pants were held up by a single suspender and his shirt had not seen the inside of a wash tub in weeks. He wore no shoes and no hat, his hair dirty and mussed. "No siree," the boy continued in a loud voice. "I'll sell my shirt first."

The crowd burst into laughter and Grant spurred his horse, galloping away. He rode hard for home, his embarrassment giving him wings. As he approached his parent's house, he noticed the stableman from the tavern across the street, staggering around in the street drunk, to the amusement of a small gathering of Grant's neighbors. The man was dressed in a parody of Grant's uniform: sky-blue pantaloons with a strip of white cotton pinned down the side, and some straw tied to each shoulder in imitation of the epaulettes.

As Grant arrived at the house, the crowd pointed from stableman to soldier. Grant hunched his shoulders and fled inside, slamming the door behind. He took off his sword and tossed it down. Then he ripped the epaulets off his coat and threw them away.

Grant searched for his father's whiskey bottle.

September, 1843, Vicinity Natchez, Mississippi

Fall came to Mississippi slowly, a lessening of the oppressive heat of summer, so slight, but so noticeable by the natives. The slaves building the large tent pavilion in front of Palatine House were certainly grateful for it and worked hard, desiring to keep the whip in John Dyer's hand from tasting blood.

None dared look up as a carriage came rolling down the lane in front of the house. Oak trees towered over the road on each side, making a green tunnel through which the carriage passed to emerge in front of the mansion. Lucius Rumble pulled back on the leads, halting the pair of horses as two slaves hustled forward, the first taking the bit of one of the horses, the other flipping down the small step on one side of the carriage.

Rumble turned in the seat. "Come children." He lifted Abigail out as Ben followed.

"Is this where you grew up, father?" Ben asked.

"Yes."

"Pal—pal—" Ben was trying.

"Palatine. Don't worry. It's hard on many people's tongues." Rumble held Abigail up so she could see the house. Her jet black eyes took in the white mansion, it's large columns lining the first floor front, the second floor porch, the slaves bustling about. "Home for a little while," Rumble whispered.

Both front doors swung wide open and there was Violet, her entrance, or more accurately, her exit, from the house, staged and grand. "Children!" she cried out. She was dressed in green, deerskin gloves gracing her slender hands, and, as always, a hat with some colorful feather topping it. She swept down the eight broad stairs to the lawn, her hoop skirt making it appear as if she floated toward them.

"Mother," Rumble said as she came to a halt a few feet away.

But Violet only had eyes for the children. She knelt, something Rumble never remembered her doing or thought possible given the skirt, in front of Ben. "My young Ben." She extended her arms. The boy took a step back in fright. "I'm your grandmother," Violet said.

"Go on," Rumble whispered. "As I told you." Although Violet kneeling had not been in the briefing.

Violet wrapping Ben in her arms and pulling him tight hadn't been either. Ben was lost in the folds of her skirt, just a tuft of his red hair poking out of the cloth. Violet hugged Ben for several long moments, then reluctantly released him and stood. She looked at her son and then the girl. "And Abigail." She stepped forward, Ben hopping to get out of the way of the hoop skirt, and embraced her son and granddaughter, albeit with a bit less ferocity than grandson.

Violet stepped back, looking between Abigail and Ben, a slight furrow marring her brow, but it was gone as quickly as it had appeared. "Come! Come in to the house. It is so grand to have y'all here."

"Get working!" a harsh voice cried out, followed by the distinctive crack of a whip and a deep hacking cough.

Rumble looked to the right and saw old John Dyer overseeing the slaves building the pavilion under which his brother would marry the woman to whom he had been betrothed so many years ago. After his exertion with the whip, Dyer was bent over, trying to get air into his lungs.

"I so despise that man," Violet said in a voice so opposite what it had just been, Rumble was taken aback for a moment, but then remembered that this was Violet, whose moods came and went like summer storms. "I wish he would die quickly although he who follows the old man might be worse, if such a thing possible."

Then the sun was back as she grabbed Rumble's arm and lightly placed the other one on top of Ben's head. "Come inside. I have rooms prepared for all of you."

"We can all stay in one room, mother," Rumble protested.

"Nonsense," Violet said and that was the end of that conversation.

Cord and King trotted their horses down the road from Jackson, Mississippi, toward Natchez, miserable from the unbearable heat and the long journey. The two had spoken little in the past few days. To the amazement of everyone, Cord most of all, he had graduated. Last in class, but who cared about that? Indeed there was a distinction to being the graduating class goat, the leader of the Immortals, the last section in every academic branch of study who eked out graduating. Cord's academic and discipline records had somehow been just enough so that his total ranking was exactly that needed to earn the diploma and commission as a lieutenant. There were whispers

Cord must have done something illegal to achieve such an impossible thing after four years of poor performance and being Silenced. But Superintendent Delafield had shaken Cord's hand at graduation just like every one else's and wished him all the best in his army career, saying the Army needed honorable men. Which was something else Cord had found strange, but he wasted little brainpower thinking about it.

King abruptly reined in his horse. Cord did the same, looking about to see the cause. Cotton fields stretched on either side of the road to distant wood lines. Dark figures toiled in the fields. The view had been the same for many miles; Cord couldn't see what was different now.

"I visited Major Lee before I met you in Pittsburgh," King said.

"Major Robert Lee?" Cord asked, wary.

"Of course. To thank him."

"For what?"

"For the opportunity he gave me."

"The *Somers* was a disaster," Cord said.

"It served its purpose," King said. He turned to Cord. "The opportunity you prodded him to give me."

"How do you know about that?"

"Sam."

"I felt I owed you something," Cord said.

"So you do believe in honor?"

Cord shrugged. "Honor, maybe. Perhaps a sense of loyalty to a fellow cadet?"

"What do you believe your destiny in the army will be?" King asked.

Cord chuckled. "I focused so much on whether I'd graduate, I've never really thought beyond."

"You have to look ahead, Elijah. My father failed to do that and it destroyed him. We're part of something that will be bigger than us." King pointed at the slaves. "See them. See how they follow orders blindly? That is part of what is necessary."

"Necessary for what?"

"For this country to grow, to become the world power it must be." King turned in the saddle and faced Cord. He raised his hands, horsewhip dangling from his right wrist. He intertwined his fingers. "The north with its industrial might and the south with its agricultural and moral might. The two can be a potent mix. The *Somers* was the most modern ship produced by the Navy. It was the crew that failed, not the ship. Specifically, it was the captain who failed. We have a code of honor in the south. And we have respect for God."

"Yes, but—" Cord began.

King cut him off. "Might is in here." He slapped his chest. "Not in this." He tapped the hilt of the heavy naval saber strapped to his waist.

Cord smiled. "But the sword could cut your heart out."

King did not smile in turn. "Not if it goes against a sword wielded by one with a stronger heart."

"I suppose that's true," Cord said.

"Major Lee thinks the same. He's a very honorable man."

Cord rubbed the badly healed burn on his right temple. He had been unwilling to go to the post surgeon and admit what had happened, so he'd treated the wound himself in the barracks with less than perfect results. "I don't think it will happen simply."

"What do you mean?" King asked.

"There are those who feel that—" he pointed at the slaves—"is an institution that should be ended. Even my own father has gone over to the abolitionists. He denounces slavery loudly. It's getting dangerous for him in Norfolk."

"I am sorry to hear that," King said. "Abolitionism is a criminal cause." He jerked on his reins and headed down the road, leaving Cord in his dust. He hurried to catch up and they rode on in silence once more.

A few miles further south they heard coughing ahead. Coming over a slight rise, they saw a thin man in dusty Army blue hunched over his mount, slowly plodding down the road. As they got closer, Cord suddenly recognized the officer.

"Sam!"

Grant looked over his shoulder, his face pale and covered with sweat. "Elijah. And King. It's good to see you both."

Cord rode up to his friend and shook his hand. King nodded a greeting.

"Are you all right?" Cord asked.

Grant coughed again, so hard that his entire body was wracked with the effort.

"Tyler's Grip?" King asked.

Cord shot King a warning look, but Grant seemed not to care. When he finished the bout, he took a deep breath, the air rattling in his lungs. "My Uncles Noah and John died of consumption, so it's possible. But I would hope not." He sat a bit taller in the saddle, which only served to accentuate how painfully thin he was. "According to the fellow I asked a few miles back, Palatine is not far ahead."

They reached a crossroads and Grant turned right. Cord followed without hesitation. King halted for a moment, then followed.

They stopped as a cluster of shacks appeared around the bend. A house, more a defensive blockhouse, crowned the top of the small knoll above the shacks. Negroes moved about the shanties, none daring to look at the three white riders.

"Samual!" Cord called out, spotting the giant man carrying a heavy load of firewood on his back toward one of the shacks.

Samual halted and turned in their direction, but kept his head down. "Sir?"

Cord halted his horse in front of the slave. "We met at West Point. In the woods. The night Ben Agrippa Rumble was born."

Samual looked up, a flash of anger in his eyes. "Agrippa be born here, twenty year ago, sir."

"What the devil are you talking about?" Cord asked.

"Don't be speaking of the devil, sir," Samual said, eyes once more downcast.

"How is Mister Rumble—Lucius?" Cord asked.

"I don' work in the big house, sir. My wife and daughter say he and children be fine."

Grant leaned forward in the saddle. "Who was this Agrippa born twenty years ago here, sir?"

Samual's head slowly came up. His coal-black eyes pierced right through Grant, chilling him with the intensity of the anger in them. "My son, sir. My son. They say he was kilt trying to escape."

"What the hell you think you doing, Samual?" The voice came from the knoll. St. George was easily recognizable at a distance by his bulk, his brown slouch hat and black sash.

Samual's head dropped to his chest as if struck by a guillotine. He'd been under the weight of the firewood the entire time without apparent effort and he turned and continued on his way. St. George stomped past him, saying something in a harsh tone the riders couldn't hear. The overseer came up on them.

"I know you, boy," he said to Cord.

Cord touched the scar on his temple. "I know you also." His hand drifted toward the pistol tucked into his waistband.

St. George placed his right hand over the top of his sash, resting lightly on his solid belly. "You now thinking something you ought not be thinking, boy."

"You shot at me," Cord said.

"Yes, but I didna hit, did I?" St. George gave his reptile smile. "I was just playing boy."

"I'm not," Cord said.

"Easy," Grant whispered. "We're here for a wedding, not a duel."

"A day of reckoning will come," Cord said to St. George.

"Oh yeah, boy. For sure. Now get on out of here."

Grant reached out and grabbed the bridle on Cord's horse. He tugged on it and they rode off.

Behind them, St. George spit into the dirt, then looked about for a slave on whom to vent his anger. But not Samual.

"They say war with Mexico is inevitable." Seneca Rumble sat in a wicker chair to the right of his father and was trying to get a conversation going in the face of Tiberius' chilly reception to their new guests. Seneca was as tall as his brother, but slender and his face was more open and friendly.

To Tiberius' left was Violet, seated in a comfortable, cushioned chair brought out from the dining room. To her left was the bride-to-be, the lovely Rosalie Little. She wore a pale blue dress, her body corseted tightly into an alluring hourglass figure that none of the men could help but appreciate. She had long blond hair, arranged in what appeared to be a haphazard pattern, which had actually taken many hours to prepare. Behind the four, a pair of slaves waved wide feather fans in a hypnotizing rhythm.

Seated across from the four on a hard bench, backs to the railing, were Cord, King, Lucius Rumble and Sam Grant. The latter was having a hard time staying awake, given his illness, the heat, and the fans waving up and down.

"It's very likely there will be war," Cord finally answered, when no one else did.

Violet Rumble was staring at him in a disconcerting manner, so he continued speaking, as if that could help him escape her gaze.

"The Mexicans are within their rights to claim Texas. I believe they have been quite lenient and generous with the Texans up to this point."

King snorted. "The Texans defeated the Mexicans soundly at San Jacinto. It's only a technicality by which Mexico still claims the territory."

Grant roused himself. "A technicality that could cost a lot of men their lives. It would be a most unjust war, if it came to that."

Tiberius raised a liver-spotted hand. "But you will fight, won't you, Lieutenant Grant?"

"Yes, sir. Lieutenant Cord and I are posted to Jefferson Barracks. We have a friend, Pete Longstreet, who's been there a year already and he's written that the regiment is well trained. We will serve in the 4th Infantry and if there is war, the 4th is certain to be in the thick of it."

"And you," Violet said, pointing with deer gloved hand, "is it Lieutenant also, my dear relative from Virginia?"

King shook his head. "No ma'am. I'm an ensign in the Navy. The rank is equivalent, but the terms different."

"Oh, men and their ranks and uniforms," Rosalie said. "It all seems so foolish."

"Hush, dear," Seneca said to her, but she ignored him.

"Where will you be going after the wedding?" Violet asked Cord. "To sea?"

"To Annapolis, Maryland, ma'am. I'm to help Commodore Perry found the Naval Academy."

"Noble endeavors all of you," Tiberius said. He looked at his eldest son. "Well, most of you. I am sure they still need someone to take care of horses at West Point."

"Now, now, dear," Violet said.

"I think," Rosalie Little began, spacing out the words which caused everyone to look at her, a not unpleasant task, "that all this talk of war is quite gloomy. I say we put a moratorium on it until at least after Seneca and I enjoy our wedding night."

Seneca Rumble blushed and Tiberius grunted a laugh. "A fair enough request from a most fair lady," he said.

Violet stood and all the men scrambled to their feet. "Gentlemen, I believe it is time for my afternoon stroll." She looked over the four young men. "A woman has rarely had such a fine array of candidates for escort." She extended her gloved hand. "Come, Lieutenant Cord, would you please accompany me?"

"Yes, ma'am."

"Oh, please would you all stop calling me that? Makes me feel like I'm running a house of ill repute. Call me Violet."

"Yes, ma'am," the four young men all said at the exact same time. Which caused a peel of laughter from Rosalie.

Violet led Cord down the majestic main staircase of Palatine and out the front door. She turned left and went around the house, Cord half a step behind her and to her right, as he had been taught in etiquette class at West Point when in the presence of a lady. He was searching for a topic to engage in conversation, as he had also been taught, but his mind could conjure nothing.

"I do so love the garden," Violet said as she led him into an opening in an eight-foot high hedge.

"It is very nice, ma—Violet."

They wove through a maze of tall hedges. Ahead was the sound of children playing. Cord was lost within seconds as Violet took a series of sharp turns and then they were in an open space with an eight-foot high fountain in the shape of an angel in the center, water spouting from her mouth, stone wings arching overhead. Several children, black and white, were splashing in the basin at the base of the angel.

"Tiberius would be quite upset if he saw this," Violet said, "but then he would have to get out of his chair and come here to see it. I don't believe in all these years he ever learned how to negotiate the hedges. It is my place, just as his is on that porch. I planted all of this years ago when I first came here to Palatine. I enjoy it, but it is also a reminder of how much time has passed since then. So it is with life."

Cord recognized Ben Rumble among the children. An older black woman was keeping careful watch, Abigail in a crib basket at the woman's side.

"So," Violet said.

Cord wasn't sure if that was a question, and if it was, what it was about, so he remained silent.

Ben recognized him and came running over, his clothes soaked. "Uncle Elijah!"

Cord hugged Ben, getting the front of his uniform wet. "It's good to see you again, Lil' Ben. Go and have fun."

Ben squirmed out of his arms and ran back to his playmates.

"'Uncle'?" Violet asked.

"An honorary title," Cord said. He ran a finger inside the collar of his uniform blouse, which was suddenly tight.

"Did you know his mother? Lidia?"

A trickle of sweat ran down Cord's back. "Yes. We all knew her."

"Did you all?" Violet sighed. "Mary," she called out to the negress.

"Yes, mistress?"

"Take the children to be cleaned up for dinner."

"Yes, mistress." She began to shoo the children out of the water.

"I understand you've met Samual," Violet said.

"Yes."

"You were in the woods watching the cabin when Ben was born."

"Yes."

"Why? Why weren't you with them in the cabin?"

"I was on quarters restriction. I wasn't supposed to be off post."

Violet turned and peered into his eyes. "Really?"

"Yes, ma'am."

"But you were off post."

"Yes, ma'am."

"So you break rules?"

"I did, on occasion. I try not to any more, though."

"You said you weren't in the cabin because it was against the rules. But then you admit to breaking the rules that night. A strange mixture."

Cord had no answer.

"Mary is Samual's wife," Violet finally said.

Cord glanced at the negress as she gathered the children.

"I own Samual. But Tiberius owns Mary. We have kept the lines of who owns what here very clear ever since I brought my dowry to Palatine. It has not been easy. Do you know what the vows for a slave wedding are?"

"No, I don't." Cord was glad the subject had changed from him.

"'Until death or distance do you part'."

Cord could hear the rustle of cloth on hedge and Rosalie Little appeared, a parasol twirling over her shoulder, keeping her long blond tresses in the shade. "Violet darling," she called out in a drawl as she came over. "I just knew I would find you here."

"That's because I asked you to meet us here," Violet said. "You don't have to pretend around Lieutenant Cord. He doesn't appear to be a man who requires pretension from females."

Rosalie swung the parasol down and jabbed the point into the grass. "You are quite correct, Violet. Lieutenant Cord, I know you might think us women to be frivolous, but we work with what power we have. Did you know that I am barren?"

Cord flushed red. "Ma'am, I did not, and there's no reason I should know such a personal thing."

"Lucius knows," Rosalie said. "But he did not tell you." She mused on that for several seconds before continuing. "Lucius always keeps his cards close to his chest. Are you his friend?"

Cord had to think about the question and Rosalie took that as his answer.

"Interesting," she said. "But there's a link between the two of you, even if it is not friendship." She tapped the ivory handle of the parasol with long fingers. "Do you know why we invited you and Lieutenant Grant?"

"To support Lucius."

"Support him in what?" Violet asked.

Cord felt like he was being interrogated at the boards back at West Point and he was unclear of the direction or purpose. Regardless, he knew he would be the Immortal of this conversation. "Mister Rumble—Tiberius—disowned him when he married Lidia. You—" he nodded at Violet—"want him to keep his connections to the family."

"And why would we want that?" Violet asked.

Cord didn't answer right away.

"Please, sir," Rosalie said. "Add it up."

"Because of Ben," Cord finally said.

"Very good," Violet commented. She took a step closer to Cord, the hem of her hoop skirt brushing up against his shoes. "Is there something we should know about Ben?"

"He's a good boy."

"Is that all?"

"Yes, Violet."

Violet glanced at Rosalie, then back at Cord. "Understand that no matter what, we have the boy's best interests at heart. He is the future of Palatine."

"Lucius might have something to say about that," Cord pointed out. "As well as Ben once he is of age."

"I am certain they both will," Violet said. "But as Lucius' friend, I ask you to help him keep an open mind about the future."

"I can do that," Cord said, anxious to get out of this maze.

"And if there were something about Ben," Violet said, "some secret, I believe only three people would know the real truth. And one of them has now passed on, has she not?"

Cord met her gaze, but said nothing.

"Ben is Lucius's son," Violet said. "And as such he is our blood."

"And he will be part of my family as of the 'morrow," Rosalie added. "So he is also tied to the future of Rosalie Plantation."

"I think that's good for Ben," Cord said.

Violet retreated a step and Cord breathed a sigh of relief.

"Very well," Violet said. "I will see you for dinner." With a rustle of her skirt, she was gone behind the hedges.

"Do you know the way out?" Cord asked Rosalie.

"I got here didn't I?" she replied, a laugh taking the edge off the reply.

Rosalie pulled her parasol out of the ground. She looped her arm in his and strolled toward a different break in the hedges. They walked in silence, twisting and turning through the greenery. When they reached the edge of the maze, Rosalie withdrew her arm and stopped.

"Tell me something, Lieutenant Cord."

"Yes, ma'am?"

"It's Rosalie. I don't feel like I run a brothel when you call me ma'am, but I would like to be your friend. Lucius always picks his associates carefully even though you don't call yourself his friend."

"Yes, Rosalie."

"Lidia. Was she a good woman?"

Cord felt a pang in his chest. "She was a very good woman."

"Did Lucius truly love her?"

Cord surprised himself by answering without having to think about it. "Yes."

"And did you?"

Now he had to think for a second, then trusted the pain he felt. "I did."

"She must have been a good woman then," Rosalie said. "Despite all."

THE MISSISSIPPI

September, 1843, Vicinity Natchez, Mississippi

ENSIGN GEORGE KING OBSERVED the paddlewheel battle its way against the Mississippi's current, en route to Natchez. He'd seen six steamers pass in the last hour and not one sailing vessel. It was a fact he filed away and planned to ponder on the journey back east.

"Without the river, none of this would exist," came a voice from behind him.

King looked over his shoulder as Seneca Rumble strolled up. Seneca was dressed in a finely tailored suit, a gold chain stretching from one pocket on his vest to the other. He carried a black cane with a lion's head knob.

King stood on a bluff, fifty feet above the muddy water. To his left, a rutted road switch-backed twice down to a wooden dock. "Do you ship your cotton directly from here?" he asked.

"We used to," Seneca said. "But now, everything is done through brokers who control the price. So we send our produce to Natchez and sell it there."

"Seems like you'd make more shipping it yourself," King observed.

"I suppose," Seneca said, "but that's the way it is."

"Still, it appears heavy wagons use that road," King said.

Seneca shrugged. "Supplies, I'm sure." He reached into a pocket and pulled out a pair of cigars. He snipped the tips off with a cutter hidden inside the open mouth of the lion.

"Very useful," King observed.

Seneca laughed. "People think me ostentatious to carry it, but it has several uses beyond the obvious." He offered one of the cigars to King who accepted it with gratitude.

King pulled a wooden match out of his pocket and flicked it on the rope-burned calluses in the web of his hand between thumb and forefinger. It burst into flame and he lit his cigar, and then offered the flame to Seneca, who took a deep puff, igniting his cigar.

King snuffed out the match with his fingers, then rubbed the end until it was nothing but dust.

"Pretty neat trick there yourself with lighting the match," Seneca said. "Why so thorough with the end though?"

"Wood burns," King said. "Ships are made of wood."

"Good point," Seneca said. "I guess I never thought of that. Watch—" he held up the cane, gripping the shaft and pulling on the lion head/cigar cutter handle. A narrow, sharp blade was exposed. "I had it specially made in Vicksburg."

"Intriguing and deceptive," King said.

Seneca frowned, but didn't get a chance to say anything as King continued.

"Congratulations on your upcoming nuptials."

"Thank you," Seneca said. "Might I ask you something?"

King nodded.

"Why did Lucius do it?" Seneca asked. "I understand you were there the morning the events transpired."

"Do what exactly?" King was observing another paddlewheel coming up-river.

"Get married to that tavern girl when he could have had Rosalie tomorrow? You've seen her. You can't tell me a serving girl can match Rosalie in any way."

"I believe," King said, "he married her because of the child."

"She can't possibly have compared to Rosalie."

"She was not ordinary, but her blood certainly can't compare to Miss Rosalie's."

"Do you know if my brother has any plans to come back here permanently?" Seneca asked.

King turned and faced Seneca. "Perhaps *you* should ask your brother. That would be a more direct and honest approach."

Seneca sighed. "I meant no disrespect. We don't speak like that in my family."

"Like what?" King asked.

"We don't speak of personal matters." Seneca shrugged. "It doesn't matter anyway. Father will never let him back."

"Fathers don't live forever," King observed.

"True," Seneca allowed. "But father might let young Ben stay here."

"Are you concerned about Ben?" King asked.

"Right now, after me, he is heir to Palatine."

"Gentlemen." Grant walked up. He wore his plain army blues, looking rather unimpressive next to King's naval dress uniform and Seneca's suit.

"A cigar?" Seneca offered.

"I prefer a pipe," Grant said. He pulled a large bowl-shaped instrument out of his pocket and went through his own packing and lighting ceremony until all three men were contentedly smoking, looking out at the water.

"Is there always this much traffic on the river?" Grant coughed after taking a puff on his pipe and his face was still pale. Overall, though, he seemed healthier than the previous day. A night of rest had done him well.

Seneca nodded. "During harvest season, yes. It's the lifeline of the country."

Grant scanned up and down the Mississippi. "To think, this extends all the way up to my Ohio River and on down to New Orleans. It's the Hudson River of the west."

"The Mississippi is much greater than the Hudson," Seneca said.

"So he who controls the Mississippi," Grant said, "controls the west."

King took a puff on his cigar and blew out a cloud of smoke. "Are you concerned the country will be invaded, Lieutenant Grant?"

"Not at all, Ensign King," Grant said. "Just before we arrived here," he said to Seneca, "a slave told us there was another Agrippa. Born twenty years ago?"

"Why was a slave speaking to you?" Seneca demanded.

"My brother had met him before," King said. "A man named Samual? He said someone named Agrippa was his son and he was killed."

Seneca almost spit out the cigar. "Samual's a damn liar. Yes, he had a son named Agrippa. And my brother was thick as thieves with him. Totally inappropriate behavior. But Agrippa, that Agrippa, tried to run away and was killed in the process. We lost a nice piece of capital that day."

"'Capital'?" Grant repeated.

"That's what they are," Seneca said. "We have over four billion, do you hear me, four billion dollars worth of slaves. We could no more afford to give that up than the North destroy all its factories."

"So it's all about economics?" Grant asked.

"Are you an abolitionist?" Seneca demanded, cigar clenched between his teeth.

"No, sir," Grant said mildly. "I think the abolitionists tend to be extremists and I am not a fan of extremists. I just wonder if perhaps the Negroes are not also people? You said your brother befriended one. Would that not indicate some level of humanity?"

"My brother's a fool. He was a fool then with Agrippa, he was a fool to get involved with some serving girl and give up Rosalie and West Point, and he's a fool thinking he can ride back here with that brat of his and try to stick his nose where it doesn't belong. He deliberately insulted all of us by giving his son the middle name Agrippa."

"That 'brat', sir, is my god-son." Grant's voice had lost its mildness.

Seneca stared at him for a second, then removed the cigar from his mouth with a wide flourish and half-bowed. "My apologies, Lieutenant Grant. My emotions got the better of me. Mentioning Agrippa—the slave—around here is a very sensitive issue."

"Apology accepted," Grant said.

"You do need to understand, sir, that things are different in the South," Seneca continued. He poked his cigar toward King. "How do you feel about the annexation of Texas, cousin?

"It's inevitable," King said. "I'm stationed not far from Washington. President Tyler is pushing hard to accomplish it."

"As a slave state, correct?" Seneca asked.

"Of course."

Grant shook his head sadly, but said nothing.

"You have an opinion on the matter, Lieutenant Grant?"

"I believe I have expressed myself enough for one day." Grant emptied the bowl on his pipe. "Is it not time to head back to the house for dinner? And for you, lucky sir, to prepare for your last evening as a single man."

Rumble adjusted the dark blue tunic and checked himself in the full-length mirror. The dress uniform would have cost a month's pay, but he had been surprised, and secretly pleased, when Benny and Letitia gave it to him as a gift before he departed West Point with their grandchildren.

His sergeant's chevrons were made of some fine material, a bit ostentatious in Rumble's opinion, but he would never say anything to the Havens, for a gift was always to be appreciated. Grant had told him of his greeting in Cincinnati and Rumble felt empathy for his friend. Some people could put on a good show with a fancy uniform and others just didn't have the constitution or capability for it. Rumble felt his uniform and the rank found a middling ground.

He heard the door creak open behind him and glanced in the mirror. He spun about as he recognized the intruder. "You should not be here."

Rosalie shut the door behind her, pressing her back against it. "You look quite dashing."

"I'm just a sergeant."

Rosalie smiled. "A sergeant. 'Doubtless it stood; as two spent swimmers, that do cling together.' That was the sergeant in Macbeth and that was you and Agrippa so many years ago, wasn't it?"

Rumble strode across the room to her. "Hush. We shouldn't speak of that here."

"But you named your son Ben Agrippa. You had to know the effect that would have."

"It is done," Rumble said.

"Lucius, Lucius. Always so dramatic. I do like your uniform." Rosalie sighed. "Tomorrow I marry. I've known the date I would be getting married for five years. The man has changed, but not the date. I have changed, but not the date. You do know, of course, that my father told your father he was willing to annul the promised marriage after my 'sickness' and its result?"

"I did not know," Rumble said. "But I could have told your father back then, that when Tiberius is set on something, he never changes his mind."

"You carry a bit of that trait," Rosalie said. "I wish you had carried it regarding me."

Rumble shifted uneasily. "I am sorry about your 'sickness and its result'."

Rosalie shrugged. "I cannot change the damage to my body." She looked up at him. She reached out her hand and lightly ran it across the scar above his right eye and then down his cheek. "The only thing I wish I could change would be to have you stand across from me tomorrow."

Rumble looked away. "I cannot. I have a family and I had a wife who will always be in my heart. There is not room for another nor will there ever be."

"I suspected as much from you, Lucius," Rosalie said, withdrawing her hand. "I respect that and I will do the honorable thing tomorrow." She was about to say something else, but paused.

"Yes?" Rumble prompted.

"Your brother."

"What about Seneca?"

"He's a fine person," Rosalie said. "Full of honor. Dashing." She stumbled out of words, not reaching her destination.

"But?"

"As a man to be a husband, I fear he lacks as much in his own way, as I do to be a mother."

"He's my brother," Rumble said. "I stand by him no matter what."

"As I will stand by my husband." She stared at Rumble and he shifted, uncomfortable. "I must ask. Did you marry your Lidia out of love for her or for the child?"

"Why could it not be both?" Rumble said.

"It could." Rosalie turned and placed her hand on the doorknob. "I want you to know, I will always love you. And I will always love your son. But you did not answer my question." She closed the door behind her as she left.

St. George tossed the bottle to Sally Skull. "Tequila."

Skull chuckled. "So you've acquired a taste?"

They were seated on the dock below Palatine. Two of Skull's men had rowed her across the river from Vidalia, where a steamer waited to take her down-river with another load of black market cotton from Palatine.

"It got a good kick," St. George allowed.

"Like a mule," Skull agreed as she sat down on the smooth top of a dock support, took a deep swig and handed the bottle back. "The load is secure." She reached into her bosom and extracted a leather pouch. "Gold as agreed. Getting a bit nervous about the dollar?"

St. George took the sack and hefted it in his meaty hand. "No. Just got some dealings coming that involves gold."

"What kind of dealins?" Skull asked.

"You a bit nosey," St. George said.

"We're in too deep to be lying to each other," Skull said.

St. George shrugged. "Traders heading west. They deal in gold. I got a couple fella's on the leash to buy goods for me off the Brits out of Yerba Buena and sell to the Injuns."

"Guns? Whiskey?"

"And other stuff." St. George was uncomfortable with the topic.

The sound of a band playing a waltz floated above them from the pavilion in front of Palatine House.

"Big party?" Skull asked, changing the subject.

"Young master Seneca getting married tomorrow."

"To the heir of Rosalie in Natchez," Skull said. She smiled at St. George's surprise. "You hear many things on the river, St. George, if you know how to listen. And I listen. So how will your young master be when he takes over the plantation?"

St. George snorted. "He be a weak man, weaker than his father. It was a lucky day when the eldest boy got that wench with child in New York."

"But he; Lucius isn't it? He has a son now, doesn't he?"

"You hear much on the river," St. George acknowledged. "Yeah. But I don' think it be his son."

"What?" Skull leaned forward. "Tell me."

"There be another man here. A friend of the elder Rumble boy. A West Pointer named Cord. I think it be his son. But no way I can prove it. And Mistress Violet, she got her eyes on the boy. She hard as nails, that old woman. She pretend different, but she hard."

"Intrigue at Palatine," Skull said, almost to herself.

St. George took a deep swallow of tequila. "I going kill both of them."

Skull's hand was reaching out for the bottle, but it froze at that last statement. "Kill who?"

"That Cord fellow. He smarted at me. And when his time come, the young Ben Agrippa. And I might kill the elder Rumble boy too, just to make it all straight."

Skull took the bottle and held it up, checking the contents against the moonlight. It was almost bone dry. "You been drinking too much and talking foolish now. You got your money. Go on home and get some sleep. I'll see you next year."

Skull left the bottle with him and got into her boat. Her two men began rowing for the far shore, angling hard against the current. Looking back at the east bank, she could see that the bluff was glowing from the lights in the pavilion and the sound of the waltz still carried across the water. Below the bluff she noted St. George's form still on the dark, a blacker shadow in the darkness.

GRANT REJECTED

May 1845, White Haven, Missouri

ULYSSES S. GRANT BARKED the order in the command voice he'd developed at West Point: "Funeral detail, attention!"

Eight officers of the 4th Infantry Regiment, four on each side of the processional path, snapped their sabers up in a smart salute, pommels in front of their faces, then slowly lowered the swords downward to a forty-five degree angle.

"Present and hold arms!" Grant ordered and the sabers were lifted to form a steel arch over the path.

The officers were outfitted in their dress blues. The thin dirt path led to a pleasant clearing overlooking a stream. A peaceful place. Grant had dug the grave alone that morning. And he carried the casket alone.

As he walked under the sabers, Grant was solemn, his eyes locked straight ahead. His fellow officers, though, couldn't maintain it. Smiles broke out here and there, but they held their sabers steady. Among the saber bearers were Elijah Cord, Richard Ewell, Charley Hoskins, and James 'Pete' Longstreet.

Watching the ceremony from the far side of the clearing were Julia Dent, sister of Fred Dent, Grant's classmate, along with two of her sisters and her mother. The Dent's were also fourth cousins to Longstreet, making the world a small place indeed. They were all at White Haven, the Dent plantation consisting of over 900 acres of bountiful Missouri bottomland, five miles from Jefferson Barracks and just south of St. Louis.

Grant knelt next to the grave, cupping the tiny yellow coffin in his gloved hands. He placed it in the hole and looked up at Julia. She was of average height, with long brown hair and, essentially plain looking. To look closely at her was disconcerting because her eyes were not quite aimed in tandem. Julia nodded.

With one hand, Grant scooped dirt over the grave of her canary. Grant stood. About-faced. "Detail, dismissed."

The eight officers lowered their sabers. Offered their condolences, as much as they could be for a bird, to Julia, and then headed for the main house to visit on 'Colonel' Dent.

Grant walked up to Julia and offered her his arm. Despite the loss of her favorite pet, she couldn't help but smile. "How did you get them all here, Sam?"

"Your father's whiskey," Grant said, as they strolled toward the house at a more leisurely pace than the other officers.

Julia shook her head. "They could have whiskey in St. Louis. They came here for you. You have something. Something special."

"I wouldn't know about that," Grant said.

Julia tugged on his arm. "Thank you. That was so sweet of you."

Behind them, Mrs. Dent, a small but energetic woman, walked with her other daughters. She tapped a fan against her lips. "That young man will be heard from some day. He has a good deal in him. I predict he'll make his mark."

One of the daughters protested. "Mother, how can you say that? Julia has so many other more dashing suitors. And father would never approve."

"He will not approve now or in the near future," Mrs. Dent acknowledged, "but time and love may tell a different tale."

The daughter persisted. "Julia has other affairs of the heart, mother, not just little Sam Grant. Some of her suitors are quite charming."

"Hush," Mrs. Dent said. "Affairs of the heart are one thing. True love is another."

"And what is true love?" the daughter asked.

"When you can count on a man, always," Mrs. Dent said. "I sense one can count on Lieutenant Grant."

Within a few minutes everyone was on the portico of White Haven where 'Colonel' Dent held court. He had no military experience, but Colonel went with the lifestyle. Slaves bustled to and fro making sure everyone's glass was full.

Cord came up to Grant and Julia. He tipped his glass. "I'm sorry for your loss, Miss Julia."

"Thank you, Lieutenant Cord. It's good to know Sam has such good friends to take a Sunday and spend it in such a way."

Cord turned serious. "I owe Sam. I would do anything for him."

Grant shifted his feet in embarrassment. "I helped you when you asked for it, that's all."

"You have done much more than that," Cord said.

Neither of the men noticed Julia staring at Grant with an admiration she'd never had before. He'd been fun to be around and a consistent caller at White Haven the past year. But she'd recently gone to a regimental ball not in his accompaniment and she'd been surprised at the distant response from the other officers. None would ask her to dance. Lieutenant Hoskins, a fellow officer in Grant's regiment, had come up to her and pointedly asked her where Grant was, as if challenging her.

"Thank you, Elijah," Grant said.

Cord bowed and walked away, heading toward Longstreet who was probably setting up bets on whether the sun would set in the west or east this evening. And getting takers.

Grant lightly touched Julia's arm. "Might we speak in the piazza, Julia? I am heading to Ohio in a week to visit my family and there is something I wish to discuss with you."

Julia Dent flushed. She swallowed hard and nodded, allowing Grant to lead her away from the crowd. They sat on a bench, alone for the moment. Grant turned toward her, his saber clattering against the stone. "Julia, I knew when I received my class ring, that I would eventually give it to a lady. The lady. As an engagement ring. I ask you to have it."

Grant extended his hand, the gold ring in his palm.

Julia Dent rapidly waved her small fan in front of her face. "Oh." She took several deep breaths and looked at the corner of the house, as if expecting an invading army to come racing around it to rescue her. "Oh, no, mamma would not approve of my accepting a gift from a gentleman."

Grant looked at her, trying to penetrate her eyes into her heart, but she turned away, still fanning herself vigorously.

"This is not a thing I do lightly," Grant said.

"I know, sir." She still would not look at him. "I have had several rings pressed upon me in the past few months. But war beckons and I believe it makes men rash and foolish and in a rush."

"I am not rash and foolish, although I do admit to a bit of a rush," Grant said in a stern voice. "I make decisions very clearly and with determination. I have made this one."

"Yes, sir," Julia said, the fan fluttering faster. "But I have not made a decision, nor can I now, or in the immediate future."

She did not tell him that she had never envisioned him as a lover or a husband. He was fun to be around. She was happy when he was present. Most of all, up until today, the most important thing had been that he was a great horseman that she could take her horse out with and ride like the wind. He had never pressed her, never pushed.

Grant sighed. "Will you at least have dinner with me in St. Louis the night before I depart for home?"

"Certainly," Julia said, willing to do anything but accede to his initial request.

Grant stood, his hand gripped in a fist around his West Point ring. The knuckles were white, but his voice was level. "Will you think of me in my absence?"

She finally turned toward him and looked up. "I will, sir."

Grant's jaw was tight. "Then I will take your leave, Miss Dent."

MASTER OF THE HORSE

May 1845, West Point, New York

Rumble rode York in a tight circle, leading the horse with a firm, but not tight, grip on the rein. The cadets assembled in the riding hall watched in utter silence. York was still the Hell Beast and in the two years since Ulysses S. Grant's record-setting jump, Rumble was the only person who had managed to ride the horse. As far as anyone knew.

"Cadets!" Master of the Horse Herschberger cried out. "Assemble, in-line, one rank, on me."

The cadets of the class of 1846 scrambled out of the bleachers and fell in to the left of Herschberger. Rumble rode to the far end of the hall and waited.

In the shadow of the entrance was Benny Havens, one hand on Ben's shoulder, come to see the spectacle. The boy was growing up fast and Abigail had just taken her first steps a few days ago. In Benny's tavern, to the delight of the cadets gathered there.

As soon as the 59 members of the class, the largest in the history of the Academy, were in a row, Herschberger strode to the front, between Rumble and the cadets, and looked down the line. "Mister Jackson. Mister McClellan. Front and center, gentlemen."

Thomas Jackson of Virginia and George McClellan of Pennsylvania double-timed to a position in front of the Master of the Horse. "Gentleman, take your place in the center of the line, relieving the two men there."

Jackson and McClellan did as ordered.

"Center two men hold, wings forward to observe," Herschberger commanded.

Using the two cadets as anchor, the lines on either side moved forward until all could see them.

"Sergeant Rumble!" Herschberger called out.

"Master of the Horse," Rumble replied.

"Advance!"

Rumble focused on Jackson and McClellan standing at attention. Jackson was almost six feet in height with piercing blue eyes that caught one's attention, even at a distance. McClellan was four inches shorter, still not grown to his full height.

Two more diverse cadets one could not find. It wasn't just their appearance. McClellan was an intellectual racehorse while Jackson was a mule. Not quick to grasp his studies, but stubborn to a fault and willing to work a problem until he wore it down with shear effort.

Rumble lightly dug his heels in to the horse's side and York began to gallop. Rumble leaned forward and whispered in York's ear: "We can do it."

"Stand fast!" Herschberger yelled as Rumble and York thundered toward the line of gray.

Ten feet from the center of the line the horse gathered underneath Rumble and leapt.

Jackson stood rock solid at attention, eyes straight ahead.

McClellan flinched but did not step out of the way.

With barely an inch to spare from the top of Jackson's head, York flew over the two cadets and landed on the far side. Rumble brought York to a halt, and turned around.

"Hold in place!" Herschberger ordered as several cadets started to break ranks to congratulate the two cadets.

"Damn it men," Herschberger shouted. "Are you going to cheer each other in battle when the enemy charges down on you and someone doesn't break and run? It's your duty to stand in place. How do you think you'll feel when it isn't just horse and rider, but a lancer wielding bright steel aiming directly toward you and he wants to ram that steel right through your chest?" Herschberger accentuated the last words by slapping one gloved hand into the other.

"Master of the Horse Herschberger," a voice called out from the reviewing stand.

Herschberger turned and snapped to attention, as did everyone, when they recognized Superintendent Delafield.

"Sir!" Herschberger acknowledged.

"I'd like to speak to Sergeant Rumble if you can spare him for a moment."

"Sergeant Rumble, you are released from current duty," Herschberger yelled.

"As you were," Delafield said to Herschberger. "By the way," he added, "a most intriguing exercise."

"Sir!" Herschberger looked confused, not sure if that were a compliment or a reprimand.

Rumble trotted York to the viewing stand and dismounted. He tied the horse off to the bar in front of the stand.

"Sir," Rumble said.

"Walk with me, sergeant," Delafield said. He had a two-foot long round leather case looped over one shoulder by a strap. He gestured for the riding door. "Young Master Ben can come with us as this concerns him also."

They left behind Herschberger shouting orders. Benny Havens straightened as Delafield approached. He touched the tip of his hat. "Major Delafield."

"Mister Havens. Still corrupting my cadets?"

Benny Havens sputtered. "Now, sir, I just give the boys a little piece of home."

"If their home was a tavern, sir, then you are quite correct." Delafield said it with a smile, removing the sting. "I know your place is needed. Just be careful dealing with my replacement. His touch on discipline regarding your tavern might not be as light."

"Your replacement?" Benny sounded resigned to breaking in another superintendent.

"I've been re-assigned. I'm off to New York City to supervise the construction of coastal defenses."

"The Academy will be poorer for your departure, sir," Benny said.

"And your business might suffer if my successor actually enforces the rules."

"True, but you've been good to my family and to me, sir," Benny said. "I appreciate it." He stuck out his meaty hand.

Delafield took it and the two men shook. "Can we borrow Ben for a walk?"

"Certainly," Benny said. He looked at Rumble. "I'll be down at the tavern. I'll see you shortly, Lucius. And you too, Lil' Ben," he added with a light punch to Ben's shoulder.

Benny Havens ambled off. Rumble, Ben, and Delafield exited the riding hall. Rumble held Ben's hand and they walked at a leisurely pace that the boy could easily match. It was March and still chilly at mid-afternoon. The trees were bare and would not bring forth green for almost two months, but at least they were emerging from the cold grip of winter. Delafield led the way up the road to the level of the academic building and the barracks. They ambled onto the Plain. To the right were the ruins of Fort Clinton, to the left, Execution Hollow, where British prisoners-of-war during the Revolution had been contained under horrid conditions, as a counter to the conditions American

POWs were being held. The tit for tat approach had achieved little except misery and death on both sides.

Delafield halted in the center of the Plain and faced the Academy. Rumble placed Ben in front of him, both hands firmly on the boy's shoulders.

Delafield ran a hand through his white beard. "You know Congress passed the joint resolution to make Texas a state?"

"Yes, sir."

"They'll wait until after Polk is in office before pushing the matter, but war with Mexico is inevitable."

"Yes, sir."

"It will be a West Point war," Delafield said.

"Sir?"

"The regular army will fight it and the regular army is led by West Pointers. Have you and Herschberger been doing that little drill for a while?"

"Ever since I could jump York, sir," Rumble admitted.

"Gotten as high as Grant?"

"No, sir. We set Grant's bar at six and a half. I was a bit concerned today about Cadet Jackson's height."

"Jackson didn't seem a very bright lad when he entered," Delafield said. "I thought he would be found in academics his first year. But I've never seen anyone work as hard to improve himself. Give him two more years here, instead of the one he has left, and I suspect he would graduate top in his class."

"He didn't blink when York jumped, sir," Rumble said.

"I saw. More importantly you saw, and you've seen all these cadets for years in many different ways. Not just in the riding hall, but also in your father-in-law's tavern. I dare say no officer stationed here knows the cadets over so many years as well as you. That's why I want to talk to you."

Rumble was puzzled. "Yes, sir?"

Delafield knelt in front of Ben. "Son, can you spare your father going away from home for a while?"

"How long, sir?" Ben asked.

"It might be quite a while, I'm afraid to say," Delafield said.

"Will he be going where mommy went?" Ben asked and Rumble closed his eyes momentarily.

"No, son," Delafield said. "Just away for a while, then he'll come back."

"If he has to," Ben said, his shoulders slumping in Rumble's hands.

Delafield stood. "Sergeant Rumble, I want you to go with the Regular Army as my personal observer when they head to Texas and on to Mexico."

Rumble's hands tightened on his son's shoulders. So much so that Ben gave a cry of discomfort and Rumble realized what he was doing. He forced himself to relax. "I'm a soldier, sir. I go where ordered."

"I know you'll follow orders, Sergeant Rumble. I know you're an honorable man. I hate to take you from your family. But this is important. What I want you to do is watch our graduates. See how they perform in combat. Then remember what they were like as cadets. I want to know which traits in a cadet make a good combat leader. Anyone can issue orders here on the Plain and polish their brass and clean their rooms. War is a very different thing."

Rumble nodded. "You want me to see how effective the Academy training is, sir?"

Major Delafield faced back toward the buildings lining the Plain: Academic, cadet barracks, officers' quarters. Above those buildings and further back in the hills loomed Fort Putnam, designed by Kosciuszko to protect the landward approaches to West Point.

"Partly," Delafield said. "Certainly, we'll need to adjust the curriculum based on lessons learned. Armies are always prepared to fight the last war, not the next one. But there's something more important."

They stood still for a few minutes. A squad of second-year cadets marched by not far away, a First Classman putting them through their paces, barking orders. They were under arms and cross-belts, muskets on their shoulders, bayonets on the end of the weapons glinting in the early spring sun.

"So young," Delafield said, almost to himself. He gathered himself. "I fear that Texas and Mexico will only be the prelude."

"Sir?"

"Imagine two locomotives on the same rail line. They're heading toward each other. At the controls are men who will not, cannot, stop their own locomotive. And even if one did, the other will still be coming on the same line. They all know that. So they pile more and more wood in the furnace, going faster and faster."

"It makes no sense, sir. But it's true."

Delafield nodded. "Slavery was an issue from the very beginning of the country, Sergeant Rumble. We all know that. Our founders decided they needed a country before they could deal with that issue. So they designed a country that was fatally flawed. That flaw is coming to fruition two generations later. And westward expansion; that's the wood being thrown in the furnace. Texas is the prelude to the collision."

"Civil War." Rumble said it as a statement.

"Inevitably," Delafield confirmed.

"Then—" Rumble paused as he realized what Delafield really wanted. "Where do your sympathies lay, sir?"

"With my oath as a commissioned officer in the United States Army," Delafield said.

"My family is from Mississippi, sir."

"I know," Delafield said. "But you will stand by the United States if it comes to it." It was not a question, but Rumble answered anyway.

"Yes, sir. Why not send an officer?"

"For the reasons I detailed earlier," Delafield said. "You have an expertise and perspective that no one else has because of your years here. And you were once a cadet. But, on top of all that, this mission is not sanctioned by anyone but me. The War Department tracks the assignment of every officer rather carefully, especially now that conflict is brewing. But you're assigned to me as of this moment and I wish to take advantage of it. I'll put you on the 'detached for special duty' roll here at the Academy. I very much doubt the new Superintendent will make anything of it, especially as I'll instruct Herschberger to say nothing of your absence."

"Yes, sir."

"Don't sound so glum," Delafield said. "The first place you'll go is Jefferson Barracks where your old friends Longstreet and Grant are stationed. Both are with the 4th Infantry and it there is trouble, the 4th will be first in line."

"And Lieutenant Cord, sir? Last I heard, he was with the 4th also."

"That's something else I have in the works," Delafield said. "A friend sent me a letter saying a special expedition is forming at Jefferson Barracks under the command of John Fremont."

"The Pathfinder?" Rumble asked.

"The same."

"Last I heard, he just returned from the west."

"And he's heading west once more," Delafield said. "The Expedition is supposed to go to the Colorado Territory and scout mountain passes, but I believe there's more to the Expedition than meets the eye. I see a reconnaissance leaving early enough to be in position in or near California in case Texas goes up in flames. Other countries, particularly Britain, have their eyes on California as ripe for the picking if the United States goes to war with Mexico.

"Fremont has a reputation as a bit of, shall we say, a wild card. Although he has orders from Washington, he tends to answer more to himself and his political connections than the Secretary of War. Fremont's father-in-law, Senator Benton, is intent on fulfilling what he calls Manifest Destiny and he has strong connections to President Polk and Polk might be hiding his hand from Congress."

"What does that have to do with Cord, sir?"

"The Secretary of War asked me to recommend an officer to accompany Fremont."

"You chose Cord?"

"Cord gave Ben his ring, did he not?"

"Yes, sir."

"Would you trust him?"

"That's not for me to say, sir."

"Lieutenant Cord will be assigned to Fremont's expedition as part of the United States Corps of Topographical Engineers."

"Cord almost failed drawing, sir," Rumble said. "Grant would be a better choice for the Topographical Engineers."

"The Secretary of War isn't concerned about that aspect of the Expedition. Fremont is more than satisfactory as a surveyor. His previous Expeditions prove that."

"Then why Cord, sir? And not Grant?"

"Sometimes it takes a wild card to check a wild card," Delafield said. "Grant always struck me as a very trusting fellow. Not the kind I would want around a character like Fremont."

"The Secretary really believes Fremont has a hidden agenda, sir?"

"Fremont is just a tool being used by others. There's a powerful faction in the government that believes it's our country's destiny to stretch from the Atlantic to the Pacific and are willing to cause a war to achieve it." Delafield sighed. "California is part of Mexico, but like Texas, the claim is tenuous. There are less than fourteen thousand Mexicans occupying that vast territory along the Pacific and a quickly growing American population that is doubling every year. As I said, some see it as ripe for the plucking regardless of what happens with Texas."

"And what can Cord do about this, sir?"

"I was ordered to recommend an officer," Delafield said. "The list I was given was not long. I chose Cord."

Rumble absently rubbed the scar above his right eye. "Sir, this is much too complicated for an enlisted man to—" he began, but his heart wasn't in the protest and Delafield cut him off.

"There is also this." He reached into a pocket and pulled out a set of rank insignia. "A promotion to Sergeant Major goes along with the mission."

Rumble accepted the insignia. "Thank you, sir."

"When you return, you will become Master of the Horse, since old Herschberger is due for retirement soon."

"That is an honor, sir."

"And this." Delafield held out the leather case.

Rumble took it and loosened the tie at one end. A brass telescope rested inside.

"So you can observe from a safe distance," Delafield said. "It is the least I can do."

"Yes, sir. Thank you." But Rumble was looking down at Ben.

"Will you leave your family with Benny and Letitia?" Delafield asked.

"I haven't had much of a chance to think about it, sir," Rumble said, but he already knew what he had to do. "I believe they might be better suited staying with their grandmother and aunt in Mississippi for a while. It would be a good place for them to see a different aspect of life than the Army."

FREMONT TO THE WEST

May 1845, White Haven, Missouri

"I have orders to follow the regiment to New Orleans," Grant told Julia Dent, while her sisters and mothers held back their laughter at his bedraggled appearance. He'd reported back from Ohio to Jefferson Barracks earlier in the day to find the Regiment gone and Lieutenant Richard Ewell commanding the stay-behind detachment of the ill and undeployable. Ewell had given Grant a pass for a quick trip to White Haven before he was to head south on the Mississippi to link up with the regiment. En route to the Dent plantation, Grant had been forced to ford a swollen creek, accounting for his sopping wet clothes. A different man wouldn't have tried to ford the creek.

Julia Dent did not share her family's mirth. She had been surprisingly shaken to hear of the deployment of the 4th, then she'd fallen into a depression. Grant's sudden arrival brought her both joy and emotional upheaval.

"How long do you have before you have to report?" Julia asked.

"I must be on my way tomorrow evening," Grant said.

"Come," Mrs. Dent said. "Let John take you to his room and give you some of Fred's old clothes. It's late. The two of you will have time tomorrow to converse."

Grant grudgingly allowed himself to be led away, leaving Julia Dent standing on the front porch of White Haven both anticipating and fearing what the morning would bring.

It brought sunlight and a very serious Ulysses S. Grant waiting for her with a carriage. He helped her into the seat, then climbed up the other side and claimed the reins. As he made to start the horses, Julia placed a hand on his forearm.

"I am but eighteen, and you twenty-two."

"I know." Grant barely moved the reins and the horses pulled.

It was a beautiful day, the roads slightly muddy from the previous day's rain. They quickly came to a bridge over a gulch that was swollen beyond its banks. Water was pouring over the wood planks.

"It does not look safe to breast," Julia said as Grant brought the carriage to a halt and contemplated the obstacle.

"We can make it," Grant said.

"I'd rather go back than take the risk of being swept away," Julia said.

Grant looked at her, a serious glint in his eye. "I assure you, I will get you across safely."

Julia twisted the kerchief in her hands. "Now, if anything happens, I shall cling to you, no matter what you say to the contrary."

Grant nodded. "All right."

And then they were across the bridge before she had a chance to say another word. Grant drove them to a small clearing, then halted the rig. He turned in the seat to face Julia. She pressed the kerchief against her mouth.

"I love you," Grant said. "A life without you is insupportable and unbearable. I want to be married."

Julia sighed deeply. "I must admit I have been in a bit of a state lately. Ever since hearing that the 4th was to be deployed." She fumbled into silence.

Grant waited.

"My father would not approve," Julia said. "Ever since Jessie, the daughter of his friend Senator Benton, secretly married that scoundrel Fremont, my father has been against marriage to a soldier, especially an older one."

"I am not Fremont."

"Father's also concerned about your health," Julia said.

"I believe the warmer climate in Texas will be good for my health."

A slight smile played along Julia's lips. "You will not back off, will you, Lieutenant Grant?"

"It is not in my nature."

Julia nodded. "I can not do marriage. Not with you leaving this evening. And with father disapproving. But an engagement. That I would welcome. And on that, I will not retreat. The engagement has to be secret until we have the proper time and opportunity to tell father."

It was Grant's turn to nod, with less vigor than Julia. "All right. We are engaged." He pulled his West Point ring off his finger and slipped it on Julia's hand.

"I will keep it safe," Julia said. "You keep yourself safe."

June 1845, St. Louis, Missouri

"Ante up," Cord said, and then took another drink from the bottle at his elbow.

The muleskinner glared at him through the smoke-filled room. Besides the three men at the 'table' consisting of an empty crate, there were a half-dozen others watching the card game. Several bottles of whiskey made the rounds and the noise from the St. Louis streets echoed through the thin plank walls of the make-shift 'tavern'. Cord had on his uniform blue pants with a plaid shirt, unbuttoned almost to his waist. It was stifling hot inside the room and the cigar smoke was thick enough to punch holes in.

The muleskinner had a knife tucked in his belt and a musket leaning against the crate, close at hand. The third player was a mountain man, with buckskin britches and a stained shirt that might have once been white and now soaked through with sweat. He had a large Bowie knife stuck in his belt and a long Lancaster Rifle resting against the table. Cord had his whalebone knife in the sheath in the middle of his back. He was realizing that getting engaged in this game, while so far yielding a healthy monetary profit, might not be so good for his health as he was woefully outgunned, having no gun.

The muleskinner threw two coins on the table. "That's all I got."

"Sorry, friend," Cord said. "It isn't enough." He glanced at the other player. "You in or out, Mister Carson?"

"Call me Kit," the man said. His smile cracked a face tanned and lined from years spent in harsh weather. For all the legend surrounding him, he was a surprisingly small man, an inch under five and a half feet. However, he had wide shoulders and a barrel chest.

"Son, I think you got something more than brass balls, so I'm out." Kit Carson tossed his cards onto the crate and folded his arms over his broad chest. His dark hair and beard were liberally sprinkled with gray and he had a patience and calmness about him that came from years of moving slowly over vast distances.

"Elijah Cord. U.S. 4th Infantry." He stuck his hand out.

"Nice to meet ya," Carson said, accepting the handshake with a firm grip.

"I've heard about you," Cord said. "Most have."

"Don't be believing all you hear," Carson said. "Only the good things."

Cord turned his attention back to the muleskinner. A couple of the men behind him, dressed in similar driving rig, leaned over and whispered in his ear. He shook his and a heated, hushed argument went on.

"I hear tell you've been assigned to United States Corps of Topographical Engineers, Lieutenant Cord," Carson said. "To be accompanying Fremont."

"How'd you hear that?" Cord demanded. "I just received word of it this afternoon."

"I scout for Fremont," Carson said. "Notice the scout and the Fremont parts of that? I know all that's going on around me."

"Yes, sir, I'll be joining you," Cord said.

"Call me Kit," Carson repeated. He turned to the muleskinner. "Gents, it's a card game, not a social meeting. You sound like a bunch of old squaws haggling over a side of buffalo."

"Mind your own damn business," the muleskinner muttered. He glared at the large pot, at his hand and then at Cord. He jabbed a finger at the money piled up. "That's three months of my wages there, mister."

Cord raised an eyebrow. "And?"

"I can't lose that."

"Then you shouldn't have bet it."

"My friends won't loan me the ante. Let me pull out what I put in and it's yours."

Kit Carson laughed. "You telling the Lieutenant he can keep *my* money but you want *your* money back after you already threw it in? How stupid do you think the man looks?" He pointed. "You've got yourself a nice Mississippi '41 musket there, don't you fellow?"

"How you know what it is?" the muleskinner demanded.

"I know weapons," Carson said. He looked at Cord. "That gun is worth everything the man put in the pot plus the ante he's lacking. You let him take his money out and put the musket up, I suggest you let him finish the hand. Where we're going, a good musket is more important than money."

Cord had a moment's doubt, wondering if he were being played. "All right."

The muleskinner bit his lip, looked at the musket, looked at the pot, then made the trade, scooping back his money and laying the musket on the crate.

"Let's see what you have." Cord took another drink.

The man put his cards down with a heavy thud on the wood. Cord couldn't help but grin. "Sorry, friend." He lay his winning hand down and reached for the pot.

"You're with him," the muleskinner declared, jabbing a dirty finger at Kit Carson.

"Never met the man before," Cord said, pocketing the money.

"But he says he knew you. And you trusted him on my musket's value."

"Easy now, gent" Carson said.

The muleskinner grabbed for his musket, but Cord snatched it first. The muleskinner threw the crate at Cord, drawing the knife from his belt. Cord was on his back, musket in hand. He cocked the hammer, aiming it at the muleskinner's gut, but didn't pull the trigger even as the muleskinner jabbed.

A Bowie knife slashed between the combating men, slicing a long gash on the muleskinner's arm, causing him to drop the blade and howl in pain. Cord scrambled to his feet as the muleskinner's two friends leapt into the fray.

Exactly as he'd been drilled on the Plain at West Point, Cord used a butt stroke with the musket to lay one of the mule-skinner's friends out. Carson thumped the Bowie's hilt on the top of the other man's head, dropping him instantly.

"Time to be going," Carson said, slowly pivoting toward the other men in the room, Bowie in front, his long rifle in his other hand. He backed up toward the door, Cord at his side. Once on the bustling street, they made quick time away.

"That musket loaded?" Carson asked, glancing over his shoulder for pursuers.

"No idea," Cord said. Under a flickering lamp, he lifted it and checked the flint, then peered down the barrel. "Not loaded or charged."

"You pointed an empty musket at a man with a knife." Carson shook his head. "Plus, you didn't pull the trigger anyways. I didn't cut him, he'd have gutted you."

"I appreciate your interceding." Cord stuck out his hand once more. "I owe you my life."

Carson shook it. "Where you from, Lieutenant Cord?"

"Virginia."

"Well, this aint Virginia and this aint West Point. You make sure any gun you got is loaded and you point it at someone, you be ready to shoot. And shoot to kill."

"Sound advice," Cord agreed. He produced the bottle, which he had somehow rescued during their escape. "How'd you know I was West Point?"

"Scout, remember," Kit Carson said. "Plus, Fremont is one of the few officers in the Topographical Corps who aint a West Pointer. He be a bit leery of them, so you be prepared for a bit of coldness from the man. But you do have some talent. Whiskey and cards and a bit of fighting skill. Not a bad combination. Let's find a quieter and less violent place to get acquainted."

A few minutes later they were seated in the lobby of a somewhat upscale hotel and had a new bottle on the table between them.

"Where's your ring?" Carson asked, pointing at Cord's hand. "Your fellow Pointers wear them like they the keys to the kingdom."

"I gave it away."

Carson grinned. "A special lady waiting for you?"

"No."

The abrupt way Cord said it was enough for Carson to stop the questions.

"Is this truly a good gun?" Cord hefted his winning.

"Yep. Mississippi 1841," Carson said. "Fifty-four caliber. Accurate out to about two-hundred and fifty yards if you know what you're doing with it. Good enough. Do you know what you're doing with it?"

"We were trained in weaponry at the Academy."

"Trained and knowing what you doing, be two separate things," Carson said.

"What's that you have?" Cord asked.

Carson tapped his much longer rifle. "Lancaster. Made in Pennsylvania. Some prefer the Hawken, but I'm happy with this." He lowered it and showed the octagonal barrel. "Fifty-two caliber. A little smaller bullet than yours, but I can hit a knothole in a tree at five hundred yards. You aint gonna find many of these anywhere. Only a few gunsmiths know how to make 'em." Carson put the rifle down and took a drink.

"Nice pig-sticker you carry," Cord said.

Carson smiled. "You know the Bowie?"

"Jim Bowie had the sandbar fight right off Natchez in the Mississippi. Gutted one man, broke open the skull of another and damn near took off the head of a third. People were still talking about it there."

"Old Bowie was a character 'til he got himself killed down in Texas," Carson acknowledged. "So, you're a spy."

Cord had been downing a shot when Carson said that and he spit out the alcohol. "What?"

"Fremont didn't ask for you to be assigned. No one asked for you. You got assigned by the government. We don't really need no tenderfoot. Stands to figure you assigned to spy on the expedition."

"If so, no one told me," Cord protested.

"That's the best kind of spy," Carson said.

"I'll pull my weight," Cord said. "I can—" he paused as he spotted someone. "Sam! Sam Grant!"

Ulysses S. Grant was escorting Julia Dent through the lobby en route to the dining room. He smiled when he saw Cord—Julia did not-- and the couple came over.

"Miss Dent, it's wonderful to see you again," Cord said.

"Good evening, sir," Julia said coolly. "And is this the famous Kit Carson, scout for Fremont?"

"It is indeed." Cord made the introductions all around and asked them to join he and Carson for a drink.

"I'm afraid not, sir," Grant said. "This is Julia's and mine last evening together for a while. I'm to be deployed south because of the Texas problem. Why aren't you with the regiment, Elijah?"

"Ah," Cord said, feeling a little light-headed from the whiskey, the near-gutting and learning that apparently, he was a spy. "I'll be heading west, not south. With my friend, Kit Carson here. To California."

Grant was surprised. "The regiment is short officers as it is."

Cord laughed. "Carson thinks I'm assigned to spy on Fremont."

"How can that be?" Grant said. "Fremont's an officer."

Cord shrugged. "Who knows? But it should be quite the adventure to go west. Although I will miss the opportunity for combat with the regiment in the south."

"Don't be so anxious to get shot at," Carson advised. "It aint nearly as exciting as most think."

"I imagine that's true," Grant agreed.

Julia tugged lightly on his arm and he turned to her. "Fremont is a beast," Julia said. "He secretly married my best friend Jessie Benton when she was but fifteen and caused her great trouble. Her father almost disowned her when he found out. He's also gone almost all the time."

"I suspect," Carson said, "that the Senator has warmed up a bit toward Mister Fremont. He's the one who gets the money appropriated for our expeditions."

"Maybe he wants his son-in-law gone a lot," Grant observed.

Carson laughed. "It's possible. People do the damnedest things for the damnedest reasons."

Julia tugged on Grant's arm once more, this time toward the dining room. He gave a slight bow. "It was pleasant to meet you, Mister Carson."

"Likewise."

Grant turned to Cord. "Since I'll be heading south tomorrow and you'll most likely be gone before I return, I wish you all the best on your journey, Elijah."

Cord stood and shook Grant's hand. "If you end up in Mexico, Sam, keep your head down and don't do anything stupid."

The two men embraced, then broke apart, Grant off to dine with Julia and Cord to continue drinking with Carson.

NEW ORLEANS

1 July 1845, New Orleans, Louisiana

NEW ORLEANS WAS THE third largest city in the United States and growing by leaps and bounds. Slaves and cotton were the principles of commerce, the former coming in through the river from other states for westward expansion, the latter going out from the Mississippi to the ocean and shipment overseas. But today, the 1st of July, 1845, the streets were practically empty. Windows and doors were shut tight as yellow fever was making a call on the city.

Sergeant Major Rumble had disembarked the steamer from Natchez over four hours ago and he was no closer to finding the 4th Infantry than he had been then. The few people he had managed to question had no idea where the army fellows who'd recently marched through town had gone.

Rumble had a haversack over one shoulder and carried a custom-made double-barreled shotgun, a bandolier of shells draped over the other shoulder. Violet had pressed the shotgun upon him prior to departing Palatine, telling him that Tiberius had no more use for it. Indeed, the last Rumble had seen of his father, the old man could not sit in his wicker throne on the second floor patio. He was flat on his back in bed, too ill to rise. He hadn't cursed his eldest son as he departed for possible war, but he hadn't given his blessings either.

Violet had given not only her blessings and a gun, but a promise to look after Ben and Abigail with her life. Drama fit Violet's personality like the deerskin gloves did her hands, but in this case Rumble had sensed a sincerity that ran deep. Seneca and Rosalie were living in Natchez, learning the cotton trading business and tending to Rosalie's father's business interests. At least that was their story.

As Rumble walked along a wide boulevard, searching for someone to ask for directions to the 4th, he remembered watching his two young ones stand on the steamer dock in Natchez, waving him goodbye. Violet had been between them, holding a parasol over their heads. Samual had stood behind the three, a mountain of a man, and a comfort to have at his children's side.

Ahead, Rumble spotted a slender fellow in army uniform walking away and ran to catch up. The man was in field blue and Rumble could see no rank insignia on his shoulders. "Hey, soldier!" Rumble called out.

The man turned and Rumble felt a surge of relief. "Sam! I mean, Lieutenant Grant."

Grant was carrying a leather folder with papers bulging out of it. "Lucius." He noted the chevrons. "Sergeant Major Rumble. I'm impressed. But whatever are you doing here?"

The old friends shook hands.

"I'm attached to the 4th," Rumble said.

"Attached, not assigned?"

"It's complicated," Rumble said.

Grant shook his head. "You and Cord. Skulking about and spying."

"I'm not a spy," Rumble protested. "I'm to observe."

"Well, it's good you brought that." Grant pointed at the shotgun. "There may a use for it."

"What are you doing in the city?" Rumble asked. "Where's the regiment?"

"The regiment is encamped in the countryside to be away from the fever. I'm the quartermaster, so I'm in town to arrange the shipment of supplies. Come with me to the waterfront where there's a broker I must speak to about some cattle and then I'll take you to the regiment."

Rumble fell in step with Grant who seemed to know his way around. The sun was setting and because of the fever, few streetlamps had been lit. A fog was rolling in off the Mississippi. It made for a most gloomy setting.

"The children?" Grant asked as he stopped outside a tavern and peered in the door.

"They're fine. I left them with Violet."

"I'm sure she'll teach them a thing or two."

"That's what I'm afraid of."

Not spotting who he was looking for, Grant moved on to the next tavern, but before they could reach the door, a knot of men spilled out into the street, angry words being exchanged. Grant stepped back into the shadows, pulling Rumble with him as the men squared off.

"I've seen two duels since arriving," Grant said, watching the men argue. "It seems to be the only thing people will congregate for. Damn fools."

"This is the south," Rumble said, as if that explained it all.

Grant shook his head. "A duelist might have physical courage to fight, but they lack the moral courage not to fight."

The two groups of men were still yelling at each other, but it was impossible to make out the words or the details of the participants at this distance and in the darkness. But then a loud voice cut through the confusion:

"Step out and face me, man to man."

Rumble gripped the shotgun tightly. "That's St. George."

At the front of the group on the right appeared the bulky figure of the overseer from Palatine. His slouch hat was pulled low over his eyes and he sported the black sash around his thick mid-section. One hand rested on the top edge of the sash.

"You speak ill of me, you face me, you yellow belly Yankee," St. George continued.

A man in a tailored suit took a step in front of his friends. "I did not speak ill of you, sir. I was pointing out that the girl you were trying to sell in there looked like a white child."

"She aint no white," St. George said.

"I said she looked white," the man said. "But I don't really care. She's got to be all of what, ten? And you were trying to sell her body to me. I knew you people were savages, but I never expected the like."

"That's it," St. George said. He spit at the man's feet. "Get you a gun, mister. And back up your words."

"This isn't a proper duel," the man protested as St. George took a step forward.

"This is the duel you got," St. George said. "You get a gun, or I shoot you down like the dog you are."

Grant tapped Rumble on the shoulder and pointed down the street where a figure appeared in the road, coming this way. "There's who I have to meet."

A tall rangy woman packing a pistol on each hip was slowly advancing toward the men.

"A woman?" Rumble asked.

"It's a strange town," Grant said mildly.

"I'm beginning to see that," Rumble said, but his focus was back on St. George.

"Skull!" St. George yelled, when he saw the woman. "Give that Yankee one of your pistols."

The woman walked between the two groups of men without any apparent concern. "What the hell are you doing, St. George?"

"He insulted me." St. George was pointing at the man in the suit.

"That's your beef contractor?" Rumble asked.

"She's from Texas," Grant said, as if that explained it all.

Skull turned to the Yankee. "You insult him?"

"He's trying to sell a young white girl—"

"She black," St. George cut in. "Her mother a slave and black as night. I know for damn sure. I seen her birthed."

"Then the father must be white," the Yankee argued.

"Don't matter who the father be," St. George said. "Any nigra blood, you a nigra. She mine to do with as I will. You can duel me or you can buy her. Don't make no difference to me."

Sally Skull pulled one of her pistols out of the holster. She held it up. "Decide mister. I aint got time to be standing around here jabbering with you fools."

"I'm not buying a young girl!" the Yankee exclaimed.

"All right then," Skull said. She tossed the pistol to the Yankee as she walked out of the way and headed for the tavern door.

The Yankee caught the gun by instinct. As he fumbled with it, St. George whipped his Le Mat out of the sash and fired. The bullet caught the Yankee in the shoulder and spun him about. Skull's revolver fell to the ground. The Yankee collapsed to his knees, back to St. George, who came striding forward. St. George stood behind the man and flipped up the hidden striker in the hammer that fired the lower barrel with the .63 caliber slug. He aimed it at the back of the man's skull.

"Hold on there." Grant came out of the shadows, pistol at the ready. "You've made your point."

Rumble was at Grant's side, the shotgun up.

St. George slowly pivoted. "This none your business." He cocked his head as Grant and Rumble became recognizable. "Young Master Rumble. You down here with the Army, eh? And you," he added, nodding toward Grant, "you jumped that horse. That was some pretty fancy riding."

"Leave the man be," Grant said.

"He insulted me," St. George insisted.

"He didn't know he was insulting you," Rumble said.

"Let him be," Grant said.

St. George shrugged. "I'll do it for you, cause of that jump." He flipped the striker back into place. "Any you other Yankees want some? I got some shots left."

There was no reply. Shaking his head he started to walk toward the tavern, reloading, when Sally Skull's voice came floating out. "Don't forget my gun."

Muttering to himself, St. George went back to the wounded man and grabbed the pistol. He also checked the man's pockets and retrieved a gold pocket-watch and his wallet. He looked at Grant and Rumble to see if they would challenge him, but they didn't. St. George went inside the tavern.

Grant looked at Rumble. "So this is the south?"

"This is New Orleans," Rumble said. "I've heard stories—" he shook his head. "You can't deal with someone who knows St. George."

"I'm the quartermaster," Grant said. "The men need beef. This Skull woman has a steamer full waiting in the harbor." He looked around and called out. "If you're this man's friend, best get him to a doctor."

A couple of figures skulked out of the darkness, grabbed the wounded man and carried him off. Grant headed for the tavern door. Reluctantly, Rumble followed and entered behind Grant.

Skull and St. George were in a corner table, engaged in intense conversation. There were only a handful of people inside, the ones who chose alcohol or business over fear of the fever. St. George saw Grant and Rumble and reached for the pistol in his sash. Skull looked up, noted the uniforms and put her hand on St. George's gun arm.

"Easy. This my business."

"He be—" pointing at Rumble—" the eldest son from Palatine."

"But now he's an Army fella," Skull said. "And I have business to conduct with the Army."

Grant stopped a few feet from the table. "You received my requisition, Mrs. Skull?"

"I did. The ship is docking as we speak. I have drovers who can off load and wrangle the cattle to your encampment. As long as I receive payment. Now."

Grant continued negotiating, but Rumble tuned their conversation out. He was looking in the corner, behind St. George, where the slight wisp of a girl had wedged herself, showing a proclivity for hiding, even in a public place. Her skin was indeed white, as the Yankee had claimed. But her facial features indicated Negro to Rumble. There was something else though, something that struck him as she dared a quick glance up at him, which caused him to shiver for a moment.

He overrode Grant and Skull's negotiations and addressed St. George. "Who was her mother?"

"You don't need know," St. George said.

"If her mother was a slave at Palatine, then you're a thief, stealing plantation property and trying to sell it."

St. George's hand headed for his vest, but Rumble caused him to freeze by swinging up the shotgun.

"Easy now, son," Skull said. "I'm in the blast of that cannon."

"Who was her mother?" Rumble said each word distinctly.

"Mary," St. George said. He held up his gun hand as Rumble pulled back the hammers on both barrels. "I aint stealing. I got Master Tiberius's legal order to sell her. I got the papers." St. George eased his hand toward his breast pocket.

Rumble was holding the shotgun so hard it was vibrating. Grant reached out and put a steadying hand on his friend's shoulder. "Be calm."

"Who was the father?" Rumble demanded. The words echoed in the now silent tavern.

St. George pulled a set of folded papers out of his pocket and placed them on the table. Then he looked at Rumble and smiled. "These here papers give me right to do whatever I want with her. As long as I don't bring her back to Palatine. You know why that is, don't you boy? I done this quite a few times."

Grant sliced his hand down between the shotgun's dual hammers and the shells, grunting in pain as Rumble pulled the trigger and the hammers slammed on the edge of Grant's palm, cutting into the flesh but keeping the gun from firing.

"We're not murderers!" he hissed at Rumble.

St. George laughed.

Grant removed the shotgun from Rumble's grip and extracted his bleeding hand. He then grabbed Rumble and shoved him toward the door. "Wait for me outside, Sergeant Major."

"Good thing you keep a rein on that boy," St. George said as Rumble stomped outside.

Grant reached into the leather folder he carried and tossed a stack of bills on the table in front of Sally Skull. "Payment as agreed."

Skull grabbed the money. "I'll get the herd moving."

"Thank you." Grant looked at St. George. "I might not be around next time."

St. George laughed. "I hope not."

Grant shook his head and left the bar and the normal muted roar of conversation resumed. Skull twisted in her seat as she picked up the pile of cash. "How much for the girl?"

St. George scratched his head. "What you do with her?"

"I can always use help on the ranch."

"What good a girl be on a ranch?"

"You run a plantation, not a ranch. Don't be asking so many questions. How much?"

St. George quoted a price, a higher one than he had offered the Yankee.

Skull peeled off the bills and dropped them on the table. She stood. "I'll see you when the next crop is ready." She grabbed the girl's arm and left the tavern, leaving a perplexed St. George in her wake.

THE GREAT SALT LAKE

October 1845, Great Salt Lake Desert, Utah

"When the natives say no one has ever crossed this desert, maybe one ought listen to them," Cord said in a low voice to Kit Carson.

Cord's tongue was swollen from lack of water, his throat parched. His skin was rubbed raw by the constant blowing sand and salt. He'd passed that point in hunger to where he no longer felt the need for food; a bad sign. He was simply starving, energy draining from his body. "There were better routes to take. Why'd he go this way? And what's our destination?"

Carson was not in a jovial mood as they watched Fremont gaze through his telescope at the desolate terrain that stretched ahead of them. And the same terrain was behind them, after a couple of days of riding and walking since leaving the Great Salt Lake. No one knew if they had passed the 'point of no return' where turning back for known water would end up being further then continuing toward the unknown. The salt flats they were crossing were indeed flat, unlike anything Cord had ever seen.

"Walker," Carson said, with a nod toward an old mountain man, "says he was out here once. He survived."

"I know," Cord said. "When he was lost. He was lucky to make it out alive. He didn't cross it. He wandered into it and wandered out of it and I feel like we're doing a bit of wandering ourselves."

Carson grimaced. "We've not only got to get across, but still have to cross the Sierras before the heavy snows if we're making for California."

"Now you sound like my friend Cump Sherman," Cord said.

"Who'ss that?"

"A fellow West Pointer," Cord said.

"Sounds like a man with vision," Carson said, as he rattled his wood canteen, confirming that it was empty. "We got two days, maybe three, before the horses go down. Without the horses, we aint gonna make it through the Sierras. We'll be caught between the desert and the mountains."

"Fremont knew it was called the *Great* Salt Lake Desert right?" Cord asked. "Not the Little Salt Lake Desert." He reached into his pocket and felt the flask. It was almost as dry as Carson's canteen and now was not the time to drain what little was left.

It had been two months since the Expedition had departed St. Louis and Cord still didn't know what to make of Fremont or what the real goal was. They'd left the city on the Mississippi with sixty men and the unit was still intact, but Cord imagined Longstreet would be betting against that lucky streak continuing.

It had taken them over a month of hard marching and riding to make it from St. Louis to Fort Bent, Colorado. Arriving there, Fremont had been put out upon hearing that five companies of US Army Dragoons under Colonel Kearny had passed through the fort just three days prior to their arrival. The commander at Fort Bent had greeted Fremont coolly, making it clear that his extended presence was not welcome.

The commander had also secretly summoned Cord to a private meeting at night. He'd handed him a sealed envelope for Fremont that Colonel Kearny had left with instructions under what circumstances to open it. The letter was weighing heavy in Cord's breast pocket.

Traveling across the Great Plains, Cord had both marveled at the expanse and grown bored with the monotony; now, swallowed by this desert on the west side of the Rockies, the eastern Plains seemed a Garden of Eden. The Great Plains had been left behind after the Fremont Expedition departed Fort Bent and struck out for the Arkansas River.

Fremont had not been very forthcoming with the exact route or destination for the Expedition, and sometimes Cord got the feeling the man was making it up as they went along. When they'd reached the Arkansas River near Pueblo, Colorado after leaving Fort Dent, Fremont had ridden his horse into the edge of the river and waved his hat dramatically: "This side, boys, is the United States. And that side is Mexico. But soon, lads, soon this will all be part of the United States."

Cord had not been impressed with the flourish, the words, or the arbitrary boundary between two countries, particularly since there were no other human beings in sight. He'd also gotten the sense that Fremont would have been more than happy to charge across the river, an international violation. Fremont had held back and they'd moved north, finally finding some life at a small settlement named Hardscrabble where the land seemed to fit the name. They'd re-supplied as much as they could buy, then punched across the Rockies, down to the Great Salt Lake, where Fremont held them in camp for two weeks of rest while making observations and hunting.

Now it was late October and all Cord could envision was snow in the Sierras if they were indeed making for California. If they made it through this brutal salt desert. The worst of both worlds.

"Carson!" Fremont called out suddenly, as if making a great decision.

"Come with me," Carson said to Cord. "Let's see what comes next."

They walked up to Fremont. He was a man of medium height with a dark black beard, now covered with sand and salt.

"We have to turn back," Fremont declared, still looking through the telescope. "I see nothing but more desert."

"Well, sir, we could turn back," Carson said, "but that would force us to spend the winter in Salt Lake."

"Waste a year," Fremont said, almost to himself. "But remember, we almost got caught in the snow last winter in the Sierras." He was still peering through the telescope, scanning the horizon for some reference point.

Cord strained his eyes, but he couldn't make out anything other than more nothingness.

"Lieutenant Cord, did you know Colonel Kearny and the dragoons were riding the Front Range of the Rockies?" Fremont suddenly asked.

In two months, Fremont had never directly addressed Cord and the question caught him by surprise.

"No, sir."

"Why do you think they were doing that?" Fremont demanded.

"Showing the flag, sir."

"To whom, exactly?" Fremont asked, slowly lowering the telescope and looking Cord dead in the eye.

"The Indians, I imagine. And to reassure the settlers."

"And what of the Mexicans?" Fremont didn't wait for an answer. "They'll have heard of the patrol by now. They always hear what goes on out here. It makes things more difficult for me. There are those who wish to sabotage me. Do you wish to sabotage me?"

"I wish to get across this desert," Cord said. "And then through the Sierras safely. If that's our path."

"Apparently you are a man of limited foresight. A shame." Fremont held out the telescope to Cord and pointed. "Look yonder and tell me if you see anything. Perhaps your eyes are better than mine."

Cord angrily peered through the scope for several moments. He spotted a slight spot of white on the far horizon. "I see a mountaintop."

"Where?" Fremont demanded. "You look, Kit."

Cord handed the scope to Carson and pointed. The mountain man held the device to his eye for a few seconds, then lowered it and nodded. "He's right. A peak. Still got snow."

"How far away do you think it is?" Fremont asked.

"Sixty, maybe seventy miles," Carson said.

Fremont frowned. "We won't make it. We need to turn back."

"There'll be water there." Cord said.

"How do you know?" Fremont demanded. "This is the first time you've been west of the Mississippi."

"If it's got snow up high, it's got water down low," Carson said.

"We must go forward, sir," Cord said. He gestured toward the western horizon, conjuring Preacher. "The pillar is a sign, just as Moses received when he crossed his own desert to reach the promised land."

"And why must we go forward?" Fremont demanded.

With a sigh, Cord reached into his pocket and pulled out the envelope. "There was another reason Colonel Kearny passed through Fort Bent. He left a sealed letter with me to give to you."

"Why didn't you give it to me then?" Fremont snapped, his face red from sun and anger.

"Because the requirements of the order relayed by Colonel Kearny were to give it to you under certain circumstances," Cord explained. "If we turn back, we won't be getting across."

"Give it to me," Fremont ordered.

"Sorry, sir," Cord said, not really sorry at all. "I'm to read the letter to you, then destroy it. There's to be no record of this."

Fremont clenched his fists in anger. "Read then."

Cord unfolded the piece of heavy paper.

"United States Congress
Washington, D.C.
3 June 1845

To Major Fremont from Senator Benton.
President Polk has dispatched an envoy to negotiate with the Mexican government to the goal of purchasing the California Territory and the Texas Territory. We believe that goal will not be achieved. Further, word has arrived in Washington that the British are preparing a Naval Expedition with their own goal of claiming California during the upcoming turmoil. It is therefore imperative that we have a presence in California as soon as possible."

Cord emphasized those last three words, before continuing to read. *"The Mexican situation in California is unstable and to our advantage. Governor Pio Pico has decamped his capital to Los Angeles. Commandante Jose Castro is reported to be in Monterrey where he controls the treasury. There is rumor of a brewing civil war between the two, which would further aid a British intervention. We have fought the British twice on this continent; we wish to avoid a third. Not only are the British assembling a fleet in the Pacific, word has reached Washington that they are preparing to resettle Irish immigrants to California and establish it as a British Protectorate. The commander of our Pacific Fleet will be receiving a similar communiqué, and his priority upon the outbreak of hostilities with Mexico will be to secure Yerba Buena, which some are now calling San Francisco."*

"We must have access to the Pacific, especially since the Treaty of Nanjing has opened five ports in China to Westerners. The British have gained Hong Kong. We cannot allow them San Francisco or they will control both sides of the Pacific. President Polk and I have spoken at length in private on this matter. The Monroe Doctrine must stand. While the President cannot proclaim this publicly, I am assuring you that you have his support. Additionally, when California is brought into the United States, as it will inevitably, you will be its first governor. President Polk has given his approval."

"While your Expedition was formed for exploration, you must see the possibilities. Although your force is small, we do not believe the Mexican government will be able to send military support to California given events that appear to be forthcoming in their home country. You must get to California and assay the situation. Exploit the rift between Governor and Commandante and also gauge the desire of the American settlers there for revolt against Mexico. If things come to blows, Colonel Kearny's scout of the Front Range of the Rocky Mountains will provide excellent preparation for a relief column to head west from Fort Leavenworth with all possible haste in the event of armed conflict. Kearny does not know the contents of this letter. Nor is he, or anyone else, to be appraised of it. This is to be held in the strictest confidence. God Speed."

Cord folded the letter and looked at Fremont, awaiting his reaction.

The explorer ran a hand through his beard, sand and salt crumbling out. His eyes were distant, as if he could see over the horizon all the way to California. He finally spoke. "It is not an order to do anything directly," he mused, "but it is an incentive to cause some havoc. And perhaps more. Much more."

"Sir," Cord pressed, "I learned something several years ago. A friend of mine told me that once you set out for some place, you get there. You don't let anything turn you aside or stop you. Because he followed that rule, he changed my life."

Fremont nodded. "Sound advice. I fear I was discouraged by the lack of support from Washington. But the letter makes all the difference. Take Carson and two other men and leave once it's dark. Head straight for what you've seen. When you find water, build a signal fire. We will follow the smoke during the day and the flame at night."

"Yes, sir," Cord said.

He and Carson quickly detailed two men, picked the strongest horses, and forged out into the desert. As soon as they were out of earshot, Carson turned toward Cord. "I didn't see no pillar of rock or snow. Just a smudge of something."

"It's out there," Cord said.

"How do you know?"

"I don't," Cord said. "But I'm not turning back until we find something." He slapped Carson on the shoulder, raising a small cloud of dust and salt. "Have a little faith, my friend."

THE NAVAL ACADEMY

10 October 1845, Annapolis, Maryland

"ATTENTION ON DECK!" Ensign George King barked the order, with less than satisfactory results. The fifty midshipmen lumbered to their feet with varying speeds, ranging from alacrity to sloth. The end result for most of them was far short of the position considered 'Attention' at West Point.

King fought the urge to retrieve the 'starter' tucked into his blue uniform sash. There had been a meeting the previous evening. The officer who had just walked in the room, Commander Franklin Buchanan, had been adamant that learning was to take priority over discipline at Annapolis. The other three officers and three civilians who comprised the rest of the faculty had concurred. King had bit his lip and remained silent.

"Sit down, gentlemen," Commander Buchanan instructed.

The midshipmen collapsed back into their seats.

"We are making history today," Buchanan began. "The 10th of October, 1846, will be remembered by generations of midshipmen to come as the date the United States Naval School was officially founded. The Secretary of the Navy, Mister Bancroft, has issued me specific instructions about my duties and responsibilities as Superintendent and those of the faculty. And what is required of you young gentlemen.

"You are to learn the science of ships and the art of naval warfare. You will spend a year on land, being instructed in the basics. Then you will go to sea for the next three years to put what you have learned into practice. Then you will return to Annapolis and spend another year finishing your studies." Buchanan looked over the young men seated in front of him. "Gentlemen, you are the leaders of the future for the United States Navy. Do your duty with pride and honor."

Buchanan walked out of the room. As soon as the door shut behind him, King shot to his feet. "Midshipmen, when an officer leaves the room, you come to attention. Is that understood?"

There was a smattering of discontent muttering. King reached into his belt and pulled out the starter. The officer to his right grabbed his arm. "That's not appropriate here, Mister King."

The midshipmen began to disperse, emptying the room.

"Don't ever touch me again," King said to the other officer, Ensign Reynolds, as soon as all the students were gone.

"You're an ass," Reynolds said.

King stiffened, a muscle in his jaw twitching. "Apologize."

Reynolds laughed. "You're a murderer, King. I heard about the *Somers*. How you betrayed a confidence. How you talked the Captain into hanging those men without trial. How you rigged the ropes. How you were first on the rope of the son of the Secretary of War. How you—"

King slapped the starter across Reynolds face, knocking him against the wall. King leapt to deal another blow but the other two officers grabbed him, pinning his arms back.

Reynolds shook his head, blood dripping from his mouth. He stepped up to King and slapped him across the face. "On my honor, I challenge you."

"Let me go," King hissed at the two officers holding him.

They released his arms.

"Challenge accepted," King said. "Dawn at the sea wall."

The next morning King put on his uniform and strode into the early morning fog to the sea wall. He was a bit surprised to see all three men already there. Each second had a wooden box in hand and Reynolds was also in uniform, his face as cold as the water battering the wall.

"You can back down," Reynolds said. "I'm an expert marksman and have stood my ground in three duels. My opponents are all in the grave."

King ignored him. He turned to the other two officers. "Seconds, are you ready?"

The two glanced at each other, then walked between King and Reynolds. They flipped open the lids to the cases. Inside each was a flintlock pistol.

"Choose," one of the seconds said. "They are identical."

King picked the gun furthest from him and Reynolds took the other.

"Your positions are marked," the other second said, indicating small stones set ten paces apart.

King marched to his and turned to face his opponent. Reynolds took his mark. "Once more, Mister King, I implore you to use common sense. Death awaits you if you continue."

"I am ready," King said to the seconds.

One of them held up a handkerchief and looked to Reynolds. "Sir?"

Reynolds nodded. "I am ready."

The second let go of the small piece of cloth.

King swung his arm up, leveled it steady as a statue, and pulled the trigger. The hammer hit the flash pan, ignited and the gun jumped lightly in his hand as the powder inside the barrel fired. He heard the pop of Reynolds' gun at the same moment.

The jump of the gun had been too light.

"Damn you!" King cursed, turning to the seconds. "You gave me an unloaded weapon."

"Reynolds' is also unloaded," one of the seconds said. "We—"

King dropped the worthless pistol and pulled the starter out of his waistband. He headed for the two seconds, intent on beating them, when a commanding voice called out of the fog: "Halt, Ensign King."

King spun on his heels and then snapped to attention when he recognized Commander Buchanan accompanied by Secretary of the Navy Bancroft walking toward them, with two armed marines as escort. "Sir!"

Buchanan stopped two paces away from King. "Gentlemen, what are you up to so early in the morning? And with pistols?"

King said nothing.

"Target practice, sir," Reynolds called out.

"And what—or who—would be the targets? Seagulls?" Buchanan asked. "Never mind. You other gentlemen are dismissed. We must speak with Mister King."

The three officers quickly gathered up the weapons and disappeared into the fog. King remained at attention, his eyes directly ahead.

"Relax, Mister King," Bancroft said, gesturing for the two marines to step out of earshot.

The best King could do was drop his shoulders a fraction of an inch and look at the Secretary. "Yes, sir."

Bancroft shook his head. "Dueling is stupid and a waste of manpower. Are you stupid?"

"No, sir."

"I've been told you aren't. Yet, you were dismissed from the Military Academy for dueling, and we have barely begun this School and once more you duel. Maybe schools are not the place for you."

"Sir, I—"

"Silence." Bancroft continued. "I read the report reference the *Somers*. And have discussed you with Commander Buchanan. He feels you are an excellent officer. But, he also feels you are not appropriate for what we want to achieve here at the Naval School and this event supports that inclination. We must educate first, Mister King. The military aspects will come later."

King opened his mouth to say something, but Buchanan cut him off. "This is not a discussion, Ensign. Do you understand?"

"Yes, sir."

"I did not come here to debate," Bancroft said. "I came here to give you orders."

"Yes, sir." King stiffened. "Sir, may I ask a question first."

Bancroft nodded. "Yes."

"The two of you set this up, didn't you, sir? The duel. The unloaded weapons. You were testing me."

"Why would you think that?" Bancroft asked.

"Because it happened and both of you were here when it happened. It is either a plan or coincidence so extraordinary that it bears attribution to the divine."

A slight smile of approval cracked Bancroft's face. "I was told you were quick. That is good. Very good. And you are brave, standing fast, knowing Reynolds' dueling record. While you might not be appropriate for the Navy School faculty, there is a mission for which I now know you are perfect. I understand your brother, a graduate of the Military Academy, is on an Expedition of Exploration to the West with Fremont."

King blinked. "That was the last I had heard, sir, in a letter from St. Louis. But—"

Bancroft began strolling toward the sea wall, Buchanan on one side, King on the other. "Walk with me, ensign, and I will tell you what you are going to do for the next few years. And, by the way, you're joining the Marine Corps for the time being. I believe it fits your temperament better."

SLAVERY

October 1845, Vicinity Natchez, Mississippi

Violet Rumble stood on the portico of Palatine House waiting for the riders. She'd spotted the dust cloud rising over the Natchez road from her sitting room window. After decades of watching the road, each plume of dust was distinctive, from that of a heavily laden wagon to a horse being pushed hard. This was the latter, and from the amount of dust, there were at least two, if not more, riders.

Violet's shoulders were slightly slumped, as if the weight of the large white house behind her and all it portended rested on them. Samual stood in the shadows of the portico, heavily muscled arms folded across his chest. Samual's daughter, Echo, stood behind Violet and to the left, as still as her father. The day had started out with serious news and Violet did not imagine good tidings were winging their way to Palatine with the horses.

The two riders appeared at the end of the lane, riding swiftly underneath the overarching branches of the oak trees. Violet recognized them immediately. Her youngest son from the stiff way he held himself in the saddle. Seneca had never bonded with horses and viewed them as a necessary evil for transportation. The flowing blue skirt billowing around the saddle of the second horse marked Rosalie, as did the glint of sunlight on her golden hair.

Violet threw her shoulders back and took the steps down to the drive. "My dear," she said to Rosalie as they arrived, "you simply must wear a hat. And you must ride sidesaddle. It's most inappropriate for a woman of your standing to be straddling a horse."

Rosalie dismounted before Samual could reach her to help. "Violet, darling, you haven't ridden further than the river in years. And the poor beast you ride can barely be considered a horse. Do you remember how much discomfort sidesaddle from Natchez could cause? I'm being practical. Plus, sidesaddle is so much slower."

Seneca accepted Samual's outstretched hand to assist getting off his horse. Feet firmly on the ground, he glared at the beast as Samual took the reins of both animals. A younger slave dashed up and relieved him of the horses, guiding them toward the stable.

Violet hugged Rosalie and then her son, his body stiff and unyielding. "What's wrong?" she asked him.

"I have a letter from Lucius," Seneca said.

Violet automatically looked over her shoulder at Echo. The young slave girl nodded, indicating that her mother was with Ben and Abigail. There had been so much excitement already today, that Violet had not had time to check on the children.

"And how is your brother?" Violet asked.

"On his way to Mexico," Seneca said.

"That we knew," Violet said.

Rosalie took her arm, just above the elbow and leaned close. "He has news that you should hear. Privately."

"Come then," Violet said, turning for the stairs. She paused on the third one and stopped. "By the way," she said over her shoulder, "John Dyer passed on this morning. I'm doubtful he is in a better place now. Tiberius has gone to make arrangements for his funeral. As if the cur deserved one. And for that—" Violet rotated on the step dramatically, "my husband is able to lift himself out of bed. Of all things."

Shaking her head, Violet reversed once more and headed into the house. Seneca and Rosalie followed. Samual and Echo trailed them. When the whites went through a door and shut it behind, Samual and Echo flanked it outside like guards.

They were in Violet's sitting room, her private sanctum in the large house. She reclined on a cushioned window seat, one arm draped across a large tasseled pillow. She lolled back, the perfect picture of wealth and leisure, although she felt neither today. Rosalie and Seneca took straight-backed chairs facing her.

"The letter?" Violet said. "What news does my eldest son send, causing you to come here by horse rather than more appropriately by carriage?"

Seneca produced a piece of paper. "Lucius sent it via steamer from New Orleans just before his regiment departed for Texas. He addressed it to me, as he must have assumed I would eventually read it, and since I was most likely in Natchez, it made more sense to do so."

"Don't assume anything with regard to your brother," Violet advised. "If he addressed it to you, then he wanted you to read it first. Lucius always does things with purpose."

A muscle on the side of Seneca's jaw quivered. "I would say his purposes have not made much sense so far."

Violet shrugged. "Who knows what the future holds? Now. What's his message from New Orleans?"

Seneca unfolded the letter to read, but Violet interrupted. "Tell me what message you think he sends, my son, then read it."

Seneca stiffened. "You don't think I can discern my brother's message?"

"I think you can discern his words," Violet allowed. "His intent might be something completely different."

Seneca looked at Rosalie. His wife leaned forward. "Violet. Please. You know why my husband and I have not been at Palatine much. As long as Tiberius let John Dyer run the plantation, there was no point being here."

Seneca spoke up. "Your news on the stairs was most welcome. A major problem has been removed by the hand of God."

Violet laughed bitterly. "You think God struck down John Dyer with consumption? If so, why didn't God do it ten years ago?"

"Hush, mother!" Seneca was shocked. "Don't speak that way."

"And you think his son will be any better?" Violet sagged back on the pillow, weariness playing across her face. "Enough. What do you believe your brother's news to be?"

Seneca licked his upper lip, his tongue brushing the fledgling mustache he was trying to grow. "Lucius saw St. George Dyer in New Orleans."

"I know St. George went to New Orleans," Violet said. "Tiberius sends him every year. For his fine liquor and his fancy cigars. As if he couldn't trust a store in Natchez. St. George is still gone, but his father must be in the ground. I sent word via steamer of his father's passing. My letter must have passed Lucius' on the river."

Seneca shook his head. "That isn't entirely why St. George was in New Orleans."

Violet sat up straight. "Go on."

"Lucius reports that St. George was trying to sell a young slave girl to some northerners. That he had the paperwork from father giving him the right to sell the girl. Lucius further reports that the girl's skin was most fair, although her features were negro."

Violet closed her eyes and nodded. "I imagined something like that must be Tiberius' answer to his problems."

"'His problems'?" Seneca asked.

Violet waved a weary hand. "What else?"

"The girl was the daughter of Mary. My brother did not say who the father might be. Lucius writes that St. George was confrontative and that he nearly shot St. George."

"Too bad he did not," murmured Violet. "Especially now." She spoke louder. "Anything else?"

"The rest is of little consequence. Lucius says that St. George was in the company of a woman from Texas. A Sally Skull. She trades cattle and was making a deal with the Army."

"That was the last thing in the letter?" Violet asked.

Seneca nodded.

Violet looked at Rosalie. "Have you read the letter?"

"I have." Rosalie had a kerchief in her hand that she was running through her fingers, a most unusual sign of nervousness.

"Speak," Violet commanded.

"I believe we now know the Dyer's hold over Tiberius," Rosalie said. "I imagine John Dyer used to take—" she searched for a word—"Tiberius' problems to New Orleans and now the task has fallen to St. George. They must have a paper trail of these transactions."

"What else?"

"I made some inquiries as soon as we received the letter while my husband was preparing for our ride here. This Skull woman is known along the river. She has a wicked reputation. It's said she deals in more than cattle. That she will buy and sell anything she can make a profit on and the law does not inhibit her in the slightest."

"Does the letter say she bought the slave girl?"

"It does not," Seneca said. "Why would you ask that?"

"I love you, son," Violet said, "but you must rely on Rosalie for advice about people. There are always manipulations being made and being planned." She looked out the window and the room was quiet for a while. Then she called out in a loud voice. "Samual!"

The door swung open and the slave filled the opening. "Mistress?"

"Close the door behind you," Violet ordered.

Samual was uncertain. "Mistress, it aint allowed for—"

"My son is here to preserve my honor," Violet said wearily. "What little I have left of it."

Samual eased the door shut, then waited.

"I know this isn't easy for you," Violet said. "But it's important. For all of us. How many other children has Mary had besides Agrippa and Echo?"

Samual looked down at the floor and did not answer.

Violet stood and walked to him. She looked up into his dark eyes. "How many?" she asked gently.

Samual's answer was a whisper. "Four."

"Why were they allowed to be born?" Violet asked. "That is not the way."

"Mary was ordered, Mistress."

"By John Dyer?"

"No, mistress. By Master Tiberius."

Violet tensed as if preparing for a blow. "And the father? It wasn't one of the Dyer's was it?"

"No, mistress."

Violet took a step back. Her shoulders slumped. Rosalie stood up and hurried over, putting a supporting arm around the older woman's shoulder.

Samual looked up. "You need know, Mistress. Mary cannot bear again. She saw to it two year ago. She afraid Master Tiberius has caught on. She afraid he looking at our Echo now."

"He can't get out of the damn bed," Violet hissed.

"He's out of the bed today, isn't he?" Rosalie said.

"With John Dyer gone," Seneca said, "we can—"

"We can do nothing," Violet snapped. "St. George is worse than his father ever was. And this is Tiberius' plantation. I brought Samual with me from Tennessee and that is the extent of my holdings." She turned back to Samual. "Is St. George stealing cotton? Selling it to this Skull woman?"

Samual met her eyes. "Yes, mistress."

"Does my husband know of it?"

"I don' know, mistress."

"How much—" Violet began, but the door to the room flew open and Tiberius stormed in, leaning heavily on a cane.

"What's he doing in here?" Tiberius demanded, jabbing the end of the cane at Samual. "I told you he's never to be in the house."

"But you don't feel that way about his wife," Violet said.

Tiberius planted the cane on the floor, hands shaking. "I have commanded Palatine for thirty years. I just buried a friend. As long as I breath, I continue to command." He glared at Violet. "Get your nigra out of here." He jabbed his cane toward Seneca. "When you are ready to be my right arm, you can return."

With that, he exited the room, slamming the door shut.

PILOT PEAK

October 1845, Pilot Peak, Nevada Territory

"You were right," Carson said.

The Expedition's horses drank from the small spring at the base of the prominent peak Cord had barely glimpsed two days ago. It was dusk and Fremont had led the rest of the column to their signal fire an hour ago. The Pathfinder seemed in a much better mood and was walking about the camp, talking to the men as they settled in for the night. The smell of elk meat cooking wafted over the campsite. Food, water and fire were the lifeblood of the Expedition and all were in abundance.

Cord rubbed his hands together over the small fire he and Carson had built up. They were on the edge of the camp, away from the main body of the men. It was Carson's way and Cord had never thought to question the habit. "Sometimes a little faith works."

"You a lucky man," Carson said. "Back in Saint Louie when—" he paused and grabbed the Lancaster long rifle near at hand.

Cord snatched his rifle. "What is it?"

Carson stepped back from the fire, into the darkness. Cord mimicked the move, standing shoulder to shoulder with the scout. When Carson gently pulled back the hammer on his rifle, Cord did the same.

A figure staggered out of the darkness, heading straight for the fire. An old Indian woman, her body emaciated, a scrap of cloth tied around her waist her only protection against the cold and decency. She held shaking hands over the flames, completely focused on absorbing the warmth for almost a minute, before she looked up with cloudy eyes and called out in her native tongue.

"Paiute," Carson whispered. "She thinks she's in one of her people's camps." He lowered the rifle's hammer. He held up one hand, palm out, and stepped into the light. *"No harm,"* Carson said in her language.

She turned to run, but one of the pickets belatedly came rushing up, weapon at the ready and barred her way, while calling out for Fremont. Within seconds, a large group of men were clustered around the cowering old woman.

"What does she want?" Fremont asked Carson.

The scout had been standing close to the woman, trying to calm her down, and talking quietly to her. He looked over at Fremont. "She been left behind by her tribe, sir. Left to die. She's too old to gather food, so she's no good to them."

"Damn heathens," Fremont declared. "White people would never treat their own like that." He gestured at the circle of onlookers. "Go back to your bed-rolls, men. Get some sleep. We've got hard traveling in the morning if we're going to cross the Sierras before the snows."

While Fremont was talking to Carson and the men, Cord had gone to the nearest cooking fire and grabbed a leg of elk. He walked up to the woman and offered it.

"What are you doing?" Fremont demanded.

"She's hungry," Cord said.

The woman hesitated, frightened, but hunger won out. She grabbed the meat, tearing away at it feverishly with her teeth as she ran off into the dark.

"That's our food," Fremont said. "We're going to need everything we've got to get through the mountains."

"I'll kill some more game tomorrow, while we're on the march," Carson said.

"Leave her be," Fremont ordered. "Her people left her to die, let her die. You're just prolonging her misery." He stalked off toward the main encampment.

When he was gone, Carson called out into the darkness in the woman's language. A few minutes later, the old woman tentatively appeared, having already gnawed the elk leg down to the bone. Cord grabbed one of his two blankets and tossed it to her. She clutched it to her chest.

"Now *that* you might well miss going through the Sierras," Carson said.

Cord shrugged. "She's probably somebody's mother."

The woman had already disappeared back into the darkness. Cord took his flask out and drained the drops of liquor that were left.

The following morning as the party set out, Cord left the small fire burning and put together a pile of food next to it.

"You a weird fella," Carson said from atop his horse, long rifle across the pommel.

"You think she's still around?" Cord asked as he mounted.

"She around. Where else she got to go?" Carson said as he spurred the horse and they headed off toward the white capped Sierra Nevada's and California beyond.

Memoirs: Ulysses Grant

Military Academy
West Point, NY
Sept U.S. Grant,
"Causes of the Mexican War"

Generally the officers of the army were indifferent whether the annexation [of Texas] was consummated or not; but not so all of them. For myself, I was bitterly opposed to the measure, and to this day regard the war [with Mexico] which resulted as one of the most unjust ever waged by a stronger against a weaker nation. It was an instance of a republic following the bad example of European monarchies, in not considering justice in their desire to acquire additional territory.

Texas was originally a state belonging to the republic of Mexico. It extended from the Sabine River on the east to the Rio Grande on the west, and from the Gulf of Mexico on the south and east to the territory of the United States and New Mexico -- another Mexican state at that time -- on the north and west. An empire in territory, it had but a very sparse population, until settled by Americans who had received authority from Mexico to colonize. These colonists paid very little attention to the supreme government, and introduced slavery into the state almost from the start, though the constitution of Mexico did not, nor does it now, sanction that institution. Soon they set up an independent government of their own, and war existed, between Texas and Mexico, in name from that time until 1836, when active hostilities very nearly ceased upon the capture of Santa Anna, the Mexican President. Before long, however, the same people -- who with permission of Mexico had colonized Texas, and afterwards set up slavery there, and then seceded as soon as they felt strong enough to do so -- offered themselves and the State to the United States, and in 1845 their offer was accepted. The occupation, separation and annexation were, from the inception of the movement to its final consummation, a conspiracy to acquire territory out of which slave states might be formed for the American Union.

Even if the annexation itself could be justified, the manner in which the subsequent war was forced upon Mexico cannot. The fact is, annexationists wanted more territory than they could possibly lay any claim to, as part of the new acquisition. Texas, as an independent State, never exercised jurisdiction over the territory between the Nueces River and the Rio Grande. Mexico never recognized the independence of Texas, and maintained that, even if independent, the State had no claim south of the Nueces. I am aware that a treaty, made by the Texans with Santa Anna while he was under duress, ceded all the territory between the Nueces and the Rio Grande; but he was a prisoner of war when the treaty was made, and his life was in jeopardy. He knew, too, that he deserved execution at the hands of the Texans, if they should ever capture him. The Texans, if they had taken his life, would have only followed the example set by Santa Anna himself a few years before, when he executed the entire garrison of the Alamo and the villagers of Goliad.

In taking military possession of Texas after annexation, the army of occupation, under General [Zachary] Taylor, was directed to occupy the disputed territory. The army did not stop at the Nueces and offer to negotiate for a settlement of the boundary question, but went beyond, apparently in order to force Mexico to initiate war. It is to the credit of the American nation, however, that after conquering Mexico, and while practically holding the country in our possession, so that we could have retained the whole of it, or made any terms we chose, we paid a round sum for the additional territory taken; more than it was worth, or was likely to be, to Mexico. To us it was an empire and of incalculable value; but it might have been obtained by other means. The Southern rebellion was largely the outgrowth of the Mexican war. Nations, like individuals, are punished for their transgressions. We got our punishment in the most sanguinary and expensive war of modern times.

WAR: 1844-1848

Camp Salubrity, LA
Near Nachitoches
July 28th 1844
To Julia Dent from U. Grant

My Dear Julia,
Mr. Higgins has just arrived from Jefferson Barracks and brings word that he saw you well on the 4th. He delivered your message and says he promised to bring some letters from you but supposes that you expected him out at the house to receive them. You can hardly imagine how acceptable your message was, but when I found that I might have expected a letter from you by his calling on it, I took the Blues so badly that I could resort to no other means of expelling the dire feeling than by writing to My Dear Julia. It has been but few days since I wrote to you but I must write again. Be as punctual in writing to me Julia and then I will be compensated in a slight degree—nothing could fully compensate—for your absence.

In my mind I am constantly turning over plans to get back to Missouri, and until today there has been strong grounds for hoping that the whole of the 4th Regiment would be ordered back there; but that hope is blasted now. Orders have arrived from Washington City that no troops on the frontier will be removed. Fred's regiment as well as mine will have to remain. We are to remain here to preserve neutrality between the United States and the belligerent parties. Who knows but Fred and me may have something to do yet? Though it may be something short of the conquest of Mexico.

Many a pleasant hour have I spent at Camp Salubrity thinking over my last visit to Mo. And its results. Never before was I satisfied that my love for you was returned, but you then assured me that it was. Does Mrs. Dent know of the engagement between us? I believe from Fred's letter that he half suspects it, although he mentions nothing of the kind.

We have big plans laid for visiting Mexico and Texas this winter.

Give my love to Ellen and the rest of the family. Again, be sure and write soon and relieve from suspense your most Devoted and Constant L
U.S.G

P.S. I have carefully preserved the lock of hair you gave me. Recollect when you write to seal with the ring I used to wear; I am anxious to see an impression of it once more.

u.s.g

At War

8 May 1846, Palo Alto, Mexico

NO PERSON, UNDER ANY PRETENSE WHATSOEVER, will interfere in any manner with the civil rights or religious privileges of the people, but will pay the utmost respect to both.

General Zachary Taylor, Commanding

Grant refolded the order and put it back into his knapsack. It had been issued before the 4th Infantry departed Corpus Christi en route to Mexico. Grant looked up and saw Rumble staring at the drawing from Kosciuszko's garden. Since the 4th Infantry had moved into drier and warmer climes, Grant's health had steadily improved, his body finally beginning to fill out and the cough that had troubled him for so long, now absent for months. Grant sometimes joked that going off to war had seemed to save his life so far.

"Why do you keep a copy of that?" Rumble asked as he slid the drawing of Lidia into his breast pocket where he kept it over his heart. "We all heard it."

Grant pretended it wasn't important. "For future reference. Some day I might actually command something instead of a bunch of teamsters, wagons and cattle."

Rumble agreed. "Some day you might. Why do you think old Zach issued it? Most armies are generally free to plunder when in enemy territory as long as they stop short of murder and rape."

It was early May and the full heat of the Mexican summer had not yet arrived to blast the soldiers. It was warm though, and the bright sun shimmered down on friend and foe.

Taylor had crossed the border after a patrol of dragoons had been ambushed by the Mexicans and sixteen men killed while the rest were captured. The fact this ambush occurred on the southern side of the Nueces River, in Mexican territory, didn't stop Taylor from sending a message to President Polk that hostilities had commenced at the hands of the Mexicans. The word among the troops was that Taylor had been secretly ordered by the President to cross the Nueces and instigate the bloodletting to get the long-simmering feud to explode into war.

Now, Grant and Rumble were with Taylor's main body of troops on the plain at Palo Alto, having finally run into the Mexican Army after marching south and relieving the siege of Fort Texas.

"I believe," Grant said, "that General Taylor realizes the Mexicans are the aggrieved party in this war and he has no desire to injure them any more than needed as directed from Washington."

"The Mexicans did a lot more than injure those dragoons," Rumble pointed out. "And why do you believe it's unjust?"

"We're acting like a European monarchy rather than a republic," Grant said. "Our government desires territory, so we start a war upon false premises against a weaker foe. There is such a thing as justice. Nations are eventually punished for their transgressions and I fear this one will cost us dearly in the future."

"I'd worry about getting through today," Rumble said as he checked the load in the double-barreled shotgun.

"I've read the news from Washington," Grant said, eyeing the Mexican line. "As we've marched into Mexico, it appears the Whigs have marched on Capitol Hill. There's a young Congressman from Illinois named Lincoln who's demanding that President Polk 'show me the spot' where the dragoons' blood was spilled."

"We know where that was," Rumble allowed. "And it was in Mexican territory."

"I don't see much of a future for this Lincoln fellow," Grant said. "A man who obstructs a war in which his nation is engaged occupies no enviable place."

"I don't envy us this place," Rumble said, hefting the shotgun.

Then he checked out the potential victims of the weapon: the Mexican army, over seven thousand strong, was drawn up across the road to

Matamoros. It was well after noon, and the sun glinted on the Mexicans' bayonets and lances. Rumble remembered old Master of the Horse Herschberger's remonstrations in the riding hall about what the cadets would face some day.

Heavy artillery pieces were positioned all along the enemy's front line and General Taylor had halted his three thousand men out of range of the guns. They were on a plain of grass reaching as high as the men's shoulders. The tops of the grass were pointy and hard, almost weapons themselves.

"Here he comes," Grant said, pointing at a figure riding along the American line.

Zachary Taylor was unpretentious for a general, dressed in blue linen pants, a long linen duster and sporting a large palmetto hat. Old 'Rough and Ready' halted his horse in front of the center of the American line and lifted one leg over the saddle, sitting sideways on Old Whitey.

In a voice that carried easily, he issued an order: "Commanders, have one platoon per company stack arms, collect canteens from the rest, and go to that waterhole—" he pointed to his right—"and fill them."

As the company commanders issued the appropriate orders, Rumble quickly drained what was left in his canteen before handing it to a soldier. "The general seems pretty calm," he noted to Grant.

"I imagine battle might be thirsty work," Grant said. "The general would know. He's been in a few hot spots over the years."

Taylor pushed back his hat and stuck a large wad of tobacco in his mouth. The entire American army watched mesmerized as he chewed and then spit. The water platoons hastened back with their precious cargo and redistributed the canteens to the ranks.

With one last spit of tobacco juice, Taylor looped his leg back over the saddle and turned his horse toward the enemy. With a slight flick of his hand, he gave the order to advance. There was no drama, no fanciful speech or exhortation. It was the business of war.

Grant looked left and right, along the line of troops stepping forward. "A fearful responsibility, commanding men in combat."

"I'd be a bit more concerned about the combat for now," Rumble reminded his friend, marching at Grant's shoulder.

Grant was a bit surprised. "Where is the Lucius Rumble who desired nothing more than to bridle York and ride him?"

"What would happen to the children if I didn't return to them?" Rumble asked.

"What about Elijah?"

Rumble snorted. "Cord is undependable."

"He might surprise you someday," Grant said. "And—" he paused.

"Yes?"

"I promised Lidia that if there were war, I would look out for you and keep you safe."

"When did you do that?"

"When I was sketching her and Lil' Ben in Kosciuszko's garden," Grant said. "She was quite insistent."

"She could be when she wanted something for someone other than herself," Rumble said. "But in war there's only so much you can do to protect yourself, never mind another."

"Regardless," Grant said, "I will do my best to look after you."

"And I you," Rumble said.

At a thousand yards, the roar of artillery firing was matched by puffs of smoke along the Mexican line as they let loose with their cannon.

"We're out of range," Rumble said to Grant. "Why are they firing?"

"Perhaps the sound makes them braver," Grant said as the cannon shot fell well short of the American lines.

As the Americans got closer, the Mexican cannons were still ineffectual not only due to their age and design, but also because they fired solid shot and the trajectory of the heavy rounds was so slow, the men could see each one come bouncing through the tall grass and step out of the way.

At five hundred yards, still out of musket range, Taylor gave the order to halt. The American 'flying' artillery came galloping up. The guns were quickly unhitched and deployed just in front of the Infantry.

"Canister and grape, Major Ringgold," General Taylor ordered, as if asking for a cup of coffee. "Give them a taste of canister and grape, if you please."

The 'flying' artillery, a concept the United States Army had just developed, light, modern guns that were moved quickly by horses, went into action. Grape was a cluster of small iron balls wrapped in canvas, thus looking like a bunch of grapes in a bag. Canister was similar, but the iron balls were encased in a tin can. Both canvas and tin disintegrated as the rounds left the barrel, spreading the balls out and spraying the target. With devastating effect on personnel in the path.

Rumble and Grant, spectators to the carnage, could see bloody paths ripped through the Mexican line where the blasts hit. The battlefield began to be covered with smoke. The screams and cries of the wounded were clearly audible in between the roar of cannon firing.

"Why don't they charge?" Rumble asked Grant.

"See—" Grant pointed to mounted men among the Mexican line swinging their sabers about and yelling—"the officers are trying. But the men won't follow."

"Then why don't they retreat?" Rumble said. "They're just standing there getting killed. It makes no sense. It's slaughter."

Just as Rumble said that, an erratically bouncing Mexican cannon ball hit a soldier standing near them, taking his head off, then ripping away the jaw of an officer right behind him. Brains and bone from the decapitated man sprayed all those in range.

Rumble dashed to the officer, Captain Page, tearing the cravat from around his neck and pressing it against the wound, trying to stop the flow of blood gurgling out of what had once been the bottom of his face.

Grant yelled for stretcher-bearers as he stood over the two of them, to warn if another ball came bounding through. Rumble looked into Page's eyes, a man he barely knew, and saw fear and pain. He leaned closer. "You'll be all right, sir. Help is on the way."

The captain was trying to speak, a difficult task given the lack of a jaw. He gripped Rumble's arm tightly with shaking fingers. With the other hand, Page pointed at his breast pocket. Rumble reached into the pocket and retrieved a blood-stained letter. It was addressed to Page's wife. Shaking his head, Rumble put the letter back into the officer's pocket with a re-assuring smile.

"You'll live, sir, and deliver that yourself." Page's eyes widened in question and Rumble nodded. "I've seen hurt worse than you've received and you'll make it. I promise."

Two stretcher-bearers came running up, dropping to their knees next to Page. They hastily slid him onto the already blood-damp canvas. Page's tongue was flopping about, having not jaw to contain it, reminding Rumble of a thirsty hound dog back on the plantation.

"Sir, you need to let go."

One of the stretcher-bearers was quicker to the need, abruptly ripping the captain's hand from Rumble's arm. And then they were off, heading toward the rear where the regimental surgeon and his gruesome tools of the trade awaited.

Rumble got to his feet. Artillery on either side was still blasting away and both lines of Infantry remained in place, the Mexicans getting the worst of it by far. Rumble flicked a piece of brain off his cheek and gripped the shotgun tightly. He took a couple of deep breaths. "Why don't we charge?"

"Our artillery is doing the job," Grant said mildly. He looked at Rumble, a perplexed look on his face. "How could you know Captain Page will live?"

"I didn't. What else to say to the man?"

"True," Grant allowed. "Strange, isn't it? I always wondered what combat would be like, but I can't say I feel much of anything, one way or the other."

"You were well trained for this at West Point," Rumble said. "I think what you feel—or you don't feel now—is what allows General Taylor to be so calm and to lead so well. You would make a much better general than I."

Grant snorted as a Mexican cannon ball came bounding past about twenty feet away, men jumping out of the way. "I'll never be a general. I just want this damn war to be over, to go back to West Point and teach mathematics, and to retire, perhaps, if I'm lucky, as a major." His eyes got a faraway look for a moment. "And marry Julia."

Then he returned his attention to the battle.

9 May 1846, Lake Klamath, Oregon

Over two thousand miles away from where Grant and Rumble experienced their first combat, Kit Carson held up a hand, halting the small party that included Elijah Cord. The four-person team was conducting a mounted patrol around the edge of Upper Klamath Lake in the southern part of the Oregon Territory. The Expedition had experienced several less-than-friendly encounters with Indians in the area over the course of their explorations. Word had just arrived in camp from two exhausted riders that an American officer with a small entourage was making his way toward the camp and Fremont had dispatched Carson, Cord and two other experienced men ahead to intercept the group before they were attacked.

Carson slid off his horse and Cord and the others followed suit. Looping the bridles over some bushes, the men made their way through the marshy terrain bordering the large lake. Fremont and the main body were camped about a half-mile behind them in a glade.

Carson held his long rifle in one hand and with the other he pointed forward and to the right. Cord gently pulled back the hammer on his rifle and aimed in that direction. Visibility through the reeds, bushes and trees was about fifty feet. The four men waited silently, weapons at the ready.

Soon all could hear the sound of horses approaching. Carson got the other three men's attention. He pointed at Cord and then held up a single finger, at the second man, held up two, at the next, held up three and then at himself and held up four. The precedence of targets based on weapons and skills of the shooters.

A mounted Indian appeared, bow looped over shoulder, lance in hand. Cord's finger slid over the trigger. He held back, waiting for at least four targets to appear so they could have the initial advantage.

A second rider appeared among the trees. A white man, dressed in a surprisingly clean white linen shirt and fatigue pants, a musket held lightly in one hand. As two more riders appeared, both whites, Cord let down the hammer on his rifle and stood, not believing his eyes. He held his musket over his head and waved it, while crying out: "King!"

The four riders halted, but then George King broke from the group, galloping forward. Cord ran from the ambush site to meet him. King skidded his horse to a halt and leapt off. In addition to the rifle, he had the boarding axe in its specially made leather sheath looped over one of his shoulders.

"Lieutenant Cord!" King exclaimed.

The two shook hands, on the other side of the country from the last place they had seen each other.

"What are you doing here?" Cord asked.

King looked weary, his narrow face even tighter. "I must see Fremont first. Deliver a message. Then we can talk."

Cord looked at the small insignia sown on the shoulder of the white shirt. "A lieutenant, not ensign?"

"I'm detached to the Marines for this mission," King said.

"And the axe?" Cord asked.

"It's a good tool."

"On a ship to cut rigging and break through wood," Cord said.

"It has other uses," King said.

Kit Carson walked up.

"This is Lieutenant King of the Marines Corps," Cord said. "King, this is our lead scout, Kit Carson."

"Always grand to see a reunion, but we best be getting." Carson was tense, his Lancaster rifle at the ready. "I'm sensing some bad air."

"'Bad air'?" King repeated.

Cord added: "We ought pay attention to what he says."

King mounted while Cord and the other scouts quickly ran to their horses. They galloped back the way they had come, arriving in Fremont's camp to great commotion.

Fremont came striding forward and actually embraced King, an extreme sign of welcome. It had been nine months since the Expedition had received any formal word from the east. For all they knew, the country was already at war with Mexico.

"Gentlemen," Fremont said to King's party, "refresh yourselves and your horses in our camp. Lieutenant King and I have some talking to do." Fremont took King by the elbow and started to lead him away, then paused. "Mister Cord, would you please join us?"

Cord was surprised both at the request and the courtesy with which it was extended. He followed King and Fremont to a spot under a wide tree. King and Cord sat on a log, while Fremont perched himself on a campstool. It was late afternoon and the sun's rays cut sharp angles through the branches and leaves overhead. It was a beautiful late May day in the Oregon Territory.

"What dispatches do you bring?" Fremont immediately asked.

"None, sir." King tapped the side of his head. "For reasons of secrecy, I was ordered to memorize the information I am to relay to you."

Fremont ran a hand through his beard. "And from whom does this information come?"

"I was initially detailed to this mission by Navy Secretary Bancroft," King said. "Then I had a private audience with President Polk of which no written record was kept."

"So I must trust your word," Fremont said.

"You should," King said. "I am an honest man."

Fremont glanced at Cord, then inclined his head in agreement. "Tell me what you've traveled so far to impart."

"President Polk's hopes of purchasing California from the Mexicans are in vain," King recited. "They will not accede to it. Therefore, the chief objective the President details to you is to take California. You are to allow no foreign interlopers a foothold in the area. And President Polk's promise to you about your station after California is taken, remains the same."

"Is that it?"

"Yes, sir."

"What do you know of that station?" Fremont demanded.

"No particulars, sir," King responded.

"So I am to wage battle against the Mexicans here," Fremont mused out loud. "Is the United States formally at war with Mexico?"

"Last I heard, no, sir," King said. "But my news is months out of date. I traveled across Mexico from Vera Cruz to Mazatlan and all I heard from the Mexican people was that war was imminent. My observation of their military is that they are ill prepared to face our army. Some of the forces are still loyal to Santa Anna; some are devoted to another general who is rumored to be planning a coup against their president."

"The situation isn't much different in California," Fremont said. "It's ripe for the picking. We've already faced several Mexican forces and they've been reluctant to press combat upon us. We could've defeated the Mexicans if I'd had the authority then that it appears I have now," Fremont said. The explorer smiled at the thought. "I won't have to pull back next time."

"No, sir, you won't."

"Good," Fremont said. "I have much to think about tonight. Thank you, Lieutenant King. Lieutenant Cord will get you settled in."

As they walked away, Cord spoke to King. "Now I know why we've been meandering around California and Oregon all these months. He's been waiting for the call to action. I gave him a similar message that had been relayed to me at Fort Bent, but it was more in the form of a defensive stratagem—to react if there was foreign action, particularly British. Now he'll go on the offensive."

"They should just make it a clear war and be done with it," King said.

They arrived at Cord's bedroll. Kit Carson was seated on the ground, next to the small fire. He rose to his feet as they arrived.

"Came a long way to deliver a message," Carson said.

King nodded. "I departed New York City by ship last year at the end of October. Landed at Vera Cruz, then traveled across Mexico to the Pacific."

"Surprised the Mexicans didn't kill ya," Carson said.

"I had a cover story that I was working for a Boston trading house," King said.

Carson laughed. "Not much of a cover. One look at you, any fool can tell you a soldier through and through."

"But I did make it," King said, a touch of anger in his voice. "From Mazatlan I took ship with Commodore Sloat, commander of the Pacific Fleet. We made it to Monterrey by way of the Hawaiian Islands."

"Aint that kind of indirect?" Carson asked.

"I was not captain of the ship," King said sharply.

"And then you made it all the way up here to Oregon," Carson said. "Quite the adventure."

"I have a feeling the adventure is yet to begin," King said. "War is coming."

"That the message you give to Fremont?" Carson asked.

"Our conversation was private," King said as he pulled a bedroll off his horse.

Carson looked at Cord, who gave a discrete nod.

"Seems like being spies runs in you fellows," Carson said.

King went for the handle of the boarding axe. "What are you saying, sir?"

Carson smiled and held up his empty hands. "Easy, friend. Just making a joke and I can see it was a poor one. I met Elijah in St. Louie when he was first slipped into our Expedition to keep an eye on us. Nothing wrong with a little scouting of things."

"I work for the President and the Secretary of the Navy," King said stiffly, but he let go of the axe.

"Well, we best get some rest," Carson said. "Probably be some heavy traveling in the morn back to California."

The three men set out their bedrolls around the fire and settled in.

Cord woke to a dead fire and darkness. He lay perfectly still for a moment, then heard movement to his left. He turned his head and in the reflected glow from the main campfire he saw Carson sitting up. When the scout reached for his long rifle, Cord grabbed the Mississippi musket next to him. With his other hand he tapped King on the shoulder. The Marine was awake in an instant, a musket in one hand, slipping the sheath holding the boarding axe over his shoulder.

Carson got to one knee, head swiveling back and forth, peering into the surrounding forest. Then he stood, rifle at the ready. Cord joined him, King at his side.

"Was you followed?" Carson whispered to King.

"I don't think so."

"Something out there," Carson said. "Near the lake. Near the horses." Without another word he stealthily began moving in that direction, Cord and King flanking him.

An abrupt crunching sound from just ahead, steel on bone, froze the three men. Carson threw his rifle to his shoulder and fired. In the muzzle flash, they could see two dozen Indians, one crouched over a body, pulling a hatchet out of the sentry's skull. Cord fired, followed by King's musket.

The three shots roused the camp, but their muzzle flashes made the firers targets and arrows whirred by, one slicing Cord on the shoulder as he quickly re-loaded.

"Stand our ground," Carson ordered, as he shoved the ramming rod down the barrel of his Lancaster, "or we'll lose the horses."

Cord and King needed little urging, both reloading quickly as more arrows buzzed by. Carson was ready first and fired. His bullet caught a charging brave in the chest and flung him back, but also revealed the precariousness of their situation as the rest of the war party was racing full speed toward the three men. Cord threw the musket to his shoulder and fired. His bullet hit an Indian in the stomach, bowling him over. He had no time to reflect on his first act of war as he dropped the gun and drew his whalebone knife. King fired another round, then discarded the musket for boarding axe.

In seconds, Carson, Cord and King were in a melee of knives, hatchets and blood. Cord ducked a war axe aimed for his head and slammed his knife just below the sternum of the attacker. He jerked upward, the blade slicing through flesh and muscle before jamming into bone. He tried to retrieve the blade but the dead man fell on top of him as warm viscera flowed over his hand and the man's last breath expelled in Cord's face.

More shots were ringing out from the camp as the rest of the Expedition was reacting. Carson was wielding his Bowie knife, carving a circle of blood around himself. King went berserk, charging forward, swinging the long handled boarding axe with ferocity.

Cord shoved the dead body off and got to his feet, rapidly reloading his rifle during the brief respite Carson and King's brutal counter-attack gained. He saw an Indian yelling commands in the center of the war party and aimed. He fired and the round hit the brave in the left chest spinning him completely around. This took the fight out of the attacking party as two other warriors grabbed the chief and ran off with him, the rest following.

Fremont was shouting commands, but Cord was watching King, bathed in blood, axe in hand, glaring about, looking for another soul to dispatch.

"Are you all right," Cord asked as he touched King's shoulder. He jumped back as King growled and whirled, raising the axe to strike.

"Easy," Carson said, grabbing King's wrist. "Your blood is up, son. It's over. Let it go. Easy, son, easy."

Sanity returned to King's eyes and Carson let go of him. They could all see the results. Indian bodies were scattered all around. There were two dead whites along with one of the Delaware Indians that had been accompanying the Expedition.

Cord looked at the first warrior he had shot. The man was writhing on the ground, hands holding his belly, blood pouring between his fingers. Fremont walked over to him, King at his side.

"Finish him," Fremont ordered.

Without a moment's hesitation, King slammed the spike end of boarding axe into the Indian's head, making the same sickening sound that had started the melee.

Carson came over and put a hand on Cord's shoulder. "The Injun was gut shot. No surviving that."

Cord shook his head. "Never shot anyone before."

"Well, it's kind of normal to be upset." Carson looked over at King who was still following Fremont, checking the rest of the bodies, swinging the axe one more time. "That aint kind of normal but sometimes it's kind of needed."

"He's seen death before," Cord said.

"He'll see it again. We all will. The day ahead is going to be the Devil's own carnage." He looked at Cord's shoulder where blood was seeping out of the arrow wound. "Let me bandage that up, before someone decides it's fatal and whacks you over the head."

Carson's prediction about the day proved accurate as Fremont moved the Expedition out at first light. He started the movement by announcing that they would destroy everything in their path. They scoured the lakeshore in a clockwise maneuver, killing every Indian they met and burning every village in their path. Cord hung back through the butchery, his rifle not needed due to the enthusiasm of the other men to avenge the deaths of their comrades. King was the opposite, always in the forefront and doing quite a bit of blood work up close and personal with his boarding axe.

By the time the Expedition departed Upper Klamath Lake, Fremont had made his point: the Indians feared and hated the white. California and the Mexicans lay ahead.

Ben Agrippa

June 1846, Vicinity Natchez, Mississippi

SALLY SKULL CIRCLED THE angel fountain and basin, wondering how much the contrivance cost. And what the purpose was, other than to say a person had money to waste on such a thing.

She smiled, imagining it on her ranch in Texas. There'd be cattle, horses, and men gathered round it all the time. The first two for the water, the latter to look at the voluptuous stone figure. Men would look with lust at a stone statue; hell, Skull knew they'd look with lust at a doorknob if they thought they had a chance with it. They were simple creatures in many ways, but anger made them dangerous.

"Why here?" St. George sounded peeved as he came around the corner of the high bushes swatting at no-see-ums. "This be the mistress's place. Damn near didn't find my way in. Not sure I can find my way out."

"You didn't leave markers?" Skull asked. The confusion on St. George's face gave the answer.

It was dusk and St. George carried a small torch, showing some forethought at least. Little bugs and no-see-ums flitted about in the early summer heat, but Skull paid them no heed. She was as used to that discomfort as breathing.

"So why here?" St. George insisted.

"Heard about all this. I wanted to see it. And the house. We always meet on the river. I wanted to see what was above and beyond the river."

"Why?"

"Don't you ever want to see what's above and beyond?" Skull asked.

St. George frowned, apparently deep in thought.

Skull didn't want him to hurt himself. "I'm sorry about your father."

St. George wasn't overwhelmed with grief. "He was old and hurting. He in a better place now."

"Where that be?"

St. George was surprised. "Heaven."

Skull held back her laughter, knowing it was one of the things that easily triggered anger in men if misplaced. "That's good for him."

"He's not in any more pain," St. George said, as true a statement as any he'd said so far.

Skull looked up at the angel. "Lot of dead folk down in Mexico."

"You called that one right," St. George said, spitting into the fountain, which bothered Skull for some reason. "But I think them Army boys bit off more than can chew. There be millions of Mexicans and just a couple thousand of them fellas."

"The Mexicans will lose," Skull said it as a fact.

"What? Why?"

"They've got no good bosses. Your average Mex, he's tough as nails. Work from sun-up till sun-down. Fight like a demon. But he needs a good boss. The Mex army got bosses like your Tiberius up on his porch. Their officers get their rank cause they born to right people, not cause they earned it. All fancy and fine, but they don't know what really be going on or how to get things done. And killing, that's a job that needs getting done well."

"It is," St. George agreed. He pulled off his slouch hat and wiped the sweat off his bald head with a dirty rag. "Not as easy as most think." He looked up at the angel. "Stupid thing."

"It's pretty," Skull murmured in a low voice, so low that St. George didn't really hear her.

"What?"

"Nothing," Skull said. "All of this, it gonna change."

"How?" St. George demanded.

"I was right about war in Mexico. I'll be right about the U.S. winning. And this, all this, the building, the slaves, the house. The way of life. It doomed."

"What you mean?"

She ignored the question. "That's why I wanted to see it. Before it all gone."

St. George shook his head, having little idea what she was trying to impart. "Say. That slave girl you bought. What you do with her?"

"Gabriel?"

"You gave her a boy's name?"

"She told me her name. The one her mother gave her."

"Slaves don get to name their children unless the master be dim."

"I like the name," Skull said. "It's an angel's name."

They both tensed as voices approached. A child's voice raised in excitement and happiness and a woman's. A young boy came running into the clearing surrounding the fountain and skidded to a halt upon seeing Skull and St. George. He was six years old, small for his age, with red hair and blue eyes.

"Ben Agrippa," St. George said, as if ordering an item off a menu.

A young black girl appeared. She halted upon seeing St. George.

"Echo," St. George said, as if the main course had appeared.

"Sorry, master," Echo quickly said, backing up a step. "Didna know you was here, master. Boy just wanted to splash. So sorry. I'll take the boy—"

"Shut up," St. George snarled.

Skull walked over to the boy and knelt in front of him. "So this is the famous Ben Agrippa Rumble. I heard of you."

Though she was kneeling, Ben still had to look up at her. "Yes, ma'am. And whom do I—" he halted, searching for the words he'd been taught—"have the pleasure of talking to?"

Skull smiled. "My name is Sally."

"Yes, Miss Sally. Pleased to meet you."

St. George snorted. "You sure, boy?"

"Where's your daddy?" Skull asked, ignoring St. George.

Ben's blue eyes locked into hers. "Why do you want to know, Miss Sally?"

Skull laughed. "So polite, yet so guarded." She looked at the slave girl. "You teach him that?"

Echo seemed to shrivel under the gaze. "No, mistress."

"I taught young Ben some of his fine manners."

Everyone turned as Rosalie Rumble walked into the clearing. She was wearing an elegant dress and carrying her parasol, but there was ice in her voice. "Pray tell, what are you doing in Miss Violet's garden, St. George? And who is your—" Rosalie tapped a finger against her lips for a moment as if in thought—"conspirator?"

"What?" St. George said.

Skull stepped in between St. George and Rosalie. "I heard enough of you to know who you are, Miss Rosalie of Natchez."

Rosalie gave a bright smile. "The knowledge is mutual, Miss Skull of Texas. Your reputation precedes you. Or is it Mrs. Skull? There was a Mr. Skull once upon a time, was there not?"

Skull took a step closer. "If you have knowledge of me, then you might want to watch that mouth of yours."

Rosalie shut her parasol and tapped the end of it in her other hand.

Skull could see that the steel tip was honed to a needlepoint. "Well, Mrs. Rumble, you sure put on a purty show and all."

"She certainly does, doesn't she?" Violet Rumble swept into the clearing with Samual just behind her right shoulder.

"What that nigra doing here?" St. George said before he thought it through.

"What are you doing in my private garden?" Violet asked. "How dare you invade my privacy?"

"I'm just visiting," Skull said.

"Not at my invitation," Violet snapped.

"My apologies," Skull said, without a hint of apology in her voice. She placed her hands on her hips, inches from her pistols. The movement was not lost on Violet who reached out and placed her hand on Ben's shoulder.

"We come here every evening because young Ben loves to play in the fountain and it does my heart well to see him do so." She glared at St. George. "It's much safer than the Mississippi, don't you agree? As Mistress of Palatine I'm entitled to this, at least. And I think as overseer of Palatine, Mister St. George, you have other places to be. Perhaps down low, across the river in Vidalia where there's a steamer docked with a load of cotton?"

St. George was befuddled, looking between Violet, Skull, Rosalie and the young boy.

"You are most correct, Mrs. Rumble," Skull said. "I was saying just that a moment ago. To my--" she paused—"friend."

"You choose your friends poorly," Rosalie said.

Skull stiffened and her hands moved toward the guns. Rosalie stepped closer, holding the parasol with one hand, the tip drifting in Skull's direction. Samual stepped past Violet, toward St. George whose hand was on top of his sash.

"Now, now, let's all be civil," Violet said. "It's a pleasant early summer evening. No need for everyone to get tense. I think this was a most intriguing meeting. For us all to finally make acquaintances and get to meet face to face. To know each other." Her voice gained an edge. "To know who is who and where they stand." She looked directly at Skull. "You did pick this place, didn't you? Because St. George, he wouldn't have thought of it."

Skull said nothing.

"I suggest," Violet's voice went back to charming, "that you all go on down to the river and do what you do and we all will just stay here and let the young boy enjoy his splashes in the fountain. And we will all await whatever else may come in the future for him. And for the two of you."

Execution

28 June 1846, San Pablo Bay, California

THE FLAG WAS HOMEMADE and new, but men were dying for the movement it represented as men often did for flags, new and old. Two men had been killed the previous day and the Bear Flag rebels who had rallied to the standard in Sonoma were in a foul and bloody mood. The Bear Flag had been completed by William Todd, a cousin of Mary Todd, married to a member of the House of Representatives, Abraham Lincoln. There was a distant irony in that fact because young Lincoln was a fierce opponent of President Polk's expansionist plans in Mexico and California, calling both a desire for *"military glory—that attractive rainbow, that rises in showers of blood."*

But there was an entire continent between speeches in Congress and the reality of battle in California.

Cord stood with Kit Carson watching the flag, tied to a tree branch over the makeshift camp of the rebels, flap in the breeze. The camp was on the shore of San Pablo Bay, just north of San Quentin, California. They were passing Cord's flask back and forth, the contents having been replenished many times over as the army made its way through the vineyards that dotted the California countryside.

The flag was made of some brown cloth on which a broad reddish stripe was marked across the bottom along with a single star in the upper left and a grizzly bear, apparently floating in air, in the upper center.

"You think that stripe stands for all the blood that going to flow?" Cord asked.

"It already been flowing." Carson spit some tobacco juice into the dirt. "Probably stands for earth or dirt or wine or some such. The star is from an old flag. Back in '36 a couple of fellows tried to capture Monterrey and call California an independent country. Call it the Lone Star State. Didn't work. Got strung up for their trouble."

"It's working now," Cord said. He noted George King was with Fremont, standing on the shore of the bay, looking through a telescope. Turning in that direction, Cord could see a small boat being rowed across the water toward the camp. "Visitors."

"Your friend thick as thieves with old Fremont," Carson said.

"Bother you?" Cord asked, knowing that the scout and the Pathfinder had a long history.

Carson shrugged. "I like John and we been through a lot together. But last couple of years he been getting, well, ambitious. I just like getting paid to travel round the land, see things no fella ever saw before. Don't need to conquer it. Especially don't need to civilize it like all these here fellas want to do to California. Grab the land; break it to make money. It aint good. I like it as it is. Wild and free."

Cord took in the lush countryside. "It's a wonderful place. A far cry from the Eastern coast."

Carson was watching Fremont and King. "You think they see the land like we do?"

"I think they believe in bigger and different things," Cord said. "Some I don't understand, but appreciating the land for its beauty isn't one of them."

It was late June, 1846, and the weather was pleasant. Indeed, Cord was finding California to be quite an oasis, a far cry from Norfolk and the High Plains and deserts they had come across to get here. He understood Carson's desire for things to stay just as they were. The large bay in front of him and the one further down south, San Francisco, made the anchorage at his birth town seem trivial by comparison. The narrow passage that opened both bays to the Pacific was a magnificent sight and Fremont had named the strait Chrysopylae (Golden Gate) since it reminded him of the harbor in Istanbul named Chrysoceras (Golden Horn).

"Mister Carson, Lieutenant Cord." King was being overly formal as he walked up to them, which put Cord on alert.

"Yes?" Cord said. He didn't bother to hide the flask and King didn't bother to hide his disdain, though he was almost the only one not drinking in the camp besides Fremont.

"I've been instructed that we have no more capacity for prisoners after all we captured at Sonoma. I've been ordered to execute whoever gets off of that boat, unless they have come to enlist in our army."

"'Our army'?" Cord said. "This isn't an army, King. And you can't be executing people who haven't done anything."

"Those are my orders," King said, avoiding eye contact. "We must continue to make a statement showing our resolve."

"I'll have no part in committing murder," Cord said.

King was reciting words given to him. "There's also the matter of revenge for our slain soldiers from yesterday."

"Armies don't do revenge," Cord said, taking a drink from his flask.

"Soldiers don't drink while on duty either." King turned to Carson. "Major Fremont specifically requested you to assist me, Mister Carson, as chief scout."

"What scouting got to do with killing folk?" Carson looked past King to the small boat, which was closing on shore. There were several rowers and three men standing. An old man from the shock of white hair, and two younger men. All definitely of Spanish descent. They were not coming to enlist.

"Let me talk to them, figger out what they want," Carson suggested.

"That was not an option I was given," King said.

"It is now." Carson hefted his Lancaster rifle and made his way to the shore, leaving Cord with a nervous King. Several of the Bear Flag rebels gathered round and the mood was turning uglier as the boat touched shore about a hundred yards away and Carson greeted the men.

There was an animated conversation, then Carson came walking back, long rifle in the crook his arm. "The old man's son was the mayor of Sonoma. He heard that we hold him as prisoner. He just wants to visit his son and go back home."

"Who are the two young men?" King asked.

"The old man's nephews," Carson said. "Twins; sons of the mayor of San Francisco. They're all peaceable and got no weapons. Just want to visit with their kin."

The three Mexicans waited by the shore, their boat back offshore about a hundred yards away. King looked at them and then over at Fremont who remained by his tent, arms folded, watching. "Wait," King ordered. "I'll talk to Fremont."

The Bear Flag rebels muttered, but complied. King strode swiftly to Fremont.

Cord observed King with their nominal commander. "Isn't good," he said to Carson. It was obvious King was arguing with their commander.

"No, it aint. Old Pathfinder wants to make a statement, not just to the locals, but to these Bear Flag jokers before we move on to the main Mexican forces." He indicated the motley crew of drunken civilians pretending to be an army.

King came striding back and the dismay on his face indicated the result of the discussion with the Pathfinder. "Are you with me?" he asked Cord.

"No. It's illegal and murder."

"You, sir?"

"Sorry," Carson said. "Can't."

King turned his back to them and addressed the dozen or so Bear Flaggers, as he slid his boarding axe out of its sheath and drew a line in the dirt with the pike. "Gentlemen, we have no room or provisions to take more prisoners.

Major Fremont has ordered they be executed immediately. It's our duty. Those who follow orders, on this line."

All the men, half of them fully drunk, the others well on their way, staggered to the line.

"Ready," King ordered.

The men lifted their rifles and pulled back the hammers on the flints in a ragged cacophony signaling imminent violence.

The three Mexicans finally became aware something was amiss. The old man stepped forward, arms upraised and called out that they had come in peace and unarmed.

"Aim." King dropped the boarding axe and grabbed his rifle, joining the firing squad.

"Lieutenant King," Cord said. "Don't!"

"Fire!"

The rattle of musketry was uneven. The old man was hit by two rounds and slammed backwards to the ground. One of the twins was hit in the head, the large caliber round exploding it and showering his brother with blood, bone and brain. The other twin was wounded in the stomach and fell to his knees, hands pressing against his body vainly trying to keep the blood from flowing out. He was crying out something in Spanish.

"Ah, Sweet Jesus," Carson cursed. "Damn stupid bastards." He lifted his Lancaster, pulling back the hammer while bringing it to his shoulder, and fired, all in one smooth motion.

The bullet pierced directly through the last survivor's heart and he toppled backwards onto the shoreline.

Cord headed for the camp, directly to Fremont who was peering at the bodies through his telescope.

"Major!" Cord stopped three paces from the Pathfinder, just as he had been trained on the Plain at West Point.

Fremont slowly lowered the telescope and looked at Cord. "Yes, Lieutenant?"

"That was murder."

"That was war."

"Against unarmed civilians? You don't have the authority."

"Do not talk to me like this in front of my command," Fremont said. He took a step closer. "Especially after you've been drinking."

"Everyone here's been drinking," Cord said.

"I have not," Fremont said. "Nor has Lieutenant King."

"I resign my commission as of this minute. Sir," Cord added.

"You cannot resign during a time of war," Fremont said. "And any action you take against me will be treason. Punishable by execution."

Cord took a step closer. "I will—"

"Easy, now," Carson said, placing a hand on Cord's shoulder. "It's done, son."

Fremont nodded. "It is indeed."

"It was murder," Cord said. "I'm going to San Francisco harbor and find Commodore Sloat," Cord said. "I'll formally—"

"Sloat is under orders to take San Francisco," Fremont said. "And then we'll move south by ship and capture the rest of the Mexican positions in California. He'll have no time for your dramatics. Also," Fremont added, a cunning smile curling under his mustache, "your good friend—and mine—Mister Carson, was complicit in what you call murder. He did fire the last fatal shot."

"He did it to put that poor man out of his misery," Cord argued, but realized that he was out-flanked.

"We head for Monterrey immediately," Fremont cried out in a loud voice. "We must beat the British to the capitol."

Cord pulled out his flask.

Battle

23 Sept 1846, Monterrey, Mexico

"MULES, MULES, AND MORE MULES," Grant muttered, in between issuing orders in functional Spanish to the Mexican teamsters trying to get the regimental baggage train unloaded and supplies sorted. The thunder of cannon fire echoed back from the front lines, a few miles distant.

Rumble ignored Sam's grousing and peered through his telescope at the Black Fort guarding the approach to Monterrey, Mexico, unaware that Elijah Cord was on the march toward Monterrey, California. The city was a formidable obstacle. On the north, in front of Grant and Rumble, was the

Black Fort, bristling with guns, built on the foundation of an unfinished cathedral. What was once to be a house of worship was now a house that dealt death.

On the south, the city was protected by the Santa Catarina River and the Sierra Madre mountains. To the east, a series of small redoubts guarded the way. And to the west, the Bishop's Palace and Fort Soldado not only protected the city, they also kept open the Mexican's supply line. It was a strategic puzzle that General Taylor had spent the last two days analyzing.

"I sent a request," Grant continued. "Written up perfectly. Asking for duty that allowed me combat. I told the Colonel I did not want a posting that removed me from sharing in the dangers and honors of service with the regiment at the front."

"Danger, I'll grant you," Rumble said, noting the muzzles of the cannon that lined the top of the massive wall of the Black Fort. They flashed as the Mexicans fired on the advancing American forces. "Honor, is another matter."

It was near the end of September, 1846, and since the victory at Palo Alto, General Taylor had been forced to delay his advance further into Mexico because an influx of volunteers from the United States had swelled his ranks. The quick war was turning into a slugfest. While the army's number was now much higher, discipline and training was much lower. Rumble noted the distinct difference between the Regular Army soldiers, many of whom were well-trained foreigners serving to gain citizenship, and the citizen soldiers who had rushed to volunteer at the prospect of 'adventure' in a foreign land and to serve the flag. Curiously, he also noted that many of the volunteer units had West Pointers as leaders; men who had resigned their active commissions, gone into the civilian world, but were now back in uniform when their country needed them.

Taylor may have spent the months training the volunteers, but it was clear from the way the army was deploying for the assault, that Taylor was counting on his regular army to do the heavy lifting as the volunteers were all being held in reserve.

"Remember in tactics class, plebe year?" Grant asked. "When they said that after forty-five days of being besieged, any fort will surrender?"

Rumble laughed. "And when the instructor asked Cord what he would do if he commanded a besieged fort—he said that he'd walk out and let the besiegers have the fort, then encircle them for forty-five days and take it back."

"That didn't go over well," Grant said. "But it has a sort of logic to it. This is a daring plan, which the General has come up with."

"'Daring'?" Rumble said. "That's an understatement. The scouts say there are over ten thousand Mexicans defending. We number a bit over three thousand. I might not have graduated, but I do remember some instructor saying that an attacking force against a fortified position needs three to one odds. We have it backwards here. And worse, our army is split. East and west of the city. If the Mexicans sally forth and attack—" Rumble didn't finish.

"You're sounding a lot like Cump lately," Grant observed. "Gloom and doom."

"I'm a realist," Rumble said.

Grant shrugged. "We're just the diversion. The main thrust is to come from the west. I believe General Taylor feels the Mexicans lack the will to assault us from their defensive positions."

"But our two forces aren't mutually supporting, while the Mexicans have the advantage of interior lines," Rumble pointed out, scribbling some notes in his 'observation pad'.

"That's true," Grant agreed, before yelling out more orders to a pair of Mexican mule handlers.

A lower melody of death underscored the cannon fire as the rattle of musketry began, initially like a few drops on a tin roof, then increasing to a full downpour.

"It sounds like a warm day in the field," Grant said, taking the telescope from Rumble.

"I'm heading forward," Rumble said. "To observe. There's only so much I can see and experience from a distance."

Grant looked at the Mexican teamsters lounging in the shadows of the few buildings of the village. "They don't need me here. I'm joining you."

Rumble didn't protest his friend abandoning his assignment. They rode swiftly toward the firing. They encountered the bulk of the 3rd and 4th Infantry regiments hunkered in a depression, out of direct fire of the Black Fort.

Within minutes of arriving, the order to advance was relayed down the chain of command. As one, the men rose up out of the depression and charged. Rumble noticed that he and Grant were the only men on horseback.

"Sam!" Rumble called as he hopped off his horse and let it gallop toward the rear, showing more smarts than any of the humans. But Grant was pressing forward and the sound of cannon and muskets was too loud for him to hear.

The fire from the Black Fort and the right flank was devastating. Within minutes, a good portion of the attacking force lay dead or wounded and officers were shouting to retreat. Due to the volume and direction of the incoming fire, the troops moved left, to the east, not backwards. The instinct to survive dictated the direction of the withdrawal.

It was a disorganized movement. Rumble saw Grant trying to rally some troops and ran toward his friend. "Sam!" He slapped Grant on the leg.

But Grant was looking past Rumble. An officer was staggering back with the troops, completely exhausted.

Rumble gripped Grant's leg as he recognized the officer. "Give Hoskins your horse."

Grant looked confused for a moment, then nodded. "Certainly."

Grant hopped off his horse and holding the bridle, stopped the regimental adjutant. "Take my mount, Hoskins," Grant said.

He received no argument and Hoskins gratefully took to the saddle.

The color bearer for the 4th Regiment came hurrying by, then cried out in pain as a musket ball hit him in the spine. He fell to the dirt, dead. Grant grabbed the standard before it struck the ground.

"Come on," Rumble urged. As they withdrew, Hoskins came galloping by, low in the saddle. It did him no good. A bullet tore though his body and he tumbled off the horse. There was no time to retrieve the body as the heavy fire continued and the horse sprinted away.

Rumble and Grant finally reached the safety of an outlying village and, along with the surviving troops, hunkered down, out of immediate danger. Over ten percent of the attacking force lay dead or dying out in the open.

Rumble spotted a church steeple and grabbed Grant, who handed the regimental colors over to an enlisted man. "Come on, Sam. We can see from there."

The two went into the church and Rumble halted, startled. The dark and cool of the interior were so different from the heat of the battlefield. Grant immediately headed toward the door to the belfry. They climbed up and Rumble extended his telescope.

He tried to make sense of what was happening. The assault of the 3rd and 4th Regulars on the Black Fort had failed. Of that they were witnesses. But further south, to the left, Rumble could spot a mass of men in blue moving toward the wall of the city.

"There," he said, handing the telescope to Grant.

"The volunteers," Grant said, seeing the unit flags. "The Tennesseans and your fellow Mississippians are over there. Colonel Jefferson Davis leads the men from your state. Class of '28." Grant stiffened, as he observed the action. "They're doing it. They're carrying the position. I see men going over the wall. The volunteers did it."

"Bet Taylor is surprised by that," Rumble said.

"The volunteers have spirit," Grant allowed. "Maybe that counts for more than we suspect." Grant lowered the scope. He closed his eyes, weariness taking over. "We might as well rest while we can. It'll be our turn again soon enough."

As the volunteers took the outskirts of Monterrey, darkness fell, bringing an end to the battle for the day. The city was surrounded, but not taken.

As soon as the sound of firing died out, Grant sought out Rumble in the evening gloom. "We need to find Hoskins' body. Bring him back before the dogs and vultures get to him."

Rumble had a metal flask in hand. An 'off to war' gift from Benny Havens, who said that his experiences in the War of 1812, confirmed that there was always a time and a place for a quick swallow, although he hoped Rumble would never experience such a time or place. Rumble took a swig and stood.

"May I partake?" Grant indicated the flask.

Rumble was going to demur, given alcohol's effect on Grant, but after the events of the day, he handed the flask over.

Grant took a deep drink. And didn't hand the flask back. Rumble grabbed a bloodstained canvas stretcher while Grant screwed the top back on the flask.

"There will be worse scavengers than vultures out there," Rumble said as he picked up his shotgun.

They departed the village, retracing the route of their retreat earlier in the day. The further they went, the more bodies they passed.

A furtive figure was off to the left, bending over a body. "Get!" Rumble yelled, pulling back the hammers on both barrels. The thief, whether Mexican or American it was hard to tell, ran off into the gathering darkness. Rumble and Grant continued forward.

Rumble couldn't help but notice something about many of the corpses: their clothes were in disarray, as if they had been pawed at.

"Damn scum have already been stealing from the dead," Rumble said.

Grant peered at the bodies. "Yes. Some. But others haven't been touched by thieves. Doesn't make sense."

A deep voice from behind startled them. "Did it to themselves."

General Taylor sat on Old Whitey, his straw hat pulled low over his eyes.

"Sir," Grant said, snapping to attention, Rumble following suit.

"Man gets shot and he isn't killed right off, he starts tearing at his clothes, looking for the wound," Taylor said. "It's a strange thing, but not so strange knowing that if you're gut shot, you're dead. Just not right away. Hell, you're eventually dead most any place you get shot." His voice was low, as if he were speaking to himself. "Saw it first time back in 1812."

Grant took a step toward Taylor. "General, isn't it a bit dangerous for you to be out here?"

"Isn't it for you also?" Taylor asked. He noted the stretcher. "Searching for someone in particular?"

"Our regimental adjutant, sir," Grant said. "He was killed during the fighting and we're recovering his body."

"Good," Taylor said. He was looking past them, at the field of dead. "A general always has to remember this before he fights the next battle. Remember the true coin of war." Taylor twitched the reins and Old Whitey started to amble back toward American lines. Taylor looked over his shoulder. "We took a beating today, boys. My fault. But we'll lick 'em tomorrow. Or the next day. But we will lick 'em."

And then 'Old Rough and Ready' was gone in the darkness.

Grant took out the flask and drank long and hard, then gave it back. Without a word, they continued.

"Hold on," Grant said, a slight slur in his voice, as they heard a moan.

Rumble remained on the road, shotgun in one hand, stretcher in the other. Grant knelt next to someone, giving him water, then wiped the man's forehead with his handkerchief. Rumble waited for several minutes, before Grant slowly lowered the man's limp head to the ground and rejoined him.

"He asked for his mother at the end," Grant said in a low voice.

"What did you tell him?"

"That she was close." Grant's tone was shaky, something Rumble had never heard before. "That she'd be here soon. Then he just died."

Rumble licked his lips and peered about, trying to get oriented. "Hoskins fell somewhere over there."

They walked in that direction and finally found the dead officer face down in the dirt, his uniform rifled, his possessions looted, his West Point ring gone. Loading him onto the stretcher, they headed back toward the village and the regiment, carrying the body between them.

"I never knew death weighed so much." Grant sounded surprised.

They made it back to the regiment and turned the body over to the grave detail. Rumble and Grant found a small dark corner of an abandoned house. They both slid to a sitting position, backs against the mud brick walls. They were exhausted beyond endurance, too tired to talk. They knew what the morning meant: bloody, close-quarters, street-by-street fighting to take the city.

"Your flask?" Grant asked.

Dawn came quicker than most of the surviving men in the 4th Infantry would have liked. Preparatory orders were issued, weapons were checked and the men assembled for combat.

But nothing happened. General Taylor was consolidating the footholds he'd gained in the city, preparing for the final assault. And letting his troops rest after the brutal battles of the first day's assault.

Outside of Monterrey, Rumble was trying to analyze what had occurred, since this was the first major setback for the Americans in Mexico, although the battle was far from over and the words among the troops was that the main assault on the west side of the city by the volunteers had had far greater success.

He was sitting with Grant on a bench outside a half-destroyed house. Not far away the screams, pleadings and moans of the wounded could be heard in a symphony of pain and despair. Men were lying on the ground all about, spent from the previous day's action, although how many would find sleep this evening was questionable, given the assault that was sure to be renewed the following morn.

"What happened, Sam?" Rumble asked. "General Taylor said it was his fault."

Grant was checking requisition forms from the companies, sending soldiers off to fulfill them. Top of the list was water, then ammunition, and then food. He paused, pencil in the air.

"First, the army was divided before the attack, as you noted. By itself that wasn't a problem. The problem came when our attack went beyond being a diversion, as General Taylor initially envisioned, into being an actual assault on the Black Fort. We should have feinted to the depression, held there while making a demonstration of charging, then pulled back once the main assault in the west had achieved it's goal. Instead we charged, with the results we lived through, but others didn't."

"Then, instead of making a quick decision to press the attack or withdraw completely, reinforcements were thrown into the fray piecemeal and I believe that's where General Taylor feels his fault lies. Our charge was ill-conceived and poorly executed." Grant went back to writing on his forms and Rumble went back to making entries in his notebook.

Inside of Monterrey, the Mexican commander ordered a tactical withdrawal, pulling his troops back to surround the city's central plaza. This tightened his lines, a sound tactical move, but had an unexpected effect on the soldiers: they were giving up terrain they had successfully defended against the American assault. The withdrawal had the bitter taste of defeat in the mouths of many of the Mexican soldiers who had fought so bravely.

As sometimes happens in war, both armies felt defeated after two days of battle.

On the second morning, the assault into Monterrey began in earnest. Grant, made acting adjutant of the 4th Infantry with Hoskins' death, no longer had to stay with the supply train and Rumble accepted his duty was at the front so they were both at the head of the regiment.

Surprisingly, the going was easy at first. The Americans moved forward, meeting no resistance. Even the Black Fort was undefended. But things changed when they came closer to the city's central plaza where the Mexicans had rallied their defense. Every house, every store, every inch of advance became a bloody affair. The roads were barricaded and many were covered by canister and grape shot. The Mexicans had learned the hard lessons from Matamoros and adapted their artillery. The roofs of the one and two story buildings had been fortified with walls of sandbags, giving the defenders the advantage of plunging fire.

It was brutal on both sides. By the afternoon, American artillery shells and mortars were indiscriminately raining down on the central plaza. The Mexicans requested a cease-fire to evacuate women and children and the battle halted temporarily while General Taylor considered the request.

Grant and Rumble heard about it from a courier as they hunkered inside a house two blocks from the plaza. They'd crawled into the house through a hole in the adobe wall from a stable next door, as far as they could go on horseback without being shot out of the saddle. The Americans had quickly learned cutting through the walls was safer than trying to fight down the barricaded streets raked with musket and artillery fire. Rumble made a note of the improvised tactics on the small pad. This had not been taught at West Point.

The room was filled with men, both regulars from the 4th Infantry and a handful of Rumble's fellow Mississippians with their rifles. Units had been jumbled together in heat of combat and the close quarters of the battle precluded reorganization.

Colonel Garland, the regimental commander, poked his head through the hole and gestured for them to join him. Grant led the way and they crawled into the stable where Garland was dusting off his uniform. "General Taylor's turned the truce down."

"Whatever for, sir?" Grant asked.

Garland edged toward the stable door and carefully peered toward the plaza. "General Taylor said the Mexicans will use up their supplies faster having to feed the civilians. Coldly calculating, but true." He turned to Grant and Rumble. "The regiment will be pushing forward soon. We're dangerously low on ammunition. The Mexicans recognize that, they'll counter-attack and we'll be forced to rely on the bayonet."

"I can go back to the supply column," Grant said. "I know how to move what we need forward."

"Going back through all the houses will take too long before we make the final assault," Garland said.

"I can ride my horse," Grant suggested. "I'll make it in no time."

"We bypassed many pockets of resistance in our push to the plaza," Garland said. "And the Mexicans are growing bolder. You'll be an inviting target as soon as you go out that door. The building across the street has a hornet's nest of snipers on the roof."

Rumble gestured toward some notches cut in the adobe wall, heading toward a wood trap in the roof. "I can give him covering fire from up there, sir. It'll only be risking the two of us."

Garland considered the plan and made the command decision. "Do it, gentlemen."

As Grant readied Nelly, Rumble lay his shotgun down and stuck his head in the hole in the wall. "I need four rifles."

The Mississippi volunteers reluctantly handed over their rifles. After checking that they were loaded and primed, Rumble slung all four across his back.

Grant had one foot in the stirrup, the other dangling free on the same side of the horse.

"Ready?" Rumble asked.

Grant nodded.

"Give me a minute, then I'll give a shout," Rumble said. He quickly climbed the ladder. A low wall topped with a double row of sandbags surrounded the flat roof. Rumble crawled to the side above the stable entrance. He un-slung the rifles, pulling back the hammer on each of them, then propped three against the sandbags.

Fourth rifle at the ready, Rumble stood and aimed toward the enemy position across the street. "Go!"

Grant and Nelly exploded onto the street below. Grant was holding himself in the saddle with the one foot in the stirrup and an arm around Nelly's neck. His body was on the near side of the horse.

A muzzle flash exploded from the opposite roof and Rumble fired at it, tossing the expended rifle to the ground and grabbing the next. As more Mexicans popped up to shoot, Rumble fired the next three rifles as fast he could, drawing the attention of the enemy as Grant raced away. The last shot struck home and blood sprayed into the air as a Mexican rifleman's head snapped back and he tumbled behind his sandbag parapet.

Rumble automatically began to reload the rifle as he had been trained. A bullet showered sand from one of the bags in front and Rumble dove behind his own wall as more shots flew overhead.

Galloping away, Grant sensed as much as felt bullets pass close by, but the firing dwindled as he got further from the center of town. Slowing the horse, he spotted a blood-stained American soldier standing guard in the doorway of a house and brought Nelly to a halt.

"What are you doing here?" Grant asked.

The nervous sentry jerked his thumb toward the house. "Full of wounded, sir. Making sure they're safe."

Grant dismounted. Hitching Nelly to a post, Grant went in the open door and was greeted with the sickly smell of fresh blood and the groans and whimpers of men in pain. He spotted a captain of the engineers that he vaguely knew just inside the door, a pistol in his lap. The left side of the captain's head was bathed in blood and Grant could see that a bullet had ripped a piece of the man's skull away. Another officer was next to him, hands preventing protruding intestines from falling to the dirt floor. There were more wounded men scattered about the room, along with several who had already succumbed to their injuries.

"I'll get help," Grant announced, the stench of blood and viscera bringing back memories of the tannery and forcing him to step back.

No one responded; all were involved so deeply in their pain.

Grant ran outside and leapt onto Nelly. He resumed his mission and soon found headquarters. Only to discover that while he had been coming back for ammunition, a courier had gone forward on a different route with orders for the 3rd and 4th Infantry Regiments to withdraw.

Grant went to Taylor's headquarters and found his chief of staff. "Sir, there's a house full of wounded that will be lost to the enemy if we don't retrieve them."

The chief of staff was busy writing out orders and barely acknowledged Grant's presence. "Lieutenant, the 3rd and 4th fought bravely, but took heavy casualties. We have Monterrey invested but not taken. We must hold our lines and can't spare the men. The western flank is pressing the battle and that's where every spare man is being sent. I'm afraid the wounded will have to fare for themselves this evening. Perhaps in the morning."

Grant reluctantly bowed to the military neccessity and went to his task as adjutant, trying to gain an accurate count of officers and men. He waited along the main road as the remnants of the 4th Infantry came staggering back, bloody but unbeaten. Rumble soon arrived, shotgun in hand, his uniform blood-smeared and his eyes distant.

"Are you wounded?" Grant asked.

Rumble shook his head numbly. "Tried to carry a wounded man back. Had him over my shoulder. Someone shot him. Shot a wounded man being carried to safety. I could feel the ball hit his body. Feel his last breath rattle out of his lungs." Rumble's hand fluttered along his left cheek. "I left him. We left many dead and wounded behind."

"I know," Grant said, still checking off names as men staggered by. "I told General Taylor's chief of staff, but he had other priorities."

"Abandoning our wounded." Rumble shook his head.

"It's war," Grant said. "There's a house crammed with wounded. You and I could—"

"I passed a house," Rumble continued, as if the word had been a trigger. "It *had* been full of wounded, but now they're all dead. The Mexicans had been through it. Every man in there had been bayoneted."

"Must be the same place," Grant said. He placed a hand on Rumble's shoulder. "Most of those men had mortal wounds. They were put out of their misery."

"You put a horse out of its misery," Rumble said, "not a man."

"War changes things," Grant said, his voice slipping into the calming mode he used on horses. "Perhaps you might partake of Benny's salve."

Rumble blinked, coming into the here, the now. He pulled the flask out and took a long drink. He offered it to Grant, who demurred. "You need it."

"This should be over tomorrow." Grant guided Rumble to an over-turned gun carriage that promised cover for the night, near the regimental headquarters. "A good sleep will do us both well."

There was no fighting the next day. A Mexican emissary bearing a white flag appeared in front of the American lines and relayed a request for a cease-fire and a parlay between the Mexican commander and General Taylor. Both were granted.

In his role as observer, Rumble positioned himself at headquarters. Grant, out of curiosity to see how generals conducted themselves, joined him. They stood behind the army staff officers as Taylor negotiated the surrender of the Mexican forces.

What they witnessed was surprising and unexpected.

Taylor's terms were shockingly lenient: The Mexicans were to depart Monterrey and withdraw a minimum of sixty miles. They could keep their arms, their horses, and six light artillery pieces. There would be no more fighting for eight weeks.

"Why did General Taylor do that?" Rumble asked Grant as they returned to the 4th Infantry headquarters. "One day we're killing our enemy, the next we're paroling them. War makes no sense."

"It makes sense in its own way," Grant said as he sat down on a bench with a barrel serving as desk in front, his makeshift office as adjutant. "To continue the fight would've been bloody. And perhaps a lasting peace might come out of this. Taylor also wishes to spare the women and children of the city from further bloodshed."

"He didn't seem too concerned about them the other day." Rumble leaned his shotgun against the wall behind the bench. "Well, I must—" he paused as a dusty rider bearing a canvas bag rode up to headquarters.

"Hey, fella, you know where I can find the headquarters of the 4th Infantry?" the soldier shouted, having no idea Grant was an officer because of his plain blue tunic.

"Lieutenant Grant, adjutant, 4th Infantry."

"Sir." The rider dismounted, untied the canvas bag, and handed it over. "Latest mail from the States." He looked about at the destruction. "Looks like I missed a heck of a fight, Lieutenant."

"Be grateful for the small favors of fate," Grant said as he opened the bag.

The courier wandered off in search of sustenance for both himself and his mount. Grant began sorting the mail by company, along with an extra pile.

"What's that one for?" Rumble asked, looking over Grant's shoulder.

"The dead." Grant paused in his sorting. "A letter for you. Sergeant Major Lucius Kosciusko Rumble, attached to the 4th Infantry," he added with a smile.

"Thanks, Sam." Rumble took the letter and walked away a few feet to read it. The purple stationery indicated the originator as much as the flowing script.

Palatine
Natchez, MS
12 August 1846

My Dearest Son,
I pray this letter finds you well and out of harm's way. We heard reports about the fighting and it all sounds quite frightful. I am glad you are just an observer and not in the middle of it.
Your brother received your missive from New Orleans. You will be heartened to learn that John Dyer is no longer among the living. I am sure he is quite at

home amongst the other twisted souls Satan can call his own. Unfortunately, his son still breathes and has taken his father's place.

Your brother spoke to Sheriff Wallace about St. George and suspicious activity on the river, unaware, or perhaps unwilling to accept, that the sheriff is cut of the same cloth as St. George. Most likely in his employee, at the very least, indebted to him. Who knows what beastly things happen in Shanty Town? It will take more than spoken words to stop St. George and get the sheriff to act. Fortunately, Rosalie is on the task.

The grandchildren are flourishing. Ben grows taller and stronger each day. He enjoys the Angel Fountain as much as you did, if not more. He will be riding soon, and I will insure he has the best possible mount and instruction.

He does not go down to the river.

Abigail is darling and I am doing my best to instruct her in the finer things in life a lady must understand. As does her aunt Rosalie.

Your father is the same.

As am I.

It is as if there is a great pause as war rages in Mexico and the entire country is holding its breath. What will happen when everyone exhales, I haven't the slightest clue. All I know is my desire for you to pass through this ordeal unscathed and return home to your children.

My prayers and love to you.

Violet Rudolph Rumble

Nothing about what he'd witnessed in New Orleans. Violet was always very particular about what she discussed and what was not to be spoken about.

As Rumble slid his mother's letter into his shirt pocket to join the sketch of Lidia and other letters, Sam Grant had finished sorting the mail and had not been rewarded with mail of his own. He pulled out a well-worn sheet of paper, Julia's last letter to him, over three months old, and opened it on top of the barrel he was using as a desk.

The tone of the letter was light-hearted and carefree. Julia mentioned being pursued by other suitors among the handful of officers left at Jefferson Barracks.

He licked the end of his pencil and began to write on the back of a blank requisition form:

4th Regiment
Vicinity, Monterrey, Mexico

25 Sept 1848

My Dearest Julia,
I received several weeks ago your letter regarding Jefferson Barracks and potential suitors. I know you are trying to lighten my heart, but you will soon learn that many of those you once knew at the Barracks are no longer with us. The toll among officers has been frightful. Lucius Rumble and I just recovered Lt. Hoskins body and--

After Grant wrote that last line he put the pencil down and tore up the piece of paper. He started anew.

My Dearest Julia,
When you write to me again, tell me if your Pa ever says anything about the possibility of our engagement and if you think he will make any further objections.
But Julia, I hope many more months will not pass over before we will be able to talk over this matter without the use of paper. How much I do want to see you again, but I know you would not recognize me. When you see me as you often do in your dreams, you see me as I was, not as I am, for climate has made a change. I mean a change in appearance, but in my love for Julia I am the same, and I know that she has not changed in that respect, for she writes me such sweet letters when she does write. Won't you continue to write to me often for it gives me so much pleasure to read and to answer your letters.
Julia, if the 4th Inf should be stationed permanently in the conquered part of Mexico would you be willing to come here or would you want me to resign? I think probable though that I shall resign as soon as this war is over and make Galena my home. My father is very anxious to have me do so.

Grant looked at that last line and closed his eyes briefly. "Lucius."

Rumble had his shotgun broken down and was cleaning the weapon. "Yes?"

"Your flask, please."

Rumble put the shotgun aside and reached into his haversack. He pulled the flask out. "Bad news from the States?"

"No news from the States. I am writing Julia."

"Ah." Rumble handed the flask to Grant, who took a quick swallow. Rumble waited a moment for Grant to hand it back, but when his friend went back to writing, placing the flask near to hand on the barrel top, Rumble went back to cleaning his shotgun.

Grant continued.

Julia, aren't you getting tired of hearing war, war, war? I am truly tired of it. I do wish this would close. If we have to fight, I would like to do it all at once and then make friends. If these Mexicans were any kind of people they would have given us a chance to whip them enough some time ago and now the difficulty would be over; but I believe they think they will outdo us by keeping us running over the country after them.

Grant took another drink.

We have just had a hard fight. Harder than any before and costlier. Twenty-Seven officers of one-hundred and twenty-two on the rolls have been killed. Many from those you knew at Jefferson Barracks. I am now the Regimental Adjutant as Charley Hoskins, whom you knew well, is no longer with us.

I wish this were the last battle. I hope it may be so for fighting is no longer a pleasure.

What made you ask the question, Dearest Julia, 'if I thought absence could conquer love?' I can only answer for myself, that Julia is as dear to me as she was two years ago, when I first told her of my love. From that day to this I have loved you constantly. You have not told me for a long time, Julia, that you still love me, but I never thought to doubt it.

Grant tilted the flask once more. Blinked a couple of times to focus on his writing, which was becoming difficult. He added one more paragraph:

Speaking of you coming to Mexico, Dearest, I do not intend to hint that it is even probable that the 4th Inf. will remain for I think it will be one of the first to leave the country. Give my love to all at White Haven and write very soon and very often to
Ulysses.

Grant took a deep breath, folded the letter and then slid it into an envelope and addressed it, ready for the next dispatch rider to begin the long journey back to the United States. He dearly wished he were making that trip along with the letter as his head drooped and then lightly landed on the barrel top.

Rumble walked over and removed the flask from Grant's slack hand. He pulled Grant's field jacket up over his head. Then he handled the business of adjutant for the 4th Infantry as best as possible while his friend slept.

California Politics

14 Dec 1846, San Luis Obispo, California

"HE SHOULD BE SHOT," Lieutenant King demanded. Throwing in a belated "Sir" as he addressed newly promoted Lieutenant-Colonel Fremont, also newly the commander of all American military forces in the California territory.

"Aint you tired of killing?" Kit Carson muttered in a voice that only Cord could hear.

Fremont sat in a high-backed chair in front of the altar inside the San Luis Obispo Mission. He wore a deerskin blouse and leggings, both of which showed much wear and tear from the constant travels of the past months. He was flanked on each side by a pair of Delaware Indians that had become his bodyguards as the fledgling army had gone up and down California, from San Francisco to San Diego and back north, sometimes by land, sometimes by sea. They'd taken Los Angeles months ago, but lost it when the native Californios revolted against the harsh military commander Fremont had left in charge: Lieutenant George King. Now King was claiming that the civilian standing tall in front of Fremont was the man who had led that revolt, been captured, paroled, and captured again.

"Don Jose de Jesus Pico, you have violated the parole so graciously given you," Fremont said. "You have taken up arms against the army of the United States."

"I took up arms to defend myself and my home," Pico said. "We have all heard what happened to Senor de Los Reyes Berreyesa and his nephews at your hand."

Fremont leaned forward in the chair. "And what have you heard?"

"That they were shot although they had committed no crime," Pico said. "That they had no weapons. Do you think any of us would be foolish enough to make the same mistake?"

"Your current mistake, sir, will cost you your life," Fremont said.

"Are you not sick of war, senor?" Pico pleaded. "God has given us life as a blessing. Do you throw lives away so easily?"

"I do yours," Fremont said coldly.

Pico spread his arms in supplication. "Colonel Fremont, you have had many victories but you have also had defeats." He glanced over at King. "I fought in Los Angeles for my family and for my relatives, not for Mexico. If we had been allowed to live as we had before there would have been no problems. Leave us Californios in peace and you will have peace. We do not care what those in Mexico say."

"Your cousin, Don Andres Pico," King said, "is commandante of Mexican forces in California. If you fight for him, you fight for Mexico."

"Country is not the same as family," Pico said.

Cord got closer to Fremont. "He makes sense, sir," Cord said in a low voice. "And it's Christmas in a week, sir. Have some mercy."

Fremont turned his imperious gaze on Cord. "Did I ask you for your opinion, Lieutenant?"

"No, sir, but we all been fighting for a long time now. We take Los Angeles, then as soon as the army moves on, we lose Los Angeles." Cord could sense King tensing next to him. Being run out of Los Angeles had not settled well with King and he was itching to go back in a fury. "The same is true all over the territory. We found a letter detailing a Californio victory over American forces at San Pasqual, north of San Diego. Also, we don't know the state of Commodore Stockton's forces down south."

Pico spoke up. "If we have to, we will leave our homes and fight you from the hills. It is a war you can never win. This is land we know and love. We will share it with you, but we must have peace and respect."

King stepped between Cord and Fremont. "We also found in those letters information that the Mexican government has offered to sell California to Britain in exchange for a war loan. As we stand here arguing, there's a priest on a British warship anchored in San Francisco Bay with a letter from Senor

Pico authorizing the resettlement of three thousand Irish Catholic families to California."

Fremont stood. "You have one hour to make your peace with God." Fremont gestured to the guards. "Take him away." He turned to King. "Prepare a firing squad. Execute the sentence after first light."

Cord couldn't stop himself as they dragged Pico out of the mission. "Sir, you go too far."

Fremont ran a hand through his beard, bags under his eyes indicating the lack of sleep all in the party were enduring. Although the California winter wasn't severe, the rain, cold and constant movement outdoors was taking its toll on the men. He slumped back down into the chair.

"I do not go far enough," Fremont said. "As you pointed out, the populace doesn't fear us as they should. I thought I'd made my point before, but it seems I must make it again. You are dismissed."

Cord walked through the wide double doors, Carson at his shoulder. "We can't let Fremont shoot that man. He's not looking ahead."

"And you are?" Carson asked.

"I am." Cord paused in the early morning darkness, campfires flickering all around. "Jesus Pico is Don Andres Pico's cousin. You think executing him is going to bring the possibility of peace in California any closer?"

You know--" Carson paused.

"What?" Cord asked.

"Fremont got a soft spot for women. And for family. Jesus Pico has some family here."

Jesus Pico refused being tied to a tree and a blindfold. He stood tall, facing the mountains and staring at the first rays of the sun slanting over the peaks. He spotted an eagle soaring effortlessly and his heart skipped a beat as he wished with all his soul he could be that bird.

"Firing detail, attention!" Lieutenant King walked down the line, making sure the eight men were in a semblance of a military rank. In the darkness, near the Mission, he could make out Colonel Fremont watching. King walked behind the men. In a voice only they could hear, he hissed: "Make sure you fire straight and true. He's to be dead on the first volley or I will take all of you to task for it."

A couple of the volunteers looked over their shoulders nervously. "Eyes front," King snapped. "Ready your weapons."

"Senor! Please!" A woman's plea tore through the chilly dawn. It caused Pico to lose his focus on the eagle as he recognized his wife's voice.

Pico's wife and children were escorted toward the firing squad by Cord. Pico's wife prostrated herself in front of King, begging for his life, while his children milled about, tired, confused and scared. The men in the firing squad shifted uneasily. King glared at Cord, uncertain how to proceed.

"Lieutenant Cord." Fremont strode up, his Delaware guards flanking him, Kit Carson at his side, whispering fiercely into his ear.

Cord snapped to attention. "Sir."

"This is insubordination," Fremont said. As Cord began to speak, Fremont raised a hand and silenced him. "But, I have reconsidered. Lieutenant King, you may dismiss your detail." Fremont looked at Pico. "Your life is spared, sir."

Pico crossed himself, then hurried to his wife who had wrapped her arms around Fremont's legs still pleading, unaware of the dispensation. As Pico peeled his wife off the Colonel he said: "I was to die. I had lost the life God gave me. You have given me another life. I devote the new life to you."

Fremont seemed startled by the declaration.

Pico escorted his wife and children away, leaving just Fremont, his guards, King, Carson and Cord.

Fremont looked at Cord. "Cross me again, Lieutenant, and I will have you tried for insubordination."

24 December 1846, Vicinity Natchez, Mississippi

Like a knight putting on steel gauntlets, Violet Rumble slowly pulled on her deerskin gloves. Then she settled the feathered hat on her head and checked in the full-length mirror that it was angled just so. It was, but the mirror also highlighted the deep crows feet around her eyes and the paleness of her skin.

That would not do.

Violet repaired to her cosmetics bureau and rectified the etchings of time and stress as best she could. She did not bother to check the full-length mirror again. She strode out of the room and flowed down the wide central staircase to the central hall where Rosalie waited.

"You look gorgeous," Rosalie said.

"Not today."

Rosalie lowered her head. "I'm sorry. It is difficult."

"This is not the Christmas I want for Ben and Abigail, so this must be done quickly and then we put on our masks and we give the children what they deserve."

Violet went to the main doors. Echo had both open before she reached them. Stepping out, Violet halted on the portico. Samual stood at the bottom of the steps, a dark tower of quiet strength. Violet hesitated, then took the stairs, her hoop skirt gracing each one. Rosalie remained on the portico, Echo behind her.

Violet stopped on the second step from the bottom. That put her eye to eye with Samual, although he, as trained, would not raise his head.

"Samual."

"Yes, mistress."

Violet reached out with her deerskin-covered hand and lightly touched his chin, lifting his face, but he still would not lift his eyes. "Look at me."

Samual swallowed hard, then his dark eyes met hers. "Yes, mistress."

"Echo has to leave Palatine."

Samual shut his eyes in pain, but he nodded. "I know, mistress."

"To save her," Violet said. "It is not as I wish but it is the reality."

Samual said nothing.

Violet dropped her hand. "I could free her, but you know that would do no good. By law, she has to leave the state if freed. And then if she doesn't make it to the north, she can be recaptured and sold. And you know she won't make it past the county line given—" she paused—"given the current state of affairs."

"Yes, mistress."

"Also, there are worse things that can happen to her if I free her." Violet's jaw clenched for a moment. "As we both know."

"Yes, mistress."

"I've arranged for her to go to a fine place, with my family in Tennessee. She'll be escorted there safely and well provided for. Her circumstances will be amiable."

"Thank you, mistress."

"Tell Mary—" once more Violet Rumble paused—"that she should understand."

"She does, mistress."

Violet paused. "Things will change here and eventually she'll be able to come back. I have stood quiet too long. We—" she nodded her head toward Rosalie standing on the landing, though Samual's head was once more lowered—"are working to change things."

"Yes, mistress."

Violet turned and walked up the stairs, not floating as she usually did, but taking each one as if climbing a steep peak. She stopped briefly and spoke to Echo without looking at her. "Go to your father, girl."

Violet and Rosalie re-entered Palatine House while Echo and Samual embraced at the bottom of the stairs.

Samual held his daughter for a long time. He heard the rattle of a wagon enter the lane. He pried his daughter loose and looked down at her, still keeping his hands on her frail shoulders. "It the right thing. You know. I know. Here." He let go of one of her shoulders and removed the worn leather covered Bible from his breast pocket. He pressed it into her hand. "This yours now."

"No, papa. No."

"You the family now. With Agrippa gone and your mama and I here, you the family." Samual shook her slightly to get her past the pain of separation. "Things be changing. Mistress Violet a good woman. You go to her family in Tennessee and be good. Do what you have to. Wait. Things be changing. I come for you when things change."

Echo looked up at her father. "Promise?"

"I promise," Samual said, placing his hand on the Bible. "As God is my witness. I come for you when they do change."

In her sitting room on the second floor, Violet Rumble was alone. She collapsed on the pillows covering the window seat and put her head in her hands. Certain no one could see her, Violet Rumble gave free rein and sobbed, tears staining the deerskin gloves.

She cried, opening up her heart to the reality that was her life. But only for a minute. Then she stopped. Went to the cosmetics table, replaced her face. She checked herself in the full-length mirror, forced a smile, changed her gloves for an unstained pair, and went to give Ben and Abigail a Christmas they would always fondly remember.

January 1847, Banquete, Texas

"Texas aint Mississippi," Skull said.

"Hotter," St. George said. "Never thought I'd be anyplace hotter than Mississippi."

A line of sweat trickled down St. George's bald scalp. It was still winter, but Texas was already as hot as Palatine in the summer. They were in the town of Banquete, outside of Corpus Christi, and the rumble of heavily supply-laden wagons moving south toward Mexico filled the air. The saloon was filled with traders, soldiers, camp followers and the innumerable 'business' people who followed an army on the move. And then there was Sally Skull.

"Why you want me to bring couple wagons full of guns and powder?" St. George asked. "Aint the army got enough stuff to shoot people with?"

Skull leaned closer. "Aint for the army."

"You selling to the Mex's?" St. George's beady eyes shifted about nervously. "Get hanged for that."

"Not for the Mex's either. There's always lots of angles in every war and plenty money to be made. You'll see."

A slender boy dressed in dungarees and a baggy khaki shirt, face shielded by a beaten forage cap walked through the front door of the saloon, leading a large, red-haired man in an out of date suit that had seen better days. The man had a big, bushy red beard and the skin on his face was almost as red as the beard. His bulbous, veined nose indicated heavy and often drinking.

St. George checked out the man, but when he looked at the 'boy' a second time, he stiffened. "She can't be in here."

"Why not?" Skull asked.

"She a nigra," St. George hissed.

"Keep your voice down," Skull said in a level tone. "She not a nigra down here. Gabriel my adopted child by Texas law."

St. George's jaw flapped as his brain tried to process that. "Daughter?"

"Yes." Skull said.

"Top of the day to you, my darling lass," the red-headed man said, giving Skull a big hug.

"Declan, meet St. George Dyer."

"A saint!" Declan stuck out a hand. "An archangel on one hand and a saint on the other. I must be blessed."

St. George reluctantly shook it, still trying to process Skull's announcement regarding the child.

"So, lass, do you have what I asked for?" Declan said.

"I do," Skull said, as Gabriel slid between her and the bar, hiding in plain sight. "Do you have the price?"

Declan reached into his suit coat and pulled out a velvet bag that jingled. "Here you be." He waited, as if daring her to open the bag and count the gold.

Skull handed the bag to Gabriel, who put it in a pocket.

"Mighty trusting," Declan said.

St. George wondered if he were referring to the not counting or giving it to the girl.

"You'll find the wagons out by the stockyard," Skull said.

"You have the Lord's blessing upon you," Declan said, with a half bow. He blew a kiss at Gabriel. "And you sweet girl, may your life always be filled with sunlight and flowers. I leave you with a blessing." He crossed himself and muttered something rapidly in Latin or a close approximation thereof.

Gabriel spoke for the first time. "Thank you, Father."

"Farewell." And with that, Father Declan made his exit.

"What the hell was dat?" St. George asked. "He a priest?"

"That," Skull said, "was a spy."

"Who for?"

"The Catholic Church, of course, since he's also a priest. But I think he's more an opportunist."

"A what?" St. George asked.

"Working for whoever pays him."

St. George understood that.

Skull picked up her drink and gestured for the bartender. "Whiskey for my daughter."

"The church?" St. George asked. "Why the church want guns? What he got planned?"

"Keep your voice down. He didn't tell me what he has planned, but I got a good idea. There are a lot of Irishmen in the Yankee army. I believe Father Declan's also a spy for the Mexican government and his job is to get as many of those Catholics to not only desert, but fight for the Mex's. Protect the sanctity of the church."

"The what of the church?" St. George was trying to follow the logic, but it didn't help if he couldn't follow the words.

Skull drained her glass. "The church always be meddling in things, 'specially down here. I'm just keeping my options open."

St. George shook his head. "And my cut?"

"Gabriel?" Skull said.

Gabriel pulled a different pouch out of her pocket and held it out to St. George. A muscle flickered in his jaw as he stared at it. After a long pause, he snatched it from the girl's hand and stuffed it into his sash.

"Mighty trusting," Skull said.

"Why you be doing this?" St. George said, jabbing a finger toward Gabriel.

"The future," Skull said. "Always got to be thinking about the future."

St. George stood up, shaking his head. "You crazy some of the time, woman."

"Maybe I am," Skull allowed. "And we need to talk about your future."

"What about it?"

"Violet Rumble is a smart woman. Your father held sway over her husband running the slave women to the house and letting them have bastards."

"So?" St. George demanded.

"When last time there was a bastard?"

St. George's eyes narrowed. He nodded his head toward Gabriel. "Her."

"Long time. When last time you ran a slave girl to the master of Palatine?" Skull asked.

"Couple years." Understanding dawned. "But Mistress Violet sent away to Tennessee the one Master Tiberius wanted."

"Mrs. Rumble gonna to make a move against you, St. George. I've heard that other bitch, Rosalie Little, been making inquiries about cotton shipments. Our cotton shipments."

"She got nothing," St. George insisted.

"How you know?" Skull shook her head. "We can't take a chance. We have to strike first."

"'Strike'? What you talking about?"

"We'll be joining you tomorrow for the journey back north," Skull said. "I'll tell you then. Now, let me drink in peace."

Colonel Fremont

16 Jan 1847, Los Angeles, California

"COLONEL FREMONT, if you persist in this manner, I will have you placed under arrest for insubordination," General Kearny shouted. "I'm the Governor of California, not you."

Fremont stood in front of Kearny's desk, inside the Government House in Los Angeles, and weathered the blast from the general. Along one side of the room, Kearny's aides hovered while on the other, Kit Carson stood as mute witness to his old friend's confrontation.

Fremont spoke in a calm tone. "Sir, I received my command, and the governorship, directly from Washington. From the President himself. It was quite explicit that at the cessation of hostilities, I was to transition from military commander to Governor of the territory. I have great deference to your professional and personal character, but until I receive word from higher authorities indicating otherwise, I will not relinquish control of California to you."

Kearny's hands clenched the edge of his desk. "Colonel, I am much older and the more experienced soldier than you. I have high regard for your wife and Senator Benton, whom I consider a great friend and who has shown me great kindness over the years. That's the only reason I have not had you placed in irons already. If you persist in this course of action, I'll be forced to send to higher command at Fort Leavenworth to have you relieved and placed under arrest."

Fremont wasn't moved. "I cannot let go of my rightful duty, sir."

"You cannot prove it is your duty," Kearny shot back. "Where are these orders from the President? I rank you, sir, and because of that, I am in command in California."

Fremont grabbed a chair and sat down. "I will prove to you, sir, that I do indeed have the President's authorization. I received a letter from Senator Benton indicating he met with the President and received such instruction."

"I would not doubt the Senator's word," Kearny said, "if you could show it to me in writing. And I did not give you permission to sit."

"The governor of California does not have to get permission to sit." Fremont turned to Carson. "Tell Lieutenant Cord that his presence is requested."

Carson touched a finger to his forehead and left the room.

An icy silence enveloped the room until Carson returned, Cord at his side.

"Lieutenant Cord," Fremont said. "Please relay to General Kearny the instructions from Senator Benton where I was to become Governor of California when it came under the control of the United States."

"What instructions?" Kearny demanded.

Fremont smiled. "In a letter you yourself brought to Fort Bent when you scouted the Front Range with your dragoons, General. Don't your remember leaving a letter there for Lieutenant Cord? Don't—"

"Stop!" Kearny ordered. "I want to *see* the letter."

"The letter was destroyed for security reasons and following specific instructions from Senator Benton in the letter itself," Fremont said. "Correct, Lieutenant Cord?"

Cord looked from Fremont to Kearny and back. "Yes, sir."

"Then—" Kearny began, but Fremont cut him off.

"General Kearny, Lieutenant Cord is a West Point graduate," Fremont said. "You would be willing to take the word of a Military Academy graduate as to the contents, won't you, General?"

One of Kearny's staff officers hurried over to him and whispered in his ear. When the officer moved away, Kearny turned toward Cord. "Were you Silenced at the Academy for a violation of honor, Lieutenant?"

A muscle rippled along Cord's jaw. "I was Silenced, sir."

Kearny faced Fremont. "Then I cannot take this man's word. I'm sending to Fort Leavenworth for orders, but I can assure you, Colonel Fremont, that your actions in this office alone are enough to bring you up on charges. Enjoy playing at governor in the interim because in six months you will be in prison. Now, get out of my office!"

Fremont almost knocked the chair over jumping out of it and lunging for Kearny. Carson placed himself between Fremont and General Kearny. "Easy now, John."

Kearny stood. "Furthermore, Colonel Fremont, regardless of whatever this supposed letter did or did not say, of more serious consequence, I have reports that you ordered the execution of three unarmed men near San Francisco. Those who took part won't speak." He pointed at Cord and Carson. "I understand you two were there and witnessed this event."

Cord met Kearny's gaze. "Sir, if you won't take my word about a letter, how can you take my word about some supposed executions?"

"I'll arraign both of you and put you under oath," Kearny threatened. "I won't have to wait for word from Leavenworth about who is governor." He pointed at Fremont. "I'll have Colonel Fremont hung as a murderer which will solve both problems quite handily."

"I'll see you in hell first," Fremont threatened.

"No," Kearny said, "it'll be your soul embracing the flames."

"Come on," Carson said to Fremont. "We need to be out of here."

"I'll put both of you under oath!" Kearny yelled.

Cord joined Carson in escorting the angry Pathfinder from the room. Once they were outside in the chill December air, Fremont exploded.

"I have the right to be governor! You both know that."

"Sir," Cord began, but Fremont cut him off.

"You could have been more forceful in there, Lieutenant. And what the devil does Silenced mean?"

Instead of answering that, Cord reached into his pocket. "Sir. Here is Senator Benton's letter."

Fremont blinked. "You were supposed to destroy it."

"It appears I didn't," Cord said.

"You are indeed not an honorable man," Fremont said. "Why didn't you produce it in there, when it would have helped?"

"I couldn't produce a letter that wasn't supposed to exist any more," Cord said.

Fremont put his hand out. "Give it to me and I will shove it in Kearny's face and—"

"You think he's going to give a rat's ass about that letter?" Carson asked. "A letter that's not supposed to exist, as Elijah points out? He could burn the damn thing, John, and then you'll have nothing for your defense if court-martialed. He wants your hide and will do anything to nail it to his wall. I been asking around while you been playing governor. Kearny sent dispatches east regarding you *before* this meeting. He just wanted to see what cards you was gonna play. I thought he just wanted you relieved, but I'm thinking now, he wants you dead."

"He puts Carson and me under oath," Cord said, "things could get mighty hot for you."

"You won't turn on me, will you?" Fremont asked Carson.

"John, you ordered those men shot."

"And you shot one of them," Fremont argued. "You'll take my side."

"You mean lie," Carson said.

"It was war," Fremont argued.

"It was murder," Carson said. "And I was part of it."

"There's an easy solution to both problems," Cord said.

Fremont turned to him. "And that is?"

"Carson and I go east. We can't testify if we aren't here. And we can show the letter to the command authority in Leavenworth."

Fremont thought it through. "All right." He put a hand on Carson's shoulder. "Would you go east for me to Leavenworth and then Washington? Rally my supporters. Contact Senator Benton and President Polk. Remind them of their promise. Make sure that letter gets seen by the right eyes to prove I acted legally?"

"You forgetting something," Carson said. "I don't have the letter. Lieutenant Cord does. And he's the only one of us who aint guilty about those killings."

Fremont's hands balled into fists, but he kept his voice civil. "Lieutenant Cord, would you accompany Mister Carson east with the letter that you possess?"

"Perhaps," Cord said.

"Don't trifle with me," Fremont warned.

"Not trifling," Cord said. "I'm negotiating." He stepped close to Fremont, looking him in the eyes. "You want me to hide the truth, which essentially means lie for you."

A muscle worked in Fremont's jaw, but he said nothing.

"I want you to say it," Cord insisted. "I want you to tell me you want me to lie."

Fremont unclenched his teeth to speak. "I want you to not talk about what happened in San Francisco."

Cord stepped back. He glanced at Carson.

"You do what you think is right," Carson said. "Don't worry about me."

Cord turned back to Fremont. "You want something from me, I want something from you."

"What?"

"You never again bring up what Kit did near San Francisco with those poor Mexicans?" Cord asked.

"I won't," Fremont said. "You have my word."

Cord laughed. "That's funny. Your word in exchange for me being dishonest. But there's more."

"How dare you—"

"You want me to be quiet about what happened and go east or not?" Cord asked.

"And what is the final price for your silence?" Fremont demanded.

"You owe me, Colonel," Cord said. "Some day, some place, you owe me."

April 1847, Fremont Pass, California

"There's luck and then there's no luck," Carson shouted as he fought his way through a four-foot high snowdrift. The wind howled about them, blowing large flakes almost horizontally. Carson coughed hard for a moment, then pressed forward.

"Don't you mean there's good luck and there's bad luck?" Cord asked, counting Carson's steps. "Five."

Carson pressed himself to the side into the snow and Cord took his place in the lead as human plow.

"I don't believe in bad luck," Carson said. "Just no luck. Which we got right now with this storm."

The snowfall had begun just after noon, calling in the cards on the gamble the two men had made to get through the Sierra Nevada Mountains this early in the spring. They were heading for Fremont Pass, hoping to make it through before another snowfall. Cord shoved forward into the wall of snow, one exhausting step after another.

"Five," Carson said and Cord now leaned out of the way, breathing hard.

"This is a hell of a storm," Cord said. "How much further to the pass?"

Given the heavy snow, one could barely see twenty feet in any direction. They were surrounded by trees and it was hard to stay on the trail.

Carson had stepped into the lead, but the older man paused and turned to Cord. "You're right. Too far. We aint gonna make it. Snow is coming down harder." He was breathing with difficulty and there was a dangerous rattle deep in his lungs. It had started the previous day and was getting worse.

Cord didn't argue. "Go back?"

"Retreat and then south," Carson said. He looked back the way they had come. The rut they had plowed through the snow was already filling in.

Cord needed no further urging. He reversed and they began to work their way down the mountain. After a few minutes, Cord sensed something was wrong and looked over his shoulder. Carson was nowhere to be seen.

Cord retraced his steps. Thirty yards up the route, he found the mountain man doubled over, coughing hard.

"What's wrong?" Cord had to yell to be heard above the howl of the snowstorm.

Carson tapped his chest. "Can't breathe."

"I'll help you." Cord reached out.

Carson shook his head. "No. Go on. It's the rule of the mountains. Got to make it on your own."

"That's not my rule," Cord said. "And I'm not renowned for following rules anyway." He took Carson's Lancaster rifle and pack, tying them off on his own pack, doubling his load. "That help?"

Carson managed a step in the right direction. "Yeah. But it's dumb on your part."

"I've been called worse." Cord removed his mittens. He took a short piece of rope and tied one end off on Kit Carson's belt and the other on his own. "Follow me." He tugged the mittens back on with difficulty, fingers fumbling. Even that short exposure had almost frozen his hands.

The minutes passed like hours as Cord struggled to push through freshly fallen snow. He could feel that Carson was attached from the pressure of his belt. They'd gone about a quarter mile toward lower ground when the rope jerked Cord to an abrupt halt. He turned. Carson lie in the snow, face down, hands clawing, trying to get up.

Carson was suffocating in the snow and Cord scrambled to help his friend. Kneeling next to him, Cord got Carson turned over on his back. The mountain man was gasping for air.

"We need to make camp here," Cord said.

"We won't make the night," Carson gasped. "Go on without me."

"Never," Cord said. He saw Carson's eyes flicker wide open, focused on something behind him.

Cord turned on his knees. Two stone-tipped spears were inches from his chest. Holding the spears were a pair of Indians, bundled in buffalo hides, their dark eyes glinting.

Carson tried calling out something, but a coughing bout precluded that. Cord raised his hands high and wide, smiling, trying to indicate a peaceful intent.

One of the braves jabbed his spear into Cord's chest, barely breaking skin, but not penetrating any further. The second one drew his spear back, preparing for a fatal strike, when a voice cried out from behind the two men. They immediately lowered their spears and stood aside. A stooped, hooded figure using a cane and assisted by a young girl, approached.

Cord helped Carson sit up.

The mountain man called out. *"We are peaceful. Just passing through."*

The stooped figure pulled back her hood. An old Indian woman stared at Carson, then at Cord. She began issuing orders. The two braves adapted their weapons to become poles for a travois to pull Carson.

"What's going on?" Cord asked, mystified by the sudden change in attitude.

Carson was laughing hysterically, the effort interspersed with coughs. Finally he got under control. "Well, son, you got good luck. Damn good luck. You remember the Great Salt Desert? The last encampment?"

"Yes." Cord suddenly made the connection. "It's her?"

"Damn good luck, son," Carson said as the old woman pulled a blanket out of the young girl's pack and tossed it over his chest. A blanket Cord also recognized.

"How can she be alive and on this side of the mountains?" Cord asked.

Carson gave a weak smile. "You gave her food and a blanket. She survived and her tribe came across her again. Surprised she was alive. They figured though she wasn't be able to forage, she sure has powerful magic. So they took her with them. Got pressed out of the Nevada territory by the white man last summer. Looking for a new home over here. Everyone's moving, getting kicked out of one place or 'nother . . ." Carson's voice trailed off.

The mountain man's head slumped back on the travois, his eyes closing from exhaustion. He rallied briefly with a smile. "You're a damn lucky man, Elijah Cord. Knew it from first time, when I tracked you down in St. Louis at that card game."

Cord woke to blessed warmth. He was ensconced in rough fur that smelled of wood smoke and grease. He opened his eyes and saw a red glow reflecting off the ceiling of a cave. Turning his head, he spotted Carson, also wrapped in a buffalo robe, a few feet to his right. He glanced left and was startled to see the old Indian woman sitting on the floor, watching him.

She reached out with a shaking hand and pulled back the robe, exposing his chest. She tapped him over the heart. Etched on the skin in black was a four-pointed compass with Mary scrolled below it.

"For my mother," Cord said. "I got it at sea to remember her."

Carson said something in her language. She replied to him, but kept her gaze on Cord. She put her wrinkled hand on the tattoo, her flesh warm. The old skin was so thin, Cord could feel her pulse beating.

"She says let it sink in."

"What?" Cord asked.

"Your remembering," Carson said. He exchanged some words with the old woman, then translated. "Your mother. Let her into your heart. Let her live there. These people believe your loved ones live on inside you."

Cord's heart constricted and he grimaced in pain. Then there was just utter weariness. "All right," he muttered as his eyes flickered shut. "Sink in."

Hanging

8 Sept 1847, Molino, Mexico

"LOOK OUT!" GRANT YELLED.

Rumble spun about, his shotgun braced against his hip, and fired both barrels. The blast abruptly altered the charging Mexican's path and his bayonet narrowly missed skewering Lieutenant Fred Dent. To make the matter certain, a sergeant stabbed the falling Mexican soldier with his sword.

They were surrounded by dead, Mexican and American. Grant was rallying soldiers hiding in an adjacent cornfield and Dent had been trying to help turn over a capsized cannon. Rumble broke open the shotgun and quickly reloaded, scanning the fields for more enemy.

It wasn't an hour into morning and the American Army was in disarray. An abrupt night assault to take Molino del Rey had turned into a meat grinder as hidden Mexican batteries poured scathing fire into the lines of blue clad infantry.

The 8th Infantry, leading the assault, had run into the fire first and lost ten of their thirteen officers in a few minutes. The remains of that regiment had come stumbling back, the men shell-shocked and chased by bayonet wielding Mexican soldiers in hot pursuit. The battle was now a melee with both sides mixed amongst each other.

Rumble clicked shut the shotgun and brought it to the ready. A flying artillery battery galloped by on the right flank. The captain in charge reared his horse and began screaming orders for the men to un-harness the guns and prepare for action. Before the artillerymen could dismount, Mexican guns did the job for them, spraying the horses and men with a barrage of grapeshot. Man and beast fell to the ground, screaming and bellowing in agony.

"Come on, men!" Grant waved his saber and pointed toward the gleaming white stone buildings that made up the town of Molino, astride the road to the Mexican Capitol.

Dent got some men to help right the cannon and prepared to fire. With a handful of soldiers, Rumble and Grant raced forward. The survivors of the flying artillery cut the harnesses off the dead and wounded horses. They hauled their cannon forward by hand, to get into position to provide enfilading fire on the Mexican lines.

An officer, his face bloodied, staggered by Rumble in a daze, pointing vaguely to the left. In between sobs, he got out: "The 5th. There's my 5th."

Rumble glanced in that direction and saw what appeared to be an under strength company huddled in a field. The men were face down on the ground, many with their arms wrapped around their head, as if that could protect them.

There was no time for Rumble to give comfort to the distraught officer. Grant had reached a building on the edge of the town. He had the men flip a cart against the side of the house, using it as a makeshift ladder to clamber to the top. Grant disappeared onto the roof, followed by the men. As Rumble started to climb, it felt as if his left shoulder was hit by a club, and he tumbled to ground.

Rumble jumped to his feet and reached for the cart handles to climb again. A red-hot spike of pain seared through his shoulder. He felt wetness and looked down to see a small black hole in his fatigue shirt, just below the shoulder blade, with a spreading stain of red surrounding it. He tried once more to climb. But now he couldn't raise his left arm above the shoulder; the pain was unbearable.

Cursing to himself, chagrined that he could not follow Grant, he spotted Fred Dent leading a squad down an adjacent street. Ignoring the pain in his shoulder, Rumble ran after them. Just before he reached the unit, a blistering scythe of musket balls from an ambush cut into the group, dropping half the men immediately. The rest ran. Except for Rumble, Dent, a sergeant and a private, who stood their ground as four Mexican soldiers charged forward, bayonets at the ready.

Dent began swinging his empty musket like a club, bashing in the head of the lead Mexican. Rumble fired his shotgun and took out a second. The private was bayoneted by the third Mexican in the stomach, but Dent immediately broke the man's skull—and the stock of his musket. The sergeant shot the fourth Mexican with a pistol and for a moment all was eerily still.

"I think you're wounded," Dent said, still holding his broken musket by the barrel, and breathing hard.

"I—" Rumble didn't get a second word out as another volley of musket balls punched through the air. Rumble felt the tug on his shirt as a ball ripped through the loose cloth at his side, but didn't hit flesh.

Dent wasn't so lucky. A ball hit his thigh, spinning him about. The sergeant tossed away his pistol and grabbed Dent by one arm. Rumble looped the sling of the shotgun over his wounded shoulder and grabbed Dent's other arm. Together, bullets buzzing by like angry hornets, they hauled Dent over a chest high stonewall into the relative safety of a courtyard.

"I'll get help," the sergeant said.

Rumble could see the fear in the man's eyes. The sergeant had gone as far as he could, fought to his limit and now he was done. He would not be back.

"Be careful," Rumble said, un-slinging the shotgun and loading it. "I'll keep the lieutenant safe."

The sergeant needed no urging. He was over the far wall and gone in a flash.

"This is a fine mess," Dent said, pressing his hands against his wound.

For the first time, Rumble took stock of his own injury. The pain wasn't as sharp, more a pulsing throb. It was a through wound, the entrance a small black hole that oozed red. The exit was a chunk of missing flesh in the rear, dripping blood freely. Thankfully, it didn't seem as if any bones had been shattered. Rumble ripped off part of his sleeve.

"Could you plug this?" Rumble asked, holding out the cloth and turning his back to Dent.

"Certainly." Dent shoved the cloth into the exit wound and Rumble clenched his teeth to keep from crying out in pain.

"Now, let's take a look." Rumble turned back to Dent. Using his knife, he cut away the cloth covering the wound. It was bloody, but hadn't severed the artery or broken bone. What they were beginning to call a 'lucky wound'.

Rumble fastened a bandage from the rest of the pant leg, cinching it down around Dent's thigh, but not too tight that it entirely cut off the blood flow.

Dent was pale from loss of blood and blinking hard, trying to stay conscious. "Write my mother if I don't make it," he told Rumble.

"You'll make it," Rumble said, more concerned about getting over-run by Mexican infantry than Dent's wound in terms of lethality.

The sound of musket and cannon fire punctuated the air in all directions. Given that the initial assault had been launched in the dark around three a.m., it was still early in the morning. Rumble looked up in the sky and saw a pair of vultures circling, immune from the carnage below and waiting to feast on the results.

"Did you know Sam is engaged to my sister?" Dent asked.

"I do," Rumble acknowledged.

"It seems I was one of the last to find out, although I did know they had feelings for each other."

"He's deeply in love with Julia."

"I am sorry about your Lidia," Dent said, his eyes closed in weakness.

The burst of pain in Rumble's heart overwhelmed the throb in his shoulder for a few moments. "Thank you. I—"

He paused as a man poked his head over the wall. Rumble lowered the shotgun and breath a sigh of relief that the newcomer wasn't Mexican. He had red hair and a bushy red beard and sported a broad smile revealing bad teeth.

"You lads hurt?" he asked in an Irish brogue.

"Yes," Rumble said.

"Drop the shotgun, son," the man said, pointing a musket over the wall directly at Rumble. Three other men clambered over the wall, dressed in ragged army blue, but sporting wide, red bandanas around both arms. They all also had large wooden crosses hung around their necks by a cord.

"What are you doing?" Rumble demanded as they disarmed him and Dent.

The redheaded man climbed over the wall. He was dressed all in black with the white collar of a priest. "Pleasure to meet you gents. I'm Father Declan. And these," he indicated the other three, "are good servants of our Lord Jesus Christ who have seen the light. We're fighting to protect the Church from infidels in this most pious of lands."

"Turncoats," Dent said.

"We serve a higher cause," Father Declan said.

"Let's be getting it over with and get out of here," one of the men said, checking the priming on his weapon.

"Put them against the wall," Father Declan ordered.

While Father Declan kept guard, two grabbed Rumble and slammed him none-too-gently against the wall. They reached down and lifted Dent, pushing him next to Rumble, but Dent's thigh couldn't support him, and he collapsed to the ground, cursing at the Irish.

Rumble reached for his breast pocket and Father Declan aimed his musket. "Easy, lad."

"Not a weapon," Rumble said. He pulled out Grant's etching. "If this is to be my death, this is the last thing I want to see."

"What do you have?" Declan came over as the other three men shifted about nervously. "She's a pretty lass. Your wife?"

"Yes."

"And your son?"

Rumble nodded.

"We need to go!" One of the men urged, peering over the wall. "Soldiers are heading this way. Let's use the steel and be done with it. They'd show us no mercy." He brandished his rifle, the long bayonet glinting in the morning sun. The man stalked over to Rumble and Father Declan. He glanced at the drawing. "Guess his mother has to be taking care of the boy forever. Or some other fella be taking care of both of them."

"Now, now," Father Declan said. "No need to be insulting."

"His mother's been dead for five years," Rumble said.

"Ah," Father Declan said. "Now that is sad. I lost my little lass many years ago. We had no children, though. Led me to the collar."

"Soldiers getting close," another man hissed, peeking over the wall.

"Let's leave these fellows with their futures intact," Father Declan ordered. He patted Rumble on the unwounded shoulder. "May the Lord bless you and your son." He hefted Rumble's shotgun. "I will be taking this pretty piece with me though."

Then the four turncoats were over the wall. Rumble slid the picture into his pocket and slumped down next to Dent.

"How are you?" Rumble asked.

"My leg hurts," Dent said. "I'd heard rumors the mutineers were executing the captured, particularly officers. War brings out the worst in souls."

"We're alive," Rumble said. "Maybe it also brings out the best of some."

9 September 1847, San Angel, Mexico

Rumble combined getting his bandage changed with a visit to Fred Dent who was recuperating in a field hospital in the town of San Angel. Grant accompanied, glad to be away from camp for a little. The mood of the troops was low after the bloody battles of the past week. Mexico City was still not taken and the confidence the army had manifested on the march here was wavering after the slaughter of the past several days. All morning church bells in the city had been ringing, extolling what the inhabitants believed to a tremendous victory in defeating a Yankee assault to seize the city, not realizing it had only been a spoiling attack.

The two found Dent on the second floor of a warehouse, the breeze from a nearby window helping to alleviate the September heat. He had a sack of cotton wedged behind him, allowing him to be half-inclined on the bloodstained army cot.

"How's the healing, Fred?" Grant asked as they gathered round Dent.

Dent had been staring out the window with a frown, but a smile broke upon his face when he saw the three. "I still have my leg and the surgeon says I will be fit for duty within a month. And you, Lucius? The shoulder?"

In reply, Rumble rotated his arm in a complete circle, suppressing a slight expression of pain. "It functions and the bleeding has stopped. No bones were broken."

"I owe you my life," Dent said. "I will never forget."

Rumble waved away the statement, this time grimacing at the un-planned movement. "Any of us would do it for the other."

"Of course," Dent said. "But you did it for me. I am in your debt."

"And I too, then," Grant added. "Julia would be most morose if I returned to White Haven minus Fred. It would put a damper on the wedding."

Dent laughed. "Your concern is touching, Sam."

"The war isn't over yet," Rumble noted.

"You're sounding more and more like Old Cump, Lucius," Grant said.

"Facing death directly has a way of making one a tad reflective," Rumble said.

Grant disagreed. "It should make you happy to be drawing a breath. All of us have faced death and all of us are still among the living. We should focus on that. Not what might or might not happen tomorrow."

"Unfortunately," Dent said, "death is happening today for some and they are well aware of it." He pointed out the window.

A row of carts carrying men trussed at the ankles and wrists was rumbling up to a set of hastily constructed scaffolds. Most of the men seemed resigned, but a few were struggling against the chains holding them in the carts. There were four carts, with four men shackled in each.

"Ah, the Battalion San Patrico," Grant said.

"The what?" Rumble asked.

"Saint Patrick's Battalion," Grant explained. "Catholic Irish soldiers who deserted and joined the Mexicans. The ones who almost killed you."

"Why did they betray their own?" Rumble asked, having been more focused on his notebooks and battle than politics.

"Several reasons," Grant said. "Most believe they serve their God before they serve their country."

"And what do the few believe?" Rumble asked.

Grant shrugged, eyes on the condemned. "Catholics are a minority in the army. Most officers are Protestant. I do think there is a case to be made that in some instances, there was prejudicial treatment toward some of these men by their officers. Combine that with the way some of our men have been treating the Catholic Mexicans and it's a difficult issue."

"They swore an oath," Fred Dent said.

"Is it that simple?" Rumble asked. He could see ropes being placed around the men's necks and tightened.

"They won't have a drop," Grant observed.

With the crack of bullwhips, the wagons lurched forward. The men's feet scrambled on the wood cargo bay until the slipped off the edge. The bodies twitched and twirled as the men slowly choked to death. Even before they were all dead, more wagons came rolling up, crowded with a different group of men. Those who had escaped a death sentence, but still had to face punishment for desertion.

Several fires had been burning for a while. One by one, held tightly between two soldiers, the Irishmen were marched up to a fire. A brand was pulled out of the red-hot embers and a D was burned into their right cheek, marking them for life. The marking was bungled on one man, the brand placed backwards on the right cheek, so the mistake was remedied by marking the left cheek correctly. It was not a day for mercy.

"Rumble," Dent said. "There. On the left."

There was no mistaking Father Declan's bulk or his black garments. He was among a cluster of American officers and several civilians, including a woman.

"Why isn't that bastard dangling?" Dent asked.

"That 'bastard' saved our lives," Rumble said.

"Saved our lives by not murdering us," Dent said. "The logic is a bit skewed. You might see if they recovered that fancy shotgun of yours. And find out why his neck isn't wrapped with rope."

Rumble left Grant and Dent in the makeshift hospital, discussing plans for life after the war as if one could dare to think of such a thing now that they were at the gates of Mexico City.

Rumble ignored the bodies dangling from the ropes. An argument was going on among the American officers and the civilians standing between them and Father Declan. The accent of the civilians was British. Politicians from the Consulate, interceding on behalf of the priest. The woman was the wife of the British Consul, an obvious ploy to add some 'decency' to the barbarity that surrounded them.

"Ah, my friend with the beautiful child and the wife who passed before her time," Declan cried out, spotting Rumble.

All negotiating stopped and everyone turned to look at Rumble. Colonel Garland spoke up. "You know this man, Sergeant Major?"

"He spared Lieutenant Dent's and my life," Rumble said. He saw his father's shotgun in the back of a wagon. Along with a noose waiting for Father Declan.

"Spared you how?" Colonel Garland asked.

"Stopped his men from executing us when we were in his power, sir." Rumble went to the wagon and took the shotgun.

"So he didn't kill a prisoner," Garland said. "Commendable." The irony was clear to all.

"Aren't you killing prisoners now, sir?" St. Declan asked.

"They've been tried and convicted," Garland said.

Rumble broke open the shotgun. Two rounds were in their chambers. He saw boxes in the wagon, underneath the rope. Marked with transit stencils. Through Natchez, MS.

"But since Father Declan did not desert from your army," the British Consul argued, "you have no right to execute him. He is Irish. A subject of the Crown. You'll be provoking an international incident if you hang him."

"Aye, and it would look bad in the newspaper, my being a priest and all," Declan threw in.

Garland rubbed a weary hand across his forehead. "Take him with you," he told the consul. "But if we find him once more on the field of battle, he will be shot on the spot."

As the British and the priest turned to leave, Rumble stepped up to Declan and showed the muzzle of the shotgun into the soft spot under the man's jaw.

Declan's eyes went wide. "Easy, lad."

"I'm not a lad," Rumble said. "What was in the boxes?"

Declan's eyes shifted over to the wagon and back. "Guns. Got to be going now."

Rumble didn't remove the shotgun. "Who sold them to you?"

Declan lowered his voice. "I can't be telling you that, lad."

"You'll tell me or you'll be losing the top of your head," Rumble said.

"Sergeant Major," Garland said, his voice more weary than commanding. "The deal is done. Let him go."

Rumble reluctantly removed the shotgun from Father Declan's chin. The British Consul dragged Father Declan to the safety of the Consulate.

Pickett's Successful Charge

13 Sept 1847, Chapultepec, Mexico

"WELL, PETE, ANY WAGERS on today's action?" Grant asked.

Using Rumble's telescope, James Longstreet kept studying the approach to the Castle of Chapultepec. Cannon balls from American heavy artillery commanded by Major Lee arced overhead and pounded the fortress, continuing a long range duel that had lasted through the night. It was as if Longstreet looked hard enough, he could penetrate the stone with just his gaze.

Chapultepec was built on a rocky hill, rising one hundred and fifty feet about the surrounding country-side and commanding the approachs to Mexico City. It was built of stone, the main portion one hundred feet above the ground with a single dome raising up another twenty feet, giving the occupants superb observation in all direction. It was an imposing edifice, surrounded by two walls, ten feet apart and each over ten feet high.

"I don't wager when blood is involved, Sam," Longstreet answered. "It's bad luck." He pointed at the castle. "That fortress is the Mexican version of West Point. The Coleio Militar. They aren't going to give it up easy."

"We wouldn't give up West Point easy," Rumble said.

Grant was checking his pistol. "If you'd have asked me my plebe year, I'd have opened South Gate for the attackers."

"Still feel that way, Sam?" Longstreet asked.

Grant shook his head. "No. The Academy prepared us well. And since wars seem to be inevitable, our country needs people like us to fight and win them."

Rumble was still focused on the objective. "There's got to be Mexican cadets in there; kids, ready to fight us."

"Some of our volunteers aren't more than kids," Longstreet pointed out. "The other day, I saw a young fellow in Jeff Davis's Mississippi unit who couldn't have been more than fourteen."

The three were crouched in a ditch as the preliminary military bombardment to 'soften up' the defensive position continued. Dawn was just beginning to show in the east and Longstreet's unit, the 8th Infantry, along with five other brigades, was to lead the assault. After fierce fighting the previous day during the approach to this position, the 4th was in reserve, but Rumble and Grant had made their way forward; Grant always desiring to be closer to the action, Rumble doing his duty as observer.

Longstreet looked like a crazy man, a far cry from the polished First Classman preparing to train plebes at West Point they had said farewell to when departing on furlough. He sported a bushy, unkempt beard and long hair that stuck out wildly, weeks removed from a bath. His uniform was dust covered and torn in places. He had two pistols stuck in his belt along with a well-sharpened saber that had seen action.

"This is dumb," Longstreet said, handing the scope back to Grant for a look. He might not be taking bets for the moment, but he was never shy about sharing his opinion. "We shouldn't be on the offensive when the enemy matches or exceeds our number and they're entrenched behind a stone wall. Why don't we cut their supply lines and make them come hunting for us? We've been chasing these rascals all over Mexico for a year since Monterrey and we're almost always the ones attacking."

"You'd rather defend?" Grant asked, slowly scanning the terrain and the enemy.

"I'd rather be sitting up there behind those walls with the 8th and have them Mex's down here in this ditch," Longstreet said. "I say we grab our spades and dig in."

"Sound strategy," Rumble agreed. "Except they are up there and we are not." He laughed. "A little while back, Sam and I were talking about when Cord said he'd give up a fortress to the enemy and then surround them for forty-five days."

"Elijah always had a different way of looking at things," Longstreet agreed. "The whole Silence thing we did to him seems childish given our current situation. What do you think?" He asked Grant when he finally lowered the scope.

"Tough going," Grant said, handing it back to Rumble. "Not much cover and no concealment. I don't like a frontal assault, but we don't have many options. Terrain dictates we can't flank the fort. It has to be subdued or else we can't take the city. And we must take the city to end this war." He glanced at Rumble. "As you once pointed out, it's not enough to defeat the enemy's army, we must indeed break their will to fight."

"What do *you* see?" Longstreet asked Rumble.

Rumble collapsed the scope and put it in the leather case. "I see a lot of bodies lying out there soon. The dead out of their misery. The wounded wishing they were dead." He shrugged, forgetting about his shoulder and immediately regretting it as he winced. "And nothing anyone can do about it, is there?"

"A bit grim," Longstreet said. "Since when do you read the future?"

"Since I gave up trying to control it," Rumble said.

"Lucius is realistic, but pessimistic," Grant said. "We had a hard go of it yesterday."

An understatement if there was one. Worth's division, of which the 4th Infantry was part, had suffered twenty-five percent casualties clearing the way for this assault on the fortress. A greater casualty rate than at Monterrey. According to what they had been taught at West Point, that made the 4th combat ineffective. Along with many other 'rules' they had been taught, that was another that had gone by the wayside in the heat of combat and become another notation in Rumble's book.

An officer of the engineers came boldly striding down the ditch, making no attempt to hunch over or duck, even though a Mexican shell occasionally flew by.

"Is that Lee?" Grant asked.

Longstreet tore his gaze away from the objective. "Yes. He's all over the place. General Taylor places the greatest trust in him. Lee found the mountain trail we used to outflank Santa Anna in the Sierra Madres and was in charge of the engineers who made it passable for the artillery."

Lee's uniform was impeccable, his rank glittering on his shoulder. "Gentlemen," he said as he walked up.

"Major Lee," Grant said, getting to his feet, as did the other two men.

Lee paused and looked at Grant, a slight frown crossing his forehead as he searched for rank, then spotted the small, dull insignia sown on the shoulders. "I don't believe we've had the pleasure, Lieutenant--"

"Grant, sir. Ulysses Grant. This is Lieutenant Longstreet. And Sergeant Major Rumble, a special observer sent from West Point."

"Pleased," Lee said, but it was clear his mind was elsewhere. He looked past the three soldiers. "This is all quite splendid isn't it?"

"Sir?" Grant was confused.

"Men at the extreme," Lee said. "It brings out the best." He pulled a pocket watch out and checked the time, then looked to the east as if confirming the sun was doing its duty. "It will be in God's hand soon."

An officer came scurrying down the trench. Another West Pointer. The opposite of Longstreet in appearance, but not quite the same as Lee. The man had long hair, curling down to his shoulders. His uniform held all the accoutrements of rank one could possibly sew or pin on and had somehow been freshly cleaned and repaired.

"Major Lee, may I present George Pickett, '46," Longstreet said by way of introduction. "Also of the 8th Infantry."

Pickett only had eyes for Lee. "Major, I—"

"Time," Lee said, flicking shut the face of the watch and heading down the trench, continuing whatever task the general had assigned.

Pickett was staring after Lee, red-faced. More concerned about the lack of acknowledgement from the West Point legend than the pending assault.

"He's an exacting fellow," Rumble noted.

Longstreet checked his own watch. "We attack in five minutes." He slumped down in the ditch, putting his back against the dirt, using the interval to get some rest.

"You'll be fine, Pete," Grant said.

Longstreet gave a crooked grin. "We both have to get back home and get married. Can't keep the women waiting."

"How'd you know I was engaged?" Grant was surprised.

Longstreet grinned. "My girl knows your girl. Women can't keep a secret worth a damn."

Rumble shook his head. "You never met my mother."

Grant relaxed. "True, but if Julia's father—" Grant stopped in mid-sentence as a bugle blared and Longstreet drew his saber. "My watch must be off. Love to stay and talk—really would, but duty calls." He jumped out of the ditch, Pickett at his side along with hundreds of men rising up out of the ground, casting long shadows in the dawn, bayonets glinting in the early morning sun.

Grant watched the advancing troops. "Your scope, Lucius?"

Rumble handed over the leather case. The rattle of musketry indicated that the advancing Americans had come within small arms range of the fortress. Despite the fire, the mass of blue clambered up the hill toward the citadel. The flashes of musket fire along the parapet and the larger blazes of cannon fire punctuated the growing cloud of smoke drifting over the battlefield.

Grant stiffened, peering through the telescope. "The standard bearer of the 8th is down! Old Pete has the colors."

Even without his scope, Rumble could see the regimental flag waving back and forth and moving inexorably toward the walls of the fort. Grant and Rumble started out of the ditch when the flag suddenly dipped to the ground as Longstreet fell to his knees, wounded. Another officer, Pickett, grabbed the colors from Longstreet and dashed forward, displaying them over his head with dash and screaming for the men to follow him. He reached the wall of the fortress and climbed up on the rubble where the cannons had done the job of breaching the stone. Pickett paused for a moment, bullets flying all about him as he waved the flag, then disappeared into the fortress, a flood of blue clad soldiers following, an inexorable tide of destruction.

Grant and Rumble found Longstreet lying with his back against a boulder, blood flowing from a wound in his hip.

"George is something isn't he?" Longstreet greeted them. "Never hesitated."

"*You* were something," Grant said. "Didn't see you stopping either, till you got hit."

"It's nothing," Longstreet said. "A flesh wound."

Rumble knelt next to Longstreet and checked the wound. "It isn't bad." He reached into his haversack and pulled out some bandages. "I put the odds at ten to one you'll be walking within a week."

Longstreet laughed through his pain. "I won't bet against myself. One of my rules."

Rumble tightened down the cloth. He spotted a couple of stretcher-bearers and called them over. Bugles blared to their rear.

"Assembly for the 4th," Grant said. He put a hand on Longstreet's shoulder as the stretcher-bearers lifted him. "Take care of yourself, Pete."

"Both of you stay safe," Longstreet called out as he was carried away.

Elijah Cord's slightly blurred focus was on a cluster of supply wagons. Four bound men were crowded on the rear of each wagon. Around their necks were ropes. The ropes were tied to wood beams over their heads. Teamsters milled around the horses shackled to the wagons. Everyone, including the condemned men, were looking to the west and up: a fortress, spouting thunder and lightning at the blue forces assaulting it, loomed in the distance. Crowning the highest part of the fortress was a Mexican flag, flapping in the breeze.

"Who are you?" A nervous, young private in blue, his hands clutching a musket, blocked Cord's way.

Cord didn't look like a soldier, never mind an officer. He sported a scraggly beard; not from fashion choice, but the result of months removed from a razor. His skin was sunburned and weather-beaten. He wore an un-tucked flannel shirt over deerskin trousers. He carried a long rifle in the crook of his arms, a bedroll over one shoulder and looked every inch the intrepid mountain man. And he was a bit inebriated.

"Elijah Cord!" An officer called out from where he lay on the stretcher and Cord had to look past the tangled beard to recognize him.

"Old Pete!"

Longstreet sat up. "I'll be damned. What are you doing here?"

"I was always assigned to the 4th," Cord said.

Cord noted the bandage on his hip. "You were injured?"

"A flesh wound. Done running around the frontier?" Longstreet asked, taking in the outfit, and the redness in Cord's eyes. Along with the stink of alcohol.

"The west coast is ours," Cord said. "The Californios surrendered in Los Angeles back in January. There was no need for me to stay. My duty there was done."

"I suppose you have some stories to tell," Longstreet said.

"Not particularly," Cord said.

"You walked all the way here from California?" Longstreet was amazed.

"I had to go to Fort Leavenworth first," Cord said. "What's going on here?"

Longstreet grimaced, from both the wound in his hip and their surroundings. "The rest of the Irish prisoners who deserted."

"'The rest'?"

"Hung the first batch yesterday," Longstreet said. "These are the rest."

"What are they waiting on?"

Longstreet pointed at a senior officer. "Colonel said the instant," he pointed now to the west, "that Mex flag over Chapultepec comes down and the United States flag goes up, they dangle."

"Rumble up there in the assault?" Cord asked.

"Yes. And Sam Grant."

Cord started forward. "I should join my regiment."

"The attack is joined. Not much you can do now. Best wait here."

"It's my regiment," Cord said.

"Was your regiment," Longstreet said. "You wouldn't recognize over half the officers and men now."

Cord stiffened. "That bad?"

"That bad," Longstreet confirmed. "Wait here a bit with me." He gestured. "Go take a look through the scope and tell me what's happening."

A large telescope was set on a tripod and officers were taking turns watching the assault.

The uniformed officers stared at Cord as he leaned over and peered into the eyepiece. The men in blue charging the castle seemed an unstoppable tide. Already, some were climbing over the wall and the defensive cannon were falling silent one by one.

"Their military academy," Longstreet said. "Rumor is some of the cadets stayed to defend it to the death."

"Then death they are receiving," Cord said. He squinted. "They're falling back on their flag. Some of the cadets are gathering at the base of the pole. Fighting to the end. Oh!" Cord pulled his eye back and wiped at it, as if dust had gotten into the orb. He leaned forward. "One is left. He's fighting like the devil. He's—he's down. Swarmed under by bayonets. One of ours, by God, George Pickett, the devil's own, is at the pole."

Everyone could see the Mexican flag begin to descend. The distant sound of cheering began to echo over the valley. The Mexican flag disappeared and then the Stars and Stripes began their ascent. Their cheering was contagious, every man roaring at the tops of their lungs.

None more so than the twenty-nine men standing in the back of the wagons.

As the United States flag reached its zenith, the Colonel cried out the command. The teamsters ordered the wagons forward and then those cheers were gone forever.

"There's no danger! See, I'm not hit!"

Lieutenant Tom Jackson stood in the middle of the road, as oblivious to the rifle and cannon fire shredding the air around him as he had been to the hooves when Rumble jumped York over his head. Jackson's gunners were hiding among boulders on the side of the road, not wishing to share the fate of a half-dozen of their fellows, sprawled lifeless about the young lieutenant.

Rumble and Grant were in the forefront of the 4th Infantry. The unit was swinging around the captured fortress of Chapultepec to finally advance on Mexico City itself. They were dashing along the road, using the embankment for some semblance of cover from the blistering cannon fire ahead. They paused and peered in dismay at the lone officer standing on the road among the abandoned cannon.

"It's a bit warm out in the open," Grant yelled to Jackson as the infantry hurried by Jackson's stalled artillery unit.

Colonel Garland came up. "Lieutenant, you may withdraw!"

Jackson frowned. "Sir, with all respect, it's as dangerous to withdraw as to stay in place. We can put fire on the enemy and aid your advance."

Garland shook his head in resignation. "That's insubordination, Lieutenant, but carry on."

They were still outside the walls of the capitol city and the army was anxious after so much time in Mexico to finish things. The end was in sight with Chapultepec taken, but the remnants of the Mexican Army still stood in the way. Rumble's notebook of observations was now four notebooks. Every evening he sat with Grant and they discussed what General Scott, who now commanded, was doing. And how the forces under Scott's command executed those orders.

The most surprising development had occurred just after the army crossed the Sierra Madre Mountains. Following the example set by Cortes centuries earlier, Scott severed his own supply line and set out for Mexico City, his troops living off the land as they passed through. It was a radical and dangerous military maneuver. For Grant, returned to duty as quartermaster of the 4th, it had meant he had to scour the countryside for food and supplies to sustain the regiment. It was an exhausting procedure and Rumble accompanied his friend on many of these foraging parties. It too was a type of warfare that had not been emphasized in the tactics classes at the Academy.

Rumble stayed close to Grant, his newly requisitioned musket at the ready. They reached a point where flanking fire from a house caused the troops to halt.

Grant held his hand out and Rumble placed the scope in the Lieutenant's hand. Grant took a moment to check the house and the terrain between.

"There's a way to get there," Grant said. He turned to the soldiers. "Follow me men, trail arms."

Grant took as much advantage of the concealment the terrain offered. As they got closer to the house, they could see the Mexicans who had been firing on the column retreating. The Americans took the building without loss. Rumble and Grant climbed the ladder to the roof of the house. While Grant scanned the terrain, several other soldiers joined them.

"The advance is still bogged down," Rumble said. He pointed. "See the enemy in those positions?"

A series of ditches filled with water and plants criss-crossed the plain in front of the walls of Mexico City. Mexican troops clustered about the main road were delivering a blistering fire at the lead elements of the American advance.

"Look." Grant had his hand on Rumble's shoulder, turning him slightly to the right.

A church was to the south of the main road, its belfry raising high above the surrounding houses.

Rumble immediately understood Grant's intent. "We passed a pack howitzer near the aqueduct."

"Would you do the honor, Sergeant Major?"

"Yes, sir." Rumble climbed down and ran back the way they had just come. He quickly found the small group of artillerymen with their howitzer hunkering down behind one of the arches.

"Lieutenant Grant requests you, and your gun's, presence," Rumble told the senior enlisted man.

The artillerymen had been fighting and moving that gun for over a year. They quickly broke it down into man-portable loads, along with a supply of shells. Rumble led the party toward the church and caught up to an irritated Sam Grant pounding on the church's door.

"If someone doesn't open up soon, I'm going to—" Grant said, but stopped as the tall door creaked open and a priest poked his head out.

"I am sorry, senor, you can not enter."

"I am sorry, too, padre," Grant responded in halting Spanish. "However, we must enter."

"You cannot."

"We must and we will."

"I am so sorry, senor, but this is a place of worship, not war."

The men carrying the parts of the howitzer and the ammunition shifted under their loads. Rumble stepped forward. "Let me convince him."

"Easy," Grant said. He smiled at the priest and used that tone Rumble recognized. "Padre, if you wish this place of worship to remain safe, you should open the door. And, if you wish to remain with your church and not become a prisoner of war, you will allow us entry." Grant took a step closer to the priest and his tone grew colder. "And finally, Padre, I intend to enter whether you wish it or not."

The priest grudgingly swung the door open. Grant led the way to the stairs. Rumble could feel the priest's glare as he passed him. He directed the artillerymen to carry the pieces and ammunition up to the belfry. It was crowded once everyone was up there. The men quickly began putting the gun together.

While they were doing that, Rumble leaned the barrel of his musket on the surrounding wall and aimed. "Wait for the howitzer?" he asked Grant.

"If you please." Grant was looking through the scope.

"You know, Lieutenant Grant," Rumble said, "why don't you keep that?"

Grant was surprised. "I'm sorry, Sergeant Major." He tried to hand it back, but Rumble waved him off.

"You make much better use of it than I do."

"No," Grant said, stepping close. "It was a gift to you—"

Rumble spoke in a voice only Grant could hear. "To direct their fire, you need it more than I do for now."

The artillerymen were experts at their job. Not only assembling the small gun, but also wedging wood under the carriage so that it could fire over the wall and toward the Mexican lines, which were about three hundred yards away.

"Gentlemen," Grant said calmly, "give me a spotting round."

The howitzer spit out a ball. Grant saw the shell explode in the air and then began to adjust. "Thirty yards further and twenty to the right, gentlemen."

As he finished the sentence, Rumble fired his rifle and began reloading. In concert, rifle and howitzer let loose. After several iterations, Grant extended the scope to Rumble. "Observe the effect."

Rumble paused in his shooting and looked through the device. The Mexican line was in turmoil. Some troops were retreating, officers chasing after them. Others were firing blindly in various directions.

"They don't know from where they're being fired on," Rumble said.

The barrage continued as the sun slid lower in the west. Around six in the evening, a courier came galloping up to the church. By now, the gunners were exhausted from hauling ammunition up to the belfry and servicing the gun. Rumble had run out of balls for his rifle and was seated with his back against the wall, sipping water from his canteen. The courier popped his head up through the door, looked around, then climbed the rest of the way.

"Captain Pemberton, sir," he said to Grant.

"You have the rank, sir," Grant replied.

Pemberton squinted and finally spotted the small bars sewn onto Grant's shoulders. "Ah, yes, Lieutenant?"

"Grant, sir."

"Lieutenant Grant, I'm General Worth's aide-de-camp. He very much appreciates the service your howitzer has been doing. Every shot has been quite effective. He wishes to bring up another gun to assist."

Rumble looked at the cramped space in the belfry, where there was barely room for Pemberton to squeeze in.

Grant gave a slight bow. "Certainly, sir. We would welcome the assistance."

"Very well," Pemberton said. He seemed about to say something else, then abruptly left, disappearing down the ladder.

"What are you doing, Sam?" Rumble asked. "We couldn't fit a rabbit up here, never mind another howitzer."

Grant shrugged. "I don't think Lieutenants have much latitude in telling Generals their ideas are not sound. He might've taken it as a contradiction. Besides, the new gun will mean more ammunition, which we'll certainly need for the morrow. And," Grant raised his voice so the other men could hear, "these gentlemen who have done such a fine job with their weapon could use a break and have their fellow gunners relieve them for a bit."

Rumble shook his head. "Sam, you are wicked."

It was too dark to keep firing and Grant dismissed the gunners, leaving the two of them alone in the belfry. Fires were burning in all directions. Some campfires, others buildings consumed by the flames of war.

Grant was staring morosely out at the flames. "I might be wicked, but war is much worse."

The Halls of Montezuma

14 September 1847, Mexico City, Mexico

"THE HALLS OF MONTEZUMA," Ulysses S. Grant said. "Cortes stood in this square three hundred years ago."

The palace of the Mexican government, and before that, Cortes, and before him, the Aztecs, surrounded the courtyard in the center of Mexico City. Along one side, a cotillion of Mexican officers in dress uniforms was lined up, ready to do the hardest task for a soldier: surrender.

On the other three sides, American troops were deployed, waiting for their commander to arrive to arrange terms and accept the capitulation.

Rumble had no comment on Grant's observations, simply satisfied that the fighting appeared to be over. Longstreet was with them, the group standing in the shade of one of the arches lining the square, watching history being made. Old Pete wore his dress uniform in honor of the occasion, even going so far as putting on his old cadet white cross belt with highly polished brass breastplate. He walked with a limp, but a flesh wound, as he called it, wasn't going to keep him from seeing the final act of the war. Grant was in his usual dusty, field uniform, his rank the same as when the war had started. The sergeant major insignia on the arms of Rumble's blue blouse were no longer golden, long faded by the Mexican sun and dirt, and less than perfect cleanings in streams and fountains across Mexico.

General Winfield Scott, who had replaced General Taylor after fierce political maneuvering, finally rode into the square, fashionably and humiliatingly late. He was followed by a massive entourage of staff officers. Scott, the polar opposite of Taylor in deportment, but equally brilliant in battle, was in full dress and wore every accouterment his rank allowed and perhaps some. His corpulent body certainly allowed extra cloth on which to pin medals. Grant felt for the horse that had to carry such a weight. Marines spread out, to guard Scott and cordon off the palace.

"We do the hard fighting and Marines get to look pretty," Longstreet groused.

"Be fair, Pete," Grant said. "They saw some hard work on the battlefield."

Longstreet rubbed his hip, the itch of the wound adding to his irritation. "Where the devil is Cord? I directed him to the quartermaster to acquire a proper uniform. And get sober."

"He didn't listen," Rumble said, seeing the man in question approaching. "When did he ever?"

Elijah Cord came walking up, still in his buckskins and plaid shirt, his long rifle in the crook of his arms. A slight sway in his step indicated he also hadn't achieved any level of sobriety. He had shaved, but his hair was still down to his shoulders. His face was hard and his trademark, mischievous grin was absent. There was a hint of Preacher Cord in the depths of his eyes.

"Elijah," Rumble said, extending his hand. "Strange this is where we meet."

"Lucius." Cord briefly shook the hand. "Sam. Pete."

Both officers greeted their fellow West Pointer, but there was a tenseness rolling off Cord that put all the men who had seen so much combat on edge.

"What is that?" Grant pointed at the long rifle, as always trying a diversion.

"A Lancaster," Cord said. "A gift from a friend."

"I've heard of those," Grant said. "Very special brand of weapon—a rifled barrel and much greater range. Must have been a good friend."

"It was a gift for saving his life," Cord said.

Rumble and Grant exchanged a glance.

"So you've fought real battles here, with real soldiers," Cord said

"Sounds like you've been in battle too, if you saved someone's life," Rumble said.

"I saw battles, mostly civilians against civilians, and I saw executions," Cord said. "I figure that's what war is. Just plain killing when you get down to it. Not at all like what we were taught at West Point. Just like those hangings yesterday."

"It's politics by other means," Longstreet said. "You studied Clausewitz at the Academy."

Cord asked Grant. "So it's all politics?"

"There's a bit more to Clausewitz than that," Grant said. He smiled at Longstreet's roll of the eyes. "I did actually read something other than novels while in the library at West Point." Grant waved a hand taking in the soldiers, the palace, all of it. "Rational decision making at the top political level, fueled, however, by violent emotions and then you have to add in the vagaries of chance. Just damn chance, sometimes, Elijah. Why did Hoskins get shot off my horse the one time he rode it and not me all the times I was on her back?"

"Hoskins is dead?" Cord asked.

"At Palo Alto," Grant confirmed.

"So, like Hoskins, we're just pawns of chance?" Cord asked.

"What's your problem?" Longstreet demanded, tiring of the angry questioning.

"I want to know why we're here," Cord said. "Why we've all done the bloody things we've done?"

"It's simple," Grant said.

Rumble, Cord and Longstreet all turned to him.

"It's our duty," Grant said.

Cord took a step back as if struck by the three words. He slowly nodded. "Yes. Duty. I understand that finally." He asked Rumble: "Ben?"

"He's at Palatine," Rumble said. "In Violet and Rosalie's care."

"And you are here."

"I'm a soldier," Rumble said. "Doing my duty."

Cord now seemed distant, like a peak far on the horizon where you could only see the cold, snow-covered top, but have no idea what lay beneath.

"So the war will be over," Cord said, gesturing toward General Scott, who was being received by a coterie of Mexican officers.

"Looks likely," Grant said.

"And we won," Cord said.

"Yes," Longstreet said.

"What did we win?" Cord asked. He seemed to be convincing himself of something more than talking to them. "Land we can tame? More people we can conquer?"

"It's over, Elijah" Longstreet said. "That's enough for now."

"Then I can be done with all this," Cord said.

"Done with what?" Longstreet asked, puzzled by the abrupt shift.

"The army, Pete. That's why I didn't draw a uniform. I won't need one."

"Don't be hasty," Longstreet advised.

"I'm not being hasty," Cord said. "I wrote my resignation before leaving California and I left it at Leavenworth. I came here to fulfill my duty to my oath, as Sam pointed out." He turned to Rumble. "Now I have to fulfill my duty to my family."

Mexican drums began playing a tattoo on the other side of the courtyard, the beat echoing off the walls as the formal surrender got underway.

"What duty?" Rumble demanded. "What family?"

"Are you staying in the Army?" Cord asked.

Rumble bristled. "What business is that of yours?"

"Answer the question," Cord said. "I've told you my plans."

"You have no right to know my plans."

"When it involves my son," Cord said. "I have a right."

"Easy now, both of you," Grant advised.

"Not your business, Sam." Cord kept his eyes on Rumble. "Answer the question."

"I'm going back to West Point and to my home there," Rumble said.

"But you're here now," Cord said. "You've been at war for a while. That's not taking care of Ben."

"And you could have done better in California?" Rumble snapped.

"As I've said, I'm resigning from the Army," Cord said. "And is Palatine a good place for Ben? You left it fast enough and insured you wouldn't have to return to take your place there. Why would it be any better for Ben? Is growing up in a tavern the best place for him?"

"Watch your tongue," Rumble warned as he took a step forward.

"Looks like you spend enough time in taverns," Longstreet muttered.

"And why would West Point be a better place for him?" Cord asked. "Won't it drive him to want to put on the gray?"

"He'll never wear the gray," Rumble said with finality.

"Why not, if it's what he wants?" Cord argued.

"He won't," Rumble said. "I will not argue this with you."

"So you're going to control his life? Send him to Palatine when it suits you, but not allow him to enter the Corps, because it suits you?" Cord plunged on. "If there's another war, I'll not be part of it. You will," he said to Rumble. "I'll take care of my son in a way you cannot."

"By being inebriated?" Rumble asked. "By being an uncivilized frontiersman? By babbling like a fool? You don't even know what you're saying." He indicated Cord's tattered clothes. "Do you have a profession other than being a drunk?"

Cord's left fist struck like a rattlesnake, a sharp, fierce blow to Rumble's nose. Blood sprayed over Rumble's face as his head snapped back. Cord's right hit the side of Rumble's head, stunning him.

Grant grabbed Cord's left arm as he pulled back for another strike. Rumble shook his head, trying to regain his senses, splashing the other three with the blood pouring out of his broken nose.

"Now, gents—" Longstreet began, but Rumble was faster. He waded forward, fists flying. He hit Cord while Grant still held his arm, knocking him back. Then the two were tumbling in the dirt, flailing away.

Longstreet glanced over his shoulder at the peace negotiations. No one had noticed the battle in the shade under the building archway yet and Longstreet kept them from being seen by the expedient method of grabbing the back of Rumble's uniform frock and tossing him further into the building. Cord followed without a toss, leaping toward Rumble on his own power.

Grant and Longstreet jumped in, pulling them apart. Longstreet held Rumble, while Grant subdued Cord. It took a few seconds, but both finally stopped struggling.

"Life's too short and brutal," Cord said. "There's only one thing in this world I care about and that's my son. I'm taking him west, where he'll have a life free of all this and where he can freely choose his own path in life."

The drum roll was picking up speed.

"I will not allow it," Rumble said. "He is my son."

"No." Cord said it with finality. "He's my son. You and I know that."

"I've raised him," Rumble argued.

"And I've paid the price for it," Cord said.

"Your choice," Rumble said. "As much as you could make a choice given the condition you were in that morning, which is not much different than the condition you're in now. There are some things that cannot be undone. I will not allow it."

Longstreet moved forward and placed an arm between the two officers. "This is not the time or place." He looked at Cord. "Lucius is right. You were drunk the morning you had to make a decision and failed to do the honorable thing. And you're drunk now. Nothing has changed."

Cord turned to Longstreet and was about to retort when he saw his reflection in Old Pete's breastplate. Long stringy hair, face flushed red from alcohol and sun, eyes blood shot.

"Elijah." Grant was at his side. "Go get cleaned up and sober and then—"

Cord walked away, passing through the Halls of Montezuma into Mexico City and then out of sight and out of the Army as the drum tattoo came to an abrupt halt, indicating peace had come to Mexico and the United States.

UNEASY PEACE: 1847-1861

What did General Lee say concerning commanders? ------ *"I cannot trust with higher command, with command of others, a man who cannot command himself. Discipline of self, as well as others, is the soul of an Army."*
    Bugle Notes: Required Plebe Knowledge, United State Military Academy

ELIJAH CORD

October, 1849, New Mexico Territory

"DAMN IT, ELIJAH!" Kit Carson grabbed one of Cord's boots and tumbled him off the card table onto the plank floor.

Cord hit with a resounding thump. Bleary, bloodshot eyes opened to the world, or, in this case, the floor level view of the Taos saloon. Which had pretty much been Cord's world for the past month during his latest binge.

"I go away for a while and you end up in here and like this?" Carson grabbed Cord's arm, helping him to his feet. "You're getting worse, Elijah."

Cord staggered and shook his head, immediately regretting that move. "When'd ya get back?"

"Last night," Carson said, propelling Cord toward the door.

"Hold on, hold on," Cord said, reaching for the bottle that was on the table.

"It's empty," Carson said. "And we've got to ride. Jicarilla Apaches attacked a party on the Cimarron Cutoff, near Point of Rocks. Killed most and word is they took some captives."

Carson propelled Cord through the saloon doors. The blast of early morning sunlight caused Cord to attempt to retreat back into the saloon, but Carson had a firm grip. Seeing him in the daylight, Carson had to reconsider his timetable. Cord wasn't just drunk, he was awash in alcohol.

"Come on," Carson growled, pulling him along the street to the adobe house he shared with his wife, Josefa, and their children.

"Coffee, black, lots of it, my dear," Carson called out as he got Cord through the front door and into a chair.

Josefa shook her head upon seeing Cord. "He is a pig."

The sudden cool darkness inside the house further confused Cord. "You say you got a job for me, Kit?"

Carson leaned over his old friend, putting a hand on each shoulder. "You get sober today. We ride first light tomorrow. Hard. The Apaches got a few days lead."

"Leave him behind," Josefa said as she carried a large black pot into the room. "He's no good to anyone."

"I need solid guns with me," Carson said. "Most fellows aint worth spit. Major Grier is rounding up some of his men and they won't be ready until the morning and most of those army fellows aren't the best shots."

"Your friend is not worth much right now," Josefa argued.

"He will be," Carson said as he took the pot from her and poured a large mug of coffee. "Drink, Elijah."

Early November and Taos' altitude brought cold at first light. Cord felt like hell had doubled down a load of pain on him. His head was pounding, his throat was parched and his hands were shaking. His horse looked like a pretty tall obstacle as he considered mounting.

"We need to get going." Carson's horse was fidgeting, sensing the rider's urgency.

Cord sighed, stuck a foot in the stirrup and swung himself on board. "I'm riding."

Carson didn't wait. He set out at a gallop and Cord followed, every movement misery. They caught up with the patrol of dragoons under Major Grier on the outskirts of Taos. Grier spared Cord a disgusted look. He was class of '35 and had been the Assistant Instructor of Infantry and Cavalry Tactics during Cord's plebe year. As par for his cadet career, Cord had been the Immortal in Grier's class, which had not been forgotten. Cord's more recent activities in New Mexico, consisting mainly of drinking, whoring, and fighting, interspersed with semi-sobering up long enough to take scouting or hunting jobs to get the money to go back to those activities didn't endear him to his fellow Academy graduate either. The only reason Grier was taking Cord as a scout was because if he didn't, Carson wouldn't go and the mountain man was a legend on the frontier.

Cord settled into a cocoon of misery, keeping Carson, Major Grier and the contingent of soldiers in sight as he followed. He had no idea what direction they were heading or what exactly they were doing. Something to do with Apaches and an attack.

It took him five days before his head was somewhat clear, but his hands still shook.

They found the site of the attack on the afternoon of that day. Six dead. Stripped naked, their bodies bloated in the sun and partially eaten by carrion. Soldiers set to work burying the dead.

"All men," Carson said. "They took the women. Supposed to be three. A Mrs. White, her daughter and a negro servant."

"What do you suggest?" Major Grier asked.

"We track them until we find them," Carson said, treating the question as ignorantly as it had been asked. He looked over at Cord. "You good?"

Cord tapped the Lancaster resting across his pommel. "I'm ready."

"Let's ride."

It took twelve more days, east across New Mexico, to track down the Apaches. It was rough country, but the Apache trail wasn't hard to follow, given there appeared to be about a hundred of them.

Finally, near Tucumcari, just forty miles west of the Texas border, the gap began closing quickly. The Apaches were moving along the bank of the Canadian River and the signs were getting fresher.

"We'll hit their camp soon," Carson warned Major Grier as they rode along the south bank of the river. "I recommend we sent a small scouting party ahead."

Grier vetoed that, believing there was strength in numbers, so they continued on, Carson and Cord in the lead, along with Grier and his adjutant, the main body of dragoons just behind.

"Do you think the women are still alive?" Grier asked.

"We haven't tripped over any more bodies," Carson said. "And there's sign here and there they got women with them. But you never know with these folk. They're--" he looked to Cord. "What's the words I'm looking for?"

"Unpredictable," Cord said.

"I assume the savages have taken advantage of the poor creatures," Grier said.

Carson shrugged. "Once someone been took a few weeks, they start losing the will to escape. They just focus on surviving. They survive a few more months, they start forgetting there any other life."

They came around a bend in the river and immediately halted as the Apache camp appeared less than two hundred yards ahead.

Carson twisted in his saddle and signaled for the rest of the men, strung out over a quarter mile to hurry up. "We need to hit them hard and fast," he advised Grier.

"I think we should try to parlay with them," Grier said. "If we go in shooting, there's a good chance the captives will get killed."

"We go in talking, there's a good chance they'll get killed too," Carson said.

"I'm in command," Grier said. "I'll take a detachment forward under a white flag—"

"Sir!" Carson had no patience. "This is gonna to go to hell quick. They already killed white people. There aint no parlaying now. We've got to charge."

"Sir," Cord said, "he's right."

"Shut up you drunk," Grier said, the command decision weighing heavy on him. The decision was taken away as Carson had predicted. An Apache on the outskirts of camp saw the riders and raised the alert. The camp became a beehive of activity, Apaches scattering in all directions.

"Get the women," Carson yelled to Cord.

The two scouts galloped forward. Behind them Grier bowed to the inescapable and ordered his trumpeter to sound the charge.

Cord raced toward the camp, leaning in the saddle to make as small a target as possible. A few braves were putting up a defense, but most were escaping. Cord saw a flash out of the corner of his eye and spotted a white woman running desperately toward the river. Behind her, a brave was drawing back on his bow. Carson jerked on the reins and snapped the Lancaster to his shoulder. He squinted down the barrel, but his hands weren't steady. He took a breath, tried to steady once more and fired.

He missed.

The brave let loose and the arrow slammed into Mrs. White's back. She dropped like a stone. The brave turned and ran.

Cord lowered his rifle as the dragoons came charging by. He lay the gun across his pommel and stared at the tremor in his hands. Then he reached into his saddlebag and retrieved his flask. He drained the entire thing in one long gulp.

There was no sign of the daughter or servant. Whether they'd been carried off or never made it here, there was no way of knowing. There were so many small trails now going in so many directions, it would be impossible to know which to follow.

Cord sat alone, not far from where a couple of soldiers were digging a hole in which to bury Mrs. White. The arrow had gone straight through her heart, killing her instantly. Grier was going through the goods that had been abandoned in the haste to abandon the camp. He was furious at Carson, believing if they had used a white flag the bloodshed could have been averted.

"You doing all right, Elijah?" Carson asked.

"I'm not."

"What happened?" Carson asked. "We got split up in the charge." He frowned. "You drinking?"

"I-" Cord began, but Grier came stomping over, holding something in his hands.

"Found this in her satchel." He held a well-thumbed pulp novel. He extended it to Carson. "Ever seen it?"

"Yeah, I seen it," Carson said, not bothering to take the book.

Grier read from the cover. "'*Kit Carson: The Prince of the Gold Hunters'* is what it says. You're a giant of a man. A hero. Been everywhere, done everything yourself." He perused the insert. "Says here in this story the frontier hero Kit Carson vows to some woman's parents that he will track down and save their daughter, no matter how long it takes."

Grier tossed the book to the ground. He pointed at it. "The myth." Then he pointed at Mrs. White. "The real Kit Carson. She must have been reading that, thinking the real deal would be coming for her. Well, you came. Didn't work out, did it?"

Carson was crest-fallen, staring at the book as if it were a rattlesnake. "I very much regret Mrs. White's death."

"It isn't his fault," Cord said.

Grier spit. "A fraud and a drunk. What a pair." He walked away.

Carson went over to the grave. Cord joined him. They helped lower her body in, then the two scouts began shoveling dirt, covering her. When they were done, Carson stood at the foot of the mound of dirt, silent and troubled.

"It's my fault," Cord said. "I had a clear shot at the brave who fired the arrow. I missed. He didn't."

Carson turned his head. "You missed?"

Cord held out his hands. The tremor was noticeable. "I killed that woman."

Carson sighed. "You didn't save her, but you didn't kill her. The Apache done that." He faced Cord. "You need help, Elijah."

The Paiute Village was nestled in the foothills of the Sierra Nevada Mountains. Snow had fallen the previous day and blanketed everything. Cord swayed drunkenly on the trail leading to the winter encampment, Carson at his side. The mountain man took the flask from Cord's hand.

"You go in with nothing," Carson said. "No gun. No knife. No food. No clothes. You go in there like you came into the world."

"What're you doing?" Cord slurred.

Carson slid the sketching of Lidia and young Ben out of Cord's breast pocket and put them in his own. Then he took the Lancaster and Bowie.

Finally, he stripped Cord, who was unable to put up much of a defense given his inebriated condition. His pale skin was whiter than the snow.

"She's waiting for you," Carson said.

Cord blinked in confusion. "Who?"

"Elijah, you got dealt some bad cards in life," Carson said. "Can't change them cards. But can change how you play them. Today's the start."

Carson gave his friend a shove. Cord stumbled, fell to his knees in the snow. Staggered to his feet. He walked barefoot through the snow toward the village. As he got closer several Paiutes came out to see this curious phenomenon enter. In the center of the village, the old woman threw open the flap to her lodge. When Cord arrived, she reached out and placed her hand on the tattoo in the center of his chest and shook her head. She had a blanket in her other hand. The same blanket Cord had given her four years ago. She wrapped it around Cord's shoulders and took into the lodge.

VIOLET RUMBLE

March, 1851, Palatine, Mississippi

FROM HER SITTING ROOM, Violet Rumble watched the plume of dust floating into the sky over the Natchez Road. A single rider coming on this early Spring day of 1851. She went over to the chest and poured herself a liberal dose of 'medicine'. She downed it, pulled on her gloves, arranged her hat on top of her head, and then went downstairs to the front parlor, where she could watch the drive to the house. The rider appeared at the end of the drive as Seneca came into the hall and joined her.

"Who is it?" Seneca asked.

"Mayfield," Violet said. "Natchez sheriff. Is your father on his porch?"

Seneca shook his head. "No. He rode off this morning."

"Where?" Violet's tone was sharper than she intended.

"I don't know, mother."

Violet went to the front door. She opened it, nodded at Samual who stood in the shadows to the right, and went to the top of the wide stairs as Sheriff Mayfield halted his horse at the end of the drive. A slave hurried up and took the reins, waiting with head downcast.

"Finally decided to do your job, sheriff?" Violet asked as he dismounted.

Mayfield was a small man, who compensated by carrying a big Colt revolver in a holster on his right hip. It slapped loudly against him as he walked to the base of the stairs. He had dark eyes that darted to and fro and rarely made eye contact. He owed his position to back room deals with the traders who ran Natchez and could get the vote out. The power elite of the plantations had ignored the position, considering it of no importance. To their own detriment.

"I got important work, Miss Violet," Mayfield said. "And the judge wasn't keen to issue a warrant."

"But you do have the warrant based on the papers Miss Rosalie gave you?" Violet pressed. It bothered her that Rosalie wasn't here, but at her family home, tending to business.

Mayfield reached into his vest and pulled out a roll of heavy paper. "I got it all. The papers and the warrant."

"Then we must ride out to Shantytown," Violet said. She gestured at Samual.

"Aint necessary for you to come," Mayfield said.

"I believe it is," Violet said.

"What's going on, Mother?" Seneca was dressed impeccably, as always, and his cane was in his right hand, as always.

"The sheriff has a warrant for St. George for black-marketing cotton from Palatine and running guns south during the war," Violet said.

"At last!" Seneca exclaimed. "It took long enough to catch the rascal."

"He isn't caught yet," Violet said. "Get your horse."

Seneca strode off to the stables. In a few minutes Samual came back leading Violet's old nag with Seneca riding beside him on his own horse. Samual helped her onto the sidesaddle and without a word she led the way down the track that led to the dark heart of Palatine. Seneca and Mayfield followed.

Violet gestured for Seneca to ride up beside her. She leaned close to her son, hand gripping the pommel of sidesaddle. "Where did your father go?"

"I have no idea," Seneca said. "He can do things when he wants, mother. You know that."

Violet shook her head. She tugged a glove tighter over her hand, a surprising sign of nervousness. They rode through a thick patch of forest, a natural wall between Palatine House and Shantytown. Violet paused as she saw St. George standing at the base of knoll, arms folded across his burly chest, as if waiting for them. And Tiberius's horse tethered on the side of the overseer cabin.

"This might not be a good time, Sheriff," Violet said.

"I came all the way from Natchez," Mayfield said. "You asked for this, you getting it."

"Afternoon sheriff." St. George touched a finger to the brim of his hat in greeting. "Whatever can I do for you?"

"Got me here a warrant for you, Mister Dyer," Mayfield said, pulling the roll of documents out of his vest.

St. George didn't seem surprised. "Don't you think the master of Palatine be told of this?"

Mayfield nodded. "Probably."

St. George jerked a thumb at his cabin. "He up there. Let's tell him."

Mayfield swung off his horse. Seneca dismounted and offered a hand to his mother. Violet's face was white. "You have to stop these men," she hissed to Seneca.

"What are you talking about, Mother?"

It was too late. St. George and Mayfield were already halfway up the knoll. Violet hurried to follow, a bewildered Seneca in her wake. He'd never seen his mother move as fast as she did now, feet flying underneath her hoop skirt. All four reached the cabin together and St. George threw the door open with a satisfied thrust of his arm.

Tiberius Rumble, master of Palatine, lie on his back in St. George's bed, buck naked, with an equally naked girl straddling him. The girl looked at the open door and the four people peering in as if they were of no consequence, not stopping her rocking motion or even slowing. Tiberius turned his head, blinking at the sudden light.

"St. George! What the hell are you—" Tiberius fell silent as he could finally make out the four. "Stop!" he ordered the girl, who ignored him. "Damn It!" Tiberius shoved the girl off and grabbed the blanket to cover himself.

The girl tumbled to the floor, then slowly got to her feet, not trying to hide her nakedness at all. Her skin was as white as the man she had been riding, but her facial bone structure indicated negro to Violet and the others. And she was young, no more than thirteen or fourteen.

"Father!" Seneca took a step into the room, but no further.

Violet brushed past him and grabbed the girl's smock, throwing it at her. "Get back to your hut."

"Oh, she aint from here," St. George said, satisfaction oozing in his voice. "Well, she *from* here, but not *of* here now."

"What are you talking about?" Seneca demanded.

Sheriff Mayfield took a step to the side. He tapped a hand on the warrant and documents. "I aint sure this a good time to be doing this. Seems you got bigger problems here."

The girl held the smock in her hands when a woman's voice pierced the air from the open door.

"What in hell have you done to my daughter?" Sally Skull stood in the doorway, her large bulk filling it. She shoved her way past everyone to Gabriel and grabbed the smock, pulling it over the girl's head. Then she turned to face the four as she jabbed a finger at Tiberius, who looked like a dying, pale fish grasping a blanket to his white haired chest. "He's raped my daughter! You son-of-a-bitch." She pulled her pistol and leveled it at Tiberius.

"Easy now," Mayfield said, without much conviction. His pistol was still in its holster. "Let's settle this peaceful."

"Arrest him!" Skull insisted, her gun still pointed at Tiberius.

Violet remained silent, watching the pieces move on the board and knowing she'd been outplayed long before arriving here.

"I'm sure there be a peaceful way to work this out," St. George said. "But you know," he added slyly, "this worse than it look."

Violet stiffened, waiting for the final blow to fall. Tiberius was sitting up now, a befuddled look on his face. Seneca was frozen in confusion and shock. Not for the first time, Violet desperately missed Lucius.

St. George reached into his black sash and pulled out a piece of paper. "This here bill of sale show that this here girl, she was sold to Miss Skull here. By me, on orders of Master Tiberius Rumble. And said girl's mother be Mary. Her father, well," St. George made a show of looking at the paper, "it not say." He turned to Tiberius. "But we know who the father be, don't we, sir?"

Tiberius' hands were shaking and his face paled.

"Your own daughter!" The outrage in Sheriff Mayfield's voice was no act. Much was allowed in the shadows, but there were some things that were considered an abomination and tolerable to none.

Gathering her shattered nerve, Violet stepped to the center of the room. "Enough!" She faced St. George and Skull. "We forget the charges, you let this go."

"Mother!" Seneca got the one word out, but beyond that he couldn't articulate a response to what was unfolding.

"You forget the charges," Skull said, "and you tear up those papers, and you never look into anything outside of the four walls of Palatine House again. You'll be kept in the life you're used to. Aint nothing really going to change. Is that clear?"

A muscle quivered in Violet's jaw, but she nodded. "Yes."

Skull smiled in triumph. "Sheriff. The fire."

Mayfield tossed the rolls of parchment into the fireplace. The smoldering embers heated the papers and they burst into flames. And with it the Rumble's nominal control over Palatine.

BEN RUMBLE

June 1857, West Point, NY

"I BELIEVE YOU have the shortest distance to travel today, yet the greatest obstacle to overcome in the next few weeks," Superintendent Delafield told Ben Agrippa Rumble.

They stood just inside the door of the tavern, flanked by Benny, who'd had one too many early morning flip in celebration, and Letitia teary-eyed, as any woman would be when her first grandchild leaves hearth and home to make their way in the world. Ben's sister, Abigail, now a bewitching beauty of fifteen, watched the farewells without quite the same enthusiasm or optimism.

Ben shook Delafield's hand. "Thank you for doing this for me, sir."

"You deserve your chance," Delafield said.

Abigail tossed some ice water on the scene. "Until father returns."

Delafield grimaced. "I sent him to Washington on official duty. He won't be back for almost a month. By then, things will have progressed to the point where he might see reason."

Abigail snorted. "You don't know him that well, sir."

"Hush, girl," Benny Havens said. "Give your brother your best wishes."

Abigail stood up on her toes to hug Ben. "I have no idea why you're doing this, Ben, but I do wish you the best."

Ben swallowed hard. He adjusted his satchel, squared his shoulders, walked out of the tavern and took the trail to South Dock.

Despite spending almost his entire life here, everything looked different to him this morning. The air smelled fresher, the water sparkled more clearly in the early morning June sun, and the trees seemed greener than ever before.

A cluster of young men was disembarking the steamer from New York and Ben joined them. The excitement was palpable as the young men began to walk up the road toward the Academy.

The fellow next to Rumble freed up his right hand from the trunk he was dragging and stuck it out. "George Armstrong Custer, Michigan." He was a bright-eyed man with flowing golden locks that cascaded around his shoulders.

"Ben Rumble."

Custer's handshake was firm. "Well, Ben, do you aspire to be a general?"

Ben blinked. "I just want to get through Beast Barracks."

Custer laughed. "I'm sure it won't be that difficult. I'm not too concerned about this place. Someone has to be at the head and someone at the foot. I'll take the foot as it will be much less work and then in four years we'll all wear the same blue uniform and start the real work when it will be time to be at the head. I see stars in my future."

"It is good to have goals," Ben acknowledged.

They reached the level of the Plain and everyone paused. Ben realized that most had never seen the Academy. Indeed, many had never been more than a few miles from their home until the trip here. Workmen were tarring the gutters of the barracks and that odor wafted over the Plain. For many, that smell would always trigger strong emotion ever afterward.

"Where to now?" Custer voiced the question on all their minds.

"There." Ben pointed. "The tents."

"Tents?" Custer was aghast. "Why tents when there are all these fine gray buildings all about us?"

"We spend the summer in encampment," Ben said. He noticed that the others were all listening to him, clinging to his knowledge in the face of the coming storm. He spotted a pair of cadets heading their way and knew the storm was going to break. "We best get moving."

"What do you think you're doing?" one of the cadets demanded.

"Taking in the view," Custer said. "A mighty fine place you have here."

The two cadets exchanged a glance. "Are you a funny man?" one asked.

"Some say I—" Custer began, but then the screaming began. Just the two at first, but like bees to honey, cadets in gray swarmed over the young men, splitting them up, dividing and subjugating.

Ben was double-teamed. Two upperclassmen, whom he recognized from the time he spent in the riding hall while his father worked and the time the cadets spent in Benny Havens.

"Drop your satchel!" one screamed.

Ben lowered it to the ground.

"I said DROP IT!" the First Classman repeated.

Ben scooped it up, then let it fall to the ground.

"Move to the adjutant's tent," the other ordered.

Like cattle to the slaughter, the small herd of new cadets was escorted with many a scream and promise of a dire future to a tent on the edge of the encampment. They were hustled into line, and sent in, one by one.

Ben was third. The adjutant seemed bored with the ritual, seated behind a field desk in the tent and looking at a piece of paper. Ben came to a halt three paces in front of the desk and waited.

"Name, new cadet?"

"Ben Agrippa Rumble."

The adjutant responded automatically. "That's New Cadet Rumble, got it?"

"Yes, sir."

The adjutant finally looked up. "We all know you and we know about you, Mister Rumble. Most of us have, shall we say, shared some libation with you at Benny Havens. We all know your father. But none of that matters now. Do you understand?"

"Yes, sir."

"Good. Then." The adjutant got to his feet and began issuing orders. "Come to attention when addressing an upperclassman. Heels together. Toes out. Hands by your side, palms out fingers closed, little fingers on the seams of your trousers, head up, chin in, shoulders thrown back, chest out, belly in, eyes straight ahead. Stay like that and don't move."

The instructions came like bullets, Ben contorting his body to comply.

The adjutant looked past Rumble as another upperclassman entered. On cue the side flaps on the tent were loosened and dropped, darkening the interior. The only light came from a single candle flickering on the field desk. The adjutant left, leaving Rumble alone with the unidentified cadet behind him.

"We have a problem with you, Mister Rumble," the newcomer said. "You've seen most of us imbibing in your grandfather's tavern. Which means you've seen most of us violating quite a few regulations. Once you sign in to the Corps, you will be bound by the honor code. Do you see the problem?"

"No, sir."

"Duty requires you tell the truth about what you've seen. You will be bound to that. If you do not tell the truth, then you are dishonorable. However, if you tell the truth, then many a fine cadet might have their futures destroyed. We can't allow that to happen."

"It won't, sir."

"We can't take that chance. I think the sooner you leave the Corps, the better," the anonymous cadet said. "You can't stay. You're a threat to too many. And if you don't tell the truth, the Vigilance Committee will come for you. I very strongly suggest you do not sign the roll, and go back down to your grandfather's tavern. We are gentlemen here."

Ben said nothing, feeling a line of sweat course its way down his back in the now-stuffy tent. The seconds passed.

"Think hard on it," the upperclassman advised.

When Rumble still said nothing, the upperclassman came so close, Rumble could feel his breath on his neck. "Don't push this. It's more than just about the tavern and the honor code. This is a place for gentlemen. We don't want your kind here. The lack of honor is in your blood."

Ben wheeled. "And what kind is that? What do you mean by lack of honor?"

"Watch you tongue!"

"Watch yours!" Ben stepped closer, chest thumping against the upperclassman's. "Are you a man? Willing to face me?"

The upperclassman laughed, even as he backed up. "You can fight as many of us as you want. It won't change a thing. It won't change your blood."

Then with a rustle of canvas he was gone.

The adjutant returned and took his place behind the desk.

"Well, Mister Rumble?"

Ben's jaw was tight, his muscles vibrating. "Yes, sir."

"Do you wish to say something?"

"No, sir."

The adjutant sighed and pointed at a piece of paper. "Sign here, indicating you are on the active roster of cadets."

Ben went to the table, quickly signed, and resumed the position.

"You will go to the quartermasters and be measured for uniform, the barber, the surgeon for exam, the armory to draw a weapon, and you will do all this within the next hour and report back here." The adjutant made a great show of checking his pocket watch and making a notation in the log. "Is that clear?"

"Yes, sir."

"You will do all this at the double. Is that clear?"

"Yes, sir."

"You know the four answers you are allowed, don't you New Cadet Rumble?"

"Yes, sir, no, sir, no excuse, sir and sir, I do not understand."

"Use the last one sparingly. Go!"

Ben ran from the tent, almost crashing into an upperclass cadet who halted him and berated him for his unmilitary appearance for almost ten minutes, eating into his hour allotment and clearly trying to provoke him into action he would not be able to take back. With every fiber of his being, Ben bore the insults and hazing.

The days passed in a blur for Ben. Within a week he learned how to march, carry his musket and some basic maneuvers. It seemed as if the drum rattled out the marching cadence all day long at the encampment. The days were long with reveille at 5:00 am. Then there was roll call to account for everyone. Then 'policing' the tent city, removing anything that wasn't supposed to there, and it seemed as if the upperclass went out of their way to place disgusting objects in the strangest places for the plebes to find. And woe unto them if they did not find the objects. Then drill from 5:30-6:30. Then arrange their bedding, raise the walls of their tents so it was open to the air, and inspection, and prepare for morning parade. They marched to the mess hall for breakfast. Ben had eaten in the mess before so he was prepared for the terrible repast that awaited.

Right after breakfast, which was wolfed down as there was never enough time allowed to properly eat, the guard was mounted. Then artillery drill from 9:00 to 10:00. Then back to the tents to clean and polish gear, a never-ending task. No matter how shiny a cadet made his brass, an upperclassman could always find fault with it. The march to lunch at 1:00. Then dancing from 3:00 to 4:00, because every cadet would be an officer and an officer was a gentleman, and a gentleman knew how to dance. Then another police call.

Then Infantry drill from 5:30 to 6:45 followed by evening parade and inspection. Then dinner. Followed by final roll call at 9:30 and lights out at 9:45.

Besides making soldiers, the strict regime forged a class of men that grew tight and developed bonds that would last a lifetime. Cooperate and graduate was a maxim beat into each plebe from the first day at the Academy, but, strangely, Ben felt his classmates separating from him as each day passed, rather than bonding, no matter how hard he tried to be one of them.

Of course, there were those who couldn't make it. By the end of the first week, three had already resigned. And more would follow.

But Ben knew he'd never resign even though it was clear the threat in the adjutant's tent was not hollow. More than any of his classmate's Ben faced the full force of the upperclass. He bore it with courage and resolve, but each day the pressure grew more relentless and a gradual silence settled onto him like a heavy, stifling blanket, keeping him distant even from his own classmates, and he knew, but could not accept, that it was the path to inevitable failure.

"He's but seventeen!" Rumble yelled, adding a belated "sir".

Major Delafield sat behind his desk and weathered Sergeant Major Rumble's outburst.

"He needed my permission to enter the Corps," Rumble added.

"He needed a parent's permission to enter," Delafield said.

"I did not give it and Lidia cannot send it from the grave," Rumble said. "Nor would she, I can tell you that for certain."

Delafield shifted uneasily as he pulled a file out of his desk. "But he did get his father's permission."

Rumble was thunderstruck. "I'm his father, sir."

"Are you?" Delafield asked gently. "I've a notarized letter from Elijah Cord. It states that he's Ben's father and he gives permission for Ben to do as he wishes with regard to the army and the Academy. It did not urge him to apply, but it did not say he could not."

"That acknowledgement is seventeen years too late," Rumble said. "It carries no legal weight."

"It is notarized."

"It could be fake, sir."

"The lawyer who notarized it is William Tecumseh Sherman, whose office is in San Francisco. And who also has some first-hand knowledge of the incident at the core of this."

"Cump?" Rumble blinked as the deeper implications hit target. "Did Ben see this letter? Does he know?"

Delafield shook his head. "No. Benny Havens wrote to Mister Cord. Apparently he wasn't easy to track down out west. The letter went via Kit Carson who still scouts for the army. He got it to Mister Cord, who then went to San Francisco to visit Mister Sherman. The return letter came to Benny, who came to me to facilitate the application. Ben doesn't know about the past."

"So Benny is behind all this."

"No. It's Ben's desire." Delafield got up and walked around the desk, putting a hand on Rumble's shoulder. "Ben's a good boy. It's what he wanted."

"It's not what I want for him," Rumble said.

"Be that as it may--" Delafield began, but Rumble cut him off.

"I made a deathbed promise to Lidia that he would not wear the gray or have anything to do with the Academy. That's a solemn promise that I must honor, sir."

Delafield looked like he'd been slapped. "I did not know of this."

"I told no one," Rumble said. "But I give you my word, sir, it was the last she spoke. I gave her my word of honor that I would make it so."

Delafield went back around the desk and wearily sat down. He rubbed his hands together. "This is most difficult." He slowly began to nod. "I see it now. Lidia was wiser than any of us."

Rumble was confused. "How so, sir?"

"Ben might not know the truth of the past," Delafield said, "but the Corps knows. The Corps always knows."

"What's happening?" Rumble demanded.

"He's being cut out from the Corps, practically silenced," Delafield said. "I didn't understand. But now I do. Lidia knew he would never be accepted."

"Sons-of-a-bitches!" Rumble was ready to head out and take on the entire Corps.

Delafield waved a hand. "Not all are treating him poorly. But enough. Enough to make it impossible for him to stay in the Corps."

"I raised Ben," Rumble said. "He has my name. I'm his father, no matter what Cord says. I'm here. Cord is on the other side of the country, doing God knows what. Sir, with all due respect. I have always done my duty. Above and beyond when you asked me to. I'm asking you now to help me honor my pledge to my wife. I will make sure Ben receives an education. A fine one. My mother has connections. We had already planned this. He will attend Bangor Theological Seminary in Maine."

"Did you tell him of these plans?"

"Not yet, sir."

"I wish I had known," Delafield murmured. "I wish I had known of your pledge to Lidia. Ah, the wisdom and truth in a dying mother's desire for her son. Women are so much wiser than us men."

Ulysses S. Grant

March 1859, St. Louis, Missouri

THE CRISPLY UNIFORMED Lieutenant from Jefferson Barracks paused in shock in the middle of the St. Louis street. "Sam? Sam Grant?"

The man he was calling out to was dressed in shoddy clothes and held a wicker basket full of firewood, which he was hawking from the street corner.

A bright smile split Ulysses S. Grant's haggard face as he recognized his friend. "Old Pete!"

Grant dropped the firewood and the two men embraced. The two had seen nothing of each other since Longstreet had stood in as Grant's best man when he married Julia Dent back in '48. Eleven years later it was clear the two men had gone down vastly different paths.

"You look quite sharp indeed," Grant said to Longstreet. "Back at the barracks?"

"For now," Longstreet allowed. "And you, you're in the city?"

Grant gestured at the wood. "Here for the week to work. I rent a room. Then walk home each weekend to see Julia and the children at White Haven."

"Walk?" Longstreet was surprised. "It's over twelve miles."

"An easy jaunt," Grant said. "I'm glad we've met. There's something that has been troubling me all these years." He reached into his pocket and emptied it of the only coin he had, a five dollar gold piece. "In all the excitement of the wedding I'd forgotten I have a debt I owe you." He held out the coin, but Longstreet didn't take it.

"There's no need," Longstreet. "I've long since forgotten it."

"It's a debt of honor," Grant said. "You loaned me the money when I needed it."

"Truly, Sam," Longstreet said. "No need."

"You must take it," Grant insisted. "I cannot live with anything in my possession which is not mine."

Face flushed, Longstreet took the coin and awkwardly shoved it into his pocket.

"Do you have the hour?" Grant asked, as if the debt had already disappeared in the current of time now that it was resolved.

"Where's your watch?" Longstreet asked without thinking.

"Pawned it two years past to make Christmas happen for the children," Grant said, as always honest to a fault. "It was a bad year," he added, as if selling firewood on the street corner was a sign of a much better one. "The hour, if you don't mind, Pete?"

"Half past one."

"Ah!" Grant grabbed his basket. "I have an appointment I must make. Would you like to accompany me?"

"Certainly," Longstreet said.

Grant set off with a purposeful stride, Longstreet at his side.

"I tried farming," Grant said. "West Pointers make poor farmers, I'm afraid. Hardscrabble I called it after some town in the Colorado Territory that Elijah Cord told me about. You remember Elijah, don't you?"

"Certainly."

"He's still out west. A mountain man or some such," Grant said. "A noble occupation, but one that does not seem suited to having a family. Now, while farming would seem to favor family life, it didn't for me. Each time it seemed as if things would work, that the crop would come in, I'm afraid nature saw it differently. A flood. A late frost in the spring. An early frost in the fall. Mother Nature is most unforgiving."

They turned a corner and the courthouse loomed ahead. Longstreet eyed it nervously. "An appointment with the law?"

Grant laughed. "Yes, but don't worry, Pete. I've broken no laws. A matter I need to resolve."

They took the steps and entered. Grant wove his way through the crowded hallways and entered a room where a harried clerk was shuffling papers.

"Sir, I am Ulysses Grant. We have an appointment."

The clerk flipped through one of the many stacks on his desk. "Yes, yes. I've got it right here." He looked Grant up and down, not impressed, but then saw Longstreet. "Is this your witness?"

"He is," Grant said.

"What am I witnessing?" A bemused Longstreet asked.

"I have a slave."

"Just one?" Longstreet asked. "My relations, the Dents, certainly have many more than one and must have bestowed more than one on Julia."

"They did to Julia, but they bestowed one on me," Grant said.

"Did he run away?" Longstreet asked.

"Gentlemen?" The clerk interrupted. "Can we get this done?" He shoved the piece of paper across his desk and pointed at the pen resting next to the ink well.

Grant took the pin, dipped it, then signed. Then he offered the pen to Longstreet. The officer leaned over the desk, pen in hand, but paused when he saw the wording. "You're freeing your slave?"

"Certainly," Grant said.

"But . . ." Longstreet grasped for words. "Sam, an able-bodied slave can fetch over a thousand dollars on the St. Louis market."

"I'm aware of the market," Grant said. "It's my decision." He said the latter with such finality, that Longstreet remembered Mexico and West Point and knew the matter was no longer to be discussed. He signed.

The clerk took the paper, shook it to dry the ink, then stamped the document. "Your property is now a freedman."

Grant turned to Longstreet. "Thank you, Pete."

Longstreet took the hand. "I've got to get back to Jefferson Barracks, but perhaps you could come out and visit?"

Grant smiled sadly. "Not for a while. But I'm sure we'll meet again."

"Mister, do you want to fight?"

Grant paused in the doorway and faced his opponent. "I'm by nature a man of peace, but I will not be heckled by a person of your size."

Nine-year old Frederick Grant charged his father, wrapping his arms around Grant's legs. The two collapsed into the room in a tumble. Grant put up a token defense, but as always, Frederick ended up the victor and Grant had to 'yield' to his son.

Seated across the room, Julia Dent, despite her anger, could not help but smile at the Friday evening ritual that occurred upon her husband's return from St. Louis. As Grant stood up and shook off dust from the long walk, she could hold it in no longer.

"Did you do it?"

"The strangest thing happened in St. Louis today," Grant said.

"You came to your senses?" Julia asked.

"I saw Old Pete Longstreet.

"How is my cousin?"

"Still in the army, seemingly well."

""But you did it?"

"Yes, my wife, I did."

Julie shook her head, frustrated. "We need the help or we need the money. You choose the worst possible course of action."

"A man is a man," Grant said.

"Negroes are not men," Julia said.

Grant picked up the newspaper and settled into a worn chair. "We may agree to disagree on this matter." He said it calmly, but in that tone that Julia recognized. Rarely used, but always final.

Grant shook the paper, perusing the headlines, preparing to read to her as she knitted, their nightly ritual. "Ah, this Lincoln fellow. They're still talking about his speech." He read from the paper to his wife, another ritual. "'*A house divided against itself cannot stand. I believe this government cannot endure, permanently, half slave and half free. I do not expect the Union to be dissolved, I do not expect the house to fall, but I do expect it will cease to be divided. It will become all one thing or all the other.*'

"'Either the opponents of slavery will arrest the further spread of it, and place it where the public mind shall rest in the belief that it is in the course of ultimate extinction; or its advocates will push it forward, till it shall become alike lawful in all the states, old as well as new, North as well as South.'"

Grant lowered the paper. Julia was watching him carefully. He looked at the fireplace. "It was strange seeing Old Pete today." His eyes were glistening. "I truly fear when I might see him again."

George King

October 1860, Harpers Ferry, Virginia

"JOHN BROWN'S MEN are armed with Sharps carbines," King warned.

Lieutenant Colonel Robert E. Lee on leave from his duty station in Texas and being close to the capitol at Arlington, and First Lieutenant J.E.B. Stuart, on leave from his post in Kansas, who'd happened to be in the war department when the bad news broke, paused in their discussion and looked over at the Marine officer who'd been standing silently by.

"How do you know, Captain—" Lee waited for the blank to be filled in.

"Captain King."

Lee frowned, as if the name reminded him of something, but immediately shifted back to the problem at hand: a group of abolitionists had seized the Federal Arsenal at Harpers Ferry. A baggage handler on a train passing through the town had been killed, the irony that the man was a free black, also of little interest to the officers. "The Sharps, Captain King?"

"I did a reconnaissance of the perimeter of the arsenal," King replied. "I saw several empty weapon's cases, labeled 'bibles'."

"Beecher's Bibles," Stuart said with contempt. "I saw plenty of those in action in Kansas when I was stationed there." He was referring to Sharp's rifles bought by abolitionist supporters and shipped to those willing to use the weapons. The name came from the rich abolitionist Beecher family, the most prominent being Harriet Beecher Stowe, author of *Uncle Tom's Cabin*.

"They have hostages," Lee said. "We can't burn them out."

"The bayonet," King said. "Let me command my Marines and we'll handle this."

The closest Federal forces Lee had been able to muster after being summoned from his house at Arlington, had been 88 Marines. King's Marines, stationed just outside Washington DC. They'd ridden hard to Harper's Ferry where there were over 100,000 muskets stored at the armory, besides other ordnance.

Lee didn't hesitate. "Lieutenant Stuart. You will go to the engine house and try to parlay them into surrendering. When-"

"They won't surrender, sir," King interrupted. "Remember, their leader is John Brown."

"Brown!" Stuart exclaimed. "I saw the results of his work in Kansas. Unarmed men hacked to death."

"We must make a good show of it then," Lee said. "We use the parlay to divert their attention. Lieutenant Stuart, you go to the door, offer Brown whatever will keep him occupied, and while he's talking to you, I want Captain King to break the door down, use the bayonet, and end this. I would prefer Mister Brown not be taken alive. A trial would just give him another pulpit from which to spread his nonsense and cause further turmoil that the country can ill afford." Lee looked around the room. "Am I clear gentlemen?"

Under a flag of truce, J.E.B. Stuart approached the double doors to the engine house where John Brown was holed up with his small army and the captives. King led a handpicked squad of marines armed with muskets tipped with bayonets and a pair of sledgehammers as close as he could get to the building without being seen.

The negotiations didn't take long, because Brown would not barter. Two of his sons were already dead, shot in exchanges with the militia that had first responded to the assault. Another man had tried to flee and been shot trying to swim the Potomac. The militia, many of them intoxicated, firing repeatedly into his body, even after it was apparent he was dead. The fire was burning and it could not be controlled.

Finally, Stuart raised his right hand, as if to wipe his brow and King jumped to his feet. "Follow me!"

They sprinted to the front door and the two marines with the hammers pounded away.

To no avail.

The thick wooden door refused to yield.

As shots rang out from the windows, King spotted a ladder lying in the engine yard. "Use that," he yelled and the squad grabbed it. As they did so, King drew the boarding axe from the sheath on his back and slammed it home, splintering wood

The squad used the ladder as an improvised battering ram, everyone putting their muscle into each swing. On the fourth attempt, the twin doors splintered open and King led the charge through, wielding his boarding axe

He spotted Brown, armed with a Sharps just inside. As the old man brought the gun to bear, King jumped to the side and slammed the axe, flat-sided, into Brown's head. Brown fired a split second before he dropped unconscious to the floor. The second marine through the door, right behind King, took the round in his belly, doubling over and screaming in pain.

Several more shots rang out as the survivors defended themselves. The marines were deadly efficient with the bayonet, spreading throughout the engine house, rapidly overwhelming any resistance.

King saw a one-armed man in a corner, reloading his Sharps with great difficulty. King charged, axe at the ready. Preacher Cord closed the breech on the Sharps and readied it, aiming. Before he could fire, King swung the boarding axe, the pike end ripping into Preacher's stomach.

Preacher Cord dropped the Sharps, grabbed the axe with his single hand and fell backward. He ended up in an awkward sitting position, pike still in his stomach.

"You cannot silence us," Preacher said.

King jerked the pike up, into Preacher's heart.

"If the arsenal had been this well guarded," Robert E. Lee muttered, "we wouldn't be going through this."

The corn-field, long since harvested, was surrounded by soldiers, over a thousand of them, mostly Virginia Militia, dressed in a wide assortment of uniforms, from red to gray to blue to various combinations of them all. A scaffold waited in the center of the field, quickly and efficiently built even before the verdict had been handed down condemning John Brown.

King said nothing in response to Lee's remark. Since the raid six weeks ago, the trial of John Brown had captivated the country, just as Lee had direly predicted. King's failure to kill the man had been written off to the heat of battle, not cold calculation. The identity of the one-armed man he had killed, had jolted King.

Disgusted with the unfolding spectacle, Lee turned his horse and rode away, heading toward a nearby hilltop to watch from a distance. King stayed in the shadow of the scaffold.

It was a cold December day, the sun chilled and distant in the clear sky overhead. A wagon came slowly down a dirt road carrying John Brown, dressed all in black, except for red slippers, sitting on a coffin. His gaze was over the field, toward the Blue Ridge Mountains, adorned with leafless trees.

A drumbeat began to King's left. A contingent of cadets from the Virginia Military Institute were lined up immediately around the scaffold, the drummer a young boy in their midst. They wore red shirts, grey trousers and crossed white belts. Their officer in charge came over to King right after Lee rode away.

"What's wrong with the Colonel?"

"Nothing," King said. "He sees no need to be close by."

"You were in the assault?" the VMI instructor asked.

"I was," King said.

"Thomas Jackson," the officer introduced himself.

"George King."

"This is God's vengeance," Jackson said as the wagon came to a halt next to the steps to the scaffold.

"It is indeed," King agreed as the tailgate to the wagon was let down. John Brown got off his coffin and quickly leapt off the wagon as if eager for his fate. The sheriff escorted him up the stairs to the platform, where he was positioned over the trap door. His ankles were tied by deputies while others slid the coffin out of the wagon and put it just below the door.

"He bears his faith well, though," Jackson commented.

"But on the wrong path," King said.

"That will be for a higher power than us to decide soon," Jackson said.

Jackson turned toward his cadets and signaled. He barked out an order and they snapped to attention as the drumbeat ceased. A heavy silence descended on the thousands of soldiers and civilians bearing witness.

A hood was place over Brown's head and then the rope was cinched around his neck.

"Do you want to know when the trap opens?" the sheriff asked Brown, his voice carrying over the silent crowd.

Brown's response was slightly muffled by the cloth, but audible. "No. Just be quick about it."

Which, of course, they were not. Like MacKenzie on the *Somers*, the officials on the scaffold now seemed uncertain as to who was in charge of the fatal moment. Minutes passed and Brown stood still as hushed conversations went on around him.

The crowd began to grow uneasy as more minutes had passed. King looked off in the distance and he saw Lee, on his magnificent stallion, watching from a hilltop a mile away.

Finally the sheriff stepped forward, axe in hand. Without warning, he swung and cut the rope holding the trap door.

John Brown fell and jerked to a halt with a resounding crack.

Not a sound came from the crowd.

The dangling body slowly twisted and turned.

The Last Written Words of John Brown, 2 December 1859

I, John Brown am now quite certain that the crimes of this guilty land will never be purged away, but with blood. I had, as I now think, vainly flattered myself that without very much bloodshed it might be done.

WAR: 1861-1862

Kit Carson

11 April 1861, Boulder, Colorado

ELIJAH CORD PEERED along the long barrel of the Lancaster, closing off the surrounding world. His focus was the sights, his breathing, and his heartbeat. The late spring snow on the Front Range of the Rocky Mountains reflected the midnight moonlight, doubling the brightness.

Cord had been moving east from California for two years, taking wide sweeps north to Canada and south to Mexico. Last fall he'd crossed the Rockies further north in Wyoming and swung down into Colorado. He had no plan, just the growing pressure in his chest to move east. He missed the beauty and warmth of California, but ever since gold had been discovered eleven years ago, the place had taken on the air of an asylum for the insane. Hordes of easterners had descended on the Free Bear territory and Cord had been glad to leave it behind.

This winter, Cord had linked up with Kit Carson at Fort Bent in southern Colorado. They'd meandered north from there, finally arriving at a small encampment called Denver, twenty miles to the southeast. They'd been hunting ever since, supplying the new gold rush towns of Denver, Boulder and others scattered along the Front Range with meat and hides. Carson was moving slowly, an accident with a horse the previous year causing him great discomfort and Cord was glad to help his friend earn some money and for the company.

Tonight was another foray to continue that job. They'd decided to hunt at night when the moon was right, to keep the tenderfoot gold rush fools from scaring off the game. As Carson put it, even Colorado was getting crowded.

The mountain man sat cross-legged to Carson's left, silent, waiting for his partner to take the shot.

Cord mentally recited the Paiute hunting prayer that he had been taught, wishing blessings upon the spirit of the animal whose life he was about to take. Not quite praying to Preacher's God, but it was a form of God Cord could kind of understand in a familiar 'I aint expecting too much from you, but I'll pay due respect' sort of way. His finger caressed the thin metal sliver as he slowed both his breathing and time-sense. The space between heartbeats lengthened. At the golden pause between beat and breath, when the blood in his veins and the air in his lungs were both still, he began to pull back.

His heart surged unexpectedly.

Cord removed his finger from the trigger. He lifted the heavy barrel from the forked stick he was using as support and shifted on the buffalo robe separating him from the snow.

"Bad air," Cord whispered to Carson.

The old scout immediately pulled back the hammer on his current rifle, a Hawken .50 caliber, and turned his head to and fro, searching for the cause. While they had a clear view toward the herd of buffalo in the grassland to the east, behind them, to the west, low trees and scrub covered the landscape as the terrain rose up to the tilted slabs of rocks the locals called the Flatirons. Beyond the Flatirons towered the peaks of the Rocky Mountains.

Forty feet away, a half-dozen figures erupted from a clump of bushes and charged down-slope piercing the air with screams and war-cries. Arrows flashed by, one piercing Cord's buckskin shirt, creasing his side and continuing through.

Cord fired. He began reloading automatically, years of practice having trained his muscles to the task without conscious thought. Carson's Hawken roared to Cord's right and the mountain man was also reloading.

Two of the attackers were down.

Both men knew how close the ambushers were, how fast they were charging, and how long it would take recharge their weapons. To keep loading correctly and efficiently while four attackers raced toward them, shouting war cries and waving hatchets, required absolute discipline. Especially when two of the surviving four suddenly fired pistols.

A bullet snapped past Cord's head, missing by less than an inch, but he didn't veer from his task. Tamping the lead ball in the barrel, he tossed aside the rod. He pulled back the hammer as he threw the Lancaster to his shoulder. His second shot hit the lead man when he was less than five feet away, the heavy lead slug throwing the figure backward in a tumble.

Cord dropped the rifle and whipped out the Bowie knife he'd purchased in El Paso. Carson's second shot rent the air and he too went for knife.

A hatchet swung down and Cord blocked it with the heavy blade of the Bowie. He whirled, dropping the blade low, letting the attacker's hatchet slice air over his head. Cord slammed the point of the Bowie into the man's gut, then jerked with all this strength, razor sharp blade severing skin, intestine and then lung as it also sliced through two ribs and came to rest in the man's heart.

With a grunt, Cord pulled the knife out of the body and spun to face where Carson was dispatching the last attacker. Cord knelt, wiping off the blade on the dead man's shirt. He slid the Bowie back into its leather scabbard and grabbed the Lancaster, cleaning off the snow. He quickly reloaded. Cord paused momentarily, as the unique stink of a degenerate drunk wafted over him, and he got a good look at the man's face in the moonlight.

"Kit."

"Yes?" Carson was also reloading his rifle, scanning the mountainside for more intruders.

"What do you have there? Arapahoe?"

Carson looked closer at the body staining the snow crimson at his feet. "Looks like. What you got?"

"White man. Drunk."

"I suspect they're all drunk," Carson said. "You must have smelt 'em even though they was down-wind of us. Aint you glad you quit the spirits a while back?"

They quickly checked the other four and discovered the party consisted of another white and four Arapahoe. And the other white was alive, crawling on his belly upslope, leaving behind his pistol and hatchet and what remained of his life in a wide blood trail. Cord and Carson ignored him for the moment, checking the others.

All the dead did reek of alcohol, which helped explain the missed arrows and pistol shots. The Arapahoe were to be expected here as the local tribe was resisting the incursions of the gold seekers. The whites were a story that needed to be explained. Carson went to the wounded man and kicked him over on his back.

The man screamed in pain, hands clasped around his stomach, dark blood oozing through clenched fingers.

"Where you from?" Carson asked.

The man had a black beard and bloodshot eyes, which had more than a hint of desperation to them. He spit at Carson, but without any conviction.

The mountain man sighed. "Son, you a dead man. You got a lead ball straight through your gut. Nothing any doctor can do for you. All you can do is make your peace and go as easy as you can."

"Damn you," the man said.

"No, son, you be damned," Carson said. "You ambushed us. Why?"

"Gold."

Cord frowned. "We're hunters, not gold miners."

"Everyone going after gold here," the man said. "Give me something to drink. Please, mister. It hurts real bad."

"We aint here for gold," Carson said. "You and your buddy aren't from around here, are you?"

"From Kansas. Please, mister?"

Cord knelt next to the wounded man and pulled out his flask. He uncapped it and trickled a bit of liquid onto the man's lips. His tongue shot out like a snake, lapping up the light flow. Then he cursed at the water. "Something real to drink!"

"That's all you get," Cord said, capping his flask. He knew it wasn't good for a gut shot man to drink anything, just sped up the bleeding, but it wasn't going to make much difference. Carson had been digging through the man's pocket and came out with a hand-printed recruiting poster.

"You and your buddy are Border Ruffians from Kansas," Carson announced, reading the poster and giving the man the label of the pro-slavery element from that state.

"Long way from home," Cord said, looking east, where the Colorado High Plains drifted off to Kansas. He looked back at the man. "What are you doing here besides trying to steal gold from the wrong fellas?"

"Colonel says we're to ambush gold miners, get as much as we can to finance our cause back in Kansas," the man said. "Bribe the Arapahoe and other Injun tribes with whiskey and the like to cause trouble with the whites. Tie down Federal troops out here."

"'Colonel?'" Cord shook his head. "Secessionist militia?"

"Please, something real to drink," the man whispered.

"Why'd you come after us?" Carson asked.

"Wanted your muskets." The man's voice was almost inaudible. "Money. Whiskey." His head slumped back into the snow and rolled to the side.

Cord stood up.

"Everyone always using the Indians," Carson said. "The British, the French, we did, and now the slavers."

Cord stood. "It's not going to end until they're all dead."

"The slavers?"

"The Indians."

Carson glumly nodded. "They aint got many more years. But the slavers aint either. Can't keep people down like that forever. It's dancing on a powder keg, while smoking a big old cigar."

Cord walked over and sat back down on his buffalo robe with a sigh. He gently lowered the hammer onto the percussion cap. He lay the weapon across his knees and looked to the east, toward Bloody Kansas where pro and anti slavery factions had been battling for years and hundreds of men had already died.

Carson walked over, rifle in the crook of his arm. "What's wrong, Elijah?"

"I've got to go," Cord said.

Carson accepted the decision without argument. "You figger it's all gonna blow up?"

"I feel it," Cord said. "John Brown hanged. Lincoln elected with only forty percent of the vote. These fellows here, coming for gold, guns, whiskey and trouble. Some think it can be worked out. It can't. It isn't just the slavery issue. I went to West Point with some southern gentlemen. They're hardheaded, but worse, they got this crazy pride. It's going to go to hell faster than most expect. I was told once to expect war by a southern officer and there was a war. But remembering my meeting with him, I know there's gonna be another."

"You worried about Ben?"

Cord nodded as he stood and rolled up the buffalo robe. "Rumble thinks he can keep my son safe, getting him out of West Point and sending him off to that church school, but Rumble is still in the Army. Things are going to be bigger than him. And this time he won't be able to ship Ben and his sister to Natchez. That would be like sending them into the storm itself. And Ben is of fighting age. This war is going to suck everyone in. I need to find out where things stand with him. Keep him safe as best I can."

Carson gathered his gear. "Guess I need to be getting back to the missus and New Mexico. I figger we won't be safe from any war there either. Damn slavery fools will be stirring up the Navajo, trying to drag the territory into pro-slavery."

Cord shouldered the pack containing all his worldly possessions. Then threw the rolled up bear robe over one shoulder, shrugging, getting all the gear to settle in place, a comfortable burden. A routine he'd been following almost every morning for thirteen years.

Cord stuck out his hand. Carson gripped it with his own rough hand. They held the handshake for several moments, then let go.

"Beware a blizzard on the Plains," Carson said. "Aint quite like crossing the Sierras or the Rockies, but one of them storms in the open can be a bugger."

"You be careful down in New Mexico," Cord said. "Give my greetings to that sweet wife of yours and all your children."

Carson smiled as he thought of her. "I will." The smile disappeared. "I smell bad air, nasty bad air, from the east. Be careful, Elijah. There are worse things than blizzards awaiting you."

11 April 1861 Charleston Harbor

It was almost mid-April, 1861 and Captain George King stood tall in the bow of a small cutter riding the Atlantic waves. He was dressed in a United States Marine Corps field uniform, his boarding axe in its accustomed place in the sheath over his shoulder. Fort Sumter was a dark hulk ahead and to the port, a few subdued lanterns twinkling here and there on the parapets. There were several fully exposed lanterns by the Fort's dock, which supply ships used.

"Ease to port," King ordered. He could see a small boat tied up to the dock and a group of officers clustered there. "Steady," King said as the cutter came within two hundred yards of the fort. With a flurry of salutes, three officers in gray got into the small boat and it cast away.

King unbuttoned his double-breasted Marine frock coat and tossed it to the deck. He stepped on it as he pulled a new gray coat out of a bag and slipped it over his shoulders. The brightly shined insignia of the Confederate States Marine Corps, organized the previous month in Richmond, Virginia, glittered on the uniform collar.

"Intercept," King ordered as the small boat headed into Charleston Harbor.

When the two vessels were close, King yelled out a greeting. "Colonel Chesnut!"

"Who goes there?" A nervous Lieutenant was in the bow of the boat, pistol in hand.

"Captain King," King replied. "Might I speak with Colonel Chesnut?"

An older officer stepped forward as the cutter and boat bumped together, four hundred yards from Fort Sumter. "What is this about, Captain?"

"A Federal ship is closing on the harbor, sir," King reported. "The *Nashville.*"

"That's a mail courier," the Lieutenant said.

"It's *supposed* to be a mail courier," King said. "Who knows what it's carrying? I fear that the Yankees are preparing to make their push to relieve the fort this very night."

Colonel Chesnut shook his head. "Major Anderson gave me his assurances the truce will continue and he expects no movement this evening. We have his terms of surrender, and although they are entirely unacceptable, they are a point of negotiation. Resupply is not part of a negotiation."

"Colonel, Major Anderson is playing for time and he's not in overall command. Whatever Yankee swine commands their flotilla is planning action."

Chesnut ran a hand through his white beard. "These are serious issues. Come with me, Captain, and relay your information to General Beauregard. He must know of this right away."

King climbed down into the boat. The cutter he'd commandeered disappeared into the darkness as the boat continued for the Battery at the tip of Charleston.

Arriving, they found a party atmosphere. Civilians mixed with militia and cadets from the nearby Citadel. There were so many lanterns and streetlamps glowing, it was almost daylight, despite the late hour. Excitement and alcohol flowed in equal and multiplying abundance.

King followed Colonel Chesnut ashore. The older officer carried a small wooden box as if there were treasure inside.

"What is that, sir?" King asked.

"Fine cigars," Chesnut said. "General Beauregard sent them with his compliments to Major Anderson. The two knew each other at West Point. In fact, Anderson was the general's artillery instructor, so let's hope he taught well. A noble gesture, but like the un-gentlemanly Yankee he is, Major Anderson refused the gift."

The gentleman who had sent the gift to his enemy, the un-gentleman, was standing on a parapet, between two large guns, arms crossed, staring out at Fort Sumter as if he could will the fort to strike its colors and give in.

King was taken aback by his first glimpse of the general whom President Jeff Davis had sent to take command of the South Carolina forces. Another West Pointer, 'Little Napoleon', as King had heard him called in whispers, was newly arrived. Previous to that, he'd been forced out of the position as Superintendent of West Point when Louisiana seceded. The rumor circulating the city was that Beauregard had had the audacity to file a mileage reimbursement to the United States government for travel from West Point back to his home in New Orleans, before being ordered by Davis to South Carolina.

It had not been paid.

Beauregard did not look like Robert E. Lee, that was for certain. His skin was olive and smooth. His eyes had a droopy, sleepy appearance, as if he were either preparing to arise before dawn or retire after a late evening. His hair was an un-natural black, and if King had been better schooled in the ways of narcissism, he might have realized that Beauregard dyed his hair to match his goatee and thick mustache. Even here, on the eve of battle there were several ladies of Charleston in attendance on his every word and gesture.

"General?" Chesnut called out.

"Yes, Colonel?" Beauregard turned, uncrossing his arms and placing his left hand on the hilt of his sheathed saber as he slipped his right inside his dress coat, where a button was conveniently unfastened. King saw the circle of newspapermen writing down every movement the general made and every word he uttered as if it were coming down from the mountain.

"Major Anderson gave me a list of conditions for surrender," Chesnut said.

"'Conditions'?" Beauregard shook his head. "The major is being unreasonable. He is in no position to give conditions."

King stepped forward. "Sir, Major Anderson is delaying. I believe the Yankee navy is preparing a sortie. This very night. My reconnaissance cutter spotted a Federal ship making way to the fort."

Beauregard frowned. "Captain . . .?"

"King, sir. The Yankees are preparing to relieve the fort. They drew off when my cutter discovered them, but I fear they will come again in force this very night. We must act swiftly."

Beauregard twisted one end of his mustache. "There is much zeal and energy here, but little professional expertise and knowledge in the art of war. It is not such an easy matter to take a fortified position."

Memories of Captain McKenzie and the debacle on the *Somers* whispered like shadows in King's brain. "General, we can take Sumter now, easily, or face a pitched battle once the United States Navy moves in. I taught at the Naval Academy at Annapolis. With all due respect, sir, while you are certainly a master of land warfare, I know battle on the sea."

Beauregard looked out at the southern belles, the reporters, the militia, and puffed out his chest to make an announcement. "Negotiations have failed. I must take action. I will give Major Anderson notification via the mouth of a cannon."

Exuberant, wild cheers rose from the crowd. Women threw their arms around the nearest man. Militia and cadets hurried to prepare their cannon.

King didn't note the few people who stood forlorn, some with tears in their eyes as the implications struck them differently, including his mother, in the shadow of the house overlooking the Battery that used to be her home. Without realizing it, King took up a vantage point underneath the tree from which his father had hung himself.

4:30 am. Dawn was not far off.

A single mortar shell from Fort Johnson arced overhead and exploded directly above Fort Sumter. There was an eerie pause, as if the ocean was waiting for what came next.

Forty-three cannon and batteries of mortars from Fort Moultrie, Fort Johnson, the Battery, and Cummings Point let loose in a barrage worthy of the start of a war.

As the first shells smashed into the brick walls of Fort Sumter, the faint sound of cheering floated across the water from the surrounding land as an undertone to the sharper crack of cannon firing.

King stood underneath the magnificent oak tree and watched the opening of the inevitable war.

Master of the Horse

13 April 1861, West Point, New York

"CADETS!" MASTER OF THE HORSE Rumble snapped as he took the familiar spot on the floor of the riding hall. "Assemble, in-line, one rank."

The cadets of the class of 1862 scrambled out of the stands and fell in to the left and right of Rumble.

When all were in place, Rumble issued his second order. "Cadet George Armstrong Custer, front and center."

With a self-confident grin, Custer stepped out of the ranks and double-timed to a spot just in front of Rumble. Custer was just shy of six feet, broad shouldered and athletic. He had blue eyes and golden hair that lay on his head in a tumble of curling locks. The word circulating in Benny Havens was that Custer was quite the lady's man off-post. The word circulating in the Academy was that Custer was not quite the academic man, the Immortal in every section, overall ranking last in his class and lingering very close to being boarded out. In some ways, Custer reminded Rumble of Cord, but there was a dark edge to Custer that disturbed Rumble.

"Double-time to the stables, Mister Custer, and bridle your horse." Rumble made a show of looking at his pocket watch. "You have three minutes."

Custer dashed off.

"Cadets, at ease," Rumble ordered.

An instant buzz of excited conversation filled the riding hall. War was in the air. And not just war, but Civil War. Many southern cadets had already left the Academy, the first as early as the previous November, when a South Carolinian had departed, in anticipation of his state's secession. He was followed by all the rest of the cadets from South Carolina, three Mississippians and two Alabamians.

The divide touched the highest ranks of the Academy as the Superintendent appointed back in January, G. T. Beauregard, had lasted only five days before being relieved for his southern sympathies after advising a southern cadet who sought consul on whether to resign: "Watch me; and when I jump, you jump. What's the use of jumping too soon?" With his departure, old Delafield resumed the post for several months before a permanent replacement was appointed. Delafield was still on post, awaiting his next assignment.

The overwhelming feeling in the press was that most of the Academy was pro-slavery. But that was only to those outside of the gray walls. Rumble knew the cadets better than they knew themselves and it was more the fact that the southerners who remained were the loudest and most outspoken, airing their opinions freely and to anyone who would listen. The northern cadets had some sympathy for the plight of their southern brethren, but that sympathy had not been put to the test. There was a sullenness and brooding among the Northerners that few could interpret.

Behind Rumble, seated in the corner of the stands, writing in a leather journal, was Ben, now a young man of twenty. He'd grown with a spurt when he was sixteen, and was now two inches shy of six feet, but as slender as Grant had been as a cadet and Rumble feared his son would never fill out. Ben had his mother's face, soft, freckled and open. His most distinguishing feature was his bright red hair. He could be recognized all the way across the Plain from that alone.

This was his first trip back to West Point since Rumble had maneuvered his son's dismissal from the Corps and his entry into college in Maine. The few days had not been enough to thaw the chill between the two and Rumble had little idea where his son's feelings lay or what his thoughts were. But he had kept his promise to Lidia and saved his son from four years of hell and that was enough for now.

Custer came galloping back into the riding hall with a flourish. He urged the large horse toward the far end of the hall. Despite it's size, the horse was no York, at least a hand smaller than the long-deceased legend of the riding hall,

"Cadets," Rumble cried out. "Attention!"

The line snapped to. Rumble called out the names of two cadets to take the center position. He noticed out of the corner of his eye that Delafield, his hair whiter than ever, had entered the hall.

"Gentlemen, hold in place, wings forward to observe," Rumble commanded.

Using the two cadets as anchor, the lines on either side moved forward until all could see the two men in the center.

Custer reached the far end of the hall and waited.

Rumble turned to the line of cadets and raked his gaze left and right. He remembered Matamoros and the Mexican line, the steel glinting in the sunlight. He shivered and focused, once more grateful Ben did not wear the cadet gray. "Mister Custer, you may—"

A plebe came running into the riding hall, uniform collar unbuttoned, face flush with excitement. "It's war! Fort Sumter has been fired upon!"

Discipline vanished as the remaining southern cadets broke into cheers.

Rumble had no desire to restore order, nor would it be possible. The southerners ran out of the stables, yelling in excitement. The majority of cadets, northerners, filed out, engaged in earnest discourse, their faces serious.

Rumble went to the bleachers where Delafield stood, arms folded, looking grim. Ben came down to stand next to him.

"So it begins," Delafield said.

"Yes, sir." Rumble climbed up the steps and joined the two.

"How many copies of your report from the Mexican War did you make?" Delafield asked.

"Three. I gave you one and I kept one."

"And the third?"

"Lieutenant Grant asked for a copy. Seeing as he was present for most of the events in it, I thought it appropriate."

"Ulysses Grant? '43?"

"Yes, sir," Rumble replied.

"Interesting," Delafield said. "I still have my copy. Gave it to some in the War Department to read, but they had little interest. We won the Mexican War, so they didn't see any point to reading a report on it. After all, whatever we did, must have worked well."

"We could have done better, sir," Rumble said. "Saved a lot of lives."

"Of course." Delafield checked his watch. "It's late. Would you care to join me for dinner?"

"Certainly, sir."

"Mister Ben?" Delafield asked.

"Yes, sir. I'd be delighted."

The three walked up to the Plain and across it to one of the officer's houses lining the wide grassy parade ground. Excited chatter echoed over the Plain from cadet rooms. Delafield let them into his small quarters, where a servant bustled about, laying out a meal.

The former superintendent sat down, his old joints protesting.

"I'm surprised they didn't keep you on after replacing Beauregard, sir," Rumble said.

"I barely turned command over to Beauregard," Delafield replied, "before the War Department sacked him. Damn fool." Delafield sighed. "I'm an old war horse. They trot me out of the stables when they need a steady hand on the Academy."

"A most steady hand is needed now, sir," Rumble said. "Why don't they keep you on?"

"Because I'm old," Delafield said. "I held the fort for a little while. I'm sure your new superintendent will fare finely." He turned to Ben. "I am sorry about forcing you to leave the Corps."

"It wasn't your fault, sir," Ben said.

"A death-bed promise," Delafield said, shaking his head. "The words are like iron chains."

"I'm sure my mother had my best interests at heart," Ben said, "and events seem to be proving her correct."

"Ah, Lidia Havens." Delafield nodded. "She was a wonderful young woman. And quite prescient. It was a shame she passed before her time. And what of your sister? Abigail, isn't it?"

"Yes, sir. She's in Mississippi," Ben said. "With Grandmother Rumble, Miss Violet."

"Natchez, is it not?" Delafield asked.

"Yes, sir," Rumble answered. "My parent's place is just south of there."

"So they are in secess country," Delafield noted.

"Yes, sir." Rumble sat a bit straighter.

"How will they go?"

"With their state, sir," Rumble said. "They are Mississippians before they are Americans. But to be more accurate, they are slaveholders before they are Americans. It's their way of life. They know no other."

"Do you have kin of military age?" Delafield asked.

Rumble reluctantly nodded. "I have a younger brother. I'm sure he'll serve the state before the country although I'm afraid he's not made of war-like material."

"Brother against brother," Delafield muttered, as if to himself. "It is so sad." He tried perking up by focusing on Ben. "So how have you been doing at your school, young man?"

"I've been at the Seminary four years," Ben said. "I returned this past week to visit father and grandpa and grandma Havens."

Delafield shook off his moroseness. "Ah, your grandfather is quite the scoundrel. I heard he and Superintendent Lee did not mix well during that tenure."

Rumble nodded. "True, sir. Major Lee enforced the rules rather strictly, but the cadets still found their way to the tavern. And Benny outlasted Lee."

"As he has outlasted every superintendent," Delafield said, "including my repeated journeys back here. Benny Havens is the one constant we can count on." He turned back to Ben as the servant came bustling in with a large pot from which she began ladling stew. "Will you continue your studies at Bangor?"

Once more, Ben glanced at Rumble. "No, sir. The plan is for me to travel to Europe this summer to further my studies."

"Ah!" Delafield smacked the table with his open palm, making the silverware rattle. "I traveled to Europe five years ago. By order of all people, the now Confederate President, Jefferson Davis, who was the Secretary of War. We went to the Crimea to observe that conflict." He pointed at Rumble. "Much as your father went to Mexico. I made copious notes. McClellan went with me. Interesting fellow. We saw the siege of Sevastopol. Bloody and brutal affair. Nothing noble about it at all. Nothing noble at all," Delafield's voice once more slipped into a murmur. "Unlike what these southern fellows here think."

"I know, sir," Rumble said. "I believe Ben will enjoy Europe greatly."

"Are you removing him further from the fray?" Delafield quickly held up a hand in defense. "Pardon me, I mean no insult. If I had a son I would send him overseas by the fastest possible means. I have done enough service to my country for my family and so have you, Sergeant Major."

"I would if I could," Rumble said, "but this plan was hatched in Natchez by my mother a while ago. She's always looking ahead."

"She sounds like a formidable woman," Delafield said as he lifted his spoon. The spoon paused halfway to his mouth as he saw the chain around Ben's neck. "You have the ring."

Ben flushed. "Yes, sir. I know I don't deserve to wear it. But I've always had it on this chain. I hope it isn't inappropriate given that I didn't graduate."

"The ring was earned," Delafield said. "You should wear it proudly."

Rumble looked out the open door and stared at the Plain.

"I wish I could remember Mister Cord," Ben said. He glanced at his father. "It must be a great bond between two men to give something so precious to the son of his friend."

Delafield coughed, his face turning red. "Ah, yes. Shall we stop this talk of war and the past and focus on our meal and discuss Europe and more pleasant things?"

"Yes, sir." Rumble said.

"Were you ever in Paris, sir?" Ben asked.

"Oh, yes," Delafield replied. "I went there before—" he paused and cocked his head. "Do you hear that?" He shoved back his chair and went to the door, stepping out into the cool April evening air.

The sound was clear now. Young voices, singing at the top of their lungs, from the vicinity of the barracks. The cadets were into the third stanza and gaining volume with each line. The Star-Spangled Banner roared across the Academy:

Praise the Power that hath made and preserved us a nation.
Then conquer we must, when our cause it is just,
And this be our motto: "In God is our trust."
And the star-spangled banner in triumph shall wave
O'er the land of the free and the home of the brave!"

"Look." Delafield pointed as the last line floated away over the Plain, over the Hudson and into the Highlands. A small cluster of cadets was staring in the direction of the barracks. Southerners. For the first time since South Carolina had seceded, they were humbled and quiet. "Now they know what they face."

The Merrimack

21 Apr 1861, Norfolk, Virginia

"ENSIGN BROOKE, what do you see?" King asked the young Naval Academy graduate standing next to him on the dock.

A Union frigate, the *USS Merrimack*, was burning so brightly it lit the skyline of Norfolk. King had supervised sinking boats in the channel earlier in the night, trapping the ship, leaving the crew of the Federal ship no recourse but to abandon it. Scattered shots echoed through the night, but in celebration, not battle, as the Federals abandoned Norfolk, scurrying like rats aboard what ships they could get to sea.

"I see potential, sir," Brooke replied. "She's settled in the mud and the flames won't reach below the waterline. The engines will be intact along with the keel. We can raise her."

"Can you build your ironclad off her keel and engines?"

"Yes, sir. I can do it."

King slapped Brooke on the back. "Good man. We'll build it, then sail up the Potomac and shell the devil Lincoln in his own home. They won't be able to stop us."

"Well, there's a fellow named Ericsson in New York, whose screw design I—"

"Ensign!" King cut him off. "We will prevail because we are the more honorable and faithful people."

8 June 1861, Mississippi River

"He killed the Matlock brothers with a two shot derringer," St. George said.

"So he's a good shot and don't waste bullets," Sally Skull acknowledged.

The steamer fought against the Mississippi, paddle wheels churning muddy water. To the right, the lights of Vicksburg glittered on a bluff overlooking a sharp bend in the mighty river. Skull and St. George sat on crates up top of the boat, just behind the pilot house, left alone by the rest of the passengers out of tacit acceptance this was the boat owner's private area.

"He more than that," St. George said. "He—"

"I know who Nathan Bedford Forrest is," Skull cut him off. "You think I was born yesterday? He one of the biggest men on the river and worth over a million Yankee dollars. I know he's mean as a rattlesnake and cold as a blizzard. I know he owns this boat we riding on. I wouldn't be here for this meeting if I didn't know who I be meeting." She took a swig from the whiskey bottle on the shipping crate that served as a table between them. "The thing you got to remember, St. George, is that he smart. Wicked smart. He started with nothing, now he one of the richest men on the river. And he didn't get it cause his pappy gave it to him."

St. George bristled. "What you saying?"

"Just what I'm saying," Skull said, earning a confused furrow in the middle of St. George's forehead. She handed the bottle to the overseer. "Listen. This war that's here now. It aint gonna be short, it aint gonna be easy, and your people, they aint gonna win."

"What do you mean my 'people'?"

"The south" Skull said. "I was down in San Anton when Texas voted to secede. I—"

"Why was you there?" St. George interrupted.

"Always deals to be made," Skull said. "Especially to armies. Some Confederate big-wigs went to the old Alamo and got the Federal commander to surrender the arsenal, hand over ten thousand rifled muskets."

"That's good," St. George said, eyes always on the immediate.

"Let me finish," Skull said. "There was another Fed officer there, Robert Lee, a Virginian. I heard of him from the Mex War and he the one that trapped old John Brown. And I could tell he was surprised things was happening so fast. Heard him talking to another officer, saying the secces was fools. When they paroled him, he went back to Virginia, back to the Union. Struck me as a sensible man. And Sam Houston, the governor, let me tell you, he fought a lot of battles and he a smart man too and he was against seceding."

"Why?" St. George asked.

In response, Skull reached into one of the many pockets on her dress and retrieved a folded newspaper article. "Here what Ole Sam said and the damn fools still out-voted him to secede: *'Let me tell you what is coming. After the sacrifice of countless millions of treasure and hundreds of thousands of lives you may win southern independence, but I doubt it. The north is determined to preserve this union. They are not a fiery impulsive people as you are for they live in colder climates. But when they begin to move in a given direction, they move with the steady momentum and perseverance of a mighty avalanche and what I fear is that they will overwhelm the South with ignoble defeat.'*"

"'Ignoble'?" St. George spit. "I don't know what that mean, but it sound bad and he damn wrong. Any southerner worth ten Yankees."

"Houston's right," Skull said. "And that's why I'm here. Your tit at Palatine is going to run dry."

"We can grow cotton forever," St. George argued.

The steamer rounded the bend and Vicksburg was behind them. The sound of revelry from whiskey, gambling and other dark arts echoed up from the main deck.

"But can you ship it to them who buy it?" Skull asked.

"Why not? New Orlean still there. Aint going no place. War or no war."

Skull shook her head and grabbed the bottle back. "You don't know what's going on and I don't mean no insult, St. George. You're bound by that plantation. I travel. Mexico, San Anton, New Orlean, St. Louis. Up and down the river and beyond. I got ears everywhere that tell me what's going on. Those pompous asses who call themself the government of the Confederacy, you know what they got planned? They're going to let all the cotton sit for a year. No more trading."

St. George sat up straighter. "I aint heard nothing of that. Why?"

"They're fools. They think they can make England and France join their side if they be hurting for cotton."

"I don't get it," St. George said. "That sound stupid."

"We agree for once," Skull said. "What we need—" she paused as three men approached. One was a big man, two inches over six feet, with broad shoulders. He had a dark beard and, in the dim lights from the boat, his black eyes glittered with intelligence and danger. He had a curved cavalry saber dangling from his waist, an incongruous image on the riverboat. The second man was not quite as tall but also big, in the way of one who enjoyed his food, his belly bulging, his face swollen from drink. The man between them was much smaller and looked like a river rat cornered and trapped.

"You must be Skull," the tall man said, sticking out a powerful hand.

Skull took the handshake, feeling the squeeze and returning it as hard as she could with her callused hand. "Forrest." She recognized the fat man. "Father Declan. It's been a while."

"Ah, now lass, I'm no longer with the church," Declan said. "I found my faith lagging and thought it best to move on with me life. Whatever happened to the pretty young thing that was with you in Banquete?"

"Why you asking?"

"Ah, she was quite the blossoming flower—" Declan began but Forrest waved a hand, cutting him off as he turned to the man between them. He gripped the back of the man's neck. The man gasped as Forrest lifted him to his toes.

"Found out this piece of horseshit has been stealing from me," Forrest said. "Running a loose table in the gambling parlor and skimming the take."

The man started to protest but Forrest silenced him by smacking him in the face with his other hand, drawing blood from a split lip.

"I'm a fair man," Forrest said, his focus on St. George and Skull. "But I'm not a man to be crossed." He tossed the thief to the deck. "Fair means you get a chance to fight. That's the law of the river." He gestured at Declan. "Give him your knife."

Declan pulled a foot long knife from his belt and tossed it to the man. Forrest reached to his own waist and drew the heavy cavalry saber. It was unusual, sharpened on both sides, so he could slash in either direction with equal effect.

"That aint fair!" the man protested.

"It's as fair as a thief gets," Forrest said. He raised the saber and the man scrambled to his feet, the knife held with trembling hand.

"Please, Mister Forrest, I swear on my mother I aint ever again going to—" he didn't get a chance to finish as Forrest swung the heavy saber. The razor sharp edge caught the man in the neck and passed through skin, muscle and bone easily, separating head from body.

The momentum of the strike threw the head out into the darkness, to splash into the dark waters of the Mississippi. The body fell to its knees, blood spurting from a still beating heart, then crumpled onto the deck.

"You think maybe his eyes still seeing?" Forrest mused as he wiped the saber off on the man's coat. "Maybe his head's drowning while his body's still bleeding?" He stepped over the body and grabbed a crate. He slid the saber back in its scabbard and took a seat. Declan joined them.

"Mister Forrest, this here St. George Dyer," Skull said.

Forrest shook St. George's hand. "Y'all know what the fools in charge got planned for the cotton?"

"Do now," St. George replied.

Forrest grabbed the bottle without asking. "So what do you have planned?" he asked Skull.

"New Orleans will soon be out," Skull said. "So we run cotton north and south overland through Mexico."

Forrest seemed bemused. "North? To the Yankees? We're at war."

Skull shrugged. "There's plenty who don't care about the war except how they can make some money."

"Like you," Forrest said.

"Like me," Skull agreed.

"You don't support the cause?" Forrest asked, arcing one thick eyebrow in query.

"The cause will need money," Skull said.

"True," Forrest said. "And guns and medicine and a lot of other gear those smart boys in the capitol haven't thought about yet while they're busy waving the flag and pounding each other on the back about how honorable they be." Forrest turned to Declan. "You can get guns, right?"

"Yes indeed, sir," Declan said. "From Europe and up through Mexico. Rifled muskets, cannon, powder and ball. Expensive though," he added, almost apologetically, but not quite.

"Of course," Forrest said dryly. "Everything's going to be expensive soon. I want enough weapons to outfit my own regiment."

"Certainly," Declan said. "I have a shipment of muskets moving up river two days behind as we speak."

"Rifled?" Forrest asked. "Good quality? Won't blow up in my men's face when they pull the trigger?"

Declan hesitated, eyes shifting to the still warm body. "Perhaps a week before I can get a proper shipment to you, kind sir?"

"A week," Forrest confirmed. "And we're going to need as many cannon you can get your hands on," he continued. "The Yankees make most of the weapons. There isn't a forge this side of the Appalachians that can turn out large guns in any quantity in the Confederacy, except maybe in Nashville, and that's a couple of rivers away."

"Consider it done, good sir," Declan said. "And I assure you, the quality will be the best."

Forrest stared hard at Declan. "Some say you were the one who got those muskets John Brown used. You travel far."

"I travel where I'm needed, sir," Declan said.

"Who you really work for?" Forrest asked.

"My avarice," Declan said.

"Well, that's something that can be counted on more than most things," Forrest acknowledged, but he didn't sound convinced.

"There's something else to be done," Skull said.

"And that is?" Forrest asked.

"We won't be able to get everything you need through Mexico. Some things, it would be best if we went right to the source."

"And you have a plan for that." Forrest made it a statement.

"By the time Jeff Davis and those others figure out their self-blockade aint gonna make the Brits or Frenchies move," Skull said, "Union ships will be doing the job." She glanced at St. George before turning her attention back to Forrest. "We can run cotton north, but we can also send cotton overseas ourselves and get top dollar. Get in return those things people are gonna be wanting."

"How?" Forrest asked. "You just said the ports will be sealed by Yankee boats soon."

"Blockade runners," Skull said. She pointed at Declan. "That's where he comes in. He got the connections in England. They can build ships. Fine ships." She turned back to Forrest. "You have the money to pay for the ships. I'll make sure you get your investment back and more. And, you'll be helping the cause. And whoever you really be working for," she added to Declan.

Forrest nodded. "I approve."

"I'll get working on my part," Declan said. "I do indeed know some English fellows who build fast ships."

St. George had been fidgeting, on the periphery of the conversation and the plans. "I want to fight. Let me join your regiment, Mister Forrest."

Forrest shook his head and spoke before Skull could. "No. We need you to keep the cotton growing and moving, both north and south."

"But-" St. George began, but Forrest cut him off, placing a hand on the overseer's arm. "And we need you to stay in the Natchez area, keep the nigras in their place. All the fancy men going to be riding off to war. We need you to do the hard work you always been doing. The dirty work. But now it's more important than ever. Some of those nigras are going to be getting ideas in their heads. You need to destroy those ideas."

"I can do that," St. George said.

"Good," Forrest said.

"But I need a favor in turn," St. George said.

Forrest crossed his arms. "Yes?"

"You right about the fancy men riding off to war. Militia be forming up. The young master of my plantation, he going to be leading the local boys from Natchez. Once they in the army, they get sent where they ordered, right?"

"That's the nature of an army," Forrest said.

"I hear a big fight brewing in Virginia. Send 'im there. You got that kind of pull?"

"Consider it done." Forrest stretched his back out. Then picked up the bottle and took a deep drink. "Killing is thirsty work." He extended the bottle to Sally Skull. "And tell your man back by the paddlewheel to lower that rifle and come on over and join us for a drink."

"Gabriel!" Skull called out.

St. George was incensed. "What she doing here?"

"She'?" Forrest was amused.

"My daughter's with me, nothing strange 'bout that," Skull said as Gabriel came out of the dark shadow of the starboard paddlewheel, un-cocking a Spencer carbine. She slid the short rifle around to her back on a leather sling. Like her 'mother', she packed a pistol on each hip. She wore dungarees, a calico shirt and ornately engraved leather boots with metal tips, which upon closer inspection proved to be tiny skulls forged out of silver. She had a black felt slouch hat pulled low over her eyes, her hair pulled tight in a bun under it.

"She always cover your back?" Forrest asked Skull.

"She does."

Forrest held out his hand for the Spencer. Gabriel hesitated, looking to Skull for permission. She nodded and Gabriel handed the carbine over.

Forrest looked at the rifle. "Interesting. How many cartridges does it hold?"

"Seven round tube," Gabriel said. Her voice was cool and low, neither male nor female.

Forrest held it out to her. "Fire two rounds for me."

Gabriel took the rifle, threw it her shoulder, cocking the hammer en route and fired, indicating there had been a round in the chamber. She charged the lever around the trigger, extracting the expended shell, loading a new one from the tube under the barrel. She fired. All within two seconds.

"Impressive," Forrest said. He looked at Declan. "Can you get me these?"

"Well, dear sir," Declan said, "they are made in the north."

"So? She got one. And," Forrest added, "you got Northern connections since you shipped those Sharps Bibles to old John Brown, right?"

"I will do the best I can," Declan promised.

"You can work both sides," Forrest said to Declan. "It's the nature of fellas like you. I can't change that. Just don't ever be working direct against me. You got to make a choice, you make it in my favor. Clear?"

"Indeed, sir. Your point has been driven home."

Forrest stood up, ending the meeting. "We dock at Natchez in the morning. Go our separate ways. But let me tell y'all something. You saw what I do to thieves. I know y'all are going to make money. But don't go too far. Deliver what's been promised. The Cause comes first." He slapped his hand on the hilt of his saber. "Always!"

<u>11 June 1861, St. Louis, Missouri</u>

Elijah Cord reached out and gently removed the just-delivered shot glass from Ulysses S. Grant's hand. "Not now, Sam."

"I've tried to re-enter the service in vain," Grant said, not protesting the alcohol disarming. "I must live and my family must live. Perhaps I could serve the army by providing bread. I did that quite well in Mexico. Surely there are some who remember that. I was a good quartermaster."

The two West Point classmates were seated in a hotel lobby in Cincinnati; a wall removed from a bustling street where volunteer soldiers wandered to and fro, many of them drunk, with an occasional courier dashing by as if on an important errand. Cord sat facing the entrance, Grant across from him.

"What have you been doing?" Cord asked.

"Inducting regiments. I've helped train a few. But nothing permanent, nothing with a future."

"Who have you petitioned for a commission?" Cord wore his buckskins. His long rifle was leaning against the wall behind him. He kept one eye on Grant and one eye on the door. Grant wore mufti, his clothes patched and dusty, a soft black hat that had seen better days resting on his head.

Grant's jaw tightened. "McClellan commands here. A major general. Can you believe that? I'm older and I ranked him when I was in the Army."

"Sam, you haven't been in the Army for a while," Cord said. "What the devil happened?"

Grant's head drooped. "I resigned. Back in '54. They had me in the loneliest place a man could be. On the northern California coast. Fort Humboldt. Half a country from Julia."

"And?" Cord pressed.

Grant looked down at the amber liquid in the shot glass, then up at Cord. "You don't imbibe any more?"

Cord shook his head. "Haven't had a drop in years."

"Why not?"

A haunted look passed over Cord's face. "The price is too high when I imbibe."

Grant sat back in the rickety chair. "You know the spirits have always been cruel to me. They thought I was hiding my drinking at Humboldt. I didn't hide it. It was the same as it had been at Benny Havens, which means not much, but with ill effect. I just couldn't stand the loneliness. Being out there, doing nothing, missing Julia."

Cord remained silent, waiting.

Grant continued. "I was sick for a while. Then McClellan came through on some mission of exploration to the Pacific Northwest. To find the best route through the Cascades to Seattle. I fulfilled all his requisitions, but you know him—" Grant paused—"or perhaps you don't. A man who spends his time on the details and cannot see the larger picture. I believe he was behind it. My commander gave me a choice. Resign or face court-martial. I wanted to be with Julia more than I wanted to fight a court-martial although many urged me to."

"Then why come to McClellan for a commission?" Cord asked.

"Where else to go?" Grant said.

"Fremont has been assigned to command the Department of the West," Cord said.

"I don't know Fremont," Grant said, "and he's said to inimical to West Pointers. Plus he has not yet arrived to take his command. They say he tarries in the east making political connections and won't be here for weeks."

"That's the Fremont I know," Cord said. "Don't worry, once he gets here, I'll get you squared away. The problem is, he won't be here for a while and you can't be sitting around as a civilian that long. We've got to get you a command." Cord gestured to a passing waiter. He put the full shot glass on the man's tray and ordered coffee. "So you resigned. Tell me what happened next."

"I came east to Julia." Grant gave a bitter laugh. "I wasn't certain she would take me back. I made it to New York City on a loan. Then Simon Bolivar Buckner, you remember him, class of '44, on the Vigilance Committee, helped me in New York until my father wired money to settle my debts."

"I remember Buckner," Cord said. "And Nathaniel Lyon. They say he saved St. Louis from going to the Secessionists."

"And killed a group of civilians in the process," Grant said. "I will not go to him for a commission either even though he currently commands the Army of the West awaiting Fremont."

"You're awfully particular, Sam."

Grant shrugged. "My father tried to reverse my resignation by writing the war department. But old Jeff Davis accepted it as Secretary of War and would hear no more of the matter. And now," he said, coming full circle, "no one will have me."

"What of our friends?" Cord asked. "I know Rumble is still at the Academy. Sergeant of the Horse."

"I haven't spoken to him in years." Grant pulled himself out of his misery. "How is Lil 'Ben? I imagine he isn't so little any more"

"I went to Palatine as soon as I crossed the Mississippi," Cord said. "Things are grim there, but Mrs. Rumble assured me that Ben is safely ensconced in Theological School and would be traveling abroad before I would have a chance to make it to the east coast to see him. Did you know he entered the Corps briefly?"

"I did not," Grant said. "What happened? Why is he not still in gray?"

"Rumble and Delafield conspired to have him removed. Turns out Lidia extracted a deathbed promise from Rumble to never allow him into the Corps. Turns out Lidia was smarter than any of us, because the Corps, even now, still has whispers of what happened so many years ago and treated Ben like an outcast. Another thing that I can add to my long list of regrets in life. But since he is safe for now, that's why I am here and not there." Cord didn't want to discuss his own affairs any more. "What of Pete Longstreet?"

"Ole Pete went with his state," Grant said simply.

"We'll miss him in the days ahead," Cord said.

"We *will* miss him," Grant agreed. "He was best man at my wedding. Who'd have thought it would come to this?"

"Cump Sherman then?" Cord asked as he thought of dark prophets. "I talked to him in San Francisco when he was lawyering. His brother is a senator."

The waiter came by and slid two barely warm mugs of coffee onto the scarred table in front of the two men, snatching up Cord's dollar, accounting for both the untouched whiskey and the coffee.

"I saw Cump in late '57 in St. Louis," Grant said, eyes losing focus as he remembered. "I'd failed once more. Failed at farming. Told Cump that and he said West Pointers make poor farmers, merchants, mechanics and bankers. Cump's lawyering days in San Francisco didn't turn out well either. Then he was down in Louisiana, teaching at a military school, something he was more adept at. When the secess demanded he turn over the arsenal, he refused and came north. He passed through St. Louis not long ago, heading east. He has connections in Washington. His brother is indeed a Senator. I heard he got command of a regiment of volunteers."

"Then ask him for help," Cord said.

Grant shook his head. "I decline to receive endorsement for permission to fight for my country. I won't play politics. I'm a soldier. That should be enough."

"What should be and what is are often two very different things," Cord said.

Grant focused on his classmate. "Are you the same Elijah Cord I last saw in Mexico City?"

Cord allowed a slight smile. "Thirteen years on the frontier can change even the most obstinate fellow. I went through a little addition by subtraction." The smile faded. "I saw things."

"Apparently," Grant said.

"It's a long story for another time and place," Cord said. "I agree with you about the politicians. Too many men are seeking a commission to gain fame so they might further their future political agendas. What did McClellan say to you?"

"He didn't deign to see me," Grant said with unusual venom in his tone. "I sat there all yesterday and today. Sitting like a fool in his adjutant's office. Was told he was in meetings or out or kept with other business. There were many officers there armed with quills, Elijah. Quite an encouraging and rousing site. All those quills wielded by such martial men."

"Men with quills can be dangerous men on occasion," Cord said. "And you need a man with a quill to sign a piece of paper so you can get into this fight."

"What about you?" Grant asked. "Will you seek a commission?"

Cord shook his head. "No. For me that's a trap I cannot allow. I meant what I said in Mexico City."

"But Ben will be safe overseas," Grant said.

"When have you ever known things to work out the way they are planned?" Cord slapped Grant on the shoulder. "What if you go about it the other way?"

"And which way is that?"

"If you won't ask the politicians to appoint you, query the men to ask for you as a commander."

"What men?"

"The men you mustered in to service." Cord gestured toward the street. "Look out there, Sam. The lack of discipline. The lack of good command of the volunteers. Men want to be led. Especially men facing combat. Find a regiment you recruited that has weak leadership and have the men petition their governor for you to command."

"That's undermining whoever commands—" Grant began, but Cord cut him off.

"You got me to jump York," Cord said. "I know you can lead. This will be between me and you and whichever of the men of the regiment you speak to. No one else need know. It's better than sitting here and drowning your sorrows in whiskey. We're both aware that goes nowhere."

Grant nodded as the idea sank in. "It's a path."

"And you always get to your destination."

12 June 1861, Palatine, Mississippi

Violet Rumble stood in the shadows and held the cleaver in her gloved hands. She watched Tiberius's sweat-soaked chest rise and fall as he slumbered in the Mississippi June heat. The snoring was going to force her hand. The longer she stood there, the more convinced she grew of that. She had not shared a bed with her husband in fifteen years and she couldn't remember if he'd made this God-awful racket back then, but she couldn't imagine tolerating it for a night. Her nerves had been fraying for years and now that there was war, it seemed as if all was becoming unraveled, so she might as well follow the country's lead.

The heavy curtains to the room were closed, preventing the morning sun from illuminating the room and keeping any semblance of a breeze from penetrating the stifling air that reeked of sweat and alcohol. Tiberius lay on his back, wearing only his leggings, the blankets and covering thrown to the side, his discarded clothes littering the floor. He'd been driven back in his carriage from a meeting of the local militia the previous evening, drunk and delirious with joy over the mustering of a local company, which Seneca would command.

It was the joy that had snapped her. She'd fumed all night in her sitting room, furiously reflecting on her life and all the golden moments when she could have made a different choice and gone down a different path, and how all those moments were now lost in the past.

All she had was the time left her.

So at first light, she'd gone to the kitchen and taken the cleaver. Violet took a step toward her husband. Another. She reached the edge of the bed and brought the cleaver up.

The door creaked open behind her.

"Mother!" Seneca's hoarse whisper was more subdued than the snoring. More afraid to wake Tiberius than have his mother split his father's head like a melon.

Violet's hand trembled. A drop of sweat crawled down her nose, causing her to shift her focus from Tiberius to the glistening bead. It fell, staining her hoop skirt. Defeated once more, Violet lowered the cleaver. She walked out of the room, brushing by her youngest son without comment. She took the back stairs to the kitchen, Seneca hurrying to keep up. Violet slammed the clever down on the cutting board with a resounding whack.

"Mother, what—" Seneca couldn't find the words to ask the question to which he did not want to know the answer. He wore a fancy gray uniform, bare of rank and insignia, his sudden induction and promotion too fast for the accouterments to be sewn on. He did, however, still have his walking stick in hand.

Violet put on her brave face and smiled at her son. "You command the company?"

Seneca blinked. "Yes."

"And you've read of war. I've seen the books you've been perusing this past year."

"I have."

Violet gestured for Seneca to follow. She walked to the back door of the house and down the stairs. Together they wove their way into her garden until they reached the angel fountain. Violet sat down on the wooden bench while Seneca remained standing, hands fidgeting with his cane.

"Are you afraid?" Violet asked.

Seneca started. "Of course not!"

"I would prefer you be afraid," she said gently. "Fear has a way of making one wiser. When your brother came back from Mexico and retrieved Ben and Abigail, he would not speak of what he'd experienced. But I could see the effect. I don't exactly know what it is like, although I have fought my own form of conflict, but I am certain war is not what your father or all those other men think it is. It is not all glory."

"I will serve with honor," Seneca said.

"I'd prefer you serve with intelligence," Violet said. "Put honor on the back shelf if need be to come home." She placed her hands on his shoulders briefly, looking up at him. "I want you to come home safely, son."

Seneca was taken aback. "We go east in two days. By rail. The word is there's going to be a great battle in Virginia soon and all this will be over after we whip the Yankees. They'll learn their lesson."

"Why are you being sent east?"

"The governor ordered it," Seneca said. "He wanted Mississippi to be represented in the battle."

Violet frowned but said no more on that matter. "And if you meet your brother?"

Seneca blinked. "He's at West Point. Teaching riding, mother. I figure he'll stay there."

"I figured that for the last war," Violet said. "I don't like this. I don't like this at all. Men are damn fools."

"We have to fight, mother. We have to protect our way of life."

"Why?" Violet waved off the question and asked a different one. "How does Rosalie feel about all that has transpired?"

"She's not pleased," Seneca admitted, "but she has her time full running her father's plantation now that her mother is ill."

"Rosalie's a strong woman," Violet said. "It's good you give her a free hand to do what she does best." She reached into her hoop skirt and her hand came back out holding a pistol from a hidden pocket. "Your father's," she said, handing it to her son.

"Mother!" Seneca took the Starr revolver in his hands. "Father will miss it."

"He won't," Violet assured her son. She sighed. "It seems my fate to outfit my sons with guns as they go off to war. Lucius came back safely. I expect the same from you."

Volunteers

13 June 1861, Springfield, Illinois

"SIR, GIVEN THAT WE ENLISTED for ninety days and have been forced to accept three years of Federal service, we respectfully submit to you that we at least go into this war with a competent commander we can rely on." The young captain who made this statement stood at rigid attention, a trickle of sweat etching its way down each dusty cheek.

Governor Yates, the de facto commander of all the regiments mustered into service in Illinois, leaned back in his chair and steepled his fingers as he glared at the cluster of young officers crowded in front of his desk. The wood surface was piled high with paperwork and Yates had only made the time for this meeting because he'd already received several reports of unruliness concerning the 21st Illinois Regiment, which had arrived in the state capitol at dawn. And it wasn't noon yet. It was bad situation, which was only going to get worse.

"I could have you shot as a mutineer," Yates said, having no idea if the term applied to soldiers in addition to sailors. Or if he could have the man shot, which seemed like it would just be a waste of an officer and a bullet, both of which were needed at the moment. A muscle twitched in the captain's jaw and the other junior officers shifted uncomfortably.

"Did you come here just to complain or do you have a plan?" Yates finally asked.

The captain kept his eyes fixed on a spot above Yates head. His words tumbled out in a rush, obviously nervously rehearsed and delivered. "Sir, we were mustered into service by Captain Grant, formerly of the regular army.

And a West Pointer, sir. And he fought in Mexico, sir. We request him as Colonel of the regiment, sir."

"You do now? You request?" Yates was tempted to look over his shoulder and find what the young man was focused on. "Dismissed!"

The officers scurried out of the office. When the door shut behind them, Yates turned to his two advisors: the state auditor and an assistant in the adjutant general's office; both men had their ear to the ground politically.

"I haven't heard of this Grant fellow," Yates said. He waved a hand over the piles of paper on his desk. "I've got requests for commissions from every favored son in the state. Why have I not heard of him?

"He's from Galena," the auditor said. "His father is Jesse Grant; runs a tannery."

"That's his father," Yates snapped. "Grant's a West Pointer, for God's sake. How many of those do we have? Why hasn't he applied for a commission?"

The assistant handed the governor a cigar. "This Grant fellow believes himself—" he searched for a word—"separate from politics."

Yates laughed. "That's a change. But still. A West Pointer. Not many of those. What else should I know?"

The assistant and auditor exchanged a glance. "It's rumored he drinks, sir."

Yates laughed again. "Who doesn't? Especially now. Hell, a drinking man may be just what the 21st needs. At least he'll understand them." He waved a hand. "Give him the commission and give him the 21st. I don't want any more complaints from the mayor about rowdy soldiers."

15 June 1861, West Point, New York

Lucius Kosciousko Rumble sat in the grass in front of his wife's tombstone. The flowers he'd planted the first spring after her death were once more rising out of the ground at the base of the stone, searching for the light. They hadn't yet blossomed and Rumble knew he would not be here for that event.

War beckoned.

"Our son will continue to be safe," Rumble said in a conversational tone. "With what has occurred recently, you were even more right to get him out of the Corps. General Delafield asked me to accompany him to Washington in a few days. I'm to brief some war department bigwigs regarding my notes from the Mexican War, although the General is not confident they'll listen. Still, if I can save a life or two, it's most certainly worth the trip. Lil' Ben will accompany me as he hasn't been to the capitol. And to be honest, I'm not ready to say farewell to him yet." Rumble held up a hand as if the stone itself were protesting. "Fear not, dear Lidia. I've arranged passage on a ship for him from Washington to Europe. It sails next month. His point of departure has only changed, not the fact of his departure. He'll be safe in Europe and the war might well be over by the time he lands on those foreign soils."

Rumble reached forward and brushed some leaves away from a new bloom. "All right. I can't lie to you and never could. I don't think the war will be over swiftly. It'll be a bloody affair, much more so than most think as I've seen the mettle of the men who will command both sides and neither will back down. We taught them well here. Perhaps too well."

Rumble's head dropped slightly and he wiped a blue sleeve across his cheeks, brushing away the tears. They always came. No matter how many springs and how many blooms.

"Ben's a fine young man, my dear. You would be most proud of him. And Abby is breaking many a cadet's heart, but I keep close watch. Given current events, I will not allow her to accept some war-bound officer's ring."

Rumble reached out and ran his fingers over the words carved in the stone:

Lidia Rumble
Mother of Ben & Abigail
Heart of Lucius
1823-1842

Rumble took a deep breath, dropping his hand, and resuming his conversation. "Abby will stay here with Benny and Letitia while I'm in Washington. No traveling to Palatine, which I'm certain you'll be glad to hear. Things on the plantation are worse than they ever were. And my mother wrote to say Seneca has donned the gray." Rumble shook his head. "My brother in uniform is a sight I'd never thought I'd see, although, knowing Seneca, he will don the finest uniform available."

Rumble bowed his head. "Sometimes I think it all started that day Agrippa saved me from the river. That all would have been as it should have been, the way mother and father planned it—"

"Who was Agrippa and why was I named after him?"

Rumble stiffened as he recognized his son's voice behind him. He didn't turn his head. "What are you talking about?"

Ben sat down next to his mother's tombstone, meeting his father's eyes. "I'm not deaf and dumb, father. You were just speaking of Agrippa and since I haven't saved you from a river, it must be someone else. And I heard the whispers and saw the looks when I was at Palatine. Even though it felt like living in a prison, never being allowed out of the great house except on special occasions, I was still able to pick up some rumors and I know there was another there with the name. That place abounds in secrets and whispers. You gave me this name for a reason. If I'm going to be parted from you overseas for several years, I need to know that reason."

"In case war consumes me and the story is lost forever?" Rumble asked.

"Let's not speak of that," Ben said.

Rumble stood, dusting the grass and leaves off his uniform. "Agreed. At least not in front of your mother." He led the way out of the cemetery. Ben walked alongside.

"Imagine growing up at Palatine," Rumble began. "Do you sense my mother's plans for you?"

"She views me as heir to the plantation unless interrupted by Uncle Seneca and Aunt Rosalie having a—"

Rumble cut him off. "That's one secret that has been withheld from you. They will never have a son. It's impossible."

"Might I know why?" Ben asked as they exited the cemetery and turned left, heading toward main post.

"You may not, as it's a personal matter between your aunt and uncle."

"Yes, sir."

"My mother had plans for me also. So did my father. Back when they spoke to each other civilly, they hatched the great plan, which they envisioned as becoming my life. Graduating West Point was part of that. Beyond that, the plantation, politics, and more."

"So marrying mother was not."

Rumble nodded. "They had other ideas. I was disowned by my father as soon as he found out."

"Why did you turn against their plan?" Ben waved a hand. "Sorry. That was a foolish question, having spent time at Palatine. It wasn't the future you wanted."

"It wasn't," Rumble agreed.

The Plain came into sight, a handful of cadets drilling. With more earnestness than in previous years.

"Father. Who was Agrippa?"

"My best friend and a slave."

Rumble didn't break stride, although his son paused in surprise for a moment, before catching up. Rumble continued. "Do you remember Mary? She passed away this past winter?"

"Of course. She practically raised me while I was at Palatine and you were in Mexico."

"Mary might as well have been my mother also," Rumble said. "She had a son, just six months older than me. Agrippa. We spent our youngest years together."

"Then it's natural he should be your friend."

"It was not natural. Not in Mississippi." Rumble stopped on the edge of the Plain and turned to his son. "You might have heard whispers at Palatine, but you never went to Shantytown, did you? You never saw the other side of the plantation. It was anything but natural for a white man and a slave to be friends. It happens, but no one speaks of it and you are supposed to outgrow it."

"What happened?"

Rumble started across the Plain. "I thought I was doing a good thing." He gave a bitter laugh. "It seems as if every time I think I do a good thing it turns out worse than I could have ever conceived."

Father and son walked in silence. They reached the stairs to Kosciuszko's garden. Rumble led the way to the small island of solitude. He gestured for Ben to sit on the bench, while he strode back and forth, unable to be still as the long bottled up story finally spilled out.

"We spent all our days together when we were small. From sunup to sundown since Mary worked in the big house and brought him with her. Of course, things changed when we came of age. Me for schooling and Agrippa for the fields. And that should have been it. No more friends, no more talking. But we'd grown too close. I was too alone in that big house as my mother dealt with my father. And Agrippa was too miserable in Shantytown and in the fields.

"So we would meet. Whenever the moon was full so we could see. On Sundays, when the slaves were given their only time off." Rumble paused for a moment sighed deeply. "He saved my life."

"The river," Ben said, startling his father.

"How do you know that?"

"The way grandmother despises it. She would never let me near it unless carefully watched. And never allowed me to go in it. Constantly warned me against the Mississippi as if it were an enemy."

Rumble nodded. "One Sunday Agrippa and I snuck down to the old dock to do some fishing. It was so damn hot, we thought a dip in the river would cool us off. I jumped off the dock first. Not ten feet from the shore. And the current took me. Agrippa didn't hesitate, he dove right in and got me to shore. In return for saving my life, I committed a crime. A most grievous crime as it turned out."

Rumble stopped and stood at the edge of the garden, on the very edge of the cliff over the Hudson River. The water from the small fountain ran by his right foot and tumbled down the rocks.

"I taught Agrippa to read. And by doing that, I killed him."

Ben opened his mouth to speak, but then shut it, waiting for the story to make its natural course much like the fountain water went to the river.

"It's a crime to teach a slave to read," Rumble said. "I knew it. But Agrippa, his mind . . ." Rumble searched for the words. "He wanted more. He wanted to know of the world beyond the fields even if he was bound to them by chains. The world he knew he would never get to see. So I taught him to read and gave him books and he traveled in his mind. But it was something he read that killed him.

"We always suspected that John Dyer and his son, St. George, were stealing from the fields. It was tacitly accepted by my father. At least that's the best I could figure, although later events proved there was much more to that than we could have ever imagined."

Rumble rushed on, the dam breached, the reservoir of darkness behind it having to be emptied. "Agrippa read an invoice on one of the wagons they loaded and shipped across the Mississippi. He read how much was being taken, and who the buyer was. Except he was caught reading. St. George shot him and tossed him in the river when they came back across from Vidalia. His body was taken by the Mississippi."

"How do you know this?" Ben asked.

"I was told what happened by another slave who was on the boat."

"Why didn't you go to the sheriff?"

Rumble shook his head. "The law? It's within an overseer's province to kill a slave as long as the owner allows. They're property. And my father allowed the Dyers anything they needed to run the plantation. I'd broken the law."

Ben got up and went over to stand beside his father. The Hudson was dotted with sails and a steamship was chugging steadily up river.

"I'm sorry about your friend."

"Thank you."

Ben hesitated, then asked. "And the ring?"

"Enough of the past for today," Rumble said.

"No," Ben said. "The way the Corps treated me. How you got me dismissed. And yes, father, I know it was you. Why did they treat me that way? What secret are you hiding from me? Who is Elijah Cord? Why do I have his ring?"

"Enough questioning!" Rumble shouted. "I'm your father. Your mother didn't want you to enter the Academy. She made me swear to that as she was dying. They were her last words. Isn't that enough?"

"Why did she make you swear that?" Ben asked.

Rumble turned and placed his hands on Ben's shoulders. "War is horrible. It uses lives up like they matter nothing. Your mother was smarter than all of us. She didn't want your life wasted like that."

Ben stared into his father's eyes for many seconds, then nodded. "I'll believe you about that, father. I'll take your word for it. There's much I don't understand, but perhaps time will give me that knowledge."

Rumble turned away from his son and looked out over the Hudson.

Ben sighed. "Grandmother wrote me. She says your brother took a commission with the Confederates."

"I know."

"What's your stand, father?"

Rumble turned in surprise. "You have to ask? I wear the blue. I swore an oath to the Federal government. I won't break my oath."

Ben shook his head. "That's not what I ask, father. For now, everyone speaks of loyalty to state or country. But few raise the deeper question this war begs to answer. Where do you stand on slavery? For when the Union wins, that institution will not stand."

"They've taught you well in Maine." He gestured up toward the Plain. "Most of the cadets here think only of the combat, of the Confederacy and the Union. They don't understand the currents underneath. Like the Mississippi, this war hides much right now, and many will be caught unawares."

"You haven't answered, father."

Rumble gave a wry smile. "You have your mother's persistence. Of course, I'm against slavery. And that's why I will be in this fight."

18 June 1861
Springfield, MO
21st Illinois Regiment

The undersigned, having been duly appointed Colonel of the 7th Congressional District Regt of Illinois Volunteers by order of Govr. Richard Yates, hereby assumes command.

In accepting this command, your Commander will require the cooperation of all the commissioned and non-commissioned Officers in instructing the command, and in maintaining discipline, and hopes to receive also the hearty support of every enlisted man.

Colonel Ulysses S. Grant, Commanding 21st Illinois

12 July 1861
Quincy, MO
21st Illinois Regiment

The Colonel commanding this Regiment deems it his duty at this period in the march to return his thanks to the Officers and Men composing the command on their general Obedience and Military discipline. Having for a period of years been accustomed to strict military duties and discipline he deems it not inappropriate at this time to make a most favorable comparison of this command with that of veteran troops in point of Soldierly bearing, general good order, and cheerful execution of commands.

Colonel Ulysses S. Grant, Commanding 21st Illinois

U.S. Grant on Traitors and Patriots

Galena,
April 21st, 1861.

DEAR FATHER:
We are now in the midst of trying times when every one must be for or against his country, and show his colors too, by his every act. Having been educated for such an emergency, at the expense of the Government, I feel that it

has upon me superior claims, such claims as no ordinary motives of self-interest can surmount. I do not wish to act hastily or unadvisedly in the matter, and as there are more than enough to respond to the first call of the President, I have not yet offered myself. I have promised, and am giving all the assistance I can in organizing the company whose services have been accepted from this place. I have promised further to go with them to the State capital, and if I can be of service to the Governor in organizing his state troops to do so. What I ask now is your approval of the course I am taking, or advice in the matter. A letter written this week will reach me in Springfield. I have not time to write to you but a hasty line, for, though Sunday as it is, we are all busy here. In a few minutes I shall be engaged in directing tailors in the style and trim of uniform for our men.

Whatever may have been my political opinions before, I have but one sentiment now. That is, we have a Government, and laws and a flag, and they must all be sustained. There are but two parties now, traitors and patriots and I want hereafter to be ranked with the latter, and I trust, the stronger party. I do not know but you may be placed in an awkward position, and a dangerous one pecuniarily, but costs cannot now be counted. My advice would be to leave where you are if you are not safe with the views you entertain. I would never stultify my opinion for the sake of a little security.

I will say nothing about our business. Orvil and Lank will keep you posted as to that.

Write soon and direct as above.
Yours truly,
U.S. GRANT.

Letter from Sidney Albert Johnston in 1862

Vicinity Shiloh, TN 23 years later
Regarding Grant's invading Army of the Tennessee

5 April 1862
To The Soldiers of the Army of the Mississippi:

I have put into motion to offer battle to the invaders of your country. With the resolution and discipline and valor becoming men fighting, as you are, for all worth living or dying for, you can but march to decisive victory over the agrarian mercenaries sent to subjugate and despoil you of your liberties, property and honor. Remember the dependence of your mothers, your wives, your sisters, and your children on the result; remember the fair, broad, abounding land, the happy homes and the ties that would be desolated by your defeat. The eyes and hopes of eight millions of people rest upon you; you are expected to show yourselves worthy of your lineage, worthy of the women of the South, whose noble devotion in this war has never been exceeded in any time. With such incentives to brave deeds, and with the trust that God is with us, your generals will lead you confidently to the combat—assured of success.
C.S.A. General Sidney Albert Johnston
(West Point class of 1826)

Mark Twain
14 July 1861, Florida, Missouri

"**F**LORIDA CONTAINED BUT one hundred people when I was born here twenty-six years ago and I increased the town's population by one percent. This is more than many of the best men in history could have done for a town."

The speaker held an old smoothbore musket in sweaty hands, and he licked his upper lip nervously, a bushy black mustache adorning the space between mouth and nose.

"Now ya get the chance to defend your town from the Yankees, Sam," the man next to him said.

Both men were dressed in civilian clothes, dirty from weeks spent foraging and traveling to and fro across Missouri following the orders of confused and amateur officers. How they'd ended up here was pure chance, the vagaries of war. It was early morning, and the dew had yet to be burned away by the mid-July heat. It was the most comfortable time of the day and would soon be gone.

"I did leave when I was four, though, so I have no particular fondness for the place," Samuel Clemens noted.

"Aint much to it," his friend agreed as they took in the muddy lane that ran through the small cluster of cabins. The two guards held a position just south of the hamlet where the road peaked a knoll, so they could see in both directions. "Why the devil does this Union Colonel want this place?"

"Probably same reason we're standing here," Clemens said. "Someone told him to."

Behind the two pickets, in a trampled cornfield, a cluster of makeshift shelters and men rolled in blankets constituted the small unit sent to defend Florida, Missouri from the Union incursion. It consisted of Clemens' own group, the self-named Marions Rangers, and other bands of men that could not quite be called a company of light infantry, although they would agree on the light: light on weapons, light on food and light on discipline.

Hush." Clemens turned his head, listening. "Riders coming." He tapped his partner on the shoulder. "Best get the Colonel."

A half mile away, on the other side of Florida, Missouri, Elijah Cord raised a fist in the air, halting the small scouting element. It consisted of him and three other men who'd happened to have their own horses when they enlisted. Colonel Grant's cavalry, Cord had dubbed the trio. He had turned down a commission and 'signed on' as scout with the 21st Illinois by dint of shaking hands with Sam Grant. Unpaid, of course. Which meant he was pretty much a free spirit, allowed to come and go as he pleased, although his allegiance to Grant bound him with greater ties than any commission or pay stub could have. He was anxiously awaiting confirmation from Lucius Rumble that Ben was safely at sea and heading toward the European continent, but the war was disrupting mail service and the past weeks spent in the field had slowed the incoming mail from a trickle to nothing.

"I smell bad air," Cord said, peering down the lane toward the small town, which appeared deserted. The road rose on the far side of the town toward a hilltop.

"'Bad air'?" one of the men repeated.

"Wait here," Cord ordered as he dismounted and handed the reins to the man.

Cord cocked the Lancaster as he wove his way through the woods on the east side of the road, every sense honed by thirteen years surviving the frontier on alert. He circumvented the town and halted at the edge of the wood line near the top of the hill on the other side. He spotted the cluster of sleeping men in the cornfield and the single, nervous picket on the summit watching the road. Cord put the Lancaster to his shoulder and took aim right at the big black mustache.

Cord felt the rhythm of his heart, the pace of his breathing, his finger on the trigger. It was an easy shot, about three hundred feet. Unbidden, the hunting prayer came to his mind and he slid his finger off the trigger.

"You a lucky fellow," Cord whispered.

Besides, he reasoned, it would alert the Confederates if he killed the picket. That was what he told himself as he let the hammer slowly back down on the cap and backed up, retracing his steps to the soldiers waiting with his horse.

"Confederates on the other side of town," Cord informed them. "Maybe a company, maybe less. We need to let the Colonel know."

They galloped back the way they had come, heading toward Colonel Grant and the bulk of the 21st Illinois.

Back above Florida, Sam Clemens was trying to shake off the unexpected chill that had suddenly run down his spine.

His fellow picket came running up. "Colonel on his way."

"You know, maybe this soldiering aint such a good idea?" Clemens suggested. "That fellow last night said there's several hundred of them Yankees coming this way and they're well equipped and trained." He jerked his thumb over his shoulder. "We aint exactly Caesar's legions."

The Colonel, their nominal commander, came striding up, hand on the hilt of his sword. "See anything, men, other than hearing some horses?"

"No, sir," Clemens said, "but I got a bad feeling."

The Colonel peered down the road. "You aren't the only one, son." He looked about. "All the townsfolk cleared out. Hell, all the livestock cleared out. My daddy taught me a lot of things, and one of them is when the livestock clears out, it's a sign."

A mile away, coming down the road at a trot, Cord met Grant, who was at the head of the long line of men in dusty blue. Grant gave the order for the regiment to halt and deploy flank security in a normal tone, the regimental sergeant major relaying it in a deep voice. Grant rode forward, out of earshot of the men, gesturing for the other three riders to join the column.

When they were alone, Grant used a bandana to wipe the sweat off his brow. "What've you seen, Elijah?"

"Less than a company of Confederates on the south side of the town, just over that hill. Not well armed and they don't look too organized, but they got guns."

Grant took a deep breath.

"Are you all right, Sam?" Cord asked. "You've faced hot lead before."

"But never in command, Elijah." He nodded his head toward the long line of blue behind him. "I'm responsible for all these men. Now I know what old Taylor felt in Mexico." Grant turned in the saddle. "Sergeant major, detail one squad from each company to fill canteens from that creek yonder, then we'll resume the march."

When the men were all well supplied with full canteens, Grant gave the order to advance. Cord rode at his classmate's side, the Lancaster balanced across the pommel of his saddle. A trickle of sweat escaped Grant's blue hat and ran down his forehead.

"That worried about the men?"

Grant replied in a low voice. "My heart is high in my chest, almost into my throat."

"Well," Cord said, "as my old friend Kit Carson once said, being nervous facing combat makes you normal."

They entered the town and rounded the bend, with a clear view of the hill.

"Picket's gone," Cord said.

Grant began giving orders, deploying skirmishers to the flanks and preparing the column to deploy into line. The essence of Infantry combat was to be able to achieve the latter task. Marching four abreast, the 21st had ten companies, each authorized one hundred men, but all short of that. What Grant had been drilling the men to do for the past month was to go from four abreast to twenty-five wide and four deep at a single command, or even fifty wide and two deep. It was much more difficult to achieve than those untrained in the military arts realized. Beyond those commands, there were numerous others that would advance, halt, wheel, pivot, and do many other maneuvers. All designed to get the mass of men with their firepower to move as one. More difficult, was to have all those men conduct those maneuvers in the face of an enemy force and incoming artillery and musket fire.

The lead company spread out as they reached the top of the hill. The other companies peeled off at Grant's commands, left and right, the woods making the maneuvers they'd practiced on the open fields more difficult.

"Sam," Cord said. "Remember Old Pete and the wolves that night? The night Ben was born?"

"Yes." Grant glanced at Cord and gave a slight smile. "Good point."

Cord and Grant crested the summit and reined in their horses.

The Confederate camp was deserted.

Cord laughed in relief. "Hell, Sam, they were as afraid of us as we were of them."

Grant slowly nodded. "I'd never thought of that. All through Mexico it never occurred to me." He turned toward Cord and grinned, the sparkle back in his eyes. "But I'll never forget it from here on out."

17 July 1861, Washington DC

Rumble was heartily sick of the capitol. Mid-July was the time when any native of the city with an ounce of sense made for the hills of Virginia for relief from the heat. But not this summer. For those hills were now enemy territory.

It wasn't the heat that bothered Rumble so much, but the sycophants who crowded the city, seeking appointments to jobs where they could draw a government salary and also keep from going into the army. It seemed as if he and Delafield were last in line to every person they were supposed to see.

"Where to today?" Ben asked.

They were housed in the sweltering attic of a private home, the best accommodations that Delafield had been able to procure for them in a city at the center of war. A window fore and aft had been thrown open, but no welcoming breeze disturbed the air as Rumble buttoned his blue tunic up to the throat.

"I'll find out when I meet the General," Rumble said. He grabbed his leather-bound folder containing the transcribed notes from all the little books he'd carried through the Mexican War. So far no one had asked to read them, never mind get a copy.

Ben stretched his arms over his head, yawning. "I believe the Founding Fathers were not as wise as I once thought for making this intolerable place the capitol. And think; Richmond is but a hundred miles distant. It seems as if one army or the other were to sneeze, they would take the other's capitol."

Rumble was grim. "It will take more than a sneeze either way."

"That's not the word on the street. They say McDowell is preparing the army for an attack on the Secessionists very soon and the war will be over before we know it."

"*They* always say many things," Rumble said, "and rarely are *they* right."

He led the way down the narrow stairs and out a side door. Exactly on time as General Delafield's carriage rattled to a halt, the driver pulling back hard on the leads.

"Sergeant Major!" Delafield called out from the back seat.

Rumble saluted. "General."

Delafield greeted Ben hurriedly, while gesturing for Rumble to climb on board and checking his pocket watch.

"I'll see you this afternoon," Rumble said as he boarded the carriage. It was moving before he was seated, leaving Ben in cloud of dust.

Rumble grabbed hold to keep from tumbling over the side. "What's the hurry, sir?"

"We've been summoned." Delafield was looking through his thin leather briefcase, checking to see if he had whatever papers it was he thought he was missing.

As they raced through downtown Washington, it seemed a city in disrepair, although it was actually a city paused in building. The monument to Washington was a stump, abandoned by a bickering Congress. The Capitol Dome was also incomplete, although cranes hovered over it, a hint that perhaps some progress might be made, some day, but not this day. Troops were camped everywhere as more and more volunteers poured in. Regiments were even being housed on the floor of Congress, which was perhaps a better use of the chamber.

"Sir, if you would tell me—" Rumble paused in mid-question as the carriage pulled up to the gate for the President's House, also called by some the White House, and whose official title was the Executive Mansion, which no one called it.

A pair of armed soldiers lounged in the shade of a wilted tree and one took a tentative step into the early morning sun to offer a token of security. He saw Delafield and Rumble's uniforms, gave a half-hearted salute and then the carriage was pulling up to the building.

A servant flipped down the step on the side of the carriage and helped General Delafield disembark. Rumble hopped down behind him and followed as they were escorted into the White House.

People hurried to and fro, a good third in uniform, and one hundred percent of them ignoring the newcomers. A one-star general was nothing to get excited over in these hallways or in this city. Delafield halted in the main hallway, as lost as Rumble.

Rumble leaned close to the old man. "Who are we to see, sir?"

"A lawyer named Stanton," Delafield said. "He works for Secretary of War Cameron and was Attorney General under President Buchanan."

"Shouldn't we be at the War Department then, sir?"

"I received a note last night to be here," Delafield said.

A large man waded down the hallway, everyone parting for him. He had steel-rimmed glasses, a fringe beard like Delafield's, and a look on his face that indicated permanent displeasure.

"Delafield? I'm Stanton."

"Yes, sir. This is--"

"Come with me." Stanton was heading back the way he'd come before Delafield could get another word out.

They went upstairs, down another crowded hallway. A young man sat at a tiny desk outside a door at the end of the hallway.

"Gentlemen, wait a moment please."

The young man opened the door and leaned in. Looking past, Rumble could see four boys pinning a man in a frock coat to the floor in a rough and tumble wrestling match. The door shut before he could make out much more and seconds later, the boys were squirting out the door, laughing and giggling.

The young man nodded at Stanton and indicated the open door.

The three men crowded into a small room dominated by an unusually tall desk. Behind which sat an unusually tall man. Delafield and Rumble snapped to attention in the presence of the President as the door shut behind them.

"Sit down, please," Lincoln said, waving toward a hard wooden bench on their side of the desk. Stanton went and stood by an open window, peering out, as if he had no interest in anything that might happen inside the room and wanted to grab as much fresh air as possible.

Lincoln looked different than the etchings Rumble had seen in the papers. His nose was the first thing one noticed, followed by the prominent cheekbones, with skin drawn tight over them. But then the eyes trapped Rumble's attention.

Rumble and Delafield sat on the bench, backs not touching the wood, much like plebes were forced to sit at meals at West Point.

"Willie and Tad like to bring their friends into the house," Lincoln said. "And it does me good to play every once in a while or I might get grumpy. Willie just received a pony the other day. I was going to refuse the gift, but he fell so in love with it, I ended up paying the benefactor out of my own pocket for the animal in order to keep it and avoid any sort of impropriety."

Rumble glanced at Delafield, unsure if they were supposed to respond to this, but the former superintendent remained silent, so he followed the lead.

"General Delafield," Lincoln said. "It was good of you to hold the reins at the Academy after that fool Beauregard displayed his southern tendencies."

"I am always glad to serve my country, sir," Delafield said.

"Would that all military men felt the same way," Lincoln murmured, more to himself than the others.

"Sir," Delafield said, "if I might introduce—"

"Sergeant Major Rumble," Lincoln said. Surprisingly, Lincoln stood and leaned over the desk, extending his hand. Rumble scrambled to his feet and met the President's firm hand.

Lincoln held the grip for a second. "I can always tell a lot about a man from his shake."

Then the President sat back down, put his feet up on the desk while leaning so far back in his chair, that even Stanton started, expecting to see the President fall over backwards. Their concern was for naught as Lincoln laced his fingers behind his head and began speaking, as if to the ceiling.

"I was in the military for a little while during the Black Hawk War," Lincoln said. "One of the proudest moments of my life was when the men in my company elected me captain. Of course, they did not do so out of any sense that I had the genius of a Mars. I could wrestle well, which they somehow seemed to believe lent itself to leadership."

Lincoln was gazing at some spot on the ceiling. Rumble was tempted to look up, but he kept his eyes on the President as he continued.

"One time we were on the march and we came upon a split rail fence. There was a narrow gate in the fence, but I fear I could not remember the proper commands to go from the march formation to the appropriate movement to get us through the gate in a military manner. So I simply called a halt, ordered the men to fall out for a few minutes and reform on the other side of the fence in formation. It worked." Lincoln dropped his feet off the desk with a heavy thud and sat up straight. "However, no one was firing at us at the time. I suppose that would have made my maneuver disastrous."

Lincoln sighed and for a moment he looked old, very old, the lines in his face falling into each other and the dark pockets under his eyes telling of restless nights.

"General McDowell will move on Richmond soon. And many say that hopefully this war will be over soon. Are you a hopeful man, Sergeant Major Rumble?"

"In this instance, I am not, sir," Rumble replied.

"Really? A rarity in this city." Lincoln looked past Stanton, out the window. "They stopped building Washington's monument in '54 when the pockets of the people donating were empty. Congress was going to appropriate the money to finish it, but then the states got to haggling. Alabama wanted the monument to have stone from every state and once that can of worms was opened Washington's tower was doomed to gather dust." Lincoln fell silent for a moment. "And then there's the capitol dome. Also incomplete. I can finish one or the other, but not both, which seems to be the theme of this war."

Silence descended in the office once more. Rumble fought not to fidget, but the sound of intense activity outside the door contrasted starkly with the stillness in side. Even the heat seemed to be at bay for the moment.

"We offered a graduate of your Academy, Robert E. Lee, command of the army. Did you know that?" Lincoln asked.

The other three men were uncertain whom the question was directed at, but Delafield answered. "Yes, sir. He was a good choice."

"Except that good choice now fights for the other side," Lincoln said. "Which means he was actually a poor choice in retrospect. As was Beauregard, whom you replaced. In fact, I'm told he commands the army in Virginia that our troops will engage shortly. And our army is led by General McDowell. The two were classmates at West Point. I find that strange. In fact," Lincoln's voice got sharper, "I find it most strange that men who swore an oath to our country, who were educated at our country's expense, who were commissioned in our country's army, are now fighting against our country. Am I the only one who finds this strange?"

"No, sir," Rumble said.

"Did you know Lee?"

"He was superintendent from '52 to '55," Rumble said.

"What kind of man is he?" Lincoln asked.

"Very smart, sir. Very precise. A very good officer. I also saw him briefly in Mexico. He comes alive in battle."

Lincoln frowned. "He's enjoys it?"

"No, sir. Not that. It just seemed his natural element."

"Woe unto us, then," Lincoln murmured. "And McDowell?"

"He's an officer, sir, and I'm but an enlisted man."

Lincoln arched an eyebrow. "Come now. Between us men."

"Before the Mexican War, General McDowell was a tactics instructor at the Academy," Rumble said.

"And?" Lincoln pressed.

Rumble looked over at Stanton, but the attorney seemed more interested in what was going on outside.

"He was a major not long ago, sir," Rumble said. "Now he commands tens of thousands. The tactics taught on the blackboard at West Point are one thing. Implementing them with an army made largely of ninety-day volunteers is another."

"The rebel army is also made of volunteers," Lincoln said. "Our soldiers are green, but they are green also. They are all green alike."

"Yes, sir."

"What else?" Lincoln prompted.

"McDowell has never led troops in combat. He was an aide-de-camp during the Mexican War."

"So he saw combat," Lincoln said.

"Seeing combat and leading men in combat are two very different things, sir."

"I imagine they are," Lincoln said. "Responsibility for the lives of others is a great burden."

The room was silent for a while, the words sinking into the walls of the President's office.

"What of McClellan?" Lincoln finally asked.

When Rumble hesitated, Lincoln's voice became harsher. "Why do you think are here, Sergeant Major? I asked General Delafield to tell me of the West Pointers, since he's been superintendent three times, more than any other. He informed me that the man who could tell me the most was the Master of the Horse. Who had once been a cadet and then taught riding to class after class of cadets. Who went to the Mexican War and wrote many notebooks full of information that no one reads.

"So? What of McClellan? He won our first battle at Philippi. Thus he now has command on the other side of the Appalachians. And he sent General

Scott a strategic plan to win the war. Very industrious and showing of initiative, don't you think?"

"You seem to have your mind made up about him, sir," Rumble said.

"I have not," Lincoln snapped. He sighed. "I'm sorry. Let me explain. There's a call to abolish West Point. So many graduates have gone over to the other side, there is a very legitimate question as to why we should continue funding the institution. But as we used to say back in Illinois, that cow has already left the barn. We're stuck with the officers we have and I need to know about them. So. McClellan."

"McClellan is a very good organizer, sir," Rumble said. "But he's not daring. And he will flinch at the critical moment, when a general needs to press on. He's not a finisher and this war will need a finisher."

Lincoln smiled. "That wasn't so hard, was it?" He didn't wait for an answer. "From all the West Pointers you've seen, as cadets and as officers, who is the best 'finisher' as you call it?"

"Ulysses S. Grant, sir."

"I like the name Ulysses. Very martial." Lincoln frowned. "Ulyssess Grant? That strikes a bell." He began sifting through a pile of papers on his desk.

Rumble plunged on. "He's solid and steady, sir, and if there's one thing he will do, it's get where he's going. I fought with him in Mexico."

"Ah!" Lincoln said, pulling out a sheet. "Here's his name. Recommendations for promotion to General from each state. He's very far down. The war might indeed be over before his name bubbles up high enough. Curious."

Lincoln reached out and grabbed a pen. He scratched through some names, then wrote a note next to Grant's name. "Well, he'll be a general within the month."

Rumble leaned forward. "If I might make a suggestion, sir?"

Lincoln paused, pen hovering over paper. "Yes?"

"Back date the promotion to May. This will allow him to rank most of the other officers on that list."

Lincoln chuckled. "Ah, the army. Certainly. Let's say, May 17th. I like the ring of that." He wrote some more and then put the paper into another pile. "I assume you'll be fighting, Sergeant Major?"

Rumble nodded. "Yes, sir. It's my duty."

Lincoln reached down to the floor, disappearing for a moment behind the large desk. He re-appeared holding a rifle in his hands. "The Henry Arms company gave me two guns. One was quite fancy and engraved in gold. Number six off the production line. Too fancy to actually be used. I'd be afraid to fire it. And they gave me this one, plain and simple." He cocked the lever. "Repeating rifle. Quite fascinating. Holds fifteen bullets." He extended it to Rumble. "I think you can make much better use of it than I. Honestly, I have had thoughts about taking it with me when I go to Congress, although fifteen bullets wouldn't be near as many as I'd need, so you'd be doing me, and a number of congressmen, a favor."

Rumble took the rifle, feeling the solid weight of it in his hands. "Thank you, sir. I'll find a use for it."

Lincoln scribbled something on a piece of paper and signed it. He folded it and extended the paper across the desk as he stood. "I'd prefer if you used the rifle to stay alive. I would want a word with you in the future, Sergeant Major. And use this," he indicated the paper, "to go wherever you desire within the army, answerable to no one but me. I want you to ride south and join McDowell tomorrow. Do what you did in Mexico. Observe. And then come back here and tell me what you've seen. You work for me now, Master of the Horse Rumble."

"You did well," Delafield said as the carriage retraced the route from the morning.

"He's not quite what I expected," Rumble said, the Henry across his lap.

"He's in for a hard time," Delafield predicted. "The abolitionists want him to emancipate the slaves immediately, but if he does so, he loses the border states. He loses the border states, we most likely lose the war. He's making it about Union, but I think that can only carry this war so far. Damned if he does and damned if he doesn't."

"I wouldn't want his job for all the money in the world," Rumble said.

Delafield pointed at the Henry. "That's a fine weapon he gave you. If only the war department would see fit to outfit the entire army with them."

"Why won't they?"

"The fools think the soldiers will use too much ammunition if they can fire fifteen shots in eleven seconds, as the Ordnance department timed it in trials."

"I thought the point of combat was to pour as much fire into the enemy ranks as quickly as possible. At least that was my experience."

"Old men move slowly when faced with change," Delafield said. "They haven't even taken the rifled musket into account yet concerning tactics."

Rumble stiffened, seeing Ben standing outside the boarding house. He knew, in the way only a parent could. He could barely mumble his parting to General Delafield as he angrily dismounted the carriage. With a clatter it rolled away as Rumble faced Ben.

"I will not allow this," Rumble declared.

"It isn't your choice," Ben said. "I'm a man and I'm of age and this time the decision is all mine."

"I can talk to General Delafield. He'll have your enlistment papers torn up."

"I'll go elsewhere and re-enlist with another unit."

"I'm going to fight; that is more than enough service for our family," Rumble said.

"And Seneca fights for the South," Ben pointed out. "Doesn't that cancel out the Rumble contribution to the northern war effort?"

"And what would you do if you had to face your uncle on the field of battle?" Rumble asked.

"I'll pray it doesn't come to that."

"And if your prayers aren't answered?"

"I'll pray harder." Ben stood fast. "What will you do, father, if you have to face your brother? Will you kill him?"

"It won't come to that," Rumble said.

"So you pray for the same thing. Father, I'm fighting whether you give your blessings or not. I'd prefer to go with your blessings."

"Your mother would not have wanted this."

"Mother didn't want me in the Corps. This is a different matter. She didn't make you promise that I wouldn't serve in the army. I believe she would've wanted me to be an honorable man and not just say words about what I believe but to take action."

"She would have wished you safe."

"All mothers want their sons safe but few are going to be granted that."

Rumble clenched his fists. "Why did you do this?"

"I had to, father." Ben reached into his pocket and pulled out an abolitionist token and handed it over.

"You got this at the seminary?" Rumble asked.

"Yes."

"So my mother's plan sending you there had an undesired effect." Rumble laughed bitterly. "So much for plans."

Ben's eyes were moist. "Think of my name-sake. Should I disavow the very legacy you placed on me with my given name?"

Rumble's shoulders slumped. "If you must do this, let me help you. A friend of mine, Sam Grant, is going to become a general out west. If you must serve, my heart would be comforted if you served under him."

"What makes Grant so special?" Ben asked.

"He's steady," Rumble said. "No matter what the pressure, he stands fast."

"Is that what a soldier is supposed to do?"

"Part of it," Rumble said. "You have no idea what war is like. It's not some noble and glorious adventure. It's blood and death and horror."

"I'm not starry-eyed, father," Ben said. "I know it'll be bad. I grew up at West Point where all they talk of is war. I did spend seven weeks in the Corps." Ben held out the token. "Take this, please."

Rumble accepted the coin and the inevitability of his son going to war.

Bull Run
21 July 1861, Manassas, Virginia

RUMBLE EXPERIENCED A GROWING sense of dread as he re-read the orders McDowell had issued the previous night. It didn't seem to occur to General McDowell that General Beauregard, whom he faced across Bull Run Creek in Northern Virginia, had sat in the same tactics classes at West Point for four years, taught by the same instructors.

He was alone in the staff tent behind Wilmer McLean's farmhouse, which McDowell had chosen as his headquarters. It was five in the morning and according to these orders, some units were already in movement. The sum of the orders comprised a complicated turning movement for the assault this morning.

While several divisions would attack the Confederate left flank for the turning movement, another element would block reinforcements coming from the Shenandoah Valley, while another element would be a diversion, and another element would protect the rear.

These were not orders for a volunteer army, roughly trained, entering combat for the first time. These were orders that Napoleon's Imperial Guard might have a chance to pull off. And they were orders Napoleon himself might have given, considering that Napoleonic tactics had been the military bible preached at West Point.

In the flickering candlelight, Rumble put the orders down and examined the Henry repeating rifle. Napoleon had not had such a weapon. Napoleon had been moldering in a grave for over forty years. In fact, during the Mexican War, the soldiers had not been armed with rifled muskets as they were now, yet the tactics had not grown with the weaponry. Rumble consoled himself by figuring Beauregard was issuing a similar set of complicated orders on the other side of Bull Run. And that Ben was heading west, to join a unit out there with Grant.

The flap on the tent twitched open and an excited young officer with a dispatch case over one shoulder rushed in. A cascade of golden locks flowed over the newly commissioned officer's shoulders. He headed right for a pile of gear, but paused upon seeing Rumble.

"Master of the Horse," George Armstrong Custer said. "What brings you here?"

"Lieutenant Custer," Rumble said. "I'm on a special assignment." Lincoln's letter was in Rumble's breast pocket, right next to Lidia and Ben's etching.

Custer didn't seem too interested. "I'm riding dispatches from General Scott to General McDowell. Just delivered a batch." He pulled a stirrup out of the pile. "Lost mine crossing a river."

A sharp crack in the distance split the air. Rumble had heard it before. A cannon firing. It was followed by a volley from a battery.

"Was that—" Custer began, but Rumble heard another familiar sound and dove for the dirt. "Get down!"

A solid shell ripped through the farmhouse, passed through the tent's canvas, and bounded onto the ground on the far side, its energy finally expended. Rumble got to his feet, dusting off the dirt.

Custer also got up, a crazed grin on his face. "Battle!"

A mile to the south, on the other side of Bull Run Creek, Seneca Rumble heard the cannon fire and paused while buttoning up his uniform blouse. He took a deep breath, noted his hands were shaking, took another breath, then finished the task. He strapped his belt on, the weight from pistol and saber pulling it low around his narrow hips. He picked up his walking stick and exited the tent he'd shared with fellow officers after arriving late the previous evening from the rail junction at Manassas.

Seneca's vastly under-strength company of forty-five Mississippians had been brusquely rolled into the 33rd Virginia Regiment, specifically, the 10th Company, the Shenandoah Riflemen. Seneca was uncertain of his role in the command structure given the scant information he'd been given the previous evening. In fact, he was uncertain about damn near everything. Shortly after arriving at the tent, he'd become aware that his, and his men's presence, was a political gesture by the Governor of Mississippi to gain leverage with the Secessionist government. No one had asked for them and no one seemed to care that they were here. The Virginians were quite convinced they could lick the entire Union Army by themselves.

The regiment was on the march. And nobody had informed Seneca. Shadowy figures flitted about in the pre-dawn, forming into columns and heading down a dirt road. Seneca quickly gathered his troops and slid them into the long snake of men moving north. He had little idea where he was and no idea where he was headed.

But the sound of cannon fire was growing louder directly ahead.

This was not Mexico.

Rumble rode his horse through forest and brush, avoiding the trails crowded with units trying to move forward. And not only soldiers filled the roads. In the early dawn, Rumble saw dozens of carriages carrying the very sycophants and civilians who had stood ahead of him in line for appointments in Washington. Today's battle was to be their entertainment. The carriages were piled high with picnic baskets and bottles of wine.

The sun was slanting through the trees, indicating mid-morning, by the time Rumble reached Sudley Springs Ford, the needle through which McDowell's main assault was to be threaded.

And threaded it was. A steady stream of soldiers marched across the ford. Their uniforms were a colorful mixture. Mainly variations of blue, but there were the Zouaves with their bright red pantaloons, and a rather large number of companies and regiments in gray

Not Zachary Taylor's regulars at Palo Alto.

But they were turning the Confederate left. McDowell's grand plan just might work.

Seneca could swear they were going in a circle. First they'd marched north. Then east, being told to prepare to attack. But that order had come to nothing. Then south. And now they were heading west and the word was they were to defend.

Seneca had unbuttoned his collar, a concession to the late morning heat. He was mounted on his best horse and bags containing his camps goods dangled from each side. It didn't occur to him how different this was from the men on foot all around him, their gear consisting of musket, ammunition box, bed roll, and whatever food they could stuff in their pockets.

There was firing in every direction, but all the 33rd Virginia had experienced so far was the sound, not the sight. There was grumbling in the ranks, but Seneca had his own complaint, one he dared not utter aloud: Most of the 33rd Virginia were clad in blue, the color their militia units had been clothed in before Secession.

The column was marching down a road covered over by tree branches, a tunnel of green. Finally, a ripple of excitement coursed down the human snake.

Battle was ahead. The Yankees had turned the flank and it was up to them to stop disaster.

"For glory, men!" Seneca cried out, waving his cane.

And for the first time since Natchez, the men responded with a cheer.

"Colonel!" Rumble rode up to his old acquaintance.

William Tecumseh Sherman was riding along a column of troops, exhorting them to move forward, to press the attack up Matthews Hill. The column was splitting, spreading a wave of blue across a green field on the south side of Bull Run Creek. Sporadic rifle and cannon fire twinkled from the brow of the hill about a half-mile distant.

Sherman wheeled his horse around. He was a different man from the young cadet at West Point. Thinner, eyes somewhat crazed, red hair cut short and a thin beard etching shadows into his face.

"Master of the Horse Rumble! What the devil are you doing here?" He didn't wait for an answer as a courier came galloping up. Sherman issued orders, and the courier was racing back from whence he came.

"We're moving them, Lucius," Sherman said. "We've got the flank and we can roll it if McDowell sends the reserves." He cursed as a bullet creased his shoulder, splitting cloth and skin. Then, without another word, he galloped forward, barking orders left and right.

Rumble put the spurs to his horse and followed, caught up in the excitement of the charge. Two batteries of regular army flying artillery galloped to his right, officers exhorting their men to get to the top of Matthews Hill.

"Get in a line, men, in a line," Seneca yelled, not quite sure of the proper order to achieve what he desired.

The rest of the 33rd was deploying, moving forward among retreating soldiers, some of whom started in fear, seeing the blue uniforms in their midst. For a moment all was turmoil, but then a colonel stood up in his stirrups, his shockingly blue eyes aglow.

"Virginians. Advance!"

The men gave a shout that made the hair on the back of Seneca's neck curl. Before he knew it, he was screaming the same inarticulate yell and pressing forward. They crested Henry House Hill in time to see a line of blue with a smattering of gray crest Matthews Hill, not quite a mile distant. The low ground in between was cluttered with retreating Confederate troops.

Union artillery suddenly began belching canister from Matthews Hill and wide, bloody swaths were cut in the men in the valley.

The blue-eyed Colonel rode along the crest of Henry Hill, now ordering the men to form and hold a line, to take the defensive and be prepared to face an attack. Seneca dismounted, handing the reins to one of his men. He saw a lieutenant in blue running by, a Virginian and grabbed him by the arm.

"Who is that?" Seneca demanded. "Why's he ordering us to stop?"

"That's Colonel Jackson, sir. Brigade commander."

Seneca looked to his right and saw a Confederate unit flowing down the hill in the assault, another officer in the lead. "And who is that?"

"General Bee, sir."

Seneca glanced once more at Jackson, weighed Colonel against General, the glory of the assault against that of the defense, then ordered his men to follow. He charged downhill, following Bee's advance as fast as he could.

The General rose up in his saddle and looked over his shoulder, waving his sword. He saw that most of the Virginians were not following. "There stands Jackson like a stone wall," he cried out.

Rumble rode toward the artillery batteries, now unlimbered and firing with deadly effect into the Confederates from the brow of Matthews Hill. He dismounted, pulling the Henry Rifle from its scabbard and Delafield's telescope from its case.

He scanned the battlefield, trying to make sense of it. Clouds of smoke from gunpowder and dust from thousands of feet and hooves obscured portions like a low-lying fog. From one of those fog banks a cohort of men in blue burst, running furiously, closing from a quarter mile.

The captain in command of the artillery shouted at his gun commanders to cease-fire. Rumble twisted the focus on the telescope.

"Sir!" he yelled, pushing toward the officer. "They're rebels!"

His words went unheard as precious seconds were lost and the Confederates halved the distance. Rumble reached the Captain and grabbed his shoulder. "They're rebels, sir!"

The Captain's face went white as he recognized his mistake.

"Fire! Give them hell!"

Seneca had his cane in one hand, saber in the other and was screaming insanely. He tripped over a body, scrambled to his feet and kept going up the hill. The Union guns were less than a hundred feet away.

The two Union batteries erupted.

Seneca was aware he was flying through the air. Everything moved slowly. Seneca saw a private hurtling back next to him, head missing, blood spurting out the carotid arteries from a still beating heart.

Seneca hit the ground on his back. He blinked dirt out of his eyes and stared blankly up at the blue sky for a moment. He raised his empty hands. His cane and saber were gone. That was the first cognizant thought that passed through his mind.

He grasped for the pistol, determined to rejoin the fight. His holster was empty. Seneca cursed and looked for it.

His left leg was gone from knee down.

Then the pain reached his brain and he screamed.

The volley of canister had decimated the Confederate lines, but they were too many and too close. There was no time to reload or limber up the guns to retreat. The wave of soldiers over-ran the two batteries.

From the flank, Rumble threw the Henry to his shoulder. He saw a General yelling orders, waving a sword wildly about. Rumble fired three rounds as fast as he could lever in the bullets and pull the trigger.

The first one shivered the General in the saddle, the second knocked him back a bit, and the third sent him tumbling to the ground.

The assault broke, rebels running to the rear in disarray, but the guns had been over-run and spiked, putting them out of action.

More Union troops came charging over the top over Matthews Hill behind Rumble and down into the low ground in front of Henry House Hill. Right into a scathing volley from the solid line of Confederates who were holding the position there. The Union officers tried to rally their men, but southern artillery was now supporting the rebel infantry and the assault wavered.

Rumble ran forward. He found the General he had shot. A Confederate lieutenant was trying to stem the flow of blood from his commander's stomach. The lieutenant didn't stop his efforts, even seeing Rumble approach with the Henry at the ready.

"Who is it?" Rumble asked, but then he recognized the wounded man. Class of '45 and one Rumble had tested with York's jump. He'd stood fast.

"Barnie? Barnie Bee?"

General Bee looked up. "Master of the Horse! Did you see Jackson? Stood fast. Didn't support me. I had to order my men to halt. To halt, damn it! Why didn't Jackson follow me?"

"He's holding the line, General. He did the right thing."

Bee raised his body off the ground and cried out in a command voice: "Let us determine to die here, and we will conquer. Rally behind Stonewall Jackson and the Virginians, boys!"

Then he collapsed.

"Take him," Rumble said to the lieutenant. "Take him back to your surgeons."

The lieutenant looked at him in surprise. "We aint got no surgeon with the regiment. Just some old country doc."

The lieutenant grabbed a couple of scared privates and got them to put General Bee into a blanket. They hurried away with him as the volume of the battle increased, the Union forces in the low ground unable to maintain their charge, Jackson's Virginians holding the high ground in front of them, pouring hot lead into the Yankees.

The Confederate left was saved.

Rumble picked his way back among the bodies littering the ground, Henry at the ready. He passed by a dead man, mouth open in a final scream that had not found voice. A man in gray was crawling, facedown, clawing at the dirt with his hands, leaving a smear of blood from a severed leg behind him.

"Easy, soldier," Rumble said, uncertain if he was Union or Rebel, not that it mattered in his condition.

Rumble grabbed the man's shoulder and turned him over.

"Brother!"

Slavery
24 July 61, Palatine, Mississippi

*V*IOLET RUMBLE PRESSED THE gun into Samual's hand. It was an old piece, a flintlock pistol her father had given her the night before her wedding, which had seen better days and better cleaning.

"I don't know if it works," she confided.

It was just before dawn and they were in the center of the garden, the wings of the angel hovering over their shoulders as if hiding their meeting from a greater power. "I loaded powder and ball. And a new flint. Here are more." She gave him a leather pouch.

"Slave with a gun means death, Miss Violet," Samual said.

"I tried to get you a certificate of registration as a free black," Violet said. "But Mississippi laws are currently so tight, it would be easier to thread the eye of a needle from a mile away by wishing. You must go."

"They catch me, they kill me, Miss Violet," Samual said.

"Things are different now, Samual," Violet said. "Go north. You'll be safe with the Yankees. There's a man with the Federals. His name is Elijah Cord. You met him at West Point delivering my note and saw him here for the wedding. Use his name when you run into the Yankees. Tell them he's a West Pointer. That might carry more weight than using the Rumble name right now." She sighed. "And Mary is gone. You have no family here any more. You stay here, you'll die alone and broken. Nothing is holding you here, Samual."

"You here, Miss Violet."

Violet turned her face away from him. "Yes. But that is my lot in life."

"Without Master St. George, you have a better life here, Miss Violet."

"Don't even think that," Violet snapped. "And St. George, devil that he is, is not my true problem." She took a deep breath and graced Samual with a brave smile. "It's time for you to find your place in the world. I don't know what that will be, but I am certain it is not here."

"And my Echo, Miss Violet?"

She reached into her skirt and pulled out some pieces of paper. "Tennessee laws are less stringent. Here's the certificate freeing your daughter. My family will honor it. And on top is a letter instructing them not to hold you under the Fugitive Slave Act. They will honor that also. You can retrieve Echo and then run to Canada to escape the Act. And here." She thrust some bills in his hands. "Yankee dollars. They might not be worth the paper they're printed on around here for much longer."

Samual didn't take the money. "Miss Violet, I can't—"

Violet's hands were on his, the money in between. "You must. Your freedom will be the only thing other than my grandson being in Europe that will allow me to survive the coming months. Both my sons are at war on opposite sides. I cannot bear to think about it."

Samual took the money.

"Go now," Violet said. "St. George is across the river in Vidalia. He's up to something. It's as good a time as any to leave."

Samual bowed his head. "God will bless you, Miss Violet."

"That would be nice and a change," Violet said. "Go east and north into the swamp. Escape this place."

Samual disappeared behind the hedges. Violet sat down on the stone bench, utterly alone except for the stone angel.

Samual didn't go east or north. After retrieving the woodcutting axe and a cooking knife, he went down to the east bank of the fog-shrouded Mississippi. Visibility was less than twenty feet. In the brush not far from the old Palatine dock, he uncovered a small dugout. Settling his large frame into the boat, he took a moment to pray.

"Lord. You please bless Miss Violet. She a good woman. And keep her sons safe, even da' one who fights for the rebs. And, if aint too much, keep me safe now. I know I not doing what she said, but I have to do 'dis. I owe the poor boy."

Then he grabbed the paddle and propelled himself into the current, muscles working furiously, going on dead reckoning. It took a while to cross and the fog began lifting. It was a race between the river, daylight, fog and his endurance.

The Louisiana bank appeared out of the mist and Samual grunted with effort to go faster. The prow of the dugout scraped into the mud and he leapt out, dragging it further ashore. He hid it amongst some trees. Then sniffed the air. He pulled the pistol out of his pocket and checked it, working on memory of what he'd seen John Dyer do years ago with a similar gun. As near Samual could tell, the gun was ready. Gun in one hand, axe in the other, knife in his belt, he made his way along the bank.

The fog was still thick, but night was giving way to day, gray light creeping through the mist. Samual began to run. A riverboat loaded with bales of cotton loomed out of the fog and Samual halted. The ship was tied to a dock, a row of empty wagons lining the shore.

Samual moved stealthily, through the brush and trees lining the bank. He'd been part of this for many years and he knew everyone had worked through the night to load the boat. The difference was the boat hadn't departed under the cover of night. It spoke of St. George's ever increasing arrogance.

Samual made his way to a clearing where dark bodies were collapsed in exhaustion. He picked his way among them until he found the young man whom he had promised 'changing times' to many years ago.

Samual knelt and shook his shoulder. "It time, James."

James eyes snapped open. Eye actually. Where his left eye should be was a scarred hole. The result of St. George moving from torture that wouldn't leave a mark, to torture that would send an obvious and permanent message since there would be no repercussions for damage to property from the big house. The wound was inflicted via a red-hot iron rod two years ago after James had tried to escape, been captured and brought back under the Fugitive Slave Act. St. George had promised that if James tried again, the other eye would be singed out and then he'd be let loose in the swamp, to be bait for the gators and snakes.

James took in the gun and axe in Samual's hand and got to his feet. "The devil over there on the dock."

Samual shook his head and pointed north. "We got to go. Now."

James grabbed the knife from Samual's belt. "Twenty year you been telling me to wait."

"We can be free."

James pointed at his head. "I been free here a long time." He tapped his chest. "I need free here. For that, I need his blood."

"No," Samual said. "Good book say 'Beloved, never avenge yourselves, but leave it to the wrath of God, for it is written, Vengeance is mine, I will repay, says the Lord'."

"You a damn fool still," James said. "Been fool all these years."

"What you mean?"

"'Eye for eye,' brother Samual. 'Eye for eye' it also say."

James headed toward the ship. Samual looked up as the first clear rays of dawn tinged the eastern horizon. "Lord, I got to save him, no matter what he do."

Samual ran after the younger slave.

St. George was tucked into the shade of an old oak tree, an empty tequila bottle held loosely in one hand, the other hidden inside his sash. His slouch hat was pulled over his face, slightly muffling the sound of snoring.

Samual arrived as James knelt next to St. George and with one hand whipped the hat off the white man's face and with the other, jabbed the point of the knife into the left eye.

St. George's scream pierced the early morning calm as both hands grabbed for the blade protruding from his face. Samual had the axe ready, one blow and the overseer wouldn't feel his pain any more and the world wouldn't bear the man any longer. He hesitated, God holding the strike as James readied a fatal blow with the knife.

A shot rang out and a bullet cracked by so close, Samual felt the breeze on his cheek and hit James in the chest, knocking him back from St. George.

"Come!" Samual yelled to James as the younger slave stumbled to his knees, blood pumping from a hole in his chest. Forty feet away the devil woman who was in business with St. George had her pistol leveled, preparing to fire again.

Samual dropped the axe and pistol, threw James over his shoulder, and ran.

More shots rang out, adding impetus to Samual's sprint. He passed through a strand of forest until he reached the edge of the massive Louisiana swamp. He splashed into the dark water without pause, pushing forward.

They wouldn't follow into the swamp right away. They'd wait on the dogs or for him to come back out. But he wasn't going to come back out. At least not on this side. And he had a little bit of time before they could get the dogs.

When he was far enough in that he could risk stopping, Samual gently laid James down on a dry hummock. A bubbly froth was coming out of the hole in James' chest as he struggled to breath. Samual pressed his hand against it, sliding his other hand underneath, to the man's back. When he drew the hand back, there was no blood, which meant the bullet was still in James.

"I got him," James gasped. "Got his eye. And I dying free."

"You not dying."

"You doctor?" James asked. He raised his head, looking down at his chest. "You take that hand away, I die. You keep it there, they catch us. Bullet got my air, my blood."

Samual took his shirt and tore it in strips. He fashioned a bandage as best he could and wrapped it around James' torso.

It did little good as blood spotted it right away and James struggled to breath. Samual once more pressed his hand hard against the wound.

"You need to get away," James said. "Leave me. I'll go north, draw 'em off. You go south. They won' think 'dat. Dogs will follow my blood."

"Won't leave you," Samual said.

"Then we both die."

"Won't."

James caught his breath. "Samual. Something you need know."

"Yes?"

"That day. On the river with your son." James coughed, blood spackling his lips. "St. George know Agrippa read what he shouldn't. Threatened him on da' boat. Agrippa jump over into the river." James paused, licked his lips, tasting the blood, his life leaving him. "St. George shot at him like it were a game. Agrippa went under. Didn' come up."

"I know," Samual said.

James gripped Samual's arm with ferocious strength. "No. You don' know. Remember he save Master's eldest boy? Agrippa mighty swimmer. I watched. Long after they go back to laughing and drinking 'bout killing uppity nigra. I saw." James coughed again, more blood. A trickle on his cheek. He closed his eyes and tried to catch his breath again.

With a trembling hand, Samual wiped it clean. "What you see?"

"I saw Agrippa crawl out on far shore. Alive. He was alive."

"Oh, Lord," Samual whispered, rocking back on his heels in shock. "Why you not tell me?"

"Better everyone think he dead. He dead, no one look for him. As long as you a slave, best for you too. You not a slave now."

With a surge of adrenaline, James shoved off Samual's hand and got to his feet. He staggered off into the swamp, heading north, his own hands on his wound.

Samual stood, his instinct to follow and help.

But then it really sunk in. Agrippa could be alive.

Samual headed south.

Lincoln
25 July 1861, Northern Virginia

"WE HEARD YOU HAD GOT OVER the 'big scare', and we thought we would come over and see the boys," Lincoln said to Sherman, both men ignoring a light drizzle that complemented the pall over the camps of the defeated Army of the Potomac.

Lincoln was in the back of an uncovered carriage, seated next to Secretary of State Seward. Lincoln's tall, brimmed hat kept the rain from his face, but his black frock coat was soaked. Rumble was on his horse, the Henry rifle across the pommel, a small piece of oilcloth keeping the trigger and chamber assembly dry. As near as he had been able to tell since leaving Washington and crossing the river into Virginia this morning, he was the sole extent of the President and Secretary of State's protection. Colonel Sherman was also mounted, but had more of an escort, a coterie of staff officers hovering behind him on the mud splattered road just outside of Sherman's series of camps containing his brigade.

"We welcome you, sir," Sherman said, with a slight bow from the saddle.

"Tell me, first," Lincoln said, "how do you feel the battle went? I hear many different tales in Washington, but since they are told by those in Washington, one might suppose those doing the telling are those who had the fleetest feet in departing the battlefield."

Sherman didn't even smile at the jibe. "Sir, it was one of the best planned and worst fought battles in history."

Lincoln nodded sagely. "The best summation I've heard so far."

"What might I do for you, sir?"

"My friend, Sergeant Major Rumble, tells me you are a grim but honest man," Lincoln said. "If I can ignore the fact your brother is a Senator."

Sherman glanced at Rumble and put the tip of his right finger to his eyebrow in acknowledgement. "Sergeant Major Rumble would know, sir. I saw him on the battlefield the other day. How's your brother, Elijah?"

"Recovering, sir," Rumble said. "He's under a civilian doctor's care, but also under guard as a prisoner."

Lincoln twisted in the seat. "Your brother?"

"Wounded in battle, sir. He lost his left leg."

"And I assume he was wearing gray?" Lincoln asked.

"Yes, sir," Rumble said.

"A shame and the curse of this war," Lincoln said. "You have my authority to end his prisoner status and send him home as swiftly as possible, as long he swears never to raise arms against the country again."

"Thank you, sir," Rumble said.

Lincoln turned back to Sherman. "With your permission, sir, I'd like to visit your camps and speak to the men. It seems they might use some bucking up."

Sherman frowned. "Please, sir, discourage all cheering, noise, or any sort of confusion; we had enough of it before Bull Run to spoil any set of men. What we need is cool, thoughtful, hard-fighting soldiers—no more hurrahing, no more humbug."

Lincoln chuckled. "I can see Sergeant Rumble spoke accurately. As you command, Colonel, I will refrain from theatrics and politicking, the two being almost the same."

The party moved out, splashing down the road. They arrived at a regimental camp, where the men were hurriedly called out to assembly. They gathered in a square around Lincoln's hack.

The President stood up, towering over everyone.

"I understand this square formation is what you men formed near the end of the Battle of Bull Run. That it was your unit that saved the entire army from annihilation. Except in that case, your weapons were pointed outward at the enemy. I am grateful you have seen fit to assemble without weapons and without pointing them at me. This is a more amendable reception than the one I receive on Capitol Hill.

"As President, I am the Commander-in-Chief. I am responsible for all. The onus of Bull Run is on me. I promise to do all I can to give you the support you need in the future. Supplies will . ."

As Lincoln went on, Sherman sidled up next to Rumble.

"I figure McDowell is out," Sherman said. "Who's next, Lucius?"

"McClellan."

"Humph," Sherman said, which was comment enough. A tic was dancing on his left cheek, underneath his scruffy beard. "Your southern brethren don't know what they're doing, Lucius," he hissed. "This country will be drenched in blood, and God only knows how it will end. It's all folly, madness, a crime against civilization! Those people speak so lightly of war; they don't know what they're talking about. War is a terrible thing, as you know. They mistake, too, the people of the North. We will fight, to the end. We're not going to let this country be destroyed without a mighty effort to save it."

"I know that, Cump," Rumble said, but Sherman was getting more and more agitated as Lincoln continued to address the troops.

"Besides," Sherman said, "where are the southern men and appliances of war to contend against us? The North can make a steam engine, locomotive, or railway car; hardly a yard of cloth or pair of shoes can southerners make. I was in Louisiana the last few years, commanding the military school. I know what they can do and what they can't do. They're rushing into war with one of the most powerful and determined people on Earth. They're bound to fail despite the recent victory. Only in their spirit and determination are they prepared for war, I'll grant them that. In all else they are totally unprepared, with a bad cause to start with. They might have made some headway at Bull Run, but as their limited resources begin to fail, shut out from the markets of Europe as they will be, their cause will begin to wane. If those damn people will but stop and think, they must see in the end that they will surely fail, but in the meanwhile hundreds of thousands will pay the price with their lives, both North and South."

"They don't want to look too deep or too far ahead," Rumble said. "I wouldn't argue with you, Cump, but I'd keep those predictions close to the chest. Not what anyone wants to hear. The five hundred or so killed during the battle has the country in an uproar."

"That will be a light day for the grim reaper in a year," Sherman predicted.

"I think the President knows that," Rumble said.

Lincoln was coming to the end. "And I also assure you that if you have a grievance, you may bring it to my attention personally. There is nothing more important to me than they welfare of you soldiers."

A cheer started, but Lincoln raised a hand, silencing it.

"Don't cheer, boys. I confess I rather like it myself, but Colonel Sherman here says it is not military, and I guess we had better defer to his opinion."

A soldier stepped forward, shaking off hands that tried to keep him in ranks.

"Mister President, we don't think Colonel Sherman has treated us very well. We was taking shelter in a barn whilst it was raining the other day, and the Colonel turned us out of it."

"Well, boys, I have a great deal of respect for Colonel Sherman and if he turned you out of the barn, I've no doubt it was for a good reason. I presume he thought you would feel better if you went to your military tasks and tried to forget your troubles."

The man stepped back, muttering. A voice cried out from behind Lincoln.

"Mister President, I have a cause for grievance. This morning I went to speak to Colonel Sherman and he threatened to shoot me."

Lincoln turned around to see the complaint had come from an officer. "Threatened to shoot you? Really?"

"Yes, sir, indeed. Threatened to shoot me like a dog."

"Come closer." Lincoln leaned over, as if passing a secret, but his voice could clearly be heard by all. "If I were you, and Colonel Sherman threatened to shoot me, I would believe he would do it and act accordingly."

The officer turned beet red and sulked off, to the laughter of the men close by.

With a few more parting words to the men, Lincoln sat down and the carriage moved out, Rumble on one side, Sherman on the other.

"Thank you, sir," Sherman said. "That officer came to me with a bit of mutiny in him. Your support is crucial to keeping discipline among green troops."

"You know, Colonel," Lincoln said, "the Confederates were green too. How was it they prevailed on the field?"

Sherman didn't hesitate. "We had three division commanders, sir. Only one had ever seen action before. Nine brigade commanders, myself among them. Only three had ever seen combat. On the other side, all the nine senior Confederate commanders had fought in Mexico."

"And all West Pointers on the gray side," Lincoln said.

"Yes, sir. Damn traitors. Ought to be lined up and shot."

"We have to catch them first," Lincoln observed.

"Sir, if I may speak?" Rumble asked.

Lincoln turned his way. "Yes?"

"When we were marching south to Bull Run we all thought the war would be over in a week. That we'd be sitting in Richmond right now. It didn't happen. These men know that now. They're sullen, they're miserable, they're defeated for the moment, but deep inside, they're angry. Angry soldiers are good soldiers. They're set for the long haul now."

Rumble continued. "I know the southern mind-set. I think the shoe is on the other foot. I think the Confederates now believe they can be in Washington within a few weeks. Which they can't. I've heard stories that some of the southern boys have gone home, thinking the victory at Bull Run was more than enough and the war is as good as over. I believe that this belief of victory by the south is going to cost them more than our defeat."

Lincoln pondered that. "An interesting twist, Sergeant Rumble. Very interesting. We've lured them into over-confidence by allowing them to defeat us."

"Sir, I—" Rumble sputtered by Lincoln waved a hand, silencing him as effectively as he had the regiment.

"I was told the army needed training. I pressed for action sooner, rather than later. I understand now. I will have more patience. I just pray the country will too."

2 August 1861, Palatine, Mississippi

A wagon or a carriage. If the former, it was not heavily laden. Violet Rumble knew the dust that rose from the Natchez Road as intimately as she knew the lines that had appeared years ago around her eyes and were conquering her middle-age.

Violet left the sitting room and went to the front door, creaking it open on hinges that needed lubrication. Many things at Palatine needed maintenance. Tiberius was ensconced in his chair on the front porch over her head, drinking constantly and speaking little, a small blessing. St. George was recuperating in his cabin, his subordinate overseers taking care of the fields, while he hatched whatever devilry would come out of the loss of his eye. And Violet took care of the big house alone.

A wagon turned into the drive and Violet felt her heart leap for the first time in weeks as she recognized Rosalie's golden hair. It had been a long time since her daughter-in-law visited from Vicksburg. Violet took the stairs swiftly, but halted on the bottom one, her happiness fading as she saw the look on Rosalie's face and that her dress was stained with sweat.

"Seneca?" Violet asked.

In response, Rosalie halted the wagon and climbed over the seat into the rear. Violet almost ran to the back as Rosalie dropped the gate.

Seneca lay on the wood planks, pale and sweating in the August heat, eyes half-lidded from morphine. His left leg was gone from the knee down and swathed in stained bandages.

"Oh, my dear Lord," Violet whispered as she climbed into the buckboard and joined Rosalie.

"Wounded at Bull Run, two weeks past," Rosalie said. "He arrived on the train to Vicksburg two days ago. I tried to talk him into staying there, but he kept insisting on coming here during his lucid moments."

"To Palatine?"

"To you." It was an indication of how upset Violet was that she didn't notice the sharp edge in Rosalie's answer.

"He must go in my bedroom," Violet said. "It's the coolest. And I will send for the doctor to dress his wound again. We will take the best possible care of him." She cried out for help and several slaves scurried up.

They carried Seneca into the house and to Violet's bed as she tore off the covers and propped pillows for him.

"You." She pointed at a slave. "Ride to Natchez and fetch the doctor."

"Yes, Mistress."

Rosalie stood silent in a corner of the room as Violet bustled about making her youngest son as comfortable as possible. She finally spoke. "Are you going to inform Tiberius?"

Violet paused. "If he wishes to know what's happening to his family, he can move off his damn porch."

Rosalie walked over and stood on the other side of the bed, Seneca between them. "His unit was practically wiped out at the battle from what I've been told. And he was captured by the Yankees."

"Then how did he end up on the train to Vicksburg?"

Rosalie held out a letter. "Lucius."

Violet used a cloth to clear the sweat from Seneca brow, and then took the letter.

Dear Rosalie,

This letter prays Seneca reaches you safely. I did not trust to the doctors in either the Confederate or Union camps. All is in turmoil here in the east after the great battle of Bull Run Creek. I took him to the first doctor I could find. The leg was gone, so it was a matter of cleaning the wound, bandaging and handling the pain. I believe the man did an adequate job.

Although he is technically a prisoner, I received dispensation from the very highest authority for his release and return back home. As part of the condition, Seneca must swear never again to carry arms against the United States. He was not coherent enough to understand this when I told him, so please remind him. If caught bearing arms for the Confederacy, he will be shot or hung if captured.

"What 'very highest authority'?" Violet asked.

"He never says," Rosalie replied. "You know Lucius."

I have been able to arrange transportation by rail on the morrow. The doctor says he is stable enough to travel and I believe it best he go home to you, for I can think of no greater care than that of one who loves.

Violet paused and glanced up at Rosalie. She was sitting on the edge of the bed, Seneca's hand in hers.

The war, at least, is over, for my brother. I came upon Seneca upon the field of battle. He had been wounded while bravely charging a Union battery.

There is other dark news. You must tell my mother that Ben is not en route to Europe. Without my permission he enlisted in the Union Army.

"Oh dear," Violet whispered.

"Ben?" Rosalie asked.

Violet nodded and returned her attention to the letter.

I have been given a great responsibility in this conflict, one that I cannot put in writing to you. My apologies. Still, Ben weighs heavy on my mind. As does Seneca's wound. And your place at Palatine in the great struggle that is coming. I fear you may not be safe at Palatine and you should consider alternative locations to remain sequestered for the duration of the conflict.

Abigail stays with Mister Havens and Letitia. I trust them and hope you understand that she will not be traveling to you any time soon. She has grown into a most handsome young woman and Mister Havens has strict instructions to keep her safe from the interest of both cadets and officers.

This war will not be as most think. Bull Run has opened eyes in the North to that. From what I hear, it has not had a similar effect in the south. Because McDowell's forces were routed, the Confederates believe victory will be swift. I can tell you from where I stand in Washington, this will not happen as it is quickly growing into a heavily fortified city. We thought we would have quick victory in Mexico and look at all the years I spent there.

Take care of my brother. Give my love to my mother.

Lucius K. Rumble

Sergeant Major, Master of the Horse

United States Military Academy

Violet folded the letter and placed a hand on her son's forehead. "This damn, damned war! It will consume us all!"

Grant
11 Aug 61, In The Field, Missouri

CORD NOTED THE TWO BOOKS RESTING on Grant's field desk as he parked a cup of coffee between them.

"Hardee's Tactics?" Cord asked.

Grant laughed, picking up the bound book. "A gift from a fellow officer who believes I need some schooling in the art."

The formal name enscrolled on the cover was *Rifle and Light Infantry Tactics for the Exercise and Manoeuvres of Troops When Acting as Light Infantry or Riflemen.* "Traitor Jeff Davis, as Secretary of War, got Hardee to write it and now General Hardee is about thirty miles south of here, fighting for Jeff. So." Grant tossed the book off the table to the dirt, and picked up his pipe from a makeshift ashtray made from a food tin lid. "I do not believe I will study his tactics, other than what I have already gleaned from it of the ways he might take action against me. I, on the other hand, have no book of my own that he can read. I believe, therein, lies a slight advantage for me."

"What's the other?" Cord asked as he grabbed a newspaper off a stack and sat down on a crate.

"Rumble's Report. My other advantage." The paper in the notebook was stained and faded with the years, but the words brought the Mexican War back to life for Grant. He was seated in a camp chair, report in one hand, pipe in the other. His command was in northern Missouri, having crisscrossed the state several times at the behest of conflicting orders emanating from whomever seemed to be in command. Cord had suggested, more than once, that they simply sit still and await reversal of whatever the next order was, as it would obviously bring them back to wherever they started from.

Grant wore a private's blouse with his rank pinned on it, as he had since the beginning of the war. The general's uniforms he'd ordered had not yet caught up with him. He presented a most unmilitary appearance, yet there was a calm presence about him that indicated to all who came by that he was the one in command.

Cord opened the *Missouri Daily Democrat*, often a more accurate source of intelligence than the muddled reports that were being brought in by couriers. "Got a new commander in the east," Cord noted.

"McDowell got sacked?" Grant asked, without looking up from Rumble's Report.

"Yes. And McClellan now reigns there. And Fremont has finally arrived to take his throne in the west."

Grant shook his head. "I am not overly fond of McClellan, but he is a good organizer and Lord knows, the army needs organizing."

"Well, well." Cord shook the paper, getting Grant's full attention.

"Yes?"

"I'm going to have to watch my words around the general now," Cord said.

"What general?" Grant was confused.

Cord folded the paper and tossed it to Grant. "Brigadier General Grant."

Grant unfolded it and read the list of appointments to the rank. "This is a surprise. First of seven to receive a star from Illinois and backdated to May. How did this happen?"

"The army works in mysterious ways," Cord said. "Sometimes bad, sometimes good. I place this in the latter category."

"I need you by my side more than ever," Grant said to Cord. "I want a man around me who can say no."

"To who?" Cord asked.

"To all who will come asking me for things. And, more importantly, to me."

"That I can do," Cord said. "And I think it's time I go visit the Pathfinder in St. Louis and get you a position that's more in line with your new rank."

Grant put the paper down and grabbed a map. "Here's the key to the west right now." He jabbed his finger at the point where the Mississippi and Ohio Rivers met in Illinois.

"Cairo," Cord said, without looking at the map.

"Yes," Grant said. "We must hold it on the defensive for now or else lose it and Kentucky. But then, when we are stronger and better trained, we must eventually take this." He slid his finger down the Mississippi, passing Tennessee and Arkansas, then Louisiana and Mississippi, halting at a sharp bend in the river.

"Vicksburg," Cord said, again without looking at the map.

Grant smiled at his friend. "How do you know without following my mighty finger?"

"I spent many years in the west," Cord said. "I understand the terrain and the importance of rivers. The Mississippi is the key to this war. All those 'On To Richmond' fellows are wrong. The rebs can just move out of Richmond and pitch government in some other town. This war is going to be won or lost out here. We take the Mississippi, we split the Confederacy just like the British tried to split the colonies via the Hudson in the Revolution."

"Vicksburg is the strategic West Point of the Mississippi," Grant said.

Cord nodded. "And you're right, we've got to keep old Sidney Johnston's Army of the Mississippi from taking Cairo. As much as we'll need to take Vicksburg, he needs Cairo and he's a lot closer to it. He's a sharp man and can read a map better than most and has the daring to take chances."

"Which McClellan won't," Grant said.

"One thing at a time," Cord said. "Let's focus on what we can do."

They were interrupted by a courier galloping up and handing a pouch to Grant's aide. The lieutenant quickly sorted the messages, bringing the bulk to Grant and a single letter to Cord.

"What news?" Grant asked as he perused the topmost report.

Cord recognized the flowing script on the envelope. "From Palatine."

He was about to open it, but Grant's words interrupted him.

"Nathaniel Lyon is dead. There was a battle yesterday between his forces and the Secessionist Missouri State Guard at Wilson's Creek. Lyon's men were driven from the field and he was shot through the head. But even in defeat, they did break the back of the secess men. Missouri will stay in the Union." Grant shook his head as he put the report down. "His men didn't recover his body. No one knows where it is. You remember Lyon from the Academy, don't you?"

"Of course," Cord said. "He spoke to me one time and then never again. But he's been a force in this state and will be missed."

"What's the news from Mississippi?" Grant asked, putting the report aside.

Cord ripped open the letter and scanned the lines. His jaw clenched as he read.

"Bad news?" Grant asked.

"Ben enlisted. Rumble sent him to come to serve under you, so he should be en route."

"We'll keep our eyes open for him then," Grant said.

"We will," Cord vowed. "It's good to know Ben has spirit, although I will sleep much less easily with the knowledge he wears the uniform."

"Lucius wrote you from Palatine?" Grant was confused.

"No," Cord said, distracted as he continued to read. "His mother. Violet Rumble."

"Ah," Grant understood. "A formidable woman as best I recollect."

"And Rumble's brother, Seneca, lost a leg at Bull Run fighting for the Rebs," Cord said.

"The war strikes home," Grant said. "At least he lives."

"Violet also says she induced a slave to run away, that Samual fellow." He looked up at Grant. "Remember? The huge negro? He's escaped with her assistance and is heading to Clarksville to claim his daughter whom she's freed and then north to Canada. She asks my assistance in any way, if I might be nearby."

"Clarksville?" Grant was looking at the map with renewed interest. "On the Cumberland."

Cord was reading the end of the letter. "She says Lucius has some big assignment that he couldn't tell her the nature of. That he was the one who found Seneca on the battlefield and that's how news of Ben's enlistment made its way west."

That drew Grant's attention from the map momentarily. "Lucius is in battle and not at West Point? He must be spying for Delafield once more."

Cord angrily folded the letter and slid it in his pocket, next to the faded sketch of Lidia and Ben, which Grant had done so many years ago. "Rumble couldn't keep Ben out of the war. I knew it! And he ran me off in Mexico. He pulled Ben out of the Corps, but still fails."

Grant stood and walked around the map table, looping his arm over Cord's shoulder. "Everyone is going to get drawn into this war, Elijah. At least he's on the right side."

"I have to go find Ben and—"

Grant squeezed the shoulder. "The Army isn't the same as it was before the war, Elijah. You must trust to providence that your son will make his way through this ordeal safely. I promised Lidia that I would allow no harm to come to him. At the time, I thought such a promise foolish, but it seems she could see the future straighter than any of us. If we have the opportunity, we'll see that promise through," Grant said. "But for now . . ." He led Cord to the map, attempting a diversion. "After we secure Cairo—if you can convince General Fremont that it is to be my job, and I have no idea how you will do that, but I do trust you on it—and before we can look down the Mississippi for the offensive, Mrs. Rumble's letter made me think of something. We must protect our flank to the east."

Cord tried to focus. "The Tennessee and Cumberland Rivers."

"Indeed," Grant said. He slid his finger along the map. "Paducah, Forts Henry and Donelson, Clarksville and probably even Nashville must be subdued first. And the Tennessee River is a dagger right through Tennessee and into Alabama."

"You're thinking far ahead, Sam."

"Someone has to," Grant said.

"Tell me something, Sam. That night the vigilance committee came for me. You were cadet in charge of quarters. That wasn't a coincidence, was it?"

Grant smiled. "After all these years, you wonder about that? I knew Fred had the duty and it didn't take much hard thought to know that's when they would come for you."

"Thank you," Cord said.

"You're welcome," Grant said, "but now I have a special mission for you. After you see General Fremont."

"And that is?"

"Go to Clarksville undercover. Find this Samual fellow. If he can make it safely from Natchez to Clarksville—and we know he made it from Natchez to West Point and back without being stopped-- then he's a man we can use. The people who are going to know the land the best are the slaves. I need someone who can talk to them. Who understands them. If I can team you with Samual, I'll have the most formidable pair of scouts any commander could desire."

"He's supposed to take his daughter to Canada. And himself."

"I'll give them protection," Grant said.

"You're breaking the law," Cord pointed out. "Fugitive Slave Act? Remember?"

"I think it's one of the negatives of seceding from the Union to believe that Federal law still applies in your favor," Grant pointed out. "I need to know the lay of the land down the Cumberland, the Tennessee and the how things go on the Mississippi."

"That's all?" Cord laughed. "Find a man who doesn't want to be found? Go behind enemy lines? Tall orders and ones that could get me hung if caught."

"Aren't you the intrepid mountain man, with all your experience in hunting and tracking?" Grant asked. "Who better to do this?"

"I'll do it. But if I discover where Ben is, I must make his safety my priority."

"He's my Godson," Grant said. "I'm with you on that."

27 August 1861, St. Louis, Missouri

There were guards on the four corners of the block, guards in front of the mansion, guards in front of the door, guards inside the door and Cord imagined there'd be guards sitting on top of Fremont's head at this rate. His dispatch from Grant eventually got him in the front door, but no further.

A lieutenant, looking very important indeed, in full dress uniform with a ceremonial sword strapped to his belt held out his hand. "I will relay that to the proper authority."

"Nope."

The lieutenant was confused. "Sir, I am the aide to the assistant to the adjutant to the chief of staff to General Fremont."

"That's a mouthful," Cord said. "You tell the assistant to the adjutant to tell the adjutant to tell the chief of staff to tell Fremont, that his old friend Elijah Cord is here to see him. He'll make some time for me."

Cord leaned the Lancaster against the wall and grabbed a chair, sinking into it, stretching his legs out.

The lieutenant still hadn't moved. "Sir, I must insist—"

Cord twitched his buckskin coat aside, revealing the foot long Bowie knife. "Son, I get irritable when I have to wait."

The lieutenant scurried off. Cord pulled an apple out of his haversack and unsheathed the Bowie knife. He sliced a piece off the fruit and popped it in his mouth.

It took a couple of minutes for an older man to appear, dressed in a uniform the like of which Cord had never seen. "I am the Commander of the Bodyguard," the man said in a heavy eastern European accent. "It is reported you have threatened one of our officers."

Cord carefully carved out a piece of apple with the Bowie, then impaled it with the needle point of the knife. He waved that at the officer. "We're going in the wrong direction. Thought at least I'd get the adjutant or maybe even the chief of staff. Commander of Bodyguard is a step of the trail sideways. Fremont know I'm here?"

The Commander gestured and two soldiers flanked him, muskets at the ready.

Cord sighed. "Tell General Fremont that Elijah Cord is here with a letter from his father-in-law, Senator Benton."

"Senator Benton is not alive," the Commander said.

"That's the point," Cord said. "General Fremont will understand and he won't appreciate you blocking my way to him and making me even more irritable than I already am."

The Commander left in a huff, but the two guards remained. Cord finished his apple, wiped the blade of the Bowie clean on his sleeve and slid it back into the sheath.

The Commander of the Bodyguard reappeared and brusquely gestured for Cord to follow, along with the two guards. They passed many officers, almost all outfitted in uniforms befitting a king's court rather than a general's field staff, and all appearing very, very busy with the papers in their hands. The three-story house was impressive, one of the hulking mansions that lined Chouteau Street in St. Louis's richest neighborhood. Impressive, but an odd place to put the headquarters of the Army of the West. Two more guards opened a set of double doors and Cord walked inside, the Commander of the Bodyguard close by his side.

"General Fremont," Cord said.

The Pathfinder was leaning over a large map that covered the entire surface of a dining table, talking to a pair of officers. So far, Cord had not seen a single officer he knew. Fremont's distaste for West Pointers was making its presence well known in his headquarters. It didn't bother Cord in the least that he was going to make his former commander swallow a bitter West Point pill.

Fremont looked up and scowled. "You've not changed in the slightest."

"Oh, I think I've changed in one or two ways over the years," Cord said. He gestured at the other men. "You want them hanging around to hear what I got to say or you want this to be private?"

"What do you have to say?" Fremont demanded, placing both hands on the map, as if by doing so he commanded all the terrain beneath them.

"Remember back in Los Angeles in late '46 with General Kearny?" Cord asked.

"Leave!" Fremont gestured imperiously and the room cleared until it was the two of them, the double doors swinging shut with a solid thud.

Cord walked over to the table, standing opposite Fremont.

"See this?" the General asked, running his finger along the map. He traced a route through southwest Missouri and northwest Arkansas into Louisiana and ending in New Orleans. "I will have it all by next summer."

"You're going to march to New Orleans on the west side of the Mississippi?" Cord asked.

"I'm a General," Fremont said. "Address me properly."

"You're going to march to New Orleans on the west side of the Mississippi?" Cord repeated. "Sure you can find your way, or someone already do the route for you, Pathfinder? Or maybe I should title you Pathmarker? Did you ever really take a trail that someone hadn't already walked on before you? Isn't the truth that you just wrote better books about those trails than the other fellows who were there before you?"

"What the devil do you want, Cord?"

Cord pulled out his Bowie knife and Fremont started, but Cord slammed the point into the map. "Before you take New Orleans next summer, you need to keep hold of this. Cairo."

"What about it?"

"I want you to give command of Cairo and all forces thereabouts to General Grant."

"Who is Grant? One of your West Point cronies?"

"Listen, I'm doing you a favor by asking you to do me one."

"Are you blackmailing me?"

"Not at all," Cord said. "I'm asking you to keep your word. Grant's the best you got out here and you put him in Cairo, he'll make the situation favorable so you can march on New Orleans next year."

"And if I don't?" Fremont demanded.

"Then you are dishonorable."

Fremont's hand went to his saber grip. "Watch your tongue."

Cord lightly touched the handle of his Bowie knife. "Ever since you had those unarmed men shot outside San Francisco, I've been itching to have a go at you. If it hadn't been for Kit being involved putting that poor fella out of his misery and knowing you'd take him down with you, I'd have let Kearny hang you. I'd have sworn on a stack of Bibles ten feet high you were a murderer." He gestured. "Try pulling that fancy blade and I'll have this pig sticker in your guts before you clear the scabbard."

Fremont took his hand off the saber. "Polk and Prentiss are senior in rank to Grant. They will not take it well to have him jumped over them."

"They'll live," Cord said.

Fremont's eyes shifted from Cord to the map, then back. "This Grant. He can fight?"

"He can fight."

Fremont's head inclined ever so slightly, a moment of awareness. "You still have that damn letter don't you?"

Cord tapped his pocket. "I do. But that aint the big thing. The big thing is whether you are a man of honor or not."

Fremont nodded. "I'll give Grant the command."

"Good." Cord turned and headed for the door.

"I under-estimated you from the time we first met," Fremont said. "When we meet again, I won't."

"We aren't meeting again," Cord said to the door. His voice dropped to a whisper. "Because you aren't going to be in command here once Ulysses gets moving."

11 October 1861, Charleston, South Carolina

"'So short-lived has been the American Union that men who saw it rise may live to see its fall.'" James Mason tapped the London Times. "The time is fortuitous for us to go to London and beseech the British to intervene on our behalf!"

Captain George King stood in the background of the Captain's cabin on board the *CSS Nashville* listening to the 'great men' talk ideology and politics, a chart tucked under his arm, waiting with the patience of a saint. London was a long way from Charleston, where the re-flagged *Nashville* was anchored.

King respected Mason and it was the only reason he kept his tongue. The rest of the upper crust of Charleston crowded into the cabin he could do without as they were the men who had shunned his father in his misfortune. Mason had been the author of the Fugitive Slave Act of 1850, which many considered the first splintering that finally led to the complete secession of the South from the North eleven years later. It was a simple law, requiring just proof of identity and two witnesses as evidence that a negro was a runaway. Then it directed that the contraband be returned to its proper owner.

The ship was riding the swell in Charleston Harbor and a cool October breeze blew in the open hatches, making the cabin tolerable. Despite the breeze, the air was full of cigar smoke and bluster.

"We're eleven states now," R.M.T. Hunter, the Confederate Secretary of States said. "If we swing Maryland, Kentucky and Missouri into the fold, we'll be fourteen and the Union won't be able to stop us."

King could stay quiet no longer. "Then why do we need to beg England for help?"

All the old men in the room turned and looked at him.

"I'm all for victory," King said, "but not at the cost of begging a foreign power and then owing them something. Our own honor and strength will be enough to overcome the Yankees. And if England wants to join the struggle against the North, have them do so for their own reasons and leave us free of any obligation."

"Young man," Hunter said, "you're a military officer and can't be expected to understand the intricacies of—"

"I understand tides and ships." King pushed forward to the Captain's table in the center of the cabin and rolled out the chart. "The *Nashville* draws too much water to take anything but the main channel. I know this from the ship's specifications. I'm familiar with the tides and channels around here. I did a reconnaissance last night in a barque. The Yankees have five warships guarding the outer markers of the main channel. The *Nashville* will never make it through."

That brought silence for the first time.

"Do you have a suggestion, Captain?" Mason asked. "We considered going south by land, through Mexico and leaving from a port there, but the journey would be time-consuming."

"I do have a solution, sir," King said. "There's a smaller steamer anchored in the harbor. She draws much less than the Nashville. She could be bought or hired to leave Charleston via shallower waterways that are not guarded and make it to open water."

"Can she sail to England?" Hunter asked.

"No, sir," King said.

"Then what is—"

King cut Hunter's protest off. "But, sir, she could make it to Havana where the British mail packet, *Trent*, regularly makes the route to London. If they leave tonight on the tide, they can get on the next sailing of the *Trent*."

Mason perked up. "Once on board a British ship, we'll be safe," he informed his partner Slidell.

The two had been chosen to head a new delegation to London to enlist England in the war effort on the side of the Confederacy. To date, the British were neutral, but that neutrality was slanted toward the south. British subjects were forbidden to fight for either side. But beyond that, the neutrality provided Confederate ships the same access to the mighty British empire's far-flung network of ports for docking and provision and to build ships to make up the fledgling rebel navy. Much to the chagrin of President Lincoln and the Union.

"Conduct the arrangements, Captain," Mason said.

"That's my decision to make as Secretary of State," Hunter said, his face red.

"Then make it, sir," King said. "The tide isn't going to wait on you."

"Watch your mouth, Captain," Hunter snapped. "I don't like this plan. It requires us to rely on outside sources to get to London."

"Then don't send them," King said. "We can win this war on—"

"Silence, you fool!" Hunter roared. "You're as ignorant as your father."

King slapped Hunter so hard, the elder man fell into the table, knocking it over, spilling the charts to the floor. As Hunter scrambled to his feet, assisted by several others, King threw his gauntlet at him. "On your honor, sir, I will face you on the Battery at dawn tomorrow. Pistol or sword, it matters not."

"For God's Sake man," Mason said as he slid between the two. "We have a large enough fight on our hands without quarrelling with each other." He pointed to the door. "Go, Captain. Make the arrangements for Havana."

King was breathing hard through his nose, nostrils flaring.

"Captain," Mason said.

King reluctantly nodded. "Yes, sir."

He exited and made his way forward, to the same transom he'd climbed over the night of Fort Sumter. A Jamaican was waiting for him, wearing a silk shirt and embroidered trousers, a cutlass stuck in his belt along with a brace of pistols.

"Get to Saint Thomas," King said. "Captain Wilkes and the USS San Jacinto will make port there on the way back from patrol off Africa. Tell him two Confederate emissaries will be aboard the Trent."

The Jamaican held out a hand and King deposited a sack of coin. The man was over the side where a skiff of similar sailors waited. They pulled away toward a small barque.

"Captain."

King turned. "Sir."

Mason walked up, puffing on a cigar. He offered one to King and they went through the ritual of lighting it.

"Well played," Mason said.

"As we discussed," King said.

"You're sure Wilkes will come for us?"

"I've met the man. He's fiery and impulsive. He's well known outside the Navy for his round the world survey from 1840 to 1841. But inside the Navy, he's more known for losing a ship on the Columbia River tidal bar and getting court-martialed upon his return for that and other actions and found guilty of illegally punishing some of his men. He won't be able to resist the bait."

"I'm not sure I like being bait," Mason said, "but unlike the men in that cabin, I know it's going to take more than words to get the British to act."

"Yes, sir."

Mason put his hands on the wooden rail. "Secretary Hunter will not bear your strike lightly."

"Then we will duel."

"No, you will not," Mason said. "We need good men. Hunter isn't a soldier but he is a politician who knows the ways of international law. We have few such men. And you are a soldier who knows how to fight and we have few of those also."

King said nothing.

"Maryland will not join us," Mason said. "Lincoln holds an iron grip there. The way he crushed the Baltimore riots indicates how far he will go. What do you think the chances for Missouri and Kansas?"

"Not good for Missouri, sir. That Lyon fellow got himself killed, but he broke the back of our resistance there and saved the St Louis arsenal. The Yankees are reinforcing quickly. Same for Kansas. The key to those states is east of them in Kentucky. If we can hold the Tennessee and Cumberland Rivers and then strike north to the Ohio, the entire war could change even more in our favor."

"Then I'll solve two problems with one move," Mason said. "I'm sending a letter to President Davis to assign you to the western theater. They need men who know the water and can help defend our forts from Yankee gunboats on the rivers."

"Sir, I'm supposed to report back to Norfolk and continue overseeing the refit of the *Merrimack* into an ironclad. If—"

"Captain, I've given you a large degree of latitude today. Understand when the leash has reached its limit. You are going west."

Sally Skull
20 Dec 1861, Banquete, Texas

"GONNA BE A WHITE CHRISTMAS here in Banquete in five days," Sally Skull said to Gabriel. She laughed. "Hell, gonna be white here all year round for a while. You never seen real snow, have you, girl?"

Gabriel shook her head. "No, ma'am."

"Well, it's sorta like that," she pointed out the saloon window, "'cept lot colder and wetter."

The main street running through town, El Camino Real, was now called the Cotton Road and bathed in white. The rumble of wagons loaded with bales was non-stop. The harsh Texas wind ripped off tufts and blew it about in such volume that every tree was laced with it and the ground was covered with a thin layer.

The doors to the saloon swung open and Declan came in, accompanied by a man sporting a large mustache with waxed tips and walking as if he had a steel rod for a spine.

"This'll be interesting," Skull muttered.

"My dear woman," Declan exclaimed. He strode up to Skull and kissed her on both cheeks. Then he turned to Gabriel. "Ah, and the precious young one who has grown so admirably." He leaned forward to give the same greeting, but Skull's word froze him.

"No."

"Ah, yes," Declan said, stepping back. "I was swept up in the joy of meeting old friends. And this," he indicated the man behind, "is Captain Arthur James Lyon Fremantle, of His Majesty's Coldstream Guards."

"That's a lot of names for one fella," Skull observed.

Declan introduced Skull and Gabriel and Fremantle bowed. "Pleased to make your acquaintance, ladies."

"You sure on that?" Skull said. She shifted back to Declan. "The news?"

"That's partly why I brought Captain Fremantle with me," Declan said. "Much has been happening. You heard about Mason and Slidell?"

"Heard there's a stir about them with the Yankees and the Brits," Skull said.

Fremantle spoke up. "They, my lady, are two of your emissaries who were pirated off a ship flying my country's flag. Under force of arms by a Union Navy captain."

"In English," Skull said wearily.

"Jeff Davis sent two fellows to negotiate with the Brits," Declan said. "But a Union ship intercepted a British ship carrying them and took them off at gunpoint. The Brits aren't happy at all with the Union."

Skull looked at Fremantle. "You here to go to war?" She looked past him. "Where's the rest of the Brit army?"

"I was already en route when I heard of the event while transferring conveyance in Havana," Fremantle said. "But rest assured, the British Empire will not take kindly to the violation of their neutrality. And it appears many in the Union are clamoring for war with my country."

"Over two men?" Skull asked.

"They were diplomats on a British flagged ship and as such their kidnapping violates international law and is a slap in the face to the Crown. I can assure you, this matter is being taken most seriously on both sides of the Atlantic. The Union Secretary of State is urging war.

"What about old Lincoln?" Skull asked.

Declan spoke up. "He hasn't weighed in on the matter."

"He aint that stupid."

"Excuse me?" Fremantle asked.

"And you were coming here for?" Skull asked.

"Ah, the business," Fremantle said. "Ships. Mister Declan here, made contact with some representatives of various English ship-builders and I am here to ascertain whether the necessary financing would follow through on the actual construction."

"But you're in the British Army," Skull said.

"Assistant Military Secretary of Gibraltar. On detached, special, secret assignment."

Skull shook her head in amazement. "Secret? You think you're being secret? You told me your name. He's the rep?" she asked Declan.

"Indeed, he is," Declan confirmed.

Skull sighed. "I got three ships loaded with cotton. I can get it for six cents a pound here, but it would cost you over thirty cents at least in Mexico. I give it to you for fifteen. The rest goes to the builders. And I can send many more ships until the Yankees wise up and shut the ports in Texas down; and then, as you can see, I'll be moving it through Mexico."

"They would want the cotton at ten cents a pound," Fremantle countered.

"I don't think so," Skull said. "Them Confederate fools already burned over a million pounds on the wharves and they aint done yet. Where else you think England gonna get it? What happens when your factories shut down with no product? Gonna be some unhappy people out of work.

"We're serious people here—" Skull continued, but paused as the swinging doors to the saloon were thrown aside and two men, covered in dust caked on by sweat, walked in.

Skull drew both pistols, Gabriel snatching up her Spencer as soon as she saw the older woman in action. Skull fired, hitting one of the men in the shoulder, spinning him about.

"Alive!" she shouted to Gabriel, a split second before the young girl fired.

The bullet from the Spencer hit the second man in the stomach as Gabriel jerked her aim down at the last second. The impact of the heavy slug bowled him back out the swinging doors onto the plank sidewalk.

Skull jumped to her feet and ran over to the man she had wounded. He was grasping for his pistol and she stopped that by firing another bullet through the arm. He screamed in pain. Gabriel rushed past, through the doors, covering the man she'd gut shot.

Skull kicked the man at her feet, making him crawl underneath the swinging doors to lie next to his partner, leaving a trail of blood.

"We got us two renegades here!" Skull yelled as a crowd gathered, half with guns drawn. "They kilt some teamsters up near San Anton. They're on those wanted posters, right here." She pulled a pair of papers out of a pocket.

A rancher bulled through the crowd, peered at the posters, then at the two men. "Sure enough. That's 'em. Murderers and thieves."

The first man looked up at Skull. "But we was here to meet y—"

Gabriel smashed his face with the butt stock of the Spencer, stunning him into silence. "Shut up."

"Hang 'em!" someone cried out from the crowd.

"Hanging's too good for these murderers," Skull said. "We'll string 'em and bury 'em and let Texas do the rest."

The crowd roared approvingly. Several men stepped forward, trussing the two renegades securely.

"You'll want to see this," Skull said to Declan and Fremantle. The Irishman sighed and drained his shot of whiskey. The Englishman was completely befuddled.

"What about a trial?" Fremantle asked.

"They already had it," Skull said. "They're on the posters, aint they?"

On the outskirts of Banquet, which didn't take long to reach, ropes were tightened securely around each man's neck as they lay in the dirt, blood seeping into the ground. Not enough to choke them, but enough to make them struggle to breath and keep them from talking. The other end of the rope was tossed over the highest branch of a mesquite tree, which meant not very high.

"There will be no drop and, besides," Fremantle said, "that's not even enough vertical distance to hang them."

"We aint hanging 'em," Skull said. "We stringing 'em."

A cluster of men wielding spades quickly dug two narrow holes about three feet deep before they hit rock. The two wounded men were jammed upright into the holes, dirt and sand packed tight around them until they were stuck. Then the ends of the ropes over the mesq uite
branch were pulled taut.

"Strung and buried," Skull said, turning back for town. The majority of folks followed but a few sadists remained to watch.

"They'll die of thirst." Fremantle was appalled. "It's barbaric."

"Nah," Skull said. "The critters will get to them first. By tomorrow there'll be nothing but bone there."

"You people," Fremantle sputtered, at a loss.

"Welcome to Texas. Still hankering to take on Americans? Now, about that price . . ."

25 December 1861, Palatine, Mississippi

Violet Rumble despised the big house. The empty rooms seemed to taunt her as she wandered aimlessly through the first level. Thirty-nine years ago when she'd arrived here as a nineteen year old bride, she'd fallen in love with the magnificent white building overlooking the Mississippi and commanding the plantation beyond. That love had gone across the spectrum from bright and burning, to faded, dried out hues, like flowers lacking water, to the grey of apathy for many years and to the bright red of rage, before sinking once more into grey.

She wearily climbed the stairs, the creak in her knees mirroring that of stairs that needed work, her breath puffing out from exertion into the freezing air. She edged open the door to her former bedroom, trying to keep the squeal to a minimum as she checked on Seneca. He was asleep, more accurately passed out from morphine, bundled in blankets against the winter cold. The fireplace was a dark hole in the wall. There was only one active fireplace, actually a tamped down pile of embers at the moment, in the kitchen for cooking and Violet dreaded having to ride out to Shantytown to plead with St. George to fill the wood bins. She'd start in on the furniture before that.

So much for Christmas morning 1861.

Violet didn't want to contemplate what 1862 might hold in store as she shut the door. She walked down the hall and halted outside Tiberius's bedroom. He too was passed out; she knew that without even opening the door. Whiskey. They might not be able to fill the wood bins, but somehow Tiberius was always able to fill his bottles.

Violet went to the top of the landing, hands gripping the railing. She remembered when she'd stood there watching guests enter for a grand party, queen of all she surveyed. She wasn't sure of the exact moment when it had begun to go wrong, and she was realist enough to know such thoughts were a waste of effort, but they were all she had. On some level she knew the key difference between youth and old age was that youth dreamed of making a future and old age dreamed of changing the past. It was hard for her to decide which was the more futile.

She retraced her way down the stairs to the kitchen. She stirred up the embers and tossed two precious pieces of wood onto the glowing red. She took the kettle and went outside to the pump. She dropped the heavy iron kettle onto the thin layer of ice in the basin, breaking through, filled it, then carried it back into the house. The wood was beginning to catch and she hung the kettle on its hook.

She went to the pantry and sighed. She might have to ride out to Shantytown anyway to get the stored produce of the plantation's own gardens. Cold they might bear, but starvation was another matter.

The sound of hooves on frozen dirt distracted her. She tamped down the leap of hope that it might be Rosalie, gone for over a month to deal with the death of her father. Ever since her daughter-in-law had left, St. George had cut off supplies to the main house. If it were Rosalie arriving, Violet knew she could count on her to send a wagon of food and wood from Rosalie Plantation, enough to get them through the winter. But Violet would not write her, begging, while her daughter-in-law mourned. Violet would rather go to Shantytown and face her penance.

Violet opened the front door. She resisted the urge to immediately slam it shut when she recognized the riders. At least she would not have to ride to Shantytown to beg. She reached into the drawer in the small table right inside the door and retrieved one of Tiberius's pistols. She tucked it in the pocket on her large skirt and went outside.

St. George came riding up the drive, a half-dozen men behind him. His subordinate overseers. They were all armed, rifles across the pommels of their saddles. Another slave must have fled, Violet thought. She remained at the top of the stairs.

St. George halted his horse at the base of the stairs and looked at her. His gutted left eye had been replaced by an orb of charred bone. The bone had been sterilized in a fire and then inserted. The bone had canals throughout its mass, allowing living tissue to merge into it, filling the hole and leaving little room for infection. An effective but painful technique, which St. George had traveled to St. Louis to undergo. Overlaid on top of the bone was a pure white porcelain cap, gleaming in the early morning sun. The white cap was pure vanity but very effective in scaring the slaves.

He sat there for a moment, taking in Violet, then shifting what remained of his gaze across the front of the house. He dismounted with a solid thud of boots meeting frozen dirt. He took the stairs slowly as his men spread out, lounging in their saddles, grins on their faces.

St. George reached into his sash and pulled out an old flintlock pistol. Violet took an involuntary step back, but gathered herself and braced for the news.

St. George tossed the weapon onto the porch with a heavy thud. "You recognize?"

Violet didn't answer.

"It got the Rudolph name on it," St. George said. "Your daddy name was Rudolph, weren't it?"

"It is."

"The name or the gun?"

"Both."

"When those nigras did this—" he pointed at his left eye—"that was left behind. So the dead one we found in the swamp had it or Samual had it. Don' matter which. How they get it? You give it? You arm a slave?"

"If you found it that day," Violet said, "why have you waited so long to produce it? How do I know you didn't come into the house and steal it?"

"Cause I got witnesses that seen it there," St. George said. "And I wait 'til I'm ready before showing my hand. And I had something to deal wit'." He pointed once more at his left eye.

"What hand do you think you're playing?" Violet asked. "If you have a legal problem, get the sheriff." That was as weak an argument as Violet had ever made and she knew it. But it might gain some time. For what, she didn't know.

"Don' need no sheriff," St. George said. "I'm Captain of the Natchez Home Guard, w' orders on down from General Johnston hisself." He stepped closer to Violet. "I'm the law now. You give 'dat nigra this gun, you be a dead woman. So you give it or Samual steal it?"

"It must have been taken from the house."

St. George laughed. "You lying. Sure as I standing here. Mighty Mistress Violet be lying. When we catch Samual, if he still alive and the swamp not take him, we'll make 'im talk. And when he tell us you give him this gun, we coming for you." He bent over and picked up the flintlock. "I be keeping this. Evidence for your hanging. I think we hang you from that angel. Watch you kick and turn for a while." He turned to leave.

"St. George."

When he turned back, he faced the pistol in Violet's hand. She pulled back the hammer. "I don't have much to live for any more. So it does me no trouble to shoot you."

"What about your lil' boy then?" St. George said. "Miss Rosalie away. You think he last long if you die now? Who give him his medicine? I took nothing. I took the pain. No need for medicine. They burn what left of this eye out while I awake and put the new one in."

Violet moved her finger to the trigger. "I'll have some satisfaction before I die."

St. George smiled and took a step closer. "You won' shoot me. You know your boy die if you do." He reached up and took the gun from her hand.

Violet's shoulders slumped in defeat.

"I'd kill you where you stand," St. George said. "But I want you to suffer. See that one-legged son of yours die. Your weak husband drink to death. Your other son killed fighting for the damn Yankees. Then I gonna come and I gonna take this place and make it mine."

He turned to go, but paused. "Something you ought know. Your lil' boy getting sent east. That was mine doing. I a powerful man now around here. You best remember that. While you still breathing."

St. George stomped down the stairs and mounted. With a whoop, he led the men on a gallop down the drive and onto the main road. The sound of the hooves faded in the distance, yet Violet didn't leave the porch, her heavy shawl wrapped around her frail shoulders.

She took deep breaths, trying to gather her energy, a chore growing more difficult by the day. She tried to develop a plan. Without the house slaves, she doubted she could harness horses to the wagon and, even if she managed, she knew she couldn't haul Seneca out and load him. She couldn't leave Seneca to go to Rosalie to get help. Tiberius was worthless. She couldn't--

"Mistress Violet."

Violet spun about. "You're alive!"

"I be," Samual said.

Violet looked over her shoulder, the dust from St. George's party hanging over the road. "You can't be here! It's dangerous."

Samual edged onto the porch, a revolver looking like a toy in his large hand. "I aint alone."

A white man came from behind Samual, someone vaguely familiar to Violet. He was dressed in buckskins, had a long rifle in his hands, and a large knife tucked in his belt.

"Ma'am, I'm Elijah Cord. We met many years ago at Seneca's wedding."

Violet nodded. "I remember. But what are you doing here with Samual?" She didn't wait for an answer. "St. George was just here. He'll hang you if he finds you."

Samual tapped a finger to his ear. "We hear, Mistress."

"Sounds like you might be facing a hanging," Cord said. "And St. George is scouting with the home guard. Probably heard some Union spies was in the area." Cord grinned. "Not sure why he'd be hearing that."

"Samual, why didn't you do what I said? Why attack St. George? Why didn't you get Echo? Why aren't you in Canada?"

Samual turned to Cord, overwhelmed by the deluge of questions.

"St. George needs attacking," Cord said. "One day I'll kill that son-of-a-bitch. If you pardon my language. And Samual didn't get Echo because she's not in Clarksville. When my friend Ulysses Grant, you'll remember him from the wedding also, took Paducah, many fled Clarksville, your family among them. I found—rather Samual found me-- in the area. From what we could pick up, your family went somewhere near Atlanta."

Violet closed her eyes at more bad news. "Yes. We have cousins in Georgia."

"Samual works with me now," Cord said. "We've been riding for weeks. Scouting. The forts on the Cumberland and Tennessee. Clarksville. Down along the Tennessee River, through Corinth and then here. Tell me of Ben. Have you heard more?"

Violet shook her head. "Little mail comes through."

Hundreds of miles of riding through enemy territory without achieving his one true goal hit Cord hard.

"Mistress," Samual said.

"Yes?"

"Something you need know. My boy, Agrippa. He might be living. James told me before he die he saw him crawl ashore 'dat day."

"Oh!" Violet fanned herself.

"Are you all right?" Cord asked.

"That's the best news I've heard in a long, long time," Violet said. She took Samual's hands in hers. "I so pray this news is true."

"We can't stand around here all day chatting," Cord said. He rubbed the stubble on his chin, trying to figure out the next move. "You need to leave. Can Seneca take a trip in a wagon?"

"He feels no pain," Violet said, "and his stump has sealed."

"I take that as a yes," Cord said. "Samual, could you please get the wagon ready?"

"What do you propose?" Violet asked.

"You got some place to go where you'll be safe from St. George?" Cord asked.

"Rosalie's plantation. But her father died recently and they're still in mourning and—"

"They'll be doing more mourning if you don't leave this place."

The implications hit Violet. "Abandon Palatine? It's our life."

"Isn't much of a life any more," Cord said, "and it's gonna get worse, ma'am. Your kin fled Clarksville. The war, no matter what the boys around here say, will be coming south. And even if it doesn't, it just plain isn't safe for you to stay here, ma'am. You did give Samual that gun." Cord glanced over at the barn, where Samual was readying the wagon. "And there's a chance the two of us might get caught. I'd get hung as a spy and they'd bring him back here and give him a lot of pain to make him talk. Then you'd be hung too."

Violet tried to rally some of her former self. "I asked you not to call me ma'am. I do not run a house of ill repute. Let me gather some things and we can prepare my son for travel."

It didn't take long to get Seneca loaded in the wagon. Cord kept a wary eye on the road, anxious to be moving. They set off down the lane. Cord rode next to the wagon. Samual drove, Violet in the back with Seneca. As they reached the end of the drive, she took one last look at the old white house.

There were no tears.

They turned the corner.

She never mentioned Tiberius.

25 December 1861, Washington DC

"Is it war or peace with England, sir?" Stanton asked as soon he opened the door to the President's office. "The Cabinet is waiting."

Rumble paused in the doorway, uncertain whether he should enter behind Stanton who had escorted him once more to the office.

"And they can keep waiting," Lincoln told Stanton. He waved at Rumble. "Come in, come in."

Stanton reluctantly stood to the side, allowing Rumble to pass and shutting the door behind. It was just the three of the men in the room and Stanton went over to window, now closed against the chill Christmas day.

"Sit, please," Lincoln said, his attention once more on a piece of paper.

Rumble sat on the hard bench and waited. It was a minute before Lincoln put the paper down and turned his attention to his visitor. "You were not a fan of General McClellan if I remember rightly."

"He's a fine organizer, sir."

"He's been organizing for a couple of months now," Lincoln said, "and with winter baring its fangs, I suspect he'll be organizing for several more. He tells me he cannot advance on the Confederates before Spring."

Rumble remained silent.

"Do you know what else he says?" Lincoln didn't wait for an answer. "'I can do it all'. Can you believe that? All encompasses quite a bit, don't you think, Sergeant Major?"

"It does, sir." The President was angry and Rumble was uncertain how to respond to the raw emotion, a drastic change from the last time he'd been in here.

Lincoln rubbed his right temple with two fingers, as if trying to press back the vein pulsing there.

"You know about the *Trent* affair?"

"I read the papers, sir."

"Should it be war?"

Rumble glanced at Stanton, who was half-turned to the room now. "We have a war, sir."

Lincoln slapped the desk and his face lightened for the moment. "Exactly! One war at a time. Perfect." He glanced at Stanton. "That will be my entire speech to the cabinet, even though almost to a man they desire to fight England. Well, they desire to declare to fight England and then send others to do the actual fighting. We'll give Slidell and Mason back to the British and they can have them, for all they're worth. Very good, Sergeant Major, very good."

The mood in the room changed like that and Rumble blinked, never before experiencing such command of emotion from another person.

Lincoln leaned forward. "You've been observing our brand new Army of the Potomac. What do you think?"

"Good men, sir," Rumble said. "They're getting organized and trained."

"And leadership?"

"It's a weeding out process," Rumble said. "Slowly, the incompetent political appointees get shelved and better officers replace them."

"West Point men?"

"Many of them," Rumble said. "They are professionals, sir."

"And the Confederates have their share." He picked up another piece of paper. "The current tally. Three hundred and six West Point graduates foreswore their oath to the country and now fight for the Confederacy. I wonder at the professionalism."

"I hadn't known the number to be so high, sir," Rumble admitted.

Lincoln dropped the piece of paper. "And McClellan? You've seen more of him than me." Lincoln laughed bitterly. "Most everyone has seen more of him than me. I went to his house a few weeks ago and I waited an hour for him to arrive and when he did he went straight to bed, not even stopping to say a how-do-you-do. Can you imagine?"

Rumble flushed red. "No, sir, I can't. That's an unforgivable breach of etiquette."

"I don't care about etiquette," Lincoln said. "I care about winning this war. The one we already have. I've tried cajoling, pleading, ordering, and threatening, and I cannot get McClellan to move south."

"He will have to eventually, sir," Rumble said. "He is planning. I've seen that. He—" Rumble paused.

"Go on."

"He wants to outflank the Confederates, Mister President. I believe he wants to do a seaborne campaign to Fortress Monroe and attack up the peninsula to Richmond sometime early next year. Probably around March or April, once the roads are dry."

"You don't sound very enthusiastic about the plan," Lincoln observed.

"I'm just a Sergeant Major," Rumble said.

"And what does the Sergeant Major think?"

"I don't understand boxing yourself in on a peninsula when you have the superior force, sir," Rumble said.

"Ah," Lincoln exclaimed, "but according to General McClellan he does not. His intelligence agency, headed by Mister Pinkerton, insists the Army of the Potomac is out-numbered by the Confederates." Lincoln waved that all away. "Young Napoleon will move when he moves and there isn't much more I can do about it for now."

"There is someone who will move as soon as he's let off his leash," Rumble said.

"Your Ulysses S. Grant?" Lincoln asked.

"You remember?"

"He took Paducah before those other fellows got to it," Lincoln said. "That's the fastest any general has moved since they opened the bar at Willard's. I had to relieve Fremont. Besides the fact he wouldn't move, he issued an emancipation proclamation on his own authority. Caused a hell of a mess and almost lost us the border states. Halleck now commands the west and says he will move. He requests I give him a month. But if he doesn't move by the end of January, I'll send an order forcing action of one sort or the other and that should get your Grant off his leash. You were right about him, it appears."

"There's something else, sir."

Lincoln raised an eyebrow. "Yes?"

"Do you remember Colonel Sherman?"

Lincoln frowned. "I heard tell he lost his mind and was relieved of command. Something about hundreds of thousands of people dying and the country laid waste. He saw Rebels behind every tree. Not a cheerful fellow by a long shot. The newspapers say he's insane."

"He's a pragmatist, sir, not insane. He's back home and I received a letter from his wife. She fears he may take his own life if he's not returned to duty. He would do well serving with Grant or even nearby Grant. They're old friends."

"Not the most ringing endorsement to bring a man back on active duty," Lincoln said. "But I'll see what I can do."

Stanton spoke for the first time. "Sir."

"Yes?"

"Your son, Willie, is riding outside."

"He is attached to that pony like nothing before." Lincoln stood and walked over to the window.

Rumble also got to his feet, to see what had caused Stanton to comment on it. The reason was obvious. The boy was ill-dressed to ride on a chilly December afternoon, wearing but a short jacket and no hat and gloves.

"Damnation," Lincoln exclaimed.

"I'll get him, sir," Rumble said.

"Thank you. Hurry, please."

Rumble ran out of the room and down the stairs of the Executive Mansion. He threw open an outer door and saw the boy galloping the pony across frozen grass. Rumble took an intercept course and got the boy to bring the pony to a stop without scaring it.

"Hello, Willie," Rumble said, putting his hand lightly on the pony's bit.

"Hello," Willie said.

"I'm Lucius Rumble."

"You're a soldier," Willie said.

"I'm Master of the Horse at West Point."

Willie's eyes got wide. "Could you teach me how to ride better?"

"I could." Rumble was leading the boy and pony back toward the stables as quickly as he could. "And one of the first rules of riding is to be properly prepared."

"I was in a hurry," Willie said.

"Being in a rush is not good either," Rumble said. "Slow and calm and steady when dealing with a horse."

They entered the barn and Rumble gave the reins to a stable hand as he helped the boy off. He escorted him into the White House's kitchen, seating him near the fire, taking off his short coat and putting a warm blanket over his shoulders.

"Do you have a son?" Willie asked.

"I do."

"Does he ride?"

"He does," Rumble said. "And quite well."

Willie put his hands out, warming them. "Is he safe right now in front of a fire like I am?"

Rumble paused. "I hope so."

"What are you doing to my son?" Mary Todd Lincoln's voice was shrill. A plump, short woman with a rather plain face, she wore a brightly colored gown as if to make up for the drabness of her physical appearance. Lincoln appeared behind her.

"Just getting him warmed up, ma'am," Rumble said.

"Get away from him now!" She punctuated the order by shoving Rumble in the chest.

"Mother!" President Lincoln placed an arm around his wife's shoulder. "Sergeant Major Rumble meant well. He brought Willie in from the cold."

Mary Todd shook the arm off and grabbed Willie by the hand. She dragged him out of the kitchen and into the residence.

Lincoln turned to Rumble with a sad smile. "The burdens of family on top of the burden of war. It can be almost unbearable."

25 December 1861
5th Ohio Cavalry
Army of the Ohio

Dear Grandmother Violet,
It doesn't have to be this way. None of it. The war. The Slavery. The factories. All men should be free. And countrymen should not be fighting each other.

But we are and believe we must fight for the cause we believe in.

I'm sorry, Grandmother Violet, but I could not keep the words inside me. None of this makes any sense, yet here I am, sitting in a field in Kentucky on Christmas morning, caught up in the great contest.

I pray this letter finds you in good health and cheerful spirits. I think back fondly to the Christmas I spent with you just before my fifth birthday. It was a magical time. As I am older, I appreciate more than ever what you and Aunt Rosalie did for Abigail and me.

The war is far north of you and I hope you will be spared any trouble because of it. You may have heard from Father that I have joined the Union Army. He was not pleased and I imagine you might not be pleased, either.

I'm sorry if you feel I'm fighting on the wrong side. But I must do what I believe is right and just. While I wish with all my heart none of this was so, it is so and I must accept it.

Father sent me west. My riding skills caught my Colonel's eyes and now I am in the 5th Ohio Cavalry Regiment. We are somewhere in Kentucky but I don't believe we'll be staying here long.

Please Grandmother Violet. Mail is precious in camp, but it appears most of us write much more than we receive. I long to hear from you.

Your loving grandson,
Private Ben Agrippa Rumble

St. George carefully folded the letter, then waved one of the men to take the usual bottle up the stairs to Tiberius. The overseer walked over to the roaring blaze in the main fireplace on the first floor of Palatine. He warmed his hands for a moment, deep in thought, then took out the letter and tossed it into the blaze.

1862
President's General War Order No. 1
EXECUTIVE MANSION, WASHINGTON, January 27, 1862.

Ordered, That the 22d day of February, 1862, be the day for a general movement of the land and the naval forces of the United States against the insurgent forces.

That especially the army at and about Fortress Monroe, the Army of the Potomac, the Army of Western Virginia, the army near Munfordville, Kentucky, the army and flotilla at Cairo, and a naval force in the Gulf of Mexico, be ready for a movement on that day.

That all other forces, both land and naval, with their respective commanders, obey existing orders for the time, and be ready to obey additional orders when duly given.

That the heads of departments, and especially the Secretaries of War and of the Navy, with all their subordinates, and the General-in-chief, with all other commanders and subordinates of land and naval forces, will severally be held to their strict and full responsibilities for the prompt execution of this order.

ABRAHAM LINCOLN.

Fort Henry

6 Feb 1862, Fort Henry, Tennessee

CAPTAIN GEORGE KING, CONFEDERATE States Marine Corps, was waist deep in freezing river water and doing his damnedest to keep the cannon's friction primer dry. The 32-pounder smoothbore was aimed north, along the Tennessee River. Coming toward Fort Henry were four ironclad gunboats, followed at a distance by three woodclads. The lead boat was over a mile away and closing slowly.

"They wait a little while, damn Yankees could just watch us drown," one of the cannoneers muttered.

"Steady, men," King ordered. He sensed a new presence on the parapet. General Tilghman, commander of the fort, was frowning at the approaching gun-boats, as if ill-will could keep them at a distance.

"How long do you think you can hold?" he asked King.

"Depends on how aggressive their commander is," King said. "Eventually, though, be it water, cannon-fire or the Infantry that's surely on its way, it'll get difficult. But if we persevere and stick to our guns, I believe we can repel the Yankees."

"The powder magazine is underwater," one of the cannoneers complained.

Tilghman didn't seem reassured either. "The men are un-trained. Their weapons are old. The fort is--," Tilghman sighed. "This is a most wretched place to build a fort. Too low, obviously." Tilghman pointed toward Kentucky on the other side of the river. "There are plenty of better positions along the river yonder, but if we had encamped on any of them during the summer we'd have violated Kentucky's neutrality."

"Which doesn't matter now, sir," King said as he peered toward the lead boat, checking the range markers he'd had emplaced along the river bank while sighting in the guns earlier in the week.

"It did then," Tilghman said.

"Permission to open fire, sir?" King asked.

"Fire away," Tilghman less an order than a bow to the inevitable.

"Ready!" King yelled.

The cannonneer pulled away the oilcloth, took the friction primer and connected a lanyard to it, which he handed to King. He stepped to the left rear of the gun, made sure the other men were clear of the recoil, then jerked the lanyard. Flame belched out of the muzzle along with a 32-pound ball, moving with such slow velocity, they could actually track its trajectory with their eyes. The other Confederate guns that were still functioning, eight in all, followed suit with a ragged volley.

The ball landed just right of the lead Union gunboat, sending a plume of water skyward. The cannon crew was at work, one man sealing the vent with his hand to prevent air from going in, the rammer jamming a sopping sponge down the barrel to make sure there were no smoldering embers that might set off the next charge of powder when it was loaded. As soon as he was done, he loudly tapped the wooden handle of the ram onto the muzzle, signaling another man to bring forward the charge and place it in the muzzle. The rammer settled the charge deep inside with his pole, then the cannon ball. King had been training the men on this routine hard for a week, ever since arriving and taking command of the artillery.

The gun was wheeled back into firing position and King once more took the lanyard, after aiming the piece. The entire process took twenty seconds. As he pulled the lanyard, King saw the flash of muzzles in the prows of the gunboats.

The battle was joined.

Three miles away, mired in mud, Cord heard the roar of cannon fire from the vicinity of the river. "I think this is going to be the Navy's battle, Sam, unless we grow some wings and fly above this muck."

Grant watched his army slipping and sliding in the low, soaked ground, making poor time in the landward advance on Fort Henry. "Nevertheless, we press on. We're committed to this course of action."

"Yes, sir," Cord said. "But Samual did warn us that the way would be hard through these woods."

"Next time, I'll listen to my scouts more closely. I'm afraid I was in a rush to get into action." Grant looked toward the sound of the firing. "I wish I knew how it goes."

"Cowards!" King screamed.

It was going worse than General Tilghman could have expected. As soon as Union shot and shell began pounding the ramparts of Fort Henry, the three thousand Confederate Infantry manning the rifle pits surrounding the fort had begun to melt away, like snow on a hot stove. It started with a man here, a squad there, but now whole companies were sliding away, toward the Dover Road and the twelve-mile trek to Fort Donelson.

No amount of exhortation from officers and sergeants could stop the flow.

King went for the radical solution. He ran to the single gun facing landward and ordered it trained on the Dover Road. "Canister!" he ordered.

The men working the gun hesitated and King drew his pistol. "We will stop this! We'll get—"

"At ease, Captain," General Tilghman ordered. "We'll not fire on our own men."

"They're cowards and deserters," King insisted.

"They're withdrawing to Fort Donelson, not running home," Tilghman reasoned, his shoulders already slumped in anticipation of inevitable defeat. "We're half underwater and in a terrible position. The situation is untenable. Sometimes the private is smarter than the general." Tilghman turned to his aide. "Inform all commanders to redeploy their men to Fort Donelson with all possible haste." He gave a wan smile. "Those of them who haven't already wisely anticipated the order, that is."

Tilghman pointed at King. "Captain King, if you would do me the favor of manning your cannons and continue firing at the Union ships for a while longer, I would greatly appreciate it. I will join you on the ramparts shortly."

King cursed the Infantry as he returned to command the river guns. Not a single one of the cannoneers dared emulate the other soldiers. King, in the short time he'd been in command of the artillery, had make clear he was not a man to be crossed. They feared him more than the Yankee guns.

However, King's will alone wasn't enough to keep submerging, ancient cannons firing. Or make ammunition appear out of thin air. One by one, the Confederate guns fell silent. On the receiving end of their shot, the Union ironclads seemed none the worse for wear, getting ever closer, their cannon ever more effective.

"Captain King, you may cease firing."

King's ears were ringing and he could barely hear the order. But he could clearly see the white flag being waved back and forth by Tilghman's aide. So could the gunboats. An eerie silence descended as one by one the cannon ceased firing.

A boat was lowered by the lead Federal gunboat. The water was so high, the boat was able to be rowed right in the gate of Fort Henry to negotiate the surrender.

King wasn't there to see it.

As soon as his last gun ceased firing, he grabbed his weapons and gear and departed the fort. The fact he was riding over mud trampled by the cowards who'd run grated on him. But he'd stayed until the white flag was shown. That at least, was some honor.

6 February 1862
Department of Missouri, Fort Henry
U.S. Grant to General Halleck, Commander Army of the West

Fort Henry is ours. The gunboats silenced the batteries before the investment was complete. I shall take and destroy Fort Donelson on the eighth and return to Fort Henry.
U.S. Grant
Brigadier General

Fort Donelson
7 Feb 1861, Between the Tennessee and Cumberland Rivers, Tennessee

"*W*HO COMMANDS DONELSON?" Grant asked Cord.

"That's a good question," Cord said as he rode next to Grant. The Union Army was moving, albeit slowly, along the Dover Road, traversing the twelve miles of land between conquered Fort Henry on the Tennessee behind them and the to-be-attacked Fort Donelson on the Cumberland ahead. "I talked to some of the fellows we captured. Seems they got a bit of a mess at Donelson trying to figure that out. Right now, it's Gideon Pillow."

Grant slapped his thigh. "I remember Pillow from Mexico. I bet I could march a squad up to within gunshot of any entrenchments he has and cause him to flee. He's not a soldier."

"Simon Bolivar Buckner is there also," Cord added.

That dammed Grant's enthusiasm. "Buckner helped me out in New York when I was attempting to get home after resigning my commission."

"He didn't help me much at West Point," Cord countered.

"That is so," Grant said. He took in the mud, the gray sky overhead and the soldiers trudging forward. "I might have been a bit premature in predicting the eighth."

"You were," Cord agreed.

"Where's your man, Samual?" Grant asked.

"He's not my man," Cord said. "He's out scouting."

"Looking for his Agrippa," Grant said.

"You have me on that. But he was right about the mud at Henry."

"And your Ben?"

Cord stared straight ahead. "The army grows faster than anyone imagined. I assume he got rolled into some unit on his way here. There's something else I learned from the prisoners."

Picking up the tone, Grant stopped his horse. "What is it?"

"George King commanded the guns at Henry. But he left when the white flag was run up. I guess he's at Donelson now. Readying more cannon."

"And so it all comes around," Grant said. "Lucius' brother losing a leg at Bull Run. And now King, Rumble's cousin, here. And Ben is out in the army somewhere. I'll make inquiries. That might be one of the advantages of being a general."

"Thank you," Cord said. "King will do better at Donelson than he did at Henry. It's much more strongly positioned. Samual and I rode the perimeter a month ago. The guns control the river, the current the gunboats will be fighting against is stronger, and the fort won't be underwater."

"But Pillow commands," Grant said.

A courier galloped up and passed Grant a dispatch. He opened it. "From Halleck. *'Hold on to Fort Henry at all hazards. It is of vital importance to strengthen your position. Impress slaves of secessionists in vicinity to work on fortifications. Shovels and picks will be sent to you. Emplace your artillery on the landward side of the fort to repel attack. Keep me informed of all you do, as often as you can.'*"

"Seems you aren't coordinated with your commander," Cord said.

Grant crumpled the message and threw it away. The soldiers following trampled it into the mud.

St. Louis, Missouri

William Tecumseh Sherman took several deep breaths before he entered the office of the Commander of the Army of the West. He looked at his hands to make sure there was no tremor in them. The tic in his cheek had not made an appearance in three weeks. He strode up to the door, knocked and entered.

"General Sherman reported as ordered, sir."

General Halleck, 'Old Brains' as he was known among the officers corps, looked up from the paperwork on his desk. "Ah, Sherman. Glad to have you assigned to me. We've got a fine pickle and I'd like your help."

"Sir?"

"It's Grant. You know him?"

"I do, sir."

"He took Fort Henry, but now the damn fool is insistent on moving on Fort Donelson on the Cumberland. He can't see he's trapped. He has the Tennessee to his back and a large Confederate garrison, well-entrenched, well armed, in an impregnable fort to his front. And he wants to attack!"

Sherman said nothing, still at attention.

"At ease," Halleck finally said. "Come, come. Look." He waved Sherman over to a field table with a map. "The proper course of action for Grant is to dig in at Fort Henry. Await the reinforcements I am gathering."

"Excuse me, sir," Sherman said. "But can't the Confederates reinforce Fort Donelson as fast as we reinforce Fort Henry? If not faster?"

Halleck blinked. "The text on warfare requires Grant to dig in at Henry and be on the defensive. It's perfectly logical. You rank Grant. I'll give you his command. Pull his columns back to Fort Henry and dig in. I'll get you more men and supplies as they become available."

Sherman snapped back to attention. "Sir. I would prefer to serve *under* General Grant."

Halleck slammed a fist on the table. "Damn-it man. Can't anyone understand proper military strategy here?"

"My apologies, sir."

"Dismissed!"

Paducah, KY
Feb 1862
General Sherman to General Grant
Command me in any way. I feel anxious about you as I know the great facilities the Confederate forces have of concentration by means of river and rail, but I have faith in you.
William Tecumseh Sherman

Fort Henry
Feb 1862
General Grant to General Halleck
There are no Negros in this part of the country to work on fortifications.
Ulysses S. Grant

Unconditional Surrender
14 Feb 1862, Vicinity Fort Donelson, Tennessee

BEN AGRIPPA RUMBLE'S rear-end hurt, he was wet, he was hungry, he was cold and he was frightened.

He was a soldier.

And better his bum hurt than his feet be soaked and sore like the poor Infantry, slogging its way through the mud toward Fort Donelson. The weather had been so pleasant during the early part of the advance after departing Fort Henry, that many men had thrown away their burdensome overcoats and blankets. They regretted that today as they shivered in a thin blue line outside the Confederate rifle pits surrounding Fort Donelson with temperatures twenty degrees below freezing. The sky was overcast and dreary, and no one seemed certain when the assault on the fort would occur.

Ben huddled close to his horse, drawing warmth from the beast, another advantage of the cavalry. His unit was behind the lines of Union infantry, ready to be deployed as needed. Battle was coming and despite all he had heard and learned, Ben was experiencing fear on a gut level that was quite disconcerting. The horse shied as cannon fire erupted in the distance.

"Gunboats," someone muttered.

"Maybe the navy will take it like they did Henry?" another man speculated.

"Where you think all the fellas from Henry went?" the first said. "There's a whole bunch of rebs in that fort. If I'd have known soldiering was such misery, I'd have—"

"Hush there!" a sergeant admonished.

Ben reached up and rubbed his chest, where the West Point ring hung on the silver chain. He knew better than to wear it openly in the Army. But the small lump of metal gave him comfort. Despite only a few weeks in the Corps, he was truly beginning to appreciate the values and training the Academy espoused.

He might be cold, tired, hungry and afraid, but he would soldier on.

King was in a frenzy, running from gun to gun, directing their barrages at the Union gunboats on the Cumberland. For many of the artillerymen it was their first time under fire and he could sense their wavering, just like the Infantry at Fort Henry.

There were three tiers of guns at Donelson: water level, fifty feet up in a trench on the front side of the rampart, and on top at a hundred feet. They were not inundated with water. They had plenty of powder and shot. The

Cumberland was narrower, denying the Yankees the ability to turn broadside. The current was faster, forcing the crews of the ships to worry as much about position as firing.

King stopped beside a 32-pounder and grabbed the gun captain. "Allow me, sir."

The gun commander stood aside and King carefully aimed the gun. "Fire!"

The cannon belched and a solid shot arced toward the lead Union ironclad. It hit the pilothouse, tearing through. A cheer rose from the Confederate artillerymen and they turned to their guns with more vigor.

"Pour it on!" King yelled as the gunboat began to yaw, giving way to the current.

Within minutes, the second of the four ironclads also began to fade downriver, riddled with shot. Then the third. The fourth put up a good battle for fifteen minutes, but the Confederates could see that it was settling lower, taking on water. And finally it too was gone, swept away by the rain-drenched river.

King leapt up on top of the parapet and waved his cap.

The men on the walls cheered their victory.

The generals inside the fort argued their future.

"Pillow is doing what I was ordered to do," Grant said, reading dispatches and writing orders at his field desk inside his command tent. "His forces outnumber me and could easily smash me if they attacked. But they're following the rules. That'll be their downfall."

Cord wasn't listening to his friend. The cannon fire had been slackening for half an hour and now it ceased. "Sam."

Cheers echoed across the clear-cut lanes of fire between the Union forces and the line of rifle pits in front of Fort Donelson.

Grant looked up from the order he had been scribbling. "Our boats have been repulsed."

"This aint gonna be Fort Henry," Cord said.

There was consternation among the guards surrounding Grant's field headquarters and Cord stuck his head out of the tent to see the cause. "At ease, men. He's authorized. Personal scout for General Grant."

The Union soldiers lowered their muskets, allowing Samual to stride through them, head held high.

"Come in," Cord said, holding the canvas flap.

Samual hesitated, then ducked his head and entered. "Masters."

"We aren't masters," Grant muttered, running his fingers across the map, searching for a new course of action, now that it appeared an easy naval victory was not in the cards. The problem was that a well-positioned fort on a river was a tough nut to crack and there was no outflanking or outmaneuvering it.

"What've you learned, Samual?" Cord asked. "Any news on either Agrippa?"

"No, sir. I went from Clarksville to Nashville. Then back up. 'Long the river. I 'member the land from when I was boy at Master Rudolph's. Met some slaves I knowed from then. They say there some talk of diggin 'round Nashville. Lots of soldiers moving this way and that. Everyone confused."

"What else?" Grant asked.

"I got insides the fort," Samual said.

Grant's eyebrows arched in surprise. "How did you do that?"

"They needed diggers, sir," Samual said. "I done plenty of digging in my time. I listen. I watch. They got no—" Samual searched for the word. "No master in charge, sir. But they got lots men. Lots guns."

"Do they have spirit?" Grant asked.

Samual considered the question. "Soldiers do. But no one telling them what to do, 'cept crazy man with big axe on his back. He got big guns ready on da river."

"We've heard that," Grant muttered, glancing at Cord.

Samual looked even more nervous than usual. "That man, he came to young master's wedding long time ago with y'all."

"It's Lucius Rumble's cousin, George King," Cord said.

"Sorry, sir," Samual said.

"Thank you, Samual," Grant said. "Get some hot food and some rest."

Samual left the tent.

"Digging at Nashville," Grant said. "That's strange. Maybe Johnston isn't going to reinforce Pillow? Why wouldn't he?"

"Maybe he's afraid to put all his eggs in the Donelson basket?" Cord said. "And he's got Don Carlos Buell's army in Kentucky to worry about. He throws everything against us here, Buell can flank him and take Nashville."

Cord went to the flap and looked out. A light drizzle had begun. "We can't sit here with the textbook forty-five days and wait for them to surrender, Sam. And I'm not quite sure the textbook is going to rule in the real world."

Grant snorted. "I understand you weren't a big believer in the siege. Maybe Floyd would be willing to switch places with us." He looked down at the map. "We need to hit the fort at the same time. Gunboats and infantry. We'll have to coordinate the timing."

Grant continued to work while Cord paced back and forth.

"I knew King would fight," Cord said. "Just didn't think he'd be out here."

Both men looked up as a naval ensign entered the tent and saluted. "Sir. Commodore Foote sends his compliments and requests a meeting with you on board his flagship in the morning at first light. He sends his regrets that he cannot come to you, but during the recent engagement, the Commodore was wounded in the foot and is unable to travel."

Grant closed his eyes briefly. "And the fleet?"

"Damaged badly, sir. Commodore Foote wishes to discuss withdrawing all gunboats to Cairo for refitting. He estimates it will take two weeks before he is able to mount another assault."

Grant didn't hesitate. "Tell Commodore Foote that I will be on board his flagship at first light. But also tell him there will be no withdrawal to Cairo. Is that clear?"

The ensign saluted. "Yes, sir."

15 February 1862, Vicinity Fort Donelson

"Come with me, Elijah," Grant said.

It was dark outside, but Cord was awake in an instant. He accompanied Grant to where their horses waited, saddled and ready, dawn still an hour off.

"No escort?" Cord asked.

"I need to think," Grant said, setting off down the thin country road. The mud was frozen, a mixed blessing. They would not be mired heading to the Cumberland above Fort Donelson where Foote's battered fleet lay at anchor. On the flip side, a misplaced hoof on the frozen ground could spell disaster.

Cord rode silently beside his friend, eyes scanning the woods on either side, aware that a nervous Union sentry could be as deadly as a Confederate patrol. They made the miles to the Cumberland without incident and were rowed out to Foote's flagship.

The naval officer was in a foul mood, his foot swathed in bandages, his fleet full of holes.

"We had the better of them, general," Foote said as they entered his quarters. "Another fifteen minutes and I'd have broken their back just like at Henry. But they hit my ship with a lucky shot. Killed my pilot, wounded me. I tried to stay the course, but was unable."

An aide offered cups of coffee to Grant and Cord, which they gratefully accepted. Foote fired up a cigar and offered one to Grant.

"I'm fond of my pipe," Grant said, but upon patting his pockets realized he was without his smoking weapon, so he accepted the cigar.

"We've taken serious damage," Foote continued. "Whoever commands the batteries knows what he's doing and they'll be better at it next go-around."

Grant glanced at Cord.

Foote continued. "My flagship took fifty-nine hits, and the others about the same. We're in rather poor shape and need to refit at Cairo."

"We cannot withdraw," Grant said, taking a seat, and firing up the cigar. "We need a plan."

The Confederates already had one. Seven miles to the south, as first light broke, rebel regiments surged out of Fort Donelson, smashing into the Union right flank along the Cumberland. They punched into the Union line, the soldiers in blue not entrenched since the spades and pickaxes Halleck had sent were still in crates on board transport craft.

Inside Fort Donelson, King watched the lines of Infantry pouring out in the assault and cursed. Next to him, Nathan Bedford Forrest was in as foul a mood.

"Retreat to Nashville!" Forrest was incredulous. "Those three damned generals argued for hours. Two are more afraid their necks will get strung as traitors if caught than fighting the Yankees."

"We could hold this place against Satan's legions," King swore as another regiment issued forth.

The rattle of musketry was increasing in volume as the Confederate forces spread out in the woods on either side of the road to Nashville. As daylight broke, it brought mixed news. The Union right was breached, so the attack was a success. Which meant that the rest of the soldiers in the fort could pack up and get ready to move out, leaving it undefended.

Apparently, even the soldiers in the assault needed to pack up, as units that had fought throughout the morning came marching back to the fort to get their kit and the heavy artillery for the movement to Nashville.

King supervised grimly as the guns that had stopped the Yankee gunboats the previous day were hauled down from their positions and hitched up to teams of horses.

"We need to do some fighting," Forrest said. "Scared and retreating can't win in the long run."

The cigar smoke gave Cord a headache. Grant and Foote had been strategizing for a couple of hours and the cabin reeked of it. Cord excused himself and went out onto the top deck. The gunboat was a far cry from the sailing ships Cord has spent his time on. Low to the water, with slanted armored sides and no sails, it would not have found favor with Preacher.

King's letter two years ago about his father's death at Harper's Ferry had not caught Cord by surprise. The fact King sent the letter had been the main surprise. Since then, Cord had not heard a word from King, which, again, was not a surprise, given he was now fighting for the Confederates.

Cord walked along the top of the gunboat, checking out the damage inflicted by King and the Confederate batteries. Sailors, many of them soldiers who had some working knowledge of water-borne life, even as scant as a raft or a canoe, had been pressed into service, and were at work on repairs.

At the bow of the boat, facing into the Cumberland's current, Cord paused. His nostrils flared. He spun on his heel and ran to Foote's cabin, throwing open the door.

"Bad air, Sam!"

Grant was startled. "What the devil?"

"There's a hell of a fight going on around Donelson," Cord said.

Grant cocked his head. "I hear no firing."

"Trust me," Cord said.

Grant shot to his feet. "Commodore, I know your ships are damaged, but draw up within your furthermost firing range of Donelson and give me all the shot you can."

Officers were issuing contradictory orders, sergeants were getting their men into formation to go in which direction no one seemed to know, and privates were swallowing their breakfasts as fast as they could. Confusion reigned, which Ben was beginning to realize was the norm for combat. It was a far cry from the precise dress parades on the Plain at West Point.

The sound of combat was eerie. The crackle of musketry in the distance, the muted roar of cannons, meant men were dying. To be swallowing a lumpy biscuit at the same time seemed surreal and Ben's stomach rebelled. He went over to a tree and doubled over behind it. The biscuit came up, having barely touched his stomach.

He scrambled back to his horse and mounted. Those who saw said nothing, each man lost in their own world. A few, the most frightened, were talking loudly, as if trying to convince themselves. They were all waiting to be told what to do as his company stood in formation next to the frozen road. The firing was to the right, Ben had no doubt of that, so he wondered why the officers were confused. There were now musket-less soldiers wandering past in retreat, eyes vacant, indicating lines being broken, men being killed, the flank turned.

A murmur rippled through the ranks. Ben looked to his left and saw two men galloping at an insane pace down the icy path. One wore a plain officer's uniform but carried himself in a way that said he was in charge. The other wore buckskin pants, a flannel shirt and had a long rifle across the pommel of his saddle.

"It's Grant," someone said.

As the two raced past, the man who looked like a frontiersman glanced to his right, making eye contact, and Ben felt a jolt.

The man jerked back on his reins, causing Grant to also rein in.

"Elijah?" Grant called out.

"Go on, General," the man yelled. "I'll be right behind."

Grant wasted no more time, continuing toward the sound of the firing.

Ben gripped his reins tightly as the man trotted his horse up. He halted a few feet away.

"Ben Rumble?"

"Yes, sir."

The man stuck his hand out. "I'm Elijah Cord. You have my ring."

The orderly withdrawal was over. The Yankees, instead of retreating like any sensible minded soldiers should have, were fighting to the death to regain control over the road to Nashville. Counter-attack after counter-attack was bashing into the Confederates outside the fort, who attacked back in turn. King ordered his men to stop pulling the artillery from the walls, sensing the battle was turning. Just as he did that, shells began arcing in from the river. The gunboats were back.

"What color were my mother's eyes?" Ben asked Cord as he broke the handshake.

Cord said nothing. He wasn't capable for the moment. After so many years, to see his son as a man in the flesh, when all he'd had were a sketch of a child, old memories, and regrets was overwhelming.

Ben raised two fingers, pointing at Cord's eyes, then he pointed at his own. "I see me."

Cord gathered himself. "Your mother had the most beautiful green eyes."

"What happened?" Ben asked.

Cord looked to his left. Grant disappeared around a curve in the road. Cord reached to his belt and unfastened it. He slid the Bowie off. "We got to fight now, son. You stay safe and we'll talk." He tossed the knife to Ben and then galloped after Grant.

King and Forrest watched as Generals Floyd, Pillow and Buckner argued. A steamboat puffing smoke was tied up to the dock outside the fort, pressing them to make a decision.

Floyd bowed to Pillow. "I turn the command over to you, sir."

Pillow turned to Buckner. "I pass it to you, sir."

Buckner didn't flinch, but he wasn't pleased. "I assume command. Get me pen, paper and ink and send for a bugler."

Floyd and Pillow scurried away to the steamer as soon as they scribbled their names on the order relinquishing command. The deckhands were tossing off the mooring ropes before the two generals were even aboard.

"How'd you know?" King asked Forrest.

The cavalry commander spit tobacco juice in a long stream. "I was in those meetings. All they talked of, except Buckner who's stuck here now, was saving their hides. Both are afraid of being hanged as traitors by the Yankees if they get caught. Should have shot them myself. Buckner seems a decent sort, but it's too late now."

"I'm not surrendering," King said as another gunboat shell exploded nearby.

"I aint either," Forrest said. "This war got a long way to go."

Grant took charge in the absence of effective subordinate leadership on the routed right flank. Many men were out of ammunition, but Grant, with his quartermaster experience, knew where stocked depots would be positioned. He issued orders to officers, to sergeants, to privates. He even corralled some frightened horses. By force of will and his single-mindedness he turned the routed regiments on the right around, even as the units in the center began counter-attacking based on the orders he'd rapidly issued on the way through.

Cord had a hard time focusing. He followed Grant with his body, but all he could think of was Ben, sitting tall in the saddle, in a blue uniform. A man.

"Fill your cartridge boxes quickly, men," Grant shouted at a group of soldiers standing in a confused group. "The enemy is that way!" Grant pointed with the now dead cigar he'd had clamped between his teeth the entire ride.

The soldiers obeyed. As they always did when Grant gave orders.

Ben tried to calm his horse. It wasn't the cannon fire or even the nearby musketry. It was the unearthly screaming of the rebels in the assault. None had ever heard the like before. It wasn't a cheer. It wasn't a shout. It was a sound that came from somewhere deep inside a man who was committed to an assault that would end in victory or death. Whose very essence was pouring up from the center of his being. The rebel yell screeched across the battlefield for the first time.

Ben felt as if a cold snake had just coiled around his spine and tightened down, while sinking its teeth into the back of his head. He gripped his rifle tighter.

The company commander came riding up, having finally received orders to maneuver. "Forward at the trot!"

The 5th Ohio moved out, passing through retreating infantry. The unit slid into a seam in the Union lines and dismounted at the edge of a patch of woods, every fourth man taking the reins for the other three and pulling the horses further back into the trees. Ben moved forward to the edge of the treeline with the rest of his unit. The regiment took a line.

For the first time they saw the enemy. Men clad in mud-splattered gray and butternut uniforms were moving across the front in an open field about two hundred yards away, unaware of the dismounted Union cavalry in the treeline.

The order to prepare to fire was given.

Ben put his musket to his shoulder, pulling back the hammer. He saw a rebel officer, pointing with his saber, issuing orders.

Ben slid his finger over the trigger as he aimed at the man.

"Fire!"

The regiment fired.

Ben couldn't.

Grant grabbed Cord's arm, shaking him out of his trance. "Are you faring well?"

Cord nodded, focusing on his surroundings. He saw a body, a man in tattered gray, lying in the field next to the road. A haversack was on the man's back. He'd pawed at his clothes, searching in vain for the bullet that had killed him.

Grant was about to spur his horse on, further into the turned flank when Cord dismounted and ran over the man.

"Elijah?" Grant called out.

Cord waved a hand, for Grant to come over. Cord pulled the pack off the man's back and opened it. He stared at the contents for a moment, and then looked up. "They aren't attacking to destroy us, Sam. They're trying to break out. He's got his personal gear in here. They're skedaddling."

It took Grant three seconds to realize the implications. "We have them!"

Cord ran to his horse as Grant galloped forward. Within a minute they spotted a Union division commander sitting under a tree, issuing orders to couriers. The commander jumped to his feet as Grant road up.

"General," Grant said to the man. "The moment is now. You must take the firing pits outside Fort Donelson. Seal them in. Can you do it?"

"My men can take the gates of hell, sir!" The division commander wheeled to his staff. "No firing caps. Bayonets only. We load and fire when we are amongst them!"

The division rose up out of the ground, blue ghosts, bayonets ready, and charged.

It was over in fifteen minutes. The firing pits were taken and Fort Donelson was cut off.

Evening was drawing its shadow over the battleground and Grant turned his stallion toward the rear to establish a new headquarters. Cord rode beside him, the horses picking their way among the dead and wounded littering the ground.

"Worse than anything in Mexico," Grant muttered.

Two wounded men lay close together on the side of the road. A Confederate private and a Union officer. Both badly wounded, now bound next to each other in pain. Most likely caused by the other. Grant halted and dismounted.

"Elijah," Grant called. "Your canteen."

Cord sighed and reached into his saddlebag. He pulled out a flask he hadn't taken a sip from in thirteen years. "They need more than water, Sam." He tossed it.

Grant knelt between the men and gave one, then the other, a sip of the brandy.

"Send for stretchers!" Grant called out in his command voice, which never seemed a yell, but always carried clearly.

Corpsmen came hurrying up and they placed the officer on a stretcher, ignoring the private.

Grant was back on his horse, but he held in place. "Take the Confederate also. The war is over for both men."

Another stretcher was produced and both wounded were carried away.

Shoulders slumped in exhaustion, Grant nudged his horse and continued on. He held out the flask to Cord.

"Keep it, Sam. Was just carrying it as a reminder."

Grant raised it to his lips, took a draft, then capped it and shoved it inside his tunic. "Let's get away from this awful place. I suppose this work is the devil's part in all of us."

They rode in silence except for the cries of wounded men all around and the quieter, but more insidious prayers of dying men, beseeching God. Some were whispering for their mothers to help them in their most dire moment.

"'Man's inhumanity to man, makes countless thousands mourn'," Grant murmured, reciting a poem Cord remembered from cow year at West Point.

"'Tis true," Cord said.

Grant gestured for an aide. "Have artillery brought up to the ridge to bear on the fort. We will make them yield in the morning."

The yielding began earlier.

King accompanied Forrest to the bunker where General Buckner was ensconced.

"Sir, me and Captain King here—" Forrest began, but Buckner waved his free hand for silence as he wrote with the other.

Headquarters, Fort Donelson, 16 February, 1862

Sir. In consideration of all the circumstances governing the present situation of affairs at this station, I propose to the commanding officers of the Federal forces the appointment of commissioners to agree upon terms of capitulation of the forces and posts under my command, and in that view suggest an armistice until 12 o'clock today.

I am, sir, very respectfully, your ob't se'v't

S.B. Buckner

Brig. Gen. C.S.A.

Buckner folded the piece of paper and handed it to a lieutenant. "Deliver this, with my respects, to General Grant."

Then he looked at the two officers. "You wish to depart to fight another day, Colonel Forrest?"

"I do, sir."

"And you, Captain King?"

"I have duties in the east," King said, "with the Navy, that I must return to."

"You may both depart, gentlemen."

"I couldn't fire," Ben said. "I let my fellow soldiers down."

Cord and Ben were seated on a log next to a blaze. They were just outside a farmhouse where Grant had set up his field headquarters. Cord had been able to track down his son rather easily, given how few cavalry units were attached to Grant's army. He'd escorted Ben back to the headquarters, not certain how to answer whatever questions would arise or how to even describe the past decades and that fateful morning so long ago. But his son didn't seem interested in any of that at the moment.

"It's normal to be scared in your first battle," Cord said. "I bet a lot of fellows didn't fire. I seen fellows who just keep reloading but never pull the trigger. End up with five or six balls in the barrel."

"I had an officer in my sights," Ben said. "I just started imagining the bullet hitting him, wondering if he had a wife, a family."

"Can't imagine like that in a fight," Cord said. "You had too much time to think before it all. But I'd rather you not shoot than take pleasure in it like some do. You know, there are jobs around the army that don't require shooting. Stretcher-bearers and such."

"And those jobs keep one in the rear and safe," Ben said, shaking his head. "You sound like fa—" he paused.

"Lucius is a good man," Cord said. "He's your true father, I know that."

Ben reached inside his shirt. He pulled out the silver chain and West Point ring he'd worn for so many years. "You should have this back."

Cord demurred. "No. I gave it to you a long time ago and it's yours."

"I didn't earn it," Ben said. "I can't wear it openly or be accused of being something I'm not." He shoved it into Cord's callused palm.

The two sat in uneasy silence for a while, which was interrupted by a pair of soldiers escorting a Confederate lieutenant bearing a flag of truce and a note. Cord waved to the lieutenant and intercepted the note meant for Grant. He read it by firelight.

"Ben," Cord said, "best be getting back to your unit. We can catch up later."

Ben stood, but before he could get to his horse, Cord hugged his son, holding him tight. "I'm sorry for all the times I wasn't there for you."

Ben could only nod, eyes moist.

Reluctantly, Cord let go of his son and went into the farmhouse. Grant was asleep on the kitchen floor.

"Sam."

Grant was instantly awake. "Another attack?"

"Come to the fire," Cord said.

They walked outside to the blaze. Without comment, Cord handed the note to Grant.

Grant read it, then reached into his tunic and pulled out the flask. He uncapped and took a long, deep drink. "Interesting it's from Buckner, not Pillow or Floyd."

"I suppose they might be elsewhere by now," Cord said.

"Well, well. What answer shall I send to General Simon Bolivar Buckner, Elijah?"

"Remember the night you took the duty to help me?" Cord asked.

Grant laughed, light-hearted for the moment. "I do indeed." He snapped his fingers and an aide brought up a writing tablet, paper and pen.

Headquarters Army in the Field
Camp Near Donelson
February 16, 1862

General S. B. Buckner.
Confederate Army.
Sir.   Yours of this date, proposing armistice and appointment of Commissioners to settle terms of capitulation, is just received. No terms except an unconditional and immediate surrender can be accepted. I propose to move immediately upon your works.
I am, sir, very respectfully,
Your ob't se'v't
U.S. Grant
Brig. Gen.

Grant blew on the ink to make sure it was dry, and folded the note. He didn't hand it to the waiting lieutenant. He held it out to Cord.

"Elijah. Would you do me the honor? I believe General Buckner will get the message much more clearly if delivered by your hand."

Cord rode through the Union lines with the Confederate officer just before dawn. They entered Fort Donelson and dismounted. All was in turmoil. Wounded men crowded the interior of the fort and men were moving to and fro, many without any apparent purpose. A cluster of cavalry was mounting up, a huge officer in the lead. Cord froze when he recognized the man next to the cavalry commander as the unit began to ride past, trying to escape.

"King."

The entire column halted behind them as Nathan Bedford Forrest and King paused.

"Cord," King acknowledged. "Come to take the fort from the cowards?"

"The official tender of surrender was made but it has not been accepted," Cord said. "You'll be fired on if you try to escape."

"I didn't come here to surrender," Forrest said, spurring his horse and moving on. "They may fire as they will and I will return hot lead in kind."

King shook his head in disgust. "You're fighting against your own state."

"I'm fighting for my country," Cord replied.

"More the fool you." King leaned over in his saddle, his face scant inches from Cord's. "You've always been the fool. Something you should know. I'm the one who killed your father."

Cord reached up and jerked King off the horse. The two tumbled into the mud, flailing away at each other. Soldiers jumped in, pulling them apart. The officer who'd brought Buckner's letter was outraged. "You're under a flag of truce!" he yelled at Cord.

"Let's go! Darkness is wasting," Forrest shouted at King.

King pointed at Cord. "We'll meet again. Count on it."

Cord wiped mud out of his eyes and off his face as Forrest's cavalry and George King galloped out of the gate. There was a scattering of shots, but no serious opposition to the fleeing forces as word had already spread like wildfire in the Union army that surrender had been offered. Few were willing to put their lives on the line when the end was in sight.

"Come on," the Confederate officer said, indicating a bunker built into the parapet. "Let's get this over with."

Cord entered the rebel headquarters. Despite the years between, he instantly recognized Buckner. The Confederate general looked up and frowned, but did not return the recognition given Cord was covered in mud.

Cord pulled Grant's reply out of his pocket and held it out.

Buckner took the note. His jaw set as he read it. "This is outrageous! These are not the words of a gentleman. This can't be from Grant."

"They're Sam's words," Cord said. He wiped a sleeve across his face.

Buckner finally recognized him. "Elijah Cord? Why would Sam do this to me?"

Cord was in no mood to argue. "Just think of this as a visit from a higher Vigilance Committee."

Lincoln
20 Feb 1862, Washington DC

"**Y**OU WERE RIGHT ABOUT GRANT," Lincoln said. "The press is saying the U.S. in his name stands for Unconditional Surrender."

Rumble sat stiffly on the bench in the President's office. The jubilation over Grant's dual victories at Henry and Donelson had swept a north desperate for good news since Bull Run. In contrast, the mood inside the White House was somber and Lincoln appeared in a particularly depressed mood. He was looking at some drawings on his desk without any particular interest and his greeting to Rumble had been perfunctory and distracted.

Rumble waited, wondering why he'd been summoned. He'd been touring McClellan's camps the past few weeks at the President's behest and assumed a report was wanted, but Lincoln showed no desire to be updated on 'Little Napoleon's' progress, or rather lack thereof. The deadline for the President's War Order #1 was two days away, and there was no sign the Army of the Potomac was within two months of moving.

Lincoln lowered his head, resting his forehead in his large hand for a moment, then rubbed his eyes. He finally looked toward Rumble, eyes puffy and bloodshot. "You will have to excuse me, Sergeant Major Rumble. We've been having a hard time of it in the residence. I suppose you've heard."

"I'm sorry 'bout your boys being sick, sir," Rumble said. "I can come back at another date."

"The war will not wait," Lincoln said, "even though McClellan acts as if it does for him." Lincoln shook his head and dismissed McClellan with a wave of his hand. "You need not report on the general. I can read the papers as well as anyone. He trains them well at least?"

"Yes, sir."

"But he will not move?"

"Not soon, sir."

"Grant moved," Lincoln murmured. He looked down at the drawings. "Something else is moving soon. Something very interesting. I want you to go with it. That's why I called for you." The President slid the top drawing across the table.

Rumble took the parchment, but could make little sense. "What is it, sir? Some kind of ship?"

"The ironclad *Monitor*," Lincoln said.

"I've never seen the like. It looks like a raft with a hat box on top."

"Two guns," Lincoln said, finally showing some enthusiasm. "They're in a turret that rotates in a circle. Most of the ship is built so low to the water, very little shows. Which means very little for the enemy to shoot at. And it's all iron up top. Of course, the wooden shoe Navy fellows are concerned she won't sail well. Or fight well."

Rumble lay the drawing back on the President's desk with a sense of trepidation. "And what is it you'd like me to do regarding it, sir?"

"Go with it," Lincoln said. "We hear the fellows from the south are building an ironclad at Norfolk to break the blockade. So the *Monitor* will be taken down there and have a showdown. I'd like you to go on board and observe the result."

When Rumble said nothing for a few seconds, Lincoln arched a bushy eyebrow. "You've never before hesitated on a tasking, Sergeant Major."

"It's just, sir, that, I'm not fond of the water."

"I would suppose you're not fond of being shot at either," Lincoln said, "yet you made it all the way through Mexico and Bull Run."

"True, sir. Why not send a navy man? I know nothing of ships."

"Which is exactly why I want you there," Lincoln said. "Pretty much every navy fellow is dead set against the *Monitor*. I had to force their hand to even have it built. They seem to want it to fail. Like most people, they fear change."

"It seems a most strange vessel, sir," Rumble said.

Lincoln sighed. "It seems as if we can invent the most marvelous machines to kill." He stood up and Rumble followed suit.

"Walk with me," the President said.

Lincoln went into the hallway, which was eerily empty. Outside the White House, darkness was descending on Washington.

"I know I ask you to go in harm's way," the President said. "I'm asking that of hundreds of thousands of men. It is not something I do lightly. I—" a clock began chiming five o'clock somewhere in the house and Lincoln abruptly halted, placing a hand over his heart, as if stricken by some unseen force deep inside. "Excuse me."

Lincoln opened a door to the right. The room beyond was dimly lit. Looking in, Rumble could see a large, rosewood bed with a tiny figure nestled in blankets. Mrs. Lincoln was hovering over the boy while a doctor stood helplessly by on the other side. The President went to his wife.

The doctor had his hand on the boy's wrist. He murmured something and Mrs. Lincoln let out a wail that penetrated to Rumble's marrow.

He reached forward to gently close the door, but slowed as he heard the President's voice clearly. "Mother, our poor boy, he was too good for this earth. God has called him home. I know that he is much better off in heaven, but then we loved him so. It is hard, hard to have him die."

Headquarters, Fort Donelson Ten
Dear Wife,
I am most happy to write you from this strongly fortified place, now in my possession, after the greatest victory of the season. Some 12 or 15 thousand prisoners have fallen into our possession to say nothing of 5 to 7 thousand that escaped in the darkness last night
This is the largest capture I believe ever made on the continent.
My impression is that I shall have one hard battle more to fight and will find easy sailing after that. No telling though. This was one of the most desperate affairs fought during the war. Our men were out three terrible, cold nights and fighting through the day, without tents.
Kiss the children for me.
Ulys.

St. George
8 March 1862, Palatine, Mississippi

ST. GEORGE HAD HIS FEET UP on what had once been a beautiful silk encased stool. It was now dirt and soot smeared. He was lounging in front of the large fireplace in Tiberius' private study, taking a long draft from the bottle of tequila Sally Skull had just given him. She was seated in a high backed chair. In one of the shadows of the room, Gabriel stood still as a rock, the Spencer in her right hand, almost a part of her.

"Miss Violet just up and left him behind?" Skull asked.

"She a cold woman," St. George said. "Rode off w' her one-legged boy to Rosalie, leaving husband behind. I got a slave taking care of him. He aint been out of his bed for a long time. Jus' drinking."

"She'll come back," Skull told St. George.

"You here ten minutes," St. George said, "and already you beating me with your words. Enjoy the fire. Musta been cold traveling the river this time year."

"The weather is the weather," Skull said.

St. George scowled. "What that mean?"

"Means I don't control it, so I ignore it. You sure she give that nigra who tried to kill you the gun?"

St. George's dead eye glinted in the firelight. "He was her special boy. Brought him here from Tennessee. She gave it to him and sent him after me. Bitch."

"Why didn't he use the gun on you, then?"

"Too dumb."

"Don't take too much smarts to use a gun," Skull argued. "Wait 'til them Yankees start handing them to the nigras."

"Never happen," St. George said.

"This go on long enough, enough Yankees get killed, it will."

"Why you always so focused on the bad happening?" St. George asked. "And your mulatto back there bothering me. Tell her put that gun down."

"She likes the gun. It gives her comfort."

St. George sighed. "You sure—"

"Damn you!"

An emaciated Tiberius Rumble stood in the doorway, gripping the frame with a sweat-soaked hand. In his other hand he held a dagger. His face was pale and his eyes were bloodshot, but he was dressed in his finest suit. He had a growth of grey beard stubbling his face. He was not looking at any of the people in the room, but at the six-foot high stone relief to the left of the fireplace. Carved into the stone were the figures of a group of Roman soldiers gathered around an altar on which was a bull. One of the soldiers was slitting the bull's throat.

Gabriel had the Spencer at the ready, but Skull signaled for her to stand down. Tiberius staggered into the room, going from doorframe to table, to a chair back, temporary anchor points to steady his drunken course. He stopped in front of the stone, his right hand sliding up the front. The hand stopped on the plumed helmet of a Roman centurion on the right side, halfway up. He slid the dagger into what had appeared to be a crack in the stone. A clicking noise echoed through the room. Tiberius removed the dagger and stuck it in his belt.

Then he leaned forward, as if falling into the carving. But the entire thing rotated with a loud screech, revealing a hidden passage. Tiberius pressed between stone and fireplace brick and disappeared into the darkness. A dry musty odor filled the study.

Skull got to her feet and grabbed a torch, lighting it in the fireplace.

"What you doing?" St. George asked.

"Following," Skull said. "I want to see the secret of Palatine."

She slid through, torch first. St. George pushed ahead of Gabriel, ignoring her glare. Two dozen stone steps led down into a brick lined cave. It was fifteen feet long and ten wide. Skull's lantern illuminated Tiberius at the far end, kneeling in front of a stone altar. His sobs echoed off the brick.

"What in damnation?" St. George exclaimed.

Skull stepped closer, lighting the top of the altar. Reddish stains covered it and extended down the front to the floor. On both sides, pressed up against the brick, were piles of bone. Human bone.

Skull leaned closer, inspecting the gruesome piles. "Children."

"What this?" St. George asked.

"I didn't do it," Tiberius was saying between sobs. "I didn't kill like you, father. I didn't."

Then Tiberius collapsed in a heap at the base of the altar. Skull knelt next to him. "He alive, but not by much."

"I don' get it," St. George said. "Who died here?"

Skull ignored him. "You lucky," she said to Gabriel. "Before this old man, his father and father's father and who knows how far back killed their 'problems' right here on this stone."

Gabriel stepped up next to Skull. She looked at the piles of bones, the blood stains. Then she knelt next to Tiberius. She placed a hand on the old man's forehead, almost tenderly. With the other she drew the dagger from his belt. Then the hand on the forehead slid up and gripped Tiberius' thinning white hair in its fist.

Before Skull or St. George could react, Gabriel drew the blade across Tiberius' neck. A crimson jet spouted forth on top of the dried blood from generations of mixed children before her.

Monitor and the Merrimack

8 March 1862, Norfolk, Virginia

"Sir, today is the Sabbath," King said. "I believe we should celebrate by killing Yankees."

"Going west didn't calm you down in the slightest," Captain Buchanan, former Superintendent of the U.S. Naval Academy, noted. He was scanning the Union fleet blockading Hampton Roads through a telescope. "Laundry day in the fleet. Their riggings are full of it. I suspect they don't anticipate being attacked on a Sunday."

Both men were standing on top the C.S.S. *Virginia*, once the U.S.S. *Merrimack*, which King had watched burn when the Confederacy seized Norfolk. The hull and the steam engines were the only things the two had in common. From the waterline up, the ship had been completely rebuilt with a radical design. The hull had been sliced along the waterline and a deck planked on. Over that deck was built an armored casemate framed with two feet of oak and layered with four inches of iron armor. The sides were sloped to deflect cannon fire. In sum, she looked like a barn's metal roof placed on top of a raft. She had fourteen gun ports, four on each side and three forward and aft. She was heavy, she was slow, but she was almost impregnable to cannon fire.

King and Buchanan were on the narrow, flat top of the ship, forward of the smoke-stack. The *Virginia* was lumbering down the mouth of the James River, toward the Yankee fleet. Their approach was noted as laundry started to get scooped out of the rigging and sails deployed. There were five Union man-of-war ahead: the *Cumberland*, the *Congress*, the *St. Lawrence*, the *Roanoke* and the *Minnesota*. The odds excited King as they extended the opportunity for a great victory, which the South desperately needed. Travelling east had been galling as the south reeled from the twin defeats of Forts Henry and Donelson and the mood of the people he met was glum.

"*'And I will execute great vengeance upon them with furious rebukes; and they shall know that I am the Lord, when I shall lay my vengeance upon them'*," King quoted.

Buchanan smiled. "Let us rebuke, Captain King. Order the gun crews to prepare to fire."

"Aren't you coming below, sir?"

Buchanan held up a Spencer rifle. "I prefer to deal my rebukes directly. I'll relay orders through you in the hatch."

"Permission to pass on the task to an ensign and join you, sir?"

"You have your orders."

King clenched his fists, but went to the hatch and climbed halfway down. He got the gun crews ready. Then as Buchanan shouted back his instructions, King relayed them, one step removed from the fray either way as a mouthpiece between captain and crew.

The *Cumberland* opened fire first. Initial shots splashed in the water, but the Union warship quickly found the range. The bang of shot bouncing off the iron plates echoed inside the *Virginia*, adding to the tumult of the steam engines. Then the ironclad's guns added to the din as King relayed the order for the forward three to fire. One of the guns was firing hot shot, the cannon ball placed in the ship's furnace long enough to be get red hot, then removed and carefully loaded, a procedure fraught with potential disaster. Fired at wooden ships, the ball not only shattered wood, it ignited it once it came to rest.

The *Virginia* bore down relentlessly on the *Cumberland*. King took a rung higher on the ladder, so he could see more clearly. Buchanan was methodically firing the Spencer at the oncoming Union ship, as if every bullet was a year he'd spent in the Union navy being sent back at it.

As the distance closed, King realized the inevitable and what Buchanan intended to do. He ducked his head down into the smoke filled interior of the *Virginia* and shouted: "Prepare for ramming!"

The *Virginia* had been outfitted with an iron ram, due to rumors the Yankees were building their own ironclad and another form of attack might be needed. While the armor was a step forward, the addition of the ram, just below the surface, harkened back to the days of the Greeks.

The *Cumberland's* guns continued to blaze away, to little effect. A cannon ball whizzed by Buchanan as he was reloading, passed over King's head so close he could feel the breeze, and punched a hole in the smokestack, the extent of the damage to the *Virginia* so far; besides all the dings in the armor plating. The *Congress* was adding to the barrage and the other three Union warships were coming closer for battle.

King could see the faces of the Union sailors over the *Cumberland* bulkheads peering at the approaching behemoth. Blood from the dead and dying was dribbling down the badly battered and splintered wooden side of the ship. Flames from hot shot were blazing throughout the hulk. But the Yankee flag still flew and the guns that were functional still fired.

The *Virginia* shuddered at the ram punched through the hull of the Union ship. Looking up, King recognized a lieutenant, an Annapolis graduate, shouting commands for a gun to be depressed far enough to fire at the attacking ship. The two men locked eyes for a minute, much as the *Virginia* was locked into the *Cumberland*. King saluted, giving credit to bravery. The lieutenant returned the salute, then gave the order to fire to the one remaining gun facing the *Virginia*. As he did so, a bullet from Buchanan caught him in the chest and he fell backward into the flames.

The cannon ball hit just in front of the *Virginia's* captain, bounced off iron plate and ricocheted away. The concussion knocked Buchanan to the deck, dazed for the moment. Not life threatening, but the situation was, King quickly realized. The ram was stuck in the side of the *Cumberland*, and as the Union ship began to sink, it was pulling the *Virginia* down with it.

King sprinted to the hatch and jumped inside. "All back!"

Levers were thrown, reversing the thrust of the propeller. The *Virginia* shuddered, still tethered by iron to the *Cumberland*. There was a loud screeching sound, then a resounding gong as the ram broke off, leaving its beak in the Union ship. King quickly clambered up the ladder to review the tactical situation. Buchanan was on his feet, using the Spencer to prop himself up. He pointed and his meaning was clear: The *Congress* was closest.

King shouted commands. The *Virginia* slowly turned toward its next victim.

The Captain of the Union ship could see the *Cumberland's* fate: sinking, survivors jumping overboard, flames consuming what wasn't already submerged. He was no fool. As the *Virginia* drew close, he ordered the Union ship into shallow water, committing a cardinal sin for every ship's captain: running aground. But at least the *Congress* would not sink.

The *Virginia* drew abreast and fired a volley from the flank guns into the Union ship. Fire was returned, as ineffectual as the *Cumberland's* had been. For almost an hour, the two vessels pounded each other. The result was that the *Congress* was slowly dismantled, blast by blast, while more dents were made in the iron skin of the *Virginia*.

It was over relatively quickly. King felt a thrill as the United States flag was struck and a white flag run up.

"Captain King!"

King shook himself out of his reverie. Buchanan was red-faced and shouting. "Can't you hear? Relay my order to cease fire!"

"Yes, sir."

King was in no rush to get below. He took each rung of the ladder carefully as another broadside from the *Virginia* belched death into the Union ship.

"Cease fire," King said in a normal voice, heard only by a few men closest to him. Slowly the word made its way through the smoke-filled interior of the ironclad and the guns fell silent, one by one.

Accompanied by several armed men, King went back up top. Survivors from the *Congress* were clambering down ropes onto the *Virginia*. Wounded men were being lowered as carefully as possible. Looking about, King could see that the *Minnesota* had also run aground, whether deliberately or not, wasn't clear.

"Captain Buchanan," King said. "If we attack now, we'll have enough light and tide to deal with her." He pointed at the third Union ship.

"The law of the sea," Buchanan countered. "Always give assistance to those who raise the white flag."

"But, sir—" King began, but was cut off as a Union shore battery opened fire.

"Damnation!" Buchanan exclaimed as Federal shots hit both the *Virginia* and the *Congress*.

A cannon ball ripped into the Union ship, spraying splinters across the top of the *Virginia*. One tore into Buchanan's leg, dropping him to the deck.

"Get the Captain below!" King ordered.

As two men grabbed Buchanan, King followed them to the hatch. Making sure all Confederates were inside, King ignored the remaining Union sailors trying to come over and those already on top of the *Virginia* desperate to get inside and out of harm's way of their own side's artillery. He clambered down the ladder, slamming the hatch shut and sealing it.

"Hot shot!" King yelled, clearly heard now. "Fire until she's blazing like Hell's inferno!"

Rumble dry-heaved, his stomach long since emptied of any substance. The seasoned sailors nearby had laughed the previous day when Rumble had first started throwing up, somewhere off the coast of Maryland, en route from New York City. No one was laughing now. The interior of the *Monitor* was smoke-filled, hot, and a claustrophobic's worst nightmare. On top of that, the vessel handled very poorly in the open sea, exactly as predicted by the traditional Navy men who had scorned her design.

A tinge of fresh air cut through the dimly lit interior and Rumble realized that a hatch had been opened. The ship was wallowing less, which meant either the storm they'd been passing through had moved on, they were in calmer water, or both. Rumble pushed his way through to the front hatch, carrying his Henry rifle.

Sailors were standing on deck, near the small metal box that poked up above the flat deck in front of the turret: the pilot house from which the Captain commanded the vessel. The first hint of dawn was showing in the east over the Atlantic. But everyone was staring solemnly to the west. The horizon glowed with an unearthly light. A tongue of flame licked into the air, followed the dull roar of an explosion.

"What was that?" Rumble asked.

The *Monitor's* Captain, Lieutenant Worden, was reading a report just brought by a skiff. "The *Cumberland* and *Congress* burning. One must have just blown up when the fire reached the powder room. At least two-hundred and forty men lost at last count."

"We're too late?" Rumble asked.

"For yesterday's fight," Worden said. "But not today's."

King held the Spencer and gave orders to an ensign positioned in the hatch, exactly as Buchanan had commanded the previous day. The ship was his; Buchanan recovering in a shore hospital. There was no one to issue him orders, no one to surrender at the slightest sign of resistance. Today was King's to own. It was time to finish the Union fleet at Hampton Roads, and open the way to the Potomac. The *Virginia* would be able to sail up that river, past the Union forts, and fire directly at the White House, where the great devil Lincoln reigned. And then the war would be over, and the South would be victorious.

The *Cumberland* was a burned out hulk. Where the *Congress* had surrendered was scattered debris and corpses floating in the water. The magazine explosion had torn apart what remained of the ship. The *Minnesota* was still aground and King directed the *Virginia* straight toward it.

"Prepare to fire!" King ordered.

The command was relayed by the ensign to the gunners. King checked the Spencer, insuring a round was in the chamber. He estimated the distance to the *Minnesota*. It appeared as if the ship were being serviced. A raft with what looked like a spare boiler on top was just in front of the warship. King squinted.

It wasn't a raft.

"Fire!" King yelled.

Rumble was jammed in the pilothouse with Lieutenant Worden and the helmsman. The metal cube poked up above the deck a few feet, with narrow viewing slits, about an inch wide, facing all four sides. Rumble was estimating how quickly he could dash down the couple of stairs into the hull of the ship and then race forward to the hatch. Then he added in trying to make that journey while the rest of the crew tried for the same exit. He wondered why no one else saw the ironclad as he did: a prison bobbing on the water, which could easily turn into an iron coffin.

Flame erupted from the bow of the *Virginia*. A second later, thunder exploded overhead as the *Minnesota* fired a broadside at the approaching Confederate ship. Worden began issuing orders to the helmsman and the *Monitor* advanced toward the *Virginia*.

"Fire!" Worden ordered and the two nine-inch Dahlgren's in the turret roared.

There was no point using the Spencer. And standing exposed to fire on top was stupid; even King had to accept that. He reluctantly retreated inside the *Virginia*, rushing from gun to gun to keep track of the Union ironclad. While his ship had more guns, the *Monitor* was much more maneuverable, running circles around the larger and more cumbersome Confederate ironclad.

The clang of rounds bouncing off the iron plates resounded throughout the ship as the Union gunners found the range. King could tell his men were also finding the target. With the same effect of much sound and fury but no real damage.

For two hours the ships battled. Sometimes so close that they collided and bounced off each other. Even firing from point blank range produced no tangible results. King grew weary of running from gun port to gun port, trying to keep the more nimble vessel in view. As the *Monitor* circled around for another charge, King leaned over a hot cannon tube and peered out the gun port.

His guns had riddled the two short smokestacks behind the turret, but that had not slowed the enemy in the slightest. He'd given the order to aim for the two openings in the turret where the Union guns fired. But given both vessels were moving, and the turret rotated, there were too many aiming variables, making it a matter of blind luck if they were to thread one of those needles. So far, no luck.

But through the smoke of battle, King noticed something. Forward of the turret was an iron box poking up above the deck, but low enough that the Union guns could fire over it. As the *Monitor* closed in, King focused on the box. As hard as it was for him to see through the gunports on his ship, he realized the Union commander would have the same problem, multiplied by having only two ports if he were in the turret. So he wasn't in the turret. The *Monitor* was being captained from that box.

King went from gun to gun and ordered each crew to focus on the box as it came to bear. They might not punch through the armor, but they'd keep the Union captain busy.

The first clash ever of metal ships was causing a lot of noise, a lot of smoke and not much in terms of results. Rumble flinched as a cannon ball hit the side of the pilothouse, the clang deafening, the shock wave jarring his teeth.

Worden grabbed the helmsman and pointed out the direction he wanted the ship to go, the ability to hear inside the metal box negated by the shot for a few moments. Angled toward the bow of the Virginia, Worden was trying to keep his two guns battling the forward guns of the Confederate ship, rather than taking on the broadside.

The two ships once more drew closer. Rumble saw one of the balls fired from the turret bounce off the sloped side of the *Virginia*, flying high up into the air and disappearing in the distance. He hoped the rebels inside felt as miserable.

A flash of light and thunderous explosion was followed by Lieutenant Worden's scream of pain. Rumble was dazed for a moment, then grabbed Worden whose hands were covering his face, blood pouring over them. A cannon ball had hit right on one of the inch wide observation slits, shattering the edges and spraying shrapnel, leaving behind a wider, jagged gap of a half foot.

"I can't see!" Worden exclaimed, pulling his hands away to reveal gashes around his eyes and burst blood vessels in them.

Rumble helped Worden sit down on the deck, his back against the support for the wheel. Behind him, the helmsman peered out the gash in the pilothouse, spinning the wheel clockwise to turn away from the Virginia.

A bullet pinged off the wall behind the helmsman. "Damnation!" the man exclaimed, keeping to the task. Another bullet zipped through the damaged slit, ricocheted twice around the interior, narrowly missing both helmsman, Rumble and Worden.

Rumble brought the Henry to his shoulder, the muzzle now able to fit through the armor. He could see a rifle poking out of the closest gun port on the *Virginia*. Rumble fired three quick rounds at the port. He saw the muzzle of the rifle spit fire in return. A spark from a bullet hitting the top edge of the damaged slit snapped in front of his eyes and he was slammed back as a fist hit his chest, right over his heart.

Rumble fell over Worden, bounced off the helm and collapsed to the deck. It was hard for him to breathe. His hand grabbed his chest where the richocheting bullet had hit and pulled it back, expecting it to be covered with blood straight from his heart and his time on this mortal coil down to seconds remaining.

No blood.

Grunting in pain, Rumble sat up, back against the armor plate. His left breast pocket was torn. Rumble reached into the pocket and pulled out the contents: a spent bullet, Lidia's and Ben's etching with a perfect round circle in it just to the right of Lidia, and the abolitionist coin Ben had given him, bent almost double from the impact of the round.

Rumble took a deep breath, relishing the pain of the broken rib in his chest.

Another bullet pinged into the pilothouse. Rumble scrambled to his feet, put the Henry to his shoulder, ignored the pain, and fired as fast as he could pull the trigger and work the lever action. He shot the remaining four rounds right at the muzzle of the rifle that had shot him.

King was sighting the Spencer on the opening once more when he was hit in the face, snapping his head back and sending him flying to the deck. The round hit his left cheek, smashed the bone, and was partially deflected through his mouth and out the right side of his jaw.

King lay on his back, trying to spit out shattered teeth. Of more dire concern was the blood filling his mouth, choking him. One of the crew saw the danger and rolled him onto his side, allowing the blood to drain out. Another jammed cloth in the wound, slowing the bleeding.

"Withdraw!" the ensign left in command screamed.

Rumble saw the *Virginia* begin a ponderous turn away.

"They're running!" the helmsman yelled in exultation. "Lieutenant," he said to Worden. "They're withdrawing."

Worden nodded, a hasty bandage Rumble had concocted from a bandana covering his blinded eyes. "Pull back to the *Minnesota* if you please."

11 March 1862, Washington DC

President Lincoln had a wet towel draped over his forehead and was leaning far back in his chair as Rumble was escorted into his office, just two days after the mighty battle of ironclads at Hampton Roads. Despite his obvious exhaustion, Lincoln peeled the towel off, got to his feet, and extended his hand.

Rumble shook it. "Sir."

"Sergeant Major Rumble. Please take a seat."

Rumble sat on the bench as Lincoln wearily collapsed back into his seat. "The newspapers say we won a great victory over the *Virginia*."

Rumble nodded, but said nothing, his chest throbbing in pain, his fingers wrapped around the bent abolitionist coin.

"So you agree?" Lincoln pressed.

"The *Virginia* still floats and is still capable of fighting, sir," Rumble said. "I may not know about naval tactics, but it seems to me the goal is to sink the opponent's ship."

"But they did withdraw from the, what is the proper word, not field, perhaps sea, of battle, first. Correct?"

"They did, sir."

"Because you used your Henry rifle that some prescient person pressed upon you."

Rumble was shocked. "Sir, how did you—"

"I get reports from many sources, Sergeant Major, and also, I get the Richmond paper and can read. I don't think it was any coincidence that the *Virginia* withdrew after you fired. The reports are that the acting captain of the Confederate vessel was badly wounded by one of your bullets. This after the first captain was wounded the day before by the shore batteries. They were running out of captains, I believe."

"A lucky shot on my part, then, sir."

"Did you know the name of the second captain?"

"No, sir."

"A former West Pointer and US Marine named George King."

Rumble's fingers tightened so hard around the token, it cut into his skin. "King is my distant cousin, sir. We were at West Point together."

"That's the nature of this war," Lincoln said. He sighed, the lines on his face collapsing on themselves and he looked ancient. "Let bravery stand where it is, Sergeant Major. I propose to put you in for a Medal of Honor. It's a new award which was proposed by Congress and I signed into law back in December."

"I can't take a medal for shooting kin, sir."

Lincoln slumped back in his chair. "Why is nothing ever easy? We need heroes Sergeant Major, so I am giving a medal. Lots of people are going to be shooting relatives by the time this war is over. Is that so hard?"

"Give it to the helmsman of the *Monitor*," Rumble suggested. "He stood fast with bullets flying all about and maintained control of the ship after Lieutenant Worden was wounded."

"So you're turning down a medal," Lincoln said. "You surely do not belong in Washington. You don't fit in."

"I don't belong in Washington, sir," Rumble agreed.

"And I suppose you are going to tell me where you do belong?"

"Instead of a Medal of Honor, sir, I'd like to go west."

"For once, fortune turns my way and the stars align," Lincoln said. He sorted through the papers on his desk. "The telegram is most fascinating. I can get news from hundreds of miles away in an instant. The problem is trying to discern if the news I'm receiving is news or if it's political maneuvering or in some cases, out-right lies. Such is the difficulty of only being able to be one place at a time. That is why I have men like you, Sergeant Major."

"Yes, sir."

"Don't look so glum," Lincoln said. "Have some faith in me. You'll go west, and I'm glad to accommodate your personal desire for that, whatever it might be; however I want you to keep in mind your primary duty is to your country."

"Yes, sir."

"I have a letter from your friend Grant's senator. He says there's quite the ruckus going on between Generals Halleck and Grant. He goes so far as to say that he's afraid Halleck might place Grant under arrest. He's already relieved him of his command."

Rumble half rose off the bench. "For what, sir! He conquered Henry. He took Donelson. His men have invested Nashville. *He* should be getting a medal."

Lincoln waved a hand. "Sit down. It appears that Halleck feels Grant has slipped his leash and doesn't follow orders. That, of course, is what Halleck says. What he means is that Grant's success has rankled his superiors. He acts while they strut and preen and do little. But Halleck does command the west. And," Lincoln stroked his chin, "there is a nugget in all of this that disturbs me. There are rumors your friend is drinking." Lincoln raised an eyebrow. "You do not leap to his defense."

"Sir, General Grant is a man who has little tolerance for spirits," Rumble explained. "However, I do not believe he would imbibe while in such a position of trust."

"They say he was booted out of the army for drinking. Is that so?"

"I've heard that rumor, but don't know if it's true or not."

"Did you see him drink in Mexico?"

Rumble fidgeted. "Yes, sir. But not much and briefly. And he was never in command in Mexico and never drunk during battle."

"A less honest man and more loyal friend might have simply answered 'never'," Lincoln pointed out. "I appreciate the honesty and that's why you're sitting there. Be that as it may, you will find out for me. Thus we strike two birds with one stone."

"Thank you, sir."

"I'm relieving General McClellan later today," Lincoln said. "He had my order and he did not move. Thus I've issued a new order."

"And his replacement, sir?"

"None," Lincoln said. "I will command through Secretary of War Stanton." Lincoln cocked his head. "You don't hide your emotions very well. You disapprove?"

"I'm not in a position to approve or disapprove, Mister President," Rumble said.

"Perhaps I will regret the decision," Lincoln said. "But in the meanwhile, as Commander-In-Chief, both figuratively and now literally, I will support your Grant." He grabbed a scrap of paper. "You have my personal order to go where you will. This is the code that you will put any telegrams you send to Washington. They'll alert me if any message comes in from you."

Lincoln stood to end the meeting. He pressed both large hands on the desktop. Rumble could see the whites of his knuckles. "You once mentioned you had a son, did you not?"

"I did, sir."

"How old?"

"He is twenty."

"Is that why you're going west?"

Rumble nodded. "He enlisted, sir. He's out west, in Grant's command."

"You trust your son with Grant?"

"I do, sir." Rumble held up the abolitionist coin. "On board the *Monitor* I was hit by a bullet, sir. This saved my life. My son gave it to me."

Lincoln leaned forward and took the coin. He ran it through his fingers. "A father's love for his son. There is nothing stronger." He gave the coin back. "I have a feeling great things are going to happen out west soon with your friend, General Grant. Go west with my blessings, Sergeant Major."

Grant and Sherman

15 Mar 1862, Palatine, Mississippi

The front doors to Palatine swung open and a single figure was silhouetted against the early morning light. St. George roused himself from his slumber and blinked his one good eye.

"Who there?"

"I have heard rumors my husband is missing," Violet Rumble said, "but that still does not give you permission to move into my home, St. George Dyer. You're trespassing. Get the hell out!"

St. George lumbered to his feet. He picked up the LeMat pistol off a table and leisurely stuck it in his black sash. "Well, well, if it aint Miss Violet."

The other overseers roused themselves from various degrees of hangover. The main hall was littered with empty bottles and other debris, the walls stained with soot from badly tended fires. St. George put on his slouch hat as the four overseers gathered behind him.

"I am not alone," Violet said.

Seneca, leaning heavily on his cane, stomped up next to her, a rough wooden prosthetic bolstering his left leg.

St. George laughed. "A toothless bitch and a crip."

Violet drew the pistol from her dress and Seneca held up a revolver. The overseers snapped their rifles and shotguns to the ready.

"You outgunned," St. George said.

"You're hasty and stupid," Violet said. "It's going to be the death of you some day. Should today be that day?"

The door to the kitchen swung open and a half-dozen soldiers in gray crowded in, rifles at the ready. Sliding past Violet and Seneca were another eight, spreading out as they entered. The four overseers lowered their weapons.

"Remember my son's company you had sent east to Bull Run?" Violet asked.

"We lost good men," Seneca said. "Many good men. Men under my command. And these men's friends."

St. George's head swiveled back and forth. The math wasn't hard. He held up his hands. "Let not be hasty."

"If I was hasty, you'd already be dead," Violet said. "Where's my husband?"

"He gone missing," St. George said. "Week or so ago. Took off on his horse."

"You lie," Violet said. "He could barely get out of bed. You did something to him. Your problem is, with my husband gone, Palatine now goes to my son."

"Be that so?" St. George said. "Which boy be that? The one wearing Yankee blue or that one-legged fella there?"

"That's not of your damn business," Violet snapped.

"Get out," Seneca ordered. "Or we'll shoot you down like the ragged dog you are."

"We be going," St. George said. "I hear tell the Yankees coming down the Tennessee River. If that so, I don' think your soldier boys here be around forever to keep you safe. I be around though." St. George turned his back to her, facing the kitchen door.

Violet thumbed back the hammer on the revolver. "All the more reason to kill you now."

"Mother!" Seneca teetered on his wood leg and cane. "We cannot murder. It is what separates us from his kind."

"More than that separates us," Violet said, "and maybe we shouldn't let that be our difference."

"You shoot me now," St. George said, over his shoulder, "you be shooting a man in da' back. Even your soldier boy can't protect you then. There still a law 'round here."

"Don't you dare talk about the law," Violet said.

"I be seeing you 'round." St. George pushed his way out through the kitchen, his lackeys following.

Seneca put his pistol back in the holster and gripped the front door frame. "And now, mother? What do we do?"

Violet looked out the front door of Palatine, down the tree covered lane. "This is our home. We will make our stand here or we will die doing so."

16 March 1862, Fort Henry, Tennessee

"I am virtually under arrest!" Grant slammed a fist onto his field desk.

"Well, good day to you and how have you been to you too," Cord said as he propped his Lancaster up against the desk and helped himself to a cup of harsh coffee from a pot simmering on the pot bellied stove. They were in the same bunker at Fort Henry from which Buckner had wielded his brief command and then unconditionally relinquished. The space was foul with cigar smoke. Ever since some reporter had filed a story that Grant had been smoking a cigar while dictating Unconditional Surrender, cases and cases of the smokes had begun arriving at camp, sent from admirers in the north.

Bowing to the onslaught, Grant had put away his pipe, feeling obligated to smoke the gifts sent his way.

"What word from St. Louis?" Grant asked. "What was General Halleck's reply?"

Cord wearily sat down on a stool and peered at his friend. "I do have to say this latest scouting venture was almost as dangerous as riding all the way to Richmond and saying howdy-do to Jeff Davis. 'Old Brains' Halleck is not happy with you at all."

"What did he say regarding my suggestion?" Grant was growing impatient.

Cord had borne a letter outlining Grant's attempt to give both men a face-saving way out of this awkward situation. It had said simply that it was the result of mis-communication and that there must be 'enemies between you and myself'.

"He was quite blunt," Cord said. "He said 'Grant is mistaken. There is no enemy between him and I.'"

Grant was taken aback. "He meant that?"

"Oh, yes," Cord said. "You're insubordinate, too full of yourself, arrogant and a drunk. And those are the nice things I heard about you at his headquarters."

"I take advantage of opportunities," Grant argued, "and I have never directly disobeyed any order I received."

"Carefully worded," Cord said. "Taking Nashville when it was undefended made sense, except for the fact Halleck told you to wait. He wanted that prize to go to Buell. Halleck also ordered you not to advance down the Tennessee River into Mississippi, yet I notice a lot less troops here than when I departed last week."

"I didn't get the order reference to Nashville until my men were already moving," Grant said.

"Did you not get it in time or did you not read it in time?" Cord asked with a smile.

"Halleck ordered me not to advance down the Tennessee," Grant continued. "He did allow me to send a reconnaissance. And my men aren't in Mississippi. They're still in Tennessee."

"So you sent practically the entire army to stop just a few miles short of Mississippi," Cord said. "Slippery Sam. Halleck hasn't changed in the slightest, except he's got less hair, if such a thing is possible and not be bald. He still hugs himself when he gets nervous and rubs his hands over his elbows. Remember that? He's doing lots of it now." He sipped his coffee and looked pointedly at the mug on Grant's desk. "A strong brew."

"It is," Grant said. "This time—" he paused. "It's coffee, Elijah. Are they really saying I'm drinking?"

"Of course," Cord said. "Listen, Sam. You won a couple of great victories. With that comes great resentment."

A new voice joined the conversation. "Of course it does."

"Cump!" Grant hopped up and greeted his old friend with a solid handshake.

"Sam," Sherman said. He nodded at Cord. "Elijah, it's been a long time."

"It has indeed," Cord shook Sherman's hand. "San Francisco is a long time and a long distance away."

"How are things up the river?" Grant asked.

Sherman moved over to the map table with Grant and Cord flanking him. "I've got your divisions encamped here." He pointed at a spot a hundred miles south of their location, just short of the Tennessee-Mississippi border on the west bank of the river. "We disembarked the steamers at Pittsburgh Landing. It's about fifteen miles from Corinth and there's a good road straight to the rail hub. We spread out the perimeter. The encampment is centered on a small church, here, called Shiloh, whatever the blazes that means."

Another new voice chimed in from the door. *"'Why did da' Lord bring defeat upon us today before the Philistines? Let us bring the Ark of the Lord's covenant from Shiloh, so that it may go with us and save us from da' hand of our enemies.'"* Samual qouted. "From One Samuel in the good book, sirs."

"Who—" Sherman began, but Grant cut him off.

"Come in, Samual." He turned to Sherman. "He's one of my chief scouts, along with Elijah."

Sherman folded his arms over his chest. "Sure you know what you're doing, General Grant?"

"I'm sure," Grant said in a tone that both Cord and Sherman recognized. This was not going to be a point of discussion.

"Shiloh mean place of peace, sir," Samual added.

Grant nodded. "What have you seen, Samual?"

Samual looked at the map. He ran a finger along the Tennessee River with a concentrated frown as if visualizing his journey on the piece of paper. His finger came to a halt. "Them be southern gents here, sir. Lots of them."

Sherman harrumphed. "Corinth. Could have told you that without having to go there. Sidney Johnston has to hold Corinth to protect the Memphis and Charleston rail line. It's the only east-west rail connection the rebels have left."

Grant ignored Sherman. "What else, Samual?"

The huge former slave shrugged. "Don' know, sir. But in da' book, the Philistines, they conquered Shiloh and got the Ark. Big defeat for the people of da' Lord."

Grant was looking at the map. "I don't believe General Johnston will attack any time soon. And the terrain looks very defensible. We have creeks to protect each flank." He looked up at Samual. "Are they flooded?"

"Yes, sir," Samual said. "Hard crossing. Lick Creek and Owl Creek. Both go into da big river. They high and if it rain more, soldier can't wade them 'cept at a couple of fords."

Grant rubbed his hands together and went back to his desk. "Good, good. Protected on each flank and we control the river to our rear and have a pair of gunboats in position. Good job, Samual."

Sherman was still eyeing the black man with distrust.

"Thank you, General."

"Samual, go get some hot food," Cord suggested.

"Yes, sir." Samual exited.

"Relax, Cump," Grant said. "He's a good man."

Sherman shook his head. "That's not it, Sam. Maybe he's right. Philistines and defeat and all that."

Grant pulled his arms back, stretching his shoulders. "Old gloom and doom Sherman. You haven't changed much."

"Let me tell you two something," Sherman said. "I was in California when the first gold was brought in from the Sierra Nevadas. Went up and confirmed the find in '48. You both know what happened with the Gold Rush. But when I tried to return to California after resigning my commission to make *my* fortune, the ship I was on failed to find the entrance to San Francisco in the fog and sank on the rocks north of the bay. I clung to the wreckage until rescued by another boat. Then that boat sank entering the bay and I arrived at San Francisco clinging to the hull. When the boat that rescues a man from a sinking, sinks, you pay attention. And, I didn't make a fortune. So don't talk to me about bad luck."

Cord laughed. "That's just no luck, Cump. I got caught in a blizzard in early '47, trying to cross the Sierras with Kit Carson. Damn near froze to death. He said there's good luck and no luck."

Grant snorted. "Every business I invested in and worked in before the war failed. So according to your friend Carson, we have three no luck fellows in this room."

"I take that as a good sign," Cord said. "Means our luck is bound to change for the better."

"That's one way of looking at it, I suppose," Sherman said. "Oh yes, speaking of a change in luck. Something I forgot." He reached inside his coat and pulled out a piece of paper and a small case. "Whatever Old Brains might be thinking, apparently someone in Washington feels differently." He put both on the field desk. Grant picked up the paper to read while Cord opened the lid on the case. A set of two stars lay inside.

"Major-general?" Grant said.

"Indeed," Sherman said. "Straight from President Lincoln. Seems like you might indeed be having a turn of good luck."

Grant fingered the stars while looking at the map. "Elijah."

"Yes?"

"I want to know what's beyond Corinth. To Memphis. On down to Vicksburg. That's the key to the whole area."

"Johnston's in Corinth with his army," Cord said. "Shouldn't that be our concern right now?"

"We've got to think ahead and plan ahead," Grant said. "I think one more victory can end this entire thing."

Cord sighed. "That'll be a long ride, Sam. Having to swing wide around Johnston, then to Vicksburg is a haul."

"We've got time," Grant said. "I don't see any action occurring for a while."

"I need a favor from you, Sam, if you don't mind, since I'll be gone for a while."

"Certainly."

20 March 1862, Savannah, Tennessee

"Sam."

Grant looked up from the order he had been writing. He jumped to his feet. "Lucius!"

The Sergeant Major and the Major General embraced.

"Sit, sit," Grant said, grabbing a pile of dispatches off a chair and clearing a space. They were in an upstairs sitting room in a mansion Grant had commandeered for his headquarters on the bank of the Tennessee River. "When did you get here?"

"Just now," Rumble said. "Via, Nashville."

"Tell me of Buell," Grant ordered. "Where's his army?"

"They're stuck at a creek just southwest of the city. Building a bridge to ford it."

Grant frowned. "According to Halleck, I'm to sit here and do nothing until Buell's army links up with me." He shook his head, dismissing the issue. "It's been a long time since Mexico, Lucius." He noted the insignia. "Sergeant Major and Master of the Horse at our old Rockbound Highland Home, I heard. So why are you out here in the west?"

"To observe," Rumble said.

Grant laughed. "Just like Mexico. For old Delafield?"

"For Lincoln."

That gave Grant pause as he tumbled that about in his brain. "And how long have you been observing for the President?"

"Since last summer."

"That solves a few mysteries," Grant said. "I appreciate your help."

"I just told the truth when asked," Rumble said. "And I wanted Ben to have the best commander the army has."

Grant flipped open the lid on a teak box. "Cigar?"

"Where's your pipe?" Rumble asked as he took one.

"I go with the wishes of the public on some things," Grant said as they went through the lighting ritual. "Speaking of Ben, I've got some good news. He's here."

"I know," Rumble said. "Fifth Ohio Cavalry."

Grant waved the cigar. "No, no. I mean *here*. Elijah asked me to keep him safe, so I had him assigned to my staff. He's probably downstairs somewhere right now."

Rumble was on his feet. "And Elijah?"

"He's on a scouting mission for me. I don't anticipate he'll be back a fortnight or so."

"Request permission to—" Rumble began but Grant cut him off.

"Lucius, just go see your son."

Rumble shook Grant's hand and hurried out of the room. The layout of the house reminded him of Palatine and for a moment he wondered about Violet and how things were there. But he forgot all that when he entered the kitchen and spotted a private with red hair scrubbing out a coffee pot.

"Son!"

Ben turned just in time for his father to embrace him. The two were still for long seconds. Rumble slowly let go of Ben and stepped back, appraising him. "You've lost weight."

"I'm gaining it back here," Ben said with a wry smile. "General Grant isn't much for special privileges but some on his staff certainly believe officers should dine well."

"That's the army," Rumble said.

"That is indeed the army." Ben sighed. "I know Mister Cord thought he was doing me a favor by having General Grant bring me to headquarters, but I want to be back with my unit."

"He wanted to keep you safe," Rumble said. "It's a normal thing to want—" he came to an abrupt halt.

"To keep your child safe?" Ben finished for him.

"You know?"

"I've pretty much known for years," Ben said. "It doesn't change anything. You married mother. You raised me, you took care of Abigail and me."

Rumble reached in his pocket. "I have something I want you to see." He retrieved the abolitionist token and handed it to Ben.

"What happened to it?"

"It stopped a bullet from entering my heart," Rumble said. "And you're a man now. If you want to go back to your unit, you get to choose to do that. I'll talk to Sam about it tonight."

5 April 1862, Pittsburg Landing, Tennessee

Cord was bone-tired. The kind of weariness that sinks so deep, a man thinks he's never going to sleep and rest enough to recover. He'd been riding non-stop for two weeks with Samual, scouting west to Memphis and south, all the way down to Vicksburg. They'd had to circle wide to east on the return, crossing the Tennessee River in Alabama to get back to Grant's army, since Sidney Albert Johnston's army was clustered around Corinth with many skirmishers and foragers scouring the land for miles about.

"Get some hot food, Samual," Cord said. "Show the idiots Grant's order if they give you any trouble."

It was a sign of how worn the big man was that he simply nodded, heading toward a cluster of fires.

Cord remained in place, in the darker shadow under an oak tree, looking at the sleeping figure curled up, an old horse blanket wrapped around him. Cord hadn't had a chance to spend more time with Ben yet. Scouting for Sam had consumed his days, his weeks and the past month.

Cord had been to Grant's headquarters earlier in the day to tell the General that no one knew what Johnston was planning, if he was planning anything at all. But it troubled Cord that he hadn't been able to slide between Corinth and the Union Army, to see what was afoot. Nathan Bedford Forrest's cavalry was covering that ground, and Cord had heard enough stories of that man to keep

Samual, and himself, well clear. And he'd also learned that Ben was back with his cavalry unit, Rumble having swung Grant's decision.

Grant was seven miles away, at Savannah on the other side of the river. Waiting to link up with Buell's column from Nashville and recovering from a nasty fall two days ago. His horse had slipped and pinned him to the ground. Only the softness of the rain-soaked earth had saved Grant from severe injury. Still, his boot had been cut off and he couldn't walk without crutches.

Cord watched Ben's chest rise and fall and wondered what it would have been like to see him like that when he was younger. As a boy. As a baby.

"Atonement," Cord whispered, gripping the rifle he'd stolen earlier in the day tight in his fists.

With all the stealth he'd learned on the frontier, Cord moved forward. He knelt next to Ben. His son's face was relaxed, peaceful in sleep. The Bowie knife was next to his son's head, within quick grasp. Cord nodded in approval. He slid the Henry repeating rifle and box of cartridges he'd stolen from Rumble's kit back at Grant's headquarters, under the loose flap of the blanket.

So intent on stealth, Cord didn't notice the beads of sweat on his son's forehead. It was a cool April night, not conducive to sweat.

Cord stood up and moved back to the darkness under the oak tree. "It's a start." And he knew a start would all he'd ever have, over and over. Making up for the years.

But tomorrow there'd be time. To sit with his son and keep up the start.

5 April 1862
To The Soldiers of the Army of the Mississippi:
I have put into motion to offer battle to the invaders of your country. With the resolution and discipline and valor becoming men fighting, as you are, for all worth living or dying for, you can but march to decisive victory over the agrarian mercenaries sent to subjugate and despoil you of your liberties, property and honor. Remember the dependence of your mothers, your wives, your sisters, and your children on the result; remember the fair, broad, abounding land, the happy homes and the ties that would be desolated by your defeat. The eyes and hopes of eight millions of people rest upon you; you are expected to show yourselves worthy of your lineage, worthy of the women of the South, whose noble devotion in this war has never been exceeded in any time. With such incentives to brave deeds, and with the trust that God is with us, your generals will lead you confidently to the combat—assured of success.
C.S.A. General Sidney Albert Johnston

Shiloh Prelude
6 April 1862, Shiloh, Tennessee

"Damn it, St. George," Sally Skull cursed. "I tol' you Violet Rumble be coming back to Palatine. And you shoulda known she not be coming back stupid. Now you lost us our easy cotton."

The two were mounted to the side of the road in the darkness, listening to lines of Confederate soldiers bumbling by. It was a heck of a racket. They were just five miles from the Tennessee River and but two from the Yankee lines. Further back from the road, Gabriel was on her horse, dressed like a man, Spencer in her hands, ready for action.

"I'll kill her and her crip son," St. George vowed.

"The crip aint the one you need worry 'bout," Skull said. "The older boy out there somewhere with the Yankees. And his false boy, named after that nigra, is the one you really need be concern with."

"That boy aint even their blood!" St. George complained. They'd ridden here with a column of Texas beef that Skull was supplying to the Confederates.

"The Rumble's claiming he blood is all the proof they need," Skull said. "You sure Ben Rumble joined the Yankee army?"

"5th Ohio Cavalry in da' letter," St. George said.

"So he out there too," Skull said. She was silent for a few moments, mulling that over. "I imagine battles can get mighty confusing. I got a couple of my drovers over on the other side, selling the Yankees some of the beef I already done sold to this side."

That was too sharp an angle for St. George's brain to negotiate. "And?"

Skull rolled her eyes, the movement lost in the darkness. "Means I can get you over there among the blue, free to roam, acting as one of my men."

"What for?"

Skull couldn't keep in the sigh of exasperation. "A bullet can come from the front or it can from the back, but no one knows really who fired it in a battle, but picking your target is a lot easier from the back. Those two Rumble's are over there. Gen'l Johnston claims his men will have their horses drinking from the Tennessee River by this evening. You do right, both Rumble's be dead by same time."

St. George remained still for a long time, as if the concept was sinking through the layers of fat and muscle. "And then?"

"Then I'll go wit' you to Palatine and do what shoulda been done in the first place. We bury Miss Violet under her stone angel along with her one-legged son. And it be ours."

"Why bury her?" St. George asked. "Just throw 'em in the river."

"Have a bit of respect," Skull muttered, but not loud enough for it to register with St. George.

"How I get over to Yankees?" St. George asked.

"Gabriel will guide you," Skull said. "She been back and forth a few times."

"I don' want no nigra—" St. George began, but Skull hushed him.

A horse came down the road, weaving through the rebel Infantry as if both horse and man could see in the dark. The rider reined in next to Skull and St. George, a flame finding a pair of moths.

"Long way from the Mississippi," Nathan Bedford Forrest said. "I suppose the two of you are making a profit out of this?"

"You suppose right," Skull said. "But we're providing some needed service to the cause."

"Big victory today, right Cuhnel?" St. George said.

Forrest was a dark shadow, but his eyes glinted in the moonlight. "Maybe. Johnston's a fighter. But they sent that fool Beauregard from the east to be his second. He made the plan for the attack. Heard an aide say he based it on Napoleon's attack at Waterloo. Thing is," Forrest leaned closer to the two, "I might not be school smart, but I recollect that Napoleon lost at Waterloo. Damn West Pointers."

"Fella in charge on the other side a West Pointer," Skull pointed out.

"Can't spit but you hit one," Forrest said. "Some of them good fellas. If Buckner had had command at Donelson from the start, we mighta held. Those rabbit politicians wearing stars are worse for the army than anyone else. And Johnston is tough as nails."

"He's a Texan," Skull said proudly. "I know't Gen'l Johnston a long time. I was but a girl when I seen him get wounded dueling Gen'l Houston for command of the Texas army. He stood fast, refusing to fire, even after getting shot in the leg. I nursed him to health when they brought him into the borde--." She abruptly stopped.

Both men stared at her, but were unable to see the look on her face. St. George had never heard that tone in her voice and Forrest encountered it every day and recognized it for what it was: adoration.

"Why'd he not shoot?" St. George asked.

"He thought it stupid for two men on the same side to be fighting each other," Skull explained.

"Makes sense." Forrest stretched out his shoulders. "They got the whole damned army coming up this one road. That don't make sense. Gonna be a big jumble once the shooting starts. A man needs to spread out to fight, not pile on top of each other."

"What they got you doing, Cuhnel?" St. George asked.

The frustration was obvious in Forrest's voice. "Right flank and hold. I told Beauregard I could cross the river with my boys and make sure Buell don't get close. But they think Buell and his army are still up by Nashville. 'Cept they don't know that for sure. They don't know anything for sure. They all think the Yankees are going to run."

"They might," St. George said, but Skull didn't comment. "Southern boy worth five, maybe ten, Yankees in a fight."

"They aint gonna run," Forrest said. "They're men, too."

To that, St. George had no reply.

Forrest looked into the deeper shadows under the trees. "Your girl with the Spencer out there, aint she?"

"She is," Skull said.

"Trust is a dangerous thing," Forrest said. He pulled on his reins. "Well, lady and gent, I got me some killing to do today. Perhaps I'll see you later in the day."

"Perhaps," Skull allowed.

"Yes, sir, cuhnel," St. George said.

Forrest rode off. Somewhere in the dark a soldier tripped, causing a chain reaction in the column of Confederate Infantry. Curses and the clank and rattle of swords, muskets, mess kits and the sundry the men carried echoed in the dark.

Skull shook her head. "Not be as many mouths to feed soon."

"Sir!"

Cord was awake instantly, one hand grasping for the Bowie which was no longer on his belt, the other for the Lancaster, fingers curling around the stock.

"What is it, Samual?" Cord sat up, the light blanket falling aside. It was just before dawn, that fleeting time when the stars disappeared in the haze of impending sunlight and it was damn near impossible to make anything out in the dark haze.

"Animals be running, sir," Samual said. "Squirrel and the like. Out of the woods and swamp to da' river."

Cord was on his feet. "Where's General Sherman?"

"Near da' Shiloh Church, sir."

Cord clapped a hand on Samual's shoulder. "All right. You go to Savannah. Tell General Grant that Elijah Cord smells bad air. Very bad."

Samual cocked his head. "Sir?"

"Just tell him, with those words: Elijah Cord smells bad air. Very bad."

"Yes, sir." Samual paused. "It's the Lord's day, sir. The Sabbath."

"I know," Cord said.

"Shouldn' be fighting on the Lord's day." Samual sprinted into the darkness.

Cord ran in the opposite direction down one of the many cow paths that crisscrossed the area. The past few days, many men and units had become lost on those paths, unable to tell one from the other, but Cord trusted his inner sense of direction, honed by years on the frontier. All around he could hear the soldier's cough. It was a constant sound that accompanied the army. Sick soldiers, trying to clear their lungs. Accompanied by a chorus of snoring from thousands of men.

Nobody had dug in or prepared defenses. Cord knew Sherman was reluctant to appear afraid after almost getting permanently removed from the Army for his proclamations of gloom and doom the previous year. And Sam Grant, well, he just didn't like being on the defensive. Besides, everyone agreed the Rebels were still in Corinth. Cord knew what Kit Carson would make of that and he felt a pang that his scouting hadn't been able to cut in between the two armies and fix the rebel positions for certain.

It was going to be a beautiful spring day. The trees were freshly leafed. Peach blossoms loomed overhead. A deer came galloping by, heading in the opposite direction, as Samual had noted. There were shots in the distance. There had been shots in the distance for days. Sporadic encounters between pickets and Confederate cavalry patrols. Or men coming off duty discharging their weapons to unload them. Those that had loaded them with powder and ball in the first place. There were a number of men who'd filled their barrels with 'oh-be-joyful', powerful moonshine to make the lonely hours on picket duty pass by that much faster by 'tipping the barrel' every so often.

This firing was different.

Like a rainstorm moving in on a tin roof, first there were the separate drops, but the volume was increasing steadily.

Cord found Sherman rolled in a blanket, underneath a wagon.

"Cump!"

Sherman's eyes flickered open. He sat up abruptly, bumping his head on the underside of the wagon. Cursing, Sherman crawled out.

"What's the report?" Sherman demanded as he buckled on his sword.

"I haven't seen anything," Cord said. "But the rebs are coming. In force."

"How do you know?" Sherman asked.

"Because we didn't expect them to be coming. I sent word to Sam."

Sherman nodded. "Wallace is at Crump's Landing. I'm sure Sam will get him moving, but we're going to need him on the double. Can you pass that message to him?"

Cord looked toward the sound of the firing, knowing exactly where Ben was.

"The best you can do for your boy, right now, Elijah," Sherman said, "is get us reinforcements."

"All right, Cump." As Sherman went to his staff, issuing orders, Cord reached in his pocket. He retrieved his West Point ring and slid it on his finger.

"Hold on there!"

The Union soldier was dangerous. Samual had spent his entire life avoiding confrontation. The soldier was scared, and that made him doubly dangerous.

"Yes, sir," Samual said.

"Where you be going, boy?" the soldier demanded.

"I got to get to Savannah, sir," Samual said. "Got a message to deliver."

"To who?"

"General Grant, sir." Samual knew that the truth was a mistake the second it left his mouth, but now it was out there, hanging in the air.

The soldier laughed. "You a dumb one, aint you? Aint never met no nigra before, but they said you people was dumb, and you sure is. You 'pect me to believe that?"

Samual started to reach into his pocket to get Grant's pass, but the soldier stuck out his rifle. "Don't you be grabbing for nothing, boy!"

More soldiers were gathering round, silhouetted by the glow from the campfires.

Taking the road had been a mistake too, Samual now accepted. He'd been in a rush. Trying to do what he was told. Elijah Cord smells bad air. Very bad.

"Sir, I got important words to give."

"To General Grant. Yeah, boy. Heard that. Who it from? Maybe Abraham Lincoln hisself?"

The soldier looked past Samual as the sound of firing made a brief appearance, a trick of acoustics, then faded to the chorus of normal camp rousing. The soldier's tongue slid over his lips. He was damn scared.

Samual took the glance as an opportunity and made a break for the woods.

He hadn't seen the other soldier. The one who'd come up behind him and laid him out cold with a butt stroke to the side of the head.

"Damn stupid nigra," the Union soldier muttered as he went back to breakfast.

Ben lay on his back, feeling each breath enter his mouth, slide down his throat and fill his lungs with difficulty. He coughed hard, a racking that twitched his body. He rubbed a hand across his forehead and it came away wet with sweat. There was a pounding inside his skull, reminding him of the one time he'd over indulged in spirits at college. Except he'd had none last night. He'd been feeling sour ever since Fort Donelson.

Beyond the snoring and coughing of other men, he could hear birds chirping, heralding a new day. He envied them. They didn't have the worries of humans. The imagination of what might lie ahead. There was here. There was now. And that's all they had.

The sound of musket firing was growing louder. That was pulling him from the here and the now, to the endless possibilities of the day ahead. Ben sat up and almost fell over. He dragged his thoughts to the present, but they slipped through without grabbing purchase, back to the long night. He'd slept some. And he'd dreamed in his fever. Of West Point. Of the Hudson River and the highlands. Of a woman with the most beautiful green eyes telling him everything would be fine. He couldn't pull her complete image out of the dream. Just those eyes. The rest of her was incomplete, hazy, like when the fog lay over the Hudson on a summer morning.

There's also been a man. Hovering over him in his dreams. Not a threat though. A comfort in some way Ben couldn't pin down.

He tossed aside the horse blanket and his eyes widened as he saw his 'father's' Henry and box of cartridges. He picked up the gun, feeling the balance, admiring the sleek lines of the weapon.

The musket fire was quicker, fiercer, beckoning. Sergeants were stirring, shaking awake men still slumbering. Ben put the rifle down and grabbed his shoes. He put them on and began to tie the laces. He wondered, a fleeting thought, if this were the last time he would ever do that. And whether someone else would remove them from his feet. He'd heard tell the Secessionists needed shoes. He'd had the same thought every day for the past couple of months, every time he put his shoes on.

Perhaps he should have gone to Europe. Ben shook his head and glanced at the Henry, decoding the message and implicit approval from his 'father'. The Bowie knife dangled from his belt in its sheath; more legacy from his birth father. Shoes ready, he stood, cradling the Henry in his arms.

Everyone was moving strangely. Long faces, tight, drawn. None of the usual early morning tomfoolery. Ben met the glance of the man next to him, a private from Cincinnati as best he could remember. The man's eyes had a shadow in them. Yesterday he'd been boasting of killing rebs.

"You don' look so good," the man said.

"A touch of something," Ben said.

"Been touched for a while," the man muttered, taking a step away.

"Lookie there!" Someone cried out.

To the south, wraiths were moving through the distant trees, tall, angular, dressed in gray and butternut. Hats pulled low over their eyes. They were close, less than three hundred yards away and there were a lot of them.

"We have to fall back and form!" the captain yelled in a voice that had a hitch in it as he reversed the proper sequence of the orders. "Mount up and pull back!"

Ben ran for the horse-line along with the rest of the men. On the left there was fire from a Union Infantry regiment, a ragged volley, and then they too began to scramble to the rear, camp fires still burning, breakfasts left uneaten.

The 5th Ohio had pulled the horse-line dozens of times in training, but this was different. As if they'd never done it before. Some men hopped on horses without saddles, galloping off. Others were grabbing the wrong gear in their haste.

Ben forced himself to do it right. Saddle. Bridle. His hands were shaking. Not from fear.

The firing was closer. Something buzzed by, like an angry hornet.

Then came that sound. Ben knew that he would never forget that sound as long as he lived: the Rebel Yell. It cut through his illness and spurred him to move faster.

Lucius Rumble paced the high porch of the house Grant had commandeered for his headquarters. It wasn't as grand as Palatine House, and overlooked the Tennessee River, not the mighty Mississippi, but it was similar enough in design. That did not give Rumble any comfort. His rifle and telescope were gone and he had no doubt who'd taken it. Damn Cord. Always thinking of himself. At least Rumble still had Tiberius' shotgun. He'd make Cord account for the Henry and scope the next time he laid eyes on him.

"You're going to wear a rut in the wood," Grant called out through the window from the table where he was eating breakfast. It was a sitting room, not a dining room, but Rumble knew better than to tell Grant that. The General was in a foul mood, his leg paining his body and the uncertainty of where exactly Buell's army was, weighing heavy on his mind.

Rumble reached the end of the porch and turned on his heel. He started to head back, but paused. Thunder in the distance, but the early morning sky was perfectly clear.

"Sam," Rumble called out.

"Yes?"

"Artillery."

"Crump's landing or Pittsburgh landing?" Grant asked.

Rumble cocked his head. "Hard to tell."

Hobbling on crutches, Grant joined Rumble on the porch. He leaned against the railing, perfectly still for several moments. Several staff officers, surprised by Grant getting to his feet, came onto the porch and joined them.

Grant tucked the crutches under his arms. "Gentlemen, the ball is in motion. Let's be off."

Rumble leaned close. "Sam, it will be easier if you let me help get you to the boat."

Grant nodded. While an aide grabbed the crutches, Rumble wrapped an arm around his old friend and half-carried him downstairs, out the front door and to the landing where Grant's steamer waited. Smoke was already coming out of the *Tigress'* stacks. Before boarding, Grant issued several orders, the most important of which was to Buell, wherever he was, directing him to come to Pittsburgh Landing with all haste. As soon as they were on board, the ship set out up-river toward the sound of the firing.

Crump's landing was closest and it became clear as they approached, that the cannon fire was further away. A steamship was tied up there, General Lew Wallace's command ship. Grant had the captain of the *Tigress* slow down a bit and pass close by.

"General," Grant called out to his division commander, "get your troops under arms and have them ready to move at a moment's notice."

"Already in motion, General," Wallace yelled back.

Grant acknowledged that with a nod and the *Tigress* picked up speed. They could now hear musket fire mixed with the belch of cannons. The symphony of all out combat, indicating this was not some skirmish.

A few inexperienced staff officers let out exclamations of shock as the *Tigress* turned a bend in the Tennessee and Pittsburgh Landing came into view. Thousands of men, so many they seemed to be a roiling mass of blue worms on the riverbank beneath the bluffs. There were even a few men trying to swim across the river in their desperation to get away. As the ship got closer, Rumble could see that many officers and sergeants had torn off their rank insignia, abdicating their duty on top of running away from the battle.

"Damn cowards," someone muttered.

"Easy, gentlemen," Grant said. "It must be hard fighting to cause this and we're going to need these men before the day is through."

The *Tigress* slid into the landing. Rumble helped Grant off the ship. With another officer, they got Grant up in the saddle, tying his crutches off to the side, where a rifle might have been mounted.

One of the division commanders galloped up. "Prentiss is attacked and falling back, trying to reform another line. Sherman's also falling back. My men are up on the bluff as a central reserve awaiting your orders, sir."

"Sergeant Major," Grant said to Rumble. "See that regiment formed up over there? Get it to form a straggler line. And that battery yonder? Move it up to the bluff and point it down the road. It'll give any fleeing men second thoughts and if need be, hold the final line."

"Yes, sir."

"Then meet me on top of the bluff."

With the division commander, Grant rode toward the battle.

The first waves of Confederates had smashed into Prentiss' and Sherman's camps, routing the Yankees, but gone no further. No amount of cussing and exhortation could get the men moving forward. There was simply too much Yankee food still hot on the cooking fires and the men's bellies were just too empty. They were soldiers, true, but they were also human.

Sally Skull watched the frustration play across General Johnston's face as he issued order after order, trying to get the stalled attack moving. They weren't far from a small church in the center of the lines.

Just before the sun had come up, Gabriel had escorted St. George around the Union left flank. St. George was somewhere ahead now on his mission of mischief and murder and Skull had decided to stick close to Johnston, figuring that was the best place to keep track of events. The general had acknowledged her presence with a tip of his hat, but there was no time for more of a greeting.

In desperation, Johnston began issuing orders to the follow on divisions, not yet engaged, shifting their assault in echelon to the left, to capitalize on the initial successes of the morning. But in doing so, he was negating Beauregard's grand Napoleonic plan, as the right flanking movement to cut the Union forces off from Pittsburgh Landing was now turning into a frontal assault into the Union center.

As they rode forward, they passed through one of the many Yankee camps. A group of soldiers were looting the tents. A lieutenant saw the general and held up an ornately engraved pipe. "A Yankee colonel's, sir! For you."

Johnston drew up stiffly. "None of that, sir. We are not here for plunder."

The lieutenant's head dropped as if he'd been pole-axed. Johnston leaned forward in the saddle and picked up a tin cup from a table. "Let this be my share of the spoils today." Then he moved on.

Skull nudged her horse forward, pushing past staff officers and the cluster of men who always seemed to gather around a commanding general. She saw a cow wandering lost across the battlefield and recognized her brand on it. One of the many she'd double-sold, first to the Confederates and finally ending up in the Union camp.

There were matters of more concern now.

Skull saw a cluster of blue in some bushes. Wounded Lincolnites. It seemed that men, like animals, crawled into bushes when mortally hurt. There were bundles all over the place, looking like clusters of rags, but they were bodies.

A courier came galloping up from the left, blood streaming from his forehead. "General! We have their right. We've knocked them off Owl Creek."

Johnston absorbed this information, then ordered more troops to press that success, the exact opposite of what Beauregard's plan called for. There was a clatter of musketry to the immediate right and everyone turned in that direction. A gaggle of Union cavalry was galloping across a field. Not charging. Retreating, some of the men shooting wildly, others wielding sabers, but most hell bent on getting away.

Skull drew her pistols and began firing.

Ben held the reins in one hand, the Henry in the other, letting the flow of his company take him away. No orders had been issued after a musket ball straight through the heart had killed the Captain. Everyone had just started riding hard, trying to get away from the unstoppable wave of Confederates. Ben knew it wasn't right, that they should be doing something other than running. The thought bounced around his brain, but couldn't find purchase on a course of action, struggling through the dullness that made any effort to think slow and painful.

To his left he saw a cluster of Confederate officers near a church. And in front of them was a woman, of all things, blasting away with a pistol in each.

Ben registered her just as a bullet struck his horse in the head, right through the ear, into the brain and the beast dropped like a stone, sending Ben tumbling forward, reins held tight.

He hit the ground hard.

Cord rode north, across Owl Creek, searching for Wallace's Division. The sound of the fighting behind him was growing louder, fiercer than anything he'd ever heard, even in Mexico.

So much for the war being about over.

He felt some comfort that Ben had the Henry. He grabbed the telescope case and pulled out the instrument. He scanned west as far as the device could reach and saw no sign of movement.

Where the hell was Wallace?

St. George didn't think much of Skull's plan. No one knew where the 5th Ohio Cavalry was and how the devil was he supposed to find two needles in this huge, tumbled bale of blue? Seemed like most of the Yankees were heading toward the river, their bodies hunched, their eyes distant. Many looked half dead already, their faces so pale. Damn bluebellies were just as he'd imagined: weak and not worth a lick in a fight.

"This way." Gabriel pointed down a narrow path through the trees.

"What's that way?"

"Savannah Landing to Corinth Road," Gabriel said. Her voice was so low, St. George could barely make out what she was saying. "Main road."

"So?" St. George demanded.

Gabriel remained still, pointing at the road. St. George finally sighed and rode in that direction. Within a couple of minutes, they did indeed reach a wider thoroughfare. Troops and riders were moving in both directions.

"So?" St. George repeated.

"We wait," Gabriel said.

"For what?"

Gabriel shrugged and pulled her hat lower over her eyes.

St. George fidgeted, anxious to do something, anything, but having no better plan than waiting here. Although he wasn't quite sure what plan this was.

After about twenty minutes, a group of riders came hustling up the road, fighting against the tide of retreating men. St. George recognized the man in the lead, despite the years since he'd last seen him. The horse jumper. Grant. He was cool and calm, with the slightest frown of concern on his forehead, just like he'd been when he jumped that huge horse. He was issuing orders left and right as he rode forward. So he was indeed a Yankee. St. George's hand drifted toward his sash, knowing, in the way predators did, that the elder Rumble wasn't going to be far away from his friend Grant.

And there the elder boy be, on the trail, riding hard to catch up.

St. George edged his horse closer to the muddy road, pulling the Le Matt out of the sash. He started when Gabriel grabbed his hand.

"Not here!" she hissed.

"Damn you—" St. George began when a rider in a hurry banged into his horse. St. George jerked his head about and looked right into the crazed eyes of a Yankee general with flaming red hair, riding hell bent for Grant. They made eye contact for the briefest of moments, then the general was past and his staff swarmed by St. George.

"Cump!" Grant reined in his horse as Sherman arrived at the same time as Rumble.

"General." Sherman saluted. Other than his eyes, he was as calm as a stone. "It's been a bit hot on the field. One of my brigades, well, it's gone. Shot all up. But the rest of the boys are fighting hard. We're giving some land, but making them pay for every step forward. I sent Elijah to find Wallace and bring him forward with all haste."

Grant pointed. "You're wounded."

Sherman held up a hand dripping blood. "It's nothing. Got hit in the shoulder too, but the bullet was spent. Didn't even break the skin."

Grant looked past Sherman at the smoke covered battlefield. "Lew Wallace's division is coming. And Buell should be here tonight. We've got to hold until then."

"My only concern," Sherman said, "is running out of ammunition."

"I've got wagons moving forward," Grant said. "Don't concern yourself with that."

Sherman pointed to the southeast. "I'd be worried about Prentiss. He's holding the center and it sounds like hell's furies have been let loose over there."

"I'll see how he's doing," Grant said. He pulled a cigar out of a pocket, cut the end off and fired it up. He clenched it between his teeth. "Let's ride, Lucius."

They galloped off, leaving Sherman with his division.

Grant turned to Rumble. "That's one commander we don't have to spend much time with."

"He's in his element," Rumble acknowledged. Their focus on the battle, neither noticed St. George shadowing them.

The Union front was not smooth and several times they came perilously close to Confederates. They rounded a thicket of blackberries, surprising a half-dozen men in gray taking turns at a pot of Union coffee they'd scavenged. Grant spurred his horse and they rode right through, Rumble firing both barrels of the shotgun, scattering them like so many geese. One of the men got a shot off, hitting Grant's scabbard, breaking his sword.

Grant didn't pause and Rumble rode close by his friend's shoulder. They found the remains of Prentiss' division spread along a half mile of old wagon trail, the ruts sinking down one to three feet, giving the men some protection. A large field fronted them. Across that field, wounded and dazed soldiers were straggling back, many coming out of a peach orchard where the sound of battle was fierce. Their faces were black from powder, the sign of men who'd fired often.

"Perfect position," Grant said to Prentiss when they found the 6th Division Commander.

Prentiss was grim. "This is the line, General Grant. We've held in the peach orchard as long was we could, but it's too exposed from the rest of the line."

Grant gave him the same news about Wallace and Buell. Looking about, Rumble could see the hard set to the shoulders of the men already in the sunken road. Their faces had the same distinctive black smear from biting off the tips of their power cartridges before pouring into the barrel. Their eyes glittered as they peered across the open space. Now veterans, no matter what they'd been this morning, they knew they had a perfect field of fire in front of them and a river to their rear.

As Grant conferred with Prentiss, Rumble went over to one of the staff officers. "Where is the 5th Ohio Cavalry?"

"What's left of them is about a quarter mile down the road," the man said. "They came back here in a hurry."

Rumble fought the urge to search for Ben, as Grant wound up his visit with Prentiss.

"How many men do you have?" Grant asked.

"Six or seven thousand," Prentiss replied. "Hard to tell. We lost many a man over the morning."

"Artillery?"

"Twenty-five pieces."

"Maintain this position at all hazards," Grant ordered.

Prentiss nodded. "Yes, sir."

"Damn it!" Nathan Bedford Forrest cursed.

With his scouts he'd just ridden the battlefield from east to west. It was all going wrong. The Yankee right was giving way, not the left as planned. And the divisions were so intermingled, Confederate generals were simply taking command of the section of the battlefield they could see, rather than the units they had started the day in charge of. Which made getting orders down to the men who actually had to do the shooting that much harder. And the success in the west was getting wasted as many of those officers were marching their men to neither flank, but toward the torrent of gunfire in the center just like Napoleon had preached: always march to the sound of the guns. Something hellacious was going on there.

Forrest spotted some dead horses in a field and turned toward them, supposing they might be from his cavalry. When he got close enough, he saw that the bodies amongst the horses were Yankee.

He jumped his horse over the body of one of the bluebellies, intent on finding General Johnston so he could get his men into the fight.

The horse's hooves cleared Ben easily. The shadow of horse and rider flashed over him, and then there was light again. Ben remained still, letting the riders put some distance between. With great effort, he opened his eyes. Then he looked about. Dead and dying. Man and beast. A peach orchard beckoned cover and the tracks of the survivors from his unit headed that way.

Ben tried to move, but the reins were wrapped tight around his right arm. He tried pulling his arm free, but the dead weight of the horse didn't give an inch. Ben grabbed the Bowie with his left hand and slashed, slicing through the leather bindings. He finally cut through the entanglement and rolled away from the dead beast. In his haste, he dropped the Bowie.

Grabbing the Henry, Ben began to low crawl in that direction weaving his way through the dead like a worm.

Having toured the entire Union front, Grant was back on the bluff overlooking Pittsburgh Landing. There was no sign of Lew Wallace's Division, nor Buell's Army.

"Too much daylight left," Grant said to Rumble.

"Prentiss will hold fast," Rumble said.

"I know," Grant said. "But can he hold long enough?"

A courier came riding up, horse panting. "General Sherman's compliments, sir!" He held out a slip of paper.

Grant took it, read, then passed it to Rumble.

We are holding them pretty well just now—but it's hot as hell.

Grant was looking to the west. "Where is Wallace?"

There was no sign of Wallace's Division coming on the road from Crump's Landing to Pittsburgh Landing. Cord clenched the reins tighter with each mile he rode. He should have met them by now. He raced through a thicket of trees and then saw a line of blue.

Heading to the left, up another road that would take them directly into the rebels, not reinforce Grant. Cord spurred his horse, moving along the blue snake, trying to find Wallace.

He found the General perusing a map two miles up, the column ahead disappearing into a swamp.

"General!" Cord didn't bother to dismount.

Wallace looked up from the map. "Yes?"

"You're on the wrong road. You should have branched left at the last crossroads. You'll run into rebels if you continue on, not Grant's flank."

Wallace slapped the map against his thigh. "Sherman's fallen back that far?"

"Yes, sir. It's rough fighting. Grant needs you in the center, not the flank."

Wallace grabbed a staff officer. "Ride to the lead. Counter-march!"

Cord took a moment to consider his own situation. Wallace would not make it before dark. Not turning his column back on itself. And if Cord took the same route back, his time would double too. Wallace wasn't going to make it before dark.

"I'll give the counter-march order, sir," he told Wallace, then he galloped forward.

It took him fifteen minutes of hard riding to reach the lead regiment and relay Wallace's order. Then, instead of heading back, he rode forward, heading toward the sound of the firing by the most direct route, counting on his buckskins and his skills to get him through the Confederate lines and to Ben.

Ben squirmed through the dead and wounded, the bodies graced with pink peach petals, as if God himself were ornamenting the bodies. The ground was moist with blood and sweat and urine. He kept his eyes averted from those he clambered over and through. There were whispers and cries from the wounded. Praying, calling for their mother, cursing the generals, the war, their fate. Someone was screaming, high pitched, an inarticulate plea. He saw a man from his unit, shot through several times like a turkey in a Thanksgiving contest, lying half-buried under his horse.

Glancing to the right, Ben saw men, blue and gray, side-by-side, clustered at the edge of a pond, like desperate animals drawn to the water, lapping it up. The surface of the pond glistened red. Ben finally cleared the orchard of the dead and dying and made it into a field. He picked up the pace as there was a temporary slackening in the firing. He could see the trail of hooves from the remnants of his unit.

He heard orders being shouted behind him. Units being maneuvered. Ben got to his knees and risked a look back. Lines of gray were spreading out about a quarter mile away, preparing for the attack. Throwing his slow approach away, Ben jumped to his feet and raced hard toward a line of trees bordering a road. He could see the glint of steel from bayonets and prayed his blue coat would keep him alive.

By the time he reached the sunken road, he was breathing hard. He tumbled into the road between two men from his company.

"How many made it?" Ben asked as he caught his breath.

"Not even half," one of the men replied.

"Best get that quick shooter ready," the other said, peering over the muzzle of his own musket. "The Rebs be coming."

Ben turned and looked back the way he'd come. A long line of gray was approaching, battle flags waving. He looked left and right. The rebels were stretched out as far as he could see. It was a magnificent sight, which under other circumstances, Ben would have marveled at.

Ben put the stock of the Henry to his shoulder and ratcheted a round into the chamber. His finger curled around the trigger. Drops of sweat threatened to blind him and he blinked his eyes clear and took a deep breath, holding in the cough.

A lieutenant from the company was pacing back and forth along the sunken road. "Let 'em come, boys. Just a little bit closer. Then we'll give 'em hell. We aint running no more. We hold here until relieved or dead!"

Shiloh

6 April 1862, Shiloh, Tennessee

"We're sweeping the field," Johnston said to General Beauregard, gesturing with his tin cup toward the sound of the heaviest firing, "and I think we shall press them to the river."

Skull had been repulsed by Beauregard the first time she saw him. She sensed his black, dyed hair and droopy eyes hid something dark buried deep inside him. She'd met the like before.

"General," Beauregard said, in turn waving his saber to the east, "we need to press the plan and slide to the right. We're being drawn into a damned hornet's nest in the center."

"Too late for that," Johnston said. He squinted up at the sun. "We've got to push them into the river by nightfall. Buell's out there somewhere. We must play out the hand the Lord has given us today before he arrives."

The sound of firing from directly ahead rose to a crescendo. For a moment everyone, generals and staff, fell silent, each man leaning slightly forward as if they could determine the outcome from the noise.

An officer, a bloodied bandage wrapped around one hand, galloped up. "Sir, we have a brigade that refuses to move forward!"

"Remain here," Johnston ordered Beauregard. Johnston paused as his personal surgeon grabbed his elbow.

"Sir, there are wounded, mostly Yankee, over yonder. I can be of service."

Johnston nodded and dismissed his surgeon with a wave of the tin cup, his focus ahead.

"Sir!" Beauregard protested. "You're acting like a regimental commander, not an army commander."

"Watch your mouth, general," Johnston snapped. He rode off with the officer who'd brought the report and Skull followed, having no desire to be around Beauregard and wanting to get closer to the fighting.

Cord crossed back over Owl Creek at the same spot. He could tell how badly the day was going from the fact that when he'd gone west earlier, the fighting had been to the south of this position, but now it was to the north, meaning he was behind rebel lines. He pulled the Lancaster out of its buckskin scabbard and laid it across the pommel, making sure it was ready for action.

A string of rags lay in the middle of a field to the right. Cord knew they were not rags, but men, mowed down while advancing, or retreating. More dead and wounded appeared as he went east. He passed through an abandoned Union camp, rebels scattered about, gorged on food, some drunk. No one spared him and his shoddy outfit more than glance.

He came upon another camp and saw a wagon marked with *5th Ohio Cav.* Swallowing tightly, Cord rode about, checking the bodies in blue. He dismounted several times to turn a corpse over. He widened his search, but didn't discover Ben. Heartened, he followed the trail of the riders who'd survived.

As he went north, he passed more over-run Union camps. A considerable number of Confederate soldiers were taking advantage of the spoils of war. The small church near where Sherman had made his headquarters just this morning was to the left.

Cord tensed as he spotted a dead horse, the rigging clearly Union. As he got closer, he relaxed when he didn't see the body of the rider. The glint of sunlight on steel caught his attention. Dismounting, Cord's breath caught in his throat as he recognized his Bowie. He picked it up, wiping the dirt off the blade. He slid the large blade into his belt. Then he inspected the horse and rigging. A single shot through the head had done the horse in. There was no sign of blood, other than the horse's.

Kneeling, Cord traced his fingers over the trail moving away, toward the north. A man crawling. No blood trail.

A positive sign.

Holding his horse's rein in one hand, Cord began to follow the track.

Ben's fever was doubled by the heat of battle. As each wave of Confederates came within a hundred yards of the sunken road, he'd begin firing as fast as he could. Sixteen rounds hit the line of gray in less than a minute. He'd sink back down and begin shoving bullets into the breech, reloading the tube under the barrel.

Ten times the Rebels came.

Ten times the Yankees stopped them.

But each time there were less and less men in blue along the sunken road, and each time, there were more Confederate battle flags crossing the field.

Shoving the last bullet in, Ben looked at the dead littering the field. There was no cheering from his fellow soldiers. Every man could do the inevitable math. Many looked over their shoulders, to the north and west, hoping to see reinforcements. In vain.

General Sidney Albert Johnston, West Point class of 1826, rode along the reluctant brigade's front line, clanging his tin cup on the men's bayonets. "I will lead you, men!"

Sally Skull watched, tears forming in her eyes, as the men roared with renewed courage, their backs straightening, a glint replacing the fear that had glazed their pupils. Johnston pointed the tin cup toward the haze of gun smoke that indicated the Yankee line.

"Men, they are stubborn. We must use the bayonet!"

The brigade, and the ones on either side, surged forward. The problem was, and had been all afternoon during every assault, was that only the three brigades charged. While the massed Confederates outnumbered the Yankees in the Hornet's nest ten to one, the attacks had never been coordinated, so each assault sent only a portion of the rebel strength at the Yankees, and thus each assault had been beaten back.

Skull spurred her horse, falling behind the ranks of gray. The rebel yell split air, but otherwise it was strangely quiet, no sparks of fire poking through the gray smoke. Perhaps the Yankees had finally broken?

Ben couldn't believe the Rebels were coming again. Eleven times already. Each charge had taken its toll on the Union side. First in dead and wounded, and then, here and there, a man would just give in. It had had happened so often, one could see the progression. A dull look came into the man's eyes, replacing the anger and courage. His shoulders slumped. He cast furtive glances at those around him. Then he eventually began walking toward the rear, not running, never running. In some ways, the walking was worse, the resignation of it. The boy to Ben's right had been giving the look for a minute. As the Confederates approached, he simply turned and began skulking away. Ben took two steps to the right, covering the hole in the line.

"Steady, steady," the lieutenant kept repeating, as if convincing himself as much as ordering the men in the sunken road.

No one said anything to the boy who left. Each knew they'd each be walking back soon or be dead.

Ben levered a round into the chamber of the Henry repeating rifle.

The Confederates were closing and there was a pattern to their actions also. The banshee screech of their Rebel Yell, the way each man leaned further and further forward at the waist as they closed, as if breasting a strong wind. How some also angled their bodies, running awkwardly, presenting slightly less of a front.

"Fire!"

Ben pulled the trigger and the Union line hurled lead.

A shiver rippled along the length of the rebel front, but they kept coming. As the men around him began to reload, Ben fired steadily, aiming each shot. He had ten rounds discharged before the others finished reloading their muskets. Aiming wasn't any particular problem as there were so many coming; so many, that maybe this time, they wouldn't stop.

Yankee cannon belched grape shot and canister, clearing bloody gaps in the Confederate lines. Thousands of little metal balls whirring through the air, little birds on flights of death. Screams, more torturous to the ears than the Rebel yells, cut through the smoke.

Still they came.

But the advancing line of butternut and gray wasn't as solid, wasn't moving as fast. Men were clustering together, instinct merging them. The Confederates were slowing, torn between courage and fear and pressed by the even stronger esprit to see it through with their fellows, which was the reverse side to the secret lure of cowardice.

A bullet hit the man to Ben's left, staggering him back a few feet. He grasped his stomach, blood pouring out of him, disbelief on his face. Ben turned back to the front. As the second volley of Union musket fire wreaked more havoc on the advancing men, Ben fired his last six rounds, then knelt to reload.

"Kill 'em. Kill 'em all," a soldier was chanting. Ben felt the blood pounding in his head as he thumbed the rounds in. The wounded man was moaning, crying something pre-speech, animal in its desperation.

Ben stood. The apex of the rebels attack was approaching his position, the foremost soldier less than twenty feet away. Mouth wide open, rebel yelling, insane screaming. Death or victory with no possibility in between.

Ben fired and the open mouth exploded in a shower of blood. As his comrades fired a volley and hastened to reload, Ben ratcheted in bullet after bullet and fired again and again, scything down the lead rebels, stopping the pinnacle of the assault that would have broken the Union line and smashed the Hornet's Nest.

Finally, another part of the pattern from the previous eleven charges held, as the Rebel line wavered, then began to melt away, retreating. Except for the last man Ben shot. He kept coming at a dead run. A tall, gangly fellow, dressed in butternut and a battered felt hat. He had no musket in his hands. And he ran stiff legged; in a way Ben had never seen. Every Union soldier who could see him paused to watch.

The reb was dead, but he was still running, the way an animal sometimes did after being killed. The legs still working, but the mind already dead, the body just not aware yet. The reb made it within ten feet of the sunken road, his eyes empty, his jaw slack, before he finally collapsed to his knees. Instead of tumbling forward, his upper torso tilted in reverse, the back of his head thumping into the ground, leaving his body in an obscene position.

Ben resumed reloading.

"They sure take killing better than any I've ever seen," a soldier near Ben muttered as he also reloaded.

St. George didn't like this skulking about much, but it seemed second nature to Gabriel. This entire war thing was quite outside anything he'd ever imagined, not that imagination had ever been his strong suit. He was leading his horse along a trail, not quite sure where he was, simply keeping Gabriel in sight.

She, in turn, was keeping the elder Rumble in sight, as she'd been doing for a couple of hours. A bloody hand reached out from underneath a bush, clawing at his boot. St. George kicked the hand away.

"Please."

A Yankee soldier was under the bush. The left side of his head was caved in, a furrow from a bullet having taken off a good part of his skull. St. George was surprised the man was alive, never mind speaking.

"Please what?"

"Kill me."

"You be dying soon anyway."

"Kill me."

St. George kicked the man, rolling him further under the bush. "Suffer bluebelly."

Gabriel knelt down next to the man. She placed a comforting hand on his forehead while she drew Tiberius' dagger with the other. She sliced it across the man's neck.

St. George said nothing as Gabriel wiped the blade off on the soldier's shirt, then slid it back into the sheath.

There was sporadic firing in every direction. St. George rubbed his forehead. That Grant fellow was issuing orders left and right, but St. George could make no sense of what was happening, so he couldn't understand how that fellow could. But he seemed mighty calm.

Rumble looked nervous. Which comforted St. George. He knew the elder boy. He knew he'd go looking for the young one, first chance he got. Some people were too easy to read.

And when father met son, St. George could finish it once and for all.

Cord watched the rebels fall back. He was flat on his belly, his horse tethered in a gully behind him. He pulled out the telescope and extended it. He saw the wounded being helped back, the fear in the men's faces. Officers screaming commands, reforming, preparing the men to go back one more time into hell.

He spotted an officer with gray hair, a weathered face and recognized Johnston from his time in the west. The General was, of all things, swinging a cup about, issuing orders to the flock of officers surrounding him.

Cord closed his eyes for a moment as he put the telescope down and picked up the Lancaster. "Lord, this is war. Taking a life is part of it. I'm damn sorry to take a good man."

He opened his eyes and pulled back the hammer on the long rifle.

Just as he pulled the trigger, Johnston's horse twisted about.

Sally Skull reloaded her pistols as she rode close to Johnston and his staff. His boot heel was dangling, a Yankee ball having torn through it during the charge. His clothes were nicked with near misses. She'd had a minie ball tear into her saddlebag, but without enough power to penetrate horseflesh.

The Yankees were tough, she'd give them that.

As he turned, Johnston reeled in the saddle, as if startled.

"General, are you hurt?" one of the staff officers asked.

"Yes, and I fear seriously," Johnston said.

Skull couldn't see a wound, but a couple of the officers hustled the General away toward a gully and she anxiously followed. She hopped off her horse and helped them lower Johnston to the ground.

"Where you hurt, sir?" Skull asked.

Johnston shook his head. "I don't know, Sally. I don't know." His face was pale and his hands were shaking.

Skull began tearing at his clothes, looking for the wound. Some lieutenant offered the general a flask, but when he poured a dribble into Johnston's mouth, it slid out the other side as the general's head lolled back.

"Where's his surgeon?" Skull demanded.

"Tending to some Yankees," the lieutenant replied.

"Damn you, Sidney Albert Johnston," Skull hissed, leaning close to the old man, "don't you die on us. We need you. Texas needs you."

Then she saw the blood filling his boot. She slid her hand along the back of that leg and found the wound. Through the artery in the back of the knee. The same damn leg in which he'd been wounded dueling old Sam Houston so many years ago. Skull ripped a kerchief off her neck and wrapped it around his thigh, preparing a knot. "Get me a stick."

When no one moved, she cursed. "Get me a stick, damn it."

"Ma'am," the lieutenant said. "Won't do no good. The general's dead."

Last Stand

"I want every cannon you have placed along the bluff here," Grant ordered his chief of artillery.

He was indicting the bluff to the east, overlooking the Tennessee and the land beyond. With Prentiss holding the center, Wallace coming from the west, one hoped, Grant could sense where his line was weakest as if the battlefield was speaking to him on some frequency those around him couldn't hear.

"This will be our last stand if it comes to it." Grant turned to Rumble. "Lucius, I've moved the regiments forming the straggler line into the fight. Gather what cavalry you can find, and form a new straggler line. Turn every man around and send them back into the battle. We stand on the precipice. We have to hold just a few more hours."

"Yes, sir," Rumble said. He fidgeted in the saddle, his thoughts elsewhere, but so were Grant's.

The General looked to the west. "Wallace should have been here hours ago. And where is Buell?"

Grant and Rumble's attention was diverted to a new development. Among the men still cowering beneath the bluff, a clergyman began berating the troops, his voice pitched pulpit, spewing inspiration and degradation. "For God and Country, men! For your sweethearts and your homes! For your flag! For your own souls, to be not be judged as a coward when you meet the most holy!"

"Lucius." Grant halted his friend. "Before you do what I asked, shut that fool up."

"General, the Union left is wide open," Nathan Bedford Forrest implored General Beauregard. "You push there, you'll have the Yankees in the river before dark."

Elijah Cord was so close, he could have hit the General with a rock, never mind the Lancaster. A cluster of officers surrounded Beauregard, who was trying to sort out the jumbled mess the Confederate attack had become. Forrest had just ridden up, his mount lathered from the exertion.

"It might well be, Colonel," Beauregard said, "but we're already engaged past the point of being able to break contact in the center."

"But, sir—" Forrest began.

Beauregard used a saber, not a tin cup, to punctuate his words. "I heard you, Colonel, and it isn't possible now." He drummed his fingers on the flat edge of his sword. "The question is, how far away is Buell?"

Cord pushed forward. "Hey there, General. I just came from the other side of the Tennessee."

Beauregard focused on Cord. "Who the blazes are you?"

"Just a traveler, sir."

Beauregard frowned. "What unit are you with?"

"None, sir."

"What are you doing here? What were you doing on the other side of the river?"

Cord decided truth could work here. "Looking for my son, General. I got no part of this fight."

"Everyone has a part of this fight," Beauregard said, "if they have any sense of honor."

"I fought in California and Mexico," Cord lied. "My fighting days are over."

Beauregard waved a hand, blowing away Cord's reasoning under the stress of battle and command. Forrest was fidgeting on his horse.

"And what did you see on the other side of the river?" Beauregard asked.

"Whole bunch of Federals stuck trying to cross the Duck River up by Columbia, Tennessee."

Beauregard leaned eagerly toward Cord. "When did you see this?"

"Yesterday."

"You believe this fellow?" Forrest demanded.

A courier came galloping up, a telegram flimsy in hand. Beauregard took it, read it, then looked back at Cord. "Curious. Regardless of where he is right now, the command in Alabama believes Buell isn't even headed here. That he's been diverted to Decatur."

Cord shrugged. "I don't know where Buell's going, General. I just know where he is and he isn't close."

Beauregard slapped the flat of his sword on his thigh. "I have Grant just where I want him." He turned to another officer. "Gather every piece of artillery, put them wheel to wheel, and blast the hell out of that pocket of resistance. Then we'll form our own line for the night and finish them in the morning."

"General—" Forrest began, but Beauregard waved him off, like he had Cord. The General and his coterie of staff rode off.

All except Forrest. The Confederate cavalryman ran a hand across the stubble on his chin. "Your boy. What side he on?" Forrest asked.

"I don't rightly know," Cord lied. "I've been out west a number of years. That's why I'm looking all over."

Forrest frowned. "I seen you somewhere."

"I been around," Cord said.

"Fancy long rifle," Forrest said.

"It does the job."

"What job is that?" Forrest's hand casually dropped to the hilt of his double-edged saber.

"Kills what needs to be killed," Cord said.

"What or who?"

Cord's thumb ran over the hammer of the Lancaster. "Whichever."

Forrest wagged a finger at Cord. "I know your type. Beauregard believes you because he wants to believe you. They all want to believe they've already won. They aint. I don't know what your game is, but I see you around this battlefield again, you won't be riding away."

Sally Skull finished fastening the top button on General Sidney Albert Johnston's coat. The old man looked almost peaceful, his face pale in the fading light. Just two officers remained with the general, the rest having ridden off to continue the battle.

"He ready," Skull told them.

The two lifted the stretcher and slid it onto the back of a wagon.

"You can take him back home to Texas now," Skull said.

"Permission to move forward, sir."

Grant looked up from the map he was perusing with his staff. "Ben?"

"Yes, sir," Rumble replied.

Grant gestured for his staff to disperse. "Things are grim, Lucius. Wallace still hasn't arrived. I don't know how long Prentiss can hold. They break through our center, they'll break the entire army."

"The 5th Ohio is with Prentiss. I'll relay that to the General, sir."

Grant's head drooped for a moment. "It's been a very bad day."

Lucius placed a hand on his friend's shoulder. "You've just got to hold until dark, Sam."

Grant took a deep breath. "Permission granted, Sergeant Major. You see General Prentiss, convey my appreciation for all he's accomplished up to this time."

"Yes, sir." Rumble put spurs to horse and raced against the tide of retreating troops toward the sound of the firing.

"Come." Gabriel kicked St. George's boot.

He pulled the slouch hat away from his eyes. They were in a narrow gully, out of the way of the troops and the bullets.

"What's going on?" St. George got to his feet as Gabriel pressed forward through the undergrowth.

"He moving," Gabriel said.

St. George followed her and they set off in pursuit of Rumble.

The world exploded around Ben and the rest of the Union men in the Hornet's Nest. Sixty-two Confederate cannons were lined up hub to hub, a quarter mile wide wall of guns hurling canister, grape shot, solid and exploding rounds. Trees were being cut down from the barrage and killing when the trunks fell on the men cowering in the sunken road. Over 180 shots per minute were tearing into the Union line. It was the fiercest artillery bombardment the continent had ever experienced.

Men broke and ran, only to be torn apart by the fierce cannonade. Every button in Ben's shirt felt massive as he pressed himself into the dirt, wishing he could burrow into the earth itself. He envied the earthworms.

A half mile away from the sunken road, a rebel skirmisher stepped onto the cow path directly in front of Rumble's horse, less than ten feet away. The soldier's musket was pointed right at Rumble's face as the man pulled the trigger.

Nothing happened.

Misfire.

Rumble swung up his shotgun and let loose with both barrels. The blast knocked the man backward, dead before he hit the ground. Rumble spurred his horse and leapt over the body, racing down the path, dodging low hanging branches. He could hear soldiers all about in the woods: southern soldiers. General Prentiss's pocket of resistance was just minutes from being completely surrounded.

The thunder of cannon fire ahead was deafening. The ground shivered and as Rumble moved forward, shrapnel began whistling through the trees, clipping off branches and leaves and causing him to hunch over in the saddle.

And, suddenly, there was silence.

Behind Rumble the pincers of the rebel attack finally closed around the Hornet's Nest. Prentiss and the Hornet Nest were surrounded.

Ben's ears were ringing, so it took a moment for the sudden stop of the bombardment to register. He was face down in the rut of the sunken road, the Henry clutched tight to his side. He blinked a few times, then shook his head, trying to clear his ears. He lifted his head.

A Union major with a white flag was standing on top of the edge of the sunken road, waving it back and forth. Ben breathed a deep sigh of relief, which brought on a spate of coughing.

Ben got to his feet. The field in front of the sunken road was paved with dead. Bodies torn to pieces, limbs scattered, men strewn in the place death had littered them. The bodies were so many, Ben felt he could walk across the field, stepping from corpse to corpse and never touch the ground.

"We done our duty," one the men nearby muttered. "No one can't say we aint done our duty and more."

"I think they done their duty too," Ben said.

At his field headquarters, Grant was immediately aware of the slackening of fire from the center and knew what it meant. He looked up at the sun, sliding toward the western horizon, then lowered his eyes toward the road from Crumps Landing, once more disappointed not to see Wallace's column. Then he looked over his shoulder. No sign of Buell's army crossing the Tennessee.

Cord rode forward through the wave of gray behind the cannons. The sudden halt of the artillery barrage chilled him as much as the firing had. It meant either annihilation or surrender.

He focused on the trail that Ben had made crawling toward the Union lines, moving through exhausted Confederate troops who lacked the energy after so many charges to advance and take their hard-earned victory and their prisoners.

Rumble could see both defeat and victory in the composure of the Union soldiers he began to encounter. Officers were ordering men to stack arms, telling them their fight was over. They'd held long enough. It was late afternoon and the sun was casting long shadows amongst the trees and over the dead.

There was pride in holding as long as they had.

There was also the reluctant acceptance of surrender.

Rumble asked for the 5th Ohio Cavalry, anxious to find Ben before the first Confederate units rounded up what remained of General Prentiss' unit. He reached the sunken road where bodies dressed in blue were sprawled in a line left and right as far as he could see, like a fence of death.

"5th Ohio?" Rumble called out.

"Yo!" a voice called out to the right.

Rumble rode that way, horse's hooves picking carefully through the dead and wounded.

"5th Ohio Cavalry?" Rumble asked a soldier's whose face was sooted with black and uniform ripped and torn. Blood dripped from the man's ear and his eyes were unfocused.

"Some of us here," the man said. He was rubbing his hands together as if washing them. "Some of us here. Some dead. Some ran. Some gone."

"Sergeant Major!" Ben was walking slowly down the road.

Rumble jumped off the horse and ran to Ben. He wrapped his arms tight around him. "I'm so happy you're alive."

Despite his exhaustion and illness, Ben smiled. "So am I. It was a hard day. But I fought." As the older man let go of him, Ben indicated the Henry. "Thank you for the rifle. I fought. You'd have been proud of me."

Rumble stared at the rifle in confusion, then collected himself. "I'm glad you did your duty."

"You shouldn't have come here," Ben said. "General Prentiss has struck the colors. We're to be prisoners."

Rumble ran a hand across Ben's forehead. "You're sweating and hot. Are you sick?"

"A touch of something," Ben admitted.

A horse and rider came flying over the edge of the sunken road. Cord, buckskins stained with smoke and sweat, jerked back on the reins, taking in the bodies, then Rumble and Ben. He gestured north. "We need to get going."

Rumble shook his head. "We're surrounded. I barely made it through."

"General Prentiss has ordered us to stack arms," Ben added.

"I don't take well to orders or surrendering," Cord said. "I just came through the entire Rebel army. Gonna take them a little bit to get organized. We can cut our way out, back to our lines."

Rumble reached out and grabbed the reins of Cord's horse. "We must follow orders."

Cord ignored him and stared at Ben. "We move fast, we can get out of here before the rebels bag this bunch. Things are pretty disorganized." He dismounted. "We can't take the roads or trails. So we leave the horses, stay to thick growth. Come on, son."

Ben looked from Cord to Rumble. Then he took a step toward Cord. "I'm not surrendering. It wasn't the way I was raised."

A twitch of a smile touched Rumble's lips and he broke open his shotgun, checking to make sure he had two live rounds. "Let's go."

Cord led the way into the woods behind the sunken road, Ben behind him, Rumble bringing up the rear. They slowly wove through the forest, staying off the paths, hearing occasional firing and the moans of the wounded they passed.

"Wallace is arriving, sir. He's filling in on the right flank, anchoring on Owl Creek."

Ulysses S. Grant took the news from the courier without comment. Wallace was hours late, but he was finally here and sorely needed. Prentiss had surrendered, giving up over two thousand men in the Hornet's Nest, but he'd held for five hours. Long enough for the army to survive today. Darkness was falling.

"General, things are going decidedly against us," one of the staff officers observed.

Grant didn't spare the man a glance. "Not at all, sir. We're whipping them now. The enemy has done all he can do today. They can't break our lines tonight. It's too late."

Unseen by the others, Grant's left hand was inside the pocket of his dusty blue blouse, fingers curled around Rumble's flask. He ached to pull the flask out, because despite his words, he knew his army had been badly battered today. He had the entire Confederate army to his front. A river to his rear. And no sign of Buell's reinforcements.

"Has anyone seen Sergeant Major Rumble or Chief Scout Cord?" Grant asked.

The replies were all negative. Grant's hand tightened on the flask and he started to pull it out, but halted as Sherman rode up, bleeding from several minor wounds.

"Cump," Grant said. "How are you faring?"

Sherman took Grant's arm and steered him away from all the other officers. "We got beat up pretty bad, Sam. Prentiss is gone with all his men."

"I know."

"Where's Buell?" Sherman asked.

"No idea."

"What are you going to do, Sam?"

"I haven't decided."

Sherman took a step back in surprise. "But—" he had no words.

Grant patted Sherman on the shoulder. "Go back to your command, Cump. I'll decide by midnight."

Grant walked toward his staff. "I want the *Lexington* and *Tyler* to commence a bombardment of the enemy lines," he ordered. "We might as well give our Southern brethren an uncomfortable night."

Hogs were feeding on the dead. Wounded men were crying out for their mothers, for mercy, for help, for death to take them. Along the edge of Bloody

Pond, it no longer mattered if one were Yankee or Rebel as men died bundled close to whatever human comfort they could get in their last moments. The still surface of the water shimmered the reflected starlight in red.

Neither North nor South had been prepared for such a day. Nor could they have been, as there were more dead and wounded on this one day around Shiloh than had been killed in all the combined wars the United States had ever fought.

Because of this, there was no system of evacuation for wounded. Across the battlefield hundreds of men who might have survived, died. Those who had not been killed had an idea they had been part of something epic, something unseen on the North American continent, but no one knew yet the magnitude of the scale. Northerners who'd survived were grateful for life and expected to be heading back over the Tennessee River soon, skedaddling back north, maybe to Nashville, maybe further to Bowling Green. Southerners were exhausted, having formed for the attack over eighteen hours ago in the pre-dawn darkness, and fighting all day. They'd pushed the Yankees from the field and could finish the job tomorrow. Tonight, most collapsed in the deep sleep of utter exhaustion wherever they were.

Wounded and dying men cried out for water and it seemed as if God heard them as storm clouds came in, blanketing the stars. A light patter at first, then a steady drizzle with the promise of a full-blown storm as the wind began to pick up.

The sound of scattered firing increased, as the three got further north. Cord suddenly halted, Rumble and Ben coming up to his side. They were near the edge of a patch of woods. There was a field ahead, but in the rain and, it was hard to tell if the ghostly figures carrying torches were wearing blue or gray.

"Rebel skirmishers ahead," Cord said. "Feeling out the line, checking the bodies."

"Might be our boys," Rumble said.

"They're not ours," Cord said with certainty.

Ben shivered and went to his knees. Cord grabbed him before he collapsed completely. "He's sick!"

"He said he had a touch of something," Rumble said. "I can carry him."

Rumble wrapped his arm around Ben, lifting him up. Cord picked up the Henry and slung it over his shoulder, keeping the Lancaster in his hands. There was a deep roar, followed by three more in rapid succession. Sounding like a train chugging by, a heavy shell from a gunboat flew overhead, the sputtering fuse marking its path. It landed a quarter mile behind them with a loud explosion. Three more shells, widely dispersed, roared by and exploded.

"Gunboats," Rumble said. "Sam's keeping the secessionists on their toes."

Cord pointed with the Lancaster. "We slide right. Toward the river. Wasn't much fighting over there, near as I can tell. We should be able to cross the lines along the river, and if need be, cross the river. There's a creekbed we can follow, keep us low and in the brush."

Thirty feet away, out of sight, St. George held the LeMat in a sweat and rain soaked hand. He wanted to wade forward and finish all three, but the odds weren't good and he didn't trust Gabriel to have his back. In fact, he more than half-suspected she might shoot him in the back.

The shells arcing overhead made him skittish. The concept that one could land on him out of the sky and kill him unsettled him something fierce. Totally impersonal.

Gabriel pointed. The trio were moving to the east and north, the elder Rumble carrying the boy. The other, the mountain man, he was different, even in the dark, St. George could see that. He would not be easy to kill face up.

St. George didn't plan on killing him face to face.

Sally Skull held her hands, palms up, out into the rain. She was seated on a log, not far from a campfire at the headquarters of the Confederate army. She watched General Jonhston's blood get washed away from her skin, drop by drop. There was a commotion to her right and she wearily turned her head to see what was happening.

There was no mistaking Nathan Bedford Forrest, nor the anger in his voice. He towered over an officer wearing a bathrobe and slippers, quite obviously done for the day. Forrest's hat dripped water and his uniform was splattered with mud. He was gesturing with one hand, his other hand on the hilt of his cavalry saber. With a sigh, Skull got up and walked over to see what the hullabaloo was about.

"We hit 'em now," Forrest was saying, "we can smash them into the river. Half of 'em will drown like rats."

The staff officer didn't even bother to stifle his yawn. "Yes, yes, Colonel. I'm sure General Beauregard is quite aware of the strategic situation. Orders have already been issued for an attack at dawn and I'm quite sure that will suffice. I suggest you go back to your picket line, sir, and keep a vigilant watch." The officer waved a hand vaguely in the direction of the front and walked into the tent from which he'd been summoned.

Forrest literally growled and had his saber half-drawn when Skull lightly touched his arm. "He's a fool and got no power. Beauregard's done for the day."

The wind was picking up and howling among the trees, sending drops almost vertical. Trees were bending and swaying.

Forrest spit, letting the saber drop back down into the scabbard. "Damn idiots couldn't find their way in the dark and storm anyways. Let's hope it's keeping Buell stopped wherever he's at."

Skull wondered if St. George had accomplished his task. She doubted it since Gabriel hadn't returned. The girl could find her way back to Skull like a hunting dog left off the leash. Dark or rain wouldn't bother her; in fact, she liked being in darkness.

"We'll know everything tomorrow," Skull said.

"Need help?" Cord asked as they pressed forward through the undergrowth, pushing their way forward toward the creek.

"I can carry him," Rumble said, breathing hard.

"Need help?" Cord repeated.

With a grunt, Rumble lowered Ben to the ground. The boy moaned and his eyes flickered but couldn't focus through his fever.

Cord handed Rumble the Henry.

"Thanks for doing that," Rumble said.

"Stealing your rifle?" Cord asked as he hefted Ben over his shoulder.

"It's something a smart father would do," Rumble said, turning away to move forward in the dark.

St. George tripped over a root and tumbled to his knees with a splatter of curses. The storm covered the sound and Gabriel waited, sphinx-like, for him to get back to his feet. St. George had no idea where the two Rumble's and Cord were ahead, but Gabriel moved as if she had a rope tied to one of them.

Soon they were sliding down into the steep gulley containing Dill Branch. Water poured along the bottom, toward the Tennessee River and St. George realized the Yankees were being smart. Letting the stream chart their course to the big river, then turn left and head for the Union lines. Except they weren't as smart as they thought, St. George reasoned, as the rain picked up intensity.

The water pouring through the gulley was gaining volume, climbing to Rumble's waist. He heard a cry and spun about. Cord had slipped and before Ben could be submerged, Rumble caught him. As they were getting closer to the Tennessee, Dill Branch was getting deeper and steeper and the rain was causing the water level to rise precipitously.

"We've got to climb out of this," Rumble said, as he hefted Ben over his shoulder.

Cord could only nod in agreement as he took the Henry rifle from Rumble, slinging his Lancaster this time. Rumble had his shotgun looped over his back. Carefully, they began to edge up the steep side of the gulley.

"Hear that?" Rumble asked.

Cord halted, going to his knees and gently letting Ben to the ground. "What?"

"Music." Rumble pointed, up and to the left. "That way. Toward Pittsburgh Landing. We must be close."

"Let me help," Cord said. Together, the two linked hands, nestling Ben between them, and continued climbing out of the gulley.

"Now!" Gabriel hissed.

With one hand braced against a tree, St. George lifted the LeMat with the other. He shook his head, trying to get the rain out of his eyes. Then he began firing. The first bullet creased Rumble's right side, a red-hot knife of pain, then the lead ball struck a rib, splintering it and exiting. Rumble gasped in agony, letting go of Ben, and tumbling down the steep slope, trying to grab hold of anything to arrest his fall.

Cord staggered under Ben's weight. The second bullet buzzed by his head, so close it singed hair. The third bullet struck Ben in his right leg, the ball hitting bone and shattering it. Cord could feel the strike, the bullet tugging the boy.

Cord dropped to his knees, holding on to Ben with one hand, while he grasped for the Henry rifle. The fourth bullet hit his waist, richocheting off the Bowie knife. Ben dangling from one hand on the muddy slope, Cord awkwardly fired the Henry with the other, aiming at the muzzle flash.

Rumble hit the creek with a splash. He tried to scramble to his feet, but the torrent of water tumbled him downstream toward the Tennessee. He fought his panic, focusing on one objective: getting back and saving Ben. His arms flailed as he tried to reach the bank.

Cord jammed the Henry down between his legs, using his free hand to lever in a new round, but then Ben slid and Cord dropped the gun, grabbing onto a sapling to anchor himself. The Henry tumbled into the ravine and disappeared into the stream as Cord desperately held on to his son.

St. George was just about to fire again, when he realized the situation.

The first of the gunboat mortars fired, followed in volley by three more explosions.

Cord could feel his muscles vibrating from the strain of holding Ben and the tree. He waited for a bullet to come out of the dark and end this.

St. George carefully scampered down through the undergrowth until he was opposite Cord and Ben, the surging creek between them. "Hey boy!" he yelled.

Cord recognized the voice and solid dark form on the other side of the creek.

"I gonna kill your boy, then I gonna kill you," St. George shouted as he thumbed back the hammer on the Le Mat.

Cord looked down at Ben. The boy's eyelids were flickering. "Your dad will get you," he said.

Then he let go of Ben. As the boy slid into the creek, St. George's gun swung down to track him. Fast as a rattler striking, Cord whipped the Bowie out of its sheath and threw it, the blade striking a split second before St. George could fire.

Stunned, St. George dropped the pistol and stared at the handle of the knife stuck his chest.

Ben disappeared into the water and Cord let go of the sapling, diving after him.

Thirty meters downstream, Rumble had managed to halt his descent by hooking an arm around a low hanging branch. He barely felt the pain in his side as he looked upstream when lightning lit up the area momentarily. He saw Ben tumbling in the water, arms weakly fighting the water. Without hesitation, Rumble let go of the branch and dove in.

Gabriel knelt next to St. George. The Bowie had struck on his right side, the heavy blade smashing through a rib, into his lung.

"You hurt bad," Gabriel said.

St. George was jammed against the tree he'd been using for support. "Help me," he gasped.

"I'm a nigra," Gabriel said. "How could I help a white man?"

She stood up and climbed out of the ravine, ignoring St. George's curses.

Behind her, St. George wrapped both hands around the handle of the Bowie. He pulled.

His scream split the night like thunder.

Cord caught up to Rumble and Ben. He linked arms with both.

"Easy now," Cord said to both. "Let the water take us."

The trio floated out of the creek into the calmer Tennessee River. The water carried them north, while Cord and Rumble kicked to stay close to the west bank. They cleared a slight turn in the river and there was Pittsburgh Landing.

A long line of steamers crowded the river, coming in from the north. As each docked, columns of men clad in blue carrying torches were pouring out of the bellies of the ships and heading up the road to the heights. Cord recognized the tune a Yankee band was playing—Dixie-- as he pulled Rumble and Ben toward the landing.

Buell's army was arriving.

6 April 1862

President Jefferson Davis,

Thanks be to the Almighty. We gained a complete victory. Driving the Enemy from his position.

General Pierre Beauregard

Lick 'Em Tomorrow

Ulysses S. Grant finally had a true idea of what had happened during the day as more reports filtered in. The losses were beyond conception. As the rain continued to fall, his generals and colonels came to him, asking about retreat. About having been defeated. Grant had been resolute, brushing aside such talk. But deep inside, he knew they were advocating the correct course of action. Even with Buell finally showing up, the casualties were staggering. The army couldn't take another day like today and hope to stay intact, and if it broke, the Union was defeated in the west.

As the storm broke, Grant sought refuge from the rain in a dimly lit cabin that was doubling as a surgery. The smell hit him like a hammer as he walked in, penetrating his resolve and flashing him back to his childhood and the odor of his father's tannery. Viscera, blood, severed limbs. An assembly line of men were being hustled in to the waiting surgeons who didn't have the time to wipe their saws clean from the previous casualty.

There were screams, begging, men cursing at the doctors, at the generals, at fate. Grant barely heard any of it. The smell staggered him back into the rain. He knew what he had to do now. He had to save the army, even if it meant retreat and defeat.

Grant reached into his pocket for Cord's flask. He unscrewed the top and was lifting it to his lips when Cord and Rumble appeared out the dark rain, carrying Ben between them. They brushed past Grant.

Grant slid the flask, untapped, back into his pocket. "How is he?"

"Leg," Rumble said as they entered the cabin. "Pretty bad."

A spot on one of the bloody tables opened up. The surgeon gestured to them and they slid Ben onto the wood. The boy was muttering, crying out in his delirium, his fever and the shock from the bullet doubling up on him.

The surgeon ripped apart the trousers, exposing the wound. Ben's right leg was badly smashed below the knee, white bone poking out of the skin. "Bad," the doctor muttered. "Hit the bone. His leg is done."

Grant pulled the flask out. "Give him this."

Cord took the flask, unscrewed the top and held it to Ben's lips. He dribbled the alcohol in, a little bit at a time, as the surgeon dipped his saw into a bucket full of blood-soaked water. Rumble was on the other side, his hand on Ben's shoulder.

"Don't you have any opium?" Grant asked the doctor.

The surgeon looked at him like he was crazy. "Used up whatever I had before noon, general. We been at this nonstop. I'll be quick."

Grant grimaced and turned for the door as the surgeon brought the saw to bear above Ben's leg. Cord reached out and grabbed his old friend. "You stay, Sam. He's your God-son."

Rumble nodded, his eyes on his son. "This is the cost of the war, Sam. You got to stay. You got to make this worth something." Blood dripped from the wound on Rumble's said, and a medic quickly wrapped a dirty bandage around it as the surgeon prepared.

Grant swallowed hard and took his place shoulder to shoulder with Cord, while the surgeon was next to Rumble. The three men held Ben down as the saw made its first cut.

That ripped Ben out of his delirium and he screamed.

Twenty minutes later, outside of the cabin, Rumble held a canvas tarp over Ben with the arm on his good side, keeping him as dry as possible. Cord was using twine to tie off the tarp to a branch. Ben's right leg was gone below the knee, a stained bandage covering the stump. Cord cinched down the last cord and they had some semblance of shelter. The storm was letting up a bit, the wind less fierce. Cord and Rumble sat down, on opposite sides of Ben.

"Bad day," Cord said.

"Bad day," Rumble agreed. "But he's alive."

"And we need to make sure he stays alive," Cord said.

Rumble nodded. "I've got to get him to Palatine. They dealt with Seneca's wound. My mother and sister-in-law will take care of him." He looked at Cord. "If that's all right with you, Elijah?"

Cord sighed. "Palatine's in pretty bad shape, but you're right. Your mother will take good care of him. We'll deal with that in the morning." He put a hand on Ben's chest, feeling the rise and fall. The hand was shaking and suddenly tears flowed down Cord's cheeks. "Damn it, that was close! I don't know what I'd do if—"

Rumble put his hand on top of Cord's. "He's alive, Elijah. He's alive."

General William Tecumseh Sherman stared warily at the glowing end of the cigar Sam Grant was puffing on. A flickering lantern highlighted the deep shadows on his old friend's face. After consulting with the other division commanders and coming to a unanimous conclusion, Sherman was going to tell Grant it was best to immediately put the river between their army and the rebels, but something on Grant's face stopped the words. Sherman stood still for a moment, rain dripping down on his hat.

"Well, Grant, we've had the devil's own day, haven't we?"

The cigar glowed as Grant puffed and in that dim light he saw Ben's blood on his hands. Then he spoke. "Yep. Lick 'em tomorrow, though."

THE END

A short excerpt from The Jefferson Allegiance, the first book in the Presidential series follows bio and book info.

About the Author

Thanks for the read!
If you enjoyed the book, please leave a review. Cool Gus likes them as much as he likes squirrels!

Look! Squirrel!

Bob is a NY Times Bestselling author, graduate of West Point, former Green Beret and the feeder of two Yellow Labs, most famously Cool Gus. He's had over 70 books published including the #1 series Area 51, Atlantis, Time Patrol and The Green Berets. Born in the Bronx, having traveled the world (usually not tourist spots), he now lives peacefully with his wife, and labs. He's training his two grandsons to be leaders of the Resistance Against The Machines.

Subscribe to my newsletter for the latest news, free eBooks, audio, etc.

For information on all my books, please get a free copy of my **Reader's Guide**. You can download it in mobi (Amazon) ePub (iBooks, Nook, Kobo) or PDF, from my home page at www.bobmayer.com

For free eBooks, short stories and audio short stories, please go to
http://bobmayer.com/freebies/
Free books include my next free book constantly updated.
And permanently free:
Eyes of the Hammer (Green Beret series book #1)
West Point to Mexico (Duty, Honor, Country series book #1)
Ides of March (Time Patrol)
There are also free shorts stories and free audiobook stories.

Never miss a new release by following my Amazon Author Page.

I have over 220 free, downloadable Powerpoint presentations via Slideshare on a wide range of topics from history, to survival, to writing, to book trailers.
https://www.slideshare.net/coolgus

If you're interested in audiobooks, you can download one for free and test it out here: Audible

Connect with me and Cool Gus on social media.
Questions, comments, suggestions: Bob@BobMayer.com
Blog: http://bobmayer.com/blog/
Twitter: https://twitter.com/Bob_Mayer
Facebook: https://www.facebook.com/authorbobmayer
Google +: https://plus.google.com/u/0/101425129105653262515

Instagram: https://www.instagram.com/sifiauthor/
Youtube: https://www.youtube.com/user/IWhoDaresWins

ALL SERIES

THE CELLAR SERIES:
1. BODYGUARD OF LIES
2. LOST GIRLS

NIGHSTALKERS SERIES:
1. NIGHTSTALKERS
2. BOOK OF TRUTHS
3. THE RIFT

The fourth book in the Nightstalker book is the team becoming the Time Patrol, thus it's labeled book 4 in that series but it's actually book 1 in the Time Patrol series.

TIME PATROL SERIES:

THE GREEN BERETS SERIES:

THE DUTY, HONOR, COUNTRY SERIES:

AREA 51 SERIES:

ATLANTIS SERIES:

THE SHADOW WARRIORS:
(these books are all stand-alone and don't need to be read in order)

THE PRESIDENTIAL SERIES:

THE BURNERS SERIES:

THE PSYCHIC WARRIOR SERIES

STAND ALONE BOOKS:
THE ROCK
I, JUDAS THE 5TH GOSPEL

COLLABORATIONS WITH JENNIFER CRUSIE
DON'T LOOK DOWN
AGNES AND THE HITMAN
WILD RIDE

NON-FICTION:
PREPARE NOW—SURVIVE LATER
SURVIVE NOW—THRIVE LATER
SHIT DOESN'T JUST HAPPEN I: THE GIFT OF FAILURE
SHIT DOESN'T JUST HAPPEN II: THE GIFT OF FAILURE
THE COMPLETE WRITER BUNDLE
THE NOVEL WRITERS TOOLKIT
WRITE IT FORWARD
102 SOLUTIONS TO COMMON WRITING MISTAKES
THE WRITER'S CONFERENCE GUIDE *(free)*
WHO DARES WINS

All my novels and series are listed in order, with links here:
www.bobmayer.com/fiction/

My nonfiction, including my two companion books for preparation and survival is listed at
www.bobmayer.com/nonfiction/

Thank you!

BOB MAYER

#2 National Bestseller
THE JEFFERSON ALLEGIANCE

THE JEFFERSON ALLEGIANCE

The Presidential Series, book I

Bob Mayer

The Historical Facts

If a book be false in its facts, disprove them; if false in its reasoning, refute it. But for God's sake, let us freely hear both sides if we choose." Thomas Jefferson. 1814.

In May of 1783, the Society of the Cincinnati was founded. A leading member was Alexander Hamilton, and the first President of the Society was George Washington, before he was President of the United States. The Society of the Cincinnati is the oldest, continuous military society in North America. Its current headquarters is at the Anderson House in downtown Washington, DC. Besides the Society of the Cincinnati, Hamilton founded the Federalist Party, the first political party.

"Can a democratic assembly . . . be supposed steadily to pursue the public good? Nothing but a permanent body can check the imprudence of democracy. Their turbulent and changing disposition requires checks." Alexander Hamilton. 1787.

Thomas Jefferson was not allowed membership in the Society of the Cincinnati.

"Your people, sir, are a great beast." Alexander Hamilton. 1792.

In 1802, President Thomas Jefferson, well known for his strong opposition to a standing army, established the United State Military Academy, the oldest Military Academy in the Americas. In 1819, he founded the University of Virginia, the first college in the United States to separate religion from education.

In 1745, the American Philosophical Society (APS), the oldest learned society in North America was founded. Thomas Jefferson was a member for 47 years and its President for 17 years. He subsequently established the adjunct United States Military Philosophical Society (MPS) at West Point with the Academy Superintendent as its first leader.   The APS has its current headquarters in Philosophical Hall on Liberty Square in Philadelphia. The MPS appears to have disappeared.

"I am not among those who fear the people. They, and not the rich, are our dependence for continued freedom." Thomas Jefferson. 1816.

Besides the APS and MPS, Jefferson founded the Anti-Federalist Party.

"The mass of mankind has not been born with saddles on their backs, not a favored few booted and spurred, ready to ride them legitimately, by the Grace of God." Thomas Jefferson. 1826.

The 4ᵗʰ of July 1826

"Is it the Fourth?" In debt, dying, and with only his favorite slave as companion, Thomas Jefferson still had one last duty to discharge.

"Yes, it is, sir," Sally Hemings said, "but it's still dark. Dawn is a half-hour off." She wiped a cool cloth across the wide forehead of the man who owned her. Not tenderly like a lover, but with the touch of a favored servant, an occasional confidant, and primarily with the suppressed and paradoxical hope of freedom at the price of her master's passing. She put the cloth back in the bowl and walked over to the drapes. She parted them and looked out into the darkness, seeing the oil lamps scattered around Monticello flickering in the pre-dawn gray.

"Is he here?" Jefferson's voice was a rasp, barely audible.

"He's been here for a week," Hemings replied, irritation creeping into her voice. "He's waiting in the Parlor."

"It's time."

Her eyes went wide at the implication. "Are you sure, sir?"

Jefferson didn't have the energy to speak again. His thinning gray hair—still holding a touch of red—was highlighted against the pillow. He made a slight twitch in the affirmative.

Hemings escorted in a frail young man with black hair and even darker eyes. His hands shook. He seemed afraid to approach the ex-President's alcove bed as if by doing so, he might bring to completion the act he was here for. Jefferson's eyes were closed. He whispered something and Hemings and the man had to come closer until they were both hovering above the President.

"Poe. It's time." Jefferson nodded toward the headboard ever so slightly. "It's there."

Edgar Allan Poe's tongue snaked across his dry and cracked lips, deprived of alcohol this long week, a sign of how serious he took this event. "Yes, sir."

Poe reached behind Jefferson's pillow and retrieved a leather bag. Something inside rattled, and Poe glanced inside, and then closed it. He held the bag with his shaking fingers.

"Sir—"Poe paused.

Jefferson's head twitched in the affirmative once more.

"Sir, where is the rest?"

"Safe," Jefferson whispered. "With an old enemy who became a friend. He will pass what he has on to the head of the Military Philosophical Society, whom you must contact. You must go to the Military Academy next."

"I understand, sir. But the Military Academy. I do not think I--"

Jefferson wasn't listening. "Hide it."

"And what is the Key phrase that unlocks it, sir?" Poe asked.

Hemings watched him lean close, his ear almost brushing Jefferson's lips. Jefferson whispered something that she couldn't make out.

Poe straightened and nodded. "Yes, sir." He glanced at Hemings, who tilted her head toward the door, wishing her master would not exhaust any more of his strength.

"Sir, you look well," Poe said. "Perhaps—"

"Leave now. Before it is light," Jefferson ordered, a surge of strength putting force behind the words. "We have enemies. The Cincinnatians are everywhere."

Poe swallowed hard. He reached down with his right hand and placed it on Jefferson's. "It has been the greatest honor, sir." He took the leather bag, and Hemings escorted him out of the bedroom, to the rear door, where a saddled horse awaited. He leapt onto it and galloped off into the darkness. She saw that he was reaching into his saddlebag for a bottle as soon as he was on the road.

She returned to the bedroom. Jefferson had closed his eyes and for a moment she wondered if he had passed, but noted the slight rise and fall of his chest.

His lips parted and he said something. She moved closer. "Excuse me, sir?"

"Do you remember Paris?" Jefferson asked.

"Oh, yes, sir."

"Maria," Jefferson whispered, a forlorn smile creasing his lips. "I should have followed my heart, not my head." His last breath rattled through his throat, and then he was still.

Sally Hemings slid the blanket up over the slack face of the third President of the United States.

*****

"Independence forever."

Five hundred miles to the northeast, the dawn came slightly earlier to Quincy, Massachusetts, than it did to Monticello in the hills of middle Virginia. John Adams needed assistance to hold up the crystal glass to give his toast to the fiftieth birthday of the country he helped found, and of which he had been the first Vice President and second President. Even that minor effort exhausted him and he barely wet his lips with the alcohol as the others in the room drained their glasses. He slumped back on the bed, his gaze raking over those hovering around his bed.

He thought it a strange group, reflecting the diverse life he'd led. Politicians, judges, businessmen, writers, thinkers, even clergy. Come to pay reverence to one of the few remaining Founding Fathers of this young country. Over the years many had forgotten that despite his speeches against the Stamp Act in the 1760s, and his fight for the Declaration of Independence in 1776, that in 1770 he'd defended the British soldiers accused of firing on the crowd during the 'Boston Massacre.' His arguments to a Boston Jury had been so persuasive, that six of the accused had been acquitted. The law, always the law, was his guiding force.

His gaze fixed on a man hovering near the doorway to the bedroom in a mud-splattered uniform. "Let me speak with Colonel Thayer alone," he ordered. The crowd shuffled out with many a curious glance, leaving the officer standing alone.

He nodded Thayer toward the mantle above the fireplace. "There. Behind the painting."

Stiff and sore after his hard ride from West Point, New York, Thayer walked over. In an alcove behind the portrait of a young woman was a packet wrapped in oilskin.

"Beautiful, isn't she?" Adams said.

"Yes, sir," Thayer replied as he took the package and slid it into the messenger pouch draped over one shoulder.

"Abigail," Adams whispered to himself. "I miss you so."

Thayer didn't react to the comment. He spun on his heel like the Superintendent of the US Military Academy ought to, and made for the door, a soldier on a mission.

"Philosopher." Adams mustered the energy to call out, causing Thayer to halt and spin about on his heel once more, stiff at attention.

"Sir?"

"To be used only as a last resort. When all other means have failed. Do you understand?"

"Yes, sir."

"Split the disks you have there with two other Philosophers. Jefferson will send the next Chair to you with further instructions. Make sure all the Philosophers who follow in your footsteps understand. It's a very, very powerful thing you are guarding. A dangerous, but necessary thing Jefferson and Hamilton did so many years ago."

Thayer nodded, his face grave. "I understand very well, Mister President."

"Power cuts both ways, Philosopher."

"I know, sir." Thayer paused. "And the remaining seven disks?"

"In the Chair's hands," Adams told the young lieutenant colonel. "You'll be contacted. The Chair is always a civilian." The voice was slight, drained.

"What, sir?"

"Always a civilian in charge."

"Yes, sir."

Adams dismissed the soldier, his old hand fluttering in farewell. "Godspeed."

Thayer left and the others came crowding back in. Adams turned his head and saw the morning light streaming in through the window. "Fifty years," he murmured to himself, closing his eyes. "We never thought what we created would last this long. The United States. At least now it can start over if need be."

His body shook and he felt the darkness closing in. He thought of the first time he saw Abigail. And then of all the time he had spent apart from her, working to make this new country come alive. He felt it had been worth it, but there was still much he regretted.

"Mister President?" Someone in the crowd leaned close.

He struggled to open his eyes. Too tired to even turn his head, he shifted his eyes, peering out the window. He saw Thayer on horseback, galloping away, the pouch bouncing on his back. John Adams, the second President of the United States, drew in a hoarse breath and spoke for the last time: "Thomas Jefferson survives."

Chapter One
The Present

Gentle swells of snow-covered ground were graced by thousands of sprouts of stone that would never grow, arranged in perfect lines, as if the dead were frozen on parade. It was a formation at parade rest. Forever. The man standing at attention was a comrade in arms, vaguely sensing his life to be a mere formality before he too joined his silent brethren. Although he couldn't quite grasp the birth and depth of that feeling and raged like the warrior he was against the hand he'd been dealt, some of the cards still face-down. The white covering made Arlington National Cemetery look peaceful, a blanket covering the violence that had brought most of the bodies here over the years.

Colonel Paul Ducharme was uncomfortable in his Class-A uniform. A black raincoat covered the brass and accouterments, which adorned his dress jacket, and a green beret covered most of his regulation, short, thick white hair. He was one of those men who ironically lost none of their hair to age, but, alas, kept none of its color. He absently touched the twisted flesh high on his cheek, just below his right eye, not aware of the gesture. His hand slid higher, pushing back the beret and rubbing the scars that crisscrossed his skull. Finally, realizing what he was doing, he shoved the beret back in place and moved forward. Always mission first.

His spit-shined jump-boots crunched on the light snow and frozen grass underneath as he marched forward. It was after official closing time, but Ducharme had entered through Fort Myer, parking in a small, deserted field adjacent to the cemetery. His old friend, Sergeant Major Kincannon, had given him access. Kincannon was somewhere out in the night, shadowing, a dark presence full of laughter and potential, and inevitably, violence.

Ducharme checked his guide map to pinpoint his location in the 624 acres of cemetery. He considered the place full of historic irony, given that it had originally been the estate of Mary Anna Custis, a descendant of Martha Washington. Custis married US Army officer Robert E. Lee, West Point graduate—the only cadet who ever graduated the Military Academy without a single demerit, a fact so odd that Ducharme, another link in the Long Grey Line, could never forget, nor could any scion of the Long Gray Line. Through the marriage she passed the estate—and her slaves—to Lee.

Their old mansion, the Custer-Lee House, now called the Arlington House to be politically correct, dominated the grounds, looking straight down Lincoln Drive toward the Lincoln Memorial across the Potomac. Thus, General Lee's former house now looked toward the statue of the leader of the country he'd rebelled against. And come so close to defeating. If only Lee had not ordered that last charge at Gettysburg on the 3rd of July 1863. Ducharme's studies of that great battle had whispered to him that Lee only ordered Pickett's Charge because he too had had trouble thinking clearly, sick from dysentery and exhaustion after years of battle. When the body failed, the mind could produce tragic results. Whether his studies were right or wrong were shrouded in the fog of history and would never be answered. As many never were.

Ducharme looked to his left and studied the mansion on top of the hill, which reminded him once more of General... Ducharme frowned and forced himself to keep from looking at the map for the name. In his mind appeared a picture of an old man with a large white beard, dressed in a grey uniform, sitting on top of a white horse. *General Lee.*

Good, thought Ducharme. His therapist would have been proud. But there was no statue of Lee at West Point, their mutual alma mater, even though Lee had done the most with the least in combat against the greatest odds of any Academy graduate. Such was the cost of loyalty to state and betrayal to country and institution.

West Point did not tolerate betrayal.

Just as randomly, yet also connected, that name triggered, unbidden, Plebe Poop—relatively useless information he'd been forced to memorize his first year at West Point: *There were sixty important battles in the Civil War. In fifty-five of them, West Point graduates commanded on both sides; in the remaining five, a graduate commanded one of the opposing sides.*

Probably why the war lasted so damn long.

Ducharme moved forward, his march going from the regulation cadence of 60 steps per minute to something much slower, as if the bodies in the ground were reaching up and wrapping their shadowy arms around him to whisper in his ear and hold onto him.

During the Civil War, the Union seized Lee's land and began using it for a pressing need: burial sites for the thousands of war dead. It had seemed darkly appropriate to someone in the Union to surround General Lee's house with Union dead.

Ducharme hunched his shoulders, bitterly resenting the pounding in the back of his skull. It was worse than it had been in a while, and this journey had a lot to do with it. Stress, the therapist at Walter Reed had warned him a few years ago after he'd woken from the induced coma, was something to be avoided. He'd shrugged it off, telling her a Special Operations soldier's constant companion was stress, and then he'd gone overseas on another deployment, into the land where the beast that raged in his chest felt at home once more. But she'd said there were other kinds of stress. He knew now she'd meant this: the unbearable stress that is closest to the heart. The beast had kept it at bay, but its true calling was now a half-world's plane ride away.

Ducharme stopped at the fresh grave and stared down at it. There was no official marker yet, just a small plate indicating the plot designation. He glanced at the number on the plate and the number he'd written on the margin of the map. On target as always. He was surprised to feel little, neither sorrow or guilt, both of which he had anticipated, but he was learning that he could not anticipate how he would feel any more. Everything was new and everything wasn't good.

This was—with a sharp intake of breath, Ducharme realized he couldn't recall the name of the man buried here. He couldn't remember his cousin's name, his brother-in-arms for over two decades. A low hiss escaped his lips as he placed his hands against the back of his head and pressed in a panic. He shut his eyes and his forehead furrowed as he forced himself to enact the memory strategies he'd been given in rehabilitation.

He could see his cousin. Numerous images in a variety of places around the world. Roommates in Beast Barracks at West Point, bonding under the bombardment from screaming upperclassmen. Drunk on the beach during summer leave in Florida, between Plebe and Yearling years, trying to convince some sorority sisters to come back to their motel. The monotony of Airborne school at Fort Benning. The thrill of graduating West Point, throwing their hats into the air. The harshness of being Ranger buddies. Serving together in Iraq. Afghanistan. After all that, to die so senselessly here in the United States under circumstances Ducharme was determined to ferret out because the beast had been whispering to him ever since General LaGrange's call to come home.

"Charlie," Ducharme said, sinking to his knees. "Charlie LaGrange."

Uttering the name cracked the emotional wall inside his chest, and he felt as if he'd been punched in the heart.

"What the hell happened, my friend?"

He was losing control. Routine. The therapist had pounded into him that routine was a route back to stability and even memory. Reaching under the black coat, Ducharme drew out his silenced MK-23 Mod 0 pistol from a holster in the small of his back. He slid the magazine out of the handle, pulled the slide back, removing the round that had been in the chamber. He placed those on the frozen ground. Then, staring at the mound of dirt, his hands moved quickly, field-stripping the gun by feel, laying the pieces out in order next to the magazine and bullet. He was done in a few seconds. He paused, his breath puffing out into the cold air, and then just as quickly re-assembled it.

He continued to disassemble and reassemble the gun, hands moving in a flurry of action, eyes on the grave as if he could see the occupant. The repetitive action was focusing his mind. On the fifth attempt, the slide slipped out of his cold hands to the frozen ground and he came to an abrupt halt, breathing hard.

Ducharme bowed forward, head almost touching the ground. "I'm going to uncover what happened, Charlie. I'm meeting your father in just a little bit to find out what he couldn't tell me on the satellite link. I'll get to the bottom of this. I swear."

The words were taken by the chill wind of the winter storm and blown across the stones, broken, splintered and then gone. Ducharme felt the beast restless inside him even as he was surprised to find that tears were flowing. He straightened, wiping the sleeve of his coat across his face. He knew the man buried here would have laughed at the tears, cracked a joke. Easy-going Charlie LaGrange, always could be counted on for a laugh, up until he died in his car four days ago. According to the General, the police had labeled it an accident, but something was wrong from the cryptic way the General had contacted Ducharme and recalled him from Afghanistan. The fact the General had sent Kincannon to meet him at Andrews Air Force Base raised more questions than it answered, because it was apparent the General had not confided in the sergeant major, yet sent him as added security. Against who or what, had yet to be revealed.

Ducharme reassembled the gun one last time, slowly, methodically, making sure there was no moisture on any of the moving parts that would cause it to freeze up in the cold. Bad form, and possibly fatal. He put the round back in the chamber, not approved for amateurs, but he was no amateur, and slid in the magazine. He was slipping it back into the holster under his coat when he heard the crunch of footsteps on the frost. He swung around, weapon at the ready, finger on the trigger.

Four tall silhouettes were backlit by the glow of Washington.

Ducharme removed his finger from the trigger as he saw they wore Dress Blues and three had archaic, but more than effective, M-14 Rifles at the ready. The fourth had a pistol in his hand. He stepped forward and raised the pistol in a sure grip. The other three, despite the ceremonial garb, spread out tactically.

The lead man spoke. "Sir. We demand you respect the grave of our fallen comrade."

Ducharme lowered the pistol.

The man warily walked toward him, weapon still at the ready. "What's your purpose here, sir?"

"Visiting," Ducharme said.

"Cemetery's closed after dusk, sir."

"I returned from overseas just an hour ago." He nodded toward the grave. "I'm visiting a friend."

In the light reflected through the snow he could see the man's face. "May I see your identification card? And please holster your weapon. My men have live ammunition in their rifles."

Ducharme slid the pistol back into its holster and pulled out his identification card. The man held up a mini-mag light and flashed it on the card, then briefly at Ducharme's face, causing him to wince.

"Colonel," the man nodded at him.

Ducharme made out the crossed rifles on the man's lapels indicating he was branched Infantry. Three gold bars and three gold rockers on the sleeves indicated his rank. The rows of ribbons on the Dress Blues, starting with the Silver Star, topped a colorful tale of combat and bravery read only by those who knew what the little pieces of cloth meant.

"Master Sergeant." Ducharme gave the man the respect he was due. "What are you and your men doing out here?"

"Our duty, sir." He nodded over his shoulder. "We're the off-shift for the Tomb. We had an incident of vandalism on a recent grave by those extremists who protest our deceased heroes in the name of their God over gays in the military. It *will* not happen again."

The determination in the Master Sergeant's voice indicated it absolutely would not happen again. They were the Old Guard, the 3rd Infantry, and the oldest unit in the United States Army. And God help any who tried to cross their line.

Another figure loomed out of the darkness, and the Master Sergeant reached for his pistol as the other three Old Guard swung their rifles about.

"At ease, men," the newcomer drawled. "Just a friend of the Colonel."

"Sergeant Major Kincannon." Ducharme introduced the newcomer. He was a tall, whipcord of a man, his face lined and wizened, indicating many years spent out in the elements. His voice was laconic and seemed on the edge of finding something to laugh at. He was also one of the most effective and ruthless killers in Special Operations, a man born in violence and never far away from it.

"We got to go, Colonel," Kincannon told him. "The General will be waiting for you."

"Give me a minute," Ducharme said.

"Roger that," the Sergeant Major replied. He went over to the Master Sergeant and engaged him in quiet conversation.

Ducharme knelt at the foot of the grave and reached inside his jacket and shirt to a chain that hung around his neck. The pain in his head was almost unbearable; a jackhammer full of deep, twisting shadows he dared not even try to shed a light on. He pulled on the chain until a small leather pouch appeared along with his dog tag. He opened the drawstring and emptied two bulky rings into his palm. One had a smooth black stone of hematite, the other a single diamond set in the center. Ducharme reached underneath his coat, feeling for the knife secreted in the center of his back. He gripped the rough handle and drew out a six-inch long commando knife. It wasn't a large, gladiator-type Rambo knife. Thin, both sides of the blade were honed razor sharp. It was designed for one purpose: killing.

Except Ducharme stuck it into the frozen ground, the blade slicing into the grave, parting the frozen soil. He dug a shallow hole. He placed both rings into the hole, and then covered them up, tamping the dirt back into place. He slid the dirt-stained knife back into the sheath. Ducharme stood and looked down at the marker. He came to attention and saluted.

"I will get the truth."

Ducharme was surprised to feel the pain in his head subside, as if high tide had been reached and it was now washing away, leaving clean sand, waiting for the sun to rise. Not likely.

He turned and walked toward the Sergeant Major. "Take me to the General."

Kincannon nodded, his rawhide, weather-beaten figure stiff in the blowing snow. "The General told me to give you something right after you came here." He reached inside his long black coat and pulled out a small package wrapped in cloth.

Ducharme unwrapped the cloth, recognizing it as oilcloth, a waterproof fabric that had been superseded long ago. Inside was a circular piece of wood with a hole in the center and a card taped to it. Ducharme recognized the name on the card instantly: his uncle, Peter LaGrange—the General. The disk was old. Etched on the rim were letters. Ducharme tried to read if there was a message, but quickly concluded there was just the 26 letters of the alphabet, randomly positioned. On one flat side the number 26 was lightly carved.

"What is it?"

"No idea, sir."

Ducharme rewrapped the disk in the cloth and slid it into his pocket. He moved forward. "Why did the General want you to give this to me now, when we'll be meeting shortly?"

"That ain't the sort of question I'd be asking the General," Kincannon said. "He tells me to do something, I do it."

"He say *anything*?"

"No, sir. Just told me to give that package to you."

"Let's go."

*****

Across the Potomac River in Washington DC, the growing darkness and thick swirling snow almost obscured the dark red object resting on the copper plate capping the Zero Milestone, due south of the White House. Drawing closer, the old man, pale in the freezing January cold, blanched as he realized he was looking at a human heart on top of the waist-high, stone marker. Rising steam fought with climate, and the warmth won, indicating that the heart still yearned for its owner. The man halted, startled as much by the living voice as the newly dead heart.

"Did you bring me flowers?"

The old man turned in the direction of the sensuous voice, in one hand holding a half-empty bottle of cognac, in the other three roses. A short, wraith-like figure followed the voice, her long black cloak matching the darkening heart behind him. Her face was hidden by a hood, all but her piercing eyes and the look. Perceptive people would recognize the look; that this was a person without a soul, without a conscience. The man was perceptive. His fate was sealed, but like all mortals, he refused to accept it.

"You are not Lucius." His shock caused him to state the obvious.

"I was sent in his place. I assume you brought the Jefferson Cipher rod and your disks." She came to a halt a few paces away. "Should I call you the Philosopher Chair?"

The wind blew cold across the man's scalp, no longer covered by his once thick hair. It hurt for him to stand tall, his body bent with the years, but he did so to face her. "You assume incorrectly."

"About which?"

"I do not have the rod or the disks."

"But you are the Chair." A statement of fact, but he felt compelled to respond anyway.

"Yes."

"The Philosopher you were to meet gave me his disks."

"You lie."

The woman pulled back her hood, revealing short blonde hair and an angelic face, incongruous with the absolute darkness in her eyes. She cocked her head slightly and stared as if he were some crossword puzzle to be solved: difficult, but one she would still do in ink, then discard, to move on to the next challenge. "Where is the Cipher rod and your disks?"

"Where is your master, Lucius?" he demanded.

"I am here in his stead."

He shook his head, glancing at the heart. "I am to meet Lucius and negotiate a deal. Things have gone too far. We must work out a compromise to keep the truce and--"

"I don't make policy," the woman cut him off.

The Chair looked left and right, his guts now as cold as his skin. A dim set of headlights made their way down 15th Street, but the brutal winter storm was keeping almost everyone at home or inside. They were inside their own enclosed snow globe.

"No one is coming to rescue you," the woman said. "The compromise I offer is a quick and honorable death in exchange for the location of the Cipher rod and your disks. And the names of the two remaining Philosophers." She drew back her cloak and revealed a short, Japanese-style sword strapped to her waist. She drew the wakizashi in one smooth motion as she came within striking distance.

The man tried to stand tall in the face of the weapon, but his legs trembled. "So you don't have the disks."

"I will find them," she allowed, signifying he'd called her bluff. "The Philosopher who was to join you here died bravely and without giving up his secrets, but I know there must still be a way to find his disks. President Jefferson would have prepared for such a possibility. I will grant him his genius."

The old man held his ground and met her gaze, even as his heart pounded wildly in his chest. On her coat was a bronze eagle medallion dangling from a small tricolor ribbon. "You are an apprentice to the Society of the Cincinnati? I didn't know they allowed women into their ranks."

"I will be the first."

He shook his head. "Behind the times as always. Our first woman was elected in seventeen eighty-nine."

"Not as a Chair, I'm sure," the woman said. "Not to the inner circle of your Philosophical Society. I will be on the inside of the Cincinnati."

"You're wrong," the Chair said, desperate to gain time. "We've had women in our inner circle. Our first female Chair was in nineteen-oh-four; the President's daughter, in fact. You're on the wrong side."

"I'm on the side I choose. The side that gives me what I want."

"And what is that?"

"This." She brought the blade close to her lips, almost kissing it.

Coldness spread through the Chair's body.

She extended the sword, holding it steady at eye level. "The location of the Jefferson Cipher rod and your disks, and the names of the last two Philosophers. I will make it easy. You will depart this mortal coil peacefully."

"But is it really the Cipher you seek, or what the Jefferson Cipher leads to?" He was trying to buy time with his babbling, which shamed him, but he couldn't stop it.

Her face was expressionless, as if carved out of unblemished white marble. "I was ordered to find the Cipher."

He leaned over, putting the bottle down along with the roses.

She looked down. "What are those?"

"All these years we have been in opposition, and you still know so little."

"I know enough to have met you here. And to have already interdicted the Philosopher who was to join you here. It is I who holds the power here."

"You hold the sword, not the power." He gave a bitter laugh, beginning to accept his fate, an inch at a time, much as he would accept the sword. "On the wall of the Thomas Jefferson building in the Library of Congress is inscribed the appropriate adage for this stand-off: 'The pen is mightier than the sword.' It has been so for a long time. The power you seek—" he shook his head—"it's the core of our Republic. Its very existence has kept the country in balance for over two centuries. You will not gain it with violence."

"I've found violence to be quite effective," the woman said with flat affect. "Where is the Cipher?"

He stood once more. "You know I will never tell you."

She cocked her head once more. She wasn't solving a puzzle now; more inputting data like a computer and then processing it.

"What is your name?" he asked, still stalling for time, giving inches but not feet. Yet. Despite the blizzard, there was a chance someone would see them.

She gave a low laugh; one that would have been appropriate in a bedroom with lights dimmed, but produced goose bumps in this situation. "The Society gave me a code name—the Surgeon."

"An odd designation." He could not help but glance at the heart on the Milestone.

"Four cuts to take the chest," the Surgeon acknowledged. "But he experienced great pain before the end. I've studied the body and I know what causes pain. You don't want to go down the same path he did. He spun a story about where his disks were and who his two fellow Philosophers were, but I knew he was lying and that cost him dearly."

"How do you know he was lying?"

She stared at him. "One of my surgical specialties was facial reconstruction. There are forty-three distinct movements your facial muscles can make, which result in slightly over ten thousand possible facial expressions. I have learned to read many of these expressions, which you cannot control. Yours tell me there is some truth in what you say, but ultimately you are lying. Just as he did and he suffered for it. As you will now."

She took at step closer and there was a flash of steel. Pain shot through him as the tip of the blade cut through his coat and shirt as smoothly and easily as if through butter, leaving a thin red line across his chest, not even an inch deep. Yet. He took a step back in shock and she took a step forward--a macabre dance of torture. Even as he was registering the pain from the first strike, the blade darted forward, tip piercing straight through flesh and muscle. Well over an inch. The Chair froze in agony as the sword skewered him in the shoulder, and then just as quickly, the Surgeon pulled it out of him. Despite the pain, he focused his mind on what had to be done.

"A non-fatal blow," the Surgeon said, looking at his blood on the blade as if it were another curiosity. "Unless you bleed to death. Which will take longer than you have. Where is the rod? Where are your disks? Who are the other two Philosophers?"

He covered the puncture wound, blood slowly seeping through his fingers. His legs gave out and he collapsed to his knees in the snow. The Surgeon stepped closer, sword at the ready. Something was alive in those eyes now. Something worse than the flat darkness. A flame of desire that would put the great lovers of history to shame.

"Never," he said. "You're wrong."

The Surgeon pulled the sword up for another strike.

"You've been lied to," the Chair cried out.

"It is *you* who lie," the Surgeon said.

He raised his hand up to protect himself, and with one blow she sliced off his fingers, causing him to cry out, the fingers tumbling to the snow, a part of him and no longer a part.

"Who are the other Philosophers?" the Surgeon asked as she leaned close.

He said something and the Surgeon put her free hand in his thinning hair, jerking his head up, and putting the edge of the blade against his neck. "Who?"

He whispered two names and she pressed the blade harder. A warm trickle of blood ran down his neck. "Who follows you? Who is your successor?"

McBride shook his head. "Never."

The Surgeon shrugged. "We already have a very good idea of who it is. We are taking steps in that direction. Where are your disks and the rod?"

He clamped his mouth shut. That was another thing he could never say. She removed the sword from his neck and jabbed it once more into his shoulder, twisting the steel. He felt it, but distantly, his nerves over-loaded.

"The disks."

She leaned close once more, her eyes intent on his face. He whispered something. She let go of his hair and stepped back. "The names are true. The location, however, is a lie. And like the Philosopher I just killed, you will continue to lie while you fight for time. Time you no longer have."

She drew back the sword.

"In the name of God, mercy, please," he cried out.

A cold smile crossed her face, amused by the pathetic attempt to reach something inside her that had died long ago. "That won't work." Her eyes locked into his. "The disks?"

"You're so wrong," the Chair said.

She lowered the sword and leaned close, her red lips next to his ear, her warm breath on his skin. "The Society calls me the Surgeon. But you can call me Lily."

He looked up at her. "Please, Lily."

Her arms moved and the last thing he saw was the flash of steel slicing through the falling snowflakes.

*****

Evie Tolliver walked into the crowded restaurant and looked neither to the left nor the right. She stood calmly, waiting for the maître d' to seat her, seemingly assured of the place and time. She was a woman of average height, but uncommon carriage; the type of body that suggests dance classes or, more likely, years of stern warnings to stand up straight. Her age would be more difficult in today's world of dermatology and expert hair coloring, but the few spots on the hands clasping the book and battered old leather briefcase suggested mid-forties—along with the self-assurance that comes with experience.

At least it appeared that way. It was a good show. Her thick, dark hair had just enough silver to make it fierce. The cheekbones, high and wide, were her only real genetic gift of youth, giving her skin an extra ten years of grip against everyone's Newtonian battle. She had the bold, blue eyes of the black Irish, bespeaking a legacy of bold adventure and high romance. A good story, perhaps.

She was dressed simply; loose linen slacks, plain top, long black leather coat and the kind of jewelry a person who traveled accumulated over a lifetime; each piece special, with a story and worn every day, but of little interest to strangers. Good bag, but years out of style. Leather boots—not stylish, but well-worn and comfortable. A bland exterior, more like a wall, to keep strangers at bay and outside interest to a minimum.

In reality, Evie wasn't as calm as she appeared. Her chest ached. Something wasn't right with McBride—he was not a man who was late. Worse, giving her his briefcase earlier in the day had been completely out of character. After being seated at a table near the wall, she glanced at her watch and then reluctantly opened the old briefcase's clasp. His sleek, ultra-modern personal laptop was in its usual spot—a computer he used to compile his articles, and a journal no one had ever read other than its author, as McBride encrypted everything he put on the machine. He joked it was a book he was writing, the Great American Story, but had always added that it would never be published—never *could* be published for some reason he never explained.

Something metallic glinted in the depths of the bag. She opened the briefcase wider. In the bottom of the briefcase was an iron rod a quarter inch in diameter and eight inches long, with brass knobs on each end. Evie was jolted when she recognized it and she could tell it was authentic, but she also knew it wasn't one of the two known originals—one in Monticello, where she had seen it safe and sound less than three hours ago, and the other locked securely in the Smithsonian.

Looking further, she spotted a thick envelope. She pulled it out. It was addressed to her in McBride's flowing script with a note in parentheses indicating she should open it if he were late—a strange and foretelling postscript. As she fingered the envelope, her mind was in turmoil as questions tumbled over each other: *Why did McBride have a previously unknown Jefferson Wheel Cipher rod? Where were the disks that went with it? And most importantly, why was he late?*

She slid a finger under the flap and broke the seal. Reaching in, she pulled out a piece of parchment folded over something round. Unfolding the parchment revealed a single, aged wooden disk about two inches in diameter and a sixth of an inch thick. She ran her finger around the rim of the disk, feeling the letters that had been carved into it, knowing its connection to the rod that was in the briefcase. The number "1" was etched very lightly into the flat side of the disk.

There was writing on the parchment. Four lines scrawled in McBride's flowing handwriting:

FIND THE CIPHER, FIND THE ALLEGIANCE
ONE PHILOSOPHER CHAIR, THREE PHILOSOPHERS
YOU ARE NOW THE CHAIR
A PHILOSOPHER WILL MEET YOU HERE

Copyright

Cool Gus Publishing
www.bobmayerc.com

This is a work of fiction. Names, characters, places, and incidents either are the product of the author's imagination or are used fictitiously, and any resemblance of fictional characters to actual persons living or dead, business establishments, events, or locales is entirely coincidental. Because this is Historical Fiction, real persons of history are woven into the story, however, they are still characterized as fictional. The author tried to make the history elements as true to historical time lines, however things in the story have been altered in the name of fiction and entertainment.

COPYRIGHT © 2017 by Bob Mayer
ISBN: 9781935712367